This signed edition of

WE ARE WATER

by

Wally Lamb

has been specially bound by the publisher.

We Are Water

Also by Wally Lamb

Wishin' and Hopin'
The Hour I First Believed
I Know This Much Is True
She's Come Undone

By Wally Lamb and the Women of York Correctional Institution

Couldn't Keep It to Myself:
Testimonies from Our Imprisoned Sisters

I'll Fly Away:
Further Testimonies from the Women of York Prison

We Are Water

A NOVEL

Wally Lamb

www.harpercollins.com

HarperCollins books may be purchased for educational, business, or sales promotional use. For information, please e-mail the Special Markets Department at SPsales@harpercollins.com.

An excerpt from "Girl Skipping Rope" was previously published in *Ploughshares*, Winter 2011–2012, Issue 37.4.

"Ghost of a Chance." Copyright © 1993, 1967, 1963 by Adrienne Rich, from *Collected Early Poems: 1950–1970* by Adrienne Rich. Used by permission of W. W. Norton & Company, Inc.

FIRST EDITION

Design by Fritz Metsch

Library of Congress Cataloging-in-Publication Data has been applied for.

ISBN: 978-0-06-194102-3 (Hardcover)

ISBN: 978-0-06-228716-8 (Signed Edition)

13 14 15 16 17   OV/RRD   10 9 8 7 6 5 4 3 2 1

This one is for two strong women:
Joan Joffe Hall and Shirley Woodka

Ghost of a Chance

You see a man
trying to think.

You want to say
to everything:
Keep off! Give him room!
But you only watch,
terrified
the old consolations
will get him at last
like a fish
half-dead from flopping
and almost crawling
across the shingle,
almost breathing
the raw, agonizing
air
till a wave
pulls it back blind into the triumphant
sea.

—Adrienne Rich

Prologue

Rope-Skipping Girl

Gualtiero Agnello

August 2009

I understand there was some controversy about the coroner's ruling concerning Josephus Jones's death. What do you think, Mr. Agnello? Did he die accidentally or was he murdered?"

"Murdered? I can't really say for sure, Miss Arnofsky, but I have my suspicions. The black community was convinced that's what it was. Two Negro brothers living down at that cottage with a white woman? That would have been intolerable for some people back then."

"White people, you mean."

"Yes, that's right. When I got the job as director of the Statler Museum and moved my family to Three Rivers, I remember being surprised by the rumors that a chapter of the Ku Klux Klan was active here. And it's always seemed unlikely to me that Joe Jones would have tripped and fallen headfirst into a narrow well that he would have been very much aware of. A well that he would have drawn water from, after all. But if a crime had been committed, it was never investigated as such. So who's to say? The only thing *I* was sure of was that Joe was a uniquely talented painter. Unfortunately, I was the only one at the time who could see that. Of course now, long after his death, the art world has caught up with his brilliance and made him highly collectible. It's sad—tragic, really. There's no telling what he might have achieved if he had lived into his forties and fifties. But that was not to be."

I'm upstairs in my studio, talking to this curly-haired, pear-shaped Patrice Arnofsky. When she called last week, she'd explained that she was a writer for an occasional series which profiled the state's prominent artists in *Connecticut* magazine. They had already run stories on Sol LeWitt, Paul Cadmus, and the illustrator Wendell Minor, she said. Now she'd been assigned a posthumous profile of Josephus Jones in conjunction with a show that was opening at the American Folk Art Museum. "I understand that you were the only curator in his life-time to have awarded him a show of his work," she'd said. I'd told her that was correct. Agreed to talk with her about my remembrances of Joe. And so, a week later, here we are.

Miss Arnofsky checks the little tape recorder she's brought along to the interview and asks me how I met Josephus Jones.

"I first laid eyes on Joe in the spring of 1957 when he appeared at the opening of an exhibition I had mounted called 'Nineteenth-Century Maritime New England.' It was a pretentious title for a self-congratulatory concept—a show that had been commissioned by a wealthy Three Rivers collector of maritime art whose grandfather had made millions in oceanic shipping. He had compensated the museum quite generously for my curatorial work, but it had bored me to tears to hang that show: all those paintings of frigates, brigs, and steam-ships at sea, all that glorification of war and money.

"On the afternoon of the opening, I was making small talk with Marietta Colson, president of the Friends of the Statler, when she stopped midconversation and looked over my shoulder. A frown came over her face. 'Well, well, what have we here?' she said. 'Trouble?' My eyes followed hers to the far end of the gallery, and there was Jones. Among the well-heeled, silver-haired patrons who had come to the opening, he was an anomaly with his mahogany skin and flattened nose, his powerful laborer's build and laborer's overalls.

"We watched him, Marietta and I, as he wandered from painting to painting. He was carrying a large cardboard box in front of him, and perhaps that was why he reminded me of the gift-bearing Ab-yssinian king immortalized in *The Adoration of the Magi*—not the famous Gentile da Fabriano painting but the later one by Albrecht Dürer, who, to splendid effect, had incorporated the classicism of the Italian Renaissance in his northern European art. Do you know that work?"

"I know Dürer, but not that painting specifically. But go on."

"Well, throughout the gallery, conversations stopped and heads turned toward Josephus. 'I hope there's nothing menacing in that box he's holding,' Marietta said. 'Do you think we should notify the police?' I shook my head and walked toward him.

"He was standing before a large Caulkins oil of *La Amistad*, the schooner that had transported African slaves to Cuba. The painting depicted the slaves' revolt against their captors. 'Welcome,' I said. 'You have a good eye. This is the best painting in the show.'

"He told me he liked pictures that told a story. 'Ah yes, narrative paintings,' I said. 'I'm drawn to them, too.' His bushy hair and eyebrows were gray with cement dust, and the bib of his overalls was streaked with dirt and stained with paint. He had trouble making eye contact. Why had he come?

"'I paint pictures, too,' he said. 'I can't help it.' I knew what he meant, of course. Had I not been painting for decades, more *in*voluntarily than voluntarily at times? 'I'm Gualtiero Agnello, the director of this museum,' I said, holding out my hand. 'And you are?'

"He told me his name. Placed his box on the floor and shook my hand. His was twice the size of mine, and as rough as sandpaper. 'You the one they told me to come and see,' he said. He didn't identify who 'they' were and I didn't ask. He picked up his box and held it at arm's length, expecting me to take it. 'These are some of my pictures. You want to look at them?'

"I told him this wasn't really a convenient time. Could he come back some day the following week? He shook his head. He worked, he said. He could leave them here. I was hesitant, suspecting that he had no more talent than the Sunday painters who often contacted me—dowagers and dilettantes, for the most part, who became huffy when I failed to validate their assumptions of artistic genius. I didn't want to be the bearer of bad news. Still, I could tell that it had cost him something to come here, and I didn't want to disappoint him either. 'Tell you what,' I said. 'You see that table over there where the punch bowl is? Slide your box underneath it. I'll look at your work when I have a chance and get back to you. Do you have a telephone?'

"He shook his head. 'But you can call my boss when you ready to talk, and he can tell me. I don't know his number, but he in the phone book. Mr. Angus Skloot.'

"'The building contractor?' He nodded. The Skloots were generous donors to the museum, and Mrs. Skloot was a member of the Friends. 'Okay then, I'll be in touch.' He thanked me for my time. I told him to help himself to punch and cookies, but when he looked over at the refreshments table and saw several of the other attendees staring back at him, he shook his head.

"He stayed for a little while longer, repelling the crowd wherever he wandered, as if he were Moses parting the Red Sea, but unable to resist the art he would stop before and study. As I watched him walk finally toward the exit, Marietta approached me. 'I'm dying of curiosity, Gualtiero,' she said, her mouth screwed up into a sardonic half-grin. 'Who's your new colored friend?'

"I stared at her without answering, waiting for her to stop smirking. When she did, I said, 'He's an artist. Isn't that the reason the Friends of the Statler exists? To support the artists of our community?' She nodded curtly, pivoted, and walked away.

"The opening ended at five P.M. I escorted the last of the guests to the door. The caterers packed up the punch bowl and cookie trays, folded the tablecloth, and moved the table they'd used back to its proper place at the entrance to the exhibit. The janitors stacked the folding chairs and began to sweep. And there it was, by itself in the middle of the floor: Jones's box. I carried it upstairs to my office. Then I put my coat on, went downstairs, and locked up the building on my way out. For the rest of that weekend, I forgot all about Josephus Jones.

"But on Monday morning, there it was again: the box. I opened it, removed Jones's two dozen or so small paintings, and spread them across my work counter. He'd used what looked and smelled like enamel house paint. Two of the works had been painted on plywood, another on Masonite board. The rest were on cardboard. The tears in my eyes blurred what was before me."

"And what *was* before you?" Miss Arnofsky asks. "Can you describe what you saw?"

"Well, he had no understanding of perspective; that was immediately apparent. Many of the figures that populated his paintings were out of proportion. He knew nothing about the technique of chiaroscuro; there was no play between shadow and light in any of his samples. Nevertheless, he had an intuitive sense of design and a wonderful feeling for vivid color. His subject matter—cowboys and Indians, jugglers and jungle animals, tumbling waterfalls, women naked or barely clothed—possessed all the characteristics of the modern primitive. Yet each gave evidence of a unique vision. And Josephus Jones was indeed a narrative painter; his pictures suggested stories that celebrated the rustic life but warned of sinister forces that lurked in the bushes and behind the trees.

"I called Angus Skloot, who told me where Joe was working that day. And so I carried his box of paintings out to my car and drove to the building site. Joe introduced me to his brother, Rufus; the two were building a massive stone fireplace inside the unfinished house. I suggested we talk outside so that I could deliver the good news about his artistic talent.

"He must have been thrilled to receive it," my guest says.

"No, quite the contrary. He was unsurprised, unsmiling; it was as if he already knew what I had to tell him. I asked him how long he'd been painting. About three years, he said. Told me he'd begun the day he awoke from a dream about a beautiful naked woman riding on the back of a lion. He had grabbed a carpenter's pencil and a piece of wood, he said, so that he could draw his dream before it faded away like fog. He wanted to remember it, but he wasn't sure why. All that day, he said, he thought about the woman astride the lion. And so, at the end of his workday, he got permission from Mr. Skloot to take some of the almost-empty cans from the paint shed. Then he'd gone home and painted what he had first dreamt and then sketched out. He said he had been painting ever since. I handed him back his box of paintings and he placed it on the ground between us. 'Tell me about yourself,' I said. He looked suspicious, I remember. Asked me what it was I wanted to know. 'Whatever you want to tell me,' I said."

"And what *did* he want to tell you?" Miss Arnofsky asks. "I realize that this was years ago, but it would be helpful to me if you can recall it as accurately as possible."

It's strange what happens next. When a painting I'm working on becomes my singular focus—when I am "in the zone," as I've heard people put it—a trancelike state will sometimes overtake me. And now it's happening not with my art but with my memory. Seated across from me, Miss Arnofsky fades away and the past becomes more alive than the present. . . .

Joe scuffs his work boot against the ground and takes his time thinking about it. "Well, my granddaddy on my daddy's side was a slave on a Virginia tobacco farm and my grams was a free woman." After the emancipation, they moved up to Chicago and his grandfather got work in the stockyards. His mother's people were third-generation Chicagoans, he says. "Mama washed rich ladies' hair during the week at a fancy hotel beauty parlor downtown, and on weekends she preached in the colored church. My daddy worked in the stockyards at first, like *his* daddy did. But sledgehammerin' cows between the eyes to get them ready for slaughter give him the heebie-jeebies, so he quit. Got work at a brickyard and become a mason—a damn good one, too. When me and Rufus was thirteen and fourteen, Daddy started bringing us along on jobs, and that was how we learnt to work with stone and mortar ourselfs." His father was a better mason than he is, Joe says, but Rufus is better than both of them. "He a artist uses a trowel and *ce*-ment instead of a paintbrush is what Mr. Skloot told him," Joe says, smiling broadly. "And thass about right, too."

I ask him how long he's lived in Three Rivers. Since 1953, he says, and when I tell him that was the year my family and I moved here, too, his eyes widen, then slowly lock onto mine. He nods knowingly, as if our having arrived in Three Rivers at the same time is more about fate than coincidence.

Both of his parents had passed by then, he tells me, and Rufus had just gotten out of the navy. He urged Joe to come east because he had a plan. They would get good jobs at the shipyard in Groton, helping to build America's first nuclear submarine, the U.S.S. *Nauti-*

lus. But the shipbuilders had shied away from hiring coloreds, fearing repercussions and race baiting from their white workers. "So we took whatever jobs we could find. Worked tobacco up in Hartford, worked at a sawmill, dug graves. We took masonry jobs when we could find them, which was just this side of never. The luckiest day of our life was the day Mr. Skloot come to visit his sister's stone at the cemetery up in Willimantic," he says. "Rufus and me was digging a grave two plots down, and he come over and the three of us got to talking. Mr. Skloot's face lit up when we told him we was gravediggers for right now but masons, mostly. He said he'd just fired *his* mason for being drunk on the job. Well, sir, by the time he got back in that big ole black Oldsmobile of his and drove away, we had us jobs with Skloot Builders. We was spoze to be on trial for a month so Mr. Skloot could see what kind of work we done, and if we was hard workers and dependable, and didn't get liquored up. But we got hired permanent after just the first week because Mr. Skloot liked what he seed us do—well, Rufus's work more than mines, but mines, too."

Mr. Skloot is the best boss he's ever had, Joe says. When I ask him why, he says, "Because he pay good and he kind. Lets us live out back on his property, and he don't even care that Rufus got hisself a white wife. Rufe married his gal when he was stationed over in Europe and brung her over here after we was working steady. She Dutch." Joe touches his work boot to the box at his feet. "I got other paintings at the house, you know. Lots of 'em. If you like these ones, maybe you want to see those ones, too." I tell him I do and arrange to meet him at his home at six o'clock that same evening.

The house is a small cottage at the back of the Skloots' property. Following Joe's instructions, I drive down the Skloots' driveway, then inch my car over a rutted path out back until I get to a brook. I park and get out, then cross the brook by way of two bowed two-by-six planks that have been placed over it. A thin white woman—Joe's brother's Dutch wife, I figure—is outside, hanging clothes in just her slip. When I ask her if Josephus is home, she sticks out her thumb and points it toward the door. Before I can knock, it swings open and Jones invites me in.

The place is filthy. It reeks of stale cooking odors and cat urine, and there is clutter everywhere. A fat calico cat is asleep on the kitchen table amidst dirty dishes, old magazines, and an ash tray brimming with stubbed-out cigarettes. The floor beneath my shoes feels gritty. Josephus's paintings are everywhere: stacked against walls and windowsills, atop a refrigerator whose door is kept shut with electrical tape. There are more paintings scattered across the mattress on the floor and on the dropped-down Murphy bed. "What's this one called?" I ask Joe, pointing to a female figure in a two-piece bathing suit standing in a field of morning glories, parakeets alighting on her head and outstretched arms.

"That one there? Thass *Parakeet Girl.*" When I pick it up for a closer look, the roaches hiding beneath it scuttle for cover.

But housekeeping is beside the point. I look closely at every work he shows me, overwhelmed by both his output and his raw talent. I'm there for hours. Some of his paintings are more successful than others, of course, but even the lesser efforts display an exotic, unschooled charm and that bold use of color. Before I leave, I offer him a show at the Statler. He accepts. When I get home, I tell my wife that I may have just discovered a major new talent.

But "Josephus Jones: An American Original" is a flop. The local paper, which is usually supportive of our museum shows, declines to publish either a feature story or a review. At the opening, instead of the usual two hundred or so, fewer than twenty people attend. Not even Angus and Ethel Skloot have come; they are on holiday in Florida. It's painful to watch the Jones brothers scuff the toes of their shined shoes against the gallery's hardwood floor and eye the entranceway with fading hope. Both have purchased sharp double-breasted suits for this special occasion, and Rufus's Dutch-born wife has apparently bought new clothes, too: a sparkly, low-cut cocktail frock more suitable for an evening at a New York supper club than a Sunday afternoon art opening in staid Three Rivers, Connecticut. Worse yet, she has neglected to remove the tag from her dress, and I have to instruct my secretary, Miss Sheflott, to go upstairs to her desk, retrieve her scissors, and discreetly escort young Mrs. Jones out into the foyer for the purpose of clipping her tag. Later, Miss Sheflott tells me she tucked the tag inside the dress rather than removing it. Mrs. Jones has confided that she can't afford it and is planning to return it to the LaFrance Shop on Monday.

In the days that follow, there are complaints about the show's prevalence of female nudity. Three members of the Friends cancel their memberships in protest. In the six weeks the show is up, the number of visitors is dismally low—our worst attendance ever. I've penned personal letters to several influential New York art dealers and critics, inviting them to discover Jones. "He is a painter of events commonplace and exotic that are shot through with an underlying sense of anxiety," I have written. "His compositions are rich with surprises, some joyful, some sinister. In my opinion, he stands shoulder to shoulder with other American primitive painters, from Grandma Moses to his Negro brethren, Jacob Lawrence and Horace Pippin, and the breakthrough artists of the Harlem Renaissance." But none of those busy New Yorkers to whom I've written has had the courtesy even to reply, let alone trek the three hours to our little museum to see Josephus's work for themselves.

The show ends. We keep in touch from time to time, Joe and I. I encourage him, critique the new work he sometimes brings by. I'm sad to learn from Joe that his brother Rufus's wife has left him, and that Rufus has taken it badly—has fallen in with a bad crowd and begun using heroin. "Mr. Skloot let him go after he found out he be messin' wiff the devil's drug," Joe says. "Booted him out of the house out back, too. I been saving up some to send Rufe to one of them sanctoriums to get hisself clean, but they cost more money than I gots. If I could sell some paintings here and there, I could do it, but ain't no one like them enough to buy any." I try several more times to interest my New York connections in Joe's work—alas, to no avail. Eventually, he stops coming around to the museum and we fall out of touch.

But in the summer of 1959, during Three Rivers's celebration of its three hundredth anniversary, I am asked to judge the art show on the final day of festivities. It's a big show; more than three hundred artists, accomplished and amateurish, have submitted work for consideration. Most have chosen "pretty" subject matter: quaint covered bridges, romanticized portraits of rosy-cheeked children, and the inevitable still lifes of flowers and fruit. As I wander the grounds, looking for *some*thing to which I can affix a "best in show" ribbon and still sleep that night, I come upon Josephus's work at the south end of the festival grounds. Delighted and relieved, I scan what I have previously admired: *Parakeet Girl, Jesse James and His Wife*, his pictures of pinup girls and fishermen midstream, ukulele players and circus curiosities. One theme seems to prevail in Jones's work: predators—lions and tigers, lynxes and leopards—attacking or about to attack their prey. Then, among these familiar paintings, I see a spectacular new one— twice as large and twice as ambitious as the others. At the center of the composition stands the Tree of Life, lush and fecund. Beneath it are a pale, naked Adam and Eve. The latter figure is reminiscent of the prepubescent Eves of Van Leyden, the sixteenth-century Dutch master. Adam, though his skin is gray rather than brown or black, bears the face of Josephus Jones himself. The benign members of the animal kingdom who surround the two human figures seem almost to smile. But trouble lurks, in the form of the treacherous serpent hanging from the tree. Joe has depicted a moment in time. Adam reaches for the forbidden fruit which Eve is about to pluck. It will be the fateful act of self-will that will banish them both from the garden. Innocence is about to be lost, and we humans, forever after, will be stained with our forebears' original sin. In *Adam and Eve*, Jones is once again exploring the theme of the predator and the prey, but he has done so in a more subtle and masterly way. *Adam and Eve* is a leap forward—a stellar achievement, and I am elated to hang the "best in show" blue ribbon next to it. The festival gates swing open to the public at 9:00 A.M. As I exit, they push past me, eager not so much to view the art, I suspect, as to fill their bellies with the pancakes that are being cooked and served inside the tent by a large black woman gotten up to look like Aunt Jemima. I admire the organizers' cunning. If you want people to flock to art, lure them with pancakes.

Later, I'm informed that the festival committee was unhappy with my selection, and I read in the newspaper the following day that an irate art show attendee rushed Jones's *Adam and Eve*, intent on destroying it, and that this would-be art critic had scuffled with its creator. This news delights me! Isn't that art's purpose, after all? To engage and, if necessary, disturb the beholder? To upset the apple cart and challenge the status quo? Was that not what the great Michelangelo did as he lay on his back, painting political satire onto the ceiling of the Sistine Chapel? Haven't artists, from that great sixteenth-century genius to Manet and Rivera, outraged the public and forced them to *think*? Now that his art has been attacked, Josephus has joined the ranks of an illustrious fellowship.

Several weeks later, I am in my office at the museum, working on the budget for the coming year and half-listening to the radio. A novelty song is playing—one that mocks "the troubles" between the Irish and the Brits.

> *You'd never think they go together, but they certainly do*
> *The combination of English muffins and Irish stew*

I chuckle at the words, thinking, well, if paintings can make political statements, then why can't silly popular songs? But I stop cold when the music ends and the news comes on. The announcer says that thirty-nine-year-old Josephus Jones, a local construction worker, has died accidentally—that he has tripped and fallen into a well behind his residence and drowned. I sit there, stunned and sickened. A promising artist has been cut down by fate just as he was hitting his stride. Unable to work, I put on my coat, walk out of my office, and drive home.

I go to his funeral service at the colored church. The Negro community has come out in impressive numbers to sing and wail and shout out their grief about Joe Jones's premature demise, but I am only one of four Caucasians who have come to mourn him; the other two are Angus and Ethel Skloot and a distraught young woman who looks familiar but whom I cannot, at first, place. But halfway through the service, it dawns on me who she is: the Eve of Josephus's painting, reaching for the forbidden fruit that hangs just below the malevolent serpent. Joe's brother Rufus is one of the pallbearers, but he looks disheveled and dazed, every bit the drug addict that Joe said he had become. The snake, I see, has bitten him, too.

None of the mourners who orate at the service, or who later gossip at "the feed" downstairs after the "churchifying," mentions Josephus's relationship to art. But I hear, over and over, their rejection of Coroner McKee's finding that Joe died accidentally. "A skull fracture and a six-inch gash on his forehead?" one skeptic stands and says. She is a loud, angry woman in an elaborate hat who looks like she tips the scales between two fifty and three hundred pounds, and as she speaks I realize that she is the same woman who played the part of Aunt Jemima at the pancake breakfast. "A six-foot man just ups and falls headfirst into a well that's seven foot deep and twenty inches across? If that was an accident, then I'll eat this hat I'm wearing, feathers and all," she declares. "That's why we got to keep fighting the good fight in the name of Jesus Christ Almighty! To get Brother Josephus some justice and right what's wrong in this sorry world and this sorry town!" From various places around the room, people call out in agreement. "Mm-hmm, that's right!"

"You tell 'em, Bertha!"

"Amen, sister!"

From the other side of the room, I hear a man's tortured sobs. It breaks my heart when I see that it is Joe's afflicted brother, Rufus. . . .

"How sad," Miss Arnofsky says, and her comment returns me from the past to the present, from the basement of the Negro church back to my studio.

"Yes. Yes, it was. Poor Rufus died not long after that, in the flood."

"The flood?"

I nod. "A dam gave way in the northern part of town, and the water it had been holding back took the path of least resistance, rushing toward the center of town and destroying a lot of the property in its path. Several people were killed, Rufus Jones included. The paper said he had been living in an abandoned car down by the river."

"When was that?"

"Nineteen sixty-two? Sixty-three, maybe?"

"And so sad, too, that Josephus never knew what a success he would eventually become. But at least in his lifetime, he had your advocacy."

"Yes, I was able to give him that much at least. But it went both ways. Joe gave me something, too."

"What do you mean?"

I pause before answering her, thinking about how to put it. "Well, Miss Arnofsky, many years have passed since the morning I hung that blue ribbon next to Joe's *Adam and Eve*. I've judged many juried shows, large and small, always asking myself just what is the function of art? What is its value? Is it about form and composition? Uniqueness of vision? The relationship between the painter and the painting? The painting and the viewer? Sometimes I'll award the top prize to a formalist, sometimes to an expressionist or an abstract artist. Less often but occasionally I will select an artist whose work is representational. But whenever and wherever possible, I celebrate art that shakes complacency by the shoulders and shouts, 'Wake up!' Not always, certainly, but often enough, this has been the work of outsiders rather than those who have been academically trained—artists who, unlike myself, are unschooled as to the subtleties of technique but who create startling work nonetheless." My guest nods in agreement, and I laugh. "And now, if you'll excuse me," I tell her, "I have to climb down from my soapbox and go downstairs and use the toilet."

"Of course," she says. I rise from my chair and stand, my ninety-four-year-old knees protesting as I do. Miss Arnofsky asks if she might have a look around at my work while she's waiting, and I tell her to be my guest.

When I return a few minutes later, she is standing in front of the shelf by the window, looking at a shadow box collage a young artist gave me years ago. "It's called *The Dancing Scissors*," I tell her. "The artist is someone I awarded a 'best in show' prize to years ago, and she gave it to me as a gift. She's become quite celebrated since then."

"I recognize the style," she says. "It's an Annie Oh, isn't it?"

"Yes, that's right. You know her work?"

She nods. "I did a profile piece on her for our magazine when she was just starting out. It was called 'Annie Oh's Angry Art.' She was very shy, almost apologetic about her work. But what struck me was the discrepancy between her demeanor and the undercurrent of rage in her art."

"Yes, I suppose that was what drew me to it as well: the silent scream of a woman tethered to the conventional roles of mother and wife and longing to break free. I predicted great things for Annie back then, and I'm delighted that that has come to pass. We've stayed in touch, she and I. As a matter of fact, she's being remarried next month, and I'm going to her wedding."

"Oh, how nice. If you think of it, please tell her I said hello, and that I wish her and her new husband all the best."

"Of course, of course. But I shall have to extend your greeting to Annie and her *wife*. She's marrying the owner of the gallery that represents her work."

"Aha," Miss Arnofsky says. "Now tell me about the other paintings here in your studio. These are your works?" I nod.

She wanders the studio, looking through the stacks of my paintings leaning against the walls, both the ones that have returned from various shows and those that have yet to leave my work space. Standing before my easel, she smiles at my half-finished rope-skipping girl. "I so admire that you're still at it every day," she says. "I see this is a recurring subject for you."

"Yes, that's right. Little Fanny and her jump rope. I've painted her hundreds of times." I explain to my guest that it was my good fortune to have received a scholarship to the school at the Art Institute of Chicago when I was sixteen years old, and how my training there helped to shape my artistic vision. "At first I merely imitated the styles of the painters I most admired. The impressionists and expressionists, the pointillists. But little by little, I began developing a style of my own, which one of my teachers described in his evaluation as 'boldly modern with a freshness of vision.' I don't mean to boast, but I began to be recognized as one of the three most promising students at the school, the others being my friends Antonio Orsini, who came from the Bronx and loved the New York Yankees more that life itself, and Norma Kaszuba, an affable Texan who wore cowgirl boots, smoked cigars, and swore like a man."

"A woman before her time," Miss Arnofsky notes. "But tell me about your jump-roping girl."

"Well, I spotted her one afternoon when Norma, Antonio, and I were eating our lunch in Grant Park. She was just a nameless little Negro girl in a shapeless gray dress, skipping rope and singing happily to herself. Her wiry hair was in plaits. Her face was turned up toward the sun in joyful innocence. As I recall, my friends and I had been arguing about whether Roosevelt, the president-elect, would prove to be a savior or a scoundrel. And as the others' voices faded away, I pulled a pencil from my pocket and, on the oily paper in which my *sopressata* sandwich had been wrapped, began sketching the child. Back at the school that afternoon, I drew the girl over and over, and in the days that followed I began painting her in gouache and oils, in primary colors and pastels and monochromatic shades of green and gray. It was as if that guileless child had bewitched me! I gave her a name, Fanny, and came to think of her as my muse. For my final project, I submitted a series of sixteen works, collectively titled *Girl Skipping Rope*. On graduation day, I held my breath as one of the Institute's capped-and-gowned dignitaries announced, 'And this year's top prize is awarded to . . . Gualtiero Agnello!' It was the thrill of a lifetime. And as you can see, capturing Fanny has become a lifelong obsession."

"Fascinating," my guest says. "You know, I Googled you before I came over here today. You've had shows at several major museums, haven't you?"

"Oh, yes. MoMA, the Corcoran, the Whitney. One of my paintings was purchased for the Smithsonian's permanent collection a while back—a study of my little rope-jumping angel over there."

"Wikipedia said you were born in Italy."

"Yes, that's right. In the city of Siena."

"Ah, Tuscany! Well, *that* was certainly fortuitous. So many great artists came from that region. Who would you identify as your early influences?"

"Well, my parents and I moved to America when I was quite young, so none of the masters. I'd have to say I was drawn to art by my father."

"He was an artist?"

"Not by trade, no. He was a tailor. But among my earliest and fondest memories is having sat long ago on his lap at a table outside the Piazza del Campo, watching, wide-eyed, as Papa's pencil turned blank paper into playful cartoon animals for me. His ability to do so had seemed magical to the little boy I was. But sadly, my parents fell on hard times after my father's tailor shop was burned to the ground by the vengeful husband of his mistress. It was Papa's brother, my Uncle Nunzio, who came to our rescue. He assured my father that Manhattan has thousands of businessmen and they all needed suits. He sent money, too—enough American dollars which, converted to lira, allowed Papa to purchase three passages to New York. And so we left Siena, boarded a ship at the port in Livorno, and traveled across the ocean. I still remember how frightened I was during that long voyage."

"Frightened? Why?"

"Because I thought we would never be free of that endless, shapeless gray water—that we were doomed to sail the sea forever. But twelve days after we left Livorno, we passed La Statua della Libertà and arrived on American soil."

"And you were how old?"

"Eight. Of course, at that age, I could only understand bits and pieces of the reasons for our uprooting. But years later, after my own sexual desires had awakened, Papa confided to me that he had not wished to be unfaithful to my mother, but that his *inamorata*, Valentina, had a body by Botticelli and hair so flaming red that she might have stepped out of a painting by Titian. You see, my father was a clothier by trade, but his *passione* was art. He was like Josephus Jones in that respect. He'd had no formal training, but he had a natural talent and an undeniable urge to draw. He was seldom without his pencil and portfolio of onionskin paper. 'A gift from God,' my mother once called her husband's artistic talent, although she would later describe it as 'my Giuseppe's curse.'"

"And why was that?"

"Because it unhinged him. Made him crazy. That's often the case, of course—that creation and madness begin to dance with each other."

"Like Van Gogh."

"Yes, Van Gogh and many others. Painters, writers, musicians."

She nods. Sighs. "So your family settled in New York?"

"Lower Manhattan, yes. We lived above Uncle Nunzio's grocery market in a four-story tenement on Spring Street. Nunzio knew someone who knew someone, and soon my father was altering men's suits at Macy's Department Store on Herald Square. And while Papa was measuring inseams, sewing shoulder pads into suit coats, and letting out the trousers of fat-bellied businessmen, I was mastering proper English in the classrooms of the Catholic Sisters of the Poor Clares and learning broken English at Uncle Nunzio's grocery market, where I worked after school and every Saturday. In warm weather, my job was to sell roasted peanuts from the barrel outside on the sidewalk. During the winter months, I was brought inside to wait on the customers." I chuckle as I recall the kerchiefed *nonnas* who came by each day to shop for their family's dinner and haggle over the prices of fruit and vegetables. Cagey *Siciliani* for the most part, who would first bruise the fruit they had selected and then demand a reduced price because the fruit was bruised. "At school, my teacher, Sister Agatha, took a shine to me and, because she thought I would make a good priest, urged me to pursue the sacrament of Holy Orders. But I was my father's son on two counts: first, when I was in the eighth grade, I surrendered my virginity to a plump 'older woman' of sixteen who was fond of roasted peanuts. And second, I loved to draw. Seated on a stool next to my peanut barrel, I began sketching the Packards and roadsters parked along Spring Street, the passersby rich and poor and the fluttering garments hanging from clotheslines, the birds who flew in the sky and the pigeons who waddled along the sidewalk, pecking away at morsels. I filled sketchbook after sketchbook, eager to show

Papa my latest drawings when he returned home from his day of tailoring. My father smiled very little back then, but he beamed whenever he looked at my pictures."

"Like father, like son," she says.

"Well, yes and no. Papa was unschooled, as I said. But when I was fifteen, one of my drawings won a prize: art lessons. And so each Saturday morning, freed from my job at Uncle Nunzio's, I would ride my bicycle up Fifth Avenue to the Metropolitan Museum of Art, where I would receive instruction from a German painter named Victorious von Schlippe. Like Uncle Nunzio, Mr. von Schlippe knew people who knew people, and the following year, at the age of sixteen, I was offered the scholarship at the Art Institute."

"Your parents must have been very proud of you," Miss Arnofsky says.

"My father was, yes. But Mama was against my going. She begged me to stay in New York—to find and marry a nice girl from the Old Country and give her grandchildren. Papa, on the other hand, urged me to go and learn whatever Chicago could teach me. I remember the tears in his eyes the morning he saw me off at Grand Central Station, especially after I unfolded the sheet of paper I'd slipped into my pocket when I'd packed the night before. 'Look what I'm bringing, Papa,' I said. He stood there, holding in his shaking hands one of the cartoon drawings he had made for me years before. Then he handed it back to me, blew his nose, and told me I'd better board the train before it left without me. And so, without daring to look back at him, I did.

"And oh, I loved the Windy City! Its crisp autumn weather, its warm and friendly people. I loved my classes, too, and was a sponge, absorbing whatever my instructors could teach me. On Sunday afternoons, it became my habit to write long letters to my parents about my exciting new life. But as autumn turned into winter, Mama's letters back to me began to describe the strange obsession that had overtaken my father. Papa claimed that Catherine of Siena, Italy's patron saint, had appeared to him in a vision, commanding him, for the edification of Italian Catholics the world over, to illustrate the story of her life: her service to the sick during the Black Death; her campaign to have the papacy returned from Avignon to Rome; her receiving of the stigmata. It was a terrible thing to witness, Mama wrote: a husband's strange decline into madness.

"That Christmas, unable to afford the trip back to New York, I stayed in Chicago and sent my parents a gift box of candied fruit, sugared nuts, and nougats. Presents arrived for me as well. Mama had sent me three pairs of socks and a week's supply of woolen underwear. Papa's gift arrived in a long cardboard tube, and when I opened the end and uncurled the onionskin paper within, there was his charcoal rendering of the mystical marriage of Saint Catherine to Jesus Christ. The lines of the drawing were as frenzied and driven as the brushstrokes of the great Van Gogh, and the paper had several tears where he'd pressed down too hard with his pencil. I pinned Papa's present to the wall above my bed, next to the fanciful drawing he had made for me when I was a little boy, and, looking from one to the other, lamented. If fate had been kinder to my father, I thought, he might have left New York, traveled west to California, and found work with the great Walt Disney instead of in a windowless back room at Macy's gentlemen's department. But as the people of the Old Country say, *Il destino mischia le carte, ma siamo noi a giocare la partita.* Destiny shuffles the cards, but we are the ones who must play the game."

"That could just as well be a Yiddish proverb," Miss Arnofsky says. "But destiny has certainly been kinder to you than it was to your father. A successful painter, the director of a museum."

I nod. Smile at my guest. "Overseeing the Statler's collection and hanging shows in its gallery hall is what paid our bills. But painting has always been my primary calling."

"And there's ample proof of that," she says, scanning the room. She asks if I have children. One son, I tell her. Giuseppe. Joseph. "And has he followed in your footsteps?"

"As an artist? In a way, I suppose. He works in television out in Hollywood. Directs one of the daytime soap operas. And that calls for a kind of artistic style, too, of course. Television is so much about the visual."

"Do you see him very often?"

"Not as often as I'd like. But I'll see him next weekend. He has to be in New York on business, and so he's coming up for the weekend. In fact, he's bringing me to Annie Oh's wedding."

"Sounds nice. And you're a widower?"

"Yes, my Anja died in 1989. Heart failure. One day she was here, the next she was gone."

"And since then? Any other women in your life?"

"No, no. I suppose you could say that in old age, my work has become my wife. Or maybe this was always so."

"Two long and happy marriages then," Miss Arnofsky says.

I nod. "Long, happy, and somewhat mysterious." My guest cocks her head, waiting for me to explain. "One's wife, one's art: you can never know either fully. After Anja died, I read her diaries and learned things about her I had never known. That she wrote verse—lovely little poems about her village back in Poland. And that once upon a time she had loved a boy in her village named Stanislaw."

"And your paintings? They keep secrets, too?"

"In a way, yes. Sometimes I'll work on a composition for weeks—months, even—without knowing what it is I'm searching for. Or for that matter, after I've finished it, what finally has been resolved. After all these years, I still can't fully explain the process. The way, when you are deeply involved in a composition, everything else in the room fades away—everything but the thing before you that is calling itself into existence. It's as if the work on your canvas has a will of its own. When that happens, it can be quite exciting. But disturbing, too, when, as the painter, you are not in control of your painting."

"Forgive me; I mean no disrespect. But the way you describe it, it sounds almost like you experience a form of temporary madness yourself."

"Madness? Perhaps. Who's to say?"

Miss Arnofsky points to *The Dancing Scissors* and says she recalls Annie Oh telling her something similar—that she began creating her collages and assemblages without really knowing why or how she was doing it.

"That was true of Joe Jones, too," I tell her. "As I said before, he told me he had begun painting because he *had* to. That something was compelling him. All I know is that at such heightened moments of creativity, I feel as if my work is coming not so much *from* me as *through* me. From what source, I can't say. The muse, maybe? My father's spirit? Or who knows? It could even be that the hand of God is guiding my hand."

"So your talent may be God-given? Is that what you're saying?"

"Well, I'm afraid that sounds rather grandiose."

"Quite the contrary," she says. "I'm struck by your humility in the face of all you've accomplished." For the next several seconds, we stare at each other, neither of us speaking. Then she smiles, closes her notebook, unplugs her tape recorder. "Well, Mr. Agnello, I shouldn't take up any more of your time, but I can't tell you how grateful I am. This has been wonderful."

"I'm just relieved to see that you still have both of your ears. I was afraid I might have talked them off." She laughs, says she could have listened to me for hours more. "Oh, perish the thought," I say. She rises from her chair, tape machine in hand, and I tell her I'll see her out.

"No, no. I can let myself out. You should get back to your work."

I nod. We thank each other, shake hands. From the doorway of the studio, I watch her disappear down the stairs.

But I do not return to my work as I'd intended.

The sun and the conversation of the past hour have made me sleepy. When I close my eyes, the images I evoked for my guest play on in my head: Rufus Jones, bereft at his brother's funeral . . . Papa's cartoon drawings coming to life before me at the piazza with the Fountain of Gaia gurgling nearby, water spilling from the mouth of the stone wolf into the aquamarine pool . . . Annie Oh's strange collages that day when I first came upon them. Suddenly, I remember something else about that day—something I had forgotten all about until this moment. I had been wavering about whether to give the top prize to Annie or to an abstract expressionist whose work was also quite impressive. But as I stood there vacillating, a gray-haired Negro appeared by my side—a man who looked eerily like an older version of Josephus Jones. It wasn't Joe, of course; by then, he had been dead for years. "This one," the man said, nodding at Annie's work. It was as if somehow he had read my mind and intuited my indecision. And that had clinched it. The "best in show" prize was hers. . . .

"Mr. Agnello? . . . Mr. Agnello?"

When I open my eyes, my housekeeper is standing before me. She says my lunch is ready. Do I want her to bring up a tray?

"No, no, Hilda. I'll be down in a minute." She nods. Leaves.

Half-asleep still, my eyes look around, then land on the unfinished painting resting against my easel. It confuses me. Why does Fanny have angel's wings? When did I paint those? I rise and go to her and, on closer inspection, realize that her "wings" are only the clouds behind her. . . . And yet, winged or not, she *is* my angel. Seventy-odd years have slipped by since I spotted her that day in Chicago, and yet she continues to skip rope in my mind and on my canvases, raising her dark, hopeful face to the sky, innocent of the depth of people's cruelty toward "the other"—those who, for whatever reason, must swim against the tide instead of letting it carry them. . . .

Well, that's enough deep thinking for this old brain. My lunch is ready and I'm hungry. I get up, balance myself. On my way out the door, I turn back and face my easel. "I'm too tired to do you justice any more today, little one," I tell Fanny. "But I'll be back tomorrow morning. I'll see you then."

On the stairs, I remember that I still have to send back that response card. Let Annie know that Joe and I are coming to her wedding.

Part I

Art and Service

Chapter One

Annie Oh

Viveca's wedding dress has a name: Gaia. It's lovely. Layers of sea green silk chiffon, cap sleeves, an empire waist, an asymmetrical A-line skirt with the suggestion of a train. I forget the designer's name; Ianni something. He's someone Viveca knows from the Hellenic Fashion Designers Association. It arrived at the apartment from Athens yesterday, and Minnie has pressed it and hung it on the door of Viveca's closet.

Gaia: I Googled it yesterday after Viveca's dress arrived and wrote down what it said on an index card. It's on the bureau. I pick it up and read.

After Chaos arose broad-breasted Gaia, the primordial goddess of the Earth and the everlasting foundation of the Olympian gods. She was first the mother of Uranus, the ancient Greek embodiment of heaven, and later his sexual mate. Among their children were the mountains, the seas, the Cyclopes, and the Hundred-Handed giants who aided Zeus in his successful battle against the Titans, whom Gaia had also birthed.

Chaos, incest, monsters, warring siblings: it's a strange name for a wedding dress.

The three Vera Wang dresses Viveca had sent over for me to consider were delivered yesterday, too. (Vera is one of Viveca's clients at the gallery.) There's an ivory-colored dress, another that has a tinge of pink, a third that's pearl gray. Minnie spread them across the bed in the guest bedroom, but after she went home, I carried them into our bedroom and hung them to the left of the Gaia. This morning when I woke up, they scared me. I thought for a split second that four women were standing over by the closet. Four brides—one in gorgeous green, three in off-white.

Viveca is abroad still. She went to Athens a week ago for a fitting but then decided to stay several more days to visit with an elderly aunt (her father's surviving sister) and to finalize the details for our wedding trip to Mykonos. She called me from there last night. "Sweetheart, it's the land of enchantment here. Have you looked at the pictures I e-mailed you?" I said I hadn't—that I'd been more in the studio than at the apartment for the last several days, which was a lie. "Well, do," she said. "Not that photographs can really capture it. In daylight, the Aegean is just dazzling, and at sunset it turns a beautiful cobalt blue. And the villa I've rented? Anna, it's to die for! It sits high on a hill above town and there's a panoramic view of the harbor and some of the other islands in the archipelago. The floors are white marble from a quarry in Paros, and there's an oval pool, an indoor fountain, a terrace that looks out on a grape arbor that's unbelievably lush and lovely." Why a pool if the sea is right there? I wonder. "The houses here are sun bleached to the most pristine white, Anna, and there are hibiscus growing along the south side of the villa that, against that whiteness, are the most intense red you could ever imagine. I just can't wait to share it all with you. You'll see. This place is an artist's dream."

"I'll bet it is," I said. "For an artist who's interested in capturing what's pretty and picturesque. I'm not."

"I know that, Anna. It's what drew me to your work from the start."

"It?" I said. "What's 'it'?"

There was a long pause before she answered me. "Well, it's like I was telling that couple that bought those two pieces from your Pandora series. Your work looks people in the eye. It comforts the disturbed and disturbs the comfortable. But this will be a *vacation*, sweetheart. You work so hard. Mykonos is my gift to you, Anna. My gift to *us*. Four weeks surrounded by what's lovely and life affirming at the start of our married life. Don't we deserve that?"

The room went blurry with my tears. "I miss you," I said.

"I miss you, too, Anna. I miss you, too."

It's not that I don't want to be with her in Mykonos. But four whole weeks? In all the years I've been at it, I've never been away from my work that long. Well, to be fair, she'll be away from her work, too. "It's not a very savvy business decision," she said when she told me she'd rented the villa for the entire month of October. "People will have awakened from their Hamptons comas by then, reengaged with the city, and be ready to buy. But I said to myself, 'Viveca, the hell with commerce for once! Seize the day!' I smiled and nodded when she said that, swallowing back my ambivalence instead of voicing it.

You do that for someone you love, right? Keep your mouth shut instead of opening it. Bend on the things that are bendable. This wedding, for instance. It's Viveca who wants to make our union "official." And *where* we'll be married: I've had to bend on that, too. Okay, fine. I get it. Connecticut has legalized gay marriage and New York hasn't. But why not book a place in some pretty little Gold Coast town closer to the city? Cos Cob or Darien? Why the town where Orion and I raised our kids? She'd wanted to surprise me, she said. Well, she'd achieved her objective, but it's . . . awkward. It's uncomfortable.

Okay then, Annie. If you have misgivings, why go through with it? Why not tell her you've had second thoughts? . . . I look up, look around our well-appointed apartment, and I see a part of the answer hanging on the wall in the hallway: the framed poster announcing the opening of my first show at viveca c. The headline, ANNIE OH: A SHOCK TO THE SYSTEM!, and beneath it, the full-color photo of my sculpture *Birthings*: the row of headless mannequins, their bloody legs spread wide, their wombs expelling serial killers. Speck, Bundy, Gacy. Monsters all.

My art comforts the disturbed and disturbs the comfortable: she'd put it better than I ever could have. It's one of the reasons why I love Viveca. The fact that she not only promotes my work and sells it at prices I couldn't have imagined, but that she also *gets* it. And yes, her apartment is as lovely as she is, and our lovemaking feels satisfying and safe. But for me that may be the foundation of our intimacy: the fact that she understands what my work attempts to do.

Orion never did. But then again, why *would* he have? I'd been so guarded all those years. A twenty-seven-year marriage of guardedness, based on nothing more than the fact that he was a man and, therefore, not to be trusted with the worst of my secrets.

But come on, Annie. You haven't told Viveca your secrets either. Why is that? Because you're afraid she might change her mind? Stop taking care of you? Be honest. Your own mother dies in the flood that night. Then your father drinks himself out of your life. And your foster parents were just stop-gaps. They fed you, clothed you, but never loved you. You wanted the real thing. Do you think it's a coincidence that Orion and Viveca are the same age? That both your ex-husband and your wife-to-be are seven years older than you?

No, that's irrelevant. . . . Or is it? Is that the real reason why you married him? Why you're marrying her? Because Little Orphan Annie still needs someone to take care of her?

I need to stop this. Stop being so hard on myself. I love Viveca. And I loved Orion, too. . . . But why? Because he had taken me under his wing? Because for the first time in my life, intimacy with a man was enjoyable? Safe? Maybe not as safe as it feels with Viveca, or as wild as it had been with Priscilla. But pleasurable enough. And *very* pleasurable for him. It made me a little envious, sometimes. The intensity of his . . .

No. I *wanted* to give him pleasure. But his pleasure had a price.

No, that's not fair. It had been a joint decision. I had stopped using my diaphragm because we *both* wanted a child. But when my pregnancy became a fact instead of a desire, I was suddenly seized with fear. What if I wasn't up to the job of motherhood? What if I miscarried again like I had that time when I was seventeen? I had never told Orion about my first pregnancy, and I held off for a week or more before I told him about this one. The night I finally *did* tell him, Orion promised me that he was going to be the best father he could—the opposite of his own absentee father. We cried together, and I let him assume that mine were happy tears, the same as his. They weren't. But little by little my fear subsided, and I began to feel happy. Excited. Until I had that ultrasound. When I learned we were having twins,

I got scared all over again. And when, in the delivery room, it looked like we might lose Andrew, I was terrified. . . .

Still, I loved being a mother. Loved them both as soon as I laid eyes on them, and more and more in the weeks that followed. Until then, I hadn't understood how profound love could be.

Not that having two of them wasn't challenging. Demanding of everything I had to give and then some. While Orion was away at work all day, I was home changing diapers, feeding them, grabbing ten-minute naps whenever—miraculously, rarely—their sleeping schedules coincided. And true to his word, Orion *was* a devoted father. When he'd get home from the college and see them, his face would light up. He'd bathe them, walk with one of them in each of his arms, rock them until they'd both gone down for the night. Part of the night, anyway. Andrew was a colicky baby, and it would drive me crazy when he'd cry and wake up his sister. And then Ariane would start crying, too. Our marriage suffered for that first year or so. Orion would come home tired from dealing with his patients and give whatever energy he had left to the twins. I resented that he didn't have much left for me. But I didn't have much left for him, either. Double the work, double the mess. Carting both of them to the pediatrician's when one of them was sick. And then going back there the following week when Andrew came down with what Ariane was just getting over. Sitting in that waiting room with those other mothers—the ones with single-tons who were always making lunch dates. Playdates. They'd ooh and ah over my two but never invite me to join them. Not that I even wanted to, but why hadn't they ever asked? They always acted so confident, those moms. It was as if everyone but me had read some book about how to be a good mother. . . .

But I *had* read the books. Consulted Dr. Spock so often that the binding cracked in half and the pages started falling out. But I had no mother of my own to rely on the way those other women did. Those grandmothers who could spell their daughters. Babysit for them, advise them. . . .

Still, I *could* have had that kind of help. How many times had Orion's mother volunteered to drive up from Pennsylvania and help out? Maria was retired by then, available. She kept offering. It's just that she acted so goddamned superior! Made me feel even more insecure. When I got that breast infection? Said I was thinking of bottle-feeding the babies because I was in such pain? She just looked at me—*stared* at me like how could I be so selfish? And then, without even asking me, she had that woman from the La Leche League call and talk me out of it.

Because she wanted what was best for her grandchildren. . . .

And she always *knew* what was best. Right? Not me, their own mother. She never said as much, but I got the message. Her son had made a mistake, had married beneath himself. He should have stayed with what's-her-name.

You remember her name, Annie. How could you forget when Maria was always bringing her up to him? "Thea's gotten a fellowship, Thea's gotten her book taken." Thea this, Thea that, like I wasn't even standing there. So no, I didn't want her help *or* her advice. Who was *she* to pity *me*?

But you showed her, didn't you? Didn't even go to her funeral. Hey, I *couldn't* go. Both of the twins had come down with the chicken pox. What was I supposed to do—leave them with a sitter?

Except I *did* leave them with one. I had just started making my art. I wanted to be down there working on it, not upstairs with two sick kids. So I hired that Mrs. Dunkel to watch them. . . . He was down there in Pennsylvania for almost three weeks! Sitting with Maria at the hospital. Calling me with the daily reports. "I don't think it's going to be long now. She seems to be going downhill fast." And then, in the next phone call, it would be, "She was better today. Awake, alert. I fed her some pudding, and she managed to eat about half of it." The twins were running fevers, crying, clinging to me. But I was supposed to celebrate because she had had a few bites of pudding? And okay, Maria was his mother. But I was his wife, the mother of his kids. We needed him, too. I was going out of my mind.

But that was no excuse. I shouldn't have hit him even *if* he wouldn't stop scratching his chicken pox. I'd tell Ariane to stop, and she would. But not Andrew. So I slapped him on his tush, harder than

I meant to. At first he just looked at me, shocked, and then he cried and cried. I was so scared. What kind of a mother hit her child that hard? It left a mark. But by the next day, it faded. If I had let him keep scratching, he would have had scars for the rest of his life.

And what was Orion supposed to do? He couldn't abandon his mother, no matter how long she lingered. But when she finally did die, there were the arrangements to make, the funeral, cleaning out her condo for resale. . . . And that babysitter hadn't worked out anyway. How could I concentrate on my work when they were up there crying, calling for me, banging on the basement door?

But I did *not* boycott Maria's funeral. I stayed home with our sick kids. And then he tells me that Thea flew in to pay her respects. That the two of them went out to dinner after the services. And I started wondering about how else she might have comforted him. . . .

Okay, Annie, you were insecure, even if, deep down, you knew he wouldn't cheat on you. But then when he finally gets everything squared away down there in Harrisburg, he pulls into the driveway and walks in the door like the returning hero. "Daddy! Daddy's home! Give us a pony ride, Daddy. Read us a bedtime story." He shows up again, they're over the worst of their chicken pox, and suddenly I'm irrelevant. The *fun* parent was back. The *good* cop. Who cares about Mommy now that Daddy's back? And I resented that. Held on to that resentment until we landed in couples counseling.

Because he didn't value my work. That's why we were having trouble. Because everything was about *his* work, and mine didn't count. I was just supposed to be home with the kids all day, at their beck and call, and then grab an hour or two after they were finally down for the night, when I was too exhausted to tap into my creativity. Half the time I'd be down there, trying to work on something, and I'd fall asleep. He'd have to come down, wake me up, and lead me upstairs to bed.

But boy, I balked at that marriage counseling idea. I thought the deck would be stacked. Me versus two psychologists. I was afraid she was going to tell me to give up my art. But instead Suzanne validated what I was doing. Helped Orion to see that my work mattered, too. And she helped *me* to realize the extent of his grieving for his mother.

"Now that my mother has passed, it's like we're *both* orphans," he said, trying hard to hold back his tears. "I mean, I was the result of my mother's affair with a married man. A Chinese man who wouldn't leave his Chinese wife for his Italian girlfriend, and then . . . took a powder. Just goddamned disappeared." He had never said much about his father's absence from his life, and until then I'd assumed he just accepted it. "The only thing I ever got from him was his last name," he said. "And it's different. I know it is. I had my mother a hell of a lot longer than you had yours, but . . ." He broke down in sobs then, and I ached as I witnessed the pain he was in. I reached over and put my hand on his shoulder. Pulled tissues from the box on the table and handed them to him. Watched him wipe his eyes, blow his nose. For the next several seconds, none of us spoke. Suzanne kept looking at me. Waiting for me to say something. And in the middle of that uncomfortable silence, I almost risked telling him *my* truths. My secrets were on the tip of my tongue. But then Suzanne glanced at her clock and said we had to wind up. That we'd gone a little bit over and her two o'clock would be waiting.

I don't know. Maybe if we had kept going to those sessions, I would have told him. But we didn't. Things were better between Orion and me—more like they'd been in the beginning. The closeness, the way he could get me to laugh. Like that time he took me to Boston—Haymarket Square—and taught me how to slurp oysters from the half-shell. Took me that first time to the Gardner Museum. . . . And being a mom had started getting a little easier by then. The twins were growing out of the "terrible twos." They had begun to amuse each other, catching bugs out in the backyard or going down to the stream out back to capture tadpoles and crayfish. That bond they'd developed gave me a reprieve. I could sit near them. Keep an eye on them while I was sketching out new ideas for pieces I wanted to make. And thanks to those counseling sessions, Orion had become more supportive of what I was doing. What I was trying to do. He began spelling me on the weekends so that I could do my work, go on my hunts for new materials. When I won that "best in show" prize? It was Orion who had urged me to enter the competition.

And then, in the middle of this better time, I got a little careless about birth control and along came Marissa. Our *unplanned* child.

He had kept promising he was going to get a vasectomy but never followed through with it. I was furious when I realized I was pregnant again, but only at first. I calmed down, just like I had with the twins. Accepted it. But my work suffered. I had to make all kinds of sacrifices because I put them first. Because I was a damned good mother. . . .

Most of the time. But then there were those times when I wasn't. When Andrew would make me so mad that . . . Because he was always *goading* me. *Challenging* me. Wasn't that why he took the brunt of it? Or was it because, of the three kids, he has the most O'Day in him? The reddish hair, the Irish eyes. He resembles my father around the eyes. And he has my father's walk.

And who else does Andrew resemble? Go ahead. Say it.

"Miz Anna?"

"Hmm?" I look up, startled. Our housekeeper is standing there. "Yes? What is it, Minnie?"

"I axed you if you got anything else needs washing?"

"Washing? Uh, no. Just the stuff that's in the basket. Thanks."

"Did I scare you just now, Miz Anna?"

"What? Oh, no. I was just thinking about something else."

Minnie doesn't say so, of course, but I get the feeling she doesn't really approve of two wealthy women marrying each other. Or maybe she just doesn't get why we'd want to. . . . *Our* housekeeper: I feel guilty even thinking it, let alone saying it out loud, which I did to Hector yesterday when he showed me the umbrella he'd found leaning against the wall downstairs in the lobby. "This isn't yours, is it, Miss Oh?" he asked me.

"No, but I'll take it. It's our housekeeper's. Thanks, Hector." I reached into my purse, took a twenty from my wallet, and held it out to him.

"No, no, that's okay. This thing don't look like it cost twenty bucks to begin with. You don't have to tip me all the time." But I waved away his resistance and made him take it. I had just withdrawn two hundred dollars from the ATM at that Korean grocery store around the corner, so there were nine other twenties in my wallet. It wasn't as if I was going to miss the tenth. Twenty dollars: what's that these days? A taxi ride up to the Guggenheim plus tip? A couple of those fancy coffee drinks at Starbucks and a slice of their pricey pound cake? I'd rather let Hector have it.

Hector's affable and he's a talker. He works construction during the week, at the site where they're building the 9/11 memorial. Works at our building on weekends. I like it when he tells me about his life. He has custody of his three kids for reasons he's not gone into with me. One boy and two girls—the same as Orion and me, although his kids are still young. They're beautiful children; he's shown me their parochial school pictures. Now that school's started again, he pays a neighborhood *abuela* to watch the kids from the time they get home until the time he does. His sister takes them on the weekends when he's here. When I asked him once if it bothered him to work every day in that hole where the towers used to be, he shrugged and said that thing everyone says now: "It is what it is." Ariane used to have that feminist poster in her bedroom: Rosie the Riveter, flexing her bicep, and beneath her, the motto: *We can do it!* Obama's campaign motto last year was a variation on that. "Yes, we can!" he promised, and we needed so much to believe him that we actually elected a black man. I remember staring at the headlines and the TV news the morning after the election, in happy disbelief. But the economy's even more of a mess than it was, our kids keep dying over there in those wars we started but can't end, and it's turned out that Obama isn't a superhero after all. Maybe that's the legacy of those fallen towers, all those lost lives: our national feeling of futility. *No, we* can't *do it. It is what it is.* And who's most affected by the way things are now? Not the people who can still afford the prices at the pump and at Starbucks. I heard on the news the other day that 77 percent of the children in New York's public schools qualify for free breakfast and free lunch. That by next year, the unemployment rate may reach past 10 percent.

Last weekend, Hector was on second shift. Earlier that day, he'd borrowed his sister's car and taken his kids to Six Flags for a last summertime hurrah. But coming back, the car broke down, and he was over an hour late. I'd just come back from a movie, and the building manager was berating him right in front of me while I waited for the elevator. There'd been complaints, he said, about the entrance being left unsupervised. Hector was mistaken if he thought he was irreplaceable; there was a stack of applications sitting on his desk. "And who do you think's going to have to stand there before the co-op board and listen to them gripe this coming Monday? You, Martinez? No, me, that's who." I wanted to walk over there and ask that stupid manager if *he'd* ever been late. If *he* was perfect. What was that thing Jesus said when he was defending the adulteress? Let he without sin cast the first stone. But then the elevator doors opened, and I got in and pressed five without having said a thing. When Viveca called me from Greece and I mentioned the incident between Hector and the building manager—told her I wish I'd spoken up—she said it was probably better that I hadn't. "The co-op board doesn't like it when tenants get mixed up in issues involving the help," she advised. . . .

My daughter Ariane wouldn't have been a wimp about it; she'd have jumped right in and stuck up for Hector. She's been a defender of the underdog ever since she was a kid. There was that time in high school when she had the party on prom night for all the girls who, like her, hadn't been asked. I can still hear them all, down in our rec room, laughing and playing music, yakking away. And then there was the time when she defended that mentally retarded boy who was being taunted by the bullies. They were getting their kicks by circling him and pitching pennies at him, and Ariane had elbowed her way past them, taken the boy by the hand, and led him out of the circle. The bullies had targeted her for a few days after that, but when they saw that they couldn't get to her, they knocked it off. It had stopped being fun. . . .

The help: it angered me, that superior tone, but I kept my mouth shut. That co-op board is like some kind of supreme body around here that everyone's supposed to kowtow to. Before I moved into the building, Viveca had to have them approve my occupancy of her guest room, which, in my opinion, was bullshit. Whose apartment is it? Hers or theirs? The co-op board: they're like those athletic boys in junior high that the principal picked to be hallway monitors. They'd put on their sashes and boss around the rest of us mere mortals. *Move to the right! No talking during passing time! I said no talking! What are you, deaf? How'd you like to get reported?* Goddamned Gestapo hall monitors. Well, it was previews of coming attractions. It's not as if, after you leave junior high, you're ever going to be free of bullies. They follow you through life. And okay, maybe I *didn't* say anything when that stupid building manager was chewing out Hector. But my art says it. What did it say in that *Village Voice* review of my last show? That my pieces are political. Howls of protest against the misuse of power. Something like that....

Coffee. I need coffee. Maybe a couple of cups of caffeine will motivate me to get to the studio today. I'm not sure why I've been avoiding going there, or why I lied to Viveca and said I was going. Is it wedding nerves? Has my creativity begun to abandon me? I take the beans out of the freezer (fair-trade, Guatemalan, thirteen dollars a pound at Zabar's). Grind them, hit the "brew" button. Everything's high end here. This new coffeemaker Viveca had sent over from Saks brews espresso and cappuccino, froths up milk for latté. I should check the manual; for all I know, it'll dust the furniture and wipe your rear end for you as well. When it arrived, I saw the price on the receipt: seven hundred dollars. Jesus! The last I checked, you could get a Mr. Coffee on sale for $19.99.... *Comfort the disturbed, disturb the comfortable.* Maybe that's it. Maybe I'm avoiding the studio because my life's become too goddamned comfortable.

To stop thinking, I put on the TV, the morning news, and there's Diane Sawyer, looking as pretty as ever. She must be in her sixties by now. Has she had work done? Have her lips always been that full, or have they been plumped with collagen? These are New York questions. Before I moved to Manhattan, I wouldn't have given a rat's ass one way or another. Well, she's probably got her burdens, too. Ratings wars, celebrity stalkers. Being that famous must be so strange.... Last week, when I recognized Diane's husband buying toothpaste at that Duane Reed, I couldn't remember any of the movies he's directed, but what I *did* recall was that his family had had to escape from the Nazis when he was a little boy, and that some childhood illness had left him without body hair. Passing him in the aisle, I glanced over to see if he had eyebrows, but when he caught me looking, I had to turn away. It's not that *I'm* a celebrity. Far from it, thank god. But I'm known in the art world now to some extent—here in Manhattan at least. How would *I* like it if some collector knew more about my shitty childhood than they did about my work?

One time on this morning show—Valentine's Day, I think it was—Diane said that when her husband travels and she misses him, she sometimes wraps herself in one of his shirts and his scent comforts her. . . . *The Graduate*: wasn't that one of his films? "Mrs. Robinson, are you trying to seduce me?" The evening Viveca came into my room, sat down next to me on the bed, and touched her impeccably manicured fingernails to my lips, kissed them, I remember feeling as confused as Dustin Hoffman was in that scene. But when we made love that night and she brought me to that long, unhurried orgasm, it reduced me to happy tears. It had been so long, and I was so grateful for the release, that I could barely catch my breath. But Viveca isn't predatory the way Mrs. Robinson was. And our relationship is about much more than good sex. She loves me, and I love her. Trust her. I've missed her so much since she's been away. Miss her the way I missed Orion when he was down there tending to his mother. The way I missed my own mother after those floodwaters carried her away. Missed my father those nights when I'd wait for him to come home from the bars. Is that what love is all about? Needing them to come back to you when they're away? To come home and keep you safe? . . .

There's the doorbell. I call down the hall to Minnie. "I'll get it!"

It's Hector. "Package for Ms. Christophoulos-Shabbas," he says, handing it to me. When I tell him he didn't have to come up, that he could have given it to me when he saw me in the lobby, he shakes his head. Reminds me that Viveca's instructions are to bring deliveries right up to the apartment.

"Oh, okay," I say. "Hold on a sec." I go get my wallet. There are a few singles in there, a five, a twenty. Five seems too little and twenty seems too much, but I give him the larger bill anyway. He glances quickly at it before putting it in his pocket. "Thank *you*," he says.

The package is from Neiman Marcus, and I know what's in it: that expensive perfume Viveca wears: Clive Christian Floral Oriental. Yesterday when we talked, she wanted to know if it had arrived yet. When I said it hadn't, she asked if I'd track the shipment on the computer. Can't blame her for that, I guess. After I found out it was en route, I went on the Neiman Marcus Web site to see what that perfume costs. I wish I hadn't. Twelve hundred dollars an ounce: that's just plain ridiculous. . . . But why *shouldn't* she buy these luxury items if she wants them? She works hard, she's inherited money from both her father and her late husband, she's generous with the charities she supports— even sits on the boards of a couple of them: Literacy Partners, God's Love We Deliver. I should stop being so goddamned judgmental. Stop feeling guilty that I love the smell of that perfume on her, the taste of the coffee that our Esclusivo Magnifica makes. I guess I'm suffering from . . . what would you call it? Lifestyle guilt? I should ask Orion to look it up in that book he was always consulting—the *DSM* whatever it was. Maybe I've got some fashionable rich lady's neurosis.

Independent of Viveca, I'm financially comfortable now—more than comfortable, actually, because of what collectors pay for my work. Well, independent of Viveca and independent *because of* her, too. My art is sold exclusively at her gallery, and I'm the featured artist on viveca.com. But I remember what it's like to live a nickel-and-dime life. To count on waitressing tips—a couple of pounds of change per shift, plus dollar bills and the occasional five or ten. I doubt Hector would be putting on that gray doorman's uniform and standing in the lobby every Saturday and Sunday if he didn't need the extra income. Still, he's always so good-natured. Hector may be the most noncynical New Yorker I've met in the four years I've lived here. . . . Unless it's an act. Maybe that big, warm smile of his hides his resentment. "The service people aren't your friends," Viveca warned me once, shortly after I moved in here. "Nor do they want to be. Be respectful of that."

One time? This was shortly after I began staying at Viveca's but before we started sleeping together. A customer at viveca c—an investment banker—had just bought one of my pieces for thirty thousand dollars, and I was feeling so flush and free that I opened a window and tossed out a hundred-dollar bill. I watched it flutter end over end toward the street below, then looked away before it landed. I didn't want to see anyone scrambling after it, or worse, two people fighting over it. I just wanted to imagine someone with a hard life happening by and getting a nice surprise. Picking it up and being on their way, a little less burdened because of that unexpected hundred-dollar bill.

I sit down at the table, unpeel a banana, and eat it while I work on the Sudoku puzzle I ripped out of yesterday's paper. The Esclusivo Magnifica plays its little snatch of classical music, signaling that the coffee's ready. I get up, grab a mug, pour, sip. Back in Connecticut, when Orion and I were first married, I'd reuse tea bags to economize. At the grocery store, I would buy whatever coffee was on sale that week: the store brand or Yuban or Chock full o'Nuts. *Chock full o'Nuts is that heavenly coffee. Better coffee a millionaire's money can't buy.* Ha! Guess again. This coffee from our high-priced machine is bracing and delicious. So shut up and enjoy it, Annie. You can't have it both ways—live like this and resent it at the same time. Stop being such a goddamned hypocrite.

I give up on the Sudoku puzzle; this one's too hard and I'm not that good at them in the first place. In fact, I stink. Numbers, logic: that's never been my strong suit. On TV, Mario Cuomo's son—the cute one, not the politician—is reading the news. I'm getting a yogurt out of the fridge when I hear him say something about Cape Cod. I look up. They're showing footage of great white sharks cruising the water. Has Orion heard about this? He loves swimming in the ocean. I'd better call him. Mario's son says that the Cape's merchants and innkeepers are worried that this last hurrah of the tourist season will take a major hit during what's already been an off year because of the bad economy.

You've reached the voice mail of Dr. Orion Oh. . . .

I don't get it. Why hasn't he changed his greeting yet? Orion left his practice at the university over a month ago, opting for early retirement—something I still don't understand. Why would a workaholic do that so abruptly? And why, all of a sudden, does he want to sell the house after he was so adamant during the divorce negotiations about *not* selling it? About staying put whether I'd left or not.

If this is an emergency, please call . . .

I was shocked when Orion took Viveca up on her offer to use her beach house for his Cape Cod getaway. He'd refused at first, but then he changed his mind. Why? Whatever's going on with him, I don't think he's shared it with the kids. I talked to all three of them this week, and none of them voiced any worry about their father. Has he met someone? No, that can't be it. If he had, Marissa would have wormed it out of him and called me. Andrew and Ariane can keep a secret but not their little sister.

There's a long, long beep, which means he hasn't been picking up his messages. "Hey, there. It's me," I say. "Have you left for the Cape yet? I just wanted to tell you, in case you haven't heard, that they've been spotting sharks up there. Be careful, okay? I hope you're well. Call me."

Marissa's probably right. I *should* learn how to text-message. "Daddy hardly ever answers the phone, Mom. But whenever I text him, he texts me right back," she told me yesterday. Well, good for her, but I'd prefer to *talk* to her father—to hear it in his voice that he's doing okay. Or not. When you've been married to someone for as long as Orion and I were, you can hear in a conversation if something's wrong—not so much in what's said as the *way* it's said. The inflections, the hesitations . . .

Is it the wedding? The fact that it will be in Three Rivers? Is that what's bothering him? I didn't want to *not* invite Orion. It's doubtful that Andrew's coming, but both of our girls will be there, and I know he'd like to see them. And Donald and Mimsy are driving up from Pennsylvania; Orion's always liked my brother and his wife and he hasn't seen them in ages. Still, I don't want him to feel that he *has* to attend. Yesterday, Viveca's assistant e-mailed me the list of who's coming and who's declined and apparently Orion hasn't sent in his response card yet. . . . I was delighted, though, to see Mr. Agnello's name on the list. I want to introduce Viveca to the man who validated my artistic efforts all those years ago when I was struggling against self-doubt, wondering if I should stop kidding myself and just give up. Mr. Agnello must be in his nineties by now. He and I have exchanged Christmas cards for twenty-something years, and when I didn't get a card back from him this past Christmas, I was worried that he might have ...

Is it because I'm marrying a woman? Is that why Orion hasn't responded? He's never been homophobic, but maybe this strikes too close to home. Bruises his male ego. That time when we met with the lawyers to negotiate the terms of the divorce, he'd already been drinking. I could smell it. And it wasn't exactly the cocktail hour; it was 11:00 A.M. I'd wanted to say something to him about it after we left, but I didn't. I was still trying to figure out what the new rules were about such things, now that we were almost divorced. The other day, I tried imagining what it would be like if the shoe was on the other foot—if *he* had left *me* for a man. It was a ridiculous exercise: picturing two hairy-chested men in bed with each other, one of them Orion. LOL, as Marissa would put it. LMFAO.

The truth, whether Orion believes it or not, is that I *hadn't* left him for Viveca. I'd left him for New York—for the opportunities it offered me, creatively and commercially. What developed between Viveca and me had been unplanned, unpremeditated. . . .

My "defection," Orion had called it on that awful Sunday back in Connecticut when I finally admitted that Viveca and I had become involved, that I'd fallen in love with her. I was "a Judas," he said. I could get my own goddamned ride back to the train station, because he sure as hell wasn't taking me there. He was through with being "a fucking sap." I'd had to hire a cab to New Haven, and on the train ride back to the city, I'd kept replaying our argument. If I was Judas, then that made him Jesus Christ, right? Well, maybe he should come down from his cross and take some of the responsibility for the fact that our marriage had failed. Which of us had practically raised Andrew and the girls single-handedly all those years when he'd leave for work early and come home late? Sit in his office all day and into the evening, counseling college kids about their problems? What about *my* problems? What about the fact that I felt frustrated and neglected all those years while he was playing savior to those troubled students of his and then coming home and feeling sorry for himself because of the toll they took? Drinking his beers and falling asleep by nine when I still had laundry to fold and put away, and three school lunches to make for the next morning, before I could go down to my gloomy little studio and grab a measly hour or two for *my* work.

Thank god the bitterness has subsided on both our parts. We have our kids to thank for that and our mutual investment in their lives, our shared worries about their unhappiness and their safety: Ariane's failed romances, our worries about where Andrew's military career might take him, where Marissa's impetuousness might take her. Our concern for our kids' well-being binds us despite our divorce. Will always bind us. And he's come around, made an effort with Viveca despite the fact that I can tell he doesn't like her. . . . Whether Viveca understands it or not, I still care about Orion, which is why I'm worried about him. Why, maybe, I *shouldn't* have put his name on the guest list—made the decision myself instead of listening to Marissa's "Daddy's an adult, Mom. He can decide if he wants to go or not." The last thing I want to do is make him feel he has to come if it will be too weird or too painful for him. . . .

I don't know. Marriage, parenting, divorce: it's a complicated equation, but there's no sense in pretending that we don't still have feelings for each other, no matter who failed who. Or is it "whom"? Fifty-two years old and I still don't know the difference. What mistake had I made that time when Marissa, in the middle of her bratty teenage phase, called me on my bad grammar? "Her and I": that was it. Ariane and I were making supper, and Marissa was leaning against the counter, trying as hard as she could to annoy me. And *I* was doing everything I could to show her that she couldn't get my goat. But when I happened to mention that I'd run into Ruth Stanley at the post office, and that "her and I" hadn't seen each other in ages, Marissa felt obliged to let me know how stupid I was. "It's *she* and I, Mother." Whenever she was mad at me back then—which was most of the time—I was "Mother" instead of "Mom" or "Mama." She went on to inform me that the way I murdered the English language embarrassed her in front of her friends, and so when they came over, would I please do her a favor and not speak to them? Well, *that* hit a nerve. I burst into tears, furious with myself for letting her see me cry. But then Ari had jumped to my defense. Had turned to her little sister and demanded that Marissa apologize to me. She did it, too. Ariane's easygoing for the most part, but she can be fierce in the face of injustice. I've often thought she would have made a good lawyer. In the wake of Marissa's remark, I'd gone out and bought one of those *Dummies* books on grammar. I studied it, spoke self-consciously for a while. I'm pretty sure it's *no matter who failed whom*, now that I think about it, although I don't remember why. . . .

Orion and Viveca have that much in common, at least: their intelligence and good educations, the way they know how to say things correctly without having to think about it. Viveca's fluent in three languages, and he used to do the *Times* crossword puzzles in pen. Complete them most Sundays. Odd how they both got mixed up with me, the girl with three years of high school and a G.E.D. It's funny. In all the years Orion and I were together, I can't remember him ever correcting me. And the only reference Viveca's ever made was that time, shortly after I started living here, when she kissed me on the forehead and called me her "Eliza Dolittle." *Do little*: I'd assumed she was implying that I didn't help enough around the apartment. But later that same day when she came in and I was running the vacuum, she pulled the plug and reminded me that that was Minnie's job. It wasn't until weeks later, when they were showing *My Fair Lady* on the old movie channel, that I finally got it: in Viveca's mind, I was unschooled Audrey Hepburn to her upper-class Rex Harrison. It was what that marriage counselor Orion and I went to that time called "ouch moments": when your spouse said something that felt hurtful. You were supposed to speak up immediately, let them know. I never called Viveca on what she'd said, though. It was weeks after the fact, and she probably wouldn't have even remembered making the comment. And anyway, Viveca's never corrected my grammar, either. She probably just cringes in silence whenever I make a mistake. Maybe that was what Orion did all those years, too. . . . That day when Ariane jumped to my defense after Marissa embarrassed me, I invited my A+ daughter to let me know whenever I said something wrong. I knew she'd be gentle about it. Clue me in privately. But Ariane never took me up on it. She was not only the best student of my three, but the kindest, too—more compassionate than either her twin brother or her little sister. She has her father's temperament, his need to help others. Which is probably *why* she's a soup kitchen manager, not a lawyer. She and her father have always been close. Ariane is Daddy's girl. When I told her that morning that we were getting a divorce, she was immediately defensive on Orion's behalf, and that was before I told her the reason *why* I was divorcing him. My god, when I *did* tell her, she was furious with me. But she came around, started speaking to me again soon enough. My mother is leaving my father because she's in love with a woman, she must have decided. It is what it is. . . .

When I called Ari yesterday to let her know I wanted to pay for her flight in from California for the wedding, she said, "No, no, Mama. You don't have to do that." But I want to. I appreciate her making the effort. San Francisco to Boston: how much would that cost? Four hundred dollars? Five hundred? She can't afford that. Not on whatever she makes managing that food bank out there. Her annual income is probably less than what Marissa makes on the residuals from that insurance commercial she's in. That thing runs so often: Marissa as a newlywed shopping with her "husband" for insurance from that blissed-out saleswoman with the headband and the big hair. How much must *that* actress make? She's on TV all the time, on the radio, in pop-up ads on the Internet. She always acts so hyped-up about the insurance she's selling, it's as if she's taken amphetamines or something. I'm just going to write Ariane a check and send it to her, no matter how much she protests.

I offered to pay for Andrew's and his fiancée's flights up from Texas, too, but he says he doubts they'll come. Can't spare the time. It bothered me that he said it with such disdain. I told him I was looking forward to meeting his bride-to-be but that I understood, of course. Still, I got the message: he doesn't approve of my marrying Viveca. I'm just not sure if he's resentful on behalf of his father, his gender, or his newfound religious conservatism.

Of my three kids, Andrew was the least likely, I would have figured, to embrace evangelical Christianity. On the contrary, he was always the one most likely to break the rules if not the Commandments—the only one of the three his father and I ever had to sit in court with. The marijuana arrest, the shoplifting arrest, the time he and his high school pals got drunk and spray-painted those school buses. And then, at the beginning of his senior year, those hijacked planes hit the Twin Towers, and it changed him. I can still see him, glued to the TV on that awful day, tears running down his face. When he started in about how he wanted to be part of America's response, it had frightened me.

I begged Andrew not to go into the military. Said all the wrong things. Argued that all those stupid *Rambo* movies he had grown up watching were all just macho Hollywood bullshit. But Orion was wonderful. He calmed me down, reminded me that the last thing we should do was make our son defensive. He was eighteen, after all; he didn't need our permission to enlist. Then Orion had gone online. Had gone downtown and talked to that recruiter. Armed with the information he had gathered, he had approached Andrew with that measured, logical way of his. Explained to him that if he went to college, got his degree, and *still* wanted to serve, he could enter as a second lieutenant and be eligible for Officer Candidate School. And so Andrew had gone off to school instead of off to war. . . . It was that goddamned organic chemistry class he was taking junior year in college that had wrecked everything. Filled him with self-doubt every time he flunked a quiz. That, and the fact that the girl he'd been dating since his freshman year had broken up with him. He hadn't even told us he'd withdrawn from school and enlisted until two weeks before he was due to report for basic training. . . .

Now he's found his Lord and Savior Jesus Christ. And my guess is that the god he's pledged himself to frowns upon gay marriage. When Ariane sent me the link to the newspaper article about Andrew's engagement, it became obvious, more or less. *Mr. and Mrs. Branch Commerford of Waco are pleased to announce the engagement of their daughter, Casey-Lee, to Mr. Andrew Oh, son of Dr. and Mrs. Orion Oh of Three Rivers, Connecticut.* Orion's and my divorce was finalized almost a year ago, and I haven't lived in Three Rivers for the last four. Either Andrew is in denial or he's lying to his in-laws and his bride-to-be. She's a pretty little thing, a petite blonde. Casey-Lee: it's a beauty contestant name. Somewhere along the way, I read or heard that Texas has had more Miss Americas than any other state. And those parents' names—Branch and Erlene. Erlene: I'd bet any amount of money that she's got big hair. There's a brother that Marissa says everyone calls Little Branch. Big Branch and Little Branch: good god. Well, if Andrew needs to hide the fact that I'm marrying Viveca, I guess I can be discreet about it. But when *they* get married, I'm not about to fly down there and pretend that his father and I are still Mr. and Mrs. If I'm even invited to the wedding, that is. Maybe I'll be expected to stay away, stay under wraps. What was that book they had us read in high school—the one where the crazy wife was locked upstairs in the attic? . . .

It's ironic, really, that my son now seems to have an aversion to lesbians. He sure was curious about them when he was in high school. I remember that time when, after I'd told him a hundred times to go upstairs and clean his pigsty of a bedroom and heard "I will, Mom. . . . I'm gonna" that I finally gave up. Decided to go up there and do the job myself. And I did—with a vengeance. Filled up three big garbage bags with crap that I was going to throw out, whether he liked it or not. I was a woman on a mission. And when I went to flip his mattress, I discovered his stash of dirty magazines and all those gym socks that never seemed to make it into the hamper, most of them stiff with I-knew-what. . . . I didn't much mind the *Playboys* and *Penthouses*. Half the teenage boys in America had those hidden away, I figured. But one of his socks was stuck to the cover of a magazine called *Girl on Girl*. I'd stood there, flipping through it—looking at all those hideous pictures of women having sex with cucumbers and other women wearing strap-on dildos. *Fake* sex, it was obvious to me, although it probably wasn't to Andrew. They all had freakishly big breasts, and one of them, I remember, had areolas as big as the rubber jar opener down in our kitchen drawer. They all looked drugged. In the photo that infuriated me the most, two women were wearing nothing but cowboy hats and holsters cinched around their hips, and one was inserting the barrel of a gun into the other's vagina. I flipped when I saw that one! Marched downstairs and out to the garage where Andrew was fiddling with the gears of his ten-speed. "Where did *this* come from?" I demanded, and when he saw what I was holding in my hand, even his ears turned red. He told me a kid in his homeroom had shoved it in his backpack without him knowing it. "Baloney!" I said. "You listen to me, young man. And look me in the eye, too." I waited until he did. "Whoever took these pictures, and whoever publishes this garbage, is committing violence against women. You got that? And whoever's looking at it is guilty, too. You have two sisters, Andrew. This junk is an assault on them and me and every other woman, including the ones in this picture." He mumbled something that I didn't catch. "What? I didn't hear you. What did you say?"

"I said they posed for them, didn't they?"

"Yes, they did. Probably in exchange for drugs. Or because they'd get beaten up by their pimps if they didn't. This is violent male fantasy, Andrew. Do you think women want to have guns stuck up inside of them?"

"Okay," he said. "You made your point."

But I was just getting started. I waved the two "cowgirls" in his face. "Do you think women really have breasts this size?"

He shrugged. "Some," he said.

"Ha! Guess again. These poor girls have had their breasts sliced open and sacks of silicone put in so that men—and *boys*—can drool over them. Do you know what happens when that stuff starts leaking inside a woman's body? I'm ashamed of you, Andrew. And if you ever bring this kind of garbage into my house again—"

"*Your* house? I thought it was *our* house."

I rolled up his dirty magazine and whacked him across the face with it. "Don't you dare smart-mouth me, Andrew Oh! What do you think your father's going to say when I show him this 'reading material' of yours?"

The shrug again. "He's probably not going to go mental about it like you're doing." The next thing I knew, the wrench he'd been using on his bike was in my hand. I took a swing at him and missed. He froze for a second or two, shocked. Then he shielded his head with his arm. "Jesus, Mom, *stop*! You're my *mother*, for cripe's sake!"

I dropped the wrench. Watched him run down the driveway and out into the road. "And from now on, put your dirty socks in the hamper!" I screamed. "And don't stick anything inside them except your big, smelly feet!" That was when I realized old Mr. Genovese across the street was standing in his doorway, watching. Fired up still, I shouted over to him. "Mind your own business! Shut your goddamned door!" Lucky for him, he did what he was told.

Fueled, still, by self-righteous anger, I pounded back up to Andrew's room, lugged those three garbage bags to the landing and flung them down the stairwell. Dragged them out to the car, drove to the dump, and took enormous pleasure in heaving them onto a mountain of trash. By the time I got back home, I had cooled down. I decided not to tell Orion about *Girl on Girl* after all, and I was grateful that Andrew didn't tell his father that I'd swung at him with the wrench—something I now felt ashamed of having done. But I have to admit that, in the aftermath of my having cleaned out his room, I enjoyed it whenever he asked me about his stuff.

"Is my Alonzo Mourning jersey still in the wash, Mom?"

"Nope. It's at the dump."

"Mom, do you know where that blue notebook is where I'm recording my weight-lifting routine?"

"I guess it's probably sitting over in the landfill."

"Mom, Mrs. Kilgallen's ragging me because I haven't handed in my copy of *Heart of Darkness*. You didn't toss *that* out, did you?"

"If it was on your bedroom floor, I did."

"Mom, that was *school property*. What am I supposed to tell Kilgallen?" I advised him to tell her he'd go to the bookstore and buy her a replacement copy. "Can I have the money for it then?"

"Not from me you can't. Use your own goddamned money."

Poor Andrew. I *was* always harder on him than I was on his sisters.

Maybe his being "too busy" to fly up here for the wedding is payback. Maybe I'm getting exactly what I deserve....

Unlike her brother, Marissa, our free spirit, is all for Viveca's and my upcoming wedding. Her mother marrying a woman: she thinks it's hip. And I'm a little concerned about the attention Viveca's been giving her. They chat on the phone. They've gone out a couple of times, just the two of them. It's not that I'm ungrateful that Viveca's made an effort with my daughter. I appreciate that she has. But both times when they got back from those lunch dates, Marissa was carrying boxes and bags from Bergdorf's. Viveca's bought her that Jimmy Choo handbag she loves, the Prada platform pumps that I'd break my neck if I ever tried wearing. Designer things that an aspiring actress and part-time waitress could never afford. As good a kid as she is, Marissa's always been a little too status conscious, and it's almost as if Viveca is trying to buy her affection. And apparently it's working. What was that thing Marissa said last week when the three of us were at the Barnes & Noble in Union Square? When she pointed out that children's book? "Look. Heather has two mommies just like me." It made me feel defensive on Orion's behalf. She's *his* daughter, not Viveca's....

What's wrong with me today? Why am I worrying about all these things that probably don't even matter? I walk around the apartment, wandering aimlessly from room to room. Passing the guest bathroom, I look in at Minnie. She's down on the floor, wearing her knee pads, scouring the grout between the floor tiles. Viveca's a stickler about clean grout; she has Minnie use some bleaching agent to get it white. I walk past my poster, ANNIE OH: A SHOCK TO THE SYSTEM! *February 1–March 31 at viveca c gallery.* She went all out for that show: ads in the *Times*, the *New Yorker*, and *New York*. Hired that publicist who got me those TV interviews that I was such a nervous wreck about.... Back in the kitchen, I grab the remote and change the channel. On the *Today* show, that Dr. Nancy lady is cautioning Ann Curry about some new medical thing we all have to worry about. I channel-surf past Cookie Monster, cartoons, cake decorating. On CNBC, they're talking about the global economy—the looming debt crisis in Greece that the Germans may or may not rescue them from. Viveca's mentioned the possibility of Greece defaulting, too, and how, for some reason I didn't understand, it could be good for her business if the euro is devalued. It's funny: she identifies so strongly with her Greek heritage. You would think she'd be more concerned about the country's balance sheet than her own. . . . The old movie channel's showing *Mildred Pierce*. There's Joan Crawford with her shoulder pads and severe eyebrows, talking to her maid, who I recognize. *Whom* I recognize? It's that little actress from *Gone With the Wind*—the slave with the squeaky voice who didn't "know nothin' bout birthing babies." Slaves, maids: it wasn't as if the studios were going to hire that actress to play anything else. At least Viveca doesn't expect Minnie to show up at the apartment in one of those old-fashioned uniforms with the little hat and frilly apron. Minnie wears the same clothes most days: her beige Sean John sweat suit and her plaid canvas sneakers. Marissa tells me that Sean John is that rap guy, Diddy or P. Diddy or whatever he calls himself. One time when she was here, she complimented Minnie on her taste. Told her she liked Sean John clothes, too. And Minnie had smiled her toothless smile and told her she picked it up "for cheap" at a street fair in Newark. . . . On the Christian channel, the pompadoured host is chatting about Jesus's love with a plump old lady in a pastel party dress and bright red lipstick. I suddenly realize it's Dale Evans. She died, didn't she? This must be a rerun. My foster mother, the first one, used to send me to school every day with an American cheese and mustard sandwich and an apple inside a rusty Roy Rogers and Dale Evans lunch box. (No Thermos like the other kids; I had to drink from the fountain.) Roy and Dale were passé by then, and I was jealous of the cool lunch boxes some of the other girls in my class carried: *Dr. Kildare*, *The Beverly Hillbillies*, and then that *crème de la crème* of lunch boxes, *Meet the Beatles*. . . .

Carrying Viveca's package down the hall to our bedroom, I glance in again at Minnie. She's seated on the edge of our soaking tub, taking a break from her grout cleaning. She's got her knee pads on, her legs spread so far apart that she could be giving birth. I wave; she waves back. When I enter the bedroom, they startle me again: those dresses. The brides.

All three of the Vera Wangs are beautiful, but none is me. What *is* me is the dress I'd already bought off the rack at that vintage dress shop I like in Tribeca: a basket-weave shift, bright yellow with bold diagonal turquoise stripes—two hundred dollars marked down to $129.99. I like those funky stripes, its above-the-knee length. The label says Mary Quant. I looked her up. Wikipedia says she was a mod British designer, popular during the 1960s. Cool, I thought, but when I tried it on and showed it to Viveca, she said, "Sweetheart, it's cute and it looks adorable on you, but to me it says sundress, not wedding dress. It's . . . youthful. On our special day, I'd love to see you in something a little more elegant and celebratory. Just think of all the lesbians over the years who *couldn't* be brides. We're honoring them, too. In another era, we would have had to pass as spinsters who couldn't find men to marry them." She'd laughed when she said "spinsters," it's so far out of the realm of who she is, who she thinks we are.

Lesbians: that's what I am now. Right? I'm marrying a woman, aren't I? And I've slept with another woman—Priscilla, the wiry tomboy I used to waitress with at Friendly's. But I don't see our marrying as something that necessarily balances the scales of justice or honors the dykes of yesteryear. . . . . *Spinsters who couldn't find men to marry them*: why had she said that? We've both been married to men. Viveca says I should pack the dress and bring it along on our wedding trip—that I can wear it when we shop or go out for lunch. She's also suggested I go with her the next time she gets a bikini wax. "There's more nudity than not on the beaches in Mykonos and hairless pussies are de rigueur," she said. Viveca gets a massage and a wax every other week. Her pubic patch is a fashionably thin vertical line that stops just above her labia. I might go topless at those beaches when we're over there, but I am *not* going bottomless. And anyway, I don't even like the beach that much. It's different for Viveca. She's Greek. Her given name is Vasiliki, not Viveca. She's anglicized the name for commercial reasons. She tans so effortlessly. But with my red hair and Irish complexion, I have to be careful. I could burn to a crisp.

I look over toward the bureau, and there's that index card I scrawled on yesterday. I pick it up and read what I'd written down. *After Chaos*

arose broad-breasted Gaia, the primordial goddess of the Earth. . . .
Among their children were the Cyclopes, the Hundred-Handed giants.
Monsters, like the monsters that are being birthed in the poster hanging in the hallway, the hundred-handed monster in my life—the shark
who swims in the waters of my memory. Whose voice I both dread
and entertain because it drives my art. . . . I'm hit by a pang of missing
Viveca: the sound of her voice, the warm safety of her body next to
mine. I approach the Gaia dress. Touch it, run the beautiful green silk
between my fingers. *After Chaos arose broad-breasted Gaia.* I sit on our
bed and open the Neiman Marcus box. Unscrew the top of Viveca's
perfume bottle and inhale her scent: orange blossoms, vanilla. I love
her. Miss her the way Diane Sawyer misses Mike Nichols when he's
away and she puts on his shirt. . . .

I read the index card over and over, and as I do, I begin to feel the
agitation, familiar and strange. Gaia . . . Gaia. Am I on the verge of
something? Is it coming?

Maybe not. Maybe my comfortable life here has begun to snuff out
my creativity. Maybe I've peaked and it's all downhill from here.

I shake my head. Shake off my self-doubt. My brain is spinning. My
fingers are flexing, making invisible art. It's exciting and scary when it
comes, like watching an approaching cyclone and standing defiantly
in its path. Maybe before this day is out, the weather inside my brain
will set *me* spinning. Maybe I'll find myself in my studio, facing my
need to scream out. Fight back against the monster. Make art.

Chapter Two

Orion Oh

The sharks and I both arrive at the Cape this first Saturday in September. As I inch over the Sagamore Bridge in this god-awful Labor Day weekend traffic, they're saying great whites are swimming the coastal waters, heading north. According to the car radio, warning signs are being posted along the oceanside beaches from Chatham to North Truro. North Truro? I reach over and turn up the volume, drowning out the annoying cell phone ring tone that's playing inside the glove compartment. *Everybody's movin', everybody's groovin', baby. Love shack, baby love shack, bay-ayy-be-ee.* "What do you want for a ring tone?" Marissa had asked me that day when she was programming my phone. "Anything," I'd said. "You pick." And she picked that awful song I've always hated.

It's not one of the kids calling me; they text me now. Before I left this morning, I deliberated about whether to take the damned cell phone with me or leave it back in Three Rivers. But what if there was an emergency? So I threw it in the glove compartment and locked it. I thought I turned the damn thing off, but I guess not. Ahh, relief. The call has gone to voice mail.

"It's a little unusual to see them in these cooler Massachusetts waters at this time of year," the shark expert tells her interviewer, a guy who, for some reason, is calling himself the Mad Hatter. "But the gray seal population's been on the rise, and we think that's what's probably luring them."

The Mad Hatter chortles. "So you're saying the problem is that there's been too much seal sex? Too many pinnipeds puttin' out?"

"Uh, well . . ."

The Diane Rehm interview I'd been listening to faded away somewhere between Braintree and Buzzards Bay. Conversely, the Mad Hatter is coming through so loudly and clearly that he might as well be broadcasting from the backseat. "Time now for traffic, news, and weather. And when we come back, we'll have more with Dr. Tracy Skelly from the Division of Marine Fisheries."

Despite my initial resistance to the idea, I'm staying rent free at Viveca's place in North Truro for the month, hoping that a Cape Cod retreat might allow me, after a summer's worth of drifting and wound licking, to anchor myself. Figure out how to shed my bitterness, forgive myself and others and start over. Orchestrate a reinvention, I guess you'd say. Thirty days has September: it's a tall order.

My game plan, once I survive this hideous holiday traffic and get settled in, is to eat healthy, cool it on the drinking, exercise. I'll jog and journal every morning, then bike to the beach for an afternoon swim. After dinner, I'll read and research—Google phrases like "new professions after 50," "change career paths." But with sharks in the water, it doesn't sound like I'll be doing a whole lot of swimming. Of course, there's always the placid bayside, but what I want is turbulence—bodysurfing along the crest of the five- or six-foot swells and getting roughed up a little by the waves I misjudge—the ones that, instead of carrying me, crack against me. I've been hoping the wildness of the water might somehow both cleanse me of my failings as a university psychologist and baptize me as . . . what?

What do you want to be when you grow up? The adults were always asking me that when I was a kid, and because I liked to draw—reproduce the images in comic books and *Mad* magazine—I'd say I wanted to be an artist. I'd enjoyed my high school art classes, had gotten good grades for my work. And so I'd entered college with a vague plan to major in art. In my first semester, my Intro to Drawing professor, Dr. Duers, had said during my portfolio review that I had a good sense of composition and a talent worth developing. But the following semester, I'd run up against Professor Edwards, an edgy New York sculptor who was disdainful of having to teach studio art to suburban college kids—who had come out and *told* us he was only driving up from the city twice a week because of the paycheck. It had crushed me the morning he'd stood over my shoulder, snickered at the still life I was drawing, and walked away without a word. But that same semester, I got an A in an Intro to Psych course I really liked. And so I had put away my sketch pad and gone on to the 200-level psychology classes. And then the summer between my sophomore and junior years, I got a job as a second-shift orderly at the state hospital.

I liked working there. Liked shooting the shit with the patients. Not the ones who were really out of it, but the ones who were in there for shorter-term stays. The "walking wounded," as the nurses called them. Some of those patients would be admitted in pretty rough shape—straitjacketed and sputtering nonsense, or in such deep depressions that they were almost catatonic. But two or three weeks later, with their equilibrium restored by meds and talk therapy, they'd be discharged back into the world.

The psychiatrists were off-putting. Tooled around the wards like they walked on water. But the psychologists were different. More humane, less in a hurry. "You're good with the patients," one of them, Dr. Dow, told me one day. "I've noticed." For him, it was nothing more than a casual observation, but for me—a kid who, up to that point, had never gotten noticed for much of anything—it was huge. On my day off, I drove up to the Placement Office at school and took one of those tests that identifies your strengths, suggests what career paths you should consider. When I got my results back, it said I had scored high on empathy and should consider the helping professions: social work, psychology. And so, at the beginning of my fifth semester, I declared psychology as my major.

I kept my job at the hospital. Worked there on weekends. They assigned me to the adolescent unit mostly: boys who had lit fires or tortured the family pet; girls who had attempted suicide or were taking the slow route via eating disorders. And then one night—Christmas Eve it was; I was covering for another orderly who wanted to be with his family—I met a new arrival who'd been admitted because of a holiday meltdown.

Siobhan was a pretty seventeen-year-old with auburn hair and pale skin. She'd been a competitive Irish step-dancer until a torn ACL had brought all that to a halt. She was type A all the way, and a big reader. *Jane Eyre, Wuthering Heights, Tess of the d'Urbervilles*: the kinds of books that, back in high school, it had been torture for me to get through. Siobhan told me, straight-faced, that she was misplaced in time—that she should have been born in an earlier, more romantic era. Fashioned herself as a tragic heroine, I guess. We weren't friends, exactly—that was against hospital policy—but we were friendly. I liked her sarcastic sense of humor and she liked mine. And believe me, humor was in short supply at that place. She nicknamed me Heathcliff—because of my "dark, swarthy looks," she said. My "big, soulful brown eyes." One time, she asked me what kind of a name "Oh" was, and when I told her, she wanted to know why I didn't look Chinese. "Because I'm Italian, too," I told her.

She reached out and touched my face when I said that. Studied it so intently that I had to look away. I was, at the time, an insecure, blend-in-with-the-woodwork twenty-year-old, not used to such focused attention. "Now I can see it," she finally said.

"It?"

"The Orient. It's in your eyes. It makes you uniquely handsome, but I suspect you already know that." Handsome? Me? I laughed. After that exchange, she stopped calling me Heathcliff. Now I was Marco Polo.

Sometimes, if things were slow on the ward after I had cleared away the dinner trays, I'd play Scrabble or Monopoly with her and some of the other patients. More often than not, Siobhan would win, and after a while I figured out how. She'd cheat. I didn't call her on it. Didn't really give a shit who won. But she knew that I knew. "Better watch out for that one," one of the old guard nurses warned me. "She's got a crush on a certain someone."

At the nurses' station one night, Siobhan's chart was out on the counter and I took a peek. It read: "Manic-depressive disorder. Psychomotor agitation during manic phase that manifests itself as oral fixation." The latter wasn't surprising. For one thing, Siobhan smoked like a chimney. And when she was out of cigarettes and couldn't bum them, she would put other things in her mouth and chew on them: hard candies, pens and pencils, the cuffs of her shirts. The covers of her paperbacks were crisscrossed with teeth marks.

One February night I was doing bed checks, and when I went into her room, no Siobhan. I walked down to the rec room to see if she was there and found her running in circles, gagging, blue in the face. We'd been trained to give the Heimlich, so I got behind her, put my fists under her diaphragm, and yanked. Out popped the plastic Checker she'd been sucking on. It had gotten lodged in her windpipe. As soon as it came out, she started crying, taking gulps of air, clawing me and hugging me so hard that, for a few seconds, it was like I'd just saved her from drowning. When she tried to kiss me, I pushed her away. After that, she started referring to me as her "knight in shining armor."

"Don't be so melodramatic," I'd say. "I was just doing my job." But secretly I was pleased. And when, at the next staff meeting, Dr. Dow presented me with a certificate of gratitude, I went down to Barker's discount store, bought a frame, and hung it on my wall.

After Siobhan was released, she started contacting me. I hadn't given her the name and number of my dorm, but she had gotten it somehow. "Hey, Orion! Phone call!" some guy would shout from down the hall, and I would walk toward the phone, hoping it wasn't her. She kept asking me to meet her for coffee. Begging me. The one time I agreed—met her at the Dunkin' Donuts just off campus—I was nervous as hell. This was the kind of thing I could lose my job over if anyone from the hospital saw us together. That didn't happen, but something else did. She was acting manic for the hour or so we sat and talked. Chewing on her coffee cup, talking a blue streak, lighting one cigarette after another. After my second cup of coffee, I told her I had a test to study for and got up to leave. That's when, out of the blue, she asked me if I was still a virgin. It wasn't until later that I thought of what I *should have* said: that her question was inappropriate, out of bounds. But what I *did* say was, "Me? Pfft. Not hardly." It was a bluff. The sum total of my sexual experience up to that point had been a drunken encounter with a so-so looking girl I'd danced and made out with at a dorm mixer and then taken upstairs to my room. Groping

her in the dark, I'd kept trying to figure out how to undo her complicated underwear until she had finally done it herself, put me inside of
her, and said, "Go. *Move*." I was done in under a minute, so technically I was *not* still a virgin. But Mr. Experience I wasn't.

When we were out in the parking lot, standing at our cars, Siobhan
announced that she had made a big decision about us. "About *us*?" I
laughed. She didn't. She had given it a lot of thought, she said. She was
ready to be "deflowered" and wanted her "knight in shining armor" to
be "the one." I stood there, shaking my head and telling her that was
not going to happen. And when she didn't seem to want to take no for
an answer—started getting a little belligerent, in fact—I climbed into
my rusted-out '68 Volkswagen with the bad muffler, started it, and
rumbled the hell away from her. Too bad I hadn't acted as professionally the night Jasmine Negron invited me in and fixed me that drink.
I could have spared myself a whole lot of trouble and shame.

That was the last I ever saw of Siobhan, although for the remainder of my semesters as an undergraduate and well into grad school
and my widening sexual experience, she occasionally starred in my
masturbatory fantasies. But years later, after I had become a licensed
clinical psychologist and landed the counselor's job at the university,
I thought I had run into her again—at the dry cleaner's of all places.

Not long before that, I had extricated myself from my three-year
relationship with Thea and was still licking my wounds from that de-
bacle of codependency. She and I had been living together for two
years at that point. She was midway through her doctoral studies
in Feminist Theory. The beginning of the end had come the night
when, postcoitally—after a go-around that I had assumed we were
both enjoying—she'd informed me that, in a way, Andrea Dworkin
was right. About what? I'd asked. That heterosexual sex was a form
of rape, she'd said, and then had drifted off to sleep while I lay there
listening to her snore. It had taken me three weeks and a couple of
sessions with my shrink before I mustered up the resolve to tell her I
wanted her to move out. "Good riddance and fuck you!" the note she
had left me said. She had placed it on top of the pile of my LPs she'd

taken out of the jackets and snapped in half: Tom Rush, Joni Mitchell's *Blue, Highway 61 Revisited*. . . .

That late afternoon when I hurried into the dry cleaner's with my armful of dirty shirts and thought it was Siobhan stepping up to the counter, I stopped cold. Same red hair and pale complexion, same petite frame. But up close, I could see that I'd been mistaken. "We're closed," she said—with attitude. So I copped an attitude, too. "Really? Because the door isn't locked and your clock up there says three minutes of six."

"Name?" she said, huffily.

"Orion Oh. *Doctor* Orion Oh."

She was unimpressed. "Starch or no starch?"

And that was how I met Annie, my *second* red-haired damsel in distress. When I left the dry cleaner's that day, our hostile little exchange might have been the sum total of our interaction had I not noticed that the only other car out front, a beat-up yellow El Camino, had a front tire that was pancake flat. I waited until the lights went out and she emerged, purposely not looking at me. I pointed. "Shit!" she said. "Shit! Shit! Shit!" She burst into tears.

I offered to change it for her. "Spare in the trunk?" I asked. She said the flat tire *was* the spare. And so I had jacked up the car and driven her and her wheel with the punctured tire over to the Sears at the mall. They said they were behind—couldn't get to it until an hour or so—and so I'd taken her to Bonanza Steakhouse while we waited. You'd have thought that rib eye and Texas toast she got when we went through the line was fine dining. Which, relatively speaking, I guess it was. In the weeks that followed, I found out that she was mostly subsisting on Oodles of Noodles and SpaghettiOs, heated on the hot plate in her tiny rented room. That was the first meal Annie ever "cooked" for me: SpaghettiOs with these tiny little monkey's gonad meatballs. "No, no, it's delicious," I assured her when she apologized, even as I pictured my Nonna and Nonno Valerio rolling around in their graves.

Well, you sure can't call Annie a damsel in distress these days, now that her work sells in the tens of thousands of dollars. That's something I never could have imagined back after the twins were born when she started making her shadow box collages. The last time I talked to Marissa, she told me that one of her mother's pieces, *Angel Wings #17*, had just sold for fifty-five thou to Fergie. "Wow," I said. "Did she pay her in dollars or British pounds?"

"Not *her*," Marissa said. "Fergie from the Black Eyed Peas."

"Oh, right," I said. When I got off the phone, I had to Google this other Fergie to find out who she was. . . .

Well, maybe now I can finally explore *my* creative side for a change. Do I even still *have* a creative side after all these years of tamping it down? Providing a service for others? To be determined, I guess. And though there's probably not much of a demand for a middle-aged ex-psychologist who can probably still reproduce the likenesses of Smokey the Bear and Alfred E. Neuman from muscle memory, there might be other artistic avenues for me to explore. Maybe I could buy myself a nice digital camera and get into photography. Or try my hand at sculpting. My Italian grandfather was a machinist, but he'd done a little sculpting on the side. Miniatures, mostly. I still have the little soapstone dolphin he made for me. To this day, I'll sometimes pick up that smiling figurine and hold it in the palm of my hand. Smile back at it. . . . I like to cook and I'm good at it. My immigrant Chinese grandfather was a hardworking, unsmiling restaurateur in Boston. And Nonna Valerio would sometimes let me help her make the sheet pizzas she used to peddle in the neighborhood. (Speaking of muscle memory, now that the traffic's come to a complete stop, I've just caught myself, hands off the steering wheel, pushing pizza dough to the edges of Nonna's scorched, warped baking sheets.) Maybe I could work up a concept, create a menu that combined Mediterranean and Asian cuisine. Open up a little bistro someplace. Call it . . . Marco Polo. But no, once the concept was figured out and the menu was fixed, running a restaurant would be full-immersion service work. Not unlike being a psychologist in that respect. People walk in the door because they need you to take care of them—to feed them or fix them. *What are you going to be when you grow up, Orion? What are you going to be, Dr. Oh, now that they've booted your ass out the door?*

God, it's been a brutal year. In January, Annie's and my three-year separation ended in divorce. That same month, I learned that I was *not*, after all, going to be named coordinator of Clinical Services. It was a position I'd been ambivalent about at first, but one I'd been assured would be mine if I went after it. That was what Allen Javitz, the dean of student affairs, had said as we stood in line at the bar at some university social function. And after he said that, I *did* want it. Felt not only that I'd earned the appointment after twenty-one years in Psych Services but also that I'd be damn good at it. I'm an empathetic listener, an out-of-the-box problem solver. But when my director, Muriel Clapp, bypassed me in favor of the far more flashy Marwan Chankar, an addictions counselor newly arrived from Syracuse University, Dean Javitz reneged and gave Chankar the nod. When the announcement was made, I felt as if I'd been sucker punched. Still, I shook Marwan's hand and tried my best to be philosophical about it. I reminded myself that *not* having to supervise sixteen clinicians was going to save me a whole lot of meetings, evaluations, and headaches.

I began to look at my endgame. Made appointments with reps from Human Resources and my pension fund. Sat down with my calculator and crunched some numbers. If I stuck it out for another four years, I figured, I'd be able to retire at 80 percent of my salary. At which point, I could sell the house, move into a smaller place, do some traveling. Maybe by then I'd have met someone I wanted to travel *with*. Every time Marissa bugged me about trying one of those matchmaking Web sites, I'd assure her that she'd be the first to know when I was ready to start dating, which I wasn't yet. And that, anyway, I was "old school." I'd much rather meet someone in person than online. But truth be told, I was still holding out hope that Annie would come to her senses. Break it off with her flashy New York girlfriend and come back home. I'd even dreamt it once—had woken up laughing, relieved. Then I'd sat up in our empty bed. Even my dreams were sucker punching me.

"Daddy, do you think some nice woman's going to just ring your doorbell someday and ask you out?" Marissa had said the last time she brought it up. She'd texted me ten minutes earlier with a seven-word message: *call me. wanna talk 2 U dude.* I can't remember when she started calling me "dude" instead of "Daddy," but I got a kick out of it. Started calling her "dude," too. "It's the twenty-first century. This is the way people meet people now, dude. You just need to, like, reboot yourself."

"Really? Am I a Mac or a PC?"

"I'm serious. And if you ask me, it's not that you're not ready. It's that you're scared."

"Hey, I thought *I* was the shrink. What am I scared of?"

She sighed. "I don't know. Being happy?"

I assured her that I was happy enough for the present time.

"Yeah, but the thing is, there are tons of women your age out there. My girlfriend Bree? Her mother was so repressed that, in all the years she was married to Bree's father, she never even undressed in front of him. Then she met this guy on eHarmony, and now she's into all this stuff she *never* would have done before."

"Like what?"

"Kayaking, motorcycling. Last week they went to a nude beach."

"Public skinny-dipping? Good god, Marissa, now I really *am* scared."

She giggled. "And you know what else? Oral sex. Bree's mom told her that letting her boyfriend go down on her was very liberating. And that giving him head made her feel empowered."

"And I bet she'd be thrilled to know that Bree is broadcasting these breakthroughs to the world. Has she tweeted it yet? Put it on You-Tube?"

"Enough with the jokes, Daddy. Mom's moved on. You should, too. And don't tell me you're happy when I know you're not."

"I said I was happy *enough*," I reminded her. "Dude."

But I wasn't. The finality of the divorce, the nonpromotion, both of them happening in the dead of winter when, by 5:00 P.M., it was already dark. I'd drive home, turn on the lights and the TV, open the fridge. The freezer pretty much told the story. I'd stare in at the frozen dinners and pizzas. The frozen top of the cake from Annie's and my twenty-fifth wedding anniversary, the bottles of Grey Goose on the door, chilled and waiting. One microwaved meal and two or three vodkas later, I'd flop onto the recliner in the family room and fall asleep too early. Wake up having to pee a couple of hours later and then be unable to get back to sleep. So I'd read, walk around the house, watch a bunch of bad TV: televised poker games, infomercials for juicers and Time-Life music collections. The latter are always hosted by some unidentified woman and an icon from pop music's yesteryear: Bobby Vinton or Bobby Vee or one of Herman's Hermits. Of course, all of the coolest icons overdosed and died years ago, which is just as well. How depressing would it be to see a gray-haired Jimi Hendrix wearing a cardigan sweater and reminiscing about the soundtrack of the Summer of Love? . . .

Some nights I'd end up staring, in disbelief still, at the empty coat hangers on Annie's side of our bedroom closet, her gardening sneakers on the floor below them. Those sneakers were the one pair of shoes she hadn't taken with her. There's not a whole lot of gardening to be done, I guess, when you've relocated to a Manhattan high-rise. On other nights, I'd wander into the kids' rooms, looking at the things they'd left behind on their shelves and walls after they grew up and moved away: sports trophies and good citizenship plaques, posters of Rage Against the Machine and Green Day, Garciaparra in his Red Sox uniform. On the toughest nights—the sleepless vigils that lasted until daybreak—I'd sometimes take out the family photo albums. Leaf through the old pictures of the kids and Annie and me—the ones of us at Disney World or Rocky Neck, or gathered around the dining-room table for some holiday dinner, someone's birthday party. In one of my favorite photos, the twins, puffy-cheeked, blow out their birthday candles. Their cake has a big number five on the top. Annie's standing to their left, holding baby Marissa. Back then when I took that picture, it wasn't as if I was wildly happy. Jumping out of bed every morning and thinking, oh man, this is the life! But it *had* been the life, I realize now. I was one of Counseling Services' young go-getters. I'd jog or play basketball with some of the grad students at lunchtime, run late-afternoon groups for undergraduates who were wrestling with anger management, stress management. I'd started those groups, in fact. Had won a university award for it. And after work, there'd be my own kids to drive home to: roughhousing and piggyback rides, Chutes and Ladders at the kitchen table. On the nights I got home in time, I'd bathe them and get them ready for bed, read them those same stories they wanted to hear over and over: *Mog the Cat, Clifford the Big Red Dog.* I drank beer back then. A six-pack would last me a week or more. I'd sleep soundly every night and wake up every next morning, reach over and find Annie's shoulder, her hip. Cup the top of her head. . . . Then the kids grew up, Annie left for New York, and her side of the bed got occupied by books and journal articles I meant to read, clothes I'd ironed and laid out for work the night before. That girl Bree's mother was straddling the back of a motorcycle, holding on to her eHarmony boyfriend and roaring through her newly liberated life. I was, on workday mornings, carrying my empty vodka bottles and microwaveable food containers out to the recycling box and then driving off to a job for which I'd lost my fire. All day long, I'd sit across from students, listening sympathetically for the most part, or feigning sympathetic listening when I wasn't feeling it, all the while glancing discreetly at the circular wall clock behind them, floating above all of those troubled heads like a full moon. "Well, that's forty-five minutes. We have to wrap up now."

And then this past March my malaise was replaced by panic when Jasmine Negron, one of my clinical practicum supervisees, walked into Muriel Clapp's office and charged me with sexual harassment. It was one of those Rashomon-like situations. I said/she said.

But you were in her apartment, right?

I was. She was frightened. I gave her a ride home and she asked me in for a drink.

And you accepted.

Not at first. I tried to beg off, but she said would I please come in. The guy she'd broken up with still had the key to her place and wouldn't give it back. A few nights earlier, she'd gotten home and he was there, sitting on her sofa. He wouldn't leave.

How many drinks did you have while you were there, Orion?

Two. And granted, she'd poured them with a heavy hand, but ... two.

I had to look away from her. Talk, instead, to my fidgeting hands in my lap. *I'm not going to sit here and lie to you, Muriel. Look, should I have gone into her apartment? Started drinking with her? No. I admit it was a stupid thing to do. Was I an idiot not to get the hell out of there when she started coming on to me? Hell, yeah.* Look her in the eye, I told myself. Say it right to her face. *But I'm telling you, Muriel*, she *came on to* me, *and if she's claiming otherwise, she's lying.* It was painful sitting there and watching the skepticism on her face.

And then, a week or so later, while Muriel was convening her kangaroo court, there was the second, more painful body blow.

Sounds like you're feeling better about things, Seamus.

Yeah. Much better, Dr. Oh. You said the new medication might take a couple of weeks to kick in, but I think it's already working. The following morning, while the other kids in his dorm were still asleep, the custodian entered the building at the start of his day and found him hanging from a rope in the stairwell. . . .

Don't! I tell myself. Four or five months' worth of self-flagellating postmortems and what good have they done that poor kid *or* his grieving parents? Think about something else. Think about where you go from here. . . .

Maybe I could write a book. I've always had a facility with language and, over the years, I've probably read a hundred or more suspense novels. There's a sameness to those page-turners that ride the best seller lists. I could study a bunch of them, take notes on what they have in common, and follow a formula. How hard could it be? . . .

Jesus, this stop-and-go traffic is driving me nuts. All summer long, the TV's been talking about how everyone in the country is cutting back because of the economy—taking "*stay*cations." But I guess my fellow travelers along Route 6 never got the memo. . . . Are the Sox playing today? Maybe there's a game on. I poke the radio buttons and get, instead of baseball, classical music, Obama bashing, some woman singing *If you liked it, then you should have put a ring on it, If you liked it, then you shoulda put a ring on it.* At the far end of the dial, some distraught-sounding guy is talking to a radio shrink about his son. "I love him so much, but he's done this terrible thing and—"

"And what thing was that?"

"He ... molested my granddaughter. His niece. Went to prison for it. And he's suffering in there. The other inmates, and some of the guards, have made him a target, okay? Made his life in there a living hell."

"And what about his victim? He's given her a life in hell, too. Hasn't he? Your son had a choice about whether or not to rob her of her innocence. But she didn't. Did this happen once? More than once?"

"It went on over a couple of years. Until he got caught."

"And how old is his victim?"

"My granddaughter? She's eleven. It started when she was eight. But anyway, I write to him, okay? Try to be supportive. But whenever I start one of those letters, I think about what he did and it fills me with rage."

"Well, that's an appropriate response. But why in the world would you write him sympathetic letters?"

"Because he's my son. I love him in spite of—"

"And that's an *in*appropriate response. Personally, I think convicted pedophiles should get the death penalty. If my son did what your son did, he'd be dead to me."

Jesus, the poor guy's stuck between a rock and a hard place. Show him a little compassion, will you?

"Yeah, but the thing is—"

"The *thing*, sir, is that your son did something so vile, so *despicable*, that it's unforgivable. You should be focusing your energies on helping your granddaughter, not your piece-of-crap son. Stop being a weenie. He's *earned* what he's getting in there."

Well, there's a counseling style for you: bludgeon the patient. I reach over and change the station. But what she's just told that guy— that he should reject his son—ricochets inside my head and transports me back to that drab, joyless room on the third floor of the Good Samaritan Hospital in Lebanon, Pennsylvania, where my mother lay dying. Where, three or four days before she passed, she and I finally touched on the untouchable subject of Francis Oh, the father who had

denied my existence. When I was a kid, from time to time I had asked
Mom about him, but she'd told me almost nothing. Had gotten huffy
whenever I inquired. How could she tell me what she didn't know?
she'd say. And so, by the time I was in my early teens, I had grown to
hate the mysterious Francis Oh. Had decided he wasn't the only one
who could play the rejection game. "Fuck *you*," I'd tell him, standing
in front of the bathroom mirror—borrowing my own face because
I had no idea what his looked like. It was around that time that my
friend Brian and I went to the movies to see that movie *The Man-
churian Candidate*. I had sat there squirming, I remember. Imagining that every one of those Chinese brainwashers in Frank Sinatra's
flashbacks was Francis Oh. It had freaked me out to the point that I
got up, ran up the aisle and out to the men's room, and puked up my
popcorn and soda. By the time I went back in, I had missed a good
fifteen or twenty minutes of the movie. "You okay?" Brian whispered.
"Yeah, why wouldn't I be?" I had snapped back. A few days later, I hit
upon the idea of being rid of my Chinese surname. I would take my
mother's and my grandparents' name instead—become Orion Valerio
instead of Orion Oh. Rather than telling my mother, I walked down
to city hall one day after school and asked in some office about how
to do it. But the process was complicated and costly, and I gave up on
the idea. Instead, whenever anyone asked about him, I'd say my father
died. Had gotten killed in a car accident when my mother was pregnant. I liked telling people that. Killing off the father who wanted no
part of me. After a while, I almost came to believe my own lie.

But decades later, after I had become a father myself and was facing
the fact that my mother's life was slipping away, I broached the subject
with her again. And this time, she was more forthcoming than she'd
ever been. . . .

*She looks terrible. Her hair's matted against the pillow and she's not
wearing her false teeth. But she's having one of her better days. They ex-
tracted a liter of fluid from her cancerous lung this morning, and she's
breathing easier. "He was a regular at the movie house where I worked
as an usherette my senior year in high school," she says. "A college student
studying mathematics—a lonely young man who always came to the*

show by himself. He liked gangster movies and started teasing me about the love stories I told him I preferred. Kidding me about how 'sappy' they were. And then one day, out of the blue, he brought me a bouquet of daisies." He was something of a mystery, she says; it had been part of his appeal. *"My parents were strict and the nuns at the girls' school where I went were advocating chastity so stridently that I gave in to his advances as a form of rebellion."* Their affair had been brief, she says, and she'd known nothing about birth control. *"Nowadays, the drugstores put condoms right out on the counter, but it was different back then. I thought it was something the man took care of, but I had no idea how."* She says it was only after she became pregnant with me that Francis told her he was married. *"Unhappily, he said, but he wouldn't leave his wife because it would bring dishonor to his family."*

She begins to cough. Points to the cup of ice chips on her tray table. I put some on the little plastic spoon and feed them to her. She sucks on them, smiles weakly, and continues. *"He tried to convince me to end my pregnancy or put you up for adoption, but I refused. I knew I wanted you despite what was to come. I already loved you, Orion."* He saw her one more time after he learned she was pregnant, she says. *"And then after that, he just disappeared. Stopped coming to the movies. Withdrew from his college. I tried to contact him there—borrowed my friend's car and drove over there. But the woman in the registrar's office wouldn't give me an address. She was sympathetic after I began to cry. I had started showing a little by then, and I'm sure she put two and two together. But she stuck to her guns. And so I surrendered to the inevitable. Went home and confessed to Mama and Papa."* The following Saturday, her father drove her to the Saint Catherine of Siena Home for Unwed Mothers, she says, and she spent the remainder of her pregnancy there. Got her high school diploma but had to miss her graduation. *"The sisters tried for months to convince me to do what most of the other girls agreed to: hand the baby over to Catholic Charities so that some nice childless couple who had prayed for a baby could adopt you. They accused me of being selfish, but I just kept shaking my head. I wanted to keep you and raise you and that was that."*

She's flagging, I can see. Exhausted and upset. Should I stop quizzing *her? While I'm trying to decide, a nurse enters. "Sorry to interrupt, Maria, but it's time for your breathing treatment," she says. Mom nods, gives her a wan smile, and opens her mouth. While Mom is puffing away on the device, I stand. Go over to the window and look out on the parking lot. But what she's told me has opened up more questions, and when the treatment is over and the nurse leaves, I sit back down again. Take her hand in mine. I remind her about that time we went up to Boston—to Grandpa Oh's restaurant. "How did you know where to find his father?" I ask her.*

"Well, Francis was a smoker," she says. "Always lit his Viceroys with books of matches that said HENRY OH'S CHINA PARADISE *on the cover. During one of the times we were at the motel where he used to take me, I slipped one of those matchbooks in my purse as a souvenir of our love. Like I said, Orion, I was naïve back then. I thought sex and love were one and the same."*

She'd gone to Henry Oh's China Paradise once before, she says, when she was six or seven months pregnant. "At first, he tried to deny that Francis was the father. How did I know this child was his son's? 'Because your son is the only man I've ever been with,' I told him. I could tell he believed me, but he still wouldn't tell me how to find Francis!" . . .

A look of exasperation had crossed her face when she said that—one I recognized. She had had that same look the day we'd walked up the stairs to Henry Oh's China Paradise so that she could present me to my grandfather as proof of my existence. Proof that, since his son had not done the right thing by me, the obligation fell on him. He needed to help finance the college education of the boy who, whether my grandfather was happy about it or not, carried his family name. Henry Oh, Francis Oh, Orion Oh: we were linked. He was duty bound. And so I practically had had to run after her that day as she exited the restaurant, her head held high, her hand clutching the check that would allow me to attend Boston University. Mom had been fierce that day, victorious. And even at seventeen, when I was still so ignorant about life and love and the repercussions of sex, I somehow knew that, whatever it had just cost her to get that money, she had done it out of a ferocious, almost feral love for the son she had refused to hand over to adoptive parents. And so—

Jesus god, there it goes again. *Love shack, baby, love shack.* . . . And
suddenly I realize who must be calling me. Annie. It's two days past
when I was supposed to RSVP. Well, if she wants to find out if I'm
going to her big gay wedding, she can go to hell because—

OH! JESUS!

Shit, that was close. If I hadn't just pulled out of my fog and
slammed on the brakes, I would have rear-ended that Subaru. That's
all I need right about now: an accident that would have been my fault.
My heart's racing, my palms have broken out in a sweat. Refocus. You
want to get there in one piece, don't you? With my eyes on the road,
I feel for the radio knob and twist it counterclockwise. Return to the
Mad Hatter and the shark lady.

"Okay then, Doc, so let's say Jaws comes upon a pod of seals that
are chillin' in the waters off of Chatham. What's his M.O.?"

"Well, first of all, 'he' is likely to be a *she*. Female great whites tend
to be larger and more dominant than males. And as to the shark's
'M.O.,' as you put it, great whites are ambush hunters. So what they
do is identify a target and then ram it hard and fast, most likely from
beneath because the underbelly is what's most vulnerable."

The Mad Hatter snorts. "That's where we're *all* most vulnerable.
Right, guys? Under our bellies and above our knees?" An *ah-ooga*
horn sounds, but the shark lady soldiers on.

"Once a shark takes hold, it whips its head from side to side, the
better to tear open a large chunk of flesh. That exposes the organs and
entrails, which will be ingested as quickly as possible. From what we've
observed, great whites may travel in small clans, but when they're on
the hunt, they separate."

"Every shark for himself, right?"

"That's right. Or *herself*."

Sharks. Ambush hunters. Viveca Christophoulos-Shabbas. . . .

Annie met Viveca through her art. She'd had a piece selected for
that Whitney Biennial, and at the opening Viveca approached her
about exhibiting at her by-appointment-only gallery in Chelsea. But
in fairness, I guess I'd started losing my wife to her art long before
Lady Bountiful came into the picture. . . .

It was strange how Annie's career had come about. She couldn't even say why, not long after our twins were born, she'd begun collecting odds and ends from junk stores, swap shops, and the curbside recycling boxes she passed while out for walks with Andrew and Ariane in their side-by-side stroller. She'd not understood it, that is, until she began creating those found-art shadow boxes. She had had no training as an artist. Something just *compelled* her to make them, she told me, but she was reluctant to explore with me the nature of that impulse. "Orion, I'm your wife, not one of your patients," she reminded me once when I tried to tease out her motivation. She made it clear that this was *her* thing. No trespassing.

Her first pieces were humorous, or so I thought: *The Dancing Scissors, The Jell-O Chronicles.* One Saturday, I remember, she requested a "mental health" afternoon. The twins had been sick, and except for trips to the pediatrician's and the pharmacy, Annie had been stuck in the house all week with cranky kids. Could I stay with them for a few hours while she went to a movie, maybe, or down to the mall? I got her coat, gave her a little swat on the rear, and said, "Go." But by the time she got back home, it was after 8:00 P.M. This was the mid-1980s, before cell phones became ubiquitous; if someone didn't bother to call in, you stared at the phone, waiting and worrying. "Where the hell have you *been*?" I demanded when she came through the door that night. But she was so jubilant, so energized, that she hardly noticed my day's worth of aggravation and worry. She had driven to Waterford, she said, intending to go to the Crystal Mall. Instead, spur of the moment, she'd hopped onto I-95 South. En route to no place in particular, she decided to get off at random exits and hunt for whatever awaited her at the dumps and secondhand shops of different shoreline towns. And it had been so worth it! She'd picked up treasures at each: a bolt of lace, a bundle of 1940s movie magazines, some wooden soda crates, a canvas bag brimming with hand puppets. Passing a billboard advertising a going-out-of-business sale at a job lot store in New Rochelle, she'd made a snap decision, signaled, and exited.

"New Rochelle?" I said. "You drove all the way into New York?"

Thank God she had, she said, because she'd struck pay dirt at that

Dollar Days. Her purchases included two large bags of deeply dis-
counted miscellany, including a twenty-four-piece box of plastic British Royal Family figurines.

I began complaining about my day with the twins—how Andrew
had kept making spit bubbles with his amoxicillin instead of just
swallowing it. How Ariane had toddled over to the dirty diaper pail,
climbed on, and tipped it over while I was at the door with a couple
of Jehovah's Witnesses—and how mopping up the mess, wet-vacing
and disinfecting their bedroom carpet, had taken me the better part
of an hour. From now on, we were buying Pampers, I told her. I didn't
care *how* much they cost. I was hoping to generate a little . . . what?
Sympathy? Remorse, maybe? But Annie just sat there, sifting through
her stuff, barely listening. And when I stopped talking, she went into
the twins' room, kissed their foreheads, and then, grabbing her new
"treasures," raced down to the studio I'd fixed up for her in the space
between the washer and dryer and the furnace. She was down there
for the rest of that night.

What had come over her? Was it OCD—some kind of hoarding
disorder, maybe? Some sort of anxiety related to motherhood? If so,
she could be treated. We could get her an antidepressant or a tranquil-
izer to take the edge off a little. But Annie wasn't accumulating stuff
solely for the sake of accumulating it. She was making art out of it,
so maybe I should back off. Give her the benefit of the doubt. . . . But
could you even call it art? Like I said, it wasn't like she'd had any formal training. To the best of my knowledge, she'd never even taken an
art course in high school. Had never even *finished* high school. Maybe
it was some sort of delayed reaction to the tough childhood she'd had.
Annie's childhood: that's always been another "no trespassing" zone.
I know the basics. She lost her mother when she was five years old.
Her father had gone off the rails as a result and she'd bounced around
in foster care. But Annie's always skirted the details of her early life.
Waiting here in stalled traffic, I can't help but wonder: has she been
more forthcoming with Viveca about her childhood? What does Viveca know?

A cruiser passes me on the shoulder, its lights flashing, its siren not

wailing but making loud little belches. There must be an accident up
ahead, which would explain why we've now almost come to a complete stop. Oh man, I haven't even gotten as far as Sandwich yet. I'll
be lucky if I get to that rental place before they close for the day—
or maybe even for the weekend. And what do I do if I can't pick up
the key to Viveca's cottage? Break into the place? Start looking for
motel "vacancy" signs? And now, adding insult to injury, this little
jerk in the Ford Focus has his blinker on and he's trying to squeeze in
between me and the Subaru. Smart move, buddy. Nothing like lane-
changing when both lanes are crawling along at about half a mile an
hour. Atta boy. Nose right in. Be my guest, you little shit. When did
you get your driver's license? Yesterday? He's talking a blue streak to
his girlfriend, oblivious that his directional signal's still blinking. To
my right is one of those big-ass campers that must get about five or six
miles to the gallon. A warning sprawls across the RV's left side: MAKE
WAY FOR MEAN DARLENE! A plump white-haired couple sits up front,
eating a snack out of a paper bag. Microwave popcorn, maybe? Their
jaws are moving in synch. When I was stuck behind them a quarter
of a mile ago, I read their back bumper stickers: LET FREEDOM RING!
and DON'T BLAME ME! I VOTED FOR THE HERO AND THE HOTTIE.

I honk at the kid in the Ford, and when he looks in his rearview
mirror, I point down at his blinker. I can tell he doesn't get it. Now the
girlfriend turns around and looks at me, too. They both shake their
heads as if I've offended them. On, off, on, off. . . . Should I? Hey, why
not? We've come to a stop. We're all just sitting here. I put my Prius in
park and get out, go up to his window and tap on it with my wedding
ring. I hear the soft clunk of his car door locks. Jesus, what does he
think I am? The traffic jam ax murderer?

"Yeah?"

"Your blinker's on."

"Is it?" He gives me this look like it's his inalienable right to drive
me crazy. But hey, I'm not about to get into a dustup about it with
Junior here. I turn and head back to my car.

He's a ballbuster, this kid. Lets about a minute go by before he finally turns it off. And when he does, it's like the relief you feel when

one of those ice cream headaches finally begins to subside. The radio's playing that ominous music from *Jaws*. "Okay, but let's separate fact from Hollywood fiction," the shark lady's saying. "These animals are carnivores, yes. But they're not evil manhunters. They hunt and eat to survive, not to kill gratuitously. That better describes *our* species than theirs."

"*Natural Born Killers*," the Mad Hatter says. "Now there's a great movie! Woody Harrelson and ... Who was the girl? Natalie Portman, right?"

It was Juliette Lewis. One of the students I was seeing at the time—when had that movie come out? 1994? 95?—she kept mentioning how Juliette Lewis and she were half-sisters, and how they looked so much alike, and if I didn't believe her, I should go see her sister's new movie, *Natural Born Killers*. She'd seen it several times herself, she said—had been invited to attend the premiere but couldn't afford the trip to California. Petra, her name was. She was a nice enough kid, high-strung but high functioning. In the honors program, if I remember correctly. But she was a sad kid who, I began to realize, had no friends. And when I *did* make a point of going to see the movie, I didn't observe the slightest resemblance between the two. I eventually diagnosed her with Delusional Disorder, Mixed Type. . . .

"No, seriously, Tracy. You should Netflix it this weekend," the Mad Hatter advises. Not likely, Tracy says. Tomorrow, she'll be part of an expedition that's hoping to locate and tag one or more of the great whites for the purpose of tracking their migratory patterns. . . .

Whatever it was that was compelling Annie to turn her landfill and secondhand shop finds into art, over the next years she created a series of assemblages she called *Buckingham Palace Confidential*. In *Elizabeth Burns the Rice-A-Roni!* Prince Philip and the rest of the royal family sit stiffly at a doll house dinette set while, standing at a toy stove on which sits a blackened toy frying pan, the Queen, wearing a coronet and a polka dot apron, throws up her jointed arms in domestic defeat. In *Lady Di Reconsiders*, the Princess of Wales, in her famously familiar wedding gown, marries Magic Johnson instead of Charles. Johnson's in his uniform, as are his ushers, the other members of the 1992 Olympic "dream team." Diana's attendants are female superheroes: Wonder Woman, Supergirl. The royal family is in attendance, too, but they've turned their backs to the ceremony. So it *was* art that was driving her, I decided—comic art at that, laced with a little feminist protest. But not dysfunction. . . . And yet, those weird scavenger hunts she was doing on the Saturdays when I was home with the kids? Whenever she came back with a good haul, she'd be wide-eyed, jazzed up, talking a blue streak and *fast*. What was that? Creative passion? Some kind of mania? I remember worrying that she might be starting to manifest bipolar disorder. But whatever Annie's behavior did or didn't indicate, I tried hard to play by her rules, encouraging her without engaging her as to why she was hunting down all this stuff, or what these 3-D collages she was making meant. But not engaging her didn't mean I wasn't watching her—trying to understand what was going on with her. Look, she was right: she was my wife, not my patient. I tried *not* to analyze her, but hey. Bottom line: I was worried about her. I'm a psychologist. I observe, make hypotheses. It's what we do.

No. Correction: I *was* a psychologist. When my license came up for renewal last month, I let the date go by. I go back and forth about whether I should have. But what's done is done. . . .

It was hard for Annie back then, I know. As the house-bound wife of a busy professional, she carried most of the burden of child care, cleaning, budgeting. She had to grab a little time here and there to work on her art. When I was down there in Pennsylvania with my mother, she hired some older woman to babysit a couple hours a day, and I applauded her for that. Told her it was a good idea. But that turned out to be a fiasco when the sitter forgot to lock the basement door and Andrew tumbled halfway down the stairs. Annie'd had to take him to the emergency room for stitches in his forehead and be grilled by the ER doc as if she were a child abuse suspect. She decided it wasn't worth it. Told the sitter not to come back. And when I got back, mentioned casually that Thea had come to the funeral, Annie'd reacted like a crazy woman. Like some spark between my ex-girlfriend and me had been reignited when the opposite was true. Seeing Thea again had been like a refresher course in why I'd ended it with her.

I'd have liked to help her out more, but the domestic imbalance was unavoidable. Counseling Services was understaffed, we clinicians seriously overworked. Students who wanted to see one of us had to put their names on a list and then wait for an appointment, sometimes as long as two or three weeks. Besides our caseloads, we counselors supervised the clinical practicums of the predoctoral students, got saddled with committee work, ran groups. In addition to all that, it fell on us to plan and implement Suicide Awareness Week, HIV Prevention Week, Alcohol Awareness Week, and so on. Most weekdays, I left for work before 7:00 A.M.—early morning was the best time to catch up on paperwork—and didn't get home most nights until six or after. On the weekends, I could help out more. Take the twins to the park, fix a cabinet door or rake leaves, make a Saturday night supper while she went off to scavenge. Saturday was our night for sex, too—a standing appointment unless one or both of the twins was up, or one of us was too exhausted for intimacy. Sometimes an extra hour of sleep seemed sexier than having sex. But weekdays? Forget it. I'd get home and my dinner would be sitting Saran-wrapped on top of the microwave, the twins would be asleep in their cribs, and Annie would be down there, creating her 3-D collages amid the basement noises, one ear cocked toward the baby monitor upstairs. . . .

Okay, here we go. The traffic's finally started to move again. Passing that camper, I put on *my* directional signal and jockey myself in front of them. Let Mr. and Mrs. Big-Ass Camper stare at *my* bumper stickers: DISSENT IS PATRIOTIC, TOO and OBAMA/BIDEN '08. . . .

Annie had been creating in basement obscurity for three or four years when I urged her to take a risk and exhibit her *Buckingham Palace Confidential* assemblages at the annual outdoor art show in Mystic. At first she resisted the idea, arguing that her kind of work wasn't what those big summertime crowds would be interested in. But I kept nudging her until, reluctantly, she changed her mind and reserved herself a space. All that weekend, people paused, smiled, and snickered at Annie's creations and then moved on to the "real" art: fruit in a bowl, seascapes. She had priced her pieces modestly—fifty dollars for the smaller assemblages, a hundred for the larger and more elaborate ones. She sold nothing. But to the surprise of many—and to the disgruntlement of the Mystic Art Association's watercolorists and lighthouse painters—the judge awarded the Best in Show ribbon to *Elizabeth Burns the Rice-A-Roni!* What was that guy's name? The judge? He'd been something of a big-deal artist himself back in the day, I remember Annie telling me. Italian guy, little pencil-thin mustache. He and Annie stayed in touch after she got that Best in Show. He must be dead by now—he was already up there back then—but I bet he'd be pleased to know where Annie's art has taken her.

Along with the five-hundred-dollar prize money Annie got from the Mystic show, she was offered a one-woman show at the Hygienic Restaurant in New London. The Hygienic had long since stopped serving food, but it had become a kind of retro coffee house—a haven for poets, interpretive dancers, klezmer bands—alternative artists of all kinds, and their equally alternative admirers. Until Annie's opening, I had never seen such a convergence of pierced, tattooed, and purple-haired people. Annie looked adorable that night in her floral dress and purple leggings, that big bow in her hair. "Oh, thank you so much. . . . You do? Really? Oh, my God," she'd respond to those who approached her to say that they loved her work or wanted to buy it. I was so proud of her that night—so happy to see her on the receiving end of some artistic appreciation, and almost four hundred dollars in sales. I knew more about psychology than I did about art, but I was becoming convinced that Annie was more talented than she or I had realized.

Her modesty about her accomplishments and her natural shyness were a big part of her charm that night at the Hygienic. Annie's brother Donald and his wife Mimsy had taken the twins for the night—their first sleepover. I'd snuck a bottle of champagne and a half-dozen chocolate-covered strawberries in the fridge before Annie and I left for the opening, and when we got home, we got into bed, drank, ate, and made love. "Good god, I'm crazy about you," I declared after we were both spent and sweaty. "Love you, too," she murmured back. If you had told me that night that, two decades later, Annie would leave me for a woman, I would have thought you were crazy. . . . Agnello: that was that judge's name. Mr. Agnello. . . . Had there been signs all along that she might be bisexual? Cues that I'd missed right from the beginning? . . .

Annie's Hygienic show caught the interest of a *Connecticut* magazine features writer who drove out to our house and interviewed Annie about her work. She'd brought along a photographer, so there was a photo shoot, too. I was happy for Annie. One door kept opening onto another door, and she deserved that. And I guess this was crass of me, but the fact that people had actually begun paying her for her work somehow, in my mind, legitimized her efforts. This was a career, not an emotional disorder. I should stop playing psych detective and just *relax*. Celebrate her accomplishments instead of stewing about her creative process. She worked so hard and with such dedication down there in our basement, to the soundtrack of the furnace's drone and the washing machine's agitation. Good for her!

But until that *Connecticut* magazine article came out, I hadn't realized the extent to which agitation fueled Annie's art. Eventually it dawned on me that her "no trespassing" rule had been *my* escape hatch, too. I'd been allowed the luxury of assuming that *The Dancing Scissors*, *The Cowgirls' Revolt*, and *Buckingham Palace Confidential* were playful. Satirical. Proof that my intense and sometimes morose wife had a lighter side, too. But in "Annie Oh's Angry Art," the writer said that my wife's compositions emerged from "the blast furnace of her pent-up rage." That they were "howls of protest against a suffocating middle-class domesticity" and the many ways in which society "tethers women to the mundane." The mundane? Had Annie been referring to Rice-A-Roni or me? Was Diana's rejection of Charles in favor of Magic Johnson metaphorical? The UPS driver who made deliveries to our house was a good-looking young black guy. Reggie, his name was. Someone she knew from way back, she said. Twice I'd gotten home from work a little early and found the two of them chatting at the front door. I couldn't quite imagine that she'd cheat on me, but was I being naïve? The scientist in me advised objectivity, but the husband in me had just been put on alert.

"Good article, don't you think?" I said, when I looked up from

Connecticut magazine to her. I was hoping she'd say she'd been misquoted. Misunderstood. Instead, she said, "Pretty good. It's weird to see yourself in a magazine, though. I feel . . . exposed, I guess."

"Well, isn't that what artists want? Exposure?"

She shrugged.

"Good picture of you."

She made a face. "I wish my hair didn't look so flat," she said. "I can't believe that, on the one day I was having my picture taken for a magazine, our hair dryer died."

"Yeah, well. . . . It's interesting what it says about your work."

No response.

"I mean, who knew you were so angry?"

"Oh, I don't know, Orion. Maybe someone who was bothering to pay attention." She walked out of the room.

I tossed the magazine onto the coffee table, got up, and followed her down the stairs to the basement. For a minute or more, I watched her yank towels out of the washing machine and slam them into the dryer. "You know something?" I said. "I don't exactly appreciate you projecting your own marital shortcomings onto me."

She turned and faced me, furious. "Do me a favor," she said. "Speak English, not psychology."

"Okay. Sure. Somebody in this marriage hasn't been paying much attention to the other person, but it sure as hell isn't me."

"Oh, right. You're just the perfect husband, aren't you?"

"No, I'm the *im*perfect husband. But I think you've got it assbackward as far as who's been ignoring who."

"Oh, really? Gee, Dr. Oh, I'm so sorry for 'projecting,' as you put it. And for having a career of my own."

It was April. I had just done our taxes. "Yeah, speaking of careers, you know how much I contributed to our income this past year? Sixty-two grand. And you know how much you made? A whopping seven hundred dollars. So I think you'd better thank your lucky stars instead of bitching about *my* career."

"Oh, you're right as usual, Dr. Oh. Thanks so much for throwing that in my face and helping me see the light." And with that, she lifted the lid of our top-loading washing machine and slammed it down. Lifted it again and slammed it. Lifted, slammed. Thanks in part to "Annie Oh's Angry Art," we had just entered the thrust-and-parry phase of our marriage.

Over the next several days, each of us accused the other of myriad slights and failures, large and small. The fighting exhausted us both, and our lives were already pretty exhausting. She began giving me the single-syllable treatment. "Good day today?" "Yup." "Want to get a sitter this weekend? Go see a movie or something?" "Nah." In the midst of that uneasy near-silence, I reread that *Connecticut* magazine article and came upon a couple of paragraphs I'd missed the first time. She'd told the reporter that, once upon a time, another artist had lived on the grounds of the house where we lived—a black laborer who'd taken up painting—and that she'd discovered one of his "compositions" that had been left behind. I knew the one she was talking about: a crazy-looking circus scene we'd found when we were cleaning out the attic. To my mind, it was strictly amateur, not to mention a little freaky-looking, and I'd wanted to throw it out along with the other junk up there. But Annie had said not to. It had "spoken to her," she told that reporter, which was news to me, and when she set up her studio in the basement, she'd brought it down there for inspiration. (Oh, *she'd* set up that work space? So much for the work *I'd* done for her down there.) In the article, she said she might even have "seen" this would-be artist, who was long dead by the time we moved in. Had seen him twice, in fact. Once out back in the yard—a big, muscular guy in overalls looking up at her as she stood at one of the upstairs windows—and another time down in her studio. Both times, she said, he'd looked right at her, nodded, and then faded away. It hadn't scared her to see him, she said; it had reassured her. Oh great, I remember thinking. Now she was seeing ghosts? Then how come I'd never heard about this? No, I figured, she wasn't seeing people that weren't there, except maybe in a dream she'd had. More likely, she had told the writer that because, hey, who *doesn't* love a good ghost story? It wasn't like Annie to fabricate stuff like that, but since she'd become an artist, she'd exhibited all kinds of new behaviors. And so I didn't challenge her on it. "Annie Oh's Angry Art" had already caused problems for us. I let it drop.

I finally got us a referral to a marriage counselor, despite Annie's suspicion that the deck would be stacked in my favor because she'd be the only person in the room who wasn't a therapist. I hired us a sitter for Tuesday evenings. (Katie had been my student coordinator for Date Rape Awareness Week.) And so for the next several weeks, Annie and I drove to Glastonbury to see Suzanne in her office full of philodendrons and ferns and hand-thrown clay pots that she had made, glazed, and fired in her wood-stoked kiln. She gave us one of those pots at the end of our first session—an imperfect one. A piece had broken off and been glued back on. "My point is this," Suzanne said, passing her finger over the crack. "This is where the pot is strongest now: at the place where it had been broken."

"How was tango class tonight?" Katie would ask when we returned home from our marriage counseling sessions. I'd invented our tango lessons so that I didn't have to tell her we were trying to fix our marriage.

"Great. How were the kids?"

"*Super* good! They're such cuties. And you know, I think it's super cool that you guys are learning the tango. I wish my parents weren't such fuddy-duddies about stuff like that. Get out of their comfort zone? Forget it. They'd rather just sit there watching TV."

Whether or not we were doing the tango up there in Glastonbury, we were definitely out of our comfort zone. But it was worth it. We *did* repair things. For quite a while, actually. Becoming less accusatory of each other lessened the tension. We practiced better teamwork with the twins and the house stuff, better listening skills, worked on more open communication. Hey, I'm a psychologist; it's not like I didn't already know a lot of these strategies. But knowing how to advise others in dealing with *their* shit doesn't necessarily mean you're going to tackle your own without having to check in with a third party once a week. And besides, my patients range in age from eighteen to about

twenty-one, twenty-two. Their relationships are more about managing
the drama than maintaining a marriage. Suzanne likened the latter to
servicing a car you love and want to last. Listen to the engine, rotate
the tires, check the oil. Things got better for us intimacy-wise, too. I
became more patient. She became more communicative about what
she wanted. She had more orgasms than she'd ever had before, and
damn if I didn't enjoy giving them to her. . . . I mean, it wasn't happily
ever after, not by any stretch. She was still distant sometimes, both in
our bed and out of it, and I still overdid it sometimes, work schedule-
wise. But it definitely got better. Our "tango lessons" went from once a
week to once a month, and then to once every three months. Marriage
as car maintenance: I was a little put off by the metaphor at first, but
as it turned out, Suzanne knew her stuff. Things were much better for
Annie and me. And then she got pregnant again and they weren't. . . .

"Their skin is covered with small toothlike scales, so they'd be vir-
tually unaware that they're being embedded," Dr. Skelly is telling the
Mad Hatter. "These tags use satellite technology, so that lets us—"

"Like a GPS system?" the Mad Hatter asks.

"Uh-huh. Pretty much. If we get lucky and the tags stay embedded,
we should be able to track the animals' migratory behavior. Which
would be fantastic! In other parts of the world, great whites have been
tracked successfully, so there's a good deal known about their migration patterns. But that's not the case here in the northern Atlantic.
Great whites in these waters have always been a bit of a mystery."

"Well, Dr. Tracy Skelly, thanks for a fascinating discussion. And
good luck tracking those great whites. Time once again to check on
news, weather, and traffic. But stay tuned, fellas, because when we . . .
two of the self-described 'guidettes' who will . . . in MTV's latest . . .
Jersey Shore, debuting next . . ." Mercifully, the Mad Hatter is finally
fading away.

Chapter Three

Annie Oh

I'm goin' to the market now, Miz Anna. Anything else you need?"

"What?"

"At the market. Anything else that ain't on your list?"

"No, I guess not. Maybe a pack of cigarettes."

"Marlboro Lights?"

"Yes, please. Do you have enough money? Here, let me get my purse and give you another twenty just in case. You can keep the change."

Last month, Viveca reprimanded me for giving Minnie an extra hundred dollars. "Sweetheart, once you start that, they start expecting it," she said, as if I were a child who didn't know better. As if Minnie were a dog I got caught feeding scraps to under the table. I kept my mouth shut, but I was pissed. I'm pissed so often lately. It's nerves, I guess. It's not that I'm *not* committed to Viveca. I am. But I've already been a bride. And I'm just not comfortable about being married back in Three Rivers. . . . But okay, I'll get through it. It's one weekend, that's all, and I'll have some time with my daughters in the house where they grew up; I'm looking forward to that. And once we return from Greece, I'll go back to my studio and Viveca will go back to her gallery and her various charity fund-raising initiatives and things will return to normal.

I've slipped Minnie more money since Viveca's reprimand—hundreds by now probably, although I haven't kept track. "Our little secret," I say whenever I press the tens and twenties into her calloused hand and squeeze.

Minnie's more guarded about her personal life than Hector is, but she's been opening up little by little, more so since Viveca's been away and I've been staying home instead of going to the studio. We've started eating our lunch together, Minnie and me, in Viveca's study because there's a little TV in there and Minnie likes to watch *The Jerry Springer Show*. I'm not sure why, because day after day, it reinforces the worst stereotypes. All the black men on *Jerry Springer* are dim-witted dogs who cheat on their women. And when Jerry brings out the brazen women these men have been cheating with, the betrayed wives rush them, slapping and punching, yanking off their wigs while the mostly white audience cheers them on. Minnie shakes her head and chuckles and thinks these fights are funny. Doesn't she realize how racist it is? That it's staged? I'm at a loss to understand what it is about *Springer* that appeals to her so much. But hey, I sit there, eating my yogurt and watching it with her.

Minnie smokes at our apartment, which Viveca would be furious about if she knew. But she's discreet. When she goes into the spare bedroom for a cigarette break, she sits in front of the open window and blows the smoke through the screen. When I walked in and caught her that time, her eyes narrowed—looked more defiant than apologetic—and she said, "You gon' tell Missuz I been rippin' smokes?" I told her I wouldn't and smiled. Asked her to please call me Annie. I thought she'd be pleased by my overture, but she just nodded, not smiling back. She hasn't called me Annie yet. To Minnie, I'm still Miz Anna, the woman who's going to marry Missuz.

Since Viveca's been gone, I've been smoking, too. The first couple of times, I bummed cigarettes from Minnie. Then I went down to the market on the corner, the one with the ATM, and bought myself a pack from that effeminate Korean cashier with the bad attitude and the Velveeta-dyed hair. He wears women's tops and pants some days—size zero, I'm guessing, because he has the narrowest waist I've ever seen. He's over-the-top hostile—resentful when you go up to the counter and dare to interrupt his magazine reading because you want to *buy* something. He sighs long-sufferingly, slaps his magazine down on the counter, and rings you up with a roll of his eyes. The other day, I got so fed up with his bad attitude that, when he went to give me my change, I grabbed his wrist, looked him in the eye, and told him that whoever or whatever he was so angry about, he didn't have to take it out on his customers. I watched his expression change from defiance to fear. He was suddenly a scared and miserable little boy, and I knew that, somewhere, in some way, somebody had abused him. I felt bad and looked away—looked down at the counter, at Oprah's beaming face on the cover of *O* magazine. He'd dropped my change when I grabbed his wrist and there were dimes on Oprah's boobs. They looked like pasties. When I looked back up at him, his mask was back on and he looked as ornery as ever. But it was too late. I'd already seen his fear. I can use it if I need to. It's part of what makes me powerful: I can sometimes figure out what other people's vulnerabilities are without revealing any of my own. It's something I learned from my family, I guess; we O'Days were talented secret keepers.

For the last week or so, I've been buying two packs at a time: Marlboro Lights for me and Newports for Minnie. On the *Today* show, that Dr. Nancy person keeps harping on the dangers of smoking. Her and her cushy doctor's life, her little brown bangs. She reminds me of those beautifully dressed girls from high school—the ones whose mothers let them borrow their credit cards and buy whatever they wanted at the Westwick Mall where I worked. That was my first real job, not counting babysitting; I'd scoop, weigh, and bag people's mixed nuts, dried fruits, jelly candies, and deluxe jumbo cashews at a kiosk called Jo-Jo's Nut Shack. My customers were fat people, mostly, who watched the scale to make sure I wasn't shortchanging them. I'd keep one eye on what I was shoveling onto the scale and the other on those girls from my school who strolled by with their bags and packages. *I* recognized *them*, but they didn't recognize me or even look my way. I hadn't had a mother in eight years, let alone a borrowed credit card to buy things with. What did any of those girls know about having to wear used clothes from Love Me Two Times or the Salvation Army store? And what does Dr. Nancy know about what someone like Minnie is up against? That day I caught her smoking? I sat on the bed next to her, lifted the window I was facing, took a cigarette out of her pack, and lit up. And the two of us sat there, inhaling and blowing smoke through our respective screens, tapping ash into the plastic cap of the

Febreze can that Minnie uses for an ashtray. Neither of us spoke until we'd each started second cigarettes. That was when she told me about her ten-year-old son, Africa. She's a single mother. It's been three years since Africa's father left, she says, and he's never paid her one single dime for child support.

Minnie drinks on the job, too. She doesn't know I know. The other night, I dropped an egg on the kitchen floor, and when I went into the cleaning closet to get something to wipe it up, I found a gallon jug of Carlo Rossi Paisano wine hidden at the bottom of a box of rags, mop heads, and vacuum cleaner attachments. It was half full. And when I checked it the following night after she left to go home, it was only a quarter full. The night after that, there was a new jug—Carlo Rossi burgundy this time. She had finished the other bottle and drunk three or four inches' worth from the new one. Well, as long as she gets her work done and Viveca doesn't find out, let her drink. Maybe I have Carlo Rossi to thank for the fact that she's been more open lately. Maybe it's not so much that she's begun to trust me as it is because she's buzzed.

Minnie has medical expenses because of Africa's asthma, and she's trying to save enough to relocate to an apartment where there's no mold. She'd like to get her teeth fixed, too, she told me, so she can find herself another boyfriend. Africa's father got remarried, she says. "His new wifey LaRue gonna have triplets is what LaRue's cousin told me on the low," she said. "Darnell don't even know 'bout them babies yet, but I do. Well, he in for a big surprise. Serve him right. That man loves his sleep better than anything 'cept hisself— lookin' at the mirror all the time so he can see how pretty he is. I hope them three babies all get colic and keep him up nights. He won't look so pretty then. He be runnin' *away* from that mirror." She chuckled at the thought of Darnell's sleep deprivation in the same way she chuckles when the black women fight each other on *Jerry Springer*. Then she snuffed out her cigarette, stood, and said she didn't suspect "Missuz's furniture gonna dust itself." I admire Minnie's flinty bitterness, and the fact that, whenever I give her extra cash, she takes it without acting beholden or even grateful. "Our little secret": it's like a contract between the two of us.

Minnie and her boy live in Newark. Africa's sickly but "sweet as sugar." For the past two years, she's paid a Spanish boy down the hall to babysit Africa in the morning "but he growin' hisself a mustache and gettin' some attitude lately." Puberty's apparently made him less dependable. "He spoze to show up befo' I leave for work. Fix Africa his breffest, make sure he gots his homework and his inhaler, then walk him to school. But half the time, I gotta go befo' he come so I don't miss my bus, and then I gotta call and call his cell phone to see if he there yet so Africa don't have to walk *hisself* to school and do his work all mornin' long with nothin' in his stomach until hot lunch. I probly gon' have to fire Oswaldo's ass pretty soon, but I ain't done it yet."

Yesterday Minnie told me she has two grown sons by another man. Twins, Ronald and Donald. Donald is doing time in upstate New York—for what she didn't say and I didn't ask. "But Ronald never been no trouble. He come outa me first, thass why. It's the second twin thass always the trouble chile." Ronald is married and works at the Friendly's ice cream plant in Wilbraham, Massachusetts, Minnie told me. "I keep axin' him to come visit us an' bring his kids so I can see my gran'babies. But he ain't come yet. Thass okay, though. I understand. He busy." When I told Minnie that I have twins, too—a daughter who runs a soup kitchen in San Francisco and a son who's stationed at Fort Hood—she nodded indifferently. And when I told her that, when I was a kid, I had worked at a Friendly's restaurant, she had no reaction at all. Minnie likes me well enough—not only because of the extra money I give her, I like to think—but she doesn't seem to entertain the possibility that she and I have anything in common.

Well, why would she? She's poor; I'm not. She's black; I'm white. Minnie says her commute takes her almost two hours either way. After she catches an early bus out of Newark, she transfers twice, then takes the ferry from Hoboken into Manhattan. At the South Ferry station, she catches the Lexington Avenue local up to the Spring Street stop, then walks over to our apartment on Elizabeth.

The trip in reverse takes longer, she says. Some nights she doesn't return home until eight o'clock or later. My walk from our apartment to my studio space at the artists' collective on Bleecker takes ten minutes when I don't stop along the way, collecting sidewalk discards that I might incorporate into my art. (On trash collection day, that ten-minute walk sometimes takes me an hour or more, depending on what people have thrown out. A few weeks ago, I had such a good haul that I had to grab an abandoned shopping cart and wheel my treasures to the studio. I was going to leave the cart on the sidewalk out front, but then I lugged that up to my workplace, too.) One night when she got home, Minnie said, she put the key in the lock, opened the door, and smelled chocolate. The Spanish kid, who's not supposed to leave Africa by himself, had done just that. Left to his own devices, Africa had gotten the bright idea to take a bath in cocoa. "He run hot water, then dump this whole big can of Swiss Miss that I got cheap at the flea market because of the gone-by date." Minnie was headachy and dog tired, she said, and when she saw Africa sitting in all that chocolate bathwater, she beat him silly, splashing cocoa every which way. "He cryin' so hard, he give hisself a asthma 'tack and I say, 'Where your inhaler at?' And he go, while he wheezin' away, he go, 'It in school, Mama.' And so we end up at the emergency for two, three hour. After we get home, I put him to bed and start cleanin' up all that mess. Seem like no mo' than a few hours go by before I had to wake up, let Oswaldo in cuz he be bangin' on the door—on time for once. By the time I got ready, I had to run to catch that bus."

That's another thing Minnie doesn't know we have in common: that I used to hit *my* boy, too. Andrew, the second-born of *my* twins. Poor, sweet Andrew, who looked so beautiful when he slept. Who, despite those wallopings, always kept my tirades from his father. His sisters did, too. Why was that? I wonder. Were they being protective of me? Were they afraid that, if they told, I might turn my anger on them, too? Or that I'd be taken away—carted off by the authorities the way I was when I was a little girl? No, that was my fear, not theirs. . . . Of the three kids, Andrew's the one with the most O'Day in him. *This? Oh, yeah, I fell off my bike and bumped my head on the sidewalk,*

Dad. . . . Me and Jay Jay were horsing around over at his house. It's just a black and blue mark, Dad. It's no big deal. If I hadn't known where those battle scars really came from, I might have believed him, too.

I didn't want Andrew to enlist; I begged him not to. Every night before I go to bed, I get down on my knees, make the sign of the cross, and ask Jesus to please, please spare Andrew from being deployed to Iraq or Afghanistan. Sometimes I get scared that God or karma or whoever or whatever's in charge of retribution will pay me back for the way I singled him out. Or because I walked away from my marriage. It amuses Viveca, I think, to see me praying; she doesn't believe in God. "What is it you're praying *for*?" she asked me one night, and I kept it vague. "World peace," I said. But mostly what I beg God for is my son's safety. Please, I pray, let me die if I have to, but spare my son. Let Andrew not have to go to either of those places and be killed.

Okay, I tell myself. If you're not going into work again today, then do something else. It's after eleven already. Go down to the lobby and get the mail. Check your e-mail.

Viveca's two-day-old message is titled *Mykonos!* I click on it. "Here's the villa where we'll be staying," it says. "Have a look." In defiance, I decide not to open the attachment—those pictures she wants me to see. . . . *Our* apartment, *our* housekeeper. What's hers, Viveca often reminds me, is mine now, too. Nevertheless, while she's away, I'm supposed to sign that prenup agreement her lawyer has drawn up. When it was hand delivered by way of messenger from Attorney Philip Liebmann's Sixth Avenue office, Viveca said, "I told Phil it wasn't necessary, but he was insistent. Got a little snippy with me in fact. I've known Phil since I was a child; he was my father's lawyer and his tennis buddy. He feels paternal toward me, that's all. But, sweetheart, it's just a boring legal formality that's going to make an overly protective old man happy. Don't read any more into it than that. What's mine is yours. You know that."

Chapter Four

Orion Oh

S he didn't just walk out on me one day; she migrated to Manhattan in stages. Day trips into the city to meet with gallery owners or important collectors turned into overnights. And after she won that NEA grant, those overnights turned into four-day work weeks because she used the money to rent studio space at a building in SoHo—a place that was owned and operated by some artists' cooperative that Viveca had connections with.

"You've worked successfully at home all these years," I reminded her. "Why do you suddenly need to make art in New York?" Because she wanted to come up from the basement and be in the company of other artists instead of our washer and dryer, she said. Because in New York she'd be able to get on the subway and, fifteen minutes later, be standing in front of some masterpiece at the Met or MoMA, or walking into some gallery in Brooklyn to see a show by some up-and-coming artist that everyone was talking about. "Sweetie, I just want to try it," she told me. "It's an experiment. It's only for a year."

"I don't know. I just don't want us to turn into one of those long-distance-marriage couples," I told her. "Look what happened to Jeff and Ginny's marriage when they tried it." For one thing, she said, she took exception to the term "long-distance" when you could get from Three Rivers to Manhattan or vice versa in under three hours. And for another, she wanted to remind me that it was Jeff's infidelity, not the geographical distance between him and Ginny, that ended their marriage. I considered making the point that being a workaholic was a kind of infidelity, too, but I held my tongue. How many times, when the kids were younger and she was housebound with them, had she leveled that same criticism at me?

"And this is something you really, really want?" I said. "Something you think is going to fuel your work?"

She nodded emphatically, no trace of ambivalence whatsoever.

"Then let me talk to Muriel. Maybe she can do some juggling in the department and finagle me a leave of absence. There's got to be plenty of sublets in Manhattan, right?"

She folded her arms against her chest. "And what would you do all day long while I was working? Hang around some tiny little studio apartment? I know you, Orion. You'd go stir-crazy."

"Yeah, you're probably right," I said. "Because I'd never be resourceful enough to get up and *leave* the apartment. Go out and engage with one of the most exciting cities in the world. I'd probably just sit around, watching soap operas and twiddling my thumbs."

I smiled when I said it, but Annie looked exasperated. For one thing, she said, Viveca had already offered her a room in her apartment, rent free. What was she supposed to do? Tell her that her husband would be moving in, too? And more importantly, she wanted to be able to immerse herself in her work without having to keep to a schedule, or even look at a clock if she didn't want to. "But how could I do that if I knew you were waiting around for me to quit for the day?" She took my hand in hers and squeezed it. "Sweetie, this is such a great opportunity for me. It would be for one year, not a lifetime. And we'd still see each other every weekend. I'd like to think we have a strong enough marriage to handle *that*."

I smiled. "Just for a year, huh? With weekend furloughs?" She nodded. "Okay, then. Let's try it."

If she was preparing for a show or had to hobnob with some wealthy art patron who was in town for the weekend, the only day she could spare me was Sunday. I'd drive down to New Haven and meet her at the train station. We'd walk over to the green, grab some lunch at Claire's or the Mermaid Bar. Compare notes about the kids—which one of us had heard from which, which of the three we were worried about that week. (More often than not, it was our wild card, Marissa. Or Andrew, who by then had entered the military and was facing the possibility of deployment.) We'd spend a couple of hours together, then head back to Union Station. Stand together out on the platform and, when the train came into view, hug each other, kiss good-bye. Then she'd board the Acela or the Metroliner and ride away. And as her one-year New York experiment turned into a year and a half after a couple of big purchases courtesy of *viveca c*, those kisses became pecks, the hugs became perfunctory. "My part-time wife" I'd started calling her, at first in jest, then in jest-with-an-edge. Later still, I hurled the term at her in outright anger.

Looking back, I'm amazed at how much in denial I was about her and Viveca. Yeah, I'd get worried from time to time, but what I thought was that maybe she'd gotten involved with some other guy. I'd imagine him, worry about him, even sometimes picture her walking hand in hand with him—some artist or musician type, some lanky younger guy with a porkpie hat and a couple of days' worth of stubble. But the only time I confronted her about another man, she got huffy—said that it was all about her work and that my insecurity was *my* problem, not hers. And hey, whenever I called her? She was almost always there where she was supposed to be—at her studio or at night at Viveca's. Once when I called and Viveca answered, she said, "You know, Orrin, one of these days you and I will have to meet in person." I let it go that she'd gotten my name wrong, and that we'd *already* met several years back at the Biennial opening. "I'd like that, too," I said. I went down to visit Annie at the apartment two or three times, but each time it was when Viveca was out of town for the weekend. I still don't know when they made the switch from roommates to lovers. Annie's told me it happened over time, that their affair wasn't "premeditated." I believe her. Interesting, though, the way she'd put it. As if it was a crime. Which it was, in a way: the murder of our marriage.

Sometimes we want something to be true so badly that we convince ourselves that it is true. How many times had I suggested that to one of the undergrads sitting across from me in my office? Some self-deluding young woman who was trying to convince herself that a boyfriend's having smacked her around was a one-time thing; some young guy's assertion that, although sex with other guys excited him, he wasn't really gay. "Put your hand out," I'd tell these students. "Now bring it closer. Now closer still." And when their hands were a half inch from their noses, I'd ask them to describe what they saw. "It's blurry," they'd say, and I'd suggest that sometimes the closer we got to a situation, the less clear it looked. And that when wishful thinking trumped the reality we might otherwise be able to see more clearly and manage, we were setting ourselves up for a rude awakening. . . . Psychologist, heal thyself. Little by little, I began to withdraw my own hand from my face, as it were. Began to face the fact that Annie and I no longer were together. That she had defected.

The showdown came one Sunday afternoon when, in the middle of an argument we were having about her absenteeism, I said, "Do you even *want* to be married to me anymore?" We were in our kitchen. I was at the stove, making dinner—frying up eggplant on one burner, simmering marinara on another. Annie was at the table, going through two weeks' worth of accumulated mail. *Of course I do*, I wanted to hear her say, but what she said, instead, was that she wasn't sure anymore. That she was confused.

"Confused?" I picked up the frying pan and slammed it back down against the burner. The noise made her jump. "Well, if *you're* confused, how the hell do you think *I* feel?" At this stage of our crumbling marriage, our battle roles had reversed themselves. Annie had always been the one who yelled and banged things when we argued; I was the one who spoke softly and civilly, maintaining the upper hand. Now *I* was the shouter, the slammer. She opened her mouth to say something, then stopped herself. Stood and walked out of the room, out of our house, and down the road. I stood at the window, watching her go. That was *my* rude awakening.

Later, when the meal I'd made was starting to go cold, she came back. We sat in silence across the table from each other. Chewed, swallowed. Each bite I took landed like a stone against my stomach. "Look, if you're confused, then go see someone," I finally said. "Or maybe we can go together like we did that other time. I can make some calls, get a referral to a good marriage counselor and we can—"

"I *am* seeing someone," she said. "Romantically, I mean, not professionally." I stared at her, a forkful of food poised in front of my mouth. "I still love you, Orion," she told me in tears. "I always will. But I'm not *in* love with you anymore. I'm sorry. I didn't mean for this to happen, but I've fallen in love with someone else."

That someone else, she said, was Viveca.

"Viveca? . . . *Viveca?*"

Annie had gone with me to see that movie, I remember—*Natural Born Killers*. It was my idea, not hers. And about ten minutes into it, when Juliette Lewis and Woody Harrelson began murdering people in a bar for the fun of it, she took hold of my arm and whispered that she needed to leave. "It's *satire*," I'd whispered back. "*Cartoon* violence. Don't take it so *literally*." But she let go of my arm, stood, and walked out of the multiplex. Walked around the mall until the film was over. I finally found her sitting at a table outside of Au Bon Pain, cardboard coffee cup in front of her, looking sad and lost. Was she thinking of leaving me even back then? Wrestling with her attraction to women, maybe, or suffering because of my insensitivity? There was that lesbian friend of hers who visited us one time—that woman Priscilla. She and Annie had waitressed together back when Annie was in her teens. They'd been close, she said, and for a fleeting moment I wondered *how* close. But I'd dismissed it. Because even if they had been intimate, it was no big deal. Some kids experiment at that age. It's how they figure out who they are. . . . No, I should have been more in touch with her feelings and her fears. Should have gotten up and left the movie with her that afternoon—been less of a therapist trying to fathom my patient Petra's psyche and more of a husband taking care of my wife. But no, I'd stayed, had sat through a film that, frankly, sickened me, too. Well, what does it matter at this point? The divorce is final. Their wedding invitations are already out. Mine, ripped in half, is in the second, smaller duffel bag I packed last night—the one filled with the stuff I've taken along for the little oceanside ceremony I'm planning to have once I get to North Truro. Or maybe I should say *if* I get there. I don't think we've moved a mile in the last fifteen minutes. Well, so what, dude? It's not like you're going to be late for work. You're unemployed, remember?

My "early retirement" from the university was an exhausted surrender, not an admission that Jasmine Negron's version of what had happened that night was accurate. Instead of giving the benefit of the doubt to a colleague they'd known and worked with for years, Muriel and her cohorts had gotten behind a doctoral student who'd received a lukewarm evaluation from me the semester before. Once upon a time, Muriel and I had been friends. Lunch pals. We'd served together on committees, carpooled to conferences. We two and our spouses had seen each other socially during those early years. But after she was named director, things changed. She informed her counselors of her intent to create a "paper trail" about everything that transpired in our department, then generated a maddening number of forms and reports. And she expected all this additional paperwork to be completed on time, not a day or two late, no matter how much our caseloads had swelled because of the policy changes she had put into place. She was a stickler about those deadlines—a pain in the ass about them— and a strictly-by-the-book administrator who expected the rest of us to recast ourselves in her image, irrespective of our own treatment styles and philosophies. She intimidated the younger members of the department, many of whom sought me out about how to deal with her demands and criticisms. And because I'd gone to bat for some of them, Muriel pulled me into her office one afternoon and accused me of undermining her authority and encouraging others to do the same. She and I had butted heads on a number of occasions and on a number of issues. And so, when Jasmine filed her complaint, Muriel appointed an ad hoc committee to investigate: Blanche, Bev, and Marsha, feminists all, none of whom could be considered my ally. Beyond a shadow of a doubt? Innocent until proven guilty? Not with *that* gang of four. Muriel went to Dean Javitz and argued that my behavior had undermined the integrity of the entire Counseling Services program.

Word got around. People took sides, and the numbers were lopsided against me. My one supporter was Dick Holloway, a holdover from the department's "good ole boy" days when men had run the show. Muriel tolerated Dick because she knew she'd outlast him, but he'd told me on more than one occasion that he was "sticking around" for the pleasure of being a thorn in her side. I'd never liked Dick, and when he stuck his head inside my office one morning to offer his support—"I hear the dykes are trying to cut you off at the knees, but hang tough" was the way he'd put it—it was small comfort. As for the other members of our department, some of whom I'd counted among my friends, they began nodding uncomfortably and looking away when we passed each other in the hall. A lot of the women in our department started giving me dirty looks. One lunchtime, I walked into the staff lounge and four women stopped their conversation, stood, and walked out in solidarity against me. It had hurt like a kick to the nuts.

Even my two best friends in the department, Marina and Dennis, began to distance themselves. Look, counseling students all day? You really care about these kids. You root for their mental health and try to promote it, but it's hard, imperfect work. You worry about the ones who are in the worst shape, and at the end of the day, you can't always shut it off like a faucet. So there's this informal support system. When it's after hours and you can't stop hearing a patient's voice or seeing the kid's tortured face? You can begin to doubt yourself. So you call a colleague you can trust with whatever vulnerability you're wrestling with. You have them listen to what's bothering you and maybe offer a suggestion or two, a little perspective. Seek out a little counseling from another counselor. Dennis, Marina, and I had done that for one another. Had helped each other out like that for years. For *years*.

"Look, Orion, I sympathize with you. I really do," Marina said when I stopped her and Dennis out in the parking lot one afternoon to ask for their support. "But I'm between a rock and a hard place with this one, okay? Because I'm your friend, yes, but I'm a woman, too. And I've been on the receiving end of unwanted—"

I put my hand up to stop her and turned to Dennis. "What about you? Because I'm telling you, this thing is a witch hunt. Was I dumb enough to give the girl a ride home when she came into my office that night like a damsel in distress? I was! Was I stupid enough to say yes when she invited me in for a drink? God, yes! But goddamnit, Dennis, she's rewritten history. Because it just did not happen the way she's claiming it did."

He stood there, nodding sadly.

"So you believe me?"

"I do."

"Then are you willing to—"

"Personally, I'm with you. But professionally? I've got to remain neutral on this one, Orion. I've got to be Switzerland."

"Yeah? Really? Then screw you, Switzerland," I said. I turned back to Marina. "And screw you, too, if you think *you're* the one who's stuck between a rock and a hard place."

"But Orion, the thing is—"

Rather than listen to their lame excuses, I turned my back on them and stormed off in the direction of my car. Looked over my shoulder and saw them both standing there, staring at me. The problem was, I couldn't *find* my goddamned car. Kept walking back and forth from row to row, on the verge of tears and thinking, Shit! On top of everything else, someone's stolen my fucking *car*? Eventually, it hit me that the Prius was in the shop being serviced. That I'd driven to work that day in a loaner. A red Saturn. I found it, kicked the bumper, unlocked it. Driving out of the parking lot, I looked over at the two of them, still standing there, talking. Justifying their reasons, no doubt, for not having my back the way I would have had either of theirs, no questions asked.

The following week, in the midst of my attempts to defend myself at humiliating meetings with the dean, the school's at-large ethics panel, and lawyers representing the university and the union I belonged to, Seamus McAvoy, a twenty-year-old engineering major with a history of clinical depression, died on my watch. A sweet kid who carried his illness around like a backpack full of rocks, Seamus had been my counselee for four semesters. I'd had to cancel our previous appointment because of one of the aforementioned ethics meetings, but I have a vivid memory of our last appointment.

So you feel you're pulling out of the quicksand then? He'd told me more than once that his depression felt like being stuck hopelessly in quicksand.

Yeah. I think I'm finally getting over Daria. I joined Facebook? And me and this poly-sci major named Kim have been messaging back and forth. She might be potential girlfriend material. His posture wasn't slumpy for a change. His hygiene and coloring had improved. For forty-five minutes, he sat there pumping his right leg up and down as if, now that he was feeling better, he was waiting for the starter's pistol to go off so he could run out of my office and reengage in life.

There was a debriefing, as there is whenever there's a suicide—a departmental review of Seamus's case. These meetings are meant to be supportive of both the therapist who'd been treating the victim and the department as a whole. Suicide is hard on all of us, no matter whose patient it is. Several of my colleagues, including some of the ones who'd been shunning me, commiserated. Even Muriel, who was running the meeting, looked right at me when she said how much easier our jobs would be if we psychologists all had crystal balls. She and Dean Javitz had talked to Seamus's parents, she said, and from the sound of it, they weren't holding the department or the university responsible. "No inquiry, no malpractice charges, thank goodness," she said. But absolved or not, I couldn't forgive myself for having been so goddamned distracted by the Jasmine mess that I had missed the red flag Seamus had waved that morning. When a potentially suicidal patient exhibits rapid improvement—becomes suddenly energized— what it *can* mean is that he's finally arrived at a plan that will free him permanently from his unbearable gloom. But I hadn't probed that possibility. I'd accepted Seamus's emergence from his emotional "quicksand" at face value. The "what-ifs": they'll do a number on you.

I went to Seamus's wake. His father stood there, stoop shouldered and dazed. His mother hugged me and thanked me for all the help I'd given her son. "He spoke so favorably about you, Dr. Oh," she said. "He appreciated how kind you always were to him." Unable to look her in the eye, I looked, instead, over her shoulder, mumbling that I wished I could have done more. Then I walked out of the funeral home, got in my car, and drove away in tears.

That evening, I called my own kids to make sure they were okay. Safe. Ariane said she'd had a tough day—that one of her soup kitchen regulars, a meth addict, had come in agitated and gotten so verbally abusive that she'd had to call the police, something she hated to do. Andrew, who's enrolled in a nursing program at Fort Hood, told me he was "stressed to the max" about an exam he was taking the next day and didn't have time to talk. Marissa told me she was bummed because she hadn't gotten the small part she'd auditioned for: a legal secretary on *Law & Order: SVU*.

"But everything's good otherwise? That disappointment aside, you're okay?" She said she guessed so. Why?

Ariane was the only one I told about Seamus's suicide. I'd kept all three of them in the dark about the Jasmine situation. Hadn't said anything to their mother, either, although Annie and I still talked every couple of weeks or so. I mean, why drag them into it? They all had busy lives, problems of their own. And frankly, I was too ashamed to say anything about Jasmine. She's twenty-nine, not that much older than the twins. Not stopping her? Not getting the hell out of there? It made me sound so pathetic.

I couldn't sleep. Couldn't concentrate. I kept forgetting to eat. In the middle of the night, a week or so after Seamus's funeral, while I was wandering around from room to room in the four-thousand-square-foot home where I now lived alone, I took on my future. Did I even *want* to keep my job? Even if I stayed and fought it, beat the charge, it wasn't like I'd ever be free of her accusation. There'd still be whispered rumors, assumptions of guilt. I'd be walking around that campus wearing the proverbial scarlet letter. And anyway, I *was* guilty, up to a point. Not guilty of what she accused me of, but guilty nonetheless. I couldn't stop seeing her withdrawing her hand from between my legs, my semen between her fingers.... Whatever was going to happen—whether the university would show me the door or not—my license to practice would still be intact. Maybe I could rent an office someplace and go into private practice. But I was weary. Dogged by self-doubt about my ability to help others fix their lives when my own was in shambles. And when a kid I might have rescued now lay buried at a cemetery up in Litchfield. . . . No, I decided, screw the 80 percent I'd be able to retire on if I stuck it out for four more years. I'd quit. Just fucking quit. Relieved, I got back in bed and began to doze. That night I slept the sleep of the dead.

My resignation was handled discreetly, classified by Human Resources as an "early retirement," rather than a resignation. None of us wanted to see it played out in the press, least of all the school, whose enrollment numbers were down in the wake of a run of negative publicity: a sports program scandal under investigation by the NCAA; a *Journal Inquirer* exposé about the epidemic of alcoholism on campus; a third consecutive downgrade by *U.S. News & World Report* in its annual ranking of colleges and universities. The agreement I signed in exchange for my willingness to go away quietly left me with a twenty-four-month extension of my health insurance coverage and a severance check that was the equivalent of two years' salary.

The Counseling Services secretaries organized a little farewell gathering for me. Coffee, cake, and testimonials from several of my colleagues who had until then maintained their silence with regard to my sexual harassment charge. That's what was reported back to me, anyway. I boycotted my own get-together. And since I wasn't there to receive my "good-bye and good luck" card and the engraved pen and pencil set with the university's logo, these were slipped into my mail slot. I retrieved them the following Sunday morning when I entered the building to pack up my office. Walking down the corridor, listening only to the sound of my own footsteps, I assumed the building was empty. Then Dick Holloway poked his head in the door and nearly gave me a heart attack. "So you caved, huh?" he said. "Well, sayonara."

Unmoored from my life as I'd known it, I didn't know how to fill up my days. That first Monday, I sat and stared at the morning TV shows, did the *Times* crossword, did my laundry. At noon, I drove over to the mall for lunch and human contact. Bought a turkey wrap at the food court and ate, a singleton among young couples, elderly cronies, and chatty young moms, their babies in strollers beside the tables. Back home again, I decided I'd read. A book a day. I walked around the house, pulling from the shelves books I'd meant to get to for months, even years. A couple of Elmore Leonards, a P. D. James, the Dennis Lehane that Ariane had sent me for Christmas the year before. Maybe I'd *re*read, too—Updike, Steinbeck, Thoreau. I stacked maybe ten or eleven books on the coffee table and ran my finger up and down the spines. I picked up *Walden*. Flipped it open to a page where someone—me?—had underlined the author's mantra: *Simplify, simplify, simplify*.

Which I interpreted as: downsize, downsize, downsize.

I dialed Annie's number and let her machine know I had decided to put our house on the market. (Our divorce settlement stipulated that I would make the mortgage payments and could live in the house for up to five years, at which point I could either buy her out or put it up for sale and split the profit 60/40.) When Annie called me back, I saw her name on my caller ID and didn't pick up. In her message, she asked me why I'd made the decision to sell. I didn't return her call, or her next one, or the one after that.

After the realtor did a "walk-through" with the first prospective buyers—a nice enough couple who nevertheless seemed like intruders—I knew I wasn't going to be able to handle a whole summer's worth of the same. Nor did I want to drop everything and evacuate at a moment's notice every time the agent called to say she was bringing someone over. So I took out a month-by-month lease on a small furnished apartment downtown. At six fifty a month, I could afford the extravagance—not that this little place where I was going to wait it out could be called "extravagant" by any stretch of the imagination. It was more bunker than luxury digs. On the realtor's advice, I left everything at our house "as is." In a market *this* tough, she said, we'd need every advantage, and a "homey" place showed more successfully than bare rooms and bare walls. She even brought over one of those scented Yankee Candles. Banana bread, it was, so those would-be buyers could smell something not really baking in the oven. Our ace in the hole, she said, was that the house was beautifully decorated. This had been Annie's doing. "Shabby chic," she called it.

On the first of July, I moved into the bunker. I hate it there. For one thing, there's a nightly racket from the bar across the street. For another, the old gal in the apartment across the hall is needy. Pesty. She seems to lie in wait and, whenever she hears my footsteps, pops open her door and wants me to talk or fix something for her. The couch in my apartment has a peculiar, not-quite-identifiable odor to it. And worst of all, the place is just too goddamned small. When I sit on the wobbly toilet seat, I can make my knees touch the opposite wall. Whatever room I'm in, I can reach up and palm the ceiling. The first night I was there, I lay awake in the dark and could almost swear the bedroom walls were closing in on me. It had been a stupid move on my part. Simplify, simplify, simplify? Bullshit! Bullshit! Bullshit!

By the third night, I decided that if I was going to quell my emotional and vocational seasickness, it wasn't going to be at *this* place. But rather than take our home off the market, I decided that what I needed was a getaway from my getaway. But where? When I'd moved into the bunker, one of the few things I'd taken with me besides the necessities was a box of stuff the kids had given me over the years: homemade cards and gifts, mostly. I pulled from the box the nautilus shell Ariane had given me one Father's Day. Held it to my ear, listened to the sound of the ocean, and said it out loud: "Cape Cod."

I looked online. Circled a few of the classifieds at the back of the *New York Review of Books*. Even though it was off-season, everything was overpriced. And later, when Annie and I finally did talk about the house, she suggested Viveca's place. Viveca herself called me later that day and offered me the house rent-free. "It's just sitting there, Orion. It's yours to use if you want to." I'd declined her offer at first but then a few days later had changed my mind. It wasn't until after I'd said yes that I learned there was a stipulation.

Deciding that a slow crawl along the scenic road might be a relief from the bumper to bumper of the main drag, I signal and exit from Route 6 to 6-A. In Orleans, I pass that Christmas Tree Shop where Annie always wanted to stop. Look for bargains, use the restroom. Needing to pee myself, I pull into the parking lot of the Hearth & Kettle where we'd eaten a couple of times. Get out of the car, stretch, and walk on rubber legs toward the restaurant. Passing a newspaper box near the entrance, I read the *Cape Cod Times* headline: GREAT

WHITES CURTAIL LABOR DAY FESTIVITIES. Inside, I head for the men's room. Some would-be graffiti artist had drawn a cartoon on the wall over the urinal I was using: a shark. "Ah, a human," it said. "Yum yum."

Leaving the bathroom, I decide to stay, get something to eat. I wait at the hostess's stand, looking around at all the families and couples in the dining room. Opt instead for a booth in the bar. A flush-faced young waitress approaches; her colonial cap and ankle-length checkered dress are offset by the snake tattoo crawling up her neck. "Somethin' to drink?" she asks, passing me a menu. She has tattoos on the backs of her hands, too, I notice, but I can't see what they say.

"Just an ice tea," I tell her. "Unsweetened."

She nods. "You ready to awduh aw do you need a few minutes?"

"I guess I'm ready. What kind of chowder do you have?"

Our eyes meet. "What do you mean, what kind?"

"New England? Manhattan?"

"All's we got is New *England*," she says. She asks me where I'm from and I tell her Connecticut. "Oh, okay. Newyawkachusetts. That explains it. You want a cup or a bowl?"

"A bowl," I say.

"Cawn frittuhs with that? They're on special. Three for a dawluh."

I tell her no, but that I'll take a Caesar salad. She nods. Writes on her pad. "So what do those tattoos on your hands say?" I ask.

Instead of telling me, she holds them out in front of me. The left hand says, *Ask me if . . .* The right says *. . . I care!*

After I've eaten and passed on dessert, my waitress brings me my bill. Eager to get back on the road, I pay in cash and leave.

At the Orleans cloverleaf, I get back on Route 6, grateful that, at last, the traffic has begun to ease. I should be getting there in another fifteen or twenty minutes. I pass that place that sells the inflatable rafts and the two-dollar T-shirts, remembering the time when we had to pull in there. Andrew had waited to tell me that he had to go to the bathroom until it was an emergency. "Sorry, no public restrooms," they'd said, and the poor kid had made a beeline for the bushes behind the place and had an accident before he reached them.

Had walked back to the car in tears with a big wet spot on the front of his shorts. And when Marissa'd started giggling, her mother had threatened to forbid her from going swimming for one whole day if she didn't cut it out. Then I'd looked in the rearview mirror at the commotion—Andrew punching his sister, her punching him back. Per Annie's order, they'd *both* spent that day on the blanket instead of in the water with Ariane. "Daddy! Mom! Look at this," she'd kept calling, so that we could watch her turning somersaults in the surf. Poor Ariane: it seems as if she was always trying to get our attention. And poor Andrew, too: he could never measure up to his twin sister's feats, and never resist being a hothead when his little sister teased him. . . .

"If you ask me, Dad, it's a *sickness*," Andrew had said in that phone conversation we'd had about his mother's wedding.

I told him I disagreed, and so did the experts. "The *DSM* stopped classifying homosexuality as a sickness way back in 1973," I said. "It's as much an inevitability as blue eyes or someone's shoe size."

"So why'd she even *marry* you then? Why did she have *us*?"

"Because she loves you guys. And she loved me, too."

"Yeah, well . . . this Vivian person?"

"Viveca," I said.

"Yeah, whatever. In that note she wrote me? When she said she hoped me and Casey can make it to the wedding because it would mean so much to Mom? Hey, sorry, lady. That ain't gonna happen."

"Fair enough," I said. "It's your decision."

"You're not going, are you?"

"No, probably not."

"You've met her, though. Right? Mom's . . . *friend*?"

"Uh-huh. You've met her, too. Do you remember that time when your mom had one of her pieces selected for the Whitney Museum show? And the five of us took the train down to New York? Stayed at that nice hotel and went to her opening?"

"Vaguely," he said. "Was that when you took us to the NBA store and we saw Rick Fox?"

"Yup. Same trip. But I've seen her two or three times since then, too."

"If you ask me, I don't even think Mom *is* gay. I think she's just mixed up. Living in New York, hanging out with all those artsy types. Who *wouldn't* get their head messed up? You know what Marissa said? In this e-mail she sent me? That she thinks *everyone's* bisexual, and that some people deny it and some people don't. Now if that's not fucked-up New York thinking, I don't know what is. And I wouldn't put it past that little twerp to be doing some experimenting with the lesbo stuff herself. You know how many gay bars there are in New York City?"

I said I didn't. Did he?

"*Plenty* of them," he said.

I told him I didn't think living in New York, in and of itself, would turn anyone gay, so we were going to have to agree to disagree on that one. "And as for your sister, she's an adult. Whatever experimenting she may or may not be doing isn't really our business, is it?"

"Yeah, but I'm just saying . . . So what's this Viveca person like, anyway? No, on second thought, don't tell me. I don't even want to know."

"It'll take some getting used to, Andrew. I realize that, but—"

"Don't defend her, Dad. Mom having a *wife*? It's messed up."

"Well, it's legal now, Andy."

"Because some asshole liberal judge back there—"

"It wasn't decided by a judge. They voted on it in the state legislature."

"Yeah, and what are they going to make legal next? People marrying their dogs or something?"

"Oh, come on now. That's kind of a specious argument, isn't it?"

"All I'm saying is, it's unnatural. Do you think that's what God wants?"

Instead of getting into an argument about God's existence, I told him I had no idea what God wants. "Hey," I said. "Not to change the subject, but I saw on the Weather Channel that you guys are getting a lot of rain down there. Right?"

"Yeah. Last couple of days there's been tornado watches, too. I mean, if women marrying women and men marrying men was God's plan, then why'd he make Adam and *Eve* instead of Adam and *Steve*?" . . .

Chapter Five

Annie Oh

Viveca has left the prenup on her desk in the study: six legal-size pages with little cellophane flags to indicate the places where my signature's supposed to go. She's signed it already in her deliberate, forward-slanting penmanship. I haven't signed it yet and may not. What's she or her father's lawyer going to do if I don't? Stop the wedding? No, she wouldn't do that. I'm not powerless in this relationship. Gallery owners need artists more than artists needs gallery owners. . . . But that's not fair. I mean more to Viveca than those commissions. She loves me. I know she does. But I also know that she envies me my creativity, my treacherous rides inside the cyclone. "Other agents have approached you. Haven't they, Anna? You can tell me," she's said more than once. That's where my power comes from. I know what her professional insecurities are, and also her personal secrets: that she terminated a pregnancy by a former lover, a man who refused to leave his wife; that she was not an only child like she tells everyone but had a mentally retarded brother who was hidden away at some training school. Profoundly retarded, she told me. She used to hate it when her parents made her go with them on those visits and she had to look at him, drooling and wearing a dirty helmet, banging his head against the wall. I've made it my business to know these things but have told Viveca very little about my own history. I hold my cards close to the vest, the way I did all those years with Orion. I may have been powerless against those floodwaters. Powerless against Kent's secret visits to my room. But I learned about power the day that I got on that Greyhound bus and the driver pulled out of the depot and carried me away from the black hole that had almost sucked me in. The black hole that my life was about to become with Albie Wignall. . . .

I'm seventeen again, stuck in Sterling because that's where my foster family lives. I'm dating Albie, not because I like him very much, but because one thing has led to another. Two of those snooty girls from my high school, Holly Grandjean and Kathy Fontaine, finally *have* noticed me—well, not me so much as what we sell at Jo-Jo's Nut Shack. "Oh, wook. Gummy bears! I wuv Gummy bears," Kathy says, and Holly says she "wuvs" them, too. I'm not sure why they're talking baby talk. Are they making fun of me? But then, I decide they aren't because Holly looks up from my merchandise to me and says I look familiar. "Don't you go to Plainfield High?" she says, and I nod and tell them that all three of us were in the same gym class freshman year. I'm so grateful that they're acknowledging my existence, these girls I thought I hated, that I shovel scoop after scoop of gummy bears into an open bag and tell them to just take them instead of paying for them. And then, at the end of my shift, my boss, Leland, points up at the surveillance camera mounted over the entrance to Jordan Marsh. It's aimed right at my kiosk. Leland tells me to take off my Jo-Jo's apron and not come back because I'm fired.

But a week later, I get another, *better* job waitressing at Friendly's. My manager, Winona Wignall, assigns me to the take-out window, which the newest waitress always gets. But within two weeks, Priscilla is the new girl, and I'm serving people at the counter and making tips. Over the next weeks, Priscilla and I become friends, bonded by the fact that, out of all the Friendly's waitresses, Winona likes us two the least.

Winona's son, Albie, is twenty-three but he acts younger. He works at the Midas Mufflers down the road. After work, he comes over to Friendly's to eat and hang around. He starts picking my section to sit at every time, and it's kind of flattering, although he's not much of a tipper. One time all he leaves me is eleven stacked pennies. Albie's over six feet tall, and he's blond and broad but not really fat, which is a miracle because when he comes in, he'll eat a Big Beef with fries and a Fribble, and sometimes after that, will have dessert, too—a sundae, usually, which, when he orders it, he always calls it the Albie Special. The Albie Special is four scoops of chocolate almond chip ice cream, strawberry sauce *and* hot fudge, and chopped peanuts, the whole thing topped with whipped cream, jimmies, and cherries (three instead of the usual one). Sometimes when I put those sundaes in front of him, our other customers look over at it, and they're probably thinking, wow, how does *that* guy rate? This one Holy Roller couple who comes in all the time? (They asked Winona once if they could leave their religious pamphlets for our other customers to take and she said no.) They always stare over at Albie's sundae while he's eating it, and I feel like going: *Thou shalt not covet thy neighbor's goods.* (My foster family sent me to parochial school, and I can still recite all the Commandments.) Instead of reminding them about the tenth commandment, though, I told the Holy Rollers that Albie pays extra for his sundae. He doesn't really. He gets all that extra stuff for the price of a regular hot fudge, *plus* you have to give him his mother's employee discount besides. Winona calls Albie "Big Boy," which fits him size-wise but also is pretty funny because Albie acts childish, especially around his mother, who he still calls "Mommy." He's not all that much younger than my brother Donald, except Donald is already married and acts like a grown-up, which he is. So is Albie, technically, but he lives in his parents' basement and still gets an Easter basket, which I know because all during Lent, Winona kept buying stuff for Albie's Easter basket and hiding it in our break room. One time, Priscilla stole two Almond Joys from one of the bags. She snuck me one, and whenever we looked at each other during that shift, we couldn't help laughing.

One night, while Albie's holding up his elbows because I'm wiping down the counter where he sits, he asks me out. I didn't expect it, and I don't know what to say at first, so I say, "Let me think about it." Then later on I tell him yes, okay, I'll go. Because, hey, I'm not stupid. He's my boss's son.

For our date, Albie takes me to the drive-in. It's a double feature: the first and second *Planet of the Apes* movies. (I've already seen the first one and thought it was stupid, but Albie picked the movie.) At intermission, he asks me do I want anything from the snack bar. I tell him yes please, a box of Good & Plenty. When he gets back in the car, he's got my candy plus, for himself, three foil-wrapped hot dogs and a big soda. In between eating my Good & Plenty, I keep shaking the box, which is partly just this habit I've had since I was little but also partly because I like the sound. It comforts me.

Albie keeps looking over at me while he's eating and I can smell that he has liquor breath. "Did you put something in your Coke?" I ask him.

"It's not Coke. It's root beer."

"Yeah, but did you?" He nods, smiles, and pulls a half-empty bottle out of his back pocket. When he hands it to me, I squint and read the label. LONG JOHN'S GINGER BRANDY, it says. Eighty proof.

"You know something?" Albie says. "You're pretty."

"No, I'm not," I tell him. I'm thinking about what I heard someone call liquor once: "Dutch courage." I don't know why. What's so Dutch about getting drunk?

"Yes, you are, and you *know* you are, too," Albie says. Ha! I think. He's either drunk or blind. But then I think, well, maybe in Albie's eyes, I'm like those girls at the mall who I got fired trying to impress. He scoots closer to my side and starts playing with my hair and my left ear. Then he leans over and starts kissing my neck. He's trying to be sexy, I guess, but it just tickles, plus now his breath smells like both brandy and hot dogs, which isn't very appealing. After a while, he reaches down and takes my hand in his. It makes me think of that song "I Want to Hold Your Hand" that's on my brother Donald's *Meet the Beatles!* album. When Donald got married and moved out of state, he gave me all of his old Beatles albums, which I still play quite a bit, even though the Beatles broke up because of Yoko Ono. Instead of watching *Return to the Planet of the Apes* or thinking about what Albie's up to, I start singing that song in my head. *And when I touch you I feel happy inside . . .* It makes me think about this girl in my fourth grade public school class named Carol Cosentino who used to wear a pink sailor hat that had all these little metal Beatles buttons pinned all over it. Carol's favorite Beatle was George, I remember. I wonder whatever happened to her. Out of the corner of my eye, I notice that Albie, while he's still holding my hand, is using his other hand to fiddle with his pants. Then I hear this snap-snapping sound and I see his belt flying into the back. From the way he just lifted his butt off the seat, he might have just pulled his pants down. I'm not sure, but I'm certainly not going to look over there and find out. But then he moves my hand over to his side and puts it down there—him and his Dutch courage. I can feel that he's still got his underpants on, which is a relief, but I can also feel that he's got a lump in there. A "boner," I've heard boys at school call it when they're talking dirty in the cafeteria. "Please?" he whispers, moving my hand up and down against his lump. I let him do it, not because I want to but because he said please, which makes me feel, kind of, that it's me who's in control of the situation, not him, and also because if Albie likes me, then maybe Winona will like me better, too, and assign me to Section A, where those lawyers from the office building next door always sit, and they're big tippers. Those booths are Althea's section, usually. Althea is Winona's pet and she used to be Albie's girlfriend. One day I overheard her telling one of the other waitresses that she broke up with him because he has no class. But according to Albie, *he* broke up with *her* because, unlike me, Althea is "a bitch on wheels who thinks her shit don't stink." That's one thing I have to say for myself: I never, ever leave a bathroom smelly; I'm very careful about that kind of thing. I keep matches in my purse even though I don't smoke, and whenever I have to use the toilet and, you know, get the bathroom smelly, I always light a match and burn some toilet paper to, what's it called? Oh yeah, *fumigate* it. Part of me wants to yank my hand away from Albie's lump, but another part of me says, what do I care? It doesn't even feel like it's *my* hand that's doing what he's making it do, and while he's over there, mouth-breathing and making my hand go faster, I try thinking of other things. I make up this game where I have to think of all the songs on *Abbey Road* in the right order: "Come Together," "Something," "Maxwell's Silver Hammer." I get all the way to "I Want You (She's So Heavy)" and then I can't think of what comes after that. It's like my mind's gone blank or something. Thinking about other things is something I learned to do on those nights when Kent would sneak into my room. I'd recite stuff they made us memorize in school: the Ten Commandments; the Joyful, Sorrowful, and Glorious Mysteries. I can still remember some of the Mysteries—the Annunciation, the Nativity, Finding Jesus in the Temple. And, let me think. . . . the Resurrection, the Crowning of Mary as Queen of Heaven. (One time, this girl who sat next to me, Tammy Tusia, had to go to the office for being sacrilegious because she leaned over and said to me, trying to be funny, "Gee if Mary got queen, who got first runner-up?" and Sister Presentation *heard* her say it. Luckily, I didn't laugh so I didn't get in trouble.) So that's how many mysteries? While I'm counting how many I've said, Albie starts going, "Oh, god! Oh, fuck! Faster!" Oh, and there's the Scourging at the Pillar, the Descent of the Holy Ghost. Albie starts to groan and now I can feel the wet stuff. I know from Kent that after the wet stuff comes out, they quiet down and stop bothering you. I finally remember the song that comes after "I Want You (She's So Heavy)." It's "Here Comes the Sun"—the one George sings. I wonder if Carol Cosentino, wherever she is, still likes George the best, even though he has long scraggly hair now and a beard that makes him look like a hillbilly. In my opinion, the Beatles looked better when they had their Beatle haircuts, like on the *Meet the Beatles!* cover.

It's after midnight by the time the drive-in gets out, and when Albie pulls up in front of my foster family's house, he asks if he can kiss me good night and I say no, it's late and I have to go in, and he accepts it. See? *I'm* in control. Not him. "Can I call you?" he asks. I make him wait a couple of seconds. Then I say, "Yeah, okay." Albie's not handsome or anything, but he's sort of cute. Priscilla from work thinks he's borderline fat and has kind of a pig face, and I can see her point, too. Upstairs, while I'm getting ready for bed, I decide Albie's ugly-cute, like Ringo. Not that he looks anything like Ringo. He looks like Winona, although he acted kind of insulted when I told him that.

On our next date, Albie and I go to the drive-in again. *Saturday Night Fever* is playing this time, and I've been looking forward to seeing it because I've had a little bit of a crush on John Travolta from when he was Vinnie Barbarino on TV. But Albie's wrecking it for me because he keeps telling me he'd bet me any amount of money that John Travolta is a homosexual. (How would *he* know?) I'm sitting there, trying to enjoy the movie, and Albie keeps saying stuff like, "Look! There's your evidence. That's a flitty walk" and "You know who dances like that? Queers, that's who. I swear on a stack of Bibles: that guy is light in the loafers."

"Do you mind?" I finally say, and after that he shuts up for a while, thank god. Then, halfway through the movie, there's lightning and thunder and it starts pouring. The movie stops and it says on the speaker that they're closing but giving everyone fog passes at the exit. When we get ours, Albie says he sure as hell would hate to sit through that faggy John Travolta movie again and, to be funny, I guess, he puts the fog passes in his mouth, chews on them, and then spits them out his window. I don't like Althea, but she's right about him: Albie's got no class.

It's early still, so we go to Kelly's Drive-Thru and get Cokes and clam fritters, and while we're eating our food, the rain stops. Albie throws out our trash, and then he starts his car and drives us out to Oak Swamp Reservoir, which is a make-out spot for kids our age. Well, *my* age. It's easy to forget that Albie's six years older than me. He parks and turns off his engine but keeps the radio on. They're playing that song "Baker Street," which I like, but when I say I do, Albie says it sucks and that he wants to listen to some *real* music. He reaches under his seat and pulls out a Judas Priest cassette and puts it into his player. "Yuck," I say. "Where's my earplugs?" and Albie says I obviously don't know good music and turns up the volume. We start making out a little, and he guides my hand down there again to that same area as last time, big surprise, and he's got his lump again. "Please, sweetie. Please," he says. It makes me think of that thing my father said to me that time when he caught me feeding veal loaf to our cat, Fluffy, under the table. "You start that, Anna Banana, and he'll pester you nonstop." One thing about my father: whenever he got finished working on our car, he always came in and washed his hands with that scratchy soap powder, Boraxo, to get the grease off. But Albie always has greasy hands, and, when he gets close to you, he smells like . . . mufflers.

Five minutes later, Albie still hasn't finished and my hand's starting to go numb. Then something unexpected happens. He puts his hand between *my* legs and starts tongue-kissing my mouth at the same time. I let him because it feels kind of strange but also a little bit good, and the more he does it, the less I want him to stop. "Mmm, you're wet," he whispers.

"No, I'm not," I say. Am I?

"Yeah, you are," Albie says. "You're so wet, I almost need a mop. You're good and ready for it, aren't you?"

I know what "it" is, and I don't want it in me, but I don't *not* want it, either. I'm confused. So when he pulls me into the backseat and gets on top of me, I let him. He pokes his thing all around down there but his aim is bad. Then he finally figures it out. He starts whispering stuff like "Oh, Jesus" and "Oh, baby" and he's pumping his hips faster and faster, and that's when, all of a sudden, I think about birth control. "Hey!" I say. "Stop. I don't want to get pregnant." He says it's no problem, that he'll pull out before he "nuts," which, I think, must mean when his wet stuff comes. There's a lot about sex that I still don't get, but I know it's their wet stuff that gets the girl pregnant. And Albie does pull out, too, going, "Oh, fuck! Oh, Jesus!" I don't appreciate the fact that he's gotten his stuff all over my stomach, and even a little of it on my new pocketbook, which I only bought the day before yesterday at Two Guys because Althea was out sick and I got assigned her section and one of those lawyers gave me a twenty for a bill that was only four dollars and seventeen cents and said to keep the change.

The next Monday in English, Mrs. Sonstroem has us read aloud from the book we're reading, *A Tale of Two Cities*. I'm trying to concentrate, but a part of me is back at the Oak Swamp Reservoir with Albie, and him making me feel that tingly way. "Miss O'Day," she says. "You're next." I hate reading out loud and have been hoping the bell would ring without me getting picked. No such luck. Plus, I'm not sure where the last person left off and Jeannie Baker has to lean over and point to where. Before I start, I see Kenny Lalla and John Marchese smirk at each other and I hear Stanley whisper under his breath, "Get ready." Get ready for *what*? I wonder, but I start reading.

And when I get to the sentence *"My father has been freed!" Lucie ejaculated*, the boys—first just Kenny and Stanley, and then a bunch of the others, all start laughing. None of the girls are laughing out loud or anything, but some of them are smiling at each other, and Betsy Yeznach's hand is covering her mouth. I don't get what's so funny.

"All right, that's enough!" Mrs. Sonstroem, who almost never yells, starts yelling. "Maybe if you're all *this* immature, we shouldn't even read Charles Dickens, who happens to be one of the very best writers of all time." Then she says something about pearls and swine that I don't get. One of the boys starts making pig snorts and she gives him a detention. Then the bell rings.

After school, and after I've changed into my Friendly's uniform and still have a few minutes before I have to leave for work, I look up *ejaculate* in my foster family's dictionary. *1. To utter suddenly and passionately; to exclaim*, it says. Then, *2. To discharge abruptly, especially to discharge semen during orgasm.* I look up *semen*. Then I look up *orgasm*. Okay, now I get it, I think. "Semen" is the guy's *milky discharge* and "orgasm" is *the highest point of sexual pleasure, marked in males by the ejaculation of semen and in females by vaginal contractions.*

The next time Albie takes me out, we skip the drive-in and go right to the reservoir. I've put my pocketbook out of range this time. He pulls out in time again, and I think to myself: he just had an *orgasm* and *ejaculated* his *semen*. Unlike the last time, I'm not feeling much of anything myself, but at least I know the names of things now.

For our next date, I have to go over to the Wignalls' house for dinner. I get embarrassed because once the food's on the table, I start eating, but Albie and his parents are just looking at me. Then Mr. Wignall says they like to say grace first. "Oh," I say. "Sorry." He and Winona hold out their hands and I take them and Mr. Wignall thanks God for the bounty that's in front of us. He and Winona have their eyes closed, but Albie and I don't and Albie's looking at me with this goofy grin on his face and making cross-eyes to be funny. When Mr. Wignall's done, he opens his eyes again and says, "Let's eat." Winona's done the cooking and it's creamed dried beef on "toast points" (which is really just regular old toast, as far as I can see) plus beets (which I hate). The Wignalls pour vinegar on their beets, so I do, too, and the vinegar soaks all into my toast so that I have to eat this mushy pink vinegar bread to be polite. Mr. Wignall has seconds and Albie has thirds. For dessert we have green Jell-O with canned fruit in it, which is something Mama used to make, too. Except at our house, everyone got their own separate dish of Jell-O, but at the Wignalls' it's in a big bowl and you pass it around and then squirt Reddi-wip on top. And in the middle of dessert, Mr. Wignall says to Winona, "Sweetness, would you pass me some more Jell-O?" I almost start laughing, thinking about how, the next day at work, I'll tell Priscilla about Winona's husband calling her Sweetness and how it'll crack her up. It's like I'm a spy or something. Then Winona says, "Would you like more cream, too, Sweetness?" and Albie says there is no more, that he ran the can dry, which is no surprise because he squirted so much cream on *his* Jell-O that, if he was my kid, I would have yelled at him for being a pig and not thinking about anyone but himself.

After dinner, Albie and I go over to my foster family's house because nobody else is home. We're watching *Dallas*, and Albie says he'd bet me any amount of money that Lucy Ewing is a slut in real life, too—that she probably doesn't even have to act. Then he tells me that, a few weeks back, he had a dream that Lucy Ewing was sucking his dick. I roll my eyes. No class, I think.

"Hey, can I ask you something, Sweetness?" Albie says. It nearly makes me puke, him calling me that. Who does he think we are? His icky parents?

"What?" I say, and Albie says he was just wondering if I would ever want to try something like that.

"Like what?"

"Sucking my dick. I bet it would really turn you on."

I get up from the couch, turn off the TV, and tell him to go home. "And if you ever say something like that again to me, Albie Wignall, I'm going to tell your *mother* you said it, and don't think I wouldn't because I would."

He says maybe I should just become a nun, and I say yeah, that's a good idea, maybe I will, and he says I'm lucky someone like him even gives me a second look, and I say "Ha, that's a laugh and a half!" and tell him again to go home. He gets up and, on his way out, slams the door so hard that he's lucky my foster father isn't home because he gets real mad when anyone slams things and he'd probably chase Albie all the way down the sidewalk.

The next night at Friendly's, Albie is all apologies, saying how he respects me, he really, really does. "Let's take a drive and clear the air after you get off work," he suggests. I tell him no three different times. Then finally I say yes just to shut him up. And when my shift's almost over, he gets up and says he'll wait for me out in his car. When I go to wipe off the counter, I see that he's left me this tip that's dimes and nickels and quarters shaped like a heart. He probably thinks he's being romantic, but all's I think is that it's pretty corny. Still, when I scoop it up and count it, it comes to two dollars and eighty cents, which is the most he's ever left me, so I guess he really *is* sorry.

But guess where we end up. In a way, he can't help it, I guess. I read in a magazine last week that, on an average, girls think about sex twice in an hour but for guys it's *seventeen* times. This time, after he puts his thing inside of me and I can tell he's getting ready, I tell him, "Pull it out! Pull it out!" and he says he can't, it feels too good, and anyways, he doesn't need to because he's taken a pill that stops the girl from getting pregnant when the guy "nuts" inside of her. A pill that men take? Here's how stupid I am: I believe him. So I let Albie have his orgasm inside of me—that night and the next two or three times after that. And then one day at work, I go up to two of the older wait-resses, Ginny and Mary Beth, who are both in their thirties. Mary Beth is married and it's common knowledge that Ginny "gets around" down at the Anchor Clanker where all the sailors go to drink and meet girls. I ask them if they've ever heard of this pill men take so that the woman doesn't get pregnant. Instead of answering me, they just look at each other. Then they both start laughing, and I feel like the idiot I am. I'm three weeks late, which is why I asked them, and now I know why I am.

It's Saturday, my day off—the day I've decided I'm going to tell Al-bie. I just wish he was in a better mood. He and Winona have just had one of their big fights, and in the car on the way over to Olympic Pizza, he's saying stuff like how Winona's "the wicked witch of the West" and his father's "pussy whipped." In the fifteen minutes since he picked me up, he's told me three times already how much he hates his mother's guts. It's quiet at the pizza place. We take the booth by the window. Albie orders a toasted salami grinder with fried onions and peppers, plus a quart bottle of Dr Pepper. I order a small Sprite and three stuffed clams. I've felt sick to my stomach all week, but suddenly I'm hungry, even though I'm nervous. When our food comes, I tell myself that as soon as I finish my second stuffed clam, that's when I'll tell him I'm pregnant. By now I'm only half-listening to his complaints about his mother, but he gets my full attention when he says that sometimes he daydreams about her getting killed in a car accident or getting struck by lightning and dying. "Winona Wignall, R.I.P.," he says. "I should be so lucky."

It's ignorance, that's what it is. He has no idea how awful it is to have your mother die. "Don't even *say* stuff like that," I tell him.

"Why not?" he says. "It's a free country." He takes a huge bite out of his grinder. There's a strand of shredded lettuce sticking out of the corner of his mouth and he's so stupid, he doesn't even realize it. "Maybe someday I'll take out my hunting rifle and put me and my dad out of our misery."

I get so mad when he says it that I kick him under the table. Not that it must hurt very much. All I'm wearing is sandals.

"What the *fuck*?" he says. "What'd you do that for?" And when I don't answer him, he lifts up his leg and stomps down hard on the top of my foot with his big clodhopper work boot. The pain shoots all the way up my leg and puts tears in my eyes. For several seconds I can't even catch my breath. I wait until the nausea passes.

Here's how I tell him. I say, "That's a nice way to treat the mother of your child, you asshole!" I didn't want it to come out that way, but I have to admit that the look of fear on his big fat face is satisfying.

"What did you just say?" he asks. I put my arms tight across my chest and don't answer him. "Are you saying what I think you're saying?"

I nod without looking at him.

"By me?"

"Oh, *no*, Big Boy," I say, real sarcastic. "It couldn't be yours because you take that pill that doesn't really exist. Remember?"

He tells me to stop fucking with him, and I tell him to pull that strand of lettuce out of his mouth because it looks disgusting.

"Are you having a kid or not?" he says, in this voice that's loud enough that a customer who's sitting at the counter swivels his stool around and looks at us. I've only eaten one of my stuffed clams, but I've lost my appetite and my foot's throbbing, goddamn him. He better not have broken it if he knows what's good for him. I get up from the booth and limp toward the door. I have first shift the next day, and it ought to be a whole lot of fun wearing my waitressing wedgies for five hours if my foot's all black and blue and swollen. Albie follows me out of the restaurant and I scream it over my shoulder, "I'm not having *a* kid, you jerk! I'm having *your* kid! Deal with it!"

Albie's scared to tell his parents, mostly his mother, so it's me who finally has to call the meeting. "It's urgent," I tell Winona. The four of us are seated at the Wignalls' kitchen table: Albie, his father, Winona, and me. There's coffee mugs in front of each of us, and Winona's put out a plate of Oreos that nobody's touching. Winona doesn't say much when she hears what we have to tell her, but her nostrils keep flaring and she's teary-eyed. Then finally she says, "Big Boy, how could this have happened?"

Albie's face is flushed and it doesn't help that he's got this naughty boy grin on his face. "The usual way," he says. "Male plus female equals baby."

Winona reaches over and backhands him. "Don't you *dare* give me that wiseguy attitude at a time like this!" she yells. At first I think he might stomp on *her* foot or something, but Albie just reaches for the Oreos. Winona tells him he has to marry me now because it's the only decent thing to do. "But I guess I better say good-bye to that beautiful church wedding that I've always dreamed about for my boy and his bride." Those tears in her eyes are probably because the bride she'd been dreaming about is Althea, not me.

Albie makes the point, feebly, that he and I have other options.

"Like what?" Winona demands, and when he doesn't answer her, she slams her coffee mug down against the table and says, "Just what do you think we are, Albert Wignall? Trailer trash? You've got obligations to this girl, and you're damn well going to meet them. And if by 'other options' you mean what I think you do, then shame on you!"

"Yeah, but Mommy . . . ," Albie says. He turns from his mother to his father. "Daddy, what do you think?"

Mr. Wignall looks back and forth between the two of them and takes his sweet time answering. "Your mother's right," he finally says. "You had your fun. Now you got to pay the piper." At this meeting, I'm more or less being treated like I'm invisible. Why is that? I'm the one who's pregnant. Don't I count? What if *I* don't want to marry *him*?

But in another two weeks now, I *will* marry Albie, not because I want to but because he's 50 percent responsible for the baby that's growing inside of me. No, more than that—75 percent maybe, him and his imaginary men's pill that stops women from getting pregnant.

Albie doesn't give me a ring; he gives me a hundred dollars and tells me to go down to Ogulnick's Jewelers and pick out something I like. None of the diamond rings are anywhere near my price range, so I settle for this little ring with a garnet chip in it that's really just a friendship ring, not an engagement ring. Winona says I shouldn't wear it to work because my male customers will give me better tips if they don't think I'm "spoken for." Ha! Like *that's* the reason she doesn't want me wearing it, not because she's embarrassed that Albie's "knocked me up," as he puts it.

When I finally call my brother to tell him about my situation, Donald says I don't even sound like I *like* this guy. What am I marrying him for?"

"Because of the baby," I tell him.

"And that's the only reason?"

"Yeah. What other reason would there be?"

But after I get off the phone, I start thinking about it, and if I really, *really* want to be honest with myself, I think I'm partly marrying Albie because, even after all these years—twelve of them now—I still miss my own mother as bad as ever. Maybe Winona isn't perfect—ha!

no maybe about it!—but in under seven months she's going to be my baby's grandmother, so she might soften toward me and maybe even start treating me like a daughter a little bit. Who knows? Maybe next Easter, I'll get an Easter basket like Albie.

My wedding dress is pastel orange with a matching headband. When Winona takes me shopping, she nixes my wearing white or wearing a veil, since Albie and I "jumped the gun" and conceived a child in sin. I have to oblige her because she's paying for the dress, which she likes way more than I do. There's no bridal shower, no fancy invitations. There'll be no graduation this coming June for me, either; I dropped out of school when I started showing. No one from my foster family or my real family is coming to the wedding, not even Donald, who says he can't in good conscience support this marriage. On Albie's side, the only people who are coming are Albie's parents—they're going to be our witnesses—plus Winona's mother, who's always clacking her false teeth and telling me to call her by her first name, Bridey, and Mr. Wignall's father, who has thick gray hair growing out of his ears and wears a hearing aid that's always whistling. The only other person I wanted to invite is Priscilla from work. I've heard Winona tell Althea that she thinks Priscilla is "one of those girls who should have been born a boy," by which she means, I think, that she's a lesbian. Which she is. Priscilla's not coming to my wedding, though, because I didn't end up inviting her after Winona gave me this stupid excuse about how she doesn't feel comfortable fraternizing with people who work under her. What she really meant, I'm pretty sure, is: no lesbians allowed. She'd probably croak if she knew about that afternoon when Priscilla drove me out to the place where she boards her horses, Lucky and Gal, and after we went horseback riding, we made out in the barn and her fingers gave me those "vaginal contractions" that it only dawned on me later was an orgasm—my first.

Even though we're going to get married to prove we're not "trailer trash," as Winona puts it, Albie keeps talking about me getting an abortion. One of the other guys at Midas Mufflers and his girlfriend had "a little complication they had to take care of" a while back, he says, and Albie's got the name of their doctor. But I am *not* getting an abortion, no matter that it's legal now and no matter how much he keeps bugging me about it.

It doesn't matter, though, because on the day we go to town hall for our marriage license they're closed for lunch, and when we go back to Albie's car to wait until one o'clock, I look down and there's blood seeping through my white shorts. "Uh-oh," I go.

"Jesus, what now?" Albie says, and I just point.

He drives me over to the emergency room and everyone there is real nice to me, real sensitive, even Albie. When I can't stop crying and my little box of tissues runs out, he goes out to the nurses' station and gets me a new box. And when we leave the hospital, he holds my hand on the way out to the car. Back at the Wignalls', Winona holds out her arms and folds them around me and I cry against her shirt, partly because I've lost the baby and partly because this is the nicest she's ever been to me. Don't let go, I want to say. Please just keep holding me.

But Winona does let go, and in the days that follow I am both sad about losing the baby and relieved that now I don't have to marry Albie after all. It's like when you're playing Monopoly and you pick up a get-out-of-jail-free card. I decide to get out of Sterling. My foster family's away at the lake for the weekend. I can pack and leave them a note—tell them I decided it's time for me to move on now that I'm almost an adult. And I can just not show up for my next shift at Friendly's. I'll just disappear.

I call Priscilla and she picks me up and drives us toward Hartford. On the way there, the car radio plays that Beatles song "Here Comes the Sun," and she and I sing along with it. *Little darling, I feel the ice is slowly melting.* . . . In the motel room we rent on the Berlin Turnpike, Priscilla and I make fun of Winona, eat pizza, and drink beer. We get drunk and crazy, jumping on the two double beds, flying past each other in opposite directions until I flop facedown on the mattress and realize I'm still a little sore from my miscarriage. It was a silly way for me to behave, especially since I was almost a married woman and a mother. But I'm not either one of those things now, and so what? I've been on a starvation diet as far as fun's concerned, and being free from Albie has made me giddy. I know that it's only for this one night. Priscilla has to get back to her horses and her job. And I have to *not* go back to Sterling, or to the stupid clod I almost married. I still feel sad about the baby, but in a way it was for the best. If it had lived, I probably would have never gotten free of Albie and his parents, and even if I did, my baby's last name would be Wignall. And my name, too. Annie *Wignall*: yuck! "Do me a favor, will you?" I ask Priscilla. "The next time he comes into Friendly's and you make him a sundae, spit on it." She kisses me and says it'll be her pleasure, and that she'll spit in his "fucking Fribble," too.

Later, in the dark, Priscilla climbs into my bed and we start making out. She does the same kind of stuff she did to me that day in the horse barn and I like it and don't even feel sore anymore. I do the same things to Priscilla, and I like doing that, too. But after we're both finished, things get quiet. I can tell from her breathing that she's fallen asleep and I get scared. Get up and go look out the window at the cars going by—the people inside them getting to wherever they're going. And yeah, I've gotten away, but I have no idea where I'm going *to*. It's like I'm a little girl again, in the backseat of that social worker's car the day they came and got me. Drove me away from Daddy. I'm crying, looking out the back window at Kent, who's running down the road after me. What Kent does to me is bad, but are these people bad, too? Where are they taking me? I don't even care that my father's drunk all the time. I just want to stay and live with him. And what about my brother? Donald's at college and won't even know where I'm going, where they're taking me. . . .

I get back in bed. Reach over and touch Priscilla's shoulder. Take her hand in mine. I keep holding on to it so that I'll feel safe and be able to fall asleep. And after a while, it works. My panic fades away and I begin to doze. The next morning when I wake up, she's still asleep. We're still holding hands.

Priscilla buys us breakfast at a diner next door to the motel, but I can't eat much. I have a stomachache. On our way out, she asks the cashier how to get to the bus station and then drives me over there. "Where to?" the ticket guy asks me. He waits. "Miss? You're holding up the line."

"Three Rivers," I say. I'm not sure why I'm going back to where my family used to live—where the flood was—except that I have to go somewhere and it's the only place I can think of. Priscilla gives me two twenties and a ten and says it's not a loan, it's a gift to help me start over until I can find a job. She waits with me until the bus comes, and when I get on it and the driver pulls away, Priscilla waves to me and I wave back. I'm crying, partly because I'll miss her but also partly because I'm doing something daring and powerful. Something life-saving, even. I've gotten the hell away from Albie, and from his mean-ass mother, too, and that's why I'm doing this. Later on during this bus ride, I realize it's my birthday. I'm eighteen. Happy birthday to me.

Getting a pay-by-the-week room in Three Rivers is easy; I manage that in about an hour after I arrive. But getting a job is harder. There's a Friendly's on East Main Street, but when I go in there to fill out an application, the manager says he only wants experienced waitresses. That's what I am, but it's not like I can put down Winona Wignall as a reference. Shop Rite says they don't need any grocery cashiers right now, but they'll put my application on file and maybe call me in a month or so. A month? I can't wait that long. My room costs forty dollars a week, and between the money Priscilla gave me and my own money, I only have thirty-three dollars left. And anyway, how are they supposed to call me when I've left the space for my phone number blank? A sign in the window of a dress shop says SEAMSTRESS WANTED. Too bad I can't sew. I go to the library and read the want ads. Some business is looking for a typist. Too bad I can't type. A drugstore wants a part-time clerk and delivery boy. Too bad I'm not a boy and don't have my driver's license. Two days later, there's a new ad. A "café" called Electric Red is looking for dancers. Okay, I think, I can dance.

The catch is: you have to dance topless on a little stage across from the bar. But my week's rent at the rooming house is almost up. I've been living on peanut butter, Wonder bread, and tap water all week. Forty bucks a night plus tips, the manager tells me. His name is Rusty. He's the bartender, too. Dancers get an extra dollar for every cocktail they can get the customers to buy them between sets (when you can put your top back on), an extra *two* dollars if the guy buys another drink for himself, too. "I give you girls ice tea instead of liquor, but the jamokes who are running up a tab don't have to know that," Rusty says. "Another girl just gave her notice, so I can start you tonight." I'm hesitant but desperate, so I decide to give it a try.

My shift goes from nine o'clock until 1:00 A.M., but we get breaks. There are three of us dancers. Gloria is kind of flat-chested, but she's a wicked good dancer. Rusty's girlfriend, Anita, is the other one, even though she has stretch marks and is kind of thick in the middle. "Some guy starts getting grabby with you, I'll give Rusty the signal and he'll handle the situation," she's promised. The sound system blares sexy disco music: "Rock the Boat," "Get Down Tonight," that Donna Summer song "Love to Love You Baby." My dancing is awkward at first because I'm so nervous and self-conscious about my boobs showing. But it helps that the spotlight on us makes it hard to see any of the men who are watching us. Older men, mostly, which somehow makes it easier. After a while I use my technique from before: thinking of things I've memorized to take me someplace other than where I am: the Commandments, the Religious Mysteries, old TV jingles. *Come and listen to my story 'bout a man named Jed, a poor mountaineer barely kept his family fed . . . Who can turn the world on with her smile? Who can take a nothing day and suddenly make it all seem worthwhile* . . . It's not so bad. By my third night, I've made enough money to pay for two more weeks' rent on my room and go grocery shopping. But on my fourth night, while I'm in the middle of dancing to that stupid song "Afternoon Delight," I look out at the crowd and can swear I see my cousin Kent out there among the old coots. I keep dancing but I'm freaking out, not concentrating, and I fall off the front of the stage and twist my ankle. The music stops and when the lights go on, I can see it's *not* him—that it doesn't even really look like him. But that ends my dancing career.

After the swelling goes down and I can walk on my ankle again, I go looking for other work. My luck is with me, and I get two different part-time jobs on the exact same day. In the daytime, I'm a fry cook at Josie's Fish & Chips. At night, I work the shoe rental counter at Three Rivers Ten Pin. Both jobs leave me kind of smelly, from cooking grease and from the antifungal spray you have to squirt into the bowling shoes after people hand them back in. I'm grateful for that spray, though, because sometimes those shoes come back smelling like the jar of Limburger cheese my father used to take out of the refrigerator and spread on crackers. But hey, work is work. Every once in a while, one of the bowlers asks me out, but I always say the same thing: "Sorry, but I already have a steady boyfriend." I'm not that interested in men, or women either for that matter. Mimi, one of my coworkers at the bowling alley, brings me to a women's bar one night, but all the public affection—kissing and dancing crotch to crotch—makes me uncomfortable. "Not my scene," I tell Mimi the next time she asks me to go with her. Priscilla and I are still in touch, though, and when she visits me those two times, we do stuff. But then she gets a steady girlfriend, a welder at Electric Boat named Robbin, and we lose touch.

It's okay, though. I like my uncomplicated single life—working during the week and going by myself to movies on weekends, or to the Laundromat, or to the art museum on Broadway. I go there every time they have a new show, and I'll even go twice to the same show if it's one I like. Sometimes if no one's looking, I reach out and touch the paintings—the hardened brushstrokes. Lean in and smell them, even. I'm not even sure why, but I like doing that. Making contact with the art. Sometimes I think about how, if my mother hadn't drowned and my father had *not* become a drunk, I might have gone to college and learned how to be an artist.

One Sunday afternoon, when I'm doing my laundry—getting fidgety just waiting for my stuff to get dry—I leave the Laundromat and start walking to nowhere in particular. But two streets over, I start recognizing things and I realize that I'm back in our old neighborhood. I approach Uncle Brendan's barbershop where my father used to work. It's called something else now, Danny's, and I wonder if Uncle Brendan died or just retired. I go up to the front window and look in. It seems pretty much the same, except there used to be a talking bird inside and now there's no cage. I walk past the grinder shop and the little grocery store where Kent would sometimes buy me gum or Popsicles. Across the street is the car lot. It's empty now; that dealership must have gone out of business. I force myself to look at the back wall that our station wagon went off of the night of the flood. I shiver a little, feeling again how wet and cold I was. Up against the wall we dropped off of is that garage thing that Kent pulled me onto the roof of. When I close my eyes, I can hear the roar of the water, and Gracie's screams. Can feel her little body bucking against mine. . . . I open my eyes and tell myself not to walk up the hill to our old house, but then my feet start taking me there.

A little girl is in front of our house, drawing on the sidewalk with chalk. Then her mother calls her and she goes running into our downstairs apartment. Standing there, I look at what she's drawn—a house, a sun with spokes, a garden with flowers that are taller than the roof of the house. What if fate hadn't made us get into our car that night and try to outrun the water? If my mother and baby sister hadn't died? What would my life be like now? That's what I'm wondering when I realize that the little girl's mother is staring out at me from the screen door. "Can I help you with something?" she calls out, and I shake my head and hurry back down the hill. . . .

On my way back to get my clothes, I think about what happened because we *couldn't* outrun the flood water: how Kent started touching me. How I had to go to Sterling and live with my foster family— the first one, not the one I lived with after that. How Albie got me pregnant. I think about when I moved back here six months ago and worked as a topless dancer at Electric Red. Last week, when I went to Mr. Big's and ran into Rusty and Anita shopping with their kids, I practically couldn't even believe I had done that—that that was me dancing up on that stage, naked on top, with guys watching me and giving me tips. . . .

The Laundromat is empty now, but someone else's clothes are in my dryer and mine have been taken out and thrown onto the table in a tangled heap. And I'm pissed because some of my clean clothes have fallen onto the not-so-clean floor. I bundle them up and put them in my basket. Then, to fix whoever it was that took them out so carelessly,

I open the dryer and it stops turning with a good thirty minutes left. That will fix *them*, I think, and I leave and head back to my rented room on Chestnut Street.

For the next two years, jobs come and go—the kinds that I either quit or get laid off from. But I'm a saver, not a spender, and so by the time I get hired as a presser at Skiba's One-Hour Martinizing and Fur Storage, I'm pretty well established. I have a driver's license now, and a used clunker of a car I picked out because it was yellow. I live in a two-room apartment on the top floor of a house on Broad Street which I've fixed up nice. I've bought myself some plants, and a little black-and-white TV, and furniture from the flea market: two yellow beanbag chairs, a coffee table with one rickety leg, and a mattress that I'm going to get a bed frame for when I've saved up a little more. I have a phone now, too. It rings every Sunday night when my brother calls me. I talk to him for a while, and then my sister-in-law, Mimsy, gets on and I talk to her. Donald has stayed in touch with our father, too. He says Daddy keeps asking for me, but Donald warns me that he's usually drunk when he goes to see him. So whenever Donald brings up my visiting him sometime, I tell him no, not yet, but that I'll think about it. . . . My name's in the phone book now, at the top of a column on page 203: *A. O'Day*. It's stupid, but sometimes I flip the tissue paper pages until I get to it. Make sure it's still there.

Mr. and Mrs. Skiba like me because I'm trustworthy and reliable. In the year and a half I've been working for them, I've never called in sick. And that time they overpaid me and I pointed out the mistake, they gave me a fifty-cents-an-hour raise to reward my honesty. One day, after Mrs. Skiba's phlebitis has gotten worse, Mr. Skiba decides it might be good for business if a pretty girl waited on customers, so I'm taken off the steam-presser and told to work up front at the counter so that Mrs. Skiba can get off her feet. They trust me to run the register because they know I would never steal from them like that other woman who used to work there and they had to fire.

Is it fate that brings Orion and me together that late afternoon when I'm trying to close? No, it's just the fact that the wall clock behind the counter has started running five minutes slow and that, on my way to work that day, I ran over a nail and got a flat tire. My first impression of Orion when he points at the clock and insists that I wait on him because it's five more minutes before closing time (which it really *isn't*) is that he's an arrogant Mr. Big Shot, the same as most good-looking guys who think they walk on water. "*Doctor* Oh," he goes, when I ask him for his name, and I'm like, Oh *please*. Big whoop-de-doo, Mr. Monogrammed Shirts.

But when I lock up and go outside, he's still there. And now he's nice. Either that or he's coming on to me. When he says he'll change my flat tire, and I tell him the flat tire *is* the spare, he jacks up my car and takes it off, puts it in his trunk, and drives us over to Sears. While we're waiting for them to fix it, he asks me do I want to get a bite to eat and I say yes, because I forgot my lunch at home that morning and I'm starving. When we walk into Bonanza Steakhouse, which I've never been to before, there's a life-size cutout of Hoss Cartwright by the front door. It makes me think of when I used to watch *Bonanza* with my brother, and how Hoss was my favorite of Ben Cartwright's sons, even though Little Joe was the cutest. At this place, you go through a line, tell them what you want, and they cook it for you right there. My meal is delicious. It's been ages since I've eaten steak. And there's a salad bar with lots of choices. Pretty fancy. The salad's so good that I go back to it a second time, which you can do without paying extra. What do I care if he thinks I'm a pig? He's just someone doing me a favor.

We talk, he asks me questions. How long have I been working at the dry cleaner's? Am I Irish? I look Irish. "Yeah," I say. "What are you?" He tells me he's half Italian and half Chinese. I can kind of see it after he says that. He's got a dark complexion and big Italian-looking brown eyes, but they're kind of Chinese-shaped. He looks a little like that actor James Farentino on *Dynasty*. When I tell him that, he says, yeah, he's heard that before. He wants to know if anyone's ever told me I look like Sissy Spacek. I say no. Not only has no one ever told me that, but I don't even know who that is.

He's pretty easy to talk to, actually. You'd think I'd be nervous in this situation, but I'm not. Well, I'm not until I ask him what kind of a doctor he is. A doctor of psychology, he says, and after that I get self-conscious about how, is he analyzing me? Reading clues about me, like that I was a topless dancer, or that my father is an alcoholic? Or that Kent said he wouldn't tell anyone *my* secret as long as I didn't tell anyone what *he* was doing. Which is stupid, I guess. He's a shrink, not a mind reader. To change the subject, I ask him if he's Chinese on his father's side or his mother's. His father's, he says, although he never knew him. "Why not?" I ask, and he says it's because his parents weren't married and his father wasn't interested in having him in his life. "Oh, sorry," I say, because I can't think of anything else. I look away from him, but when I look back, I notice that his eyes aren't totally brown. More like yellowy brown. What do they call that color? Hazelnut?

"When I was five years old?" I say. "My mother drowned in a flood. But at least I remember her." I can't even believe I've just said it. Not even Mr. and Mrs. Skiba know about that.

"Rough, huh?" he says. I nod. Eat some more salad. "Hey, listen to us. Pretty heavy-duty conversation for a first date, huh?"

Is that what he thinks this is? A date? Because it isn't and he better not be getting any big ideas. I go, "I wonder if my tire's ready yet."

"Only one way to find out," he says. Slides off his seat, gets up from the booth. When we pass Hoss Cartwright on our way out, I smile at him and nod, almost forgetting that he's only cardboard. What do I think? That we've just eaten at the real Ponderosa Ranch instead of at this restaurant? Not that the Ponderosa is even real. In the scenes where they go outside, the trees in the background all look fake. Hey, come to think of it, the Cartwrights' cook, Hop Sing, was Chinese, too. Or Japanese. I always get those two mixed up. My tire *is* ready when we go back. "No, no," I tell Orion when he offers to pay for it, but when I realize I'm six dollars too short, he has to chip in the rest. What I'll do is pay him back next time he comes in for his shirts, and if he gives me a hard time about it, I'll *insist*.

Back at One-Hour Martinizing, I hold Orion's sports coat while he puts my wheel back on, tightens the bolts, and lowers the jack. "Well, I had a nice time," he says. "Watch out for nails now. See you on Friday."

Friday? Wait a minute. Is he asking me out? "What do you mean?"
"My shirts," he says. "Didn't you say they'll be ready by Friday?"

"Oh, right," I tell him. I'm relieved and disappointed—a little of both.

Later on at my apartment, I put on TV and it's weird because *Dynasty*'s on and there he is: Dr. Nick Toscanni, otherwise known as James Farentino. It's just a coincidence, I guess, but just the day before at the dry cleaner's, one of our customers, Mrs. Chudy, said to me—I forget what we were even talking about, but she said, "My dear, there *are* no coincidences. That's just God's way of remaining anonymous." And I was like, to myself not to her, yeah? How do *you* know? But hey, maybe she's right.

Anyways, after *Dynasty* gets over, I put on my pajamas and get ready for bed. In the dark, I lie there wide awake, thinking about Dr. Orion Oh. Is it some kind of weird omen that first I told him he looked like James Farentino, and then there James Farentino is on my TV? Except I can't remember Orion Oh's face, exactly; all's I can picture sitting across from me in that booth at Bonanza is James Farentino. I'm jumpy, sort of, and I start thinking about Orion Oh kissing me, and me kissing him back. It gets me kind of excited, and I reach under my pajamas and start touching myself—something I've only done once before when I was in the tub, except I got embarrassed and stopped doing it. This time I keep going, though, picturing other guys I think are sexy. Tommy Ianuzzi from high school, Andy the UPS guy who teases me when he comes into the store, Little Joe Cartwright . . . James Farentino . . . It feels too good to stop so I don't. I close my eyes and press my lips together and it's coming, it's coming. And then, oh god, I'm there. I've just given myself orgasm number three. Priscilla gave me my other two, but I didn't even think about her at all while I was touching myself. It's kind of confusing because, given my experiences with both Albie and Priscilla, I kind of thought I might be a lesbian. Which, maybe I am. But maybe not. Maybe I'm . . . what do they call it? AC/DC? Which, in a way, is a good name for it because sex is kind of like electricity going through you—in a good way, I mean. Well, whatever I am, if he asks me out on Friday when he picks up his shirts and I give him his six dollars back, maybe I won't say yes but maybe I will.

Except he doesn't ask me. I'm waiting on someone else when he comes, and Mrs. Skiba takes his receipt, gets his shirts, and rings him up. "No more flat tires?" he calls over to me, smiling.

"Nope," I say, strictly business. And it isn't until after he's left that I realize I forgot to pay him back.

But the next week, when he comes in with more dirty shirts, he's also got a pair of dress pants that's got a stain. "Salad dressing," he says. "Think it will come out?" I tell him we'll try. "Hey," he says. "Do you like Woody Allen?"

"What?" I go.

"Woody Allen. He's got a new movie out. I was wondering if you'd like to see it with me this weekend." I tell him yes, okay. And after he leaves Mrs. Skiba says something about how I look like the cat that ate the canary, whatever that's supposed to mean. Why am I the cat, not the canary?

The movie is *Manhattan*. It's kind of a coincidence that it's about Woody Allen having a relationship with a younger girl. A *high school* girl. I'm not sure how old Orion is, but I turned twenty-two last month and he's what? Thirty, maybe? Meryl Streep is in the movie, too. She's Woody Allen's snotty ex-wife who left him for a woman. AC/DC, I think. Except I relate more to the younger girl than to her. Mariel something. She has a pretty voice and a nice body. Nicer than mine, that's for sure. In some of the scenes, she's walking around in just a shirt and her underpants. I could see myself having sex with her, but not with Woody Allen. Yuck. Why would *she* want to? Probably because it's his movie. In real life, I bet she's got a boyfriend who's younger and cuter. Near the end of the movie, after Woody's broken up with her and she's going off to Europe, Orion reaches over and puts his arm around me. Which I like. And which, come to think of it, my father used to do with my mother sometimes when they were sitting on the couch watching TV together. When the movie's over, I get up to leave, but Orion wants to stay and look at the credits, so I sit back down. It was okay, not great. Or else I didn't totally get it. Like, why was it in black and white? You'd think that for tickets that cost six dollars each, you'd at least get a movie that's in color.

Walking out of the theater, it makes me feel a little stupid when Orion starts talking about what a genius Woody Allen is. He asks me if I'd be up for ice cream. And where does he drive us to? Friendly's! But it's kind of nice being a customer for a change instead of the scooper. We get cones at the take-out window, then go back to the car. And just when I'm thinking about how I don't have any business going out with someone who's so intelligent and sophisticated— someone who's got the word *doctor* at the front of his name—he takes his first lick of the cone and his ice cream falls off it and into his lap. It strikes me funny—nervous funny—and I try not to laugh. But then *he* starts laughing, so I let it out. And when he puts his empty cone on his forehead and says look, he's a unicorn, I laugh so hard that I'm kind of snorting. "Sheesh, how *old* are you, anyway?" I ask, and he goes that he's twenty-nine going on six. So I was close. Albie would have thrown a fit if he did something this spastic, but Orion just thinks it's funny. And he's a *psychologist*, for cripe's sake. His father never even *wanted* him.

When he drops me off back at my place, he doesn't try to kiss me or anything, but he asks for my number so he can call me again. I tell him yeah, that would be nice. And two nights later, when the phone rings and I know it's not my brother's time to call, I run so fast to the phone that I stub my toe on my stupid coffee table.

For our second date (I don't count the time he helped me with my tire and took me to Bonanza as a real date), he picks me up on Sunday morning because he's taking us on a hike. His hair is still wet from his shower, and when we get in the car, I can smell his clean smell, which I like. And recognize. It's Irish Spring soap. I buy Irish Spring, too, when it's on sale. Otherwise, I buy the store brand. I like those TV commercials for Irish Spring, where the people talk with Irish accents like my ancestors must have talked with. Our great-grandparents on my mother's side were Irish immigrants, Donald told me once. She was a maid at some rich family's house and he delivered coal there, which was how they met. It's funny how people meet. Orion and me, for instance. If he got his shirts washed, starched, and pressed at the Troy Laundry instead of where I work, we'd still be strangers.

On our third date, Orion does kiss me, and two dates later we make out. I like it—his lips on mine, his tongue in my mouth, his hand up inside my blouse. "Okay?" he keeps asking, and I keep nodding yes. It's more like what I've done with Priscilla than what I used to do with Albie. Mostly what I did *for* Albie, I mean. He never really cared about how *I* was feeling. But with Orion, it's more like . . . what? Sharing, I guess. Like, when we went out to eat earlier that night and got one dessert with two forks.

The first time he asks me over to his apartment for dinner, I'm nervous. But he seems a little nervous, too. Not slick or anything. He pours us some wine, and when he hands me my glass, his hand is shaking a little. He goes into the kitchen to check on what he's cooking, and I look around. His wall-to-wall carpet has lines in it, which means he's just vacuumed, probably because I was coming over. He's got nice furniture and nice posters in metal frames. *Arty* posters, like the stuff at the museum I go to. The door to his bedroom is open. It's a little messy in there, which I kind of like. It makes him less perfect. Not that *I* keep a messy bedroom, just the opposite. I like to keep things neat, everything in place. But his kind of reminds me of Donald's old room. "Time to eat," he says. "Come on in." He's got a round oak kitchen table which he's already set. His plates are that Fiestaware I've seen in shopping circulars. The napkins are cloth, not paper. Cla*ssy*.

Dinner is salad, pasta, and these rolled-up meat things that have cheese and herbs and chopped nuts inside. Braciole, he calls them. "Want a little more gravy?" he asks. That's what he calls tomato sauce: gravy. He says he's had the braciole simmering in it all afternoon, which is why they're so tender. And I'm like, oh my god, this is the best food I've ever tasted. While we eat, he starts telling me about how he's a runner—that he runs three miles a day during the week on his lunchtime and five or six miles on the weekend. And about his work—about the students who come in to see him. Kids who have just broken up with their boyfriend or girlfriend, overachievers who have just gotten their first C–. "But then there are the tougher cases."

"Like what?" I say.

He says some of the kids he counsels are trying to survive some serious childhood trauma. "A house fire that took someone's life, a really bad car accident. Or physical abuse, sexual abuse—incest in particular."

I drop my fork when he says that, and I'm furious with myself. I don't want him psychoanalyzing me like he does his patients. "Whoops, clumsy me," I say, trying to laugh it off. But he's just looking at me, not smiling.

"Did I hit a nerve just then?" he asks me.

"What? No!" But he's still looking at me. Still not saying anything. My mind is racing. I told him about my mother, didn't I? Yeah, I did. "Well, kind of," I say. "When you just said that thing about childhood trauma. I started thinking about the flood. The one my mother died in."

"Ah," he says. "Do you ever go back there? Find yourself reliving that night. Because there's something called post-traumatic—"

"What? No." Stop looking at me! "I don't . . . I wouldn't say I relive it. I just think about it sometime. That's all."

"Have you ever seen anyone about it? Gone to a therapist?"

"Me? No. I don't need to do that."

"How about when you were a little girl? Right after it happened. Did anyone take you to see a counselor?"

"A shrink, you mean?" I shake my head. "Gee, you're not going to make me lie down on your couch and tell you about my childhood, are you? I thought this was a date, not an appointment!" I was trying to make it sound like a joke, but it comes out kind of snotty.

He tells me he's sorry, that he hopes he hasn't made me feel defensive. "And you're right. I'm off the clock. The doctor is *out*." He's smiling.

I smile back. "By the way, this meal is really delicious. You'll have to give me the recipe."

It works. He starts telling me about how he doesn't really follow a recipe. That he cooks "intuitively" the way his nonna did.

"Your what?"

"My grandmother. A little of this, a little of that. More wine?"

"Yes, please," I say and slide my glass over to him.

By my third glass of wine, I'm feeling warm and relaxed. Happy to be here with him again. And it's not just the wine. It's also because, except for when he asked me that thing about childhood trauma, he makes me feel safe or something. In a way, it's like being with my brother, Donald, who I could always trust. I start telling him about Donald, how he could be funny sometimes. How he used to wiggle his ears to make me laugh. He says oh, he can do that, too, and I tell him no he can't, and he does it. Not as good as my brother, though. When he did it, his forehead didn't move the way Orion's does. When I tell him I need to use his bathroom, he says sure, go ahead. It's right off his bedroom. "Just excuse the clutter," he says.

After I flush the toilet and wash my hands, I pull back his shower curtain and sure enough, there it is. A bar of Irish Spring. He uses Prell shampoo, too, I see. I'm tempted to peek inside his medicine cabinet before I leave, but I don't. I'm not a snoop.

When I go back to the kitchen, I see that he's already put dessert on the table—slices of ice cream with nuts and cherries in it. There's also a bottle of some bright green liquor on the table, and he asks me do I want him to pour some on my ice cream. "No way," I tell him. "Liquor on top of ice cream? That's like when one of our dry cleaning customers who comes from Maine told me that people up in Maine drink Moxie with milk in it, and I was like *bleagh*." He laughs. Tells me he finds my "unvarnished honesty" refreshing. Which, I'm pretty sure, is a compliment.

When we've finished with our ice cream, Orion says he's gone to the video store and rented us a Sissy Spacek movie so that I can see my "doppelgänger."

"My what?" I go. My double, he says.

The movie is *Coal Miner's Daughter*. After we start watching it, he puts his arm around me like he did when we went to see *Manhattan*, and I rest my head on his shoulder. "She won the Oscar for this," he says. "She's got dark hair here, but she's actually a strawberry blonde with freckles. Like you." He reaches up and touches his finger to my nose. "So what do you think? See the resemblance?" I don't but tell him

I do, a little. "Except you're much prettier," he says. Which is funny, because I've just been thinking how much prettier she is than me.

A few minutes later, he turns my face to his and starts kissing me. And a few minutes after that, neither of us is really watching the movie anymore. Then, out of the blue, he goes, "You know, Annie, I'd really like to make love to you tonight, but only if you're ready. I don't want to pressure you." And out of the blue, instead of telling him I'm *not* ready, I tell him I am. Am I? Or is it the wine? The Fiestaware and the smell of Irish Spring? I'm confused. I can feel my heart beating fast and I'm not sure if it's from excitement or fear. Or both.

We leave the dishes on the table, and holding my hand, he leads me into his bedroom. We sit on his bed and start kissing again. He unbuttons his shirt and takes it off. Pulls his undershirt over his head. This is the first time I've seen him with no shirt on—his chest with the little brownish nipples, his belly button (an outsie) at the bottom of his hard, flat stomach. I like what I see. He unbuckles his belt. "You're trembling," he says. "You sure about this? Because we don't have to if you're not sure." When I tell him it's okay, that I *am* sure—which I'm not, really—he holds my hand against his warm chest muscles and starts massaging the back of my neck. I touch my fingertips to his wrist and feel a pulse. Calm myself to its steady rhythm. "Excuse me," he says and reaches over to his nightstand. Takes out a condom, rips open the foil with his teeth. While he's putting it on, I lie back on the bed, crawl beneath his green plaid sheets, and undress myself. It's kind of like walking out to the end of a diving board just before you jump off. . . .

With Kent, and later with Albie, I had to go someplace else until it was over. But with Orion, I stay right here in the moment. His hands are all over me, massaging my shoulders, my back, the insides of my thighs. His fingertips are fluttery against my clitoris, and it feels as delicious as the meal he's made. I don't deserve someone like him, but Orion doesn't know that. . . .

I don't have an orgasm or anything, but when he gets on top of me and enters me slowly, it feels good. No, better than good. I've never really understood before why a woman would want a man inside of her, but now I get it. With each of Orion's thrusts, I want the next one, and the next. I lift my legs and put my heels against the small of his back to take him in even deeper. We rock together, slowly at first, and then faster, and then crazy fast. His fingers are pressing hard against the back of my shoulders. His breath starts coming out in quick blasts against my neck. Then, abruptly, he stops. Shudders. He stays on top of me until I can feel him lose his hard-on. "Phew," he says and rolls off. For a minute or more, we just lie there, side by side, not talking. Then he takes my hand and squeezes it. "You good?" he asks.

"Uh-huh. That was nice."

"Yeah, for me, too," he goes. "Do you know what I love about you? Why I think I may be falling *in* love with you?" Wait. He's falling in love? With me? He *must* mean me because I'm the only other one here. He says something about my lack of pretense, and something else I don't catch because I'm thinking about something Candace, the woman who cuts my hair, said the last time I was at her shop: that most men are scared to even say the word *love*. That they think if they do, it's somehow going to put a hex on them. But Orion's just said it. I heard him with my own ears. And who knows? Maybe I'm falling in love with him, too. Only I'm not even sure I know what love is. What does it mean when you say you love someone? And who have I ever really loved? Mama, that's who. And Daddy. And Donald. But Mama most of all. And maybe now Orion.

I guess I must be in love with him, because the next night when my brother calls me, he says I sound like I'm in a good mood and asks me what's new. "I have a boyfriend, that's what," I tell him. Which, despite who I am—and maybe only because of the secrets I'm determined to withhold from Orion—I do. I have a handsome Italian-Chinese boyfriend who has a nice apartment and a good job and who keeps calling me. A boyfriend who's had sex with me three times now and has a nice body and is not afraid to say the word *love*.

For the next several weeks, things go great between Orion and me. He takes me out to nice restaurants, or else we stay in at his place, eat takeout or the meals he cooks, and then watch TV. Sometimes we have sex afterward, and sometimes we just get in his bed, cuddle, and drift off to sleep. He's only been to my dinky apartment twice, and both times I've felt embarrassed and a little bit scared about what it might say about who I really am. The first time he came over, he noticed the wobble in my coffee table, turned it upside down, and said he could fix it. The second time, he brought a screwdriver with him, tightened the screws, and now it's good as new.

I've told him some stuff: about how, after my mother died, my father turned into an alcoholic and I had to go into foster care. When I tell him about how scared I was having to go and live with strangers, he says something weird but really sweet. "Too bad I didn't know you back then. I would have come and rescued you." Like he was Prince Charming or something. Which he is, in a way, because he's rescued me from the simple, uncomplicated life I thought I liked until I realized how much I was missing. How lonely that life had been: going to work, going home and watching TV, going places by myself on weekends. He knows I didn't go to college, but not that I didn't even graduate from high school and got my G.E.D. instead. I've told him nothing about Albie or my miscarriage. One Saturday, after I've mentioned how much I like museums, he drives us up to Boston and we go to this *amazing* museum which used to be some rich lady's mansion and now is open to the public. The Isabella Stewart Gardner Museum: it's one of the most beautiful places I've ever been to, and when I tell him that, he says he can't wait to show me *more* stuff. Take me to *other* places that he knows I'll love. That this is only the beginning. Maybe that's what love is. Having someone who guides you through different experiences, coaxes you to try new things but still makes you feel safe. But that's only *my* side of it. What I still don't really understand is what's in it for him. Why *he* keeps saying he loves *me*.

I get nervous when Orion tells me he's going to introduce me to his mother. She lives in Harrisburg, Pennsylvania, and works at a ritzy private school teaching talented and gifted kids—the kind of student I *wasn't*. There's some big summer conference at the university where Orion works, and she's coming up for it. We're driving over there, picking his mom up at the dormitory where she's staying and taking her to lunch.

When Orion goes in to get her, I move to the backseat. Maria is plump but pretty, and real Italian-looking. She sticks her hand between the front seats, shakes mine, and says she's happy to meet me. "Happy to meet you, too," I say. When I tell her I like her blouse, she laughs and says she's had it for years. So? I can still like it, can't I? It was a *compliment*. Orion kind of resembles her but kind of doesn't because of his Chinese-shaped eyes.

On the way to the restaurant, he asks her how her conference is going, and she tells him a bunch of stuff that I'm not really listening to because I'm thinking about some of the things he's told me. How his father wouldn't marry his mother after she got pregnant. God, even Albie wasn't *that* much of a heel. Poor Maria! After Orion was born, he said, he and his mother had to go live with her parents, which they did all while he was growing up. . . . Orion's told me about the first time he met his Grandfather Oh. It was when he was going into his fourth year of high school. He and his mom went up to the restaurant he owned in Boston because Orion wanted to go to Boston University, and Maria needed him to help pay for it. Which he agreed to do, even though he wasn't too happy about it. That was pretty brave of her, to do that. Pretty *ballsy,* as Priscilla used to say. Shit, I wish I hadn't just thought about Priscilla. What if, in this car, I suddenly go temporarily insane and say something like, "Hey, Maria, I'm not only having sex with your son, but I've had it with a woman, too—orgasms and everything." Thinking about saying that makes my stomach do flip-flops and I have to crack open my window and get some air. It's just nerves, I guess. I'd never, *ever* say something like that, even if I *did* go crazy because I'm so . . . what do you call it? Not depressed, but it sounds like that. I've heard Orion say it about some student he's been seeing. Oh, I know. Not *de*pressed. *Re*pressed. . . . Orion said his grandfather was real rude to his mother that day when they went to see him, but that he was nice to him. And that, after Orion was *at* Boston University, sometimes him and his friends would go to his grandfather's restaurant for Sunday dim sum and they always got to eat for free. When I asked him what dim sum was—I was starting to ask him stuff by then without feeling like he was going to think I was stupid—he said he'd rather show me than tell me. And the next weekend he drove us back to Boston, to Chinatown, and we ate at the place his grandfather used to own before he died. It was upstairs in this big, noisy dining room where these little, unsmiling Chinese women wheeled the food around in carts and you chose whichever of the little hors d'oeuvrey things you wanted and most of them were delicious, except for the batter-fried chicken feet which, when I realized what they were, I spit out in my napkin and made him laugh. He laughed some more after he showed me how to eat with chopsticks but I kept dropping things. Then he had one of the Chinese women get me a fork. She nodded but acted kind of put out and when she came back with my fork, she *threw* it on the table instead of placing it. And Orion said, "Excuse me. Don't *throw* it at her. Please pick it up again and *hand* it to her." And after she did and walked away, I thanked him and he said no thanks were necessary. That he liked coming to the aid of damsels in distress. Which, even though it's not like I was tied to the railroad tracks or anything, I thought was so sweet. Protective, kind of. . . . After we ate our dim sum, instead of driving right back, we walked around the city. And when we got to the Prudential tower, Orion took me on this zooming elevator ride to the top. When we went over to the windows and I looked down, I felt a little dizzy and went, "Whoa." He put his arm around me to steady me, and the two of us looked out at all the buildings and the boats on the river. And when I said that I'd never been this high up before, Orion said, "No? You've never ridden in a plane?" I shook my head and he said, "Well, we'll have to see to that." Then he said again how much he liked showing me things, and that that was one of the reasons he loved me. And that maybe someday he would hire someone to take us on a ride in one of those balloons so that we could float through the sky. Like Dorothy at the end of *The Wizard of Oz*, I thought, but didn't say it. Then he started talking about the kinds of things astronauts must see when they go on space flights, but I wasn't really listening because I was thinking: balloon rides, plane rides, dim sum: Yikes! . . .

And so, sitting in the backseat of Orion's car and looking at his mother's head on our way over to the restaurant we're going to, I think about how I really want to like her, and more than that I want *her* to like *me*. I just hope he hasn't told her that we're having a sexual relationship because, you know, it's his *mother*.

Our lunch is at this place, The Depot, that used to be a train station but now it's a restaurant. We sit in the little caboose that's attached to the main building, at a table that's really just for two people. Orion sits across from Maria and me, and me and her are kind of squashed in together, which is a little uncomfortable, especially since I'm left-handed and she's right-handed, and our arms keep bumping into each other. Mostly, it's just the two of them talking because I feel so self-conscious, and also because I can tell that whenever Maria asks me something, it's only because she's being polite. "Oh, I heard from Thea a few weeks ago," she tells Orion. "Her dissertation has been approved and she's already gotten a job. At Emory University, tenure track." When I ask who Thea is, Orion says she was an old girlfriend of his. "Well, she was a little more than that," Maria tells me. "They were engaged." They were? Orion was engaged? "Brilliant girl," Maria tells me.

"Huh," I go. "Wow." Because I can't think of anything more "brilliant" to say. And then, reaching for the bread basket, I knock over Maria's water glass and the water spills into her lap. I'm dying about being such a klutz, but Maria says that's all right, it's only water, it will dry. Except she keeps dabbing at it with her napkin even after our salads come, and asks the waitress for extra ones because of "our little mishap." By which she really means *my* little mishap. "So tell me, Ann, what is it you do for a living?" she asks me. Orion answers for me—tells her how we met at the dry cleaner's where he gets his shirts done. "Yeah, but that's just my temporary job," I lie. "I'm saving up to go back to school. College."

Orion looks at me funny. "You are?" he says.

"Yeah," I say, looking over his shoulder. "Yup." When his mother asks me what I'll be studying, I say the first thing that comes into my mind. "Art."

"Art history?"

"No, just . . . art."

And she goes, "Aha. Interesting."

After we finish our meals, the waitress asks us if we've left any room for dessert. I shake my head because I can't wait to get out of there, but Orion and his mother decide to share this custardy-looking thing with a crust on top that they break with their spoons. Orion keeps telling me to try some, but I keep going, "No, no thanks. I'm stuffed." Which I'm not, really. If his mother wasn't here and it was just me and him sharing it, I'd be digging right in, maybe even as much as his mother is. She's eating like 75 percent of their dessert instead of 50 percent. Boy, she sure likes *her* sweets.

When we drop Maria back off, I tell her again that it was nice to meet her. "Likewise, Ann," she says. They get out and walk to the front door of the dormitory. I watch them share a laugh about something (me?), and hug each other good-bye. Ann, I think: not Annie or my real name, Anna. To her, I'm just some random Ann that he's wasting his time with. She's probably just told him he should end it with me and go back to that Thea person—that he's making a mistake. When Orion gets back in the car, he asks me how I liked her. "Great!" I say. It comes out fake, a little too enthusiastic, but he doesn't seem to notice. He says she liked me, too, and I think, ha! That's a laugh. Tell me another one. He wants to know if I want to go back to his place and I tell him no, that I'm kind of tired. Which I am. All this effort with his stupid mother has exhausted me.

Back at my apartment, I flop down on my mattress and fall right to sleep. Which was something I hadn't done much of the night before because I was so nervous about meeting his mother. It's dark by the time I wake up, and I sit up and start thinking about the dream I've just had. Well, more of a nightmare than a dream, I guess. Orion was screaming at me, saying with this angry face that he doesn't love me—that he *never* loved me. And for some reason, I was standing at an easel, painting a picture with my own blood.

A few nights later, I'm over at Orion's. After we make love, I get up to go but he grabs my arm and tells me not to—that he wants me to stay over, even though it's not the weekend. So I do. Except I can't get to sleep. Instead, I just lie there, wondering what that Thea was like, and why they broke their engagement. I decide it must have been her decision, not his, because Orion's too kind to break someone's heart. Which is probably why he hasn't broken up with me yet. He's restless tonight, tossing and turning in his sleep and mumbling mumbo jumbo. Maybe he's wrestling with wanting to dump me but not wanting to hurt me. The last time I look at his clock radio, it says 3:13. . . .

But I must have fallen into a deep sleep after that, because the next thing I know, it's light out and I'm waking up to the sound of him in the shower. My panic's gone now. Why would he say he loves me, wants to show me new things and take me to new places, if he doesn't? That was just my scared middle-of-the-night thinking. My worrying for nothing. "Morning," he says when he comes out of the bathroom wearing just a towel. I smile. Watch him. Sometimes in the middle of making love, he whispers that I have a beautiful body and I have to stop myself from correcting him, pointing out all my flaws: stubby legs, smallish boobs. The truth is that *he's* the one with the beautiful body. Those wide shoulders and runner's calf muscles. The little line of hair that starts beneath his belly button and goes down. When he pulls off the towel, I watch him walk across the room to his dresser, his penis bobbing. In the months we've been together, I've gotten to know his body inch by inch. And then I think about Thea—how she must have known it as well as I do. How, maybe when she thinks about him now, she realizes she made a mistake. Wishes she hadn't ended it with him. She could call him tomorrow—today, even!—and tell him she wants him back.

Tying his tie in the mirror, he tells me he has to go in early for some meeting. The coffeemaker's gurgling in the kitchen, and I ask him if he wants me to get him a cup. No, he says. I should stay in bed and relax. "You don't go into work until noon on Tuesday. Right?"

It touches me that he knows my schedule. "Right." A few minutes later, he brings *me* a cup of coffee, kisses me on the forehead, and reminds me to lock up when I leave. He goes out the door whistling.

I've been alone in his apartment before, but until this morning I've never snooped. I don't know Thea's last name, so I go through his whole Rolodex and there's no Thea in it. There's no evidence of her in his bedroom closet, either. But when I think to look under his bed, I pull out the plastic storage bin that's under there and take off the lid. It's mostly his old college stuff—papers he's written, notebooks with notes in them. But there's a thick envelope in here, too, and I take it out. Spill what's in it onto his bed: pictures, letters. Most of the photos are of him and this same woman who must be Thea. She's thin and beautiful and has long brown hair, long fashion model legs. There's one of Orion and her in dress-up clothes, and a bunch of pictures of the two of them at some fancy resort or something. The one of him kissing her has writing on the back in what must be her handwriting because it's not his. *O and me at the Ocean House, July '77.* O, she called him instead of Orion. Even her penmanship is pretty. In the picture I hate the most, Orion's between Thea and his mother, his arms around them, the three of them smiling. I hear Maria say what she said at that lunch we went to: *Brilliant girl.* Talented and gifted, I think. The kind of girl she thinks her son deserves.

When I'm done looking at the pictures, I notice that one of the letters he's saved has a return address that says *Thea Kingsbury, 64 Egmont Street Apt. 3-C Brookline, MA.* I take it out of the envelope and read it. They must have just had a fight or something, because she says she's sorry about what she's said—that she's been under a lot of pressure lately and didn't mean to be such a "dolt." Until we had that lunch with his mother, I'd been thinking that maybe—*maybe*— he and I might have a future together. Ha! If she wrote him another letter like this one, he'd drop me like a hot potato. I stuff everything back in the bin and shove it under Orion's bed. Everything, that is, except the picture of him and Thea with his mother. I rip that one up and bring the pieces into his kitchen. Turn on the faucet and the garbage disposal and watch them disappear down the drain. There's a bowl of peaches on his counter. I grab one, bite into it hard, and my teeth hit the stone. This peach is like life, I think. Juicy and delicious on the outside until you get to the pit.

After I leave his apartment and go home, I call work and say I'm sick. Which I am, except not with a stomach virus like I tell Mrs.

Skiba. It's my first sick day since I started working there. "Bananas and toast," Mrs. Skiba says. "That will settle your tummy." All day long, I go back and forth about what I should do. Or shouldn't do. And by late afternoon, I've reached my decision.

It would be too painful to break up with him in person, so I do it over the phone. At first, he doesn't say anything. Has he hung up on me? No, because I can hear his breathing. "I just don't get it," he finally says. "Have I been missing something? Because if I have, let's talk about it. Work through it." Like he's my psychologist, which he *isn't*. I tell him I can't talk about it. He goes, "Why not?" Because if we did, I might start telling him everything. That I snooped around in his apartment and found those pictures. That his mother doesn't think I'm good enough for him. I might keep going until I told him every single thing I've kept from him. "I thought things were going so well for us. Jesus Christ, Annie, the least you can do is give me an explanation."

"It's just that . . . we're a mismatch. And it's better we face it now than later. I have to go now. Bye." I hang up on him and start to cry. And when he calls right back, I don't answer the phone. I don't answer it the next two times either. Or the next day. Or the one after that. Then the phone stops ringing.

He usually comes in with his shirts on Tuesdays, my late day, except the following Tuesday, he's a no show. I've been dreading seeing him all afternoon, but now that it's closing time, I'm disappointed. When Mrs. Skiba asks me what's wrong, I tell her I don't want to talk about it and she backs off. I miss him so badly that it's like I hurt physically. And hey, I *do* hurt physically: headaches, stomachaches, diarrhea. I keep thinking about calling him and telling him I was being a dolt, but I don't. Better that *I* ended it before he could have. Or that he didn't end it but wished he had. He's probably already reconnected with Thea by now, his *real* girlfriend. Which is probably why he's stopped calling me and started going to a different dry cleaner's. Every day when I go into work, I check the slips to see if he's brought his shirts in and I just missed him, but I haven't. He's probably getting them done at the Troy Laundry now.

The night he shows up at my door, he looks awful and his breath smells boozy. "Have you been drinking?" I ask him.

"Yeah, every fuckin' night since you lowered the boom," he says. He's got the same mad face he had in my dream and says he needs to come in. When I ask him why, he says because I owe him a better explanation than that we're a mismatch. *Why* did I just cut and run like that? *How* are we such a mismatch? He pushes the door open and barges past me, makes a beeline for one of the beanbag chairs, and sinks down into it. It sighs under his weight; it's weird how they do that, these chairs. I sit down on the other one.

"It just wasn't going to work," I tell him.

He shrugs. "Why not?"

"Because I'm me and you're you, that's why."

He shrugs again. "What the fuck does that even *mean?*"

"It means you're a psychologist and I never even went to college. And I'm not *going* to go either. I just said that to make your mother like me."

"She *does* like you," he says. "And I don't give a shit whether you went to college or not. I love you, Annie, not your freakin' curriculum vita." My what? "So come on. Don't leave me in the dark like this. What else?"

There were a million other reasons. Where should I start? "Because . . . because you have nice furniture and I don't even have a bed frame yet. Because I buy my clothes on clearance and you wear fancy monogrammed shirts." He laughs. "It's not funny! I just don't deserve you, Orion. Thea deserves you. I bet you any amount of money she's sorry she broke up with you. And that if you picked up the phone right now and called her, she'd—"

He kicks over my coffee table. First he fixed it for me, now he's trying to wreck it. "What the fuck does Thea have to do with anything?" he wants to know. "And for the record, *she* didn't break it off. *I* did."

"Oh," I say. "You did? Why?"

"Because she was a narcissistic bitch! A spoiled little trust fund baby! And because I could feel the noose tightening around my neck! Annie, *she and I* were the mismatch, not you and me. I want to be with you. Take *care* of you. Was I just deluding myself? Because I thought you wanted that, too."

"I did," I say. "I do."

"Then what the fuck is the *problem*?"

We end up on my mattress, and the makeup sex is pretty intense. When Orion comes, he says, "I love you . . . love you . . . love." And I burst into sobs of joy and relief. Hold on to him so tight that it's like he's saving me from drowning.

He proposes to me two days later. Instead of saying yes, I ask him if he's told his mother yet. He looks at me like I'm weird. Wants to know why he'd do that. "No reason," I say, "Uh . . . when are you thinking you'd like to—"

"Soon. As soon as possible. I don't want to wait unless you do. Do you want to wait?" I shake my head.

We go ring shopping and I pick out one of the smaller diamonds. "Really?" he says. "Because I kind of like the one three down from that one." He means the one that's my real favorite but looks like it costs way too much.

"Yeah, that one's gorgeous."

"Exquisite," the jeweler says. I try on both of the rings, but I stick to my guns and say the other one's fine. Then I get my finger sized and we leave the store and go to town hall to apply for our marriage license. I blush a little when the clerk tells us we're a cute couple.

The next night, Orion comes over with a pizza. And while we're eating it, he reaches into his pocket, takes out the little blue velvet box, and hands it to me. I open it and there it is: the beautiful, more expensive ring. "Don't give me any arguments," he says. "I know which one you really wanted. Try it on. I want to see how it looks." And when I do, he looks up from my hand to my eyes and smiles. Takes me in his arms and kisses me. "I love you so much," I tell him. And I do, whether I deserve him or not. While he's holding me, I look at my ring finger resting against his shoulder and sparkling in the overhead light. Am I still plain old Annie O'Day from foster care who almost got trapped into marrying Albie Wignall? Because I don't feel like that girl right now. I feel more like Cinderella. Who, come to think of it, had a shitty life, too, until she went to that ball. And who almost blew it like I did until they put that glass slipper on her and it fit.

Cinderella and her glass slipper? Happily ever after? No, I've long since stopped believing in fairy tale endings. But if what I have now with Viveca isn't perfect, it's still special and real, despite my misgivings. I love her. She loves me. I walk over to her desk, sit down, grab a pen. Flip the prenup to the places that need my signature and scrawl my name. There. It's done. So much for that.

Chapter Six

Orion Oh

That Sunday afternoon when Annie lowered the boom? Told me she would always love me but that she was in love with Viveca? After she left—took a cab because I refused to drive her back to the train station—I didn't call her and she didn't call me. But after a month or so of silence, I e-mailed her to let her know I was going to be in New York for a three-day psych conference the following week, and that I wanted to see her. Talk to her. Since she was the one who'd left, it was she who was calling the shots. Was reconciliation on the table or should I get a lawyer? We needed to talk because I needed to know.

She e-mailed back to say she wanted to see me, too. Suggested we meet for dinner at Milos, a Greek restaurant in Midtown. Eight P.M., say? If I'd let her know, she'd make a reservation. I clicked on "reply." *Sounds good. I'll be there. Love you, Orion.* I stared at that "Love you" for several seconds. Replaced it with *See you soon* and sent it into cyberspace.

I arrived at the restaurant twenty minutes early and, to calm myself, ordered a Grey Goose and tonic at the bar. Jesus, we'd been married for almost twenty-seven years. Why was I feeling first-date nervous? I was on my second drink when they arrived, twenty minutes late—Annie *and* Viveca. My anger was visceral, but I tried hard to swallow it back. Apparently, Viveca still didn't remember having already met me that time at the Whitney because her opening shot was that I looked nothing like what she had pictured. "No?" I'd said. "What had you pictured?"

"For some reason, I thought you'd be more . . . *psychologist*-looking."

"Meaning?"

"Oh, I don't know. Balding with an earring and a little ponytail, maybe. Shorter." She laughed as if what she'd just said was funny, and I felt like saying that she looked nothing like what I had pictured, either: that other Greek monster, Medusa. Annie told Viveca that I was six foot three, which was no longer true. At my most recent physical, my height had been recorded as six one and a half. I'd shrunk.

We made it through drinks and dolmades with lemon sauce cordially enough, and I managed not to wince whenever Viveca referred to Annie as Anna, twisting the knife a little more by pronouncing it pretentiously: *Ahna*. But halfway through our entrées—and, for me, a *third* vodka and tonic—Viveca asked me if she could ask me something.

"Shoot," I said.

She wanted to know if I was accepting of Ahna's and her relationship.

I tensed. Sipped my drink. "Define 'accepting,' " I finally said.

Viveca said she wasn't trying to be "fractious," but that for the past hour I had had very little eye contact with her, had directed almost all of my remarks to Annie, and it made her feel invisible. "Maybe I'm just misreading things," she said. "But it feels like I'm getting a passive-aggressive vibe from you."

"Sweetie, please," Annie said, reaching across the table. She placed her hand on top of Viveca's hand. Comforted her, not me. *She* was Sweetie now.

"Passive-aggressive?" I said. She wanted eye contact? Okay then. I'd give her eye contact. I stared at her in silence until she looked away. Then I downed my drink, stood, and tossed my napkin onto the table. "Gotta go," I said and started for the door.

"Orion?" Annie called. "Orion, come back." Without turning around, I raised my hand and waved her a backward good-bye.

Annie's handwritten letter of apology arrived in Monday's mail. She had thought, mistakenly she realized now, *stupidly*, that it might be easier for me to meet Viveca if I didn't have to anticipate it beforehand. "But I can see now that it put you in a really awkward position, Orion. I'm so sorry."

I e-mailed her, not to say that I accepted her apology but to tell her I'd made an appointment with a lawyer to see about a legal separation, and that she might want to do the same. And that if she hadn't already done so, she should let Ariane, Andrew, and Marissa know about her decision to end our marriage in favor of her new lesbian lifestyle. "I think it should come from you, not me. Just don't expect them to be thrilled."

I pass the signs for Eastham, North Eastham. The T-shirt and lawn ornament shops. Both the Blue Dolphin Inn and the Four Points Motel have their NO VACANCY sign up, probably because it's Labor Day weekend, the last hurrah of summer. But the traffic's much better, finally; I'm going forty now, pretty much. I'm gaining on it. I just hope I get to that rental office in time to pick up the key. . . .

All three kids checked in with me soon after she told them, which she did when they came home for Christmas, but not until just before each of them was about to leave. Marissa, who lives in New York and had met Viveca, was totally accepting of her mother's decision. Ariane wasn't happy with Annie, but she was sweetly sympathetic to me. "Daddy, why don't you take some time off and come out here for a visit? I'll show you around San Francisco." Andrew was furious. He'd leapt to my defense when Annie told him, he said—had yelled at her, stormed out of the house. I was the one who drove him back to the airport. His mother had wanted to come, too, but he told her he didn't want her to.

"I mean, Dad, how long have you guys been married?" Andrew said, outraged on my behalf. "Twenty-something years, right?"

"Going on twenty-seven," I said.

"And she just wakes up one day and decides she's *gay*?"

I told him I thought it was a little more complicated than that. That *two* people were responsible for a marriage's survival, not just one. He didn't seem to be listening. . . .

My second meeting with Annie and Viveca occurred just about a year ago. By then, our divorce was in the works but had yet to be finalized.

"The San Gennaro festival starts this weekend," Annie told me over the phone. "We were wondering if you'd like to come into the city and join us. Walk down there together. The weather's supposed to be beautiful." We? I remember thinking. Really?

I'd become resigned to the dissolution of our marriage by then, but I wasn't exactly relishing the idea of seeing Viveca again. I *did* want to see Annie. "I won't have to dance the tarantella with Lady Bountiful, will I?" I joked.

Annie laughed a little. "Be nice," she said. "What do you say?"

"Yeah, okay. Why not?"

From Penn Station, I took a cab down to Elizabeth Street. Viveca's apartment building had a doorman. He buzzed them for me. "She said to go on up," he said. I shook my head. Asked him to tell them I'd wait down there in the lobby. I'd been there once before, back when I was still in the dark about their affair, and I wasn't eager to see Viveca's place with fresh eyes now that I knew the full extent of their "cohabitation." Didn't want to have to go home and picture it. So while I waited, the doorman and I talked baseball. Yankees versus Red Sox, that kind of thing. It might not have been New York's year, he said, but if Boston thought they were going to kick Tampa Bay's ass in the playoffs, they were dreaming.

When they came downstairs, I took both of Annie's hands in mine and kissed her on the cheek. Viveca, too, leaned in for a kiss—or, specifically, a pair of those New Yorky air kisses that don't quite land on either cheek. "It's good to see you again," she said. All I could manage in response was a nod, a smile.

We headed over to the festival, Viveca noting while we walked that as Chinatown had expanded, it had taken over Little Italy, which had pretty much shrunk to a couple of streets, Mulberry and Mott. *Taken over*, I remember thinking: interesting choice of words.

But at the street fair, sharing a bottle of chianti at an outdoor café and watching the crowds stroll past the calzone and cannoli stands, we three were on our best behavior. Annie and I were telling Viveca stories about the kids when they were small. How, the longer Ariane, our type A, had lasted in the third grade spelling bee, the farther south her tights kept drifting and how, when she won, she jumped up and down and they fell to her ankles. How, on a dare from his cousin, Andrew had swallowed a dime that, luckily, he'd pooped out the next day. "But the twins were a piece of cake compared to their little sister," I said. Annie nodded in agreement but added that Andrew had had his moments, too.

Telling the stories was fun and, on my part, satisfying. A little facetious, I guess. It reminded Viveca that Annie and I had shared a life. Had raised a son and two daughters together. Whatever she had with Annie now, she would never have that. But when Viveca said she was looking forward to getting to know her other two "future step-children," I felt myself clench. My smile didn't waver, though. I picked up the wine bottle and replenished our glasses.

They both looked lovely that afternoon, Viveca's glossy dark hair and long tanned neck contrasting opulently with her blindingly white blouse, Annie's porcelain complexion and strawberry blond hair aglow in the early autumn sunshine, the small, delicate fingers of her left hand curved around the bowl of her wineglass. For twenty-seven years, she had worn her wedding and engagement rings on one of those fingers. Now, instead, she was wearing a gold band etched with the Greek key pattern—those interlocking right angles and vertical lines, rendered in Aegean blue. Viveca wore a matching ring.

Our conversation turned from the kids to our respective ethnicities, and the extent to which family heritage had influenced our lives. Viveca volunteered that, despite having become a successful business-woman, she had never quite won the approval of her father, an Athens-born banker with ties to Chase Manhattan. "He was very patriarchal. Expected me to get my college degree and then become a good Greek wife like my mother. Raise children, cook and keep house, and limit my outside activities to the *Philoptochos*."

"What's that?" I asked.

"A charity. The Friends of the Poor. That's what good Greek wives did: helped the downtrodden and left the serious stuff—business, politics—to their husbands. My father was none too happy when I opted for a master's degree in art history instead of what he had planned. He'd even hand-picked a nice Greek husband for me: a cousin of a cousin who owned a chain of drugstores in Long Island and New Jersey. Don't get me wrong. Papa was proud of my accomplishments. But he was disappointed, too. Abe and I held off getting married until after he died. A career was one thing, but an Arab husband? A town hall ceremony instead of a big Greek Orthodox church wedding? It would have been too much." Annie had told me in a prior conversation that Abe had been Dr. Abdul Shabbas, a prominent Manhattan oncologist who'd been on Ronald Reagan's short list for surgeon general. Nixed by Nancy, according to Viveca, for astrological reasons. Viveca had inherited her wealth from both Dr. Shabbas and Papa Christophoulos.

"Well, at least you're not Irish," Annie said. "All that Catholic guilt and good-natured blarney to hide our real feelings."

Viveca turned to me. "And how about *you*? Half Italian and half Chinese, right? Now *that* must have been interesting."

I smiled. "Interesting? Oh, yeah." I took another sip of my chianti without saying anything else. Maybe Annie had told her about how my father had abandoned me and maybe she hadn't. But *I* sure as hell wasn't going to go into it with her. To shift the subject a little—to spare me, maybe—Annie noted that if we walked south down Mulberry Street and came to Canal, the bustling main artery through Chinatown, we'd be at the intersection of both my mother's and father's heritage.

"That's right," I said. "Add a little green beer into the mix and we've got our kids' heritage, too."

She and I were looking at each other, sharing a smile, when Viveca said, "Ah, here they come." My eyes followed hers to the approaching procession. And for the next several minutes, we drank our wine and watched with bemused interest as the faithful rushed and jockeyed to pin dollar bills to Saint Gennaro's passing effigy in hopes of warding off the misfortunes that God or fate or others might deliver. Bodily harm, say. Or vengeance. Or betrayal. . . .

*   *   *

I drive past the old, familiar sights: the Wellfleet Drive-In, the Box Lunch, Moby Dick's. There's the minigolf place where Ariane once got two holes in one and beat her brother, reducing him to angry tears. There's Outer Cape Health, where we had to bring Marissa for stitches after she cut her foot on that razor clam shell. Passing the sign for Paine's Campground, I recall the fun we had there when the kids were young: toasting marshmallows, playing war and slapjack at the picnic table, walking down the pine needle path to that crystal clear pond. I smile, seeing once again, Andrew and Marissa chasing after all those pale green frogs and Annie, sitting at the water's edge, braiding Ariane's hair. Ari didn't make it home for the holidays last December, so I haven't seen her in almost two years now. If I drive down for the wedding, at least I'll be able to spend some time with her. Or if I don't, maybe she can come up here and see me. I miss her. Miss all three of them. Next time I talk to them, I'll have to ask if they remember that camping trip. Annie had already started turning those junk store finds into art by then, but her work hadn't yet begun to consume her the way it did later. The way it swallowed her whole.

My third close encounter with Annie and Viveca was on home turf this past April. I was in the middle of the sexual harassment mess and battling insomnia over Seamus's suicide when Viveca called me out of the blue. She and Annie were en route to Boston to visit the Isabella Stewart Gardner Museum. "The Gardner is one of Annie's favorites," she said. Did she think I didn't know that when I'd been the one to take her there that first time? The one who had driven Annie to the Gardner all those other Aprils, when the nasturtium vines hanging from the museum's indoor courtyard balconies were in full saffron bloom? Since Three Rivers was on the way, Viveca said, she was wondering if they might stop by and say hello. "Anna would love for me to see the house where you all lived when the children were growing up and she was starting out as an artist. And we'd both love to see you, too, of course."

Then why hadn't Annie called? I asked. I had spoken to her just

the day before; she'd called concerned about Ariane, whose boyfriend
had broken up with her. That poor kid: she'd had so much heartbreak
when it came to men. "And how are *you* doing?" Annie had asked me.
I'd told her about Seamus's suicide but not about the Jasmine mess. I
complained about my insomnia. Melatonin and Sleepytime tea, she'd
advised. As if *that* was going to let me off the hook.

"Oh, you know how unassuming Anna can be," Viveca said. "She
didn't want to put you on the spot if it wasn't a good time. We're stopped
at one of those awful turnpike places. I'm out in the car and she's run in
to use the ladies'. If it's not convenient, Orion, I understand."

It had been six or seven months since San Gennaro. I told her it
would be nice to see them, by which I meant that it would be nice
to see Annie. "Wonderful!" Viveca said. Now I wasn't to fuss. They
would only stop by for half an hour or so. No, no, they wouldn't stay
for lunch. They'd probably be there sometime around eleven.

By the time they pulled into the driveway in Viveca's Escalade, it
was a little after noon. Between the call and their arrival, I had run the
vacuum, run out and bought scones, some pricey coffee, and a dozen
daffodils. Daffodils were Annie's springtime favorite.

"Orion, your home is charming," Viveca said, after Annie had
walked her through. I told her it was all Annie's doing; she had done
the decorating, chosen the colors for the walls, refinished the antiques
she'd picked up on the cheap at auction sales and secondhand shops. I'd
changed nothing since she left, telling myself it would be a comfort to
the kids when they came home for visits—something which happened
a lot less frequently now that Andrew and Ariane had dispersed to different parts of the country. Marissa worked most weekends at that place
where she waitresses and tends bar. When she did come home, it was
usually a peck on the cheek and a quick conversation before dashing
off to some local watering hole to meet up with her hometown friends.

"Well, it's just lovely, Anna," Viveca continued. "I adore the accent
pieces, the way you've offset the neutral shades with splashes of color.
Blended traditional New England with 'shabby chic.'" (Until she said
that, I'd assumed "shabby chic" was an expression that Annie had
coined.) "It's all very homey, very welcoming. And it's a *perfect* comple-

ment to the architecture." She turned from Annie to me. "Now who did you say the builder was, Orion?"

I hadn't said. "His name was Angus Skloot. He built a number of homes in this area during the 1920s and 1930s. This is the one he and his family lived in."

"Well, you were wise to invest in a builder's home, I'll tell you that much. Has your Mr. Skloot ever been written up in any of the architectural magazines?" *My* Mr. Skloot? I said I doubted it. "Well, he certainly *should* have been. His use of stone and brick, the inside finish work: it's masterful! And the upstairs and downstairs fireplaces are to die for! You don't often see this level of fine craftsmanship from regional builders. It's a gem—quintessential Colonial New England."

Annie and I exchanged bemused smiles. When we'd bought the place from Skloot's daughter back in 1984, we'd been more attracted to the brook out back and the acreage behind it than we were to the house itself. We'd always liked the house but had never thought of it as a "quintessential gem."

"The masonry was done by a couple of guys who worked for Skloot," I said. "They were—"

"Let me guess. Southern Italian immigrants, right?"

I shook my head. "I was going to say brothers. The Jones brothers. They lived right here on the property, in a little house out back. Until their big falling-out, that is."

"Over what?" Viveca asked.

"A woman." I turned to Annie. "Sweetie, you probably remember the details better than I do. You're the one who talked to that gal from the historical society who had the scoop." After the fact, I realized I'd just called her what we had called each other during most of our married life. Sweetie: it had come out of my mouth as if the last three years had never happened.

"They were black," Annie said. "When one of the brothers married a white woman—she was foreign born; European, I think—the three of them lived together in the house out back. The falling-out happened when whichever brother was the husband found the other brother in bed with his wife."

"Oh, my. Miscegenation *and* a love triangle." Viveca chuckled. "Quite the small town scandal, I imagine."

I nodded. "Especially after one of the brothers drowned in the well behind their house. They found him stuck in there head first. The coroner ruled it an accident, but apparently there was some speculation that he'd been murdered. If you saw how shallow that well is, you'd know why. He would have had to try pretty hard to 'fall into' it."

"Do they think he was murdered by the other brother?" Viveca asked.

"Or the people in town who didn't like blacks mixing with whites," Annie said. "From what Miss Galligan at the historical society told me, there was a KKK chapter in Three Rivers back then, and the Grand Dragon or whatever he was called lived just up the road."

"And now we have an African-American family living in the White House!" Viveca noted. What was she implying? That Obama's election had eradicated racism? Ordinarily, I would have challenged her on that assumption, but I didn't have the energy. It was still a mystery to me what Annie saw in this woman. Was it money? Prestige? For as long as I'd known her, neither of those things had ever mattered that much to her. But maybe they did now.

Annie told Viveca she used to be a nervous wreck when the kids played in the woods out back. "They knew they weren't supposed to go inside that dilapidated old house, but they'd sneak in there anyway. Their 'clubhouse,' they used to call it. One day I caught Andrew and his friends running across the roof, and all I could think of was that it was going to collapse under them. That, and the old well where the brother had died: that scared me, too. I was always afraid one of them was going to fall in and drown. It still gives me the creeps, thinking about that thing out there," she said.

"The well wasn't really a hazard," I reminded her. I turned back to Viveca. "For one thing, it wasn't very deep. And for another, Annie's brother, Don, and I had lugged a heavy stone slab over the opening. No kid was going to budge that thing."

"But still," Annie said. A shiver passed through her. "Okay, that's enough about that creepy well. Let's talk about something else."

It was a beautiful spring afternoon: blue skies, seventy-five-degree sunshine. We sat out on the back deck, having our coffee and scones. It had rained steadily the day before, and so the grass glistened and the stream made its music. In the middle of Annie's updating me about Ariane, Viveca let out a quiet gasp. I followed her gaze. A doe and her freckle-backed fawn had wandered from the woods into the clearing. We three sat there in silence, watching them.

Shortly before they left, Viveca reminded Annie that she'd said she wanted to show her something. "Oh, that's right," Annie said. "It's in the basement. Orion, do you mind if I go down there and get it?"

Her asking permission seemed strange. "Of course not."

"Should I go with you?" Viveca asked. Annie said no, she'd bring it up. She'd be right back. Find *what*? I wondered but didn't ask.

Viveca and I gathered up the plates and coffee cups and went inside to the kitchen. "Anna doesn't know anything about this yet," she said, her voice lowered to a conspiratorial whisper. "But I have an ulterior motive in driving up to the Gardner today."

I looked over at her. "Do you?"

She said she was meeting informally with one of the museum's board members about seeing if Annie and she might exchange their vows in the museum's courtyard. "They have a 'no weddings' policy, but they may make an exception for two women from the art world and their guests, some of whom have recognizable names and deep pockets. Wouldn't Anna just love that? Being married at the Gardner?"

Looking away from her, I said yes, she probably would, then changed the subject. Asked her if they had ever recovered the paintings stolen from the Gardner several years back. "No, not yet," she said. "From what I understand, it's still an open case with the FBI."

"Wasn't that one of the biggest art thefts on record?"

"Indeed. They made away with a Vermeer, some Degas drawings, a Rembrandt self-portrait."

"Then it's probably just a matter of time before they crack the case, I imagine. I mean, it can't be easy to unload works that are that valuable."

"Oh, there are ways," she said. "Art theft is a very lucrative business, Orion. But I hope you're right. It's heartbreaking to go there and see the empty frames where those priceless works used to hang—placeholders waiting for their eventual return."

"What kind of ways?" I asked her.

"Excuse me?"

"You just said there were ways that even famous works can be fenced. I'm just curious about how they'd—"

"Well, they could change hands a few times until they ended up with an unscrupulous dealer who'd make sure they disappeared into someone's private collection. Or they could be disbursed and resold on the international market. I wouldn't be surprised if they were hanging somewhere in Saudi Arabia or Dubai, one of the oil-rich countries. Or in the palace of some dictator who decries Western values but craves Western art. It's a big world, Orion, with a multitude of hiding places."

"Huh. Poor Isabella Gardner must be turning in her grave."

"Indeed she must be. Her philanthropy was genuine. She meant for her collection to be enjoyed by the public after she died. It's tragic, really."

When Annie rejoined us, she was holding that strange painting I'd forgotten was even down there. "Found it," she said. "One of those brothers we were talking about earlier had been an amateur painter. Obviously, he hadn't had any training. But this picture has always intrigued me. It was up in the attic when we moved in—left behind by the Skloot family, I guess. Look at the colors, the composition."

Viveca took it from her and held it at arm's length. In the painting, a woman, her head and body strangely disproportionate, leers at the viewer. Outfitted in a risqué bikinilike costume, she sprawls lasciviously against the head of an elephant whose trunk snakes out from between her legs. The background is bucolic—a white picket fence, a grove of trees with painstakingly painted leaves, each leaf rendered so distinctly that the trees compete for attention with the figures in the foreground. Strangest of all is the malevolent, midget-size circus clown who peeks out from behind the trunk of a tree on the painting's right side. He's holding a spearlike pointer which he seems to be aiming at the woman's crotch.

I was standing behind Viveca, looking over her shoulder. "The

Freudians would have a ball with all the psychosexual goings-on in *this* thing," I joked. Annie smiled. Viveca seemed not to have heard me.

"It's unsigned," she said. "But my god, it looks an awful lot like—" Annie interrupted her. "Look at the back."

When she did, Viveca read aloud what was written there. *This painting is a gift to Mr. and Mrs. Skloot. I call it 'The Cercus People.' I hope you like it. Joe J. November 1957.* Annie noted that he must have meant *circus* people.

Apparently, the Skloots hadn't liked their gift. *The Cercus People*, painted on cardboard, not canvas, was unframed, and there was neither wire nor hook on the back. My guess was that they'd exiled it to their attic as soon as they received it.

Viveca looked from the painting to me. "What did you say the brothers' name was?" she asked.

"Jones," I said.

"Oh, my word, I thought so!" she said. "Do you know what I think you have here? An original Josephus Jones!"

She had been interested in Josephus Jones for years, she told us— had researched him but had never been able to track down or acquire any of his works. Still, despite the odds, it all fit. She knew that Jones had lived in rural Connecticut, that he had died under questionable circumstances, that he had been employed as a laborer. He had created his art using whatever was available to him: oil-based house paint, particleboard, shirt cardboard. "One source I talked to several years ago, an elderly man who knew him, said he had been prolific—had painted obsessively. But very few of his works have ever resurfaced. A collector in Santa Fe owns two, I know, and the American Museum of Folk Art in New York has three. And now, apparently, we've discovered another. Orion? Do you own this painting?"

I said I guessed so. I didn't go into it with Viveca, but Annie, during our divorce mediation, had relinquished the contents of the house to me. And as far as I knew, the Skloots' daughter was their only heir, and she had died a spinster several years back. I remembered reading her obituary.

"Check with your attorney," Viveca said. It came out more like an

order than a request. She had shifted gears and was all-business. "And
if you do own it, which I imagine you do, if it was left behind, I'd like
to buy it." I held up my hand like a traffic cop. "No, no. You're right.
Take your time deciding. I'm just very excited about this find." She
must have been. For the rest of their visit, she looked mostly at the
painting instead of Annie or me.

As I walked them out to her car, Viveca handed me her business
card. She said she'd call me midweek to see what my lawyer had said
and what my thoughts were about selling *The Cercus People*. She
advised me that, whatever my decision, I should have the painting appraised and insured. I shouldn't hesitate to e-mail her with any questions, and if I needed a referral to a top-notch appraiser, she could
certainly provide me with that. I nodded. Closed their car doors for
them and waved them off.

I was struck by what had happened in the last fifteen or twenty
minutes. Viveca had gone on the hunt and Annie had gone silent—
had become almost opaque. I wandered out to the backyard, wondering why, when I suddenly recalled something she'd said in that
once-upon-a-time *Connecticut* magazine article. How, when she'd
just started making her art, she'd seen something mysterious out here.
Some*one*: a black man in overalls who, a second or two later, was gone.
Was that why she'd gotten so quiet just now? Was she remembering
that she'd told that reporter she might have seen a ghost? . . .

When I looked up at the deck, I saw the daffodils. The sun was
shining so brightly on those yellow blooms, they looked almost electric. Before, while we were having our coffee, I'd gone back into the
house and gotten them—had put them on the table in front of Annie.
She'd said nothing but had smiled, fingering them. I'd meant to wrap
them in wet newspaper and give them to her to take with her, but in
the excitement about the painting, I'd forgotten.

Back inside, staring at Joe Jones's freaky painting, I recalled something else I hadn't thought about in years—something that had happened when Andrew was what? Fourteen or fifteen, maybe? When
I'd gotten home from work that afternoon, Annie had met me at the
door, fit to be tied. "Do you know what I caught your son and his

friends doing out at their 'clubhouse' this afternoon? Sitting up on the roof, smoking marijuana! I made them come down and I could smell it all over them—in their hair, their clothes. I sent the other boys home. Then I picked up the phone and called their mothers. I told Andrew he was grounded for a month. And you'd better back me up on this, Orion! Don't you dare pull any of this bad mom, good dad stuff!"

I assured her that, although I wished we could have discussed Andrew's punishment before she doled it out, I would back her. Still, Andrew and his buddies hadn't done anything *that* terrible. God knows, I'd done my share of experimenting when I was their age. But Annie had her Irish up, so I didn't dare suggest that she might be overreacting to the situation.

"You know what *I* think we should do?" she'd said. "Pay someone to go out there and bulldoze that goddamned house down to the ground. Have you noticed how the roof sags in the middle? Do you know what could happen if they started horsing around up there and it fell in under them? Somebody could end up with a broken back or a broken neck or worse! Can you imagine the lawsuit if something like that happened? Or if one of those boys—Andrew, even!—had gotten killed? We'd never forgive ourselves."

"Sweetie, relax," I said. "Take some deep breaths."

"Oh, you and your deep breaths! *You're* not the one who has to worry about what goes on around here all day long. *I* am. And if I want to get worked up, I'll get good and goddamned worked up!"

I told her I'd go up and read the riot act to Andrew. And that the next day—Saturday—I'd go out there and board up the windows, put a padlock on the door. She nodded, still scowling. Climbing the stairs to Andrew's room, I thought, well, this is just what I need after a long day's worth of listening to the college kids' tales of woe: to come home to a half-hysterical wife and a kid who may be turning into a doper.

"Yeah, but Dad, it's like having the Gestapo for a mother!" he protested.

"That's bull. You're just mad because she busted you."

"But a whole *month*? Nobody else's parents are this strict!"

"No? Well, I guess you got the short end of *that* straw."

He flopped facedown on his mattress, squashed his pillow over his head, and groaned. I heard Marissa before I saw her standing in the doorway. She was harassing her big brother with an impromptu ditty. "Ha, ha, ha, ha, ha. Andrew's in troub-le."

"Hey, you," I told her. "Am-scray."

But Andrew had bounded off his bed and was chasing her down the hallway. "Shut the fuck up, you little brat!" he screamed, flying after her down the stairs. Marissa was screaming, too—more theatrically than from fear.

"Mom! Help! Andrew's trying to hurt me! And he's swearing, too!"

And from the kitchen: "Andrew Joseph Oh! You're in *enough* trouble with me as it is! Don't you dare lay a hand on her!" I had to grab her wrist to stop her from whaling on him, and when I did she freaked. Yanked her arm back and stumbled backward, sobbing. "Hey," I said. "Annie? It's okay."

"Don't you *ever* grab me like that again!" she screamed.

At supper that night, Ariane shared the good news that she'd gotten a 96 on an algebra quiz and that, in her French class, her group had placed first in their Parisian culture presentations. "That's great, honey," I'd said, a little less enthusiastically than I'd intended. Pouting into his plate, her brother mumbled, "Yeah, way to go, Brainiac." Annie's attention was drawn to Marissa who, with her straw, was blowing bubbles in her milk. "What have I told you about not doing that?" she asked, slamming her hand on the tabletop. "If you don't cut it out, I'm going to reach over there and smack you one!"

"Go ahead," Marissa said. "I'll just report you for child abuse."

Annie's lower lip poked out and she left the table in tears. "Well," I said. "I don't think we're ever going to be mistaken for a Norman Rockwell family." One of the kids asked me who Norman Rockwell was, and instead of going into it, I told them to get their butts off their chairs and clean up the supper dishes. Addressing Marissa, I said, "And *you*, Little Miss Smart Mouth, sweep the floor and then sit down and write an apology to your mother." Marissa wondered why *she* was the one who had to apologize, when it was Annie who had threatened to hit her. I stared her down. "Okay, *fine*," she muttered. Then she turned to her brother. "What are *you* smiling at, Dogbreath?"

At the entrance to our bedroom, I looked over at Annie. She was facedown on our bed. The lights were off. "Hey?" I said.

"Hey what?"

"Rough day, huh? You all right?"

I waited. "I just need to be alone," she finally said. Later, after I'd turned off all the lights and climbed into bed myself, she rose and left the room. The next morning when I woke up, I realized she hadn't come back to our bed all night. I found her asleep on the window seat that looked out on the back of the property. My suspicion was that the events of the day had triggered some old, unresolved stuff for Annie. Something from that rough childhood of hers that she was always so unwilling to talk about. Concerning my wife's history, I had long suspected that she'd been abused, either physically or sexually. Most likely when she was in foster care. But from the start, Annie's rule about her childhood was crystal clear. She didn't want to go there, and she was adamant that I not go there either. I knew precious little about her life before the day I walked into the dry cleaner's that first time, and that was the way she wanted it.

But anyway, good for my word, the next morning I loaded up our van with plywood and two-by-sixes, hammer and nails, and a padlock I'd picked up at the hardware store. I inched the car down the narrow packed-dirt footpath to the Jones brothers' old cottage, steering around rocks and ruts, bending tree branches as I went. When I got to the cottage, I laid the planks across the brook, but there hadn't been much rain that season. The water was down to a trickle. Out behind the place, there was evidence galore of Andrew and his buddies' clubhouse shenanigans: spent firecrackers, empty pint bottles of applejack, a rain-wrinkled *Hustler* magazine. Someone had toted a hibachi out there. In the grass beside it were a rusty can opener and three or four scorched aluminum cans with blackened food on the bottom.

Inside, on the windowsill by the back door, marijuana seedlings were sprouting from half a dozen flowerpots. So those little shits were cultivating, too. The floor was littered with playing cards, someone's ripped and stained backpack, several more skin magazines, and half a dozen roaches at the bottom of an empty Pringles tube.

There was something else in there, too, I now recalled: a number of strange-looking paintings on cardboard, similar in style to *The Circus People*. There was one larger painting: Adam and Eve naked in the Garden of Eden. When I looked at the back, I saw that he'd painted it on a legless old card table. From that one and the ones on the floor, I realized that Andrew and his buddies had propped up the four or five that featured naked or bare-breasted women. The paintings were garish, amateurish; the women looked misshapen, more bizarre than sexy. But then again, to pubescent fifteen-year-old boys, female top-lessness of any kind could rev up the testosterone. Hadn't those saggy-breasted native women in *National Geographic*, some of them smiling toothlessly, stirred *my* ardor way back when?

I had never paid much attention to this ramshackle old place at the rear of our property, but now I looked around at what had been the Jones brothers' home. I rocked back and forth on the buckled lino-leum, ran my fingertips over the water-stained wallpaper, the enamel kitchen tabletop with its coating of dust and grit. I walked over to the ladder that led up to the crawl space in the eaves. Looked at the rope and pulley system that they had rigged up to raise and lower it. When I climbed that ladder, I squinted into the crawl space and saw them: another couple dozen or more of what I assumed were worthless paint-ings, plus stacks and stacks of old magazines: *Look, Life, Coronet*, the *Saturday Evening Post*. I climbed back down the ladder, stacked the paintings Andrew and his buddies had carried down, and put them back up there where they belonged. Then I raised the ladder, wound the rope around the hook in the beam, and cinched it tight. Outside again, I saw what she meant: that roof was sagging dangerously. Some-one *could* get hurt. So I hammered, padlocked, and secured the place. And as far as I knew, ten years later, it was *still* secured.

Viveca called me the following Monday with two proposals, one ex-pected, the other a surprise. If I decided to sell *The Circus People* and could verify with my attorney that I was the owner of the painting, she would pay me forty thousand dollars for it. It was a very generous offer, she assured me; I'd see that when I had the painting appraised. Then she moved on to her second proposal: a September swap—her apartment in New York or, if I preferred, her place at the Cape, in exchange for my home in Three Rivers for their wedding. "Please say yes, Orion. It would be such a lovely surprise for Anna." God, the nerve of this woman.

"What about the Gardner Museum?" I said.

"They wouldn't budge. They told me that if they made one exception, it would open the floodgates. So I thought of Plan B: a quiet country setting that would be a reasonable commute for our Manhattan friends, and your place would be perfect. I can't tell you how many times I've thought about those deer we saw. It would be such an idyllic setting."

I told her I was sure there were idyllic places in Greenwich or Westport, and that the commute for the New Yorkers would be even shorter. Or, closer to Three Rivers, there was the Altnaveigh Inn or Bella Linda. "Besides," I said. "I doubt Annie would feel comfortable being married here. I imagine if you ran it by her, she'd tell you that."

Viveca sighed. "Okay, Orion, I have to confess to a bit of benign subterfuge. This *is* what Anna wants, but she's too shy to ask you herself." After they had gotten back from Boston on Saturday, Viveca said, Annie had told her how much it would mean to her if they could be married at the place she'd called home for so many years, with her family gathered around her. "And that includes you, of course," she assured me. I thought of that thing Marissa used to say when she was in high school: *Gag me with a spoon.*

I told her no.

Would I at least think about it?

I said I didn't need to think about it. "Find someplace else."

After I hung up, I stood there, staring at the phone. Why did I always let this woman flummox me? And why was she pushing this idea? Was it about *The Cercus People*? Was she hoping to poke around the property and maybe find more of Jones's paintings? It wasn't that I thought she'd do anything unethical, but that conversation we'd had about the art theft at the Gardner Museum was still on my mind. It was like that expression the college kids always used: I'm just saying...

When she called back two days later, there was no more mention of the house or the wedding. It was all about the painting. If I sold it to her, she could go as high as forty-five thousand, no higher. With the economy as unstable as it was, the art market had destabilized as well. If she could find a buyer for *The Cercus People*, she had to make sure she could make back her investment.

I told her I'd have to get back to her—that I hadn't had time to get it appraised. Did I want that referral? she asked. I said no, I'd take care of it on my end. Fine, she said. Whichever way I wanted to handle it.

I brought Jones's painting to two nearby museums. Sondra Zoë, the director of the Hitchcock, said I shouldn't hold her to it—outsider art was not in her area of expertise—but that forty-five thousand dollars seemed to her like a fair offer. Sal Tundra, the director of the Benson Museum, *did* know outsider art, although his specialty was voodoo artists from the Caribbean. He'd heard of Josephus Jones, he said, but didn't know much more than what I could probably find out on the Internet. Tundra, however, also surmised that Viveca's purchase price was fair. "But you could always counteroffer. Tell her you need fifty thousand and see what she says."

When I called her back, I told her I would consider selling her *The Cercus People* for fifty thousand. Agreed, she said. For an additional five thousand dollars, she wasn't going to quibble. Would I be sending her the letter from my lawyer verifying ownership? I didn't have a lawyer, I told her, and I wasn't going to go looking for one. But I'd dug up all the paperwork from when we bought the house, and our agreement stipulated that we owned whatever contents had been left behind. "Still," she said, "I'd feel more comfortable if I had a letter verifying that." When I told her I wasn't going to pay some attorney to state what I already knew, she said all right then, fine. She'd FedEx me the check that day and would hire a courier service to come and get the painting. Would Friday morning work for the transfer? It wouldn't, I said. I reminded her that I'd said I would *consider* selling it, but I still hadn't made up my mind and didn't want to be pressured about it. There was a long pause on her end. "All right," she finally said. "How much more time do you need to decide?"

"Well, let's put it this way, Viveca. If and when I want to sell it, I'll let you know."

I heard her exhale. She asked if she was competing with another collector. "Are you trying to engage me in a bidding war? Is that it?"

"No," I said. "I'm not that cagey and it's not about the money."

"Then what *is* it about, if you don't mind my asking."

If I'd been honest, I would have told her it was about leverage. About taking back some of the power from the woman who'd caused my wife to leave me. "I just like the painting," I said. "It's about my keeping it, not about my selling it to someone else."

"Very well then. Let me know." *Click.*

In the end, I said no to selling the painting but yes to her second proposal—partially, anyway. They may be getting married in Three Rivers, but the ceremony's not going to be at *our* house. Marissa and Ariane will be bunking there, and maybe their mother, too; I'm not sure about that. But Viveca *won't* be. She'll be staying at the Bella Linda Inn, where their wedding's going to be. That was where I had to draw the line, whether or not she's letting me stay at her place up here free of charge. She *won't* be sleeping in the bed I used to share with Annie. And if she goes over to the house and pokes around, she won't find *The Cercus People* or any of those other Josephus Jones paintings, either. I've made sure of that. So I guess you could say I'm like that sagging roof of the Jones brothers' little house down in back. I partially caved, but mostly not. . . .

Here's the sign for PAMET HARBOR and TRURO CENTER. I put on my blinker and, at long last, exit Route 6. I should be there in just a few minutes; the real estate office is less than a half mile off the exit. But the drive up here has taken me five hours instead of the usual three. It's almost seven thirty. They've got to be closed by now. . . .

D'Andrade Realty—here it is. I pull into the crushed clamshell parking lot. No lights on inside, just like I figured. But when I get out and walk toward the building, I see that the rental agent has left the key inside a business envelope taped to the office door. "Christophoulos-

Shabbas Cottage" is scrawled across it in red Sharpie. Viveca would not be pleased with this casual a system. In a five-minute phone conversation, she mentioned to me twice that some of the artwork at her summer place is extremely valuable, so whenever I go out, I should make sure to lock the doors and windows and put on the alarm system—instructions in the loose-leaf folder on the coffee table.

Viveca's "cottage" turns out to be a stunning split-level contemporary—a far cry from the rustic beach bungalow I've been imagining myself hunkering down in for my soul-searching retreat. I slip the key into the double lock, turn the knob, and enter. Walk down the three steps into the foyer and look around.

Jesus Christ, what a place!

Chapter Seven

Annie Oh

Remembering my past has riled me up. Minnie's left for the day, and I could use a drink. But rather than helping myself to one of those fine wines that Viveca buys, I go instead to the utility closet and take out Minnie's jug. Grab a coffee mug from the kitchen and carry my mugful of Carlo Rossi into Viveca's bedroom. I pour, drink, pour some more, drink some more. I sit on the edge of her bed—our bed—and stare at those four bridal dresses. I should be getting up, walking down to my studio instead of thinking about the wedding. . . .

Nothing's ever neat and tidy. Perfect. If the girls want to be there and Andrew and Orion don't, well, I just have to accept that. It's their prerogative. And maybe Andrew *is* too busy. Maybe that's all it is. And Orion? Well, I can appreciate why he wouldn't want to be there. I think it was generous of him to say yes, the girls and I could stay at the house the weekend of the wedding. His only condition was that Viveca *not* stay there, and I can appreciate that, too. When I explained it to Viveca—how it must feel from his perspective—well, she didn't like it but she accepted it. Had her assistant book her a suite at Bella Linda, where the reception's going to be anyway. It'll be more convenient for her. . . . And anyway, who knows? He hasn't said one way or the other if he's coming. He may drive back down from the Cape and be there after all. And if he does come, I'll feel . . . relieved. It will show me that he loves me more than he hates me because I fell in love with her. Because I fell out of love with him.

And if my born-again son isn't coming to the wedding because he's standing in judgment of me—assuming that Viveca and I are subverting God's plan or whatever—well, it's my life, not his. I became an artist, moved to New York. I've earned what's come to me. I work hard at what I do. . . .

But so did Josephus Jones. A bricklayer by day, a painter by night. It's strange that Orion and I bought the property where he used to live and work. Is it just a coincidence that two unschooled outsider artists just happened to . . . or was that God's plan, too? What was it that woman said to me that time? That coincidence is God's way of staying invisible? Could it have been Josephus Jones I saw out in our yard that day? . . . And that other time I've never told anyone about, when I was down it the basement, working on one of my pieces. When I looked up, that same man I'd seen before was standing there. Watching me. I jumped, looked away for a second. And when I looked back, he wasn't there. Was that just something I imagined? Or dreamt, maybe? Sometimes when I was working down there late at night, I'd start to doze. . . . No, it's ridiculous. I don't even believe in ghosts. . . .

But I believe in the resurrection of Jesus Christ. How can I believe in one and not the other? Well, if Josephus Jones has been tracking my success from the Great Beyond, I'll bet he's a resentful ghost. He ended up stuffed in that well out back and I ended up here in this luxury apartment.

I can feel it approaching: the cyclone. I grab my mug and drink some more of Minnie's wine. Sometimes when the weather in my head changes, I can hear his voice. And I don't want to. Not today, when I'm already feeling so vulnerable. When I'm here instead of at my studio, working.

Tell me something, Annie. And be honest.

Shut up! Go away!

What is it that you want?

I want this: my life here in New York with Viveca.

Anything else?

I want my kids to be safe. I want Orion not to hate me.

Ah, very nice. Very unselfish. But you can't fool me. What is it you really want?

I want . . . to make my art.

And aren't I an integral part of that? When the cyclone comes toward you, isn't that because of me? After all, Annie, I know your secrets, your shame. Like it or not, I'm in your head. It's me who starts the cyclone.

I shake my head. Grab Minnie's jug and refill the mug. I drink, stare at Viveca's wedding dress. . . . When she married Abe, she told me, everything was so spur of the moment that she'd had to wear an off-white Oscar de la Renta pantsuit that was hanging in her closet. She carried a bouquet that Abe's secretary had ordered. They'd lived together for years on the Upper East Side. Attended dinner parties with people like the Kissingers, Alan Greenspan, and Andrea Mitchell. They'd held off marrying because both families opposed it. Because Viveca's father hadn't wanted his daughter to marry an Arab, and Abe's grown daughter had made no secret of the fact that she didn't like Viveca. So they'd waited until after her father's passing, and even then Abe had wanted to keep things streamlined and simple, for his daughter's sake: a civil ceremony at City Hall, a small wedding luncheon at the Four Seasons for immediate family and a few friends and colleagues. At that luncheon, Viveca said, she'd overheard Abe's daughter refer to her as "the barracuda" and it had ruined her day. Tears welled up when she told me that, I remember. Since Abe's death, she and the daughter have had as little contact with each other as possible, even after the daughter's husband died. Viveca sent her flowers and a letter of condolence, she said, but didn't attend the funeral. "I just couldn't go there and hug her, offer her sympathy," she said. "The barracuda: after I had tried as hard as I could with that spoiled little princess."

Viveca is pleased that Ariane and Marissa are going to be my attendants. She won't meet Ariane until the weekend of the wedding, but she and Marissa have grown fond of each other, and I'm glad for that. When the two of them went shopping for Marissa's bridesmaid's dress, Marissa saw what she liked at Stella McCartney's shop over there in the Meatpacking District. Viveca bought it for her. I told them both that I wanted to pay for it, but when I asked them how much it cost, they wouldn't tell me. Viveca said that was a secret between her stepdaughter and her.

Ariane's picked out something online from Coldwater Creek. "Do you think it's all right, Mama?" she e-mailed me, along with the link. Ari's never been that sure of herself when it comes to fashion, and she's self-conscious about the weight she's gained since she moved to San Francisco. Poor Ariane. She's unlucky in love, and every time she gets dumped, she eats.

I e-mailed her back. Told her I thought she'd look beautiful in that dress, and if she liked it, that was all that mattered.

She e-mailed me again. What about the color? Was burgundy going to clash with anything?

Absolutely not, I wrote back.

"Burgundy?" Viveca said when I told her about Ariane's and my exchange. "Maybe it's me, but I've always thought of burgundy as such a matronly color. Can't you talk her into something a little more fun? A little more age appropriate?" It made me feel defensive: her disapproval of Ariane's choice. Viveca hasn't even met Ariane yet and she's trying to tell her how to dress? Now I'm not *just* defensive. I'm mad! Before I can stop myself, mug in hand, I throw my wine at her pale green wedding gown.

It lands halfway down the skirt. The red wine against the green silk makes it look like Gaia, the primordial earth mother, is having her period. I know I should feel guilty. Contrite. I should be rushing to the fridge and grabbing a bottle of club soda before the stain sets, or rushing Viveca's dress down the street to that dry cleaning place. But I'm *not* contrite. I'm a little giddy, in fact. I pour another mug of wine and throw it at the other three dresses. In some places the wine seeps in and it dribbles down to the hems in others. I do it again: pour, splash. I feel like Jackson Pollock must have felt, except I'm not dribbling paint; I'm staining beauty with blood.

I laugh. I feel powerful. The cyclone is swirling, coming closer, and I'm meeting it head-on. It enters me, travels down my arms. I grab all four of the damaged dresses and rush out of the bedroom, out of the apartment. Downstairs in the lobby, our weekday doorman, Rocco, is on duty. "How you doing, Miss Oh? You need a cab?"

I'm in too much of a hurry to answer him. He swings the door open for me and I rush out into the street.

Chapter Eight

Orion Oh

The kitchen counters are black granite, the lights are motion sensitive. The side of the house that faces the ocean is floor-to-ceiling glass. The artwork hung throughout the downstairs is edgy and wild—and, I have to admit, pretty fucking spectacular. Some beach bungalow, Viveca.

After I've done an upstairs and downstairs walkabout, I go back out to the car. Leave my bike on the roof rack but retrieve my other gear: laptop, groceries, Grey Goose. On my second trip in, I grab the duffel bag I've stuffed with Ts, shorts, and underwear. The little marble dolphin my grandfather made for me when I was a kid is in there, too; I'm not sure why I packed that. I leave the second duffel in the backseat of the car—the one that holds my history. It takes me three more trips to carry in the twenty-two paintings I removed this morning from the crawl space in the Jones brothers' ramshackle little house. I'll be goddamned if she's going to get her hands on them, as unlikely as that would have been. Let the art shark cruise other waters.

I find where she keeps her glasses, grab one, fill it with ice. Pour myself a stiff one and flop onto a beige leather sofa—the kind they describe in those high-end catalogs as "buttery soft." I sip my drink and remember. . . .

It's after nine on that March evening when Jasmine knocks on my office door. I've just finished my paperwork and am ready to go home. "Come in."

I don't recognize her at first. She looks different. It's her hair, I guess. It's longer than it was the previous semester, and lighter—honey-colored instead of dark brown. She's in tears and shaking badly. Her winter coat's flapping open, and she's wearing a red V-neck sweater underneath. She's pacing, speaking so rapidly that I'm not getting half of what she's saying. I stand. Go over and close the door, then lock it at her request. "Have a seat," I say, but she says no, she's too nervous to sit. She goes over to the window and takes a furtive peek out at the quad below. When I ask her to tell me again what has her so upset, she says, "Not what. *Who.*"

Her ex-fiancé has been scaring her, she says. Stalking her. He won't return the key to her apartment she gave him. Last week, she went home and there he was. And tonight, as she walked toward her car in the student lot, she saw his car a few parking spaces away from hers. Saw him sitting there with the lights off and the motor running. She panicked and ran back toward the Psych Services building and saw the light on in my office.

When I ask her if she wants some water, she nods, and so I grab one of the plastic cups in my desk drawer and tell her I'll be right back. At the doorway, I look to my right, my left. The hallway's empty. I fill the cup from the drinking fountain and bring it back to her. She's taken her coat off now and has sat down after all. "Thanks," she says when I hand her the water.

She drinks it too fast and water dribbles down her front. The sweater she's wearing fits tightly across her breasts. She brushes the water off her skirt and takes another sip. Her fingernails are painted deep red. Her oversize hoop earrings rock back and forth. Were her breasts always this size? It seems as if half the young women on campus these days have gotten implants. Earlier that day, when one of my patients told me she felt her new breasts were helping her with her self-esteem issues, I was at a loss about how to respond. I could almost hear a whole generation of feminists sighing in defeat.

When I ask Jasmine if she's considered taking out a restraining order against him, she shakes her head. She just keeps hoping he'll get involved with someone else and leave her alone. But when she saw his car out there—or what *might* have been his car, she's not even sure now—she panicked.

"Maybe you should call campus police," I tell her. "And if I were you, I'd definitely have your locks changed." When she asks how she would go about doing that, I suggest she look online and call a locksmith.

"Oh, right," she says. "Duh." She'll do both of those things, she says, but right now all she wants is to go back to her apartment, deadbolt the door and put the safety chain on, and try to get some sleep. She can leave her car here overnight and get it tomorrow. Could I please give her a ride home?

I nod, pack up my briefcase. At the door, I look both ways before entering the hallway. "Let's go," I say. She follows me out. Walks down the hallway behind me.

En route to her apartment, I try to distract her by asking how her semester is going. "Better," she says. The evaluation I gave her the semester before upset her at first, she tells me, but she's come to see it as useful criticism. She's grateful. She'll be applying soon for an internship. There are a couple of places in Boston that look good. Can I write her a recommendation?

Her work was poor, but maybe it's improved. I'll ask some of my colleagues, see if that's the case. "I might be able to do that for you," I say. "But let's just get you home safely. Take one thing at a time."

When I pull up in front of her building, she asks me if I'd like to come in. I decline, but when she asks if I'd *please* come in for a few minutes—she's still feeling shaky and doesn't want to enter her apartment alone—I say okay. When we're inside, she tells me to have a seat. I watch her go from room to room, checking, I guess, to make sure the ex-boyfriend isn't hiding anywhere. She returns from the kitchen holding a bottle of white wine in one hand and, in the other, a fifth of Captain Jack. "I have this and this," she says. "Which would you like?"

Neither, I say. I really have to be getting home.

"Please, Dr. Oh."

I nod. Point to the whiskey. "Just a short one."

There's Coke in the fridge, she says. Do I want a Jack and Coke?

Good god, no. All I want is to get home, get something to eat. I squeezed in a patient at lunchtime, so all I've eaten since breakfast is a pack of peanuts from the vending machine. "Just some ice if you've got it." She nods and, a few minutes later, returns with a Jack and Coke for herself and, for me, a tumbler three-quarters filled with whiskey, two little ice cubes floating at the top. Jesus, if I drank all this, it would knock me on my ass.

She sits beside me on her green leather love seat. We sip our drinks. She tells me about her father's defection and her miserable four years of high school, her dating history with the menacing ex-fiancé. Seth is ten years older than she, she says. He makes good money and has sophisticated tastes, and that was what appealed to her. She enjoyed going out with an adult for a change. In the two years they dated, he never hit her. His abuse was mostly just verbal.

"That's still abuse," I say.

She nods. Gets up and puts her iPod in the dock. Turns up the music.

"Cassandra Wilson?" I ask.

"Uh-huh. Do you like jazz?" I say I do. She says she does, too—that Seth took her to a number of jazz clubs when they were first going out and got her into it. We sit there in silence, listening to Wilson's rendition of Chet Baker's "Let's Get Lost." Jasmine thanks me for my help, says she feels better. "She's got such a sexy voice, doesn't she?" she says.

"She does," I say, but her comment is a red flag. The liquor and the music have shifted the mood, and I've just caught myself thinking about how beautiful she is. It's time for me to go. She stands and says she's going to fix herself another drink. Do I need mine refreshed? "No, no," I say. "I really should be going."

"Okay," she says. "Just wait a sec."

While she's in the kitchen, I look down at my glass, surprised to see that I've drunk half of what she poured, something I hadn't meant to do. I stand. Feel a little woozy. At the entrance to her kitchen, I open my mouth to say good-bye but instead ask her, does she mind if I get myself a little more ice?

I'm reaching into the freezer when I feel her come up behind me. She slips one hand inside the back pocket of my jeans and begins massaging my neck with the other. Pulling free, I turn and face her. Her top is off. Her breasts are beautiful, her nipples rosy pink and erect. There's a tattoo over the left one—a tiny blue dragonfly. "No, no, Jasmine," I say, looking away. "You're feeling confused right now. It's understandable, but—"

She says I should call her Jazzy. That's what her friends call her, and we're friends, aren't we?

I shake my head. "I'm your superior," I say. "Look, you got really scared tonight. I can imagine how vulnerable you're feeling, but we can't . . . or *I* can't—"

"Can't what?" she says, smiling. I can tell she's tipsy.

"Take advantage of your situation."

"I'm a consenting adult, Orion," she says. "If you want, you can check my driver's license." She takes my hand and places it on her breast. Leans in and places her mouth against mine. She pushes my lips apart with her tongue and flicks it against my tongue.

I put my hand on her shoulder to push her away, but she smells so good. She's such a beautiful girl. I start returning her kisses, telling myself as I'm doing it that I have to stop. Have to get out of here *right now* since I haven't gotten out already. She reaches down and cups her hand against my crotch, starts rubbing me there. And I let her. There's my crucial mistake: I let her. For the past several minutes, I've been flirting with the edge of the cliff and now I'm falling off of it.

"You're getting hard," she whispers. She unzips her skirt and shimmies. It drops to her ankles. She guides my hand to her pubis. She's wet.

My heart is pounding. My breathing is fast and shallow. And then my zipper's down. She slips her hand through the slit in my shorts and wraps it around my cock. Starts running her finger around the ridge at the base of the head. God, it's been so long. It feels so good. But I have to stop her or . . . "Hey, Jasmine? Jazzy? I . . ."

"Shh," she whispers. "Just enjoy it."

She laughs when I come. Withdraws her hand and looks at her semen-covered fingers. I tell her I'm sorry, ashamed of myself. Babble about how I've been separated from my wife for some time and am out of practice. That I hadn't realized I was going to—

"It's okay, Orion. I'm a big girl. It's fine."

Fixing my pants, I make my way toward the door, mumbling assurances that nothing like what just happened has ever happened between me and a student before. She says it's not necessary for me to apologize. I nod. Glance down at her hand and get the hell out of there.

On the drive home, I grip the steering wheel to stop my hands from shaking. I try to unsee her breasts, the dragonfly tattoo. My mind's ricocheting with shame, guilt, anger at myself. But *she* seduced *me*, right? *I'm a big girl. It's fine.* But how many times have I counseled students who had slept with their professors and then come into my office shaken and confused? How many times have I tried to point out to these kids, guys as well as girls, that they'd been taken unfair advantage of? Sometimes I'll see one of the offending profs on campus and think, what a shit you are, what an abuse of power. And now I've joined their ranks.

The next day, she e-mails me to thank me again for my help and to remind me that I promised to write her a recommendation, which I didn't exactly do. The following Monday, there's a Post-it note stuck to my office door. *Reccomendation letter for Jasmine,* it says and I stand there, stupidly, thinking: it's one *c,* two *m*'s. How's she supposed to go on, become a therapist, when she doesn't even know that?

For the next few weeks, nothing happens. I'm relieved not to run into Jasmine in the building or anywhere else on campus. I tell myself that it's blown over; that it's amounted to an embarrassing cautionary tale, that's all. I'll just never put myself in a situation like that again. But each time I try to write her that letter, I revisit my humiliation. I've started it half a dozen times. Look, stop torturing yourself, I tell the tortured face in the bathroom mirror. Just finish her goddamned letter and be done with it. So she gets an internship someplace? Let her inadequacies catch up to her there. And if she squeaks by, so what? The profession's already got plenty of incompetent shrinks. What's one more? But instead, I look up her schedule to see which of my colleagues are supervising her now. When I seek them out, they're universally negative about Jasmine's work. Did I actually promise her I'd write her a recommendation, or had I only said I'd consider doing it?

She e-mails me to ask if I have her letter yet. I e-mail back to say I haven't. In her return e-mail, she asks me if I can get it done in the next few days because her applications are coming due. She'll stop by my office to pick it up. And when she does come by, I tell her I've talked to some of her other profs and have had to reconsider. "I think it would be a mistake for you to apply," I say. "At least for now." She frowns. Asks why. "Because these internships tend to throw you into the deep end of the pool. I just don't think your work is strong enough yet. If I were you, I'd reconsider." She glares at me for several seconds, then turns and leaves.

The next day, Muriel summons me to her office to tell me we have a problem. "We?" I say. . . .

When I wake up in the dark, I don't know where I am. I rise too quickly, stumbling and bumping into unfamiliar furniture. My movements make the lights go on. I squint and sit back down, waiting for the seasickness to pass. For several seconds, I'm confused and scared.

After I've oriented myself—realized I'm at Viveca's beach house—I recall the dream I just had: Annie and I are sitting on the couch in our Three Rivers living room, holding hands in the middle of some crisis. Maya Angelou is sitting across from us, consoling us. "Our thoughts and prayers are with you at this difficult time," she says. Is one of our kids hurt? Has one of them died?

Annie, sobbing, turns to me. "Is it because of me?" she asks.

"No," I say. "It's something I did." I turn back to Maya Angelou. "Right?" But she's become Obama.

"We're doing all we can," he says.

At daybreak, I rise and go outside. I'm still wearing what I wore yesterday during my long drive here, what I slept in on that sofa. I need coffee, need a shave and some mouthwash, but there's another need I have to see to first. On my way to the car, I'm stopped by the sound of the ocean in the distance—the same sound I heard when I placed Ariane's nautilus shell against my ear and knew this was the place where I had to be. A gull calls. A small brown rabbit scurries from the clearing into the woods. Something rustles behind the bushes, sight unseen. I can smell the ocean as well as hear it.

I pull that second duffel bag from the backseat of my car. Open the trunk and grab the box of rocks that's in there. Yesterday before I left, I walked around the property, picking up nine or ten of them for my private ceremony. I place the rocks, one by one, into the duffel bag. It already contains my license to practice psychology, the university awards I've received, my farewell pen and pencil set, and the mushy, now-melted top of Annie's and my twenty-fifth anniversary cake. There are photographs in there, too: Annie and me on that cruise we took to the Virgin Islands; the two of us seated with Muriel Clapp and her husband at some social function. . . .

Well, some of what you're saying jibes with what Jasmine contends, Orion, but there are crucial differences in your stories, too.

I'm not telling you a story, Muriel. I'm telling you the truth. What did she say?

That she went to your office that night because she was afraid for her safety and she thought she could trust you. That you drove her home and, when you got there, you asked her if she had anything to drink. That you more or less invited yourself in.

That's a lie. She asked me to come in and have that drink.

But you were inside her apartment?

I was. Because she said she was afraid to go in there alone. Her boy-friend wouldn't give her back her key and . . . I said no at first, Muriel, but then . . .

Did you seduce her?

No, what happened was—

How many drinks did you have while you were there, Orion?

One. And granted, she'd poured it with a heavy hand, but . . . one drink. That was it. Look, the bottom line is that she's lying about who seduced who. I swear to god. What happened was—

Did you ejaculate in her presence? Just tell me that.

When I get to Long Nook Beach, I park, get out of the car, grab the duffel bag. I walk the path to the top and look out at the rolling ocean, the surf crashing at the water's edge below. It's somewhere between high and low tide. Something down there is lying half in and half out of the water. The surf washes over it and then retreats. I climb down the steep dune path and walk toward it.

It's a dead seal. Its organs have been eaten away. The frozen grimace on its face is the same as Jesus's as he looks up toward a heaven, a Father, that doesn't really exist. *My God, my God, why have you forsaken me? . . .* That letter? The one I wrote Francis Oh, the father who'd wanted nothing to do with me? Who had *died* instead of facing me? That's in the duffel bag, too. Unopened, with the word *deceased* scrawled across the front of the envelope. I should have gotten rid of that thing long ago.

Standing beside this dead, devoured seal, I rear back and hurl the bag, as far as I can, into the gray-green water. I watch it sink. Then I jimmy my wedding ring back and forth until it slips over the knuckle and off my finger. I fling it into the sea. Am I crying? Laughing? Both?

Who am I, now that I've thrown my life into the ocean? Who will I be?

Chapter Nine

Annie Oh

Hurrying toward my studio with the wine-stained bridal dresses, I pass the grocery store where that hostile Korean boy works. I stop, turn around, and rush in. He's there, behind the counter. "Hey!" I say. "Spray starch!"

"Aisle four," he says without looking up from his magazine. I throw the dresses onto his counter and race to aisle four. Grab the three cans on the shelf and hurry back to him.

"Do you have more in back?" He shrugs. "Then go look. It's urgent." He doesn't budge; he just sits on his stool and stares at me. "Goddamnit! Move!" He flips over his magazine and heads toward the back room. Lucky for him, he's hurrying. Leaning on the counter, my elbows on the dresses, I call to him. "I'll take whatever you've got!"

The spray starch, twenty-four cans to the box, plus the three I've already grabbed off the shelf, comes to sixty-nine dollars. I dash over to the ATM machine in aisle one, do what the screen says, and grab the hundred dollars that come shooting out. I'm feeling frenzied. I need to get to the studio and start. I put four twenties on the counter and tell him to keep the change. Then I give him the remaining twenty, too. "Here," I say. "Buy yourself something pretty."

Carrying the dresses and the starch, I run toward the studio without even bothering to look at what people have left out on the sidewalk. In my head, I'm inventorying the storehouse of accumulated stuff that's waiting for me to use: mannequins and tailor's dummies, rubber hands and rubber hearts, a bolt of pink net, a bust of Medusa.

A couple of blocks before I get to my destination, I catch myself mumbling an old prayer I learned in parochial school.

Hail holy Queen, Mother of Mercy,
Our life, our sweetness, and our hope.
To thee do we cry, poor banished children of Eve;
To thee do we send up our sighs,
Mourning and weeping in this valley of tears . . .
Pray for us, O Holy Mother of God,
That we may be worthy of the promises of Christ.

Wait. What's Jesus got to do with it? I'm praying to Gaia.

I work all night on the disturbing and evocative piece that, by week's end, will become *The Titan Brides of Gaia*, the largest and most ambitious assemblage I have ever made. The day after it's finished, Viveca will return from Greece, come up the stairs to my studio, and stand at the entrance, staring in at it. At first, I'll not be able to read her face as she looks at the wedding dresses, stiff with starch and bloody from battle because I've turned them into art. Is she angry? Sad? But then she will walk toward me, in tears, and take me in her arms the way Winona Wignall did the day of my miscarriage. The way my mother used to. Viveca will pronounce this latest creation of mine "stunning," "sensational," "a tour de force." Three weeks later, there will be a feverish auction among art patrons, and *The Titan Brides of Gaia* will sell for a hundred and seventeen thousand dollars, the highest price anyone has ever paid for one of my works. A venture capitalist will be outbid by some new singer named Lady Gaga who Marissa says she loves and dances to at the gay clubs she and her friends frequent. Viveca will invite Lady Gaga to our wedding, but she'll send her regrets, much to Marissa's disappointment.

But all that will happen in the days to come. Right now, exhausted and spent after having been up all night—having seen in my head and begun creating *The Titan Brides of Gaia*—I stumble out of my studio, down the stairs, and through the streets toward our building on

Elizabeth Street. It's early morning, a weekday not a weekend, and so Rocco is on duty at the front door and Hector is probably arriving at the 9/11 site for his day's work there. Minnie must be en route to our apartment—on a bus or a ferry or a subway train. Hopefully, her babysitter has gotten himself out of bed and is helping Africa get ready for school. It's a lovely late summer morning. The sky is blue, the air is crisp and dry. Mykonos is better than this?

Inside the apartment, I open four of Viveca's expensive bottles of red, then grab the kitchen funnel and, one by one, pour each bottle into Minnie's jug. I'd hate to have her realize I know her secret, and that I drank her wine.

Later that sunny morning, too agitated, still, to sleep but too exhausted to return to the studio, I decide to take one of my scavenging walks. I'm on Delancey when she passes me at a brisk pace, going the opposite way, a study in self-satisfaction. It's her, all right: that Dr. Nancy woman from the *Today* show. Without really knowing why, I pivot and start following her. A few blocks later, she stops and reaches for the door handle of a Starbucks. At first I only *feel* like saying it, but then I *do* say it. Shout it, in fact. It's as surprising and sudden as when I threw that wine at Viveca's dress. "Hey, Dr. Nancy!"

She stops, turns to see who's calling her. When she notices me, she smiles a patient smile in the name of fan recognition. Then she starts into that Starbucks. "You know what goes good with one of those overpriced chai lattés you're probably going in to buy?" I yell. "A *cigarette*, that's what! Live a little! Light up!" The smile drops off her face.

It's a beautiful, blissful day. My two canvas bags are brimming with people's sidewalk discards: faded yellow silk roses, a Pee-wee Herman doll that talks, a painting of Saint Martin de Porres with purple sequins glued to the frame, a dented bicycle fender, a skein of yellow yarn. My new finds have reenergized me, and those four bloodied brides—Gaia's daughters, their dresses stiff with starch—are waiting for me. I turn and hurry toward my studio, walking as fast as I can. But that's not fast enough. I break into a run.

Part II

Mercy

Chapter Ten

Ruth Fletcher

March 12, 1963

We buried my husband, Claude, today, finally. Me and Belinda Jean. His emphysema took him nine days ago, but the wake and funeral had to be put off because of the flood. McPadden's Funeral Parlor was in the water's path.

I cried when Mr. McPadden called to say they had to postpone things. The flood water had rose up to the windshield of his hearse, he said. He went on about sparkplugs and distributor caps, but car talk is Greek to me. He also said the wool rugs in the two rooms where they wake the dead got soaked and probably would take their sweet time drying out, even outside on the lawn in the warm sun. The weather's been so strange lately. For three days, it rained like the dickens—a cold rain it was, just this side of snow. But the day after the dam broke, it got sunny and warm and it's been that way since. *Too* warm, if you ask me. Seventy-seven degrees in the middle of March? The TV said yesterday's temperature broke some record.

Claude's wake was last night, from seven to nine o'clock. Sixteen people showed up to pay their respects, not counting Belinda Jean and me. I know because when we were the only ones left, I counted the names in the signing book. Claude's sister Verna come over from Rockville, which I appreciated because she's wheelchair-bound from her diabetes. Her daughter Carol brought her. My second cousin Wanda Brautigan came, too—her and her husband, Clifford. And a few of the men Claude worked with at the icehouse. Not that foreman, though; there was never any love lost between Claude and him. Oh, and our neighbors, Mr. and Mrs. Skloot: they came. I thought it was kind of them to pay their respects, especially since Claude had made that big stink about Mr. Skloot letting those colored brothers, the Joneses, live out back on his property. I never liked it that Claude was a member of the Connecticut Ku Klux, and that he was a part of the window-smashing that night out back on the Skloots' property. My feeling when it comes to the coloreds is: if they don't bother me, I won't bother them. That's not to say that I approve of whites and coloreds marrying each other, which was what Claude and the others were so hot under the collar about: when Rufus Jones, the older brother, was living with that white wife of his from Germany or wherever she came from and drove her all around town in his flashy convertible. Gerta van Hofwegen: that name sounds fancy, but she was cheap goods. Still is, I guess. She was in the arrest report a few months back on a morals charge—something about performing immoral acts on the men at Electric Boat during their lunch break. Well, that's what she gets for marrying out of her race, I suppose. Her husband come to a bad end, too, of course. Got hit by the flood water and drowned in the river behind the movie theater. Divine justice, I guess. I don't think the Good Lord ever intended for coloreds to mix with whites, because if He did, why would He make us so different? Our noses and hair and such, and the fact that Negroes rut like animals from being oversexed? Back when I was twelve years old and bled for the first time, my mama, with her shy ways, couldn't bring herself to explain the birds and the bees to me, so she had her sister Bitty take me aside and explain the particulars. And that was the first thing Aunt Bitty told me: now that I had reached womanhood, I wasn't to look a colored man or a colored boy in the eye because if I did, it would stoke their fire and I'd get raped. When she told me what rape was, it was all I could do not to put my hands over my ears and run from the room. Then she told me about what husbands did to their wives in private, which was how babies got made, and that for some women this felt natural and pleasurable and for other women it was something they had to do out of duty. I asked her what the difference was between that and rape, and she said the difference was that the one was natural and decent, the way God designed things so that His people would

populate the earth, and the other was *un*natural and *in*decent. . . . I
don't call them niggers anymore, like I used to; I've made an effort to
stop doing that after I learned that it was disrespectful and ungodly to
use that word. And I don't contend, like some do, that them and us are
two different species, or that we have souls and they don't. We *can* in-
terbreed, I know that, but I don't believe it's what the Good Lord ever
intended. We're different is all I'm saying, the coloreds and us. Maybe
that's why Rufus Jones drowned that night. The Good Lord works in
mysterious ways, so maybe it was divine justice.

But jeepers, that flood was a terrible thing—seven lives lost and
half the downtown stores ruined. All the next day, there were helicop-
ters flying overhead, and Walter Cronkite talked about Three Rivers
on the news that night. Governor Dempsey traveled over from Hartford to look at the damage and talk to the families. I thought that
was a merciful thing for him to do. I didn't vote for him last election
because he's a Catholic and a Democrat. We got one of them living in
the White House, and one's enough for me, whether what they say is
true or not: that if it come down to it, a Catholic would be loyal to the
pope in Rome rather than to the Constitution. But I did appreciate
the effort the governor made. They closed the high school for three
days in a row so that the students could go downtown and help with
the cleanup. The radio's been saying those boys should all make sure
their shots are in order, though, because the water might have bacteria
in it. I'm not sure what the danger is. Typhoid, maybe.

Two of the flood victims were waked at McPadden's last night,
same as Claude. It was that young mother and her baby. Claude's coffin was laid out in the smaller room, theirs in the bigger one across the
hall. Belinda Jean and I got to calling hours early, and when I looked
in the other room and saw that baby's casket next to her mother's,
it nearly broke my heart. Myrna O'Day, the woman's name was, but
the paper said everyone called her Sunny because she had a sunny disposition. The baby's name was Grace. They found that poor doomed
child's body tangled up in a tree that got knocked over. And this was a
strange thing: they found the mother floating in the basement of Mc-
Padden's of all places, where Claude's corpse was waiting to be waked

and buried. It said in the paper that the printing company down the street from McPadden's had a lot of flood damage, too, and that the water was so powerful, it moved two heavy printing presses from one side of the floor to the other. I suspect Claude got moved around some, too. I could see it in my mind: his coffin floating around down there like a boat with him in it. I didn't ask if that was the case, though, and Mr. McPadden didn't say. But at least Claude was in his coffin, or so I choose to believe.

The paper said that, after the dam broke and all the water in We-quonnoc Pond went racing toward the downtown, the ice on top of the pond cracked and broke into big chunks that traveled along with the rushing water. It's been a cold winter and the paper said those blocks of ice were a foot thick and as long and wide as cars, some of them. That's what caused a lot of the damage in town, I guess: all that ice smashing into things, storefronts and such. I read that one of those ice chunks stove in the double doors at McPadden's where they bring the bodies in. What I figure is that the water must have carried poor Sunny O'Day through those open doors, and that's why they found her in McPadden's basement. It's hard to understand a peculiarity like that—a drowned woman coming to rest inside a funeral parlor. It's like Reverend Frickee always says: The Good Lord moves in strange and mysterious ways that aren't ours to understand.

Sunny O'Day: it just don't seem like a name you'd associate with tragedy. Her surviving children had their picture on the front page of the newspaper the day after it happened. Those two, plus a nephew who lives with the family. The photo was taken at the hospital after they got rescued from that tree they were in and had to be examined by the doctor. The boys—the son and the nephew—looked gloomy, and the little girl looked like she was in a daze. That poor child: five or six years old and now she's got to grow up without a mother to guide her. That would have been Belinda Jean's fate, too, if Claude hadn't married me soon after his first wife died. He never said as much, but I know that was why Claude asked me for my hand: not because he loved me and couldn't live without me, but so that I could mother Belinda Jean. I've done right by her, too; that's not pride, it's fact. I was thinking about something on the ride to the cemetery this morning: that Claude was a widower when he married me, and now I'm his widow.

Those wool rugs at McPadden's last night weren't what you'd call wet, but they were still damp. At one point during Claude's wake, when nobody new was showing up, I slipped off my shoes and felt the moisture on the bottoms of my stockings. They had a bit of a smell about them, too, and wet wool's not the pleasantest of odors. But I suppose that couldn't be helped. Maybe if I'd bought both the spray of carnations *and* the casket blanket like the florist wanted me to, the smell of the flowers might have cut down on the smell of the wet wool. Carnations have such a nice fragrance to them. Sometimes on my birthday, Claude would give me a few extra dollars so that I could go downtown and buy myself a present. I'd almost always buy carnations and that pretty smell would fill up the house. He'd come home from work, bend and smell them, and say, "Mm-mmm. These sure stink pretty. Happy birthday, Ruthie Pie."

They're Catholics, I guess, the O'Days. A priest come by and said a rosary with everyone. I could hear them all murmuring their Hail Marys across the hall. I recognized the priest. It was that Father Fontanella who was over at the collapsed mill the night of the flood, helping the firemen dig for survivors. Four people got buried alive in the wreckage, and the radio said a fifth is hanging on by a thread. Paper said that if the mill had given way during the day, twenty people or more could have lost their lives, but the night crew's smaller. Thank the Lord for that. . . . The O'Days' side had a line of people paying their respects that went all the way down the hall and out the door. Hundreds of mourners, it looked like, when I got up to use the restroom. Compared to that, the number that came to Claude's wake was puny, but it's like I told Belinda Jean: the circumstances were so different. Sunny O'Day died unexpectedly, still in her twenties, and the flood took one of her children, too. Claude died from his emphysema, and truth be told, nobody ever said *he* had a sunny disposition. But he had his good points, too. He wasn't a drinking man or a womanizer; I thank my lucky stars for that. Our bedroom's so quiet now. Too quiet.

It's odd; I never in a thousand years would have figured I'd miss the sound of his wheezing in the next bed over. Two packs a day: that was what claimed him is what the doctor told me. Sunny drowned and Claude smoked himself to death.

It said in the paper that Sunny O'Day's husband is a U.S. Navy veteran and a barber. And it wasn't till the middle of yesterday that I put two and two together and realized he was the same barber who cuts hair at the place Claude goes to. Used to go to, I mean. It's on Franklin Avenue: the Shamrock Barbershop on one side of the building and Cirillo's Grinders on the other. It's the uncle who owns the barbershop, but Claude was always talking about how that nephew who had the second chair was such a cutup. How he kept all the customers entertained while they were waiting for their haircuts. He'd be sweeping hair off the floor, Claude said, and then, in the middle of it, turn up the radio and start dancing with the broom. Claude said the uncle and him each have a sign above their mirror. The uncle's says HEAD BARBER and the nephew's says HEAD SCREWBALL. They keep a mynah bird in the shop, Claude told me, and the nephew trained it so that, after he says "Shave and a haircut," the bird will say "Two bits." On the Saturdays that Claude went down there to the Shamrock, he'd come back with his hair all neat and trimmed and smelling good, and he'd have bought himself a meatball grinder for his lunch. He'd sit there at our kitchen table, eating his grinder and telling me what crazy thing the nephew did or said that day. Claude wasn't usually partial to those show-offy types that call attention to themselves, but he sure got a kick out of that guy.

Charles "Chick" O'Day. Chick and Sunny. He's so young to be a widower, that poor man. Twenty-nine, the newspaper said. I got a glimpse of him last night at the funeral home. The poor fellow looked like he'd gotten the wind knocked out of him, which I guess he has. He'd best find some nice girl to marry so those kids can have a mother. And maybe he can send the nephew back to where he come from. He looked like trouble to me with that Elvis Presley haircomb and the Elvis Presley sneer to go with it. Back when I worked in the high school cafeteria, I could always pick out the troublemakers when they come through the line—the ones who'd try and swipe an extra pudding or apple goodie. Hide it under their napkin or some such. I'm not saying I caught all of them, but I caught a fair amount. I had an eye for spotting the troublemakers. . . .

The other boy—the son—looked like a nice young man, though: dark suit, shirt and tie, his hair in a crew cut like his father. But the child I keep picturing in my mind today is the little girl, the way I seen her at the wake last night. While they were saying the rosary over there, she come wandering across the hall to our room, looking so lost and sad, her eyes moving back and forth between Claude's open casket and us. But then Belinda Jean smiled at her and gave her a wave and she gave Belinda a wave right back. "I got peppermint candies in my pocketbook," I said. "Would you like one?" She nodded and started walking toward us. But then that cousin come in and said, kind of cross like, "What are *you* doing over here? Get back where you belong."

I told him I was just about to give her a peppermint. Could she have one? "Maybe later," he said. He come over to me and held out his hand. I dropped three peppermints onto it, one for her, one for her brother in the other room, and one for him.

"What's your name, sweetheart?" I asked the little girl.

He answered for her. "Her name's Annie."

"Well, that's a pretty name. And what's yours?"

"Kent," he said. He closed his hand tight around the candy and pointed his chin over at Claude. "Who's in the box?"

"My late husband," I said. I touched Belinda Jean's arm. "Her father."

"Oh," was all he said. He took the little one's hand in his.

"My daughter and I are very sorry for your losses, Kent," I told him. I turned to the little one and smiled. "And you, too, Annie." I reached out to touch my hand to her cheek, to comfort her a little, but he yanked her away from me. Then he walked her out of the room, with her looking back over her shoulder at us. I don't know. I could be wrong. I *hope* I am. But to me, that Kent seems like trouble.

After they left, Belinda told me she remembered the little girl from when her mother used to bring her into the library in a stroller. It's a crying shame Belinda probably won't ever get married and have children of her own now that she's let herself go to lard and become so housebound. She always loved children and was good with them. When she used to work at the library, doing the story hour for the young ones was her favorite thing to do. For a while there after she graduated high school, I used to urge her to go on to normal school and become a teacher, but that suggestion fell on deaf ears. *I* believed she could do it, but *she* didn't. And her father was always suspicious of education, so that might have been part of it, too, I guess. . . .

That little girl, Annie, was wearing a blue gingham dress with a lace collar and a petticoat underneath, and patent leather Mary Jane shoes and white anklets. They had her dressed up the way I used to dress Belinda Jean for church when she was little. If someone doesn't step in and mother that child, it'll be a crying shame. . . . Belinda Jean took it hard when *her* mother died, and poor Claude was at a loss as far as how to raise a motherless child. Well, I didn't know anything about being a parent either, especially to an eleven-year-old girl who was pulling out her eyebrow hair and picking her nose so hard and so much that she'd give herself nosebleeds. First time I met her, all I could think about was one of those sad songs my daddy used to sing whenever he took out his guitar: *Motherless children have a hard time when the mother is gone.* That was back when we lived in Alabama. I don't recall Daddy ever playing his guitar after our farm failed and we moved up here to Connecticut so he could work in the mills, instead, like his brother Emil had already done. Emil was my cousin Wanda's father. Wanda and I become friends as well as cousins after we both became northerners. I stood up for her when she married Clifford, and she stood up for me when I married Claude. . . . The first thing I did after I told Claude yes, I would marry him, was go down to Cranston's and buy two books on how to care for a child. One book was saying things like, "Never, ever kiss your child and never hold it on your lap." As if children were "its" instead of girls and boys. The other book, by that Dr. Spock fellow, said, right off the bat on page one, "Trust yourself. You know more than you think you do." It was a comfort to read that. I threw out the first book and read the Dr. Spock one so much that the pages come loose and had to be held together with a rubber band. But anyway, I stopped those scabby eyebrows and bloody noses of Belinda Jean's in short order once I come into the picture. I only had to whip her twice with the strap before she quit that foolishness.

Reverend Frickee put on a nice service for Claude today. Earle Potter played the organ and Martha McCoy sang some of the songs I'd asked for, "The Old Rugged Cross," "Rock of Ages," "How Great Thou Art." I made a list of what I wanted. The only one they didn't do was "On the Wings of a Dove," that Ferlin Husky song I always like when it comes on the radio. *On the wings of a snow white dove, He sends His pure, sweet love. . . .* Pastor Frickee said that song was too modern and for funerals they like to keep things traditional, which I understood, of course. The pastor spoke some nice words about Claude: how he was a good man who had his faults like all of us but was a hard worker and a good provider. Both the newspaper obituary and Pastor Frickee mentioned how Claude won our house the Three Rivers Christmas decorating contest back in 1956 for all that stuff he put out in our yard. I have the electric bill to prove it. I'm a saver, or as Claude used to call me, a "pack rat," which I never much appreciated because of all God's creatures, rats are the ones I like the least. Well, rats and weasels and snakes—the one because they're filthy and carry diseases and the others because they're mean and treacherous. Once when I was a little girl, I saw a weasel kill a cat—hold it in its jaws and whip it from side to side and then, after the cat went limp, eat it. Some of it, anyway. The turkey vultures swooped down and finished the job. It still riles me whenever I remember seeing that. It was our neighbor's cat, Winky. It always used to come over to our backyard because I'd put a saucer of milk on the back step. It was early morning when that weasel attacked Winky. No one else was up yet. I got out of bed and looked out the window to see what those ungodly screams and howls were all about, and to this day, I wish I'd of just stayed in bed and not seen what I seen because I can *still* see it. And hear it, too—those screams coming out of poor Winky, whose only crime was that he'd come over to lap up a little bit of milk, poor thing. . . .

Claude wasn't much of a churchgoer, but Reverend Frickee was kind enough not to mention that. It brought me to tears when, at the cemetery, he looked at Belinda Jean and me and told us we had to be strong for each other in the coming months, and that we would see Claude again someday in the Sweet Bye-and-Bye. I wasn't crying from comfort at the pastor's words; I was crying because I guess by now Claude has met His Maker, and I doubt he's been let into heaven. Claude took his secret to the grave and I intend to take that same secret to mine. But he died unrepentant with blood on his hands. I suspect that right now and for all eternity he'll be suffering Hell's tongues of fire for what he done. And maybe, because of my silence, I'll join him there when my time comes.

I worry about Belinda Jean—about the guilt I suspect she's feeling. Since her father passed, she hasn't shed a single tear, not even when Mr. McPadden and his son came out to the house and carried Claude's body down the stairs and out the door. And Belinda's a crier. She bawls at sad movies and TV shows. Why, when Elvis Presley had to go into the army, seems like she cried for days. But for her natural-born father: nothing. It's not normal. And neither was the two of them, father and daughter, living under the same roof and not speaking to each other for almost three years because of what happened with one of those Jones brothers. The artist is the one I'm talking about, if you could even call that crazy stuff he painted "art." Not the brother who was married to that white tramp. (Common law, I suspect; from what I know of the coloreds, they're likely to skip the church service and head right for the bedroom.)

It drove me crazy, that uneasy silence between Belinda Jean and Claude, on account of that colored brother's painting and what happened because of it. Of course, for Claude the trouble with those Jones brothers started way before that. To begin with, he wasn't thrilled when the Skloots bought the land next door to ours and built that big, fancy house of theirs; Claude thought it stuck out like a sore thumb and made the rest of our homes on Jailhouse Hill look puny. But then when Mr. Skloot hired the Joneses as masons for the buildings he was building around town and let them move into that little place in back of his big house, well, Claude was fit to be tied. And that was *before* he realized they had a white girl living back there with them besides. Swapping her back and forth between them is what Claude figured. The funny thing was, when they were first settling Jailhouse Hill back in the eighteen hundreds, the coloreds was who lived there, kind of like it was just the coloreds who lived on Goat Island back in Alabama. They were poor, but it was *educated* Negroes, a lot of them, that lived here on Jailhouse Hill back then. That's what Belinda Jean told me. When it was quiet down there at the library, she liked to read up on the history of the town. She said the colored community settled here on this hill because none of the white folks wanted to buy property so close to where the criminals were. There was no trouble, though, because the blacks kept to themselves and didn't try to mix in with whites—even had their own store where they food-shopped and their own grammar school, but not their own high school. Belinda Jean said there was a colored boy in the first graduating class at the Three Rivers Free Academy, back in eighteen eighty-something. "Good lord, don't mention that to your father or it'll set him off and there'll be hell to pay," I told her and she didn't. . . .

They planted a garden that first summer they moved in—those Jones brothers, I mean, not the Skloots. One August day Rufus and his white wife come by and knocked on the door to give us some of their tomatoes. They were just being neighborly, and I didn't see any harm in taking them. But when Claude got home from work and I told him where those tomatoes had come from, he took the bowl of them outside and fired each and every one at the trunk of our big oak tree. Took satisfaction, I guess, in seeing those tomatoes explode against the tree. "She's got an accent," I told him. "Maybe it's different where she comes from. Maybe whites and colored mix over there in Europe."

"Well, they ain't living in Europe, are they? They're living *here*." He was shouting it more than saying it, like I approved of race-mixing, when all I was saying was live and let live. That tomatoes are just tomatoes. Well, he fumed a while, and I'm pretty sure he was mixed up in that window-busting out at that little house of theirs, though he never said as much and I never asked him.

But for Claude things come to a boil in the summer of 1959. That was when Three Rivers was having their three-hundred-year celebration and Joe Jones won that art contest. Lord, what hoopla there was that summer! The outdoor history pageant, the big parade, the fireworks, the beauty queen contest. Belinda Jean shocked me when she put herself in the running for Tercentenary Queen. It was out of character, on account of her shy ways. I'm still not sure what possessed her to do it; she was sweet as sugar back then but wasn't what you'd ever call the beauty queen type. I knew she wouldn't make the final five—the ones who got their pictures in the paper so that everyone in town could vote for who they wanted. But it was a rude awakening for poor Belinda Jean, particularly when she overheard one of the judges say how easy it was to separate the beauties from the "bow-wows." After she heard that? Good Lord, she cried a whole weekend from hurt feelings! But then she got picked to be a trumpeteer in the history pageant, and that smoothed her feathers some. Her father give her some guff about her costume: tuxedo with tails and matching short shorts. But when Claude found out that one or two of his Ku Klux brothers were letting their daughters be trumpeteers, too, and that *they* didn't seem to mind their girls showing their legs up on a stage, he gave in and said she could participate after all. In the dark from the other side of our bed, he said he still didn't like his daughter "parading her wares for all of Three Rivers to see," but that he was sick and tired of trying to go to sleep at night to the sound of her sobbing her fool head off down the hall. He was wheezing to beat the band that night, I remember; I guess that was maybe when all those Lucky Strikes started gaining on him. His breathing always got worse when he got worked up over something.

Claude had some involvement in the town's Tercentenary, even though he told me every night when I put his supper in front of him that he thought the whole thing was stupid. There was a contest sponsored by the *Evening Record*, the Three Rivers Savings Bank, and Hendel's Appliance Store because they sold Frigidaires. That contest involved ice, and Claude's foreman put Claude in charge of it. What he had to do was drive a two-ton cake of ice downtown and park it in the traffic island on Franklin Square, right in front of the five-and-ten. There was a five-hundred-dollar prize for the person who could guess how long it would take for that block of ice to melt in the summer sun and trickle down finally to just water. Mathematics students from as far away as Yale University entered the contest with their fancy arithmetic about time and temperature, but the surprise winner was Rufus Jones. He got his picture in the paper, accepting the check for the five hundred. A few days later, he was driving around town in that big white convertible with the red leather seats—him and his white wife. Throwing it in people's faces is the way Claude felt. He was fit to be tied.

The history pageant was held on a Saturday night, I remember. It was me who brung Belinda Jean to the dress rehearsal the night before and Claude who brung her to the pageant the next night. The cast members had to get there an hour early and assemble behind the big outdoor stage while the bleachers filled up. Claude was halfway home when he looked in his rearview mirror and saw that Belinda Jean, who was nervous as a bushy-tailed cat in a room full of rocking chairs as my daddy used to say, had forgot her trumpet in the backseat. (They weren't real trumpets, of course. They were just cardboard fakes painted gold and covered with glitter that the trumpeteers were supposed to put to their lips whenever they played the trumpet music through the loudspeakers.) Well, Claude figured that if Belinda Jean was a trumpeteer without a trumpet, they wouldn't let her get up on stage and he didn't want her bawling for the next week. So he drove back there with her trumpet and went behind the stage looking for her. And what does he see back there but his daughter and two or three of the other trumpeteers talking and laughing with Joe Jones. Jones was dressed up like a Wequonnoc Indian in buckskin pants and no shirt. Claude went a little crazy is what happened next. He reminded Jones that he was a Negro, not an Indian, and told him if he ever caught him talking to his daughter again, he was going to be "one sorry coon." He made an awful scene, I guess—humiliating poor Belinda Jean in front of all the other cast members. Grabbed her by the arm and drug her back to the car and wouldn't let her be in the show after all. I felt so sorry for the girl. She'd told me just the night before that she'd made friends with a couple of the other trumpeteers, and one of them was having a party at her house after the show was over and that Belinda Jean was invited. I was a nervous wreck the next morning when I had to drive over to the festival headquarters and turn her costume back in, because I don't like to drive downtown where it's trafficky. I'm always afraid I'm going to sideswipe some parked car or hit someone who's just jumped into the crosswalk without waiting for the "walk" light.

After the pageant, Belinda Jean and her father gave each other the silent treatment for over a month. I finally went to Reverend Frickee and asked him for help. He come out to the house and talked to Belinda and me first, and then when Claude got home from work, he talked to him in private and then had the three of us pray with him as a family. Claude kept looking over at me all the time Pastor Frickee was there, and if looks could kill . . . Before he left, Mr. Frickee read some little poem about the world coming to an end either from fire or ice, and he give us a little sermon about how ice between family members caused more harm than fire. Which I interpreted as him saying that it was better to have a fight and get things out than to give people the silent treatment and let things keep festering. I could have been wrong, though; poetry's hard for me to understand because it never says things plain and simple. Well, Claude did not appreciate that I'd involved Pastor Frickee in our family business, and after he left, I was told in no uncertain terms that what went on in our house *stayed* in our house, did I understand? But the funny thing was, by the next day, the ice began to thaw between Claude and Belinda Jean, so the pastor's visit had done some good. The only problem was: Claude gave *me* the silent treatment for the next week or more. My forty-seventh birthday come up in the middle of that week, I remember. No money for carnations that year!

I knew Belinda Jean and Joe Jones had become friendly in spite of Claude's warning, or maybe even because of it. I kept my mouth shut, though. I didn't want Claude finding out and starting World War Three. Truth be told, I was afraid to tell him—afraid for Belinda Jean and for Claude, too. I was scared Claude might fly off the handle and do something he'd get arrested for. March over to the Joneses' place next door and do more than just break some windows. So I decided I'd keep my mouth shut and deal with the situation in my own way.

This was *how* I knew she and him had become friends. After they laid me off from the school cafeteria, I got another, better job through the classified advertisements in the *Evening Record*. What I did was spy for this California company that distributes movies to the Loew's Poli on East Main Street. (The movie theater's just a one-mile walk down Jailhouse Hill and over the Sachem River bridge, so I didn't have to drive downtown to get to work. I could hoof it.) What I had to do was go to the movies and count the number of people in the audience. It's what's called "spot checking." They wanted to see if the number of tickets the theater reported being sold matched up to the number of people I counted. They were checking to see if those theater managers were on the up-and-up, or if they were underreporting ticket sales and pocketing the difference. For every show I went to and reported back on, they give me nine dollars, so I'd do four or five spot checks a week and make, most weeks, almost fifty dollars. Which was about ten dollars more than I'd made at the school cafeteria, plus I'd get to watch all those movies. I liked that I was my own boss with no one breathing down my neck and me not having to stand on my feet all day long. Claude knew what my job was, but Belinda Jean didn't because her friend Peggy Konicki's mother sold the tickets at the Loew's Poli. (Peggy'd run for Tercentenary Queen, too, but she didn't make the cut either. It was the big shots' daughters who did: Anita Graves whose father was a doctor, and Sally McWilliams whose mother was a big chunk of cheese on the city council. It was rigged, I figured, because Sally got voted queen, and she could have used a diet and some pimple cream. She wasn't any more of a beauty than Belinda Jean or Peggy.) When I was on the job, what I usually did was scoot upstairs to the balcony, where no one else went in the middle of the week except maybe an amorous young couple or two. If that was the case, I'd do this nervy thing that was very out of character for me. I'd say, like I was an employee at the theater, "Excuse me, but the balcony is closed. You have to go downstairs." And they'd get up and go. After the previews were over, and the cartoon if there was one, I'd look below and count the heads and write the number in my little notepad. Of course, the balcony hung over the rear seats downstairs, so I'd have to lean over the railing and count the people in the back rows, too. Then I'd just sit back and, if it was a hot summer day, enjoy the refrigerated air and watch whatever was showing that week: *Rio Bravo* or *Lover Come Back* or *I Want to Live!* (Susan Hayward played a good part in that one.) Instead of buying the refreshments they sold at the concession stand, I'd bring my own: some Peek Frean or Hydrox cookies, or some peanut butter and Saltine crackers I'd put in a wax paper bag before I left home, plus the pint of Old Grand-Dad I would buy at Patsy's Package Store on the way downtown and slip into my purse. I admit it: I liked a little nip while I was watching those movies up there in that empty balcony. It was very relaxing and helped me to get lost in the stories. Of course, after I'd done my count (counting myself, too, but they always added the cost of my admission onto my pay, long as I included my ticket stub), I would have to keep my eye out for stragglers and add them to the number I'd already recorded. To my way of thinking, if you have to come late to a movie, then don't come at all. Those latecomers were a nuisance.

But anyway, this was how I found out about that friendship that was brewing between Belinda Jean and Joe Jones. When I bought my ticket that day—*West Side Story* was what was playing—Peggy Konicki's mother told me that Belinda Jean had already gone in and was probably waiting for me in the lobby. "Oh, thanks," I said, pretending like what she assumed to be true *was* true: that my daughter and me had made a plan to meet at the show. There was no one in line behind me, and that Mrs. Konicki has got a gift for gab. She was telling me all this stuff like how *West Side Story* was a Broadway show before it was a movie, and that Natalie Wood didn't do her own singing for the picture—that she just mouthed the words to someone else's voice. I was getting a little impatient with her, but when you're a spy, you have to act nonchalant so no one gets suspicious.

Mrs. Konicki said, "Natalie Wood is Peggy's favorite actress. That girl will go to see whatever picture Natalie Wood is in."

"Oh, Belinda Jean, too," I said. "They're two peas in a pod." Which was an out-and-out fib. Belinda likes Debbie Reynolds the best—all those *Tammy* movies. But while I was chatting with Mrs. Konicki, I was worrying that Belinda Jean might see me before I could get up to the balcony because, like I said, she didn't know about this job of mine. And also I was wondering why Belinda was at the movies instead of at the library where she said she was going. She'd started her part-time job there that summer, but it wasn't one of her regular days. One of the other girls had called in sick, she said, and they'd asked her to fill in. "Well," I told Peggy's mother. "I guess if Belinda's already in there, I better not keep her waiting."

Up in the balcony, after my eyes adjusted to the dark, I made out Belinda Jean from her silhouette. She was sitting by her lonesome in one of the middle rows. The movie had already been going for about five minutes when I see some boy come in and sit in the row behind Belinda and one seat over, even though there were plenty of empty seats all over the place. Well, more a man than a boy, it looked like to me. He was more solid than skinny like a high school boy, tall and wide-shouldered. I just hoped he wasn't some masher. But I figured that wasn't the case when he leaned forward with his elbows resting on the seat in front of him, the one next to Belinda Jean's, and him and her started shooting the breeze. Kept it up, too. They were doing more giggling and talking to each other than watching the movie, and of course, neither of them realized that *I* was watching *them*. I didn't know yet that it was Jones that was sitting right behind her. That come later, after I had to sneak down and use the ladies' room and I saw him out at the snack bar buying popcorn and two sodas. I was a little bit tipsy from the Old Grand-Dad by then, and when I realized who it was, I missed a step and had to catch myself. The refreshments lady looked up at me, but thank God Joe Jones didn't turn around. Not that he would have even recognized me, probably, but I didn't want to chance it. Whether you're spying for a movie company or spying on your own daughter, the last thing you want to do is get noticed.

When I got back to my seat, all I could think about was what would happen if Claude found out that Belinda Jean was sitting in a public theater and acting so chummy with a colored man. It give me the shakes, I got so worked up. Well, that afternoon I finished the Old Grand-Dad before I slid the bottle under my seat; usually, I put the cap back on and leave some for home. But it didn't matter how much I drank. I still couldn't concentrate on the movie. I knew it was about two groups of dancing hoodlums, but that was about all. And later, after the credits come on and everyone started walking out, I realized I'd been so distracted that I'd forgotten to count the number of people in the audience. So in addition to all my fretting, I was going to be out my spot-checking money. I could have just made up a number, I suppose, but I'd never do such a thing. I'm as honest as the day is long and I'd like to think my good character's worth more than nine dollars.

That night, before Claude come home, I told Belinda Jean that I'd gone shopping downtown and had stopped in at the library to say hello but hadn't seen her. "They had me downstairs, shelving books in the stacks," she said.

"Oh, then I guess it *wasn't* you I saw coming out of the Loew's Poli after all," I said. "But boy, it sure looked like you. Same blue checked skirt and white blouse with puffy sleeves. You two could have been twins."

Oh yeah, she said. That *was* her. She forgot. The girl she was supposed to cover for came in anyway, so they let her go early. She didn't feel like coming home yet, so she went to the movies instead.

"You know, Belinda Jean," I said, "you are judged by the company you keep. Just remember that."

She asked me what that was supposed to mean. Said it defiantlike. But I could see the blood drain out of her face.

"It means just what you think it means," I told her. "You should always pick your friends wisely and act the way you would if you were out in public with your father and me." She stood there, clenching her fists and jutting her chin out like she was gunning for a fight. Then she lost her nerve, I guess, because she stormed out of the kitchen, stomped up the stairs, and slammed her bedroom door behind her. That was when I first suspected that she and Jones might have gone past the "friends" stage. I got down on my knees and prayed on it that night, and for the next several nights. Prayed that it wasn't so, because if it was and Claude got wind of it, he'd raise holy Hell and then some.

It was me who brought the whole thing to a head. Not on purpose, Good Lord! If I had only known, I would have avoided that art show like the plague. The Tercentenary celebration had been going on all summer and was having its final event that Sunday: a pancake breakfast inside the festival tent and a big art show outside of it. Between Rufus Jones winning the ice-melting contest and that incident at the history pageant, Claude had been a stick-in-the-mud about anything having to do with the Tercentenary—hadn't wanted us to go to the parade, or the fireworks, or the firemen-versus-policemen rope pull, or either of the two concerts, the one with Les Paul and Mary Ford or the other one with Johnnie Ray and that Tommy Sands fellow who married Frank Sinatra's daughter. I suspected it was because, after he'd made a scene that night at the history pageant and humiliated Belinda Jean, Claude was embarrassed to show his face at any of the other events. But both those things had happened in June and now it was August. I wanted to go to *something*. So I went on and on about pancakes and arts and crafts, and finally Claude gave in and said he'd take me if I'd just stop my "goddamn belly-aching." We went right after I got home from early church, and the crowd was already so big, we had to park four streets over from the tent.

When we got there, we had our pancakes and coffee. Then we walked around looking at the booths inside, the pottery and homemade jewelry and leather goods and such, and I could tell that Claude was bored to tears. The paintings were all outside, hanging up on chicken wire fencing. When we started walking around out there, Claude kept making comments like "You call this art?" and "Some kindergarten kid could have made a prettier picture than that," and there were the artists, sitting right there on stools and webbed chairs and most likely hearing what he said. Not all of the artwork was my cup of tea either, but I knew each person had tried their best. So I was relieved when Claude run into someone he knew and started talking with him. "I'll just keep going and look at the rest and then we can leave," I said.

Claude said, "Hallelujah for that," and the other man laughed.

Joe Jones had his pictures set up at the south end of the show. Most of the other artists were chitchatting with the passersby, but he was standing there all by his lonesome, waiting for people to stop and look, I guess, which nobody was doing. It was hot and humid out, and his dark skin was shiny with sweat. He had on canvas pants and canvas shoes and a tight red-and-white-striped T-shirt that showed off his muscles. Whenever he moved, you could see them shifting under his shirt. He glanced up at me for a second or two, but I could tell he didn't know who I was. His sign said JOSEPHUS JONES, ENAMEL PAINTINGS ON POSTER BOARD AND MASONITE BOARD. SMALL ONES $5, BIG ONES $20.

To my eye, those paintings of his were crazy-looking. In one called *Hunting Day*, two men were out in the woods and one was holding his rifle to the back of the other one's neck. In another called *The Cercus People*, a clown was pointing a stick at a woman in a bathing suit who was riding on top of an elephant. I looked away from the one called *Three Nude Women in a Garden* and another called *Taking a Bath with the Seneoritas*. I wished he had shown better judgment than to put those naked ones up; there were a lot of families with children at that art show. And I'm no great shakes when it comes to spelling, but I was pretty sure that *senoritas* only had one *e* in it, not two. Lord, but he'd sure brought enough of his pictures to show—forty or fifty of them, it looked like! There were paintings of colored cowboys and colored Indians, jungle animals fighting each other, a mountain lion up in a tree getting ready to pounce on a mother deer and her fawn. They were all very colorful, I'll give him that much, but not one of those paintings was something you'd want to pay good money for and then go home and hang up behind the sofa in your living room.

But I guess I must not know art that well because Jones's biggest painting, *Adam and Eve*, had a blue ribbon hanging next to it that said BEST IN SHOW. I stopped and looked at that one, trying to figure out why it was a prizewinner, my eyes bouncing from the blue ribbon to Adam and Eve in the all-together, except for the fig leaves he'd been decent enough to paint on their privates. Adam was reaching out for Eve and Eve was reaching up to pick herself that apple that would cast them out of the Garden of Eden. And this was curious: they both had gray skin instead of flesh-colored skin—as gray as cement. There were some ghostly-looking baby goats at their feet and cows behind them, and the snake was coiled up in the apple tree. A shiver ran through me when I looked at Adam's and Eve's faces. Despite that gray skin of theirs, Adam had Josephus Jones's Negro face and Eve had Belinda Jean's! Good God Almighty, I said to myself. If Claude sees this, he'll go berserk. But when I looked from that painting to where I'd left him talking to that fellow he knew, I saw him walking straight toward me.

I reached him first and tried to turn him around. "Come on," I said. "It's hot out here and I've seen enough. Let's go." Except he *wouldn't* turn around.

"Our car's parked this-a-way," he said.

I watched him look over at Jones, and then start scanning his paintings, snickering. But when he saw *Adam and Eve*, the smile dropped off his face. He went right for it, aiming to destroy it, I guess.

When he done that, Jones went right for Claude. The two of them rassled with each other and fell to the ground. Claude's punches weren't connecting, but Jones's were. He was getting the best of Claude and then some. When I started screaming, a crowd come rushing over. And then the cops were there. They pulled Jones off of Claude and separated the two. One of the cops talked to Claude and the other talked to Jones. I could hear Jones say something about having a right to defend his work since it was under attack, and the policeman he was talking to kept saying, "Yes, sir. I understand, sir. He was clearly the perpetrator." Claude was throwing around words like "nigger" and "kill the black son of a bitch," and I was scared to death they were going to arrest him. But they didn't, thank the Lord. They just escorted him off the fairgrounds with me hurrying behind them. If Claude came back to the art show, one of the policemen warned him, he'd be cooling off in jail for the night. "You can't attack someone's artwork just because you don't like it," the other one told Claude. Of course, it was about much more than that. It was about Belinda Jean and Joe Jones, naked as jaybirds in the Garden of Eden, on display for those crowds of people to see. And it was about *how* that painting got painted—who'd gotten naked with who, and why, and what else might have happened. Not that Claude told those police that "Eve" had his daughter's face and body. He was mum about that, figuring, I guess, that he'd rather have them think he was a crackpot than that his daughter'd been with a colored man that way.

When we got back to the house, Belinda Jean wasn't there, thank God. She and Peggy Konicki had gone down to Ocean Beach for the day. I tried to calm Claude down, but he wasn't in any mood to listen to the likes of me. And when I suggested that maybe Belinda and me could go see Pastor Frickee and he could talk some sense into her, he grabbed my arm and squeezed it and said I was to leave that do-gooding minister out of our personal business or else. All day long, Claude kept walking around the house and out in the yard, short of breath and slamming things and mumbling to himself about "killing that black bastard." I'd never seen him so mad, and I was scared skinny for Belinda Jean.

When Belinda come home around seven or so, she was wearing that terry cloth poncho I'd sewn her and her bathing suit underneath. He hair was in a ponytail and she was looking sunburnt and healthy. Claude come right at her, backhanding her in the face and splitting her lip. He called her "a disgrace" and "a coon's whore" and told her to pack her things and get out of his house.

"And go where?" she sobbed. I was crying. She was crying. Claude was wheezing like he'd just run all the way up Jailhouse Hill.

"I don't care where," he said. "Plumb to Hell for all I care, because that's where you're headed sooner or later anyway. Or why don't you go next door and live with those two niggers and that white slut they share."

"Daddy," she kept sobbing. "Daddy, *please*. We're just friends, that's all. I didn't do anything wrong."

"No? Letting him see you the way only a husband's got a right to see his wife? Letting him make a dirty picture of the two of you and hang it up for everyone in town to ogle? I don't know what devil spawned you, little girl, because you sure ain't my child. Not anymore you ain't. Now go! Get out of my sight! You don't live here no more, period." He wouldn't back down. Wouldn't listen to reason. And so she put a few things in a paper bag and left.

I was sick to my stomach all night long with worry about her. Where was she? Was she safe? Should I call the police? I would have, but I was afraid it would set him off again. I didn't sleep a wink all night with him in the other bed, wheezing and cursing and muttering terrible things about having a score to settle with the nigger who'd ruined his daughter.

Belinda called me the next morning after Claude left for work. What she'd done, she told me, was walk five miles over to Peggy's house wearing just her flip-flops and her poncho and bathing suit underneath. She'd slept there the night before, and would sleep there that night, too. Then Mrs. Konicki got on the line and said something about how Belinda Jean's problem reminded her of *West Side Story*. Whatever she meant by that I didn't know, but I just agreed with her to shut her up. I was grateful to her, nonetheless. As long as Belinda was staying with the Konickis, I figured, she was safe.

It didn't turn out *so* bad, though. Because on the third night, he let her come back home. See, she'd written him a letter and snuck back here and tucked it in the *Evening Record*, so that when Claude come home from the icehouse and sat down to read his paper, Belinda Jean's letter fell out. I read it after he did. In the letter, she said Jones and her were nothing more than "acquaintances," and that she had never disrobed in front of him, nor he in front of her. All that had happened was that he'd come into the library one afternoon while she was working at the front desk and drawn a picture of her face. A pencil sketch that looked just like her. She hadn't even known he was doing it until he showed it to her, she said. She had no idea he was going to bring that sketch home and use it to paint her face on Eve's naked body. Whether what she said in her letter was the truth or a lie, I couldn't tell. But Claude took it as gospel. When I looked up from reading what she'd written, I saw something I'd never seen before: my husband's tears. "Why are you crying, Claude?" I asked him.

"Because my little girl's still pure," he said. "He didn't foul her after all, except in his filthy mind."

I pulled the tucked-up hanky from the sleeve of my dress and handed it to him. "Here," I said. He wiped his eyes, blew his nose, stood and shoved the hanky into the pocket of his overalls. Then he walked out the door.

When I heard him start his truck, and then heard those truck tires on our gravel driveway, I knew where he was going: over to the Konickis' to bring his daughter back home. And while he was gone, I sat in the rocking chair, rocking and thinking about what I'd seen that day in the movie theater: their two silhouettes down below me in the middle rows. They were talking and laughing easily with each other, like they were more than just acquaintances. Then I thought about what else I'd seen: that picture of his, Eve reaching up to pick that apple. Well, I thought, if it brings us peace around here, then let him believe what he wants to believe. But in the Bible, that's not the way it went. Once Eve bit into that apple and got banished, there was no coming back. Paradise wasn't hers no more. Life was hard for her and Adam and all of us who come after.

Still, I figured it was over at that point. For the next several weeks, I thought that, and after a while, I stopped thinking about it at all. Except it *wasn't* over. The worst was coming. Claude had just been biding his time.

It come on the radio first. The noontime news said how a local man, employed as a mason by building contractor Angus Skloot, was found dead on the Skloots' property. Found stuck headfirst down a well. All afternoon, every hour on the hour, the radio kept saying that same thing, just those couple sentences in the middle of the rest of the day's news. I was so scared that I couldn't even get my housework done. I just walked around from room to room, letting everything go. Claude had been sullen the night before, but that was nothing new. Then he'd had trouble sleeping. I woke up in the middle of the night and heard him walking around downstairs. When I put the light on and looked at the clock, it said it was two something. I woke up later and lit the light again. It was quiet downstairs now, but his bed was still empty. But that didn't prove anything. Claude had trouble sleeping lots of nights. One minute I'd tell myself no, he wasn't capable of murder. The next minute, I'd start worrying that he might be.

In the morning, before I went downstairs to make Claude's breakfast, I prayed on it—asked Jesus Christ Almighty not to let my husband have done what I was afraid he might have, and if he *hadn't* done it, to please forgive me for even thinking along those lines. Claude didn't say more than two or three words to me while he was eating his eggs and toast. Well, that doesn't prove a thing, I told myself; he never *was* the talkative type in the morning. But after Claude went off to work, I decided to go out to his garage and look around. The work I did down at the Loew's Poli made me a detective of sorts, didn't it? I'd just go out there and poke around a little, like a detective would do. But when I went out there, I saw that he'd padlocked the garage door. Usually that lock just hung open unless we were going away someplace for the day. And when I went back in the house to take the spare key off the hook, it was gone. All our other extra keys were there except that one. By the time Belinda Jean come downstairs for her breakfast, I was good and worked up. "What's the matter with you?" she asked me.

"Nothing," I said. "Not a thing. Why do you ask?" She shrugged and shook a little more shredded wheat into her cereal bowl.

She was working that day. It was her long day because the library doesn't close until 8:00 P.M. on Thursdays. From the normal way she'd been acting before she left, I could tell she still didn't know about Jones's death. But halfway through the afternoon, the front door banged open and I could tell from the look on her face that she knew. "I'm sick," she said and ran right upstairs. Two or three times, I heard her in the bathroom, upchucking from the sounds of it. I made her a cup of tea, put some milk crackers on a plate to go with it, and went up there. She was back in bed, her face against the pillow. "Here," I said. "This'll settle your stomach."

She turned and looked up at me, her face bright pink from crying. My heart was breaking for her, she looked so pitiful. "I had two friends in this whole wide world," she said. "And now one of them's dead."

I hated to ask it, but I did. "Is that all you and him were, Belinda Jean? Just friends? Because I heard you vomiting. You're not baby sick, are you?"

"No!" she shouted. "He was nice to me was all. He was easy to talk to and he said he thought I was pretty. That's all there was to it." She put her face to her pillow again and wailed.

After she'd quieted down, I said, "Drink your tea and eat a little. It'll make you feel better." Then I left the room. That was all we've ever said to each other about Joe Jones, from that day to now, four years later.

That night, the *Evening Record* run a picture. It showed Jones's shoes sticking up out of that shallow well. And the headline above it— FOUL PLAY SUSPECTED IN LOCAL MAN'S DEATH—nearly stopped my heart. I held my breath as I read through the article. It said that it might have been an accident, that Joe could have tripped and fallen into that well headfirst, but that the victim's brother was wanted by the police for questioning. They'd questioned Angus Skloot, too, it said, and he'd told them the brothers had had a violent quarrel after Rufus's wife had took off and left him. The paper didn't come out and say there'd been hanky-panky between Joe and Rufus's wife, but I thought that was what it was saying between the lines. Well, good, I thought. If it was murder, it wasn't Claude who done it. It was one brother killing the other brother, same as Cain had killed Abel in a jealous rage and been made "a fugitive and a vagabond in the earth." The coroner, Mr. McKee, would be conducting an inquest over the next several days to figure things out, the paper said. There was nothing in that article about Josephus Jones being a picture painter. I was relieved about that. I didn't want anyone who might have seen the scuffle between him and Claude putting two and two together and getting seven. As far as I recalled, when the police stopped their fight at the art show and walked Claude to the exit gate that day, they hadn't even asked him for his name. That was a relief, too.

Usually, Claude finished work at five o'clock and was home by five fifteen wanting his dinner. But the day that story about Jones's death broke, he didn't show. I held his supper until eight or so, then wrapped it up and put it in the Frigidaire. By the time I heard his truck come up the driveway, it was after ten and I was upstairs in bed, staring into the pitch-dark and praying as hard as I could. It had been quiet down the hall for an hour or more, so I figured Belinda had finally gotten to sleep. I got up and went downstairs. Everything was still dark, but when I looked out the back window, I saw the light on in the garage. I went out there in bare feet with just my nightgown on.

"Where you been?" I asked him.

He didn't answer me. Didn't even look at me.

"What are you doing out here, Claude?"

He told me it was none of my business what he was doing, but I just stood there, looking at him. "If you must know, Miss Nosey, I'm cleaning some of my tools," he said then. But his toolbox was shut, still up on the shelf. He had his crowbar in one hand, a kerosene-smelling rag in the other. A pair of his coveralls was in a heap on the workbench. I walked over to them. "These dirty?" I said. "I'll take them in. I'm doing wash tomorrow." But when I went for them, he batted my hand away.

"Don't bother," he said. "They're no good anymore. My boots neither."

It made no sense. I'd bought him those boots for his birthday the month before and they were hardly broken in. "No? Why not?"

He turned and faced me. Gave me a long, hard look. "Because they got nigger blood on them. The overalls, too." When he said that, my heart sunk.

I said nothing. Just stood there, staring back at him for the longest time until a shiver run through me. Then I turned away and walked back toward the house. A little while later, I stood at the window and watched as he burned those coveralls and boots in the barrel, the flames leaping up and lighting his face like he was Lucifer himself. Like I was married to the devil.

And maybe I had some devil in me, too, because every morning

and night for the next several days, and sometimes even in the middle
of the day, I'd get down on my knees and pray that Rufus Jones, not
Claude, would be arrested—that an innocent man would pay for the
crime instead of a guilty one. It was a shameful thing for a Christian woman to do: asking the Good Lord to cover up a lie for selfish
reasons, and a terrible lie at that. He didn't grant my request, either.
I found that out the day the radio said that Rufus had been found,
questioned, and cleared. That he'd gone off on a three-day toot was all,
and witnesses at the places where he'd been had said so.

But at the end of that same long week, the paper and the radio
said that Coroner McKee's report concluded that Joe Jones's death
was accidental—that he'd probably tripped in the dark, stumbled
and fallen into the well headfirst, and drowned. The well was made
of stone, it said, and was most likely responsible for Jones's banged-up
skull and forehead.

There was some guff about Jones's death from the colored folks.
That big colored woman, Bertha Jinks—the one who's mixed up in
that group, the N Double A C P, and is always stirring up race trouble? She wrote a letter to the editor of the *Record* saying that everyone in town, black or white, knew how unlikely it was that a six-foot
man would fall into a five-foot-deep well and manage to get himself
drowned. And that if Josephus Jones had been a Caucasian instead
of a Negro, the coroner would have concluded otherwise, and the police would have worked overtime until they'd solved his murder and
gotten the victim some justice. My heart was near to stopping when
I read that letter, and I got so scared that I didn't even finish it. I just
ripped it out of the newspaper and tore it into a million little pieces
and burned them in the sink. Other letters to the editor went back
and forth for a week or so after that, most of them in support of the
official findings, and one or two saying how the coloreds were always
finding *some*thing to complain about. After a while, the whole thing
died down.

But not in our house. In our house, it kept festering in silence, like
an untended-to wound that never quite heals and eventually kills you.
Belinda Jean quit her job at the library, stopped speaking to her father,

and started staying home all the time. Whenever her friend Peggy called, she'd have me tell her she was out, and after a while Peggy got the message and stopped calling. Claude's suffering and breathing got worse and worse. And then, nine days ago, he turned purple, gasped for his last breath, and died—unrepentant and undetected in the matter of Josephus Jones's murder. May God grant him mercy for what he done, I pray each night, and may He grant me mercy, too, for having kept my silence these four years. In the Bible, it says that Jesus told the Jews, "You shall know the truth, and the truth shall make you free." It's in John 8:32. But knowing the truth and telling it are two different things, and knowing the truth about how Josephus Jones met His Maker and not *saying* how hasn't set me free. It's put me in a kind of prison. Me and poor Belinda both. . . .

At Claude's wake last night, it broke my heart the way Belinda Jean kept jerking her head up every time someone appeared at the doorway of the room where we were sitting. I suspect she was waiting for Peggy Konicki to show. Peggy, the only friend she ever had that didn't get murdered. . . . Her mother come into Benny's the other day, where I work now, running the cash register. Mrs. Konicki opened her wallet and showed me Peggy's wedding picture, and a picture of her cute little grandbaby. I hate my Benny's job, because it keeps me on my feet all day long, and because the manager's always hanging around, making sure that I ask whoever I'm ringing up if they want the stuff that's on the counter. "Can I interest you in a can of these deluxe mixed nuts?" Or, "Need any flashlight batteries today?" Or, "How about some bubble stuff for the kiddies? You know how children love to blow bubbles." . . . I looked at that picture of Peggy's baby quick. Then I had to look away and pinch my leg hard so that I wouldn't cry in front of Mrs. Konicki, who was already a grandmother and I was never going to be one.

I still count heads for that movie distributor, Axion Entertainment, and between that and Claude's Social Security and my Benny's paycheck, we get by, Belinda and me. Of course, she doesn't work. Doesn't leave the house hardly ever, either. Just hangs around all day from morning till nighttime, watching TV in her housecoat. She's big as a house now, poor thing. Has those two or three double chins and breathes like she's out of breath, even when she's just sitting on the couch, knitting and watching her TV shows. I remember when I first come on the scene and laid eyes on her. She was eleven. Half of her eyebrows were missing and she had a wad of paper towel plugging up the bloody nose she'd given herself. Then I took charge and she got better. And now she's bad again. *Real* bad. She don't turn off that television at night until after Johnny Carson's over. I get down on my knees and pray for her every single night.

Tonight, after I've gotten myself ready for bed, I'm going to pray for that other little girl, too—the one I saw across the hall last night at McPadden's Funeral Home wearing her blue dress and Mary Jane shoes. Chick and Sunny O'Day's little daughter, Annie. She could use some prayer, I think. It's like that song Daddy used to sing back in Alabama. I heard it on the radio just the other day. Johnny Cash was the one singing it, I'm pretty sure. *Motherless children have a hard time when the mother is gone. . . .* There's more truth than poetry in that line. When I heard that song again, I sat down and cried a river.

Another thought just come to me: how, even though the circumstances of their dying were different, both Sunny O'Day and Claude died because they suffocated. Because they couldn't draw enough air into their lungs—her from drowning and him from his emphysema, and maybe because of the terrible thing he done, too. And then they both ended up together in the basement of McPadden's that night, floating in floodwater.

I'm down on my knees now, asking God why, if He's merciful, He had to put so much meanness in the world He made. Weasels pounce, snakes bite, dams break, men kill other men. And why would a merciful God let a little child's mother die? I'm crying now and praying both, for Belinda Jean and that little O'Day girl. And for the souls of Sunny and Claude. And for Joe Jones's soul, too, and the soul of his brother who died in the flood. Dear Lord, have mercy on all of them, and on me, too, if it is Thy will.

Part III

Family

Chapter Eleven

Andrew Oh

I tidied up my point of view
I got a new attitude . . .

I'm Dr. Laura Schlessinger and I do welcome you to this hour of the program. Our number here is 1-800-Dr. Laura. That's 1-800-D-R-L-A-U-R-A. I'm here with Kimberly Neill who screens your calls, Benjamin Pratt who orchestrates our music, and me. I am my kid's mom, ready to preach, teach, and nag you into doing the right thing. . . . Casey-Lee, welcome to the program."

"Hi, Dr. Laura. Thank you for taking my call."

"Thank *you*."

"I've been listening to you since my mom used to pick me up from grade school, and I just wanted to say what an honor it is to speak with you."

"Thank you. How can I help?"

"I'm . . . well, the thing is . . . Sorry. I'm a little nervous."

"That's okay."

"Do you want me to give you some background, or should I get right to my question?"

"Well, why don't you just start and we'll see where it goes?"

"Okay. Actually, I'm calling for my fiancé. He's got a family situation that he's struggling with, so I suggested we call Dr. Laura and see what she has to say about it."

"And your fiancé's name is?"

"Andrew. His problem—well, his parents are divorced, okay? And his mother's getting remarried. To a woman."

"Uh-huh. And your question for me is?"

"Whether or not we should go to their wedding. See, he grew up in a family that wasn't very religious, but since we've been going out, he's found His Lord and Savior. We already said we couldn't go, but now he's getting pressure from one of his sisters about how we should, because it'll hurt their mother if we don't. And yesterday his mom's partner sent us plane tickets so that we can surprise her. And, well, the thing is . . . Don't you think gay marriage is sinful?"

"What *I* think is beside the point. What do *you* think?"

"Me? I think it is."

"Okay. Now a minute ago, you said this was your fiancé's problem. So why is it that you're calling me instead of him?"

"Oh. Well, because I said I would. He's right here, though."

"Ah. Then why don't you put him on?"

"Oh, okay. [*sotto voce*] She wants to talk to you."

Muffled voices.

"Hello?"

"Hi, Andrew."

"Hey. How are you?"

"Fine, thank you. Now, first of all, I have a note here from Kimberly that says you're a member of the military."

"Yes, ma'am. United States Army, Specialist E-Four."

"And what's your specialty, soldier?"

"My . . . I'm in a nurses' training program."

"Ahh. Well, thank you for your service to your country. And hoo-ya!"

"Yes, ma'am. Thank you, ma'am."

"Casey-Lynn says you're conflicted about going to your mother's wedding. Why don't you tell me about it?"

"Okay, well . . . Like Casey said, she's getting married to a woman, okay? She's . . . my mother's an artist. Kind of a free spirit, you know?"

"And?"

"And her and this woman have been living together for a while, and now they're going to get married. Which, you know, they can do.

Legally. Because the wedding's going to be in Connecticut. And so, part of me thinks I should go because, you know, she's my mom."

"And what's the other part telling you?"

"Uh . . . what?"

"You just told me that *part* of you is telling you to go, so I'm assuming there's another part that's telling you not to. Right?"

"Yes, ma'am."

"Because?"

"Because I don't, me and Casey don't . . . we feel that marriage should just be between a man and a woman. Whether, you know, it's legal or not."

"So this wedding flies in the face of your values."

"Yes, ma'am. Plus, I don't know. I just think that going would be disloyal to my dad. I mean, him and my mom are divorced, but—"

"Divorced for how long?"

"Over a year now. But they've been separated for, like, three years."

"And how long had they been married?"

"My mom and dad? Maybe twenty-six, twenty-seven years?"

"And they decided to end their marriage because?"

"Because of *her*, I guess. This woman she's marrying. She started working in New York, okay? Because of her art? And she was renting a room in this woman's fancy apartment, okay? So one thing led to another and . . ."

"And what? Your mother decided she liked women better than men? Fancy apartments? New York deli? Ha, ha, ha."

"I think it was about living in New York at first. Because of the art scene there. She does these crazy, experimental . . . installations she calls them."

"Not the kind of art you'd hang over your sofa then. Okay. Got it. Have you discussed your conflict with your father?"

"Yeah, and he's pretty cool about it. At least he says he is. He may even go to the wedding."

"Really? Wow! I'm not sure if that makes him the most forgiving man in the universe or the most masochistic. Ha, ha, ha."

"The thing is, I don't even think she's really homosexual. I just think—"

"Andrew? *Andrew?* You need to face the facts. You told me that your mother left your father for a lesbian hookup. That makes her a lesbian. And now she wants to make it legal so that she and her shack-up honey can—"

"I don't know if I'd put it that way."

"No, of course you wouldn't. Honor thy mother, right? But did your mother honor the solemn covenant she made with your father? No, she didn't. It doesn't really *matter* what this other person's gender is. What matters is that she forsook her vow to love, honor, and cherish her husband. To be *faithful* to him. Right?"

"Well, yeah. I guess."

"Then for whatever reason your *father* doesn't want to 'man up' and say screw you, babe, if you think *I'm* going to your big gay wedding, I see no reason why that obligates *you* to—"

"Well, my dad's a peacemaker. Plus, one of my sisters keeps bugging me to—"

"Andrew? You and your girl called me for my advice, so why don't you stop talking over me and *listen* to what I have to say?"

"Okay. Sorry."

"It doesn't *matter* what your father's decision is, or what this silly sister of yours wants *you* to do. If your values are telling you that this marriage is wrong, then going to the wedding would say otherwise."

"So you're saying I shouldn't go."

"No, I'm saying that if you decide to go, your presence makes a statement. And if you decide *not* to go, that makes a different statement. It's up to *you* to decide which statement you want to make."

"Right. But I just feel—"

"Doesn't matter what you *feel*. What matters is what you *do*. Suppose your commanding officer gave you a direct order to do something. What does he care about? Your *feelings* or your actions?"

"Yeah, exactly. But she sent us these plane tickets. See, the thing is, I already told my mom we weren't going because we couldn't afford the trip. But then we got these tickets. With a note that says my mom and her—"

"So *what*? If she wants to waste her money, then let her. The fact that she's trying to manipulate you—*guilt* you into going—doesn't obligate you."

"Yeah, that's what Casey-Lee says."

"And she's right."

"But family's family, you know? Both my sisters are going. I'd be the only one of her kids who—"

"Then go. Have a great time, and if one of the brides throws the garter, I hope you catch it. Not sure if they throw the garter or two bouquets at a lesbian wedding. Ha, ha. But if you don't want to go, I'd suggest you call your mother, tell her you love her very much, and say that you can't attend her wedding because you don't condone this kind of union. Just be honest with her."

"Yeah, but I don't want to hurt her feelings."

"So what's more important? Sparing her feelings, or being true to your own and your fiancée's moral code? Just don't forget: there are *two* women to consider here. The one who birthed you, and the one you're marrying."

"Yeah. Okay. . . . Wait a minute, Dr. Laura. Casey's handing me a note. Oh, okay. She wants to know if we should send them a gift."

"Sure, if you want to. Something modest, a Crock-Pot or a cut-glass vase. Or, if you don't want to spend the money, send them a pretty card."

"But wouldn't that be the same as—"

"No. *Acknowledging* their wedding is different from having to go there and *witness* it. Right?"

"Yeah, okay. We can do that."

"Good. Now put Casey-Lynn back on."

"It's Casey-*Lee*."

"Excuse me?"

"You just called her Casey-Lynn, but it's Casey-Lee."

"Uh-oh. My bad. Thirty lashes with a wet noodle for me. Ha, ha, ha."

"Here she is."

"Hi, Dr. Laura."

"Okay, sweetie, I think we've got this all straightened out. By the way, when are you and your man getting married?"

"A little over a year from now. Next October."

"And tell me. I'm just curious. Are *you two* shacking up?"

"Us? Oh, no. He lives on the base and I'm living with my parents. Partly to save money, but also because, well, I want to save myself."

"Wow! Good for *you*! And Andrew's okay with that? Because a lot of men think differently about these things than women do. They're more interested in slam, bam, thank you, ma'am than deferred gratification."

"No, Andrew's . . . he respects that I want to wait."

"Excellent! In that case, you go out and buy yourself a pretty white dress when the time comes because white will actually *mean* something when *you* walk down the aisle, unlike ninety-nine percent of today's brides. Especially the ones with baby bumps. Ha, ha, ha."

"Um, Dr. Laura? Can I ask you one more question?"

"Sure. Go ahead."

"When we do get married, should we invite his mom and her . . . partner to the wedding?"

"Do you want to?"

"No. Well, his mom, I guess. But not both of them. I just think it might make the other guests uncomfortable."

"Fine then. Invite his mother, but have Andrew make it clear that you two expect her to leave her spouse at home. And if she's willing to attend under those conditions, then be polite and respectful to her. Be gracious. And then go ahead and have yourself a lovely day and one hell of a honeymoon. Put on a pretty little negligee for the wedding night and rock his world. And tell that man of yours from me that he's getting a good woman. That's rare these days. We're becoming an endangered species, ha ha. Okay?"

"Yes, okay. And thank you *so* much."

"You're welcome, sweetie. Good luck. And you know what? Don't hang up. I'm going to transfer you back over to Kimberly so that she can take down your address. I want to send you copies of two of my books, *The Proper Care and Feeding of Husbands* and *The Proper Care and Feeding of Wives*. An early wedding present for each of you. All right, sweetheart?"

"Yes. Thanks again, Dr. Laura."

"*You're* welcome. . . . Gloria, welcome to the program! Oh, oh, wait a minute. Looks like we've got to take a break. Be right back."

It felt so wrong, it felt so right . . .
I kissed a girl and I liked it, I liked it

"Welcome back. Our number here is 1-800-Dr. Laura. That's 1-800-*D-R-L-A-U-R-A.* You know, over the break, I was thinking about that last caller. You see what pain and confusion it causes for the rest of the family when a husband or a wife doesn't respect the covenant of their marriage? The children, especially. Even adult children. I still can't believe that that husband's going to attend. What's he going to do? Walk his ex-wife down the aisle and give her away to her new bride? He's a peacekeeper? More likely, the poor guy's probably been so beaten down by the feminist agenda that he's surrendered his man pants, ha ha ha. Remember a while back when the feministas got all bent out of shape because the bride was supposed to say she would love, honor, and *obey* her husband? Good lord, what outcry! 'Obey? Oh, no, we can't have that. That might interfere with my *happiness*—my *fulfillment*.' So now we have divorce rates hovering around fifty percent, and Heather has two mommies and no positive male influences in her life. You know, I've been attacked in the media, accused of being antigay, but the truth is: I've counseled many gays and lesbians on this program, and also when I was in private practice. I'm not antigay. I just happen to believe that the sacred institution of *marriage* means one man and one woman. . . . Gloria! Welcome to the program."

"Hi, Dr. Laura. First of all, I just want to say that, thanks to you, I'm my husband's girlfriend and my kids' mom."

"Excellent. And how many kidlets, and what are their ages?"

"We have two sons, ages four and two. I'm a stay-at-home mom, and I'm planning on homeschooling my boys when the time comes."

"Excellent, excellent. And what can I do for you today?"

Chapter Twelve

Marissa Oh

I hear the buzzer and run to the door. Look through the peephole. It's Bree, thank god. I undo the chain. Turn the lock, slide the bolt back and let her in. "Hey," I say. "Thanks for coming."

"Sure. What's going on? You sounded so freaked-out on the phone."

I take off the ball cap, remove my sunglasses. Watch her eyes widen. "Oh shit, Marissa! What happened?"

I try to strangle my sobs but can't. She waits. "The motherfucker beat me up. That's what."

"Who? Matthew?"

I shake my head. Matthew's a bartender where I waitress, a guy I've gone to bed with off and on. "Tristan McCabe," I say.

"The actor? Jesus, Rissa. What the . . . ?" When she takes me in her arms, I hold on for dear life. It happened on Friday and now it's Sunday afternoon. It's been a long, scary weekend. I don't want to let go of her because this is the first I've felt safe. "Okay," she finally says. "Start from the beginning."

I flop onto the couch and she sits down beside me. Takes my hand in hers. "You know my friend Ebony from acting class?" She shakes her head. "Yes, you do. I introduced you two at that Anthropologie in the Village?"

"The one who works there?"

"Yeah. She called me Friday afternoon. Asked me . . ." Bree pulls a Kleenex from the box on the coffee table and hands it to me. I wipe my eyes. Blow my nose.

"You want a glass of water or something? A Xanax?"

I shake my head. Tell her I took one of my roommate's an hour ago.

Bree asks where she is. "In Cancun with her boyfriend, thank god," I say. "If she knew about this, she'd probably get on Twitter and tell the whole world."

"Okay. So Ebony called you."

"She's been having trouble making her rent. Plus, she's way overextended on her credit cards. So she took out an ad on Craigslist."

"What kind of ad?"

"You know."

Bree's eyes widen. "With all that 'Craigslist killer' stuff in the news? What is she? Crazy? God, I wouldn't even put a listing in there when I was trying to sell my futon. Complete strangers coming up to my apartment. I don't *think* so. But go on."

"So she called me and asked if I wanted to make some easy money. And maybe some contacts."

She frowns. "I don't think I like where you're going with this."

"Bree, I haven't had an acting job in like six months. And do you know why? Because in this shitty business, it's all about who you know, who you can network with. Plus, Ebony said she had hooked up with Tristan the last time he was in town, and that he was really nice. Respectful. She met him at the hotel where he was staying and they had a few drinks in the bar. Then they went up to his room and all he wanted was a blow job. He paid her three hundred and tipped her an extra hundred on top of that."

"For a 'respectful' blow job? Jesus Christ, Marissa." She grabs a pillow and hugs it. "So?"

"So he called her this past Friday. Said he was in town to do some promos for that cop show he's in, and could they hook up again? But this time he wanted her to bring a friend with her, preferably an Asian girl. That he had a thing for Asian girls."

"Oh, please. What does he think? That he's ordering off a menu? And you *agreed* to this?"

"Well, yeah. Because Showtime is casting for a new series they're planning to film here in the city next year, okay? I had called about it, but they said they were only doing closed auditions. But Tristan told

Ebony that the casting director is the sister of his college roommate, and that he could maybe make a call and get her in. So I thought that if I went there with her, it might open a door for me, too. He's on network TV, Bree. He was in *Band of Brothers*. Do you know who produced that series? Tom Hanks!"

"Are you out of your mind, Marissa? Exchanging sex for six degrees of separation from—"

"Don't fucking judge me!"

"Okay, I'm sorry," she says. "It's just . . . you're scaring me."

"And anyway, it *wasn't* sex. Not really. Ebony said all I'd have to do was get naked and make out with her a little while he watched, and maybe make out with him a little, too. And maybe, you know, let him watch me touch myself while they . . . But that was all. She'd take care of the rest, she said. They'd already agreed on a price. A thousand dollars, which we could split fifty-fifty."

Bree gets off the sofa and goes over to the window. Stands there with her back to me. "Marissa, do you know what they call women who make business arrangements like that?"

"Yeah, and do *you* know how many casting calls I've been to in the past month? Seven. With zero callbacks. Look, I don't expect you to understand. You go to work every day, sit up there in your office on the umpteenth floor of corporate headquarters, nice and safe. But acting is a tough business."

"And finance isn't?"

"Yeah, I'm sure it is. But it's not like you have to go out and hit the pavement all the time, looking for jobs that you don't get, and then go waitress at night. Put up with a bunch of bullshit from assholes with money to burn so you'll get bigger tips. And hey, it's not like you didn't sleep with your supervisor before you got that promotion."

"Because I *liked* the guy. There's a difference, Marissa."

"Yeah, and you like your new salary, too."

As soon as it's out of my mouth, I'm sorry I said it. The last thing I want to do right now is make her mad. Alienate her so that she leaves. "No, I'm sorry. You're right. It *is* different. And it was stupid of me to go there with her. I *know* that now, okay? But at the time, it seemed like an opportunity. It's like what Ebony says. In this business, it's all about who you know and who you blow."

"Jesus Christ, Marissa!"

"Look, all I'm saying is that if you want acting work and you're not Scarlett Johansson, you've got to make compromises. Take risks. That's just the way it works. And it wasn't like there was going to be any penetration. I was clear about that."

She turns and faces me. "Wasn't *going* to be? Just tell me, Rissa. Did he rape you in addition to using you as a punching bag?"

"No! He was . . ."

She comes back and sits down. "Okay, just tell me what happened. God, you're making me a nervous wreck."

"He was staying at the Mondrian down in SoHo, okay? I met Ebony in the lobby and we were both a little early, so we went to the bar and had a drink. You know who we saw in there? Kate Hudson."

"Yeah, whatever. Then what?"

"So Ebony was explaining how it would play out. What she was going to do, what I'd do. I asked her if it would be cool to talk with him about representation—if, like, he thought I should try to get an agent or wait until I had a few more acting credits, maybe ask him who *his* agent is. I already knew he's represented by UTA, one of the big gorillas out there, but I figured, hey, if I could get him to talk about it, he might even give me a referral to *them*. But Ebony said I shouldn't bring any of that up until after we were finished, and only if, you know, he had had a really good time. 'Let's play it by ear,' she said. And I was nervous, you know? Part of me was like, okay, I can handle it. Ebony will be there. It's not like I'm going to be alone with him. And another part was like, I can't believe I'm going to do this."

Bree shakes her head. "That was the part you *should* have been listening to, Marissa," she says. "So?"

"So we went up to his suite. And at first, everything was cool. He paid Ebony and ordered up some sushi and a couple of bottles of Cristal. And after they delivered it, we were just sitting and talking, drinking champagne. Tristan and Ebony were eating the sushi, too, but I didn't because I'm always so spastic with chopsticks. Didn't want to hear, 'You're part *Asian* and you don't know how to use *chopsticks*?' But then he starts feeding me. Putting maki in front of my mouth and going, like, 'Open up, Ming.' "

"Ming?"

"Yeah, Ebony had given us both fake names. She was Karina and I was Ming. She said the only real information she gives these guys is her cell phone number. It's a safety precaution."

"Oh. So at the end of this little session he's going to give a referral to someone named Ming?"

"No! But I figured that, if we gave him what he wanted, I'd tell him my real name afterward." She's staring at my swollen face. "Look, are you trying to make me feel like a bigger idiot than I already—"

"No. I'm sorry. Go on."

"He . . . he asked us if we wanted to do a line of coke with him, and we did that. I wasn't going to, but I was feeling a little tipsy from the champagne, and I figured the coke would get me, you know, refocused. But I wasn't out of control or anything. I know my limits."

She reaches over and touches the bruise on my cheek. "Well, apparently Mr. Hollywood doesn't know *his*," she says. "Does it still hurt?"

I nod. Go on. "He put some music on, some Jay-Z, and he said he wanted us to dance for him. So we did that. Then Ebony started doing this striptease for him. So I did, too. We hadn't discussed that downstairs, but I mean, the guy was paying us a lot of money, so I figured okay, I can do that much. Ebony started kissing me and I was like, well, this was what I agreed to. It was just acting, you know?"

"Oh, yeah. Sounds very Shakespearean." I give her a look. "Okay, I'm sorry. I get sarcastic when I'm nervous. You know that. Then what happened?"

"He was . . . he was sitting there, smiling and watching us and . . . touching himself. Under his shirt, between his legs. Then he got up and got naked and the three of us were dancing. He started getting a little free with his hands, but it wasn't over the top or anything. But then he . . ."

"He what?"

"Went into the bedroom. Said he had to call California and ask his agent something. And I was like, his *agent*, so I was trying to listen to what he was saying. But the only thing I could make out was him going, 'Are you shitting me, Jenny? Then fuck Universal! And grow a dick while you're at it!' And after he hung up, he was in there for another ten minutes and we were just sitting there, waiting for him. And when I asked Ebony what was going on, she was like, 'Shh.' . . . I don't know, Bree. I think maybe his agent gave him bad news about something. Or that maybe he took something else while he was in there. Because when he came back out again, he looked wild-eyed and was acting all pissed off at us. He goes, 'Come on, let's go!' like *we* were the ones who'd been keeping *him* waiting. It was like Jekyll and Hyde, you know? He started getting rough. Grabbing at us, bumping up against us. He reached over and pinched my nipple and I was like, 'Ow!' Ebony told him to cool it, and he said he hadn't paid her for a fucking lecture. So she got down on her knees to . . . you know. But he batted her head away and said *he* was calling the shots. And she said, no, *she* was—that they'd already agreed on the terms. He went ballistic! Started screaming that she and her 'slant-eyed sidekick' had better do what he wants or else. Then he starts walking around the suite and has this . . . *tantrum*. Pushes over the table where the champagne and sushi were. Picks up a chair and smashes it against the wall. He was like, 'Do you bitches know who I *am*? Do you think I'm giving you a grand for fucking *amateur* hour?'"

Bree flinches. "God, you must have been so scared."

"I *was*. And I was like, okay, let's just give him his money back and get out of here. He had paid Ebony in cash, okay? And I could see the bills sticking out of her bag. So I grabbed the money and held it out to him. And when I did that, he got so mad that . . . He grabs the money out of my hand and throws it on the floor. Then he gets all up in my face and . . . starts *screaming* at me. I kept backing up, you know? Until I was against the wall. Ebony kept saying, 'Come on, baby. Come over here so I can make you feel good.' Except he wouldn't back away from me. There was this big vein popping out on his forehead, and his face was all red and contorted. His spit's flying out at me. Then he starts . . . he makes a fist and starts . . ."

Bree covers her mouth with her hand.

"*Punching* me! In my face, my stomach. At first I was like dazed. Doubled over, you know? I felt like I was going to throw up. And when I looked up again, I saw him forcing Ebony facedown on the arm of the sofa. She was struggling to get up, but he had his hand on the small of her back and he wouldn't let her. And she was like, 'Use a condom, please just use a condom.' And he goes, 'Fuck condoms. I want it back door.'"

Bree's blinking back tears. "This is a nightmare. What did you do?"

"Got behind him and tried pulling him off of her. But he swiveled around and shoved me so hard that I fell backward. Onto the floor. One of the champagne bottles was right there. And I thought maybe if I hit him over the head with it. . . . But I was scared that, if it didn't knock him out, it would make him even crazier. So I figured, okay, I'll get help. Grabbed my clothes. Got dressed as fast as I could. But when I was almost to the door, I was like, 'Oh, shit! My purse!' I went back to grab it, but he saw me and yanked it away. Started whacking it, over and over, against the wall. And everything went flying out. My wallet, my phone. While he was busy beating the shit out of my bag, Ebony grabs her clothes and points at the door, like come on, *let's go*. But what was I supposed to do? Leave without my phone? My credit cards? Only, when I went to pick them up, he *tackled* me. Got on top of me and . . . Oh god, it's . . . it's like I'm back there again."

"No, you're not," Bree says. "Look around. You're here with me in your apartment. You're safe."

"Look what that son of a bitch did to me!" I pull back my hair so she can see the bruise on my neck. Pull up my shirt and show her his teeth marks on my stomach.

"He *bit* you?"

I nod. "Ebony ran out of there. And when he heard the door, he jumped up. Started to go after her and . . . that gave me enough time to get up and get to the bathroom. Lock the door. But then he starts slamming himself against it. I was down on my knees on the floor, watching it push in like that movie where Jack Nicholson goes crazy. Except it *wasn't* a movie. It was really happening, Bree. I've never been so scared in my whole life. I thought . . . I thought, now he's going to bust in here and kill me."

A shiver passes through her. "*Did* he get in?" she asks. I shake my head. "Then how did you get out of there?"

"When Ebony got out in the hall, she saw this room service guy. He called security and they came right up. He wouldn't answer the door, but they had a pass key, Ebony said. And some tool to push back the bar that secures the extra lock. When they got in, I could hear them out there like, 'Okay, Mr. McCabe, let's calm down before this turns into an incident. Why don't you put your clothes back on? It's not worth it, is it? If we have to notify the police and they come up here and see . . . what is that over there? Cocaine? You don't want the media to get a hold of something like this, do you?'

"After they got him under control, they told me to come out. And when I did, I couldn't even look at him. I just glanced at the security guys. They looked like ex-military or something. I grabbed my stuff and went to leave. I just wanted to get out of there, you know? But they said they needed to talk to me and my friend out in the hall. One of them stayed in the suite with Tristan and the other one had Ebony and me go with him down to some office on a different floor. He asked us a bunch of embarrassing questions and wrote down our answers. Wanted our contact information. He asked for mine first, and like an idiot, I gave him my real name and phone number. Ebony just made up a name and number. She did most of the talking. She was like, 'Look, we're not going to call the cops or anything. We just made a mistake. There wasn't any money exchanged. Can we please just get out of here?' And I was thinking like, oh, no, there wasn't any money exchanged. It was just all over the floor. But the guy said okay, they were willing to overlook what happened—that they'd contact us if they needed to. But that from now on, we were banned from the Mondrian."

"Oh, *you're* banned, but Mr. Celebrity isn't? They probably apol-

ogized to the pig and sent up a fruit basket because of the inconvenience. So then what did you do? Go to the emergency room, I hope."

I shake my head. "It's not like I needed stitches. He beat my purse
up worse than he did me. We just . . . just left. Got into one of the cabs
waiting outside the hotel. Neither of us said much. I just sat there with
my hands over my face, trying to stop shaking. It took forever to get
across town. Obama was in the city and the traffic was horrible. The
driver dropped me off first, and when I got back up here, I locked and
bolted the door. I just kept walking around in here, trying not to see
it all over again. Bree, I can't eat, can't sleep. All day yesterday, I was
too scared to leave the apartment or even answer the phone. You're the
first person I've talked to since it happened."

"Did you call your therapist at least?"

"Sandie? No! She's already on my case about my risky behavior."

"Then maybe you ought to start listening to her. Jesus, Marissa,
you are so fucking lucky."

"I know, I know. But now what am I supposed to do?"

"Get yourself as tetanus shot for one thing," she says. "And if I were
you, I'd go to the police and press charges."

"And tell them *why* we were up in his room? Get arrested for . . . ?"

"Solicitation," she says.

"Oh yeah, that would look good on my résumé, wouldn't it? Never
mind the cops. I don't even want to talk to Ebony. She's called and
texted me like five or six times since it happened, but I haven't answered any of them."

"Good," she says. "You shouldn't. Your friend is a hooker."

"No, she's not. She's just . . . Bree, look at my face. I've got my
mother's wedding next weekend. And I was planning to see my father
at the Cape first. Surprise him. My sister's going to be there and—"

"Okay, calm down. The swelling should go down by then."

"Yeah, and these bruises he gave me are going to turn all purple
and yellow. I can't just show up and have them ask me about them."

Bree says she's more concerned about the bite mark. Do I want her
to go with me to a clinic and get that tetanus shot?

I shake my head. "Those places are always jam-packed on weekends. I don't want to have to sit in some waiting room and have every-one look at me. I'll get one tomorrow."

"Have you been cleaning it at least?" she asks.

"Yeah, with peroxide."

"Well, we should get you some antibacterial cream to put on it. And some gauze and tape. You need to cover that wound before it gets infected."

"I'm more worried about my face," I say. "I can't let my father or my sister find out what happened."

Bree says she's heard about some homeopathic stuff that's supposed to be good for bruises. "Arnica or something. It acts like an anti-inflammatory. And my friend Karen? The one who works the cosmet-ics counter at Bloomingdale's? She says there's this great cover-up they sell there. Karen said some model she recognized came in last week wearing sunglasses and a kerchief. She told Karen her boyfriend had roughed her up, and she had a shoot the next day. Karen says she fixed her up so that you couldn't even notice. She's working today. Why don't we go uptown and—"

"I can't! I don't want to leave the apartment. Not yet anyway."

She gives me this look like I'm pathetic. Which I am. "Okay," she says. "Then why don't I go get it for you. I'm sure it's expensive, but maybe Karen can use her employee discount. And while I'm out, I'll pick up the other stuff, too—the Arnica and some Neosporin or something. Okay?"

I tell her I don't want her to leave yet.

She says okay, she'll stay for a while longer, but I have to *promise* her I'll get that tetanus shot. "All right, I promise," I tell her, but I already know I won't. It's not like he was a rabid dog. Not in that way.

When she asks me if I've eaten anything today, I shake my head. "Then let me go over to that place across the street and get you some-thing. Some soup, maybe, or a sandwich."

"No," I tell her. "But on second thought, can I have that Xanax? That one of Allegra's I took was the last one she had."

Bree nods, reaches into her purse. "Want some water with it?"

"No. Some wine, maybe. There's some chablis in the fridge. Pour yourself some, too. Let's get drunk."

And so we do. Or I do, anyway. I lose track of how much Bree has drunk, but she's taken a Xanax, too, because she says just *hearing* about what happened has made her so anxious, she needs to even herself out.

After the wine and drug kick in, I don't feel so scared anymore. Wasted, we start complaining about our lives, our respective careers. "Why is it that in corporate America, the ones who wield the most power are the biggest douche bags?" Bree asks.

"Kate Hudson," I say. "She does movies, commercials. Gets herself on Leno and Letterman, *Access Hollywood*. Why her? Why not me?"

"Because your mother's not Goldie Hawn."

"No, my mother's an *artiste*." I say it as much to myself as to Bree. "An *edgy lesbian artiste*. Next weekend, I'm going to be in my mother's *lesbian wedding*." For some reason, this makes me laugh. I picture Mama working in her studio, surrounded by all that scary art she makes that rich people pay insane prices for. Like that piece she made out of ruined bridal gowns. How much did Gaga pay for that thing? And I can't even get acting work that pays scale?

I ask Bree if she wants to see the bridesmaid's dress I'm wearing to the wedding—the black strapless Stella McCartney that Viveca bought me when the two of us went shopping. But Bree just looks over at me vacantly, like she's deaf or something. So yeah, she *is* wasted. Maybe if I showed her.

I go into my bedroom. Take the dress out of my closet and hold it up against myself in front of the mirror. I slip out of my shirt and jeans and put it on. Look in the mirror at the girl in the chic black dress with the black-and-blue face, one side puffed up like a fucking baseball glove. . . . Maybe if I were my mother, I could rip the dress, stain it, and sell it as art. But I'm *not* Mama. I'm an out-of-work actor so desperate for a connection that I sold myself. Could have gotten myself killed. Then I'd be famous: Tristan McCabe's victim. I'd be like that blond girl who got killed in the Caribbean on her school vacation—the one whose mother is on TV every two seconds. *I can't get work, but that dead girl's mother has turned herself into a celebrity? . . . Maybe I'm not cut out for this meat grinder of a business. Or maybe I am. Maybe if I stick it out, my big break will happen next month, or even next week. . . .*

When I walk out of my bedroom wearing the dress, I see that Bree has fallen asleep. I pour myself the last of the chablis. Sit down next to Bree. I see him again, his face contorted with anger, screaming at me the way my mother used to scream at my brother. . . . I hope he dies. Gets hit by a car or shot by some crazy fan. Gets killed in a plane crash on his way back to Hollywood. It would serve him right. I sip my wine. Rest my head on Bree's shoulder. I'm getting drowsy now, too. . . .

When I wake up, Bree is standing over me, taking the empty wineglass out of my hand. She smiles, I smile back. Then I remember what happened on Friday. "I have to go," she says. "I'll get you some of that cover-up and the other stuff. I'll come back tomorrow."

I stand. Teeter a little and follow her to the door. Watch her while she waits for the elevator. When it dings and she gets in, I close my door and lock it. Slide the bolt back in place. Put the chain on. My roommate's not coming back from Mexico until when? Wednesday? Thursday? . . .

I see the rage in his eyes, feel his blasts of breath, his spit hitting my face. My heart is pounding and I start to shake again. My head aches. My face is still sore to the touch. The bite mark on my stomach hurts like a motherfucker.

Chapter Thirteen

Ariane Oh

Oh god, I feel so sick, and of course they've assigned me the middle seat. Mr. Businessman is on the aisle, where I wish I was in case I have to run to the lavatory. He's a big man, and his legs are spread wide. One of his knees is out in the aisle and the other's trespassing into my space. The Holy Roller woman's got the window seat. When she was coming down the aisle during boarding, I read her sweatshirt: GOD IS GREAT. Where's that sickness bag, just in case? There's everything but in this seat pocket. How long is this flight?

Click click. "Good morning, folks. This is Captain Tom Moynihan. Wanted to let you know that we've reached our flying altitude. We're expecting smooth air on our way to Boston this morning, so I'm going to go ahead and turn off the seat belt sign. But while you're seated, we'd like you to . . ."

All right already. Blah blah blah. My stomach's rolling and I'm shaking. If he doesn't stop talking, I'm not going to make it to the bathroom.

"Our super duper flight attendants will be starting the beverage service in just a few minutes, and—"

Shit! I've just retched and had to swallow back my own vomit. Mr. Aisle Seat turns away from me. Well, tough. It's not like *I* can help it. "You okay?" the Jesus woman asks. I nod rather than say anything. I don't want her to have to smell puke breath. My throat is burning. My stomach's gurgling. This is horrible.

"On behalf of my wing man, First Officer Bill Brazicki, and our entire Chicago-based flight crew, I'd like to tell you how glad we are to have you aboard today. And now we invite you to sit back, relax, and enjoy the flight." Finally! I unbuckle, stand up too fast, and clunk my head.

"Excuse me! Excuse me, please!" Mr. Business unbuckles and stands, looking annoyed. "Thanks," I say, accidentally stepping on his foot. "Sorry." Hurrying toward the bathroom, I push past another woman to get there first.

"Well, pardon *me*," she says in this bitchy voice.

"It's an emergency!" I call over my shoulder. "I'm pregnant!"

When I reach the lav, I step in, slam the door, and slide the "occupied" bolt. Holding back my hair, I bend my head low and regurgitate some more. It's just bile, mostly. I've been vomiting ever since my alarm went off at five this morning: at home, on the way to the airport, twice in the bathroom during the layover. Dr. Rosinsky said the sickness should subside in another month. "I hope she's right for your sake," Cicely told me. "With Sha'Quandria, I was only sick for the first trimester, but DeShawn had me upchucking the whole nine months. Then to top it off, he breeched and I had to get a C-section." DeShawn is a senior in high school. I guess it's not true what everyone says: that once you see the baby, you forget all about the pain and the inconvenience.

I go to flush but can't find the button. Well, I guess I'd better try to pee as long as I'm here, although I don't really have to. I pull down my pants and suspend my rear over the bowl. Manage a little bit of dribble, find the flush button, pull up my pants. I could have held off a while on buying these pregnancy jeans, but I'm glad I didn't. My sister would probably be mortified by the elastic waistband. I can just hear her: *You're twenty-seven years old and you're already wearing old lady pants?* Well, so what? They're comfortable. Those old ladies have the right idea. I turn and face the sink. Look at myself in the mirror, which is a mistake. Bags under my eyes, chapped lips, pasty complexion. I cup my hands beneath the faucet, swish, and spit. Do it again. And again. I wish I had a mint to suck. Ow! I just whacked my elbow. What did Axel tell me they call it when people have sex in these cramped little bathrooms? I forget. God, why would anyone want to do *that*? It's got to be horribly uncomfortable, plus it's gross, especially for the poor people who have to use it afterward. You go in there to pee and walk out with an STD. . . . *I'm pregnant*, I announced on my way in here. Haven't even told my parents yet, but now a bunch of strangers on a plane know. How weird is that?

When I step out into the cabin, there's a line. A stylish woman, a guy in a ball cap, a young couple with their hands in each other's back pockets. The mile-high club: that's what it's called. Gross . . .

Back at my row, I stand and wait but finally have to tap Aisle Seat Guy on the shoulder. "Sorry to bother you again. Is your foot okay?" Does that grunt mean yes or no?

"Feel better?" Jesus Woman asks when I'm in my seat again.

"Yes, thanks." There's stuff all over her tray table: beads, little medals, a spool of . . . what? Fishing line? Oh, I get it; she's making bracelets. Hey, if we hit some turbulence, her little cottage industry will be all over the floor. Why doesn't she just knit?

"So what's your due date?" she asks.

"Hmm? Oh, March. March twenty-sixth. How did you know?"

"Well, for one thing, I figure that's not pleasure reading you're doing." She chuckles, points. The book I've brought, *Home from the Hospital: Now What?* is poking out of my seat pocket. "That, and I heard you say you were on your way to the john," she says. "This your first?"

"Yes."

"Morning sickness?"

"More like morning, afternoon, and evening," I say.

"Oh, honey, that's tough." She reaches over and pats my hand. "March, huh? So you're only a couple months along?"

I nod. She's older than my parents. Short, teased hair dyed jet-black. It's probably the same style she wore back in high school. Axel's mother is about this woman's age and she wore her hair like that, too. A lot of women do that, I've noticed: hold on to the hairstyles of their youth. Her GOD IS GREAT sweatshirt probably means she's one of those family values types. To fend off any questions about a husband, I ask her if she has any kids.

"Oh, good golly, yes. Three sons by my first husband, What's His

Name, and three daughters by my second, What's His Name Number Two." Her laugh is a pleasant cackle. "Grandkids now, too. Seven of 'em. That's why I'm flying in from Colorado: to see my latest grand-baby and help my daughter out. My youngest. She's just had a nine-pound baby girl—*her* first, too. She was in labor for eleven hours, poor thing. Lisa's narrow-hipped, like the women in her father's family." She extends her hand. "Dolly Cantrell, grateful alcoholic." We shake.

A *grateful* alcoholic? If she saw some of the winos we serve at Hope's Table, she wouldn't be so grateful. "Glad to meet you. I'm Ariane."

"Glad to meet you, too. You flying for business or pleasure?"

Neither, really. I'm going to Mama's wedding out of obligation. "Pleasure," I tell her. "I'm visiting my parents." What am I going to say? That I'm seeing my father first, then going to my mother's gay wedding?

"Oh, that's nice."

I nod. I think about that Christmas vacation two years ago, the last time all five of us were together as a family. I'm back there in my room, packing for my flight back to San Francisco, when Mama comes in....

"Is this yours, Ariane?" she asks, handing me my cell phone charger. I thank her for spotting it. It would have complicated things if I'd left it here in Connecticut. Instead of leaving my room, Mama lingers. Straightens some of my old stuffed animals on the shelf, looks out my window. Then she turns and faces me. Asks me to sit down. There's something she needs to tell me, she says. Whatever it is, it's bad. I can tell from the look on her face. Is she sick? Is Daddy? I'm scared.

"Ariane, your father and I are separating."

My tears start spontaneously, partly because she hasn't just said that she or Dad has cancer, and partly because of what she did *just say. "Separating? Why?"*

They've grown apart, she says. Her work, her life in New York. His life here.

"But it's a trial separation, right? Are you guys going to marriage counseling?"

She shakes her head. Says she's already seen a lawyer about a divorce.

"Is this Daddy's idea or yours?"

She lies. Says it was a mutual decision.

"*Mama, I've been home for six days. Why are you just telling me this now?*"

Because she and Daddy didn't want to ruin our Christmas, she says. My thoughts ricochet. How long has this been in the works? Was it a snap decision?

"*Do Andrew and Marissa know?*" *I ask.*

"*We told your sister last night before she went back to the city. Asked her not to call you or your brother until after we'd had a chance to speak with you ourselves. Daddy and I figured we'd sit down with you two after breakfast this morning, but it hasn't worked out that way. Andrew texted me late last night to say he was sleeping over at Jay Jay's because he had too much to drink and didn't want to drive. And then your father got a call this morning and had to rush off. One of his patients left a message on his voice mail. Apparently, she came back to school early and has been walking around the empty campus having suicidal thoughts. We'll talk to Andrew this afternoon when he comes home, I guess. His flight doesn't leave until five o'clock. Hopefully, your father will be back by then. It depends on whether or not this patient of his—*"

"*Mama, stop! Never mind about Daddy's patient. Why aren't you and Daddy at least going to try and save your marriage?*"

"*Because it's gone beyond that point. Ariane, I just want you to know that this isn't—*"

I put up my hand to stop her. "*Would you please just leave me alone?*" *She nods, invites me to ask whatever questions I have. When she gets up and goes, I close my door and lock it. Flop facedown on my bed and hug my pillow.*

It should have taken me all of fifteen minutes to pack my stuff, but the task has become overwhelming because of Mama's news. An hour later, I'm still not done. Mama's back upstairs again; I hear her coming down the hall. Thankfully, she stays on the other side of the door and doesn't try to open it. "*Are you almost ready, Ariane? We should leave pretty soon.*" *Oh? Why is that, Mama? So you can dump me off at the airport and rush back to your hip life in New York? I almost say it but, instead, tell her to give me five more minutes.* "*Ready?*" *she asks when I come downstairs with my suitcase. Instead of answering her, I open the door and head out to the car.*

On the way to the airport, she makes small talk while I stare out the side window. Once she's taken the exit from I-84 to I-91, she tries broaching the subject of their separation again, but I stop her. Tell her I don't want to discuss it with her until I've spoken to my brother and sister. "And my father," I add. I'm not even sure why I'm more angry with her than I am with Daddy. Later, I'll know why, but I don't at this point. For the rest of the ride, we're silent. At the airport, she puts on her blinker to signal she's going to short-term parking. "You don't have to check in yet," she says. "I thought maybe we could grab a quick cup of coffee and—"

"No thanks," I say. "Just drop me off in front. I'm flying Delta." She complies, pulls up in front of Delta's outside check-in. With the engine running, she gets out. Stands by the trunk while I pull out my luggage. "Hug?" she asks, holding out her arms. I nod but just stand there—make her come *to* me. *I don't hug her back. I know I should, but I can't. I'm sick of being the good daughter—"Saint Ariane," as my brother used to call me. Entering the airport, I can sense that she's waiting for me to turn back and wave. I don't.*

Check-in goes okay, and the security people aren't too obnoxious. Waiting at my gate, I try calling Marissa, but she doesn't answer. Call Daddy's cell. "You've reached the voice mail of Dr. Orion Oh. If this is an emergency . . ." I don't leave a message. I think about calling Axel but decide not to. He's still in Wisconsin with his family, and we've only been going out for a month. Our relationship is too new to dump this on him. Alone with Mama's news, I try to reason with myself. It's their *marriage, their* decision, *not mine. But our family's never going to be the same. If they go through with this divorce, what will* next *Christmas be like? When I finally look up, most of the seats around me are empty. When did they start boarding us? Did they even announce it? I'm one of the last people to walk through the jetway and onto the plane.*

I'm glad I've been assigned a window seat. Relieved, too, that the seat next to me is empty. I spend most of the flight staring out at the sky, at the distant ground below. I wonder how many of the people in those little

Monopoly houses down there have been affected by divorce. At least they didn't split up while we were still kids. I'll give them that much.

My layover's in Atlanta. When we land, I put my phone back on. I've missed a call from Daddy, but when I try to call him back, I get his voice mail again. Marissa's still not answering either. I start dialing Axel's cell but change my mind and shut the phone. Get up and stand in line at Cinnabon instead.

The flight to San Francisco takes forever, and the woman sitting next to me is a mouth breather. I'd like to get up and slap that whiny little boy across the aisle. I keep trying to get lost in the movie they're showing, but I can't concentrate. Why haven't *they gone to see a counselor? A marriage of almost thirty years isn't worth even* trying *to save?*

"Ma'am?"

I look over. It's the flight attendant. "Hmm?"

"Something to drink?"

"Oh. Sure. Do you have Coke?"

"We do. Coke, Diet Coke, and Coke Zero."

"Regular Coke, please. No, wait. Ginger ale." Maybe it'll settle my stomach. I don't need the calories, but I'm supposed to avoid diet soda while I'm pregnant. Jesus Woman says she wants black coffee, and Aisle Guy wants Bloody Mary mix, "the whole can, no ice." My stomach heaves a little at the thought of drinking spicy tomato juice.

"And would you three like peanuts, pretzels, or Biscoff cookies with those?" the flight attendant asks us. He wants peanuts, she wants cookies. "Nothing for me, thanks," I tell her. I've long since heaved up my breakfast and I'm starved, but I don't dare eat anything because—

"Uh-oh. Looks like I'm out of Bloody Mary mix, sir. Be right back." I watch her walk toward the front of the plane. Who's fatter, I wonder. Me or her? Back when they were called stewardesses, they were all as thin and glamorous as models. At least that's the way they make it look on *Mad Men*. It's fun at work on Mondays, when we're preparing for the lunch crowd and talking about what happened on *Mad Men* the night before. When I'm on maternity leave, I'll miss those mornings, cooking and chatting with my volunteers. But six weeks will probably fly by, and I'm sure I'll visit once I get my bearings. Everyone will want to see the baby. . . .

It's a little after five California time when the plane lands and taxis toward the gate. Eight o'clock back in Connecticut. All around me, I hear people's cell phones go on. Hear their shorthand conversations with their loved ones. "Hey, it's me. I'm here." I've missed another call from Daddy but decide to wait to call him back. I don't want to have a private conversation in this public place. It takes longer than ever for our baggage to come out. When I finally grab my bag and go outside, climb into the back of a taxi, I try my brother. No answer. He must still be in the air. He must know by now, too. Is he taking it better than I am? Worse? Andrew has Mama's temper. I bet he's pissed at both of them.

I'm at the door of my apartment, putting my key in the lock, when I hear the phone ringing inside. I enter and rush to it, figuring it's Daddy or Andrew. But it's her again. She asks me how my trip back went. "You drop your bombshell, then I have eight hours to just sit with it by myself on planes and in terminals? How do you think it went, Mama?" I'm never snotty like this. That's Marissa's thing, not mine. But right now, I don't even care.

She tells me how sorry she is. Then she apologizes for something else: for not having told me the whole truth earlier. "I was going to," she says, "but when I saw how hard you were taking it, I lost my nerve."

"What's that supposed to mean? What 'whole truth'?"

Listening to her, I stare down at the photo of Axel and me on my coffee table. It was taken at that crab restaurant we went to down near Fisherman's Wharf. I've left it out because I want to put it in that little frame I bought. "I was the one who asked for the divorce, Ariane," she says. "There's someone else in my life now."

"Who?"

"Honey, it's Viveca, the woman whose gallery represents my work." I don't get it at first. Why does she have to divorce Daddy because of some professional relationship? "I didn't mean for it to happen. I didn't even see it coming at first, but I've fallen in love."

"With who?"

"With Viveca." She says other things: how she tried at first to deny her feelings. How the last thing she wanted to do was hurt Daddy.

"Mama, stop it. You're being ridiculous."

"I know it's going to take some getting used to this, Ariane, but I hope that after a while, after you've had time to think it through—"

"I mean it. Just stop. You're not leaving Daddy for a woman."

"Yes, I am, honey. I already have. I'm sorry."

Axel and I go blurry from my tears. I reach down and turn the picture facedown. "This is bullshit!" I tell her. Hit the button to shut her up and fling my cell phone across the room. I've never been this mean to her before, but she deserves it. It's crazy, what she's saying. How dare she do this to Daddy! To all of us!

A few minutes later, I follow the ring tone to where my damn phone landed. It's underneath the couch. Figuring it's Mama calling back, I ignore it and head for the fridge. There's got to be something in there that hasn't gone bad yet. A half-carton of cold lo mein later, I pick the phone off the floor and see that it's Axel who was calling. It's bad news: his grandmother, a massive stroke, a decision to take her off life support. He'll stay in Wisconsin until after the funeral. His semester doesn't start for another two weeks and he's brought his laptop, so he can work on his syllabus while he's out there. "Talk to you soon, babe. Sorry I have to scrap our New Year's Eve plans, but I know you understand."

And I do. I'm sympathetic. But the timing couldn't be worse. Should I fly out there to be with him? No, we haven't been going out long enough. I'll send flowers or donate to a charity if they've designated one. . . . Shit! I was really looking forward to us seeing in the New Year together. Now I guess I'll be spending the night with my last year's New Year's dates, Ben and Jerry. Eating Cherry Garcia and trying not to think about my mother and that Viveca woman. About poor Daddy by himself in Three Rivers . . .

When Marissa finally answers, I can tell from her slurry voice and the background noise that she's at some bar getting drunk. "Yeah, I was surprised at first, too, but hey. People change, Ari."

"From straight to gay? When they're in their fifties? And we're just supposed to accept this little adventure of hers?"

She starts in on this stupid theory about how rigid categories like gay and straight are imposed by society. "Scratch the surface and we're probably all bisexual, Ari."

"Oh, for Christ's sake, this is our mother and father we're talking about! Stop being so hip about it, will you?"

"Stoli and pomegranate," she says, throwing me until I realize she's halted our conversation to order herself another drink. "I've gotten to know Viveca a little. She's awesome, Ari. You should see her apartment."

"I don't want to see her apartment. I just want Mama to come to her senses."

"What did you say? God, it's so fucking loud in here."

"Nothing. Never mind. I'll talk to you tomorrow."

"Yeah, okay. Just try not to be such a tight ass about it, okay? People evolve."

"Oh, shut up."

After a nearly sleepless night, I call my father. It's 8:00 A.M. where he is, almost sunrise here. Yes, he's unhappy about it, he says. Yes, he feels angry and betrayed. But what can he do? Insist that she stay married to him when she doesn't want to? When I ask him how Andrew took the news, he tells me he didn't say much. Then he went up to his bedroom and punched a hole in the wall. That was what Daddy was doing when I called, he says: trying to see if he could patch up the damage instead of having to replace the Sheetrock.

After about a week, I start answering Mama's calls again. Start coming around. Good old Saint Ariane, she always does. But accepting the fact that she's having a lesbian affair doesn't mean I have to like it. . . .

I loosen my belt a few inches and rebuckle it. I'm starting to show a little, but I can still conceal it. I hope, anyway. When I ordered my dress for Mama's wedding, I'd already had my procedure but wasn't sure if I was pregnant yet. I'm glad I thought ahead and got the empire style instead of the dress I liked better. I just hope it won't make me look too dumpy. Marissa said Viveca took her shopping and bought her a designer dress—a strapless black mini. We'll be quite a contrast: Annie's thin, striking daughter and the dowdy older one. The do-gooder. Well, what's new? In high school, Rissa was a homecoming princess and I was president of the Let's Discuss It Club.

Jesus Lady reaches inside the neck of her sweatshirt and fiddles around in there, adjusting her bra straps. When we went shopping for my pregnancy pants yesterday, I probably should have gotten a few new bras, too, instead of listening to Cicely about waiting until I was ready for nursing bras. When I tried my dress on last night before I packed it, it felt a little tight in the bust. My boobs are definitely bigger now. Axel would have liked that. Well, too bad for him. What was that crack he made when I was getting out of the shower that time? That I belonged to the Itty Bitty Titty Committee? As if I wasn't already self-conscious about my body. Hey, it's not like *he* was Mr. Perfect Physique. Like he didn't have that muffin top above his pants. When I bought him those cargo shorts with the thirty-eight-inch waist instead of thirty-six, he acted so touchy about it.

When the flight attendant returns, she's forgotten that I didn't want anything to eat. Drops two packets of peanuts onto my tray. My stomach lurches. "Would either of you like these?" I ask my seatmates. The woman smiles and shakes her head, but Mr. Business snatches them from me without saying thanks. From the corner of my eye, I watch him rip open the packets with his teeth and pour them into his empty plastic glass. He shakes the glass and brings it to his mouth as if he's drinking the peanuts. Next, he burps open his can of Bloody Mary mix, takes a long drink, and slurps the excess off the top of the can. Guy's got no manners. And an oral fixation, too. Right, Daddy? Well, I should talk. The night Axel broke up with me, I went home and ate an entire roll of Girl Scout cookies. Sometimes when I wake up in the morning, I still catch myself sucking my thumb like I did when I was a little kid. . . . Out of the corner of my eye, I watch Mr. Business take two little bottles of vodka from his briefcase and pour them into his can of juice, swish it around. How the heck did he get his little stash past security? Well, these businessmen fly all the time. They must know all the little tricks.

"There. Finished," she says. What's her name? Dolly? She puts her beading materials into her big canvas carry-on, takes a sip of coffee, and opens her cookies. "Gee, can they spare it?" She chuckles. Is she thinking out loud or talking to me? "These are more like crackers than cookies, aren't they?"

Okay, me. "Really," I say. Normally, I don't get all buddy-buddy with the people in the other seats when I fly, but she seems nice enough. Maybe it'll make the trip go by faster. "Every time I fly, things get a little cheesier."

"Isn't *that* the truth!" she says. "And now with all this pain-in-the-neck security stuff. Put your toiletries in a clear plastic bag, take off your jacket, remove your shoes. Last time I flew, they confiscated a perfectly good pair of Millers Forge nail scissors that I'd had for years. Had to go out and buy another pair that don't work half as good. I know they've got to take precautions, but do I look like the type who'd hijack a plane with nail scissors?" She chuckles at the thought of it and points down at her shoes. "I bought these ugly things at Wal-Mart just so it'd be a little easier to slip them off and on when I went through check-in." I look down at her black wedgies with Velcro straps. She's right about them being ugly. Maybe she's wearing elastic waistband pants, too. I ask her what kind of work she does.

"Oh, I'm retired now. Used to work in the billing department at Memorial Hospital in Colorado Springs. I was the office manager there. I'm the bossy type, so it fit me to a T. What about you, dear?"

"I'm a manager, too. I run a soup kitchen in San Francisco."

"Well, good for you, honey. That's God's work you're doing. I bet it's challenging, though."

I nod. "Especially in *this* economy. Donations are down, our budget's been frozen for two years now, and our numbers keep increasing."

"Oh, my. What do you do? Serve a noontime meal?"

Breakfast *and* lunch, I tell her. "Plus, we do a dinner on alternate Fridays, with entertainment. Folk singers, usually, but last week we had a magician."

"Sounds like fun. How many meals do you put out in a day?"

"Last month we averaged about a hundred for breakfast and over two hundred for lunch. This past Thursday, we cooked eight good-size pork roasts, and we still ran out. The last twenty or so guests had to make do with egg sandwiches. Open-faced ones after we started running low on bread."

"Well, an egg sandwich will fill you up as well as anything." She tells me she helps out twice a week at the Salvation Army store near where she lives. "Been doing that for four years now, and I still can't get over the things people don't want: brand-new clothes, sofas that are as good as new, mattresses that look like they haven't even been slept on. Course, with the furniture, you've got to be careful." She lowers her voice. "Bedbugs."

"Eww," I say. "Gross."

"Other day, I got myself a Broncos sweatshirt that someone didn't want. Had the tags still on it. Lord, I love my Broncos. You must root for the Forty-Niners out where you are. Or are you an Oakland fan?"

I tell her I don't really follow football.

"No?" She looks shocked. "Well, I'm a football *fanatic*. Every year after the Super Bowl's over, I go into a little slump."

"My husband follows football," I say. Why did I just lie like that? What's the matter with me?

"Most men do," Dolly says. "It's in their blood. You know the sex yet?"

I'm dumbstruck for a second, thinking she's just asked about my sex life with my imaginary husband. Then I realize she means the sex of the baby. I shake my head. "The doctor says she'll be able to tell me after I have an ultrasound, but I'm not sure I want to know."

"Well, if I'm any indication, I'd guess it's going to be a boy. I was sick with my boys but not my girls." Same as Cicely, I think. "I blame it on that damn Y chromosome, ha-ha. Everyone says how much easier boys are to raise than girls, but that wasn't my experience. I used to have a sign over the toilet for my guys when they were growing up: I AIM TO KEEP THIS BATHROOM CLEAN. YOUR AIM WILL HELP. SIGNED, THE MANAGEMENT."

God, I wish I could laugh as easily as she does.

"No, my boys gave me a run for my money during their teen years, but all three turned into decent fellas, thank the Lord. Course, Lisa, my youngest, wasn't any picnic when she was a teenager, either. Drinking and drugging. Shoplifting. Straightened herself out, though. She's in AA now, too."

"What did she name her baby?" I ask.

"Nineliez. Nineliez Maria. Her partner's Puerto Rican."

"That's pretty," I say. "Different." She's just said "partner," not "husband" or "boyfriend." Maybe her daughter's gay. Maybe she used a sperm donor, too.

"At this point, you can't really tell what that new little munchkin's going to grow up looking like, but I suspect it'll be Spanish. Her mother's got some Dutch from her father and some German and British from me, but the Spanish will most likely be dominant. What are you?"

"Me? Well, I'm Irish on my mother's side and Italian and Chinese on my father's." I think about how Andrew, Marissa, and I look so different from one another. He's got Mama's red hair and green eyes, her fair skin. I have Daddy's dark hair and Mediterranean complexion. Marissa's the only one who you can tell has some Asian in her.

"Heinz fifty-seven varieties, eh?" Dolly says. "I can see the Italian in you but not the Irish or the Oriental." Oriental? In Berkeley, you could probably get fined for saying something so politically incorrect. "Good lord, if it wasn't for my high blood pressure, I could eat Chinese food every day of the week. Too much sodium, though. A few years after I got sober, I asked my Higher Power to remove my craving for alcohol and He did. But I still crave egg foo yong and General Tso's chicken. I'd pray on that, too, but I figure the Good Lord's got a few more important things on his agenda."

"Oh, okay. When you said before that you were a grateful alcoholic, I assumed, well . . . "

"That I was an active drunk? No, ma'am. I've been sober for thirty-one years. Best decision I ever made, joining AA—next to divorcing those two lunkheads I was married to. Both of 'em drank like fish. Problem was, I used to try and keep up with them. After I quit, I gave Number Two an ultimatum. 'It's either me or the booze,' I told him. And when he went out and got soused that same weekend, I packed his bag and showed him the door. Lucky for me, I had a good job and the house was in my name. I'd gotten it in the settlement from my first divorce."

"Huh," I say, unable to think of anything else. Mr. Aisle Seat has already polished off his cocktail, I assume, because he's just bent his can in half and stuck it in his seat pocket. Oh, wow, you're strong enough to bend aluminum. What a he-man! Turning back to Dolly, I ask her how her daughter's doing—the one who's had the baby.

"Well, she's having a little trouble with breast-feeding," she says. "Getting the baby to latch on. But she'll get the hang of it. Course, I'm no expert on the subject. Back when I was having mine, the doctors were pushing formula instead of breast milk. You planning on nursing yours?"

I tell her I am because all the baby books say it's better for them. Builds up their immunity. "And I'm not going to rush into giving my baby solid food either," I say. "I read this article online said that feeding babies solid food too early can lead to obesity and diabetes later on."

"Well, take it from me, honey. You can read up on the subject all you want, but the best way to learn how to be a mother is by being one. When I brought my first home from the hospital, I wasn't even sure how to pin a diaper. Had to have my cousin Etta come over and show me. On-the-job training: that's what mothering is." She reaches over and pats my knee. "But you'll learn quick enough, same as everyone. Did your mother breast-feed?"

Did she? I don't know. I don't remember her nursing Marissa. "I'm not sure," I say. "Maybe not, though. I have a twin brother."

"Well, I guess that's why the Good Lord equipped us gals with two breasts instead of one," Dolly says. "Course, some women have triplets, so that busts my theory." She chuckles some more. Mr. Business lets out a fed-up sigh. Well, excuse us. And by the way, I can smell your booze breath.

"I like your bracelet," I tell Dolly. She slips it off and hands it to me for a better look. The little dime-sized medal hanging off of it has a butterfly on one side, three words on the other: SERENITY, COUR-

AGE, WISDOM. In my peripheral vision, I see Aisle Seat Guy take a peek at Dolly's bracelet, too. "This is from the serenity prayer, right?" I ask.

"Uh-huh. You know it?"

"Sort of. At the soup kitchen, they have AA and NA meetings right after lunch twice a week, and when they say that prayer at the beginning, sometimes I stop and listen to it. It's so simple, but it says a lot." Listen to me: the agnostic who hasn't prayed since she was a little girl.

"Well, the Good Lord wants our lives to be simple," Dolly says. "Love one another: that's all He wants. It's us that makes things complicated."

She smiles. I smile back. We're both quiet after that, but when my thoughts wander back to breast-feeding, it reminds me of something. "Oh, shit!" I say. It just slips out.

"Something the matter?" Dolly asks.

"No, I just thought of something I forgot to do before I left work yesterday. Sorry for swearing."

"Didn't hear a damned thing," Dolly says. "What'd you do? Forget to turn off the coffeepot?"

"No, nothing like that. I was supposed to order more cases of nutritional supplements from our pharmaceutical supplier, but I got distracted. The freezer in the basement had gone on the blink, and some of the meat had begun to thaw, so . . . well, let's just say I never went back to my desk."

"Nutritional supplements? Like vitamins?" Dolly asks.

"No, no. Enfamil for the crack babies and Ensure for our elderly guests and the ones with HIV AIDS. We got a grant last year that lets us buy and distribute them, and I'm trying to stockpile as much as possible. The funding runs out at the end of the year."

"And they won't renew it?"

"Maybe, maybe not. Nothing's a sure thing anymore."

"Well, good luck," Dolly says. "Canned formula's gotta be better than mother's milk with crack in it." She tells me she drank during her first couple of pregnancies. "My doctor recommended it, in fact. Told me to have a glass of wine or two in the evening to settle myself.

I drank and *smoked* with my oldest. Course, back then they didn't
have all the warnings they do now. I wish they had. My Jimmy was the
puniest of my six, although you'd never know it now. He goes six one,
six two, and could stand to lose twenty or thirty pounds. So who's
picking you up when we land? Your parents?"

"My father." When I told Daddy I was flying in to Logan instead
of Hartford, I said I didn't mind renting a car and driving out to the
Cape. But I was relieved when he insisted on picking me up. . . . Andrew says he thinks Daddy's taking Mama's remarrying hard, but Marissa says he's fine with it. Now I'll be able to see for myself how he's
doing. Sometimes he seems okay when I call him, and sometimes he
seems, I don't know, distracted or something. "Actually, my parents
are divorced," I tell Dolly. "I'm spending some time with my father
first. Then I'll visit my mom." And meet her wife, I think.

"Well, I'm sure they'll both be tickled pink to see you. This their
first grandchild?" I nod, smile. "I bet they're excited."

"Oh, yes. Very." Will they be?

Dolly asks me how much time I'm taking off after the baby's born.
"Six weeks," I say. "I could take more time than that, but it would be
without pay and I can't afford it. I'm just making ends meet as it is."

"What about your hubby? Doesn't he work?"

Oh, shit. My husband. I borrow Axel. "He, uh . . . he teaches at a
community college, but only part-time. He's looking for a full-time
position, but no luck yet. The job situation's pretty tight right now."

"So what'll you do once your maternity leave's up? Use day care?"

"No, I can't . . . we can't afford that, either. I'm planning to bring
the baby to work with me." Dolly wrinkles her nose and tells me
that will be difficult. "Well, if the bus stop near my apartment is any
indication, half the new moms in Berkeley are toting their infants
to their jobs. And I'm sure my volunteers will be glad to help out
when I get busy with other things. . . . Berkeley's expensive, and we
could probably get a cheaper apartment in Oakland. But it's not as
safe there, and I've heard that the schools aren't very good. Besides,
raising a baby is going to be a big enough change without worrying
about moving, too."

"Right," Dolly says. "Well, you'll figure it out." And with that, she takes her newspaper from the seat pocket, puts on her glasses, and starts to read.

Rather than sitting there feeling guilty about lying to her, I pick up *Home from the Hospital*. Fish around in my purse for the yellow highlighter. I'm in the middle of the chapter on nursing—what to do about breast infections—but I just keep reading the same paragraph without absorbing anything. Dolly's got a point about overpreparing. Why read about some infection I might not even get? . . . Her daughter's lucky that Dolly's coming to help her with the baby. I wish Mama wasn't going to be so far away when my baby comes. Maybe she could fly out and stay with me for a few weeks. I won't ask her, though. She has her work, and she'll still be a newlywed. But if she volunteers . . .

Mama: a newlywed and a grandmother, all in the same six months. And me: an unwed mother. When my friend Cindy Soucy and I were in middle school, we would sit at lunch and plan our futures: how we'd meet our boyfriends at college, get married after graduation, and start our careers. Then we'd have kids; she wanted two and I wanted three. We were in fifth grade, I remember, and both of us had just started menstruating. . . .

"Mama, something's the matter with me. I think I better go see the doctor." I point to the evidence: the bloodstained crotch of my pajama bottoms. She frowns, says nothing's wrong. "Go down to my studio and wait for me. I'll be right down. I just need to get something."

While I wait for her, I look around at her artwork. It's weird, kind of scary-looking. I don't like it, but I would never tell her that. It would hurt her feelings. Sometimes when it's my turn to do the laundry and I go down here while she's working on some new piece, she's concentrating so hard that she doesn't even seem to realize I'm there. And I try to be as quiet as I can because she's concentrating and has this angry face. It's the same face she gets when Andrew's done something to make her mad and she goes off on him. Goes mental, kind of. It's scary when she gets like that. But yeah, she makes that same face when she's working on her art. No wonder it comes out like this. Mama's art is . . . angry.

When she comes back down to the basement, she hands me the "some-

thing" she had to go get—that awful booklet with the cartoon drawings, "From Girl to Woman." "The most important thing you have to remember now that you've started ovulating," Mama says, "is that from now on, you should never, ever put yourself in a situation where you're alone with a boy or a man. Because you just can't trust them."

"Not even Daddy? Or Andrew?"

"Of course you can trust them. But otherwise you have to be very careful from now on." Other men flash in my mind. Mr. Genovese across the street? My English teacher, Mr. Fogel, who told me he thinks I'm a good writer? "What about Uncle Donald?" I ask her.

"Oh, Ariane, don't be silly. Of course you can trust your uncle."

Mama's nervous. I can tell by the way she's picking away at her finger. While she's in the middle of explaining why I can expect to bleed once a month from now on, the basement door bangs open and Andrew comes clomping down the stairs. Mama's mad. "Didn't I just tell you that your sister and I needed some privacy?"

"Yeah, but Gary just called me. A bunch of us are going to ride our bikes down to the field to play baseball. I need to get my glove."

"Not now, Andrew!"

"Yeah, but I need it now, or else I'm going to get there after they choose up."

Shaking her head, she gets up and goes to the big box where he keeps his sports stuff. Instead of tossing him his glove, she hurls it at him. It hits him in the face.

"Ow! Jesus Christ, Mom. You didn't have to nail me with it."

"What did I tell you about that 'Jesus Christ' stuff? Now go! Get out!"

She glares at him as he takes the stairs. When the door at the top slams, she turns back to me. "Any questions?"

I ask her why I can't trust men anymore.

"Because males have a kind of built-in instinct that females can trigger once they get their period. A kind of sexual radar. Animals, humans: all males. You remember how we sometimes had to keep Missy in the house before we got her spayed? How all those male dogs would congregate in the yard and wait for her to come out?"

"Yeah, but . . . ?" I don't get the connection.

"And do you remember what happened that time when Missy got out and that boxer down the street jumped on top of her and started humping her?"

"Yes."

"Well? You know what rape is, don't you? . . ."

God, why did she have to put it that way? Scare me like that? Males were horny, dangerous dogs: that was her message. I remember going upstairs to my room with that booklet she gave me, my hands trembling as I turned the pages. I didn't calm down until Cindy Soucy told me what *her* mother had said: that once a man and a woman fell in love and got married, sex was a beautiful part of their life together, not just the way that babies got started. . . .

It's so weird the way life turns out. For me, at least, maybe not for Cindy. Until she tried to "friend" me on Facebook last month, I hadn't heard from her in years. I'm too busy for social networking, I told myself. Told Marissa, too, when she tried to "friend" me. From what people who are on Facebook say, it's a colossal waste of time, but what I don't get is why they're always on it anyway. . . . *You should never put yourself in a situation where you're alone with a boy or a man.* Did Mama decide she was a lesbian after she met Viveca, or was she always one? And if she was, why did she marry Daddy? . . .

I'm nervous about meeting Viveca. I want her to like me, and I really want to like her—to show her that I'm cool now about her and Mama's marriage. Marissa's always saying that Viveca's awesome, but that time when I asked her why, all she talked about was their shopping trips, and how Viveca has taken her to the Plaza Hotel for tea. Last month when Rissa got all spastic because Jimmy Choo was on the guest list for the wedding and I asked her who he was, she was like, "Oh my god, Ariane, what planet do you *live* on?" It wasn't until after we'd hung up that I thought of what I *should* have said: that I pretty much live on Planet Soup Kitchen, where the needs are a little more basic than the need for designer shoes. I didn't dare pack my Birkenstocks when I was getting ready for this trip, which was ridiculous now that I think of it. I live in Berkeley, for Christ's sake! It's not that I'm intimidated by my little sister, but from everything she's said, and from the pictures I've seen, Viveca seems so chic and glamorous. I guess I just don't want her to look down on me: Annie's shlumpy older daughter. The fat one. No one to share her life with, no prospects on the horizon. . . . I wonder what Mama has told Viveca about me. Does she know how angry I was at first when I found out about their affair? Does she know I'm fat? At my last ob-gyn appointment, my weight had gone up to one seventy-seven—my high school weight. And I'm bound to gain a lot more in the upcoming months. God, I just hope I don't go over two hundred. That would be more than I've *ever* weighed. I think back to that conversation I once heard my mother and father having about me when they thought I was out of earshot. . . .

"I mean it, Annie. I want you to get off her about her weight. Half the girls who come into my office are obsessed about it. They were chubby as kids and now they're anorexic, some of them. I don't want her to think her value depends on what the scale says. It's unhealthy."

"So you want her to keep gaining until she develops diabetes? Because that's unhealthy, too. And what about her social life?"

"Her social life is fine. She's got friends."

"And don't you think she'd like a boyfriend? You know boys that age. Their eyes slide right past the girls who are overweight."

"She's doing just fine, Annie. I mean it. You keep harping on her weight and she's going to develop a complex about it."

Too late, Daddy, I think. I already had developed a complex about it, and I fed it daily. And Mama was right. I did want a boyfriend back then. I still do. Sipping the last of my ginger ale, I look past Dolly at the clouds we're flying over. It looks like a thick covering of snow—as if you could step out onto it and those clouds would hold you. Last week there was another suicide off the Golden Gate Bridge. The third this year, the paper said. When Daddy told me one of his college kids killed himself this past year—a boy he'd been treating for depression—I could tell from the shakiness in his voice how hard he was taking it. Was that why he resigned so abruptly? Maybe. But that doesn't explain why he wants to sell our house now, too. To get away from the memories, maybe—to pack up and move on. . . .

I think Mama and Daddy will be okay with my decision, once I tell them both. Get that part over with. I'm pretty sure Daddy won't have a problem with it. He didn't know his father, but he turned out fine. And yes, I'll explain to them if I have to, I *am* younger than most of the women who get pregnant this way. And maybe the right guy *could* still come along. But I don't want to keep playing the wait-and-hope game until I'm forty. What if my eggs are too old by then? The chances for birth defects are a lot greater for older moms. And yes, there's always adoption if you want to gamble on the genetic cocktail of two strangers. At least this way, I was able to read the donors' histories. Weed out some of the potential for problems. It's not foolproof; I know that. And they pay these guys to do what they do—about a hundred dollars, I've heard. So I guess they could lie on their forms if they needed the money. Well, I'm going to love this child, no matter who he or she turns out to be. But being a single mother is going to be challenging enough without increasing the chances of raising a kid with special needs. . . .

The flight attendant comes by with her plastic bag and we deposit our refuse. The ginger ale must have worked, I guess, because my stomach feels more settled. I give up on *Home from the Hospital*, and when I slip the book back in my bag, I see the red folder in there. Take it out. I'm not sure why I brought it with me, or for that matter, why I didn't shred what's in it once I made my decision. It's innocuous-looking, though; as long as I hold it close to myself, neither of my seatmates will be able to read what's in there: the photocopied fact sheets of my prospective donors. For the millionth time, I look over the forms of the two I narrowed it down to. Should I have picked number 251 instead of number 311? Brown hair and eyes, five foot nine, no history of cancer in his family, college educated, no alcohol or drug issues other than "recreational use of marijuana, occasional." He was the one I *thought* I was going with. Then at the last minute, I picked number 311 instead: Brazilian ethnicity, two years of college instead of four, a mother who died at forty-six. The reason listed isn't cancer or heart disease. "Boating accident" it says. I look at the math I did in the margin of his fact sheet; he was only thirteen when he lost her. Why did I change my mind? Was it because I felt sorry for him, this motherless boy who's now almost thirty? Well, whatever the reason, it's a done deal. Number 311 has fathered the life that's growing inside me—this child I already love who will give me a purpose besides feeding the poor, and who will love me no matter how much I weigh. . . .

Of course Axel would have been my first choice. Okay, stop it, I tell myself. Don't go there again. But I do. After we passed the first anniversary of our being together, I began to think—hope—that everything was finally going to work out for me. For us. We'd get married, have kids; it wasn't the perfect life I'd planned with Cindy way back in middle school, but it was close enough. So I didn't see it coming the night he took me to that Thai restaurant and started talking about how it wasn't me; it was him. How he still cared about me and hoped we could stay friends. How many times had I heard *that* line? I'd started sobbing, humiliating myself in front of the other diners. Humiliated myself a second time when I went to him three months later and asked if he'd please just impregnate me, no strings, no obligations. I'd begged him not to answer me right then and there, to just *think* about giving me his sperm if he couldn't give me anything more than that. I can still see him sitting there, shaking his head and probably thinking how glad he was to have gotten himself out of his relationship with this desperate, pathetic woman. . . .

Then Desmond, the group home supervisor, said no, too. He and his Prader-Willi clients with their big, cumbersome bodies and almond-shaped eyes had been volunteering at Hope's Table for a few years, and we'd become friends. Had gone out for coffee a few times. Desmond was divorced, no kids—his ex-wife's decision more than his, he said. Because of their food issues, he would bring his Prader-Willi guys in after all the meals had been served and the guests had left. They'd wipe off the tables, sweep and mop the floor. I liked Desmond's dry sense of humor, and the way he interacted with the guys he supervised. His "kids," he called them, although some of them were in their thirties and forties. He always seemed so fatherly toward them— so unflappable, even the time he caught that one guy eating soap in the men's room. He sure didn't look unflappable at that Starbucks we went to when I asked him if he'd father my child. He looked shaken. Then, right after that, he stopped coming. He had called Cicely, not me, and told her they'd started volunteering someplace else. "I wonder why," I said, even though I knew. . . .

I can't predict how my brother and sister are going to take my news. Marissa will either think it's cool or that it's weird. No one in the family but me knows about the abortion she had last year. I don't judge her for making that decision. She wasn't ready to have a child and, frankly, I'm not so sure she would have been a very good mother. But I will be. I want this baby as much as I've ever wanted anything in my life, and as sick as I've been, I haven't regretted my decision for one second. I wonder if Marissa ever wishes she hadn't terminated her pregnancy. Does she ever even think about what her life might be like now if she hadn't? . . .

I just hope Andrew's not going to give me grief, now that he's become Mr. Born Again. It's weird how he's done this turnaround. Andrew was always the rebellious one in the family. Who knows? Maybe he still is. Maybe all this "Lord and Savior" stuff he's into now is his way of rebelling against growing up in a liberal household. The last time I talked to him, he was saying how great it is that he and Casey-Lee go to church with her family. Then he started complaining about how our parents put us at a disadvantage because they didn't give us a religious foundation. I had to remind him that Mama used to bring us to Mass when we were little, and that it was *he* who raised such a stink about going to church that she finally gave up and let us stay home with Daddy on Sunday mornings. "Exactly," he said. "She went to church and we got to stay home with the atheist. What kind of role-modeling was that?" I didn't argue with him. I just changed the subject so I wouldn't have to listen to his proselytizing. I still can't tell if this Christian soapbox of his is his own idea, or his fiancée's. Those couple of times they Skyped me, she hardly said a word, except to note that my brother and I look nothing alike. . . . And if Daddy didn't believe there was a god, what was he supposed to do? Fake it? I wonder if Mama's stopped going to Mass. Probably. Why would she keep going when the Catholic Church is so dead set against same-sex marriage? . . .

I put away the red folder and pull the in-flight magazine out of the seat pocket. *Sky Mall*: it's ridiculous. Who in the world would ever buy luggage and "wireless talking barbecue thermometers" while they're on a plane? Well, somebody must, I guess. God, I'm so tired. I didn't sleep for shit last night, and then I had to get up so early to catch my flight. I'm just going to close my eyes and rest. . . .

I'm in the studio audience watching Mama. She's a contestant on a game show—she and some other new brides. They're sitting beside their husbands. For some reason, Mama's gotten married to that detective on Law & Order: SVU—*the one with the anger management issues. The host asks him what's the one thing in Mama's purse that people would be surprised to find in there. "A baby?" he says. Then Mama reaches into her purse and takes out a little pink plastic baby. And when she puts it in the palm of her hand, it starts moving, coming alive. . . .*

Whatever Dolly's just said to me, I didn't catch it. "I'm sorry. What?"

She's holding up her *Denver Post* and tapping her finger at a front-page picture of the president. "I asked you what you think of this guy?" she says.

"Obama? I like him. He sure has inherited a mess, though."

"Uh-huh," she says. End of subject. She must be a Republican. Well, so what? I like her. She's a hoot. And anyway, I've been making an effort not to be judgmental about other people's politics, as long as they don't try and cram it down your throat like my brother does.

"Sorry if I woke you up just then," Dolly says. "Looks like you were taking a little catnap."

"No, no. Just resting my eyes." But no, I must have been dozing because I was having that weird dream.

"Well, why don't I shut my trap and let you rest them some more?"

Under his breath, but loud enough for us to hear, our other seatmate says, "Thank god for small favors."

Dolly turns to him. "Amen to that, sir. For all His blessings, large and small." Looking at me, she mocks him by making a grouchy face.

Closing my eyes again, I replay the dream. God, my dreams have been so strange lately. Where did *that* one come from? . . . Oh, I know. Part of it, anyway. The other night, nervous about this trip, I couldn't get to sleep. I put on the TV, grabbed the remote, and landed on the Game Show Channel. They were showing that old program, *The Newlywed Game*. From the 1960s or 1970s, it looked like from the clothes and the hairstyles. First they asked the wives a bunch of questions. Then they brought back the husbands and had them guess what they'd said. A shiver runs through me when I think about that creepy, fetus-size toy baby coming alive. . . .

The intercom clicks on. "Captain Moynihan again, folks. Wanted to tell you that we've begun our initial descent. We'll be touching down in Boston in about another twenty minutes."

I'm disappointed that Andrew's not coming to the wedding. I was really looking forward to seeing him. But it's probably just as well. I wouldn't want to look over at him while Mama and Viveca are exchanging their vows and see him scowling, clenching his jaw the way he does when he's mad. The way he did that night at dinner when we were in high school—tenth grade, it was. Andrew was going through that phase where he acted like he couldn't stand me. Like, suddenly, *I* was the bane of his existence instead of Marissa. It hurt, I remember. It was confusing. Was it because I'd gotten fat? Up until then, my brother and I had always been close. . . .

"Just do me a favor, okay?" he says to me. He's hunched over his meal, shoveling it in as if someone's going to snatch his plate away if he doesn't. "When you see me at school with my friends, don't come over and start talking to me." Earlier in the day, at lunchtime, I had committed the terrible sin of asking him if he had his house key because I wasn't going home on the bus. I was going over to Cindy Soucy's house so that she and I could work on our campaign posters. Cindy's running for president of our class and I'm running for treasurer. Last year I ran for the same office, but Beverly Bundy beat me. Beverly and I used to be friends in elementary school, but she's really changed. Andrew's told me that her boy-

friend, Digger, has been bragging in the locker room lately about how, on weekends when her parents go out, she lets him come over and get into her pants. When I told Andrew it was none of my business, he rolled his eyes and called me Saint Ariane.

"She's your sister, for crying out loud," Daddy says. "Why can't she talk to you?"

Because she's fat, I think my brother's about to say. Andrew's been lifting weights since last summer and he's getting muscular. He's always walking around the house with his shirt off, admiring himself in whatever mirror he passes. Not me. I avoid mirrors, except to fix my hair. "Because she's in honors classes with all the other brains," he tells Dad.

"So?" Daddy says. "You could be in those classes, too, if you spent as much time with your books as you do with your barbells." *Andrew was in honors algebra and honors earth science the year before. Mama and Daddy think the school dropped him down because his grades were just mediocre, but that wasn't it. Andrew went to his guidance counselor and begged her to put him in easier classes.*

"Yeah, like I'd even want to," Andrew tells Daddy. "I hate those honors kids. And so do all of my friends."

"And why is that, Andrew? Enlighten me, will you?" *I look over at Mama. She's staying out of this exchange, but I can see from her face that she's mad.*

"Because they think they're better than everyone else. And because they're always sucking up to the teachers so they can get better grades."

Daddy nods toward me. "And that's true of your sister? She gets A's not because she works hard for them, but because she butters up her teachers? She thinks she's better than—"

"No, not her, but . . ."

"But what?"

"Nothing. Never mind. Just forget it."

Marissa chimes in. "The brains in my school act all stuck-up, too," *she tells Daddy. You'd never know it from the way she goes out of her way to bug Andrew, but she idolizes him. She's told me that all her friends have crushes on him.*

"*You stay out of it,*" Dad tells her. Then he turns back to Andrew. "*Don't you dare tell your sister to ignore you at school. And don't ignore her, either. You understand?*"

"*Okay, okay. I got it. Can I be excused?*"

"*Yeah, you can be excused to clear the table and wash the dishes. And when you're finished, you can skip the weight lifting and get right to your homework.*"

"*It's not my week to do the dishes!*" Andrew protests. "*It's the twerp's week. Look on the refrigerator if you don't believe me. It says it right on the schedule.*"

"*I don't care what the schedule says. When I tell you to do something, you do it.*" Daddy stands up and thanks Mama for the very nice meal she's cooked. "*Now if you'll all excuse me, I have to go make some phone calls.*"

That ends it, I assume. Mama and Andrew start clearing the table. Freed from her responsibility, Marissa heads for the living room to watch TV, the little brat. But when I get up and carry the rest of the dishes into the kitchen, there's Mama, armed with our big soup spoon and whacking Andrew on the back of his head and his neck. Once, twice, three times. My brother's just standing there, shoulders scrunched up, taking it as usual. "*Don't you ever, EVER make your sister feel like a second-class citizen!*" she yells.

"*Mama, stop. It's not that big a deal,*" I say.

"*It is to me!*" When she hits him again, I hear the sound of metal against skull. Then she throws the soup spoon and it lands with a clatter in the sink. I rinse it off, put it in the drawer. She's struck him so hard that she's bent the handle.

Poor Andrew. Mama never hits Marissa or me. But ever since we were little, my brother's been her whipping boy, even when we were both in trouble for something. I'd get yelled at, and Andrew would get yelled at, hit, and put in the bad boy chair.

Later that evening, I stand at my brother's doorway and ask him if he's okay. Why wouldn't he be, he says. When he gets off his bed and approaches, I assume he wants to tell me something without Marissa's big ears hearing it down the hall, or maybe even to apologize. But that isn't it. He's only gotten up to close the door in my face.

The next morning at school, Cindy and I get excused from first period study hall so that we can put up our campaign posters. And two periods later, passing one of my posters in the hall outside the library, I see that it's been defaced. "ARIANE OH FOR CLASS TREA$URER!!" it says in the block letters I've drawn and filled in with different colored markers. And on the bottom, someone's scrawled, "She's Tons of Fun!!" In tears, I pull the poster off the wall, tear it up, and stuff the pieces into my purse. I don't get it. I don't ever act mean or stuck up. I try to be friendly to everyone. I don't know who would do this. But Andrew does.

I love my brother. I always have. And even if he acts snotty toward me when we're at home, I know he loves me, too. So I'm scared for him when, in the cafeteria at lunchtime, I see him rush Digger Blankenship from behind, and put him in a choke hold. I run toward them. "Andrew, don't!" I beg him. "You'll get in trouble!"

When he screams at me to shut up and stay out of it, Digger takes advantage of the distraction and breaks free from Andrew's hold. He takes a swing, but my brother grabs his arm before it connects and wrenches it back. Digger screams out in pain, so that now even kids on the other side of the cafeteria know something's going on. Andrew punches Digger in the temple, where, if you hit someone hard enough, I've heard, you can kill them. Oh, god! Stop it, Andrew! Stop it! When he lands a punch in Digger's face, blood sprays out of his nose and onto the floor.

Kids are out of their chairs, yelling "Fight! Fight!" and forming a circle around my brother and Digger. Both boys are on the floor now, rolling around and pounding each other. I'm relieved when I see Mr. Driscoll and Mr. Scarlatta running over to stop the fight.

They're both suspended, Digger for two days and Andrew for a whole week because he started it. Because Andrew can't come to school, he can't compete in the wrestling quarter-finals, which probably means our school will get eliminated by Fitch, our biggest rival. Andrew's the team's second best wrestler. It's because of me. Because Andrew was defending his fat twin sister. "Your brother should go see a shrink!" Beverly Bundy tells me when I'm at my locker a few days later. "He's psycho!" She deserves a really mean comeback for saying it, but the only thing I can think of is, "No, he's not."

On the day of the elections, Andrew's still on suspension. During first period, there's a sophomore assembly so that everyone can listen to the class officer candidates' speeches. Our class adviser, Mrs. Masterson, is introducing us in alphabetical order; the candidates for president first and so on. Kevin Formiglio, our class president last year, stands at the podium, and just like last year, he makes all these ridiculous promises: he'll convince the school to start selling McDonald's for lunch, he'll bring back the smoking area. He gets a standing ovation from some of the general studies kids when he says that, but not many of those kids ever bother to vote anyway. Then it's Cindy's turn. When she and I helped each other with our speeches last weekend, I suggested she not list as one of her credentials that she's made the honor roll each semester since we've been students here. My brother's right; the majority of our classmates hate honors kids. Cindy said she'd think about cutting out that part, but she hasn't, and when she mentions the honor roll, the same section of kids who cheered about the smoking area start making kissing sounds. Voting doesn't start until next period, but in my opinion, Cindy's already lost the election. Seth Sugarman's next. He says that when he gets elected president, he'll represent our whole class, not just the college prep students, so he hopes that not just college prep kids vote today. I wish I had thought to say something like that. Seth says that being in sports has taught him how to be a good team player. He's wearing a tie and his basketball jacket with the leather sleeves instead of a tie and a nice sports coat like the boys were told to wear, and when he goes to sit down, a bunch of the other boys on the basketball team stand up and start chanting, "Seth! Seth! Seth!"

There are three candidates for all the other offices, but it's just Beverly and me running for treasurer. When it's only us left to speak, Mrs. Masterson says, "And now you'll hear from your two candidates for the important office of class treasurer." It's B before O, so Beverly goes first, and when she walks to the podium in her tight pink sweater and black leather skirt, she gets whistled at. Her speech is terrible; it's not even really a speech. "I didn't prepare anything because I didn't want to bore you guys to death," she says. "All I want to say is that I'll work wicked hard for our class like I did this past year. I promise! Okay, that's it. Thanks, you guys!" Well, I think to myself, at least my remarks are going to be substantive. I have my index cards with me, but I've pretty much memorized my speech so that it won't look like I'm reading.

"And last but not least, Ariane Oh," Mrs. Masterson says.

On my way to the podium, I accidentally drop my index cards on the floor and, when I bend over to pick them up, someone makes a really loud and disgusting noise that makes it seem like I've just passed gas. Everyone laughs, even a lot of the girls. When I start my speech, I speak too closely into the microphone and my words come out like an explosion. I'm so nervous by now that I do have to read it instead of saying it from memory, except that I didn't number the cards and now they're all out of order, so that I have to stop twice to organize them and then start again. I tell my classmates that I'm responsible with money, and that I'll work really hard to make our fund-raisers a success. I've thought up some really good ideas for fund-raising—a doughnut sale every Friday during homeroom, a dance where we fill out forms about ourselves and the computer matches up boys and girls who are compatible—but that index card's not in the right place and I won't even realize I didn't mention my ideas until afterward. When I wrote my speech the weekend before, I meant every word of it, but I can hear in my voice that I don't even want to be class treasurer anymore. All I want is to get off this stupid stage.

After the assembly's over, I go into the girls' room instead of class, lock myself in one of the stalls, and cry into a wad of toilet paper. At lunch, Hillary Hopfer tells me it was Butchie Evanko who made the breaking wind sound. It figures. Beverly and Butch are first cousins. But I feel better as the day goes on. By last period, so many of the kids in my classes have told me I did a good job—that they couldn't even hardly tell how nervous I was—that I start thinking it might be close, or that I even might have won if the voters saw past that leather skirt of hers and took into consideration that she couldn't even be bothered to write a speech, so how hard was she really going to work for our class?

That night, Mrs. Masterson calls with the election results. Cindy and I have both lost. When I ask her how close it was for treasurer, Mrs. M says she's not really at liberty to say, so I guess I have my answer. "Think about it this way," I tell Cindy when we console each other over the phone. "It's our class that's really lost. You and I would have worked a hundred percent harder and made way better leaders."

Later, after my homework's done, I'm lying facedown on my bed feeling sorry for myself when someone says, "Hey." I think it's Daddy, but when I look up, it's Andrew standing at the door. "Sorry you lost," he says.

"Just tell me," I say. "If you weren't suspended, would you have voted for me?"

"Shit, yeah," he says. "And I would have made sure all my friends voted for you, too." I get up and walk toward him. But when I put my arms out to give him a hug, he takes a backward step. "All right already," he says. "Don't go overboard."

God, I was so young back then. So naïve. I thought the harder you tried to be the best and most useful person you could be, the more you'd succeed. I wonder whatever happened to Beverly Bundy. And Digger. And Cindy, who was as earnest and eager to serve back then as I was. Did she get married and keep her maiden name? Is she still single? Does she have some great career? I guess I'd know if I had become her Facebook friend like she wanted me to. The real reason I didn't, I realize now, is that I didn't want to suffer by comparison. What would I tell her about how my life turned out? That I'm pregnant by a sperm donor? Working my head off at a job that pays thirty-eight thousand dollars a year? That my parents got a divorce because my mother's decided she's a lesbian? Well, who cares? Me, I guess. High school was a million years ago. Why in the world am I still letting it rent space in my head?

When the plane lands and taxis to the gate, Dolly slips her wooden bead bracelet off her wrist and hands it to me. She says she wants me to have it.

"Oh, no, I can't," I tell her. "It's yours. You should keep it."

"Honey, I've got a dozen more just like it in my bag. I make them for my AA friends, and for people just coming into the rooms. I'll be going to meetings while I'm helping out at my daughter's, so I brought some with me."

"But I don't have a drinking problem."

"Didn't think you did," she says. "New mothers need serenity as much as drunks do."

I smile and thank her. Slip on the bracelet and shake my wrist a little, watch the dangling medal rock back and forth. "Before?" I tell her. "When I said my husband liked football? I wasn't telling you the truth."

"No?" She waits.

"I'm not married. I *had* a boyfriend but . . . I got artificially inseminated at a clinic. I just . . . I didn't want you to think. . . ."

She reaches over and places her hand on my belly. "Honey, all that counts is this little one in here," she says. "Doesn't matter a fiddler's fart how it came about. Artificial insemination, huh? Wish they'd have had that available when I was your age. I could have saved myself a peck of trouble."

There's a chime; the seat belt sign goes off. When we stand up to deplane, the guy in the aisle seat opens the overhead, pulls out his bag, and then slams it shut with my stuff and Dolly's still in there. I've had it with this self-important jerk. At Hope's Table, when guests are being rude, I don't take *their* crap, do I? Why should I give this idiot a free pass just because he's wearing an expensive suit? "Hey," I tell him. "Our luggage is in there, too, you know. Open it back up." He looks shocked but does what he's told. "Now take our bags out and hand them to us." He does that, too. Then he starts up the aisle, pushing past the passengers in front of us.

"Congratulations," Dolly says. "That knucklehead had it coming."

"No problem," I say, feeling light-headed and liberated—better than I've felt this whole trip. Dolly and I wish each other good luck. I step aside to let her go first. Then I follow her toward the exit, walking on rubbery legs.

Inside the airport, I head toward baggage claim, which is where Daddy said he'd meet me. I hope he's there. It'll freak me out if he isn't. I step onto the escalator and descend, scanning the crowd. I don't see him, and there are no messages on my cell phone. Waiting at the baggage carousel, I text Cicely about ordering the nutritional supplements. From the opposite side of the conveyor belt, I watch Dolly lift her new grandchild out of her daughter's front pack and hold her to her chest, pat her tiny back. The baby's father is handsome. Tall and tattooed, a ponytail.

"Ariane!"

And now here's Daddy after all, smiling and waving, coming toward me. He's wearing shorts, sandals. There's a breaching whale on the front of his T-shirt, sunglasses folded and hanging from the neckline. He's tan, slimmer than when I saw him last.

It's only when he approaches that I realize he hasn't come alone. There's a woman with him—a pretty, slim brunette. Fortyish, maybe. Nice tan. She's wearing a loose-fitting blue top and paler blue cropped pants, the kind I'd wear if I wasn't so short and stubby-legged. Is she Asian? Who is she? Why is she smiling at me? What's going on?

Chapter Fourteen

Orion Oh

When I get back to Viveca's with the groceries, Ariane's already up. Out on the deck, staring at the snatch of ocean you can see from where she's standing. The sliders are open, so I can hear the birds singing in the trees, the surf lapping the shore in the distance. It's cooler this morning, and breezy. She's wearing her hair longer these days, and the breeze is lifting it a little, fluttering her nightgown. Pregnant: I still can't believe it. Wasn't it just the day before yesterday when I was down on my hands and knees in the living room, giving her and her brother pony rides?

I glance over at the microwave clock. Five after nine. I'm glad she slept in a little. She had a long travel day yesterday, and by the time we got back here, she looked beyond exhausted. Crashed early, even by East Coast time. We talked a little about her decision to get pregnant and then went up to bed. . . . She's heavier now, and that can't be all baby weight. Not at this stage. She took that last breakup pretty hard, and she's always been an emotional eater, poor kid. But she's such a pretty girl, as pretty as she is sweet. Of the three of them, Ariane's always been the kindest and most level-headed, although I'm not sure how well thought out this big decision of hers was. Raising a child is hard enough when there's two of you, let alone just one. My mother didn't have it easy. And neither did I, for that matter. My *nonno* did his best, but it wasn't the same. No dad to help me with my Pinewood Derby car or teach me how to ride a two-wheeler. The pain in my gut about my absentee father had gradually curdled into a hatred of him because of his defection. But it's her life. I just wish she lived a little closer to home so we could pitch in after the baby gets here. Gets *there,*

I mean. She's so committed to that soup kitchen of hers that she probably won't consider coming home. I can at least suggest it, though. I'm still her dad. I don't *have* to sell the house.

"Hey there, Sleeping Beauty," I call out to her.

She turns, looks in and gives me that beautiful, brave smile of hers. "Hi, Daddy. Where have you been?"

"I drove down to the little market in Wellfleet for a few things." Sleeping Beauty: wish I hadn't just called her that. Last night, she told me the reason she decided to go the sperm donor route was because she came to the conclusion that a handsome prince was probably never going to show up.

She comes inside. Walks into the kitchen and gives me a hug, rests her head on my shoulder. "It's so good to see you," I tell her. "I've missed you."

"Missed you, too, Dad." As she breaks away, I see that her eyes are glistening with tears. She pulls out one of the stools at the counter and sits.

"So anyway, I got you some bananas. And this." I hold up the box of Cream of Wheat. "When your mother was pregnant with you and your brother, that was about all she could stomach for a while. She ate so many bananas that, after you guys were born, I was relieved to see you weren't monkeys."

She smiles. "Thanks, Daddy. I can't promise I'll be able to keep them down, but I appreciate the effort. Mama had morning sickness, too?"

"With you and your brother, yes. Not so much with Marissa." Ariane says something about someone's Y chromosome theory, which I don't get. But before I can ask her about it, she wants to know if Annie breast- or bottle-fed her and her brother. "She breast-fed all three of you. Andrew gave her a little trouble at first, but you took right to it. You were a regular chow hound."

"Still am." She laughs. There's another thing I wish I hadn't said. We haven't seen each other in almost two years, and so much had happened since then. Think before you open your mouth, Dr. Oh, I advise myself. Proceed with caution the way you did with all those college kids you sat across from in your office. . . . But hey, she's my daughter, not one of my patients. I need to relax, let this initial awkwardness between us subside. I may be her *divorced* dad now, and she may be pregnant, but we both just need to get reestablished. And if I'm too tentative with her, she might get the wrong idea—assume I'm judging her about her pregnancy. Which I'm not, really. It's her life, not mine.

Unpacking the groceries, I hold up the bottle of ginger ale I've bought her. "Picked this up, too. It's supposed to be good for upset stomachs." She nods. Says she had some on the plane yesterday and it helped. "Well, let me get your breakfast started. I think I'll make myself some scrambled eggs. You want some? With some toast, maybe?"

She shakes her head, says she's still pretty squeamish. "My doctor says not to worry, though—that my body gives the fetus what it needs first. Pregnancy's sort of amazing that way, isn't it?"

"Oh, it is. Nothing more amazing than the human body." I take out a saucepan, scan the directions on the Cream of Wheat box. "You look rested, hon. Did you sleep okay last night?"

She nods. "My head hit the pillow and I didn't wake up until twenty minutes ago, not even to pee. That mattress is so comfortable, I probably could have stayed in bed all day."

"Pretty good accommodations here at Chez Viveca, eh?"

"I'll say. I didn't really notice so much last night, but when I walked around this morning, I was like oh, my god. This place is beautiful."

"The best that money can buy. How do you like the artwork?"

"It's incredible. Before you got back, I was looking at those floral photographs over the fireplace. They're signed Mapplethorpes. I can't imagine what those must have cost. What kind of flowers are they? Orchids?"

"The one on the left is. I'm not sure about the other one. Jack-in-the-pulpit maybe. Or jonquils. Your mom's the expert in that department."

She nods. Says that, other than Mapplethorpe, she doesn't recognize any of the artists' names.

"Me neither. That's her specialty, I guess: painters and sculptors who were untrained, out there on the periphery. She collects them and promotes them like crazy. Drives up the value of their work."

"Like she did with Mama," Ariane notes.

"Exactly."

She gets off the stool and walks over to the table in the living room. Smiles at the sculpture sitting on top of it. Political satire in papier-mâché, I guess you'd call it. Three two-foot-high figures, their heads and bodies transposed. Bin Laden's wearing a white late-Elvis jumpsuit. Kim Jong-il's suited up in an NBA uniform. Ahmadinejad's a cross-dresser in a Madonna getup, complete with conical bra. "This is funny," she says.

"Yeah, isn't it? Especially in light of what Ahmadinejad said in his speech at Columbia. You hear about that?" She shakes her head. "Apparently, there's no such thing as homosexuality in Iran. Maybe that's why your mother and Viveca have decided not to honeymoon there."

The smile drops off her face, Annie's late-in-life lesbianism having just entered the room with us, thanks to me. "Yeah, right," she says.

To rescue the mood, I tell her that one of the late night hosts—Jimmy Kimmel, I think it was—referred to Ahmadinejad as Scruffy McWindbreaker. It restores her smile. "Late night TV, Daddy?" she says. "That doesn't sound like you. You were always such an early bird."

"Well, when you're an old retired geezer who doesn't have to get up and go to work anymore, you can be the master of your own schedule."

She tells me I'm not a geezer. Asks if it feels weird not to work.

"It did at first. But I've kind of been getting my bearings since I've been up here. Going to bed when I want, running, reading. And thinking about things I never had much time to think about before."

"Like what?"

"Family stuff for one thing—my paternal side. I know a lot about my Italian relatives, but almost nothing about the Ohs. Mainly because my father didn't want to have anything to do with me." She nods, but I wish I hadn't put it that way. Does that furrowed brow mean she's comparing my situation to the one her child will have? "So since I've been up here, I've been getting kind of curious about that. The only Chinese relative of mine I ever met was my grandfather. My father's father."

"Didn't he own a restaurant?"

"Uh-huh. A dim sum place in Boston. I used to eat there some-times when I was in college." There's a question on Ari's face and I'm pretty sure I know what it is. If I had a connection to my grandfather, why had I had none with his son? But I don't want to go into all that with her: my mother's withholding information until the end of her life, the contempt I'd felt for the father who had wanted nothing to do with me. So I shift the conversation a little because I don't want my daughter to pick up on my pain, my vulnerability. "So yeah, I've been looking into the ancestry thing a little, poking around on those genealogy Web sites. It's a new thing for me, this curiosity about my Chinese heritage. To tell you the truth, I never gave it much thought before now." Which is *not* the truth. It's a bald-faced, knee-jerk lie. "I've found a cousin I never knew I had. Ellen Wong. She lives out in Cincinnati. Her grandfather and mine were brothers, the only two who emigrated from the old country. She and I have been communi-cating, swapping information. So that's been kind of cool."

Ari says she wishes she had gotten to know *her* grandparents.

"Yeah, the only one who was still alive when you were born was my mother, but you were too young to remember her. You would have liked her, too. In fact, you resemble her a little. It struck me yesterday at the airport. Of the three of you, you're my little *paisana*."

She smiles. "Your little meatball, you mean."

"Hey, your Cream of Wheat's just about ready over here. You want me to put a little milk in it? Sprinkle some sugar on top?"

"Okay."

"And the magic word is . . ."

"Pleeease." She says it like she's six years old again, and I stand there at the stove, smiling, thinking about the breakfasts I used to make the kids on those Sunday mornings when Annie went off to church—pancakes with surprises inside. Coins I'd wrap in foil and stick in the batter, like my Nonna Valerio used to do when I was a kid.

"So what do you want to do today, kiddo? Hang out around here? Go down to the beach and ride the waves like we used to?"

She clutches her belly. "No waves, thank you. But a walk on the beach sounds nice. Can we go to Long Nook?"

"Sure. Or over to the bayside beach if you're still into shell collecting. That's closer. But I like Long Nook better. I've been running there mornings. Between six and seven o'clock when I can get my lazy ass out of bed. I like it when I have the whole beach to myself. Looks different than it did when you were kids."

"Different how?" she asks.

"There's more ocean and less beach. Erosion, I guess. They've got 'no climbing' signs posted every hundred yards or so at the base of the dunes. And now, on top of that, there's all these posted warnings about the great whites they've been spotting lately. Which is unusual, I guess."

"What's that about, Daddy? Global warming?"

"No, not directly. Tracy says it's about the seals."

"She said she's a marine biologist?"

"Uh-huh. Apparently there's been a population explosion among the seals, and the eating's too good for the sharks to pass up. So they're sticking around later than they usually do, cruising closer to the shore."

"Have you seen any?"

"No, but I've seen a couple of seal carcasses along the beach, which I imagine is their doing. Pisses the gulls off when I run by them. Disturb them while they're picking over the leftovers. Couple of days ago, this one gull started dive-bombing me, squawking like he was giving me hell."

She smiles. "So that's why Tracy's up here? Because of the sharks?"

"Yup. She's part of a team that's hoping to track them. Embedding homing devices in them when they spot them so they can study their migration patterns once they start heading down to warmer waters."

"By the way, I like Tracy, Daddy. I hope she wasn't too uncomfortable when I got sick at that restaurant we stopped at and just blurted it out about being pregnant."

"No, no. She understood."

"Cooking smells make me nauseous lately—fried food, especially. It was so nice of her to help me out in the ladies' room like that after we'd known each other for what? An hour? It was kind of weird that I told her I was pregnant before I even told you."

"Doesn't matter. She just felt bad because it was her idea to stop and get something to eat."

"Tell me about her," she says.

"About Tracy? What do you want to know?"

"Well . . . she said she teaches at U.R.I., right?"

"Uh-huh. Associate professor in biology. Sharks are her specialty. She did her doctoral thesis on them."

"And how did you guys meet?"

I laugh. "At the sushi counter, actually. I was up in P'town doing my grocery shopping. We exchanged a few pleasantries while we were looking over the seaweed salads and spicy tuna rolls. Then I got behind her in the checkout line and we started talking some more. I kept glancing down at the ID badge she was wearing, trying to remember where I'd heard her name before. Then when we were both out in the parking lot, it dawned on me. I'd been listening to her on the radio when I was driving up here a few weeks back. She was being interviewed about the sharks. Holding her own with this doofus deejay. Which I congratulated her for."

"And since then?" she asks. She's fishing, I realize, but I'm going to make her work for it.

"Since then what?"

"Are you and she . . . ?"

"Are we what?"

"Dating?"

"Dating? Yeah, I took her to a sock hop down in Hyannis. We went to the malt shop afterward. Shared an ice cream soda with two straws. That woman can wear a poodle skirt like nobody's business."

"Come on, Daddy."

"Where we going?" She rolls her eyes the way she used to at her dad's corny jokes. "We're just friends, honey. We went out to dinner a couple of times. That's all." Three times, actually. And out for breakfast the morning after she came back here and spent the night. But I'm not about to go into that with Ariane. She'd probably pick up the phone and tell her sister, and then I'd *really* get the third degree. Marissa's been hounding me about getting a girlfriend since before the ink was dry on her mother's and my divorce decree.

"Would you *like* to be more than just friends?"

I shrug. Remind her that Tracy and I are both up here temporarily.

"Daddy, you live in Connecticut and she's in Rhode Island. That's not exactly insurmountable. Is she already in a relationship?"

"Nope. Divorced, no kids."

"She's Asian, isn't she?"

"Half. Hawaiian on her mother's side."

She gives me a mischievous smile. "She likes you, Daddy."

"Does she? What makes you say that?"

"I could tell from the way she was looking at you on the ride back here, and at that place where we stopped to eat. Not to mention that she went with you to the airport in the first place."

"Well, Detective Oh, it just so happens that she had business in Boston yesterday anyway. Had to drop off some report at the New England Aquarium. So we carpooled. I gave her a ride there, and then we drove over to Logan to pick you up. Now what's that Cheshire grin for?"

"It's the twenty-first century, Daddy. People don't usually 'drop off' reports in person these days. They e-mail them in an attachment."

"No kidding? Well, then, I guess she *must* have the hots for me. Can't blame her. You know what a chick magnet I am." I dish out our food and bring it to the table. "Come on, detective. Breakfast is served. *Mangia.*"

We sit. I eat my eggs; Ariane takes a bite of banana. She asks me if I've heard from Andrew lately. "Couple of days ago," I tell her. "Says he's doing okay." She tells me she wishes he was coming to the wedding. "Yeah, well, he's still struggling with your mother's . . . lifestyle change. I guess it's just as well."

She nods. Puts her bare feet up on the empty chair between us.

"You still like going barefoot, I see." She nods, says the bottoms of her feet are so impervious by now, she could probably walk on hot coals. "Yeah, well, best not to test *that* theory," I tell her. I reach over and grab her big toe. "This little piggy went to market, this little piggy stayed home. Remember?"

She smiles. "This little piggy had roast beef, this little piggy had none."

"Must be a vegan," I say. But she's teary again. "What?"

"Nothing."

"No, tell me."

"It's just that . . . my baby won't have a daddy to play that with."

"No, but he'll have a granddaddy." Neither of us mentions the obvious: that I'll be doing my grandfathering long-distance. Still, I don't want to push it—the idea of her moving back.

Ten minutes later, I've finished my breakfast and she's had all of six little bites of her Cream of Wheat. I've counted. Well, I can't really blame her. Even with sugar on it, it's like eating wallpaper paste. We get up, carry our dishes to the sink. When she says she'll do them, I tell her no. She's my guest.

"Hey, Daddy?" she says. I look over my shoulder and see her over by the Mapplethorpes again. "You've met Viveca. Right?"

Ah, Viveca. I figured we'd be getting around to her sooner or later. "I have." I put the last of the dishes in the drying rack. Start scouring egg off the frying pan. "You have, too, actually. Remember that Whitney Biennial show that your mother had a piece in when you guys were kids? We all went down to New York City for the opening, stayed overnight in a hotel?"

"I think so. Was that the trip when we went to the NBA store and that guy yelled at Andrew for trying to shoot three-pointers?"

"Don't remind me. One of his wild shots from downtown almost wiped out a whole display of team mugs. I saw that ball go flying and thought I was going to be buying about a thousand bucks' worth of broken ceramic. Ah, yes. Those fun Oh family outings."

She's wandering the living room, going from one piece of art to another. "That was a really big deal that Mama's work got selected for that show. Wasn't it?" she asks.

"It was. But yeah, that opening was when we all met Viveca. She came up, introduced herself. Told your mother she was interested in representing her. And the rest is history. The big commissions, that article in *Newsweek* that put her on the map as an up-and-comer."

She comes back to the kitchen. Leans against the counter next to me. "You don't like Viveca, do you?" She's watching my face in profile, studying my reaction to her question.

"Hey, she's letting me stay here, right? So I guess she can't be all bad."

"No, seriously, Daddy," she says.

"Well, let's just say she's not really my cup of tea. But don't let my feelings color yours. I think you'll like her when you get to know her. Your sister does." Okay, she says. She'll keep an open mind. "Good. Hey, let's go sit down for a minute, okay?" We move back into the living room, face each other on opposing love seats. "Now about this baby you're having. What are you hoping for? Boy? Girl? One of each?"

Her eyes widen. "Oh god, I'm not sure I could handle twins. But don't multiple births run in families?"

"Sometimes. But I wouldn't go out and buy doubles of everything just yet. You'd run more of a risk of that if you'd had in vitro. Have you had an ultrasound?"

"Next month," she says. "My doctor says they only do it earlier if it's a higher-risk pregnancy. Women over thirty-five."

"Well, you'll know soon enough, but I think you can relax. Odds are you're having one, not two."

She asks how her mother and I felt when we found out we were having twins. I tell her it was a surprise, but that we were excited about it. Why mention how upset Annie was at first? "In fact—"

"Oh, jeeze!" she says. "Excuse me, Daddy." She gets up and rushes to the bathroom off the kitchen. To drown out the sound of her retching in there, I reach over and put the radio on. They're playing some old song I half-remember. *It's a strange, strange world we live in, Master Jack.* . . . There's a flush. She opens the door looking pale and miserable, poor kid. But she flashes me that brave smile.

"You okay?" She nods. Sits back down. When I ask her if she lost her breakfast, she says just a little of it. "Well, that's good. Are you still up for the beach, or do you want to take a rain check?"

"No, let's go. If I have to vomit again, I can do it there just as well as here. Puking at the beach will be a new experience."

"Well, I know one thing, kiddo," I tell her. "This baby's going to be one lucky kid to have such a damned good mother."

"You think so?"

"Oh, I *know* so. Name one thing you're *not* good at."

"Dieting," she says. "Delegating responsibility at work. Remembering to water my plants. Oh, and keeping boyfriends. I wasn't too good at that."

It breaks my heart to hear her say that. I want to tell her that she surrendered too soon to this artificial insemination thing—that a lot of people are in their thirties before they find someone, settle down, and have a family. That if what she wanted was a traditional marriage, the right guy might very well have come along. But I hold my tongue. This is an argument I might have used if she'd talked to me about her plans *before* she got inseminated, which she didn't choose to do. So now it's a fait accompli—this baby whose father is some nameless, faceless Brazilian guy who sat in a room with a skin magazine, did his thing, and sold them the spunk they injected into her. *It's a strange, strange world we live in, Master Jack.* Can't argue with that.

"You know," I tell her, "if you want, you could always come back home to have the baby. Stay with me at the house and—"

"Daddy, you're *selling* the house. Remember?"

"Just say the word and I'll take it off the market."

She shakes her head, says her life's out there in California. And besides, she doesn't expect Annie or me to juggle our lives because of her. "But I *was* thinking that maybe Mama could come out and be there for the delivery. Stay with me for the first week or so when I come home with the baby."

"I bet she'd be happy to do that," I assure her.

"Well, first things first," she says. "I haven't even told her I'm pregnant yet. I'm a little nervous about doing that."

"Don't be, Ari. She'll respect your decision. I'm sure she'll be very happy for you once she gets used to the idea."

"Hope so," she says. She stands, says she's going to go change for the beach. But halfway up the stairs, she stops and looks back at me. "Daddy?"

"Hmm?"

"Do you think Mama was a good mother?"

The question comes out of nowhere. "Well, why don't *you* tell *me*?"

"No, she was," Ari says. "I just wanted to hear what you thought."

"Because?"

No reason, she says. She was just wondering.

While she's up there, I pack her a snack in case she gets hungry while we're at the beach: another banana, a granola bar, a couple of paper cups and the ginger ale. I wish I'd bought a plastic bottle instead of glass, but I can wrap it in a towel and it should be fine. . . . *Was* Annie a good mother? Yes, overall. Sure, the kids frustrated her sometimes—Andrew more than his sisters. There were those evenings when she'd meet me at the door when I got home and start her litany of complaints before I could even put down my briefcase and take off my coat. But I couldn't blame her. I was so work-driven back then. I'd leave the child care to her pretty much, then try to spell her on weekends. It got harder for Annie once she started making her art. She'd be upstairs with them all day long when what she really wanted was to be down in the basement working on those shadow box things she was doing. . . . And it wasn't like she'd had much role-modeling to draw on either. Her own mother had died so young. And after her father hit the skids and they removed her from the house, those foster moms probably weren't the best role models, either. But given all that, Annie did fine by our three. . . .

And hey, it's not as if *I* was Father of the Year. Things would come up at work and I'd end up missing one of Ari's recitals or Marissa's gymnastics meets. One of Andrew's Little League games or, later, one of his wrestling matches. The night the twins graduated from high school, I remember, there was a crisis with one of my patients, and I ended up getting there late. Annie was so pissed at me, she hadn't even saved me a seat. I missed the speeches, but at least I was there to see them get their diplomas—sitting by myself up in the balcony of the auditorium. It didn't seem to bother the kids, but Annie gave me the silent treatment for the next couple of days.

I'm just not sure why, out of the blue, Ariane asked me that about her mother. Is it nerves? Hormones? Or maybe she's promising herself she's going to be a different kind of mother—less high-strung, less fly off the handle. Fear of the unknown; that's probably all that she's feeling. Annie felt that, too. And when she was in labor, she was mad as hell. . . .

We're in the delivery room and her labor's not going well. "Do you see what you've done to me? We're never having sex again! . . ."

But as soon as Ariane was born, she was crying tears of joy. And a few minutes later, when things became touch and go with Andrew— the umbilical cord had gotten wrapped around his neck—she pleaded with the doctor to save her baby. By the time we took them home from the hospital, she was madly in love with those two kids. Possessive of them, even, when my mother came up to help. Mom had planned to stay two weeks, I remember, but she went home after the first one. They'd had a fight while I was at work. "In all my years, no one's ever spoken to me like that," Mom told me when I was carrying her suitcase out to the car. She was in tears. "I was just pointing out that they'd be safer on their stomachs when she put them down, and she turned into a crazy woman." Being a mom just took Annie some getting used to, that was all. Some fine-tuning. It wasn't the first time she had had one of those little bouts of hers, and it wasn't the last time either. But when she'd get like that, I'd remind myself about all the upheavals she'd had to weather as a kid. Unexpected change was what always seemed to rile her up. Frighten her. I think that was what was always underneath that anger of hers: her fear. I wonder if Viveca's ever seen that side of Annie.

"Daddy?" Ariane calls down. "Do you think I need a sweatshirt?"

"No, you should be good."

But when I go upstairs to change into my trunks, I stuff one into my backpack for her just in case. She's still my little girl. I like taking care of her, and I love it that she's here. . . . And hey, I can understand why, when she's ready to have the baby, she'd want her mother to go out and help her instead of her old man—that maternal thing. But I'm a free agent now. If Annie can't swing it, I could go out there and pitch in. . . . Okay, Grandpa, you're getting ahead of yourself. First let's see how Annie reacts. I just hope she'll be as cool with it as I *said* she would be. Should I call and give her a heads-up? No, it's Ariane's news. She should be the one to tell her.

Let's see. Do I have everything? Sweatshirt, towels, snacks, sunblock. The beach chairs are already out in the car. I guess that's it. I grab my stuff and walk down the hall. Poke my head in her room, but she's not there. "Ariane?"

"In here," she says. I follow her voice to the unused bedroom where I've stashed those paintings I hauled up here. When I unpacked the car after I got here, I stacked them against the wall, but Ari's laid them out on the king-size bed. "Have you seen these, Daddy?" she asks. "They're amazing."

"I not only saw them," I tell her. "I brought them up here."

"*You* did? Why? As a favor for Viveca?"

"Nope. She doesn't even know about them." She looks at me, confused. "You know that ramshackle old cottage out in back of our house?"

She nods. "Andrew's secret clubhouse."

"It was until your mom caught him and his friends messing around down there and had me board the place up," I remind her.

"I forgot about that. God, when they'd come back up from there, they reeked of weed so badly that you could almost get high from the fumes. Didn't someone die at that old house once? Drown in a well or something?"

"Yup. The artist who painted these, as a matter of fact. Poor guy couldn't sell any of his work in his lifetime and now they're worth big bucks, according to Viveca."

"Wait. Didn't you just say she doesn't know about them?"

"She doesn't."

I tell her about the day her mother and Viveca came to the house on their way to the Gardner Museum. About Viveca's discovery of *The Cercus People*. "Read the back."

She does. "And Joe J was . . . ?"

"The guy who painted all these. You see that big one leaning against the chair over there? The Garden of Eden painting? Look at

Adam's face. Now look at the men's faces in some of the others. Notice anything?"

"It's the same face," she says.

"Right. Jones's face, I'd be willing to bet. He paints the skin gray in a lot of them, but look at the facial features and the texture of the hair."

"He was black?"

"Yes. Had a white woman living down there with them—him and his brother. Back then, of course, that would have rattled people's cages." She says that sounds more like the South than Connecticut. "Ha! Don't kid yourself."

She puts *The Cercus People* back on the bed. Scans the others. "They're creepy but kind of cool, too," she says. "Like scenes from dreams you have but can't quite get the meaning of. I like how he distorts the figures—almost as if you were looking at them in a fun house mirror."

"Yeah, well, I'm not sure that was intentional. He was self-taught, had had no training. Which is what Viveca specializes in, you know? Outsiders, primitive painters. I thought her eyes were going to pop out of her head when she saw that painting we had. She'd been looking for works by Jones for years, she said. She wants to buy it from me, but I've held off selling it to her."

"Why?"

"You want the truth? Because she wants it so badly." I look away from her look of disapproval. Maybe she's right. Maybe I *am* being childish.

"Are you going to let her know about all these other ones?"

"I don't know yet. Haven't decided."

"But why did you bring them up here with you?"

I begin to gather them up, stack them. "Because the house is on the market. People traipsing in and out, walking the grounds. And then, with the wedding coming up, who knows who might be over there poking around?"

"Daddy, the wedding guests will be at Bella Linda. The only people who'll be at the house are Mama, Marissa, and me." I carry the stacks over to the other side of the room, lean them back against the wall. Turn and face her.

"But I'm sure Viveca will be over there with you guys. I just figured if I brought them up here with me, I wouldn't have to deal with it."

She gives me a skeptical look. "Daddy, I'm sure she's not an art thief. Are you going to keep them? Sell them?"

I shrug. "Don't know yet, honey. Hey, I thought you and I were going to the beach."

Chapter Fifteen

Andrew Oh

Casey-Lee's in a pissy mood because she suggested we go to that new Japanese hibachi place for dinner and here we are at the Olive Garden instead. "Oh, I don't really care, sugar," she'd said when I picked her up. "We can go there if you want." So we did and now she's got an attitude. Well, it's not going to get any better when I tell her I'm reconsidering my decision—that I might cancel our weekend plans and go back there after all. Use one of those tickets she sent. There's a part of me that's curious about this Viveca. The woman Mom changed her whole life for. But I don't know. Maybe I should just stay put. Either way, I'd better make a decision pretty soon. Their wedding's only four days away.

A waitress approaches—a pretty, dark-eyed Mexican. Nice, fleshy body. A C-cup, maybe. "Hi, folks. I'm Xan and I'll be your server tonight. How y'all doin'?"

"We're just fine," I tell her. "How are you?"

"Great! Well, I'm a little nervous, actually. I've been shadowing another waitress all week. This is my first night going solo." I ask her how it's going. "So far so good," she says. "Can I get y'all something to drink to start you off?"

I turn to Casey-Lee. "White wine?" She nods. "A glass of pinot grigio for the lady and a Lone Star for me." Casey-Lee likes things traditional. Likes me to order for both of us.

"You got it," the waitress says.

Casey's off tonight. Fidgety. Going out in the middle of the week's probably a mistake. She's already told me she's tired, and that she still has her lessons to plan for tomorrow, and things to cut out for some bulletin board she needs to put up before the school's open house on Thursday. "Hey," I say.

"Hey what?"

"You look very pretty tonight. Is that a new dress?"

She rolls her eyes. Says I asked her that the last time she wore it.

"Oh. Sorry."

"That's okay," she says. "By the way, you look handsome in that shirt. When I was in Brooks Brothers, I couldn't decide between the blue check and the green check. But I'm glad I went with the green. It's a great color for you."

"Well shucks, darlin'. That's mahty nice of you to say so." She cracks a smile. Gets a kick out of it when I talk Texan to her. I reach across the table and take her hand in mine. "So how are things going with your new class?"

She makes a face. Says she wishes she was still teaching third grade. "Kindergarteners are still such babies at the beginning of the year. I had two of them crying today because they missed their mothers and another who wet her pants. And that boy I was telling you about? Jett?"

"The one with the 'alternative' parents?"

"Uh-huh. He kicked another child while they were in line at the drinking fountain. A *girl*, no less. Epiphany, and she's as sweet as they come and hadn't done a thing to provoke him. When she started crying, he stood there denying it, and I told him I'd seen him do it with my own eyes. He's going to be trouble, that one. And when I called home and talked to his mother, she was like, 'Did he have something sugary for snack? Because sugar makes him ornery.' Instead of, 'We'll give him a consequence' or 'Did he hurt that poor little girl?'"

"Did he?"

"Just her feelings," she says. "But that's bad enough. I mean, last week Jett's mom complained because I was having her son recite the Pledge of Allegiance along with the other children, but now it's okay for him to assault another child because the room mother brought in Apple Newtons and Hi-C? I can just imagine what *she's* gonna bring in when it's her week to be room mother. Tofu, probably. Edamambo or whatever they call it. Like *that'd* go over big with the children."

"Crazy, huh?"

"Meet the mother halfway, Marian said. Have him stand with the others but just not recite the pledge. So what can I do? She's the principal. I just wish she wasn't so wishy-washy. I been thinking more and more about getting my master's in administration instead of reading. I tell you one thing. If *I* was in charge at that school, things would be different. I'd back my teachers, not tell them to bend over backward to please the parents. I mean, if she doesn't want me to teach her son to show some respect for the flag, maybe she should homeschool him out at that organic farm thing they're part of. But anyway, that's enough about school. How was your day?" I open my mouth to tell her, but notice that she's looking over my shoulder. "Oh . . . my . . . *Lord*," she says.

"What?"

"There's Miss Bascomb, my old earth science teacher."

I turn to see who she's looking at. "The woman in the red dress?"

"No, the next table over." I spot two heavy-set women, both of them in jeans and orange T-shirts, matching close-cropped gray hair. They're drinking Lone Stars, too. "Well, I guess I owe my girlfriend Janisse an apology. She always used to insist that Miss Bascomb was one of *those*."

One of those lesbians, she means. It feels like a gut shot. Like she's slamming my mother, even though she's probably not even making the connection. "Got your gaydar up, huh?" I say.

"I used to tell her, 'Janisse, just because she wears pants all the time and has posters of the Cowboys and the Spurs all over her classroom, that doesn't prove a thing. Maybe she's just a sports fan. Maybe skirts make her look too hippy.' And Janisse would go, 'Girl, you're just naïve. She's got a *softball* trophy on her bookcase. Drives a *muscle* car for crying out loud.' Whenever Janisse had to go to her room for extra help, she'd make me go with her even though I was getting straight A's in science. She was afraid Miss Bascomb would try and recruit her."

Okay, that's enough, I feel like saying. But what the hell am I getting so defensive about? *She's* not the one who's connecting the dots between those two dykes over there and my mom. *I* am. It's *my* problem.

Our drinks arrive, and when the waitress goes to put down Casey's wine, she spills a little on her. "Sweet Jesus, look what you just did!" she says, loud enough so that the people at the next table look over. Casey's sopping at the spill like she's gotten half the glass dumped on her instead of just a little dribble. The waitress apologizes and rushes off to get her some extra napkins. "It's okay," I assure Casey. "White wine's not going to leave a stain."

"It most certainly will, Andrew. Do you realize how delicate silk is? That's what I hate about these chain restaurants. It's not only that the food is so-so, but the service is unprofessional." In other words, this never would have happened if we'd gone to that hibachi place.

"She's new," I remind her. "She's nervous."

"Oh, then I guess that gives her the right to slop whatever she wants on her customers. Well, there goes *her* fifteen percent tip."

When Xan returns with more napkins—a stack of them—Casey instructs her to make sure she reports the spill to her manager. "I'll try and treat the stain when I get home, but if it doesn't come out, I'll have to bring it to the dry cleaner's and give y'all the bill."

Xan yes ma'ams her. Apologizes again. She asks if we need a few more minutes or we're ready to order. "Babe? You know what you want?"

She slaps her menu shut. "Just a Caesar salad," she tells me.

"Appetizer- or entrée-size, ma'am?" the waitress asks, short-circuiting Casey's preferred ordering process.

"What?"

"Did you want the smaller Caesar or—"

"That's all I'm having. A Caeser salad, dressing on the side."

"Yes, ma'am. Dinner size then. Did you want anchovies on that?"

Casey shoots her a look like she's an imbecile. "No, I do *not*, thank you."

"Okay. Got it. And you, sir?" I order the seafood ravioli, Alfredo sauce instead of marinara. "Good choice," she says. "That's my favorite dish on the whole menu. Any appetizers for you guys?" Ooh, boy. She's just hit another nerve. Casey hates it when people refer to women as "guys." Blames the "feministas" for the fact that everyone does that now. I've heard her pal, Dr. Laura, use that word, which is probably where she got it. Casey thinks that woman walks on water.

"What do you think, babe?" I ask her. "You feel like splitting an order of calamari?"

"Those deep-fried rubber band thingies? I don't *think* so." Now I'm an imbecile, too.

I sneak the waitress an apologetic look. "Guess not," I tell her.

"Okay then. I'll put this right in for you guys." Ouch.

When she walks away, Casey-Lee starts in about fried food and fatty sauces. "You keep eating like that and you'll have a coronary by the time you're forty. Why do you think Daddy had to get that triple bypass last year? Clogged arteries from eating the same kind of thing you just ordered."

Plus the fact that Daddy's fifty or sixty pounds overweight and twice my age. And I doubt all those bourbon and branch waters are all that good for his ticker either. "I did a six-mile run this morning," I tell her. "I'm guessing my heart can handle a little cream sauce every once in a while."

"Fine," she says. "What do I know? I'd just like to be your wife, Andrew. Not your widow."

Yup, bad idea: a midweek meal. "You should have just told me if you were too busy to go out tonight. You seem so stressed-out."

"I'm fine," she insists. "I *wanted* to see you. We've gotta eat, don't we?" She sips her wine. I drink my beer. "So what was your day like?" she asks again. Maybe this time she'll let me answer.

Crazy, I tell her. "We got six new patients on the ward that I had to do intakes for. They're just back from Afghanistan. Got deployed over there for the troop surge."

"Oh, you mean the troop surge our 'antiwar' president ordered?" She makes little quotation marks with her fingers when she says "antiwar." "Maybe now he realizes what poor George W was up against."

What George W created and Obama inherited, I feel like saying.

Although I've let her assume otherwise, I voted for Obama last year. Not that I'm too happy with the way he's been handling things so far. The economy, the wars. "A couple of these new guys we got had to be medevaced out of there," I tell her. "They're in bad shape. Some of the worst I've seen."

"The worst how? Physically?"

"One of them, yeah. He's got a TBI. A gunner, twenty-one years old. Took shrapnel in his head and his neck. He's already had three operations. Brain surgery, facial reconstruction. Poor guy doesn't even remember the day he got hit."

"Well, that's probably good. Right?"

"Maybe. But at least it'd give him a context, you know what I'm saying? Why he's struggling to put sentences together. Come up with the names of simple objects on cards. Today when I was doing his assessment, I held up this one card with a picture of a banana on it. 'I know what it is,' he told me. 'Give me a minute.' But you should have seen the look of defeat on his face when he finally gave up. When I told him what it was, he started to cry. He's probably never going to be a hundred percent."

"That poor thing," she says. "When I was volunteering at the V-A with my women's fellowship last year, it broke my heart to see some of those boys. Bandaged heads, missing limbs. I know they have an important job to do over there, but still. I get down on my knees every single night and pray for them."

See? She's in a bitchy mood tonight, but she's got a good heart.

Casey's cell phone chimes inside her purse, and when she takes it out and reads the text message she's just gotten, she says it's from some woman on some committee she's on—that she'd better respond. Watching her text her back, I recall the day I met Casey-Lee. She was sitting in the solarium, reading some Stephen King story to a couple of our walking wounded. Engaging those guys who would otherwise be sitting in their rooms, absorbed in their misery. Stephen King and a beautiful blonde paying attention to them: it probably did those soldiers more good than all the medication and talk therapy our team was providing. And then a few days later, when I walked into that church service hungover from the night before, there she was again. . . .

Casey believes that there's no such thing as coincidence. That it was the Good Lord's plan to bring us together. Which was why it hadn't worked out with that *other* guy she'd almost gotten engaged to: the up-and-coming attorney her father had hand-picked for her. The first time I went over to their house, they still had a picture of him and Casey on their refrigerator: Waco's answer to Barbie and Ken, they looked like. Not that I'm complaining about her looks. When she stopped me outside the church that day—surprised me by saying she recognized me from the hospital—and I took a chance and asked her out, I was shocked when she said yes. I'm *still* shocked, sometimes. I like it when we walk into a club or a restaurant and heads look up. . . . But more than once, I've imagined Big Daddy's reaction after that first time I went over there. *His last name's what, Casey-Lee? Oh? What kind of a name's that? He got some chinky-Chinaman in him? What's that? Irish and Eyetalian, too? Well, that boy's a real mongrel then, idn't he? . . . A first lieutenant? Well, that's fine, honey. I've got nothing but respect for the U.S. Army. You know that. But a nurse? Kind of a nancy-pants career choice, don't you think? And what can nurses make? Fifty thousand, maybe? Fifty-five tops? That may be a decent salary for a woman. But for a man? A breadwinner? . . .* Yeah? Well, what's that thing I heard at our last training? That one out of five of the ones coming back from Afghanistan and Iraq are suffering from some kind of mental illness? Sounds to me that mental health's more of a growth industry than real estate lawyering, wouldn't you say, Big Daddy? Not that I'm being fair. Just because I can *imagine* him saying that shit doesn't mean he said it. I'm just glad they took that picture off their refrigerator, that's all. And maybe Casey's right. Maybe we *did* come together because of some divine plan. She brought me to Jesus, didn't she? Helped to ground me in a spiritual life when I was flapping around in the wind? Getting wasted on beer and weed, wasting my time and money on porn. My sister can argue all she wants to about how it wasn't our parents' fault that none of us grew up godly, but we'd been raised to be skeptical about religion. Love thy neighbor, sure, but not because Jesus Christ said so. Support the Democrats because they work for the common good and Republicans are just out for themselves. But it's not that black and white. Casey's plenty charitable: reading to the walking wounded, volunteering with Big Sisters. Whenever she talks about that little girl she used to take places, she lights up. . . . My parents, my sisters: voting for Obama was a foregone conclusion for them, but not for me. I remember standing there in that voting booth at the base, looking at both those levers, still undecided. It was McCain's cancer that finally convinced me to pull the lever for Obama. Palin was just too inexperienced. I couldn't see her being a heartbeat away from the presidency.

"Earth to Andrew," Casey says. "Where have you just been?"

Looking over at her, I realize she's finished texting and put her phone away. Rather than tell her what I was thinking about, I get back to what my day'd been like. "No, I was just thinking about this other guy that came in today. He's got PTSD something fierce. I'm in the middle of doing his intake, right? And there's this loud crash somewhere else on the ward. He jumps up, starts going all crazy on me like we were being fired on instead of someone out on the floor just dropped something. I couldn't talk him down. Couldn't even keep him in the room we were in. He runs out on the floor, wild-eyed and screaming. Ended up, me and LeRoy had to straitjacket him and get one of the docs to sedate him."

"It's so sad," she says. "I just wish these wars weren't necessary. I hope those 9/11 hijackers are burning in hell."

I nod. "This guy's my age. He's got two kids already and a third one on the way. Makes you wonder if the ones coming back in bad shape are *ever* going to get their heads back on straight again. Or if they're gonna end up on the scrap heap like all those Vietnam burnouts. You know?" But I can tell her mind's gone someplace else.

"So did you get someone to cover for you this coming weekend?" she asks. Here's my opening—my chance to tell her that I might be going back for my mom's wedding.

"Yeah. I switched rotations with Josette. Her boyfriend's coming down the weekend after, so it worked out great. I've got tomorrow through Monday now. So I was thinking—"

"Good. Don't forget the prayer breakfast on Saturday morning. It starts at nine. You better write it down."

Maybe I should wait until after we eat. Or at least until I decide for sure what I'm doing. Why get her upset if I'm *not* going? "No, I'll remember. You have to speak at that breakfast, don't you?"

"I'm giving the opening greeting. Remember? Which is why I don't want to see you walking in late. By the way, you know who's sitting at our table? Mayor DuPuy and her husband. And did I mention that John Ashcroft and his wife will be there? Traveling down from Missouri? My mother says the Ashcrofts are big in the Assemblies of God Church. They're sitting just one table over from us, so I'm sure we'll get to meet them. You should wear your uniform, not your civvies, okay? What was Ashcroft again? Secretary of state?"

"Attorney general." Gee, maybe he'll sing that song of his at the breakfast—the one they're always making fun of on *The Daily Show.* Jon Stewart, Colbert: they go over the top about the conservatives sometimes, but they can be pretty funny.

"Oh, and I have to go early and help set up the table decorations, so you won't need to pick me up. You just need to *get* there."

I nod. "And that thing with your parents is the same night, right? What time does that start?"

"Six o'clock. Drinks first at the house, and then we're heading on over to Diamond Back's for dinner. The reservation's for seven thirty, but my parents want you there for the cocktails, too, Andrew. This is a real big deal for Daddy. His top clients and their wives are going to be there, so you can't be late for that either. I'd feel a lot better if you wrote this stuff down. Or I could e-mail it to you. Why don't I do that?"

Yeah, why don't you, darlin'? Wouldn't want to screw up Daddy's schedule. I guess I'd just better stay put this weekend. It's not like my mom's expecting me. "Good idea," I tell her. "Hey, did you just say 'client*s*?' Plural? I thought it was just that one couple, the Hatchbacks or something?"

"The *Hal*bachs," she says. "It was supposed to be just them, but now he's invited the Rutherfords, too. Cubby Rutherford isn't exactly a client yet, but Daddy's been working on it. Cubby's a big real estate guy. His company's building that new high-rise that's going up on Highway Six."

"The one past the Richland Mall?"

"Uh-huh. He owns lots of properties here in Waco, and in Fort Worth, too. Daddy got wind that he's unhappy with his present firm, so he's been getting chummy with Cubby. Playing golf with him, taking him skeet shooting at his hunt club. If Cubby decides to switch to Commerford and Crouse, he'll be Daddy's biggest client. So the stakes are high. Mommy's as nervous about Saturday night as a kitty cat in a room full of rocking chairs."

Texas talk, I think. Give her a smile. "Why's that?"

"Because Cubby's wife is a Reformed Baptist deacon and Judie Halbach's got a mouth on her. Gets a few drinks in her and starts cussing like a ranch hand. Talking about gun control, and how going to that clown school cured her depression. In the last election, she campaigned for the Democrats against Governor Perry. Mommy says she'll just die if Judie gets lit and starts in about that. I mean, the Perrys and the Rutherfords are personal friends. But Daddy says they can't uninvite the Halbachs at this point. Johnny Ray Halbach's a big client, too."

"Well, maybe I could sit next to this Judie and, if she starts mouthing off, spill some wine on her."

"Ha-ha, very funny," Casey says. She looks down at her dress again. Presses a fresh napkin against the stain which, to my eyes, isn't even visible. "I keep thinking club soda'd be good to treat this with before it sets, but I'm not sure because it's silk." To change the subject, I ask her how our wedding plans are coming along. Big mistake. "Ugh," she says. "Don't remind me. My mother got a call yesterday from my girlfriend Abilene?"

"The bridesmaid I haven't met yet, right? Your college roommate?"

"Abby's my maid of *honor*, Andrew," she says. "I'm glad at least *one* of us is focused on what's only going to be the biggest day of our lives."

"Yeah, point taken," I tell her. "Because hey, it's only another four-teen months till showtime. I'd better get with the program, huh?"

She gives me a look. Hitches her hair behind her ear in that way I used to think was so cute. Now I find it annoying. Last time when we went out and I started counting how many times she did it, I got up into the teens.

"Are you making fun of me?" she asks.

Yup. "Nope. Just trying to offer a little comic relief."

"Well, let me tell *you* something, Andrew Joseph Oh. You men have it easy. What's the groom got to do other than rent a tuxedo and show up at the altar? But it's different for the bride. If my mother and I hadn't spent most of this summer going around to places, locking things in and putting down payments on . . ." *You listen to me, Andrew Joseph Oh!* I hear my mother say. That was always my cue to tune her out. Go someplace else in my mind while she stood there screaming at me. Unless, that is, she'd crossed over into lunatic land—was gearing up to hit me. Whack me with something. She never knew how lucky she was that I never hit her back. How close I came to doing that once or twice when—

"*Have* you?" Casey-Lee says.

"Have I what?"

"Asked any of your friends yet about being groomsmen? Are you even listening to me, Andrew?"

I nod. Tell her I'm working on the usher thing, which I'm not. Not to her satisfaction, anyway. I'm thinking about asking my buddy Jay Jay from back home to be my best man. Or my dad, if Jay can't get out here for the wedding. And I suppose I'll have to ask her doofus little brother to be an usher. But where I'm going to scare up five more "groomsmen" I can't imagine. "So anyway, Abby called your mother. What did she say?"

"That she and some of the other girls in the wedding party have been texting back and forth. And that they thought maybe they'd try and book my shower at one of the downtown restaurants that's got a private room with a bar. Make it, like, more of a bachelorette's night out than a bridal shower. And get this! She asked my mother did she mind if they hire a male stripper."

I laugh out loud thinking about Mean Erlene with her proper ways fielding *that* question. And then about that *Saturday Night Live* rerun Casey-Lee and I saw a few weeks back—the one where Chris Farley and what's-his-name, the *Dirty Dancing* guy, were auditioning for Chippendales. I was practically falling off the chair laughing, and Casey just sat there, stone-faced, talking about how fat and disgusting Chris Farley was. Which was the whole point of that skit.

"Boy, I'm really amusing you tonight, aren't I?" she says. "What's so funny now?"

"Nothing. I was just thinking about something else."

"Well, my poor mother didn't think it was funny. She was horrified. She was like, 'Well, Abilene. There'll be a lot of Casey-Lee's family there. I don't think her aunts or either of her grandmaws would appreciate that kind of party.' And neither would *I*, and I'm the guest of honor. Does Abby think I want to see some man dancing around in one of those G-string things? And a bunch of my girlfriends drunk as skunks and stuffing dollar bills in there? Groping his . . ."

"Meat and potatoes?" I suggest.

"That's enough, Andrew. There's no need to be crude. I mean, my poor MawMaw Clegg would probably have a stroke."

Or a hell of a good time, I feel like saying. Rise up from that motorized wheelchair of hers and start dirty-dancing with the stripper. But I keep that thought to myself. Cover my smile with my hand.

"I mean, when we were rooming together at the U, Abby was such a quiet girl. And spiritual. Whenever I'd get nervous about some test that was coming up, or hurt because another girl in our sorority said something mean about me, she'd go, 'Give it to Jesus, Casey-Lee. Just pray on it and give it up to God.' And now that she's a big shot buyer for Dillard's, she's turned into a . . . *party girl.*"

"So I take it your mother wants a swankier affair?"

"A more *dignified* one, yes," she says. "High tea at some nice inn, maybe. Or something nice at the Hilton. Mommy'd already called the Hilton before Abby called. Did some research. They've got an outdoor garden pavilion where they do showers. And a poolside patio with a fountain if it's a bigger group. But when she told Abby what she thought, and even offered to *pay* for the place, she said there was this silence on the other end. So now she's in a bind. She doesn't want to seem pushy, but she doesn't want her only daughter's bridal shower to be just some excuse for my girlfriends to get drunk and act improper. And neither do I, for that matter. This is supposed to be about *me*."

"Then why can't you just talk to Abby and tell her how you feel?"

"Because it's a surprise! I'm not even supposed to know about it!"

I sit there thinking about something to say that won't dig me in deeper. But here comes our waitress with a tray on her shoulder. "Ah, here we go," I say. "Good. I'm starved."

Xan puts down our meals and grabs my empty beer bottle. "Another Lone Star, sir?" Is she wearing a bra under that blouse? It's a toss-up. I tell her I don't mind if I do. As she walks away, I check out her pear-shaped ass.

"Doin' some window-shopping?" Casey asks.

Busted. "Now why would I do that when I've got the prettiest girl in the joint sitting across from me?"

"Hmph," she says, but smiles. Nice save, Mr. Smooth Talker.

And I'm not the only one checking out Xan. Casey's teacher and her pal are following her movements across the floor, too. Does my mother do that? Check out women? Okay, Andrew, knock it off. Don't even go there.

Casey-Lee's looking at my meal. "Those ravioli are drowning," she says. "Could they *put* any more of that glop on them?" To appease her, I pick up my fork and start scraping away some of my Alfredo sauce. Only, when I look up to see if she's registering the gesture, she's picking through her salad. Looking to ferret out anchovies-in-hiding is what I'm guessing.

"Speaking of weddings, my mother's is this coming weekend," I say.

She looks right over at her teacher and her friend. So she *is* making the connection. "I know it is. You never did say whether you wanted me to order them the Steuben glass figurines or that bud vase from Tiffany's, and I had to send them *some*thing. I went with the vase."

"Great. Thanks for doing that. Did you use my charge card?"

"No, I had to use mine. The Web site said they needed some other four-digit security number on top of the long one, and you didn't write that down. Or the expiration date either."

"Oh, jeeze. Sorry about that. I'll write you a check. How much was it?"

"With express shipping, it came to two ninety-five."

"Three hundred bucks for a bud vase?"

"It's from Tiffany's, Andrew. What did you want me to do? Send them something from Target?"

"No, no. I just didn't figure it would cost—"

"And then I didn't know if I was supposed to send it to that New York address or the Connecticut one. I tried calling you to find out, but you didn't answer your cell phone."

"Well, like I said. We were crazy busy today."

"And then, while I was calling, waiting for you to pick up, the screen timed out and I had to start all over again. I ended up sending it to your-all's old house in Connecticut. Isn't that where the wedding's at?"

"No, it's at some inn. But that's where my mother and sisters are staying, so it's fine. She'll get it. Thanks again."

"You're welcome. Have you talked to your sisters lately?"

"Spoke to Ariane last night, yeah." I think about what she told me during that call: artificial insemination, single motherhood. I haven't mentioned it to Casey-Lee yet. I'm still trying to wrap *my* head around it. "She's visiting my dad for a few days. He's staying up on Cape Cod—the town where we used to go for vacation when we were kids."

"Cape Cod's different towns?"

"Yeah. Ari says my other sister's going up there, too. Wants to surprise my dad. Then on Friday, they'll head down to Connecticut for the wedding."

"Even your *father*?"

"No, he's taking a pass." Am I taking one, too, like she thinks? Or am I going? Not deciding's making me a little nuts.

"Well, I should hope so. Why would he put himself through that? I just feel sorry for your poor sisters. Good Lord, they've got to witness their mother marrying someone of her own sex? Going against nature like that? It's weird." I can feel myself tense. Because yeah, it is weird, but she doesn't need to beat it into the ground. She starts fiddling with her salad again, picking out the croutons and piling them on one of those extra napkins.

"What's the matter?" *Now*, I feel like adding.

"They're stale," she says. "These things must be older than Methuselah."

Xan comes back with my new beer. "How is everything?" she asks. Fine, I tell her. Great.

"Yeah, like I said, I love that dish. Enjoy." This time I'm careful not to watch her go.

We eat. Neither of us says much, except when Casey mentions again that she still has her lesson to plan, those bulletin board letters to cut out. And now, on top of that, she's got to go online and find out how to take a white wine stain out of silk. "Tell you what," I say. "When we get back to your house, you can work on your lesson and I'll cut out your letters for you." She says thanks but no thanks. That the last time I helped her cut stuff out, I didn't stay on the lines. "Because I'm left-handed and all's you had was right-handed scissors."

"That's because no one in our family is left-handed," she says. "I'd bring home a pair of the left-handed ones from my classroom if I thought you could stick those big sausage fingers of yours through the holes." I can't even believe we're having a conversation about scissors.

When Xan returns to clear our plates, she's got dessert menus. I'm about to tell her no thanks, just the check, but Casey-Lee asks her how the tiramisu is. Delicious, Xan tells her. The best dessert on the menu. Casey says, okay, she'll have that. "Good choice. How about you, sir?"

"Nothing, thanks. Just the check."

"Coffee, maybe? A cappuccino?"

"No, but you know what? If she's having dessert, why don't you bring me a Captain and Coke?"

"Sure thing. Oh, and the bar's running a special this week. You can get a double shot for just a dollar more."

"Can't pass up a bargain like that," I tell her. Maybe Captain Morgan can help me get through the rest of this damned meal.

When the bill comes, Casey's gone off to the ladies' room. I pay in cash and add an extra twenty to the tip because of the way Casey treated her when she spilled that little bit of wine. Xan swings back by and grabs the folder. "Any change?" I tell her no, we're good. When I see Casey coming back, I chug the rest of my drink and stand.

"Ready to go?" I ask. She nods and we head for the door. But as we pass by that old teacher of hers, she reaches out and touches Casey's arm. "Well, my word, is that Casey-Lee Commerford all grown up?"

"Oh, Miss Bascomb!" Casey says, fake surprised. "Nice to see you again. This is Andrew, my fiancé." As proof, she holds up her ring.

"Ooh, that's purty," Miss Bascomb says. "This here's my friend, Margaret." We exchange glad-to-meet-yous. When Miss Bascomb asks me where I'm from, I tell her Connecticut.

"Enemy country," her friend says. She points to the Tennessee Lady Volunteers logo on her orange T-shirt. Until then, I'd assumed they were both wearing U.T. Longhorns shirts. "That little Eyetalian coach you got up there is a burr in poor Pat Summitt's saddle, but y'all got some damn good players. Hate to say it, but Maya Moore's gonna pay off big time for y'all."

"Her and her women's basketball," Miss Bascomb says. "She's a fanatic. So when's the wedding, you two?"

November, Casey tells her.

"Not this coming one," I say. "The following November."

"Well, I'll be. And what are you doing with yourself these days, Casey-Lee?" She tells her she's teaching kindergarten. "Oh, that must be fun. They're such cutie pies at that age. Margaret was an elementary school teacher, too."

"Got out two years ago," Margaret adds. "Exchanged the classroom for the golf course. I miss my third graders, but not all the b.s. bureaucracy of those last years. All that state-testing and such. I feel sorry for you young teachers. It's not like the good ole days." Come on, Casey, I think. The woman's speaking to you. The least you could do is have the courtesy to look at her. They're nice, these two.

Margaret gives up on Casey and turns back to me. "Played basketball myself when I was in college. Course, that was back in the stone age when they'd only let us dribble it in from half-court because we were such delicate flowers."

"Ha!" Miss Bascomb says.

"Yeah, I didn't realize that until I went to the Basketball Hall of Fame," I tell her. "Hard to believe now, huh?"

"Thank God for Title Nine. That's all *I* can say. The Basketball Hall of Fame's up in Massachusetts, idn't it?" I nod. "I'd like to get up there and see it myself if I could ever get this stick-in-the-mud here to take a trip."

"I'm a homebody," Miss Bascomb says.

"Well, we gotta go," Casey says. "Nice to see you again, Miss Bascomb."

"Nice to see you as well. You two sure make a handsome couple, I'll tell you that much."

I smile and nod at her. "Thank you, ma'am," Casey says. "Bye-bye now."

At the door, she notes that she called us a *handsome* couple, instead of a nice-looking one. "Like we're two men." Last Sunday at family dinner, her father said that in his "humble opinion," signing the Defense of Marriage Act into law was just about the only useful thing Clinton ever did during his two terms as president. "Far as I know, the Book of Genesis didn't mention anything about Adam and *Steve*." We all chuckled, as if he'd just made it up instead of that it's stuck on every other back bumper around here.

"Did you notice those matching rings on their fingers?" Casey says. "What does that tell you?"

"I don't know. That they went shopping together? That they like the same kind of jewelry?"

"Oh, yeah. Sure." She laughs that laugh of hers—the one I used to think sounded so pretty. Sounds snarky now. Casey's told me more than once that she admires Sarah Palin's grit. "Wait'll I tell Janisse."

"And maybe you should call the *National Enquirer* while you're at it. Give 'em a scoop. They like to out the gays, don't they?"

She says she doesn't know—that she never reads those trashy papers. Which is bull. Last time we were waiting in line at the grocery store, she was thumbing through one of them, tickled to death. Looking at the "gotcha" pictures of movie stars at the beach, caught with their cellulite and potbellies showing. "Eww," she kept saying. "Eww." We walk out into the parking lot, me almost fed up enough to accuse her of being homophobic like her father. But that'd be the liquor talking, I suspect. I keep my mouth shut.

At the car, she asks me if I'm okay to drive. Says she wouldn't feel comfortable operating my car, but she will if she has to. "I'm fine," I tell her. "I only had a couple of beers and a cocktail."

"Two cocktails," she says. "That Captain and Coke was two drinks in one." We get in. I start her up and back out of the space. "Put your seat belt on," she says. "Are you *sure* you're okay to drive?" I answer her by not answering. Was she always this naggy? No, this is something more recent. Back-to-school stress, probably. Wedding planning. Or maybe it's previews of coming attractions. Maybe now that she's got that ring on her finger, she feels she can yank a little harder on the leash. I reach down, buckle my belt. Look over at her to see if she's satisfied. And when I look up again, I just miss the black Escalade that's pulling into the parking lot. "See?" she says. "But go ahead, Andrew. Get yourself a DUI if that's what you want."

It comes out as shouting. "Jesus fucking Christ, stop harping at me!"

"And you stop using the Good Lord's name in vain!" she shouts back.

She's right about that at least. Sorry, Lord. That was just a slip. I'm thankful for all Your blessings. But Casey's not finished. "Whatever the bug is that crawled up your backside tonight, it's not *my* fault."

"Look who's talking crude now," I shoot back. "And for your information, *you're* the one who's got the bug up your ass. 'I hate chain restaurants. I better e-mail you a reminder because you're too irresponsible to get there on time by yourself. Wear your uniform, not your civvies.' You didn't give it a rest that whole damned meal. And it's not like I'm *that* irresponsible."

"I didn't say you were irresponsible, Andrew."

"Not in so many words, but that's what you meant."

"Oh, hush up."

"No, *you* hush up." It's the kind of exchange I used to have with my kid sister. Maybe I *will* get on that plane and go to the wedding this weekend. That'd fix her.

But a mile's worth of silence later, she says she guesses she *is* kind of "off," tonight. That that open house coming up at her school's got her in a tizzy. "I'm sorry," she says. I mumble a knee-jerk apology, too.

When we get back to her parents' place, I pull into their circular drive. Her mom's Mercedes is there but not Daddy's Beemer. "Your parents out?"

"Uh-huh. They're at Little Branch's school for a sports boosters meeting. You want to come in?" When I tell her I better get going and let her get her work done, she says she wants me to come in. "Please, hon? I don't want us to leave things like this." So I cut the engine. Get out and go around to her side and open her door. Sometimes when we're alone in there, she lets me get a little frisky with her. One time, after we'd had an argument and made up, she even unzipped my fly and went down on me. She's done that a couple of other times, too. I guess in Casey's mind a b.j. doesn't count as premarital sex. That it's just a service she's willing to provide. Guess I've got Bill and Monica to thank for that. So there's another of Clinton's accomplishments besides the Defense of Marriage thing, Daddy. Not that it's all that pleasurable: her head pumping up and down like the cylinder of a car going eighty miles an hour, box of tissues at the ready next to her knee.

"I'm going upstairs to change," she says. "Be right down."

"Yeah, okay."

She'd go ape shit if she knew I'd gone to that place with LeRoy a couple of times. What was it called? The Pink something. Pink Flamingo? The first time we drove out there, I stayed in front and watched the pole dancers while he went in the back with that bleached blonde with the fake torpedo tits. But the second time, I succumbed. Rented myself some time with that girl Claudine who talked dirty while she was riding me bucking-bronco style, one arm up in the air, the other holding onto my hip. I start stirring a little just thinking about it. No big surprise. Three double shifts in the last ten days. By the time I get back to the barracks, I've been too whipped to go into a stall and give myself some relief. At least I got some shut-eye this afternoon. Which is probably why, despite that fiasco of a meal, I'm feeling horny for her. Wanting one of her put-him-out-of-his-misery blow jobs . . .

Last time me and him went to that place—the Pink *Lady*, that's what it's called—when we got out to his car afterward, LeRoy goes, "Hooey, I got my pipes cleaned out *real* good tonight. That gal oughta work for Roto-Rooter. How 'bout you?" When I told him I wasn't the kiss-and-tell type, he'd laughed. Produced a joint, lit it up, and took a hit. "Nah, I'll pass," I'd said when he held it out to me. I was already feeling calm and mellow after that workout with Claudine. Dozed a little on our way back, even. The guilt came later. . . .

I'd ask LeRoy to be an usher if I thought he'd get the Commerford family seal of approval, which I know he wouldn't. "Hillbilly trailer trash" was Casey's verdict that time the three of us went bowling. She'd taken offense at the profanity he used whenever he got a pin-split or a gutter ball, which was plenty. Even with the way she lobs the ball, Casey beat him two strings out of three. She'd gotten *really* pissed when he started rating some of the other women at the alley from one to ten. "He'd better not ever rate *me*," she'd said on the phone later that night. Which, the next day on the ward, was exactly what he'd done. "How'd an ugly sumbitch like you ever snag a fox like her?" he'd kidded me in that West Virginia drawl of his. "That purty lil thing's a tin outa tin, you lucky fuck. I bet she's a she-devil in the sack." I'd smiled, told him I had no complaints. That's a laugh. I'm probably the only guy left in the state of Texas that's still waiting for the wedding night to tap his girlfriend. So that, when she says "I do," she'll still be a virgin. Technically, that is. I've gone down on her a few times, too, without hearing any objections.

When she comes downstairs again, she's got her dress slung over her arm. We go into their family room. Casey sits cross-legged on the couch and starts cutting out her paper letters. I'm given an assignment, too: get on Google and find out how to remove wine stains from silk. "Says here cold water and salt. You wet it a little and then rub salt into it."

"Salt? Are you sure that's for silk?"

No, it's for burlap. "Uh-huh."

She gets up and grabs the dress. "Okay, come on."

In the kitchen, she's at the counter treating the stain according to my directions with a kind of . . . how would you describe it? Delicate intensity? I come up behind her. Reach under her T-shirt and up to her braless breasts. Cup them, move against her a little, and then a little more. Feel myself rising and bend my knees so that it's between her butt cheeks. She lets me for several seconds, then turns around. "Andrew, now quit."

"Why? Don't you like it?"

"I like it fine, but you're distracting me. And besides, my parents and my little brother could walk in here any minute. Why don't you go into Daddy's den and watch TV or something? I think there's a Rangers game on."

The Rangers: I've been stationed here for almost two years now without ever getting into that team. Still, I head down the hall to Big Branch's man cave. Flop down on one of those oversize leather couches in there and scan the room: big-ass cherrywood bar, big-screen TV. Deer head on the wall, and next to it that stuffed and mounted marlin he's always bragging about having caught down in Key West. My eyes move to their family portrait, a museum-size oil painting that Casey's told me some artist made of them from a professional photograph. Big Branch sits in his red leather chair, wearing a tan suit with Western-trimmed lapels, those custom-made cowboy boots that he said he paid six hundred bucks for. A teenage Casey-Lee and her mom, in gowns, stand on either side of him. Little Branch, a chubby kid in a crew cut and string tie, is down on one knee in front of his dad. God, I hate that kid. Thinks his shit doesn't stink now that he's turned into a no-neck high school fullback. I recall the Sunday dinner a few weeks back after we'd all gone to church together—the one when Big Daddy made that crack about Adam and Steve. Little Branch had just come back from football camp and most of the conversation revolved around that. Then Big Branch turned to me, as if it dawned on him that I existed, too. "You play sports in high school, son?"

"Yes, sir. I was a runner. Cross-country in the fall, track in the spring. And I wrestled in the wintertime."

"Wrestling, huh? That so?" he says, more polite than interested.

Casey-Lee tells him I qualified for the state meets in high school three years out of four. And then that dipshit brother of hers chimes in. "At my school, the guys that go out for track are all a bunch of pussies."

"Branch Commerford Junior!" Erlene says. "You mind your mouth."

Big Branch points his fork at him, a chunk of meat stuck to it. "Your Mama's right, sonny boy. You'd best remember you're at the dinner table, not in the locker room." But I catch the smirk before he turns to his wife. "This is a fine dinner you've put on the table, Mama. If there's another woman in the great state of Texas that can roast a chicken as good as Erlene Commerford, I'd like to know who she is." Actually, I made states *four* times out of four. Only the third freshman in our school who'd ever done that.

Staring at that oversize family portrait, I try and picture myself in it: a Chinese-Italian-Irish mongrel among these blue-blooded Texans. It's a stretch. I picture our wedding day, me looking out at Casey coming down the aisle with her dad, a picture-perfect bride. Full pews on her side and half-empty ones on mine. I picture our reception at that big, fancy hotel ballroom they've booked, everyone chatting and drinking, doing the Texas two-step and the Cotton-Eyed Joe. Having a grand old time, except for my family, huddled together at a table, watching everyone. Why'd she say yes that first time I asked her out? Was it God's plan like she said, or was she just on the rebound? Rebelling against her father by dating a guy he *wouldn't* have picked out for her? A blue state northerner? A nurse? . . . And why, if I'm the one she wants, is she trying to change me into someone I'm not? A husband who'll order for her in restaurants and adopt the Commerford family values? Someone who'll belong in that picture up there? . . . Does she love me? She says she does. And I love her, too. Enough to spend the rest of my life with her? Shit, do I even know what love is anymore? I thought my parents' marriage was rock solid until. . . .

I turn on the TV to get my mind off all this heavy-duty shit. Find that Rangers game. Watch a little of it with the sound turned down. I'm bored and keyed-up both. First she wants me to come in with her. Then she wants me to sit in here by myself. I look down at the coffee table book in front of me. *Frederic Remington: The Complete Prints*. Look over at that brass Remington sculpture sitting on Daddy's bar: a broncobuster, one hand on his bucking horse, the other up in the air. I start thinking again about that hooker at the Pink Lady. Her saying those filthy things while I was fucking her. I look over my shoulder to make sure the coast is clear, then put my hand between my legs. Make myself hard. Sitting here in Daddy's den, it's as much about defiance as it is about pleasure. But it's too risky. I get up and head for their downstairs bathroom.

Go in and lock the door. Look around at the gleaming white fixtures, the blood-red walls. There's a red orchid blooming on the windowsill, the same color as those walls and the matching towels. Above the towel rack, there's a picture of the Last Supper, Jesus looking like the lead singer of Pearl Jam. It's not the Son of God watching me, I tell myself. It's only Eddie Vedder. I close my eyes, unzip. Start stroking myself to my memory of that night at the Pink Lady. But I was weak that night. Gave into temptation. Whoring's a sin. So I replace Claudine with Casey-Lee: the way she looked that time standing there in her black bra and black panties when I walked in on her. Walked over and unhooked her bra. Put my mouth to her breasts. . . . But then I see her at the Olive Garden tonight, complaining, hitching her hair behind her ear. I want to keep feeling good. Want to finish. So I put that waitress we had in Casey's black underwear. "Xan," I whisper. *Thou shalt not covet thy neighbor's wife.* But there was no wedding ring on her finger. There's no husband. And she wants it as much as I do. Wants to spill wine on me and lick it off. When she takes off her bra for me, her beautiful brown breasts spill out. I slide her panties down. Reach out and caress her there. Feel her warm, wet pussy.

But when I open my eyes, there I am in the mirror over the sink, having sex with just myself. And there's Jesus on the wall behind me, looking not like Eddie anymore. Looking sad and disappointed because He knows Judas is going to betray Him. That *I'm* betraying Him, too, doing what I'm doing. And man, if that's not a buzz kill. What's Jesus doing in the bathroom, anyway? And what the fuck am *I* doing? . . . *Two women marrying each other? It's unnatural*, she'd said before. Well, what's so natural about her out there and me in here, jacking off with the door locked? Limp now, I zip and buckle back up. Unlock the door and head back to the kitchen.

She's at the computer. Does she think I was lying to her? That I made up those instructions? "I told you exactly what it said to do," I tell her. "I checked two different Web sites."

"I treated it already," she says. "I'm on Facebook."

"Facebook? I thought you had all that work to do?"

"I do. I'm just sending Janisse a quick message about seeing Miss Bascomb and her 'friend.' I have to tell her she was right all along. She's going to die laughing."

And that's when I know, beyond a doubt, that I *don't* love her enough. I tell her I need for her to turn around and look at me, and when she does, I say, "I've changed my mind."

"About what?"

"Marrying you. I'm sorry. I can't go through with it. I'm never going to fit into that picture."

"*What* picture? What are you talking about?"

"No matter what else she is, she's my mother. I can't just—"

"Yes, you *are* going to marry me! I'm wearing your *ring*! You're going to be my *husband*!"

The next several minutes are bad. Her sobbing, following me through the house as I head toward their front door, pulling on my arm so that I'll stay and talk some more. So that she can talk me back into it. "Can we at least pray on it before you go?" she pleads. "Would you please just get on your knees and pray with me, Andrew? Maybe

the Lord will take away your confusion." I tell her I'm not confused—
that I was, but now I'm not anymore. "Please, Andrew. Please don't
humiliate me like this. What am I supposed to tell everyone?"

"I don't know," I say. "I'm sorry. I don't want to hurt you, but I just
can't do it. I would if I could, but I can't."

"Yes, you can. Of course you can, Andrew. The save-the-date cards
are already back from the printer's. What am I supposed to say to my
family and my friends? What about all those places where we made
down payments?"

"I'll pay you back," I tell her.

"I don't want you to pay me back! I want you to keep the promise
you made to me! You have to!"

She follows me outside, pulling on me some more. If I don't get out
of here, get away from her, my head's going to explode. "Can you just
think about it for a day? What about Saturday night? Daddy's counting on us being there. Mommy said the Halbachs are bringing us an
engagement present."

"I can't," I keep saying. "I'm sorry."

"Can you please just go to the prayer breakfast on Saturday morning then? Maybe being in that big room with all those prayerful
people—"

"I won't be here on Saturday," I tell her. "She's my mother, Casey. I
need to see my family."

"Is this about her wedding? Because if you need to go to it, I'll go
with you. We can go together. You still have those plane tickets, don't
you? Let me go with you, Andrew."

I shake my head. Get in the car and start it. "Take your hand off
the handle," I tell her. "I don't want you to get hurt."

"Well, it's too late for that!" she screams. "And I'm not giving you
your ring back, either! You gave it to me! It's mine!"

"I don't want it back. Now stand away from the car." And when I
begin moving it forward, she finally does.

"Please, Andrew! Please don't go!"

Gunning out of the driveway and onto the road, I shoot past Erlene, Big Branch, and Little Branch coming home. I feel relieved to

be rid of them all, their daughter included. Feel, for the first time in a long time, like I've slipped that leash and can breathe again. . . .

Driving back to the barracks, I pray. Help me, Lord. Help her, too. Show her Your precious mercy. Thank you, Jesus, for all your blessings. Forgive me my sins. Show me the way so that I may do Your will. Forgive me my trespasses, Jesus. Please forgive me and help her to forgive me, too.

After I'm prayed out, I put on the radio. They're playing something off of that Rage Against the Machine CD I bought back in high school. I crank up the volume and let the bass shake the car. Because yeah, I'm sorry for what I had to do. But I'm pissed as hell, too. Furious enough to hurt someone. Nobody back at the barracks had better cross me or give me shit, because the way I'm feeling, I'll take their fuckin' head off, so help me god!

Chapter Sixteen

Orion Oh

When we get to Long Nook, there are only three other cars in the lot. We walk the path to the top of the dune and look out on the blue sky, the rolling gray-green sea below us. "Oh, my god, I forgot how beautiful it is here," Ariane says. "But I can see what you mean about the erosion."

"It's high tide, or just about," I tell her. "Yesterday when I ran here, a wave came in and soaked my sneakers. So I took them off and—"

"Daddy, look!" she says. I follow her pointing finger to the horizon where a whale is spouting. We continue to stare out there for another minute or more, and the whale obliges us—this time with a beautiful breach.

The beach below is nearly empty. I jump the two-foot drop, then take her hand and help her down. We walk single file down the foot-path that beachgoers have trampled into the dune. At the bottom, we trudge a couple hundred feet then drop our stuff. I spread the blanket, unfold the chairs. We put on sunblock and sit, smiling, looking out at the rolling surf. "You chilly?"

"A little," she says. "It's windy here."

"Then here you go," I say, reaching into the knapsack for the sweat-shirt I've brought for her. I toss it to her and she puts it on.

"Much better," she says. She points to the four or five people way down the beach. "The nudies?" she asks.

"Yup. They still camp out down there. I see them in their glory when I run that way."

She laughs. "One time? When we were kids? I walked down there looking for sand dollars, and when I realized no one was wearing bathing suits, I was *shocked*. But the next day, I walked down there again. And the day after that. I'd never seen grown men naked before, and I was fascinated."

I laugh. "Remember how your brother used to call you Saint Ariane? I guess you weren't so saintly after all."

"No, I wasn't. This one time Marissa started whining about going with me to find sand dollars, too, and you or Mama said I had to take her. I always tried to be cool about looking, but she sure wasn't. I had to tell her to stop gawking. Then I had to bribe her not to tell you guys about what we saw."

"Bribe her with what?"

"Sand dollars."

"Sex Ed 101, huh?" I said. "And all this time, I thought it was shells you were interested in. But you already knew some stuff, right? I remember how nervous your mother was before you and she had 'the talk.' She wanted me to do it, but I said no—that I'd talk to Andrew and she could talk to you."

"Yeah, and you know what the first thing she said was? That I should never, ever let a boy touch me below the waist. Or go someplace alone with a boy or a man because they couldn't be trusted."

"God, that's weird. You sure she put it that way?"

"Oh, yeah."

"Well, she couldn't have scared you too much if you went on those sand dollar expeditions."

"Yeah, but that was later. By then, I'd found out all kinds of other interesting things about sex from my girlfriends. When Mama and I had 'the talk' and she started telling me how women bleed every month, I was terrified. I got mixed up and thought that if a male looked at you with sex on his mind, it would happen spontaneously. Like those holy statues you'd hear about."

"Stigmata instead of menstruation, huh? Good thing she stopped making you guys go to church with her then. You probably would have followed the nuns out and disappeared into the convent."

She laughs. Gets up and goes down to the water. I watch her shield her eyes with her hand, stare out at the horizon. Looking for that whale again, probably. She starts playing that game she used to do as a kid—backing up as the surf comes in so the water can't catch her feet. Seeing her doing that makes me happy. Whoops, one of those waves just tagged her.

When she comes back to the blanket, I ask her if she wants a snack. "Got a couple of bananas in my duffel. And some crackers." She says okay, she'll try a banana. I'm pleased when she eats over half of it.

"What should I do with the peel?" she asks.

"Just bury it in the sand. It's biodegradable. You thirsty? I've got waters, ginger ale." She shakes her head. Her doctor wants her to keep hydrating, she says, but she doesn't want to have to go in the water to pee. She suggests we try that walk now. "Okay, sure. Just tell me when you want to turn around." I get up, put on my sunglasses. "Which way, boss? Toward the nudies or not?"

"Not," she says, and we start out.

After we've walked a while, she asks me what I've found out about my Chinese family. "Well, let's see. They were peasant farmers in the south—a village called Guangnan. I looked it up on a map; it's not too far from the Vietnamese border. That cousin I've been communicating with says her grandfather came over here first. Entered the country in your neck of the woods, actually. San Francisco. Just made it, I guess."

"What do you mean?"

"Well, apparently Chinese immigration was unrestricted in the years when the railroad lines were being built. They needed the labor. But once they were done, California started grumbling about all those pigtailed heathens polluting the good old American gene pool. So Congress shut the door on them. Passed something called the Chinese Exclusion Act. Your great-grandfather had to come here by way of Canada."

"So much for 'Give us your tired and hungry, your huddled masses yearning to breathe free,'" Ariane says.

"Yeah, well, that melting pot stuff was always more about what this country *wanted* to believe about itself than the way people really felt. But anyway, my cousin says her grandfather had two families, one here and another back in the homeland."

"He was a bigamist?"

"I guess. Apparently, it was a pretty common practice back then. 'Split-household' families, they called them. According to Ellen, his wife over there had only produced daughters, but his concubine here had had a son, so that gave her preferred status."

"Oh, you men," Ari says, shaking her head. "Plant your seed wherever and then wave good-bye." It's ironic that she'd put it that way, given how she got pregnant. Ironic, too, because that's what my father did. But I'm not going there with either of those thoughts.

"Ellen's got some old letters and pictures that she's going to send me after she gets them scanned. She's had the letters translated."

"From what? Mandarin?"

"Cantonese, more likely. Mandarin was the language of the upper classes. But it's the photographs that I really want to see. She says there's one of your great-grandfather taken shortly after he arrived, when he was in his late teens or early twenties."

"Cool," she says. Shakes her head. "The Chinese Exclusion Act. Boy, racism was right out in the open back then, huh? How about when you were a kid? Did you ever experience any of that anti-Chinese prejudice?"

"Here and there. From other kids in school, mostly. Slant-eyes, Charlie Chan. Stuff like that. One time I was playing basketball at the playground, and when I blocked another kid's shot, he called me a 'fucking gook.'"

"And you don't even look very Chinese. Did you call him on it?"

"Not verbally. But when I went for a layup a few minutes later, I threw him an elbow. Gave him a bloody nose that, to tell you the truth, I'm still kind of proud of. How about you? Ever on the receiving end of that kind of stuff."

She says the only thing she can think of was one time in high school when she was trying out for the math team. "Just before they passed out the tests, this boy told me I had an unfair advantage because I was Asian. Wayne Ogilvie, his name was."

"How did he even know you were?"

"Because of those registration forms we had to fill out at the beginning of every school year, where you had to put what nationalities you were. He sat in front of me in homeroom, and when we passed them in, he had looked at mine. He was such a pain, that kid."

"You made that math team, didn't you?"

"And Wayne Ogilvie didn't." She shoots me a mischievous look. "I guess you could say I threw him an elbow with my test score."

"Atta girl. Hey, what do you say we head back to the blankets? I don't want you to overdo it." She nods. Says she's getting kind of thirsty, that maybe she'll have one of those waters I brought after all.

"Good. Your doctor's right about keeping yourself hydrated. And hey, you wouldn't be the first one who's ever peed in the ocean."

When we're back at the blanket, I decide to go in for a swim. "Watch out for the sharks," Ari says. I bare my teeth and tell her *they* better watch out for *me*. "I'm serious Daddy. Be careful."

"Yes, ma'am."

The water is gorgeous. Cleansing. Whenever a wave comes, I stick my head into it and let it pass over me. Floating on my back, I think about becoming a grandfather. About my grandfather, my absentee father. I really want to see that picture she's going to send. . . .

When I come out, I see that she's fallen asleep. I watch her for a while. When the kids were little and I'd come home late from work, I used to love to go into their rooms and watch them while they were sleeping. Then I'd come back out and have to listen to Annie's complaints about them: who'd fought with whom that day, who'd spilt their milk at lunch, which one she'd had to put on the time-out chair. One time, to short-circuit her bitching, I asked her if she ever enjoyed her time with the kids, or if it was just torture all day long. She'd poked out her bottom lip and run off to our bedroom to cry. Wouldn't talk to me for the rest of that night, wouldn't accept my apology. The ice didn't start to melt until the end of the week when I'd handed her the flowers I'd bought on my way home from work and got her to smile. But that night in bed, I remember, when I reached for her in anticipation of some makeup sex, she kicked me, hard, and jumped out of our bed. And when one of the kids called for her as she was hurrying down the hall, she'd screamed, "Shut up! Shut up! Shut up!" Andrew, I guess it was; he was the one who sometimes suffered those nighttime fears.

Daddy, do you think Mama was a good mother? . . .

Ariane's out for the next hour or so. Doesn't wake up until the sun starts sinking behind the dune. It's cooler now in the shade. "Have a good nap?" I ask her when she stirs, opens her eyes.

"Mmm. But it feels cold now. You want to go?"

When I pull in at Viveca's, there's a van parked in the driveway. The sign on the side says LOWER CAPE CLEANERS. A guy and a girl get out—midtwenties, maybe. Well-scrubbed, tanned and fit. "Cleaning service," the guy says.

"Oh, okay. Sorry to keep you waiting. I didn't expect you."

"No problem. We just got here." He explains that the realty company hires them on behalf of the owners. They come in once a week.

"Oh. Jeeze, I've been here for the last two. Did I miss you?"

He shakes his head. "We were away. Family stuff." He looks over at the girl. "This is my sister." I introduce myself and my daughter. "Glad to meet you," they both say. Tell us their names. "Well, we'd better get to work," the guy says. They open up the back of their van, take out cleaning supplies, an upright vacuum cleaner. When I tell him there's one in the front hall closet, he says they like to use their own. "The industrial vacs pick up way better."

"Okay. Right. Well, give us a minute and we'll get out of your way. We'll be out on the deck if you need anything."

"No problem."

Inside at the sink, I get us drinks. A ginger ale for Ariane, a vodka and tonic for myself. Ari whispers that she was looking forward to a shower. "There's one outside in the back," I say. "But you can look down on it from the dining room window." She glances at the cleaning guy and says she'll wait.

Out on the deck, with the vacuum cleaner droning away inside, we sip our drinks. The breeze ruffles the leaves on the trees, exposing their silver undersides. The clouds are playing peekaboo with the late afternoon sun. I'm about to ask her about dinner when Ariane starts bitching about her brother. "The way he talks, it's like Manhattan is Sodom and Gomorrah. I mean, we've *all* had to process Mama's new lifestyle. But they've been together for almost three years now. Why is he still so *mad* about it?"

I shrug. "He's worried about Marissa, too, you know. Apparently she told him she goes dancing in gay clubs sometimes. Probably just to shock him, if I know your sister. She still doesn't get that God thing he's into now. He thinks New York's Sin City and she thinks Texas turns you into a Jesus freak."

"Yeah, well . . . Marissa did have a little thing with a woman when she moved to New York. One of her acting teachers."

"Really? Well, she's not the first young woman to try a same-sex 'thing,' as you put it." I smile, thinking about something else. "When I was in grad school, I did a practicum at a women's prison. They had a saying down there: straight at the gate, gay for the stay. But Marissa? The girl who used to climb out her bedroom window so she could meet that boy she was so madly in love with? The one who worked at the Dairy Queen. What was that doofus's name?"

"Derek," she says. "God, I forgot about those little rendezvouses. You grounded her and Mama marched her down to Dr. Zahl's office and had her put on birth control. But anyway, Marissa's experiment didn't last very long. She told me sex with a woman was okay, but that she missed cock. Her words, not mine."

"Yeah, well, that's a little too much information for dear old Dad." She turns away, a little embarrassed, I think. The breeze blows the hair away from the nape of her neck and I spot a bug there. But when I reach over to brush it away, I see that it's a small tattoo. A dime-size ladybug. "And when did milady get inked?" I kid her. "Pray tell."

"After Axel broke up with me," she says. "My girlfriend Melanie and I went into San Francisco for dinner. She had just gotten dumped, too, so we both decided to do something a little crazy."

"And fashionable. So many people have tattoos these days, I'm thinking of getting one myself."

She's looking at me as wide-eyed and gullible as ever. "Seriously?"

"Hell, yeah. A skull and crossbones, maybe. And under it, I'll have them put, 'Don't mess with Grandpa.'"

She smiles, rolls her eyes. "Oh, yeah. I'm sure Tracy would love that."

I smile, too, thinking about the tattoos Tracy has: a little butterfly above her left breast, a starfish at the small of her back—both of them highly kissable. I finish my drink, get up off my chair. "I'm going in for a refill. You good?"

"Uh-huh."

Inside, the girl's scouring the kitchen sink and the vacuum's droning upstairs. The house doesn't really need it; I just vaccumed yesterday. But hey, they've got to make a living, too. And it's not like *I'm* paying them. "So how long have you and your brother been in the cleaning business?" I ask her.

"Us? Since our mother got sick. It's really her business, but she's got cancer." I ask her how she's doing. "Better," she says. "But the chemo kind of wipes her out. My brother's taken over the business mostly, but I help him out during the summer. I'm in grad school."

"Really? What are you studying?"

"Business administration."

"You must be getting ready to go back pretty soon, huh?"

"Uh-huh." She goes back to her scouring. Guess she'd rather get her work done than chitchat with the clientele. Can't blame her for that.

I go a little easier on the vodka this time. I'm starting to get a nice little glow from the first one. But then I hear Ari's question again. *Daddy? Do you think Mama was a good mother?* I change my mind. Tip the bottle and pour myself a little more.

Back outside, I ask her again why she was asking about her mother's parenting. "Oh," she says. "I don't know. No reason, really."

No? Then why can't she look at me? I wait.

"It's just . . . the way she used to go off on Andrew sometimes."

"Meaning?"

"The way she'd get so mad at him. Hit him."

"Hit him? As in, give him a swat on the tush, or we'd better call Child Protective Services?" I meant it as a joke, but she's not smiling.

"She just . . . She got abusive sometimes. Not with me or Marissa. Just with him."

"Abusive? That's a little strong, don't you think?"

She shakes her head. "She was different when you were at work, Daddy. Not all the time, just sometimes. She'd get furious at something he did. Or didn't do. And then . . ." I stand there, waiting for her to finish. She takes a sip of her soda. Looks out at the trees instead of at me. "I don't really want to go into it. Okay?"

But no, it's not okay. "You're talking about her yelling at him mostly, right? Verbal abuse, not physical. Except for a slap here and there."

She shakes her head. When she looks back at me, she's in tears.

"Then how come Andy never said anything?"

"Because he used to cover for her. You'd come home and ask about some bruise he got and he'd say he fell down or something. Or bumped into something. That he was being clumsy."

"Well, he *was* pretty clumsy." No smile, no nod in agreement. "Right?"

"Daddy, please. Why does it even matter now?"

"I mean, granted, she may have had her faults, but it's not like she was a child abuser. Was she?" She looks at me but doesn't answer. "*Was* she?"

"Not with Rissa or me."

"Look, kiddo. I'm a trained psychologist. If something like that was going on in my own home, don't you think I would have picked up on it? Whether he was 'covering for her,' as you put it, or not. I would have read the signs. Or one of you would have come to me. That's the pattern with kids in an abusive situation. If one parent is dangerous—*physically* dangerous, I mean, not just hotheaded—the kids may try to hide it for a while, but eventually they disclose it to the 'safe' parent."

"No, you're right. Forget I even said anything. I was just being stupid."

"Stupid? You? No way. But I bet I know where this is coming from. You're getting ready to be a parent yourself, so naturally you're analyzing everything about *your* parents. Deciding what you want to recreate in your relationship with your own child, and what you want to do differently."

"Yeah, but . . . that's what I'm afraid of."

"Meaning?"

"What if I lose control? Hit *my* child? Don't kids who grow up in abusive homes become abusers themselves?"

"Sometimes. But you *didn't* grow up in an abusive home. Look, your body's changing. It's probably just your maternal hormones kicking up—sending you into overdrive so that you start worrying about all the what-ifs that are never even going to happen. And sure, your mother might have swatted him once or twice when he was bugging her. God knows, he was good at *that*. But it's not like she was . . . dangerous."

"Daddy, you don't have to defend her. Not from me. And yeah, my hormones probably are—"

"Trust me, honey. If she had been abusive, I would have known." But she's looking at me skeptically. "Okay, you're not convinced. So let's examine it a little more. Give me an example."

She frowns, thinks about it. "Well, one time—"

"Knock knock," someone says. When I look back, there's Tracy standing behind the slider. "Am I interrupting something?" she says. "You both look so serious."

"No, no, come on out," I say, standing. And then to Ariane, "To be continued." Tracy slides open the screen and steps onto the deck. When I ask her if she'd like a drink, she shakes her head.

"I've spent the afternoon analyzing the contents of a twelve-foot basking shark's abdomen. Trust me. I need a shower more than a cocktail. Don't get too close." Turning to Ariane, she asks her how she's feeling.

"Okay, thanks," Ari says. "Daddy's been very solicitous."

"Well, I should hope so. Hey, I went online this morning and looked up morning sickness remedies. Made a list and had Megan, my grad assistant, pick up some stuff that might help. She was pregnant last year and had a go-around with morning sickness, too. So she added a few things that helped her."

"Oh my god, that's so nice of you," Ariane says. She takes the bulging plastic bag that Tracy's holding out to her. Reaches inside and pulls things out one by one. Ginger candies, peppermint tea, Saltines, a box of something called Preggie Pops.

When I ask Tracy what we owe her, she points a finger at me. "Don't even go there, buster," she says. I throw up my hands in surrender. She turns back to Ari. "I've also written down some of the foods they recommend—things that are rich in Vitamin B-6. Fatty fish, baked potato, oatmeal, spinach. Oh, and there's a little bottle of lemon oil in there, too. Megan says during her first three months, certain odors would make her queasy. So she'd sprinkle lemon oil on a handkerchief and keep it in her pocket. When some smell was bothering her, she'd take it out and sniff that instead."

"That's a great idea," Ari says. "Tell her I said thanks."

Again, Tracy declines my offer to get her a drink. Says she really wants to go clean up. "Then come back after you do," I say. "Join us for dinner."

"Not tonight," she says. "I'm teaching that online course, and I've got a bunch of my students' lab reports to get to. I'll take a rain check, though. How about tomorrow night?"

"Sounds good."

"And thank you so much," Ariane says. "I really appreciate it."

"No big deal. I just hope it helps. Okay, I'm out of here."

I walk her back through the house. The cleaning woman's dusting now. When we're out the front door, Tracy says, "My, my, maid service? Some guys really know how to live."

I shrug. "Not my idea. The realtor sent them." We head over to her car.

"Hey, I hope I didn't barge in at the wrong moment back there," she says. "Whatever you two were talking about, it looked heavy-duty."

I shake my head. "Just some old family history." I thank her for helping Ariane. Reach over and kiss her. She gets in her car, starts it and backs up. I wave to her as she drives off.

Back on the deck, Ari's holding her Preggie Pops—reading the back of the box. I ask her about dinner. "We can go out for a bite, or I can run up to P'town, get some groceries and cook us something. Maybe buy some of the things on Tracy's list."

Ariane chooses option number two. "If you don't mind, Daddy."

"Nope. Not at all. Now let's get back to what we were talking about." She shakes her head. Changes the subject to how much she likes Tracy. Okay, message received, but we're not finished with this yet.

Inside the house, my phone goes off. *Love shack, baby love shack, bay-ayy-be-ee.* Ari gives me a quizzical look. "Cell phone," I say. "I should have known better than to have your sister choose my ring tone."

She smiles. "Don't you need to get it?"

"Nope. Whoever it is can leave a message."

But then, another interruption. The cleaning guy's at the screen. "All set," he says. "See you a week from now."

"Okay." I reach into my wallet and pull out two tens for a tip. I grab the register receipt from Tracy's bag of stuff. "Let me jot down my number for you. If you call the night before and let me know when I should expect you, I'll make sure I stick around."

"Will do," he says. He takes the number and stuffs it in his pocket. "All right then. Later." He waves the two tens at me. "Thanks, man."

I wait until I hear their van start up, the tires crunching against the clamshell driveway. But Ari gets up and starts toward the house. Says she's going to take that shower now. "No, wait. Sit down," I tell her. When she does, I pull my chair closer to hers. "Okay, help me out here. You said your mother was abusive toward him. So give me a specific."

"Daddy, please. It's been such a nice day. Can't we just drop it?"

"No."

She sighs, resigned. Struggles to begin. "This one time, Mama and I were making supper and . . ."

"And what?"

"Andrew was sitting on the kitchen stool, okay? And he started bugging her. He wanted to skip supper and go off someplace with Jay Jay. I don't remember where. But Mama said no. And when he asked her why not, she just ignored him. So he got off the stool. Went over to her and said it again: 'Why not?' And instead of just saying something like 'Because I said so' or 'Because I want you home for dinner,' she just kept not answering him. So he *kept* asking her. You know, like goading her. I could tell she was getting madder and madder, but she still wouldn't say anything. So he got even closer. Right up in her face, you know?"

Annie's always hated that. Close talkers, people whispering in her ear: it makes her skittish. "How old were you guys when this happened?"

Sixteen, she says. It was right after she'd gotten her driver's license. "You and Mama wouldn't let Andrew get his until he brought his grades up," she reminds me. "And he was so mean to *me* about it. Like it was *my* fault. If he needed a ride someplace, instead of asking me, he'd *order* me to take him. And when I did, he'd tell me all the way there about what a bad driver I was. How *he* should have been the one who got his license, not me."

"Yeah, okay. Back to the kitchen. He was goading her."

"He just kept repeating it over and over, right into her ear. 'Why not, Mom? Why not? Why can't I?' And then . . . and then . . ." She's shaking. Her breathing's fast and shallow, as if she's back there. "She just snapped."

"Hit him?"

She looks down at her lap. "You know that wooden mallet she used to use to pound out meat if it was tough?"

"Yeah. You're not saying . . . ?"

"She had that mallet in her hand and . . . she went after him with it. He put his hands up over his face to protect himself, but his forehead was . . . She hit him on his forehead. Hard! I heard this sound and . . . It was awful, Daddy. He went staggering across the kitchen. Grabbed onto a chair like he was going to pass out. I was so scared. I thought she had really hurt him. Cracked his skull or something."

For the next several seconds, I'm speechless. "And you're telling me you actually saw this?"

"Yes! I was standing right there!"

It's hard to watch the pain she's in, but I have to know. "Deep breaths," I tell her. She obeys. Calms down a little. "It's okay, Ari. Just get it out, and then you'll be done with it."

"Don't be mad at her, Daddy," she pleads. "She couldn't help it."

"I'm not mad." But I am. I'm furious. She took a weapon to our son and I'm just hearing about it *now*? "What happened after—"

"She reared back and was going to hit him again with it, but I grabbed it away from her. And I was like, 'Stop it, Mama! If you don't stop it, I'm calling Daddy!' When I said that, she just looked at me. Stared at me like . . . like she was coming out of some crazy trance or something. She looked over at Andrew. And when she realized what she'd just done, she . . ."

"What?"

"Dropped to her knees and started . . . *wailing*. It was horrible."

"But your brother was okay? He didn't pass out?"

"No. He was just holding on to that chair and looking at her."

"What about Marissa? Was she there when this happened?"

"In the house, yes, but she didn't see Mama hit him. She came into the kitchen when she heard her crying. I remember her just standing there, staring down at Mama like she was a freak or something. When Andrew and I finally got her up off the floor, she was like, 'Just get away from me! All of you! Leave me alone!' Then she ran upstairs to your bedroom and locked the door."

I can't believe what I've just heard. Don't want to believe it. "And what did you kids do?"

"Andrew left," she says. "Got on his bike and took off."

"Which was the last thing he *should* have done. He could have had a concussion and . . . What about you and Marissa?"

"I finished making dinner. Put it on the table. Mama wouldn't come down, so the two of us ate without saying anything. Did the dishes. Then Andrew came back and he ate. You got home late that night, I remember, and by then things were back to normal, almost like nothing had happened. I was at the kitchen table doing my home-work, and Mama and Marissa were in the den watching TV. I don't remember what Andrew was doing. Probably up in his room, playing his music."

"And none of you said anything to me." She shakes her head. "Did she tell you not to? Threaten you or something?"

"No. Nothing like that. We just . . . I don't even really know why we didn't tell you. When she got like that, I guess we wanted to protect her."

"From *me*? What did you think I was going to do?"

She shrugs. "We *should* have told you. But we felt . . . sorry for her."

"Sorry for *her*? For Christ's sake, Ariane. Your brother was the victim, not your mother."

"I know but . . ."

"If one of you had come to me—if *she* had come to me—I could have done something."

"I think that's what we were afraid of, Daddy. That if you knew, you might send her away someplace and—"

"No! I could have gotten her put on medication. Depakote or something. Insisted she see a therapist. Do you realize what could have happened if she had seriously hurt him? There might have been police involvement, an arrest. How many times did she lash out at him like that?"

"That bad? Just twice, Daddy."

"Twice? What happened the other time?"

"I . . . wasn't home, but Marissa was. She told me they were upstairs, arguing with each other and—"

"Who? Who was arguing?"

"Mama and Andrew. She started chasing him down the hall, whacking him from the back with a hairbrush. And when he got to the top of the stairs, trying to get away from her . . ."

Oh god, don't say it. "Tell me."

"Marissa said she saw her shove him. And he fell. Landed upside down at the bottom of the stairs. And then Mama came to her senses again like the other time. Marissa said she ran down there and . . . and got down on the floor and was just holding him in her lap. Rocking him and telling him over and over that she was sorry. That she loved him and didn't mean it."

"But you didn't see this."

"No. By the time I got home, they had already gone to the emergency room."

"Who? The three of them?"

"No, just Mama and Andrew. That was when Rissa told me what happened. And when they came back, he had a cast. He was okay, though. They'd taken an X-ray. He had just broken his wrist."

"No, *she'd* broken it. What about the doctor who treated him? Didn't he question them about it?"

"Yeah. Andrew said he told the doctor that he tripped and fell down the stairs. That's what he told you, too, I remember. Daddy, it was Andrew who always made us promise not to say anything. He'd say that he had asked for it. Deserved it. Then he'd make up some story about how he'd gotten hurt so you wouldn't question it. He felt sorry for her, Daddy. We all did. It wasn't like she could help it when she got that way. And after, she'd feel terrible about it. Try to make it up to him. To all of us. She'd take us out for ice cream, or over to the mall. She felt so *guilty*."

I shake my head. Tell her it's the classic pattern for an abuser: lash out and then act remorseful. Buy the victim's silence. "Victim*s*," I correct myself. "Plural. Your brother was the primary victim, but you and your sister were victims, too."

She shakes her head. "That makes her sound diabolical, and she *wasn't*. She just . . . she couldn't *help* it. I'm sorry, Daddy. You're right. I was the oldest. I should have gone to you. It's like you said before: you were the safe parent."

"No, your mother was the one who should have . . . And even if she didn't. Goddamnit, I used to treat kids that had come from violent households. Used to read the signs and get them to confront what they'd been through."

She stands. Goes over to the railing and looks out. I get up and go to her. Put my arm around her and tell her how brave she's been for

finally telling me. She leans against me. Apologizes again for keeping
it from me. Says she just didn't know what to do.

"Why would you? You were just a kid. I should have read the signs.
Picked up on *some*thing." She begins to cry. For the next few minutes,
we just stand there, me holding on to her, reassuring her. The poor
kid: it happened ten years ago, but she's still clearly traumatized. All
three of them must be, Andrew most of all. Her target. Her victim.

When we go back in, Ariane heads upstairs. I hear the shower
going. Mix myself another drink and pace through the downstairs
rooms. They're damaged. They've got to be. And Annie just gets away
with it? Causes all this emotional wreckage and then goes off to her
New York life? I think about how pretty she looked that sunny afternoon at the San Gennaro festival, and the day the two of them came
by on their way to the Gardner Museum. My wife, the woman I'd lost
and still longed for. . . . Then I see her going after him with that mallet.
At the bottom of the stairs she's pushed him down, cradling him in
her lap like she's the Virgin Mary in a fucking pietà. Well, guess what,
Annie? The secret's out. You *didn't* get away with it. I don't care about
your hip, highbrow wedding, or the fact that it happened all those
years ago. You're going to account for what you did to them. You and
I are going to have a long-overdue conversation, and it's not going to
be pretty. I go over to the sink and pour the rest of my drink down the
drain. I'm not sure what I'm going to do yet, but getting smashed isn't
going to help. Not with Ari here.

When she comes back down again, she's wet-haired and scrubbed
clean—the way she used to look when she'd get out of the tub as a kid.
She looks drawn, though. Exhausted. When I ask her if she's all right,
she shrugs. I suggest that we get in the car. Drive up to P'town and get
those groceries. "Some steaks, maybe, or some fish. I can fire up the
grill when we get back."

She says no, she'd rather stay here. Be alone for a while. "Maybe I'll
take a walk while you're gone. How far is the bay beach from here?"

"About half a mile. Tell you what. If you're not here when I get
back from the store, I'll drive the car down there and pick you up."

"Okay," she says.

I grab my keys and head for the door. "Oh, and lock up before you leave, okay? Viveca's orders. There's a spare key in one of the kitchen drawers. The one below the silverware drawer, I think—where the other kitchen utensils are. The spatula and nut crackers and stuff." Is there a mallet in there?

She nods. "I might not go, though. I'll see how I feel." I tell her not to overdo it if she feels tired—that we can always walk down there tomorrow. "Yeah," she says.

Driving along Route 6, I replay what she's disclosed. Start to back-pedal a little. Memory's not that reliable. Maybe she's remembering it worse than it actually was. . . . But Jesus Christ, how could I have been so blind? I'd helped everyone else's kids and left my own three in the lurch.

In the supermarket parking lot, a woman grabs the space I was about to turn into. Asshole! I find another spot two cars down. She gets out of her car, I get out of mine. Following her into the store, I glare at her back as if she's guilty of something far greater than taking my parking space. But it's Annie I'm furious with, not this random woman. At the entrance, I grab a basket and go in. It's so brightly lit that it feels like a police interrogation room. *You didn't know your wife was abusing your son? Or did you just look the other way?* The strawberries are achingly red, the piles of bananas insanely green. When I bump into a cart someone's left in the middle of the aisle, I apologize to it. What the fuck, Orion. Get a hold of yourself. A woman in a cap and apron approaches me with a tray of free samples. Says something. But I walk right past her. She might as well be speaking in a foreign language.

It dawns on me that I've forgotten the list Tracy made. What foods did she say? Spinach was on there, I remember. Salmon would be good, I guess. Or chicken. That's it: I'll pick up one of those rotisserie chickens. Make a spinach salad. Buy some frozen veggies and zap them in the microwave. It'll be quick, easy. But after I've gotten these and head to the checkout, I see that the lines are four or five people deep. Six P.M. and they've only got three registers open? Ridiculous! While I wait, I glance at the tabloids' screaming headlines: all those disclosures of celebrities' bad behavior. . . . She *did* single him out more than the girls when they were growing up. I knew that. But he was more challenging, too. Always testing, pushing her buttons. Hey, it wasn't like *I* never lost my temper with him. But still. Physical abuse? Cracking him in the head with a mallet? Pushing him down the stairs? . . .

He's twelve or thirteen, sitting across from me at the dinner table, his wrist in a cast. We're eating the pizza, his favorite, that Annie's picked up on their way back from the hospital. "You must be on a first-name basis with those emergency room doctors by now," I say, nodding at his cast.

He glances over at his mother then looks back at me. "Yeah. What can I tell you, Dad. I'm a spaz."

"What did you say you tripped on?"

"What?"

"You told me you took that tumble because you tripped on something. What was it?"

"I don't remember."

"You don't remember something that happened this afternoon?"

"His sneakers," Marissa volunteers.

"Oh yeah, that's right," he says. "My sneakers. I left them on the stairs."

"Well, don't be in such a hurry next time," I tell him. "And from now on, don't leave your stuff on the stairs. That's an accident waiting to happen. That goes for the rest of you, too. How many times do I have to tell you kids not to do that?"

"Yeah, okay, Dad," Andrew says. "You're right. I'll try and be more careful."

"Sir?" someone says. When I look up, there's no one else in front of me. I place my stuff on the belt. Apologize to the kid at the register, the people waiting behind me. *When you got home that night, everything was back to normal,* she said. But goddamnit, I should have known something was wrong. It was probably staring me in the face.

When I load the groceries into the car, I realize too late that the cover of the rotisserie chicken's not on tight. The juice has spilled all over the other things in the bag, onto the backseat, the carpet. It's a mess. I say it out loud—"Fuck!" I snap the top back on, ignoring the dirty look I just got. Open the car door with greasy fingers. Get in and slam it shut.

Driving back to Viveca's, I approach a family riding their bikes in the shoulder. A mom and dad, two kids, all of them wearing helmets. . . .

I'm in the bathroom shaving when he barges in. He's what? Fifteen? Sixteen? I've taken him to empty parking lots a few times so he can practice his driving. He swings open the medicine cabinet door like I'm not even standing there. "Hey, do you mind?"

"Oh, sorry. I've got a headache. Mom says to take some aspirin."

When he closes the medicine cabinet, I see his banged-up face in the mirror: a cut over his eyebrow, a goose egg on his forehead. "How'd that happen?"

"What?"

"That bump on your forehead."

"This? I dunno."

"What do you mean you—"

"I fell off my bike. Hit some sand and went into a skid, then bam! Fell head first against the blacktop."

"And I don't suppose you were wearing your helmet."

"Nah. I forgot. Sorry."

"You feeling groggy? Nauseated? Because from the size of that lump you've got, you could have gotten a concussion."

"Nah, I'm okay." And he's out of there. . . .

Did he have a bike accident, or was that the time she clobbered him with the mallet? All those bumps and bruises. All those trips to the emergency room, and what do I do? Lecture him about wearing a helmet, leaving his shit on the stairs . . .

Looking at the road ahead, I'm disoriented for a few seconds. Then I realize I've missed my exit and the two after it. Driven all the way to Wellfleet.

When I get back, Ariane's on the couch, reading. "Decided not to take a walk after all, huh?" I ask.

"I was going to, but I couldn't find that key," she says.

"Oh, sorry. I thought it was in there with that jumble of other stuff. Guess not. Let me start supper, then I'll look for it."

"Do you want some help?"

"Nah, piece of cake. Relax. What's that you're reading?" When she holds up her book, I squint and make out the title: *Home from the Hospital: Now What?*

"Daddy?" she says. "You know when you were asking me before about whether I wanted a boy or a girl?" I nod. "I guess I want a girl."

"Yes? Why's that?"

"I don't know. I think maybe boys are harder."

I can guess what's on her mind. She's worried that if she has a son, she might take after her mother. Which she wouldn't. They're nothing alike, temperament-wise. Ariane's sensible, measured. Whereas Annie was *always* strung tight, even before the kids came along. She could fly off the handle at things that anyone else would take in stride. She's just hot-tempered, I'd tell myself. Thin-skinned. Over-the-top angry sometimes? Sure. But not sick. Not pathologically angry. . . . Were they *that* good at keeping it from me, or did I have blinders on? Doesn't really matter, I guess. What matters is that I failed them, Andrew most of all. Good god, my poor son.

We eat in semisilence, our earlier conversation a weight between us. The TV's on, murmuring in the background: Sarah Palin's latest pronouncement, Lindsay Lohan's shenanigan du jour. Ari's pushing her food around on her plate more than putting it in her mouth. The weather guy promises that tomorrow will be bright and sunny with low humidity—a perfect beach day, ten out of ten. "Hey," I finally say. "Do we need to talk any more about what you told me?" She shakes her head. "Okay, but if you change your mind—"

I stop. A car's just pulled up outside. Tracy, maybe? Has she decided to come over after all? I get up, look out. But it's not her silver Saab. It's a taxi. A young woman gets out of the back. Sunglasses, jeans, a pork pie hat. Suddenly it hits me that it's Marissa.

"Hey, guess who's here?" I call back to Ari.

"The prodigal daughter," she says. "I had strict orders not to tell you so that it would be a surprise."

The front door bangs open. "Hey, dude!" she shouts. "Bet you didn't expect to see me here." She's got a travel bag in one hand, a garment bag draped over her other arm. She puts them down, walks over, and gives me a hug. "Hey, can I borrow a twenty? I forgot to go to the ATM before I left the city, and I'm a little short." I take out my wallet. Ask her if she's taken the cab all the way up here from New York. "Dude, I'm not *that* stupid," she assures me. "I took a bus to Provincetown and got a cab from there." I give her the twenty and she goes outside again.

"Good luck getting it back," Ariane says. It's a family joke: Marissa's famous for "borrowing" money she never pays back.

When she's back inside, she scans the downstairs. "Nice digs."

"Why don't you take off your hat and shades and stay awhile?"

"Oh, Daddy," she says, dismissing me. She spots the half-eaten chicken on the counter. Goes over to it, peels off some skin and pops it in her mouth. "I'm freakin' *starved*," she says. "What else you got?"

I make her a plate. The three of us sit at the table and catch up while she eats. Marissa tells her sister to stand up, and when she does, she reaches over and feels her belly. "Nice little baby bump you got there," she says. "Still getting sick?"

Ariane nods. "I had a pretty good day today, though."

"Cool. Maybe you're over the hump." She looks over at me and smiles. "Look at the dude," she tells her sister. "He's like *beaming*."

And I guess she's right. In a few days, they'll be heading down to their mother's wedding, but for now the two of them are all mine.

I make Marissa and me some coffee, Ari a cup of Tracy's peppermint tea. We talk for an hour or more, then sit down to a *Law & Order* rerun that Marissa wants to see because her friend from acting class has a couple of scenes and she missed it the first time this one ran. He's the scumbag ex-boyfriend of the murdered girl. It's the same old, same old: he *looks* guilty but it's a red herring. The real killer won't surface until the halfway point. "It's going to be the woman she ran the nursery school with," I tell the girls.

"You've seen this one before?" Ariane asks.

"No, but I've watched so many of these shows, I could probably write their scripts." A few minutes later, I'm proved right. "I rest my case," I tell my daughters. "Me and Jack McCoy. Hey, by the way, Marissa, the sun's gone down. You can take off those dark glasses now."

"They're prescription," she says. "My contacts started bothering me." She turns to her sister. "He's still bossy, I see."

A few minutes later, Ariane gets up and says she's going to bed. "Yeah, I think I will, too," Marissa says. "I'm beat. That bus ride was exhausting."

I offer to get her some sheets, figuring I'll put her in the bedroom where Joe Jones's paintings are stashed, but when Ari says her room has a queen-size bed, Marissa decides she'll bunk in with her. That way, they can talk some more. "Have a pajama party."

"Okay," I say. "But don't make any crank calls, you two. I'll be up in a little while. Beach tomorrow?"

"Sure," they say in unison. Watching Marissa follow her sister up the stairs, I think about the difficult conversation I'm going to have to have with her about her mother: read her reactions, compare her version of the things that happened to Ariane's. Try as best I can to assess the damage our homelife left our kids with.

I've left my laptop on, and before I go up, I decide to check my e-mail. There's one from my cousin Ellen. It's got two attachments. She says the first picture she scanned is one of my grandfather taken shortly after he arrived in California. There's a date on the back: July 1, 1897. The second photo was taken in the forties at an Oh family reunion, she says—something her older sister Doris had. Doris thinks my father is the boy in the striped polo shirt kneeling in the front row.

I click on the first attachment. Study the formal black-and-white portrait of Grandpa Oh when he was a young man barely out of his teens if that—a "coolie" laborer at a fishing cannery, according to Ellen, who would eventually travel across the country and become a successful restaurateur. His posture is erect, his expression sober. Am I reading into it, or is that fear I see in those almond eyes? Well, why wouldn't he be afraid? He's left everything he's ever known to start over half a world away.

I hesitate before opening the second attachment. I've never seen any pictures of my father, and I'm not sure I'm ready to see one now. But taking a deep breath, I aim the mouse and click. This photo is in color, slightly out of focus. I find Francis Oh among his twenty or so relatives—a skinny, unsmiling boy of about twelve or thirteen. He's looking directly into the camera. Directly at me. But his face betrays no expression; he's as unknowable as ever. And so the gush of emotion I expected would overtake me doesn't happen. I stare at him, this cipher of a father, and feel nothing. . . .

I locate Grandpa Oh in the picture, too, standing behind and a little to the right of his son. White shirt, wide red tie, pleated pants held up with suspenders—a younger version of the man I saw five or six times when I was a college student in my late teens. Is the petite woman with the 1940s hairstyle standing next to him his wife, my father's mother? My Chinese grandmother is as much of a cipher as her son. I don't even know her first name. Grandpa Oh was a widower by the time I met him, that day when my mother exacted from him his promise to contribute to my college fund. When, during another of my visits to his restaurant, he hesitated but then wrote down my father's work address: *Francis Oh, c/o Oh and Yang Accountants, 502 Stewart Street, Dayton, Ohio.* I held onto that address for another seven or eight years before I mustered up the courage to write to him. Ask if I could meet him. I close my eyes and see the envelope that came back to me unopened, the word *deceased* scrawled over my own handwriting. A second rejection, this time due to death. . . . The palm trees in the yard behind the group suggest that my father and grandfather, for the sake of family connection, must have returned to California for this reunion. Among the gathering of adults and children, there are no half-breeds like me. No husbands or wives of different nationalities. Everyone is unmistakably, uniformly Chinese. Well, my Italian grandparents had been the same. Hung out with family members and other *Siciliani* for the most part. I can't recall that they had any *non*-Italian friends. . . .

I close down my computer, lock the doors, turn off the lights. I'm halfway up the stairs when I remember that phone call I got before when Ari and I were out on the deck. Well, whoever it is can wait, I tell myself. But a few more stairs later, I change my mind and head back down.

"Hi, Dad, it's me." I see him in the kitchen, shielding his face as she comes toward him with that mallet. "I changed my mind about going to the wedding. Got someone to take my weekend shift and . . . Casey's not coming. Just me. I get into Bradley at about two tomorrow. Rented a car so I can drive up there and hang out with you guys for a few days. Ari says the twerp's going up, too, I guess. You're in Truro, right? Call me back and give me the address, will you? I have my GPS. . . . Well, okay. See you soon."

When I go upstairs, I can hear my girls yakking away down the hall. I brush and floss my teeth, stare at myself in the medicine cabinet mirror: the guy who tried all day long to help the kids who came into his office, and then went home and ignored the signs that his own kids needed help. That their mother flew into those violent rages. Attacked her own son. *Our* son. . . . Well, okay, maybe I *was* asleep at the wheel. But at least I hadn't cut and run like my father had. I raised them, read to them and bathed them, helped guide them into adulthood. And they turned out okay, didn't they? They're solid, self-supporting adults. . . . Except, in that voice mail he left, Andrew sounded troubled. Nervous. When he gets here, I'm going to have to have a sit-down with him. With the three of them. Talk to them about their mother, whether they want to go there or not. Find out what kind of baggage they're still hauling around because of their two highly imperfect parents. Well, hey. Whose parents *are* perfect? Who's *not* carrying around baggage from childhood? Who among us is immune from family pain?

I close my bedroom door, turn off the light. Undress in the dark and crawl under the sheet. Lying there, I close my eyes and see my grandfather—both the old man I knew and the solemn-looking immigrant boy in the picture. He must have had to carry his burdens, too. Poverty, hunger. Why else would he have left what was familiar and launched himself into the unknown? . . .

"Grandpa Oh." I say it out loud in the dark. Say it again. "Grandpa Oh." In another seven months or so, that's who I'll be, too.

Chapter Seventeen

Andrew Oh

A t the Sturbridge tolls, I take a ticket. Take the ramp onto the
Mass. Pike. "Proceed on Interstate-Ninety East for fifty-six
miles to Interstate-Four Ninety-Five South, Exit Eleven-A,"
the GPS voice says. It's just me, her, and this Egg McMuffin I've been
chewing and swallowing without really tasting it. Now that I've gotten something in my stomach, I don't want any more. I fist the rest of
it inside the paper and toss it onto the passenger's seat floor. When I
catch myself worrying about how Casey's doing, I stop myself. Turn
on the radio. Metallica at 6:00 A.M.? Uh-uh. . . . Kanye? Nope. . . .
What I could use right about now is some New Testament wisdom,
but I doubt there's any Christian stations up here in politically correct
Massachusetts. Hey, Toto, I don't think we're in Texas anymore.

I kill the radio. Put on my signal and shoot past the red Nissan and
the two sixteen-wheelers in front of it. One's a Sam Adams truck, the
other's a Dunkin' Donuts. None of the bars in Waco have Sam on tap,
and the closest Dunkin' Donuts is eighty miles away in Round Rock.
Kinda nice, actually—being back here. Driving a V6 again. In all the
drama and heartbreak of the past few days, I forgot to make a reservation at the car rental place and had to choose between what they had
left: a Jetta or this big-ass Chrysler SUV. I'm just lucky I was able to
exchange that ticket she sent for a red-eye. Gives me a little more time
up there with Dad before we have to head down to the wedding. The
traffic's light at this time of the morning and I gun it. Hit eighty and
set the cruise control. I'm anxious to get there and see the three of
them, even pain-in-the-ass Marissa. Not that I'm looking forward to
telling them what's happened. . . .

* * *

"In two tenths of a mile, turn right," the GPS lady says. "Turn right."

I do what it says. Take the Pamet Road exit, then follow the next two or three commands. Travel a mile or so up the country road it's put me on. "In one tenths miles, turn right. . . . Turn right." I drive onto a dirt road. Pass two or three houses nestled in the trees. Unpainted shingles, white trim: typical Cape Cod. "Arriving at destination. On right." But which one is it? The bungalow with the weather-beaten shakes or the big white house up there on that bluff? I don't see Dad's car at either one. Then I remember that he bought a new car last year—a Prius. And there's a black Prius, parked at the big house. I turn the wheel and head up the driveway, my tires crunching broken clamshells bleached white by the sun. The front door bangs open, and there they are, rushing toward me. Marissa first, then Ariane, and then my dad. I take a deep breath and get out of the car. Here goes.

Chapter Eighteen

Orion Oh

Becuse sharks are more intelligent than seals," Tracy tells them. The five of us are out on the back deck at Adrian's, having breakfast before the kids head back home for the wedding. We've arrived at the restaurant in three different cars: mine, Tracy's, and that big SUV Andrew rented. It's packed up with their stuff. The twins and their sister are taking off from here: rehearsal dinner tonight, the ceremony tomorrow. But for another hour or so, I've still got them here with me. And Tracy's shark stories have got them, too. The three of them are wide-eyed, fully attentive, like when I'd read them bedtime stories and ham it up, take on the voice of Long John Silver or whoever. "I've seen them breach right out of the water and come down hard," Tracy says. "Slam the seal to stun it and then go in for the kill."

"Bullies!" Marissa says, touching her face. I hadn't even noticed that bruise she's got until Andrew said something to her yesterday, but it's more evident out here in the morning sun.

Andrew tells Tracy he saw an attack like that on TV—something called Shark Week. "But it would be the shit to see it in person." Tracy says it's too bad he can't stick around longer. She'd take him out on the boat with her.

Marissa sulks, gulps her Bloody Mary. When Andrew kidded her about that bruise yesterday—*Was it really a cabinet door or did somebody pop you one?*—she'd told him to go fuck himself, then had gone into the kitchen and fixed herself another drink. Something's up with her: the way she's been knocking them down, even this morning. Two Bloody Marys to everyone else's one. But she's not volunteering anything. Not to me, anyway. Maybe to her sister. They were out on Viv-eca's deck yesterday, deep in some private conversation that stopped abruptly when I stepped out there. "Hi, Daddy!" Ariane had said, re-placing the worried frown on her face with a counterfeit smile. *Had* someone hit Marissa? Why else would she have gotten so testy when her brother said that? Maybe I can take Ari aside for a minute before they leave and ask her if she knows anything—if that's what they were talking about out there. But no, it probably did happen the way she said. I'm probably just being hyperalert because I'd missed the signs that their mother had hurt their brother. . . .

Except what about that bar where she works? Her apartment's only a couple of blocks away, she says—a five-minute walk home after her shift. Still, things can happen even in that short a distance, especially late at night. Someone could know her patterns, be waiting in some alley. Jump out and surprise her like those sharks surprise the seals.

Someone must have just said something funny, because they're all laughing. I join in, unaware. "Right, Daddy?" Ariane says.

"Oh yes, that's right."

The kids look relaxed and healthy; all three of them got some sun at the beach yesterday. It's been a good visit, overall. Just a few rough spots: when he needled her about that bruise, and when she teased him about being a Bible thumper. And when I sat them down and tried to get them to talk about their mother's assaults on Andrew. I blew it when I used that word: assault. They clammed right up, the three of them. . . . But yeah, overall, it's been good. Too short, though. When we were getting ready to come here and I told them I didn't want them to leave, Ariane suggested I come down with them. "You can stay at the house while we're at the wedding. Mama and Viveca are going back to New York after the reception. Getting ready for their trip to Greece. We could hang out together on Sunday until Andrew and I have to leave for the airport." I was tempted. Considered it. But no, it's better to leave things the way they are.

They like Tracy. She had already won over Ari with that stuff she bought her. It really has seemed to quell her nausea. But when she came over for dinner last night, Andrew and Marissa were reserved with her. Before she got there, those two were up to their old tricks: him chasing after her with one of the live lobsters we'd picked up at the wharf, her fending him off with couch pillows. But when Tracy arrived, they'd put the brakes on that behavior. Turned back into cautious adults. This morning's different, though. Everyone's at ease. They can't resist her shark stories.

Ari asks why the great whites are so interested in hunting seals when they could eat whatever's swimming around under the sea.

"It's the layer of blubber they're after," Tracy tells them. "It's rich with nutrients. We suspect that's why they've been sticking around so late in the season. Consuming what they can so that they can convert it into energy for their long migration down to warmer waters. They ought to be heading out pretty soon now. It's going to be fascinating to track them en route with those devices we've tagged them with. Hopefully, they'll stay embedded for the duration. I'm excited about it."

Marissa says if she was on that observation boat and saw one of them attacking some poor seal, she'd take out her gun. Her gun? She's got a gun?

"Better the seals than us," her brother says.

"Well, actually, sharks aren't really cruising around looking for humans to devour," Tracy says. "I think we can blame Steven Spielberg for that misconception. He and whoever wrote that book the movie was based on."

"Peter Benchley," Andrew says. "Back in high school, I handed in that same book report for my summer reading assignment three years running. Didn't get nailed until I got to Mrs. Jennings's class."

"Mrs. Jennings hated my guts," Marissa says. "Probably because I was related to *you*." Andrew concurs, smiling proudly. But Ariane says she learned a lot from Mrs. J's class. That she was an awesome teacher.

"Have you figured out which one of us was always the teacher's pet?" Andrew asks Tracy.

She laughs. Says she has a pretty good idea. "I was no angel in grade school, either. I got kicked out of the Brownies for smoking a cigarette."

Marissa tells her about the time at Brownie camp when she got in trouble for singing that song "Bad to the Bone" the night of the talent show. "Too bad we weren't in the same Brownie troop," she tells Tracy. "If we'd have joined forces, we probably could have taken down the entire Girls Scouts of America organization."

Tracy calculates that she would have been in high school by the time Rissa was in Brownies. That she's not sure she would have still been able to fit into her uniform. "Hey, who sang 'Bad to the Bone' anyway?" she asks. "George Thorogood?"

"And the Destroyers," Andrew says. "I had that CD until my bratty little sister scratched it to shit." He starts singing. "Bad to the bone, I'm b-b-b-b-bad." He points his thumb at Ariane. "Or in her case, I'm g-g-g-g-good."

"Hey!" Ariane protests. "I'm going to be an unwed mother. That's pretty bad-ass, right?" Nervous smiles all around, Ari's included.

Unaware that he's just broken off his engagement, Tracy asks Andrew how he likes Texas. "S'all right," he says. "It's got its good points."

"Like what?" Marissa quips. "Armadillos? Jesus jamborees?"

His nostrils flare a little at the Jesus remark. She's pushing it, and I'm relieved when he doesn't take the bait. "Armadillos are cool," he says. "Kinda slow and stupid, though. I've hit so many of them on the road that I've probably thinned out the population."

"Not on purpose?" Ariane asks. He says sure, that he's an armadillo serial killer. Rolls his eyes.

Tracy tells him she did some research in the Gulf of Mexico once. "Down around Padre Island. That's one of the things I remember most: the armadillo roadkill all around Corpus Christi."

"Is it armadillos or arma*dildos*?" Marissa says. She looks expectantly from face to face, but nobody thinks it's funny. She downs the rest of her Bloody Mary and starts swishing the ice around at the bottom of her glass. For the next few minutes, she sits there sulking.

When our waiter comes by, he asks if he can get us anything else. Marissa opens her mouth to answer him, but before she can order another one, I cut her off. "Just the check, thanks."

Ariane glances at her watch and says they'd better get going.

"And I've got to get over to the lab," Tracy says. "But hey, this has been fun. Thanks, you guys, for letting me share your time with your dad." The other two acknowledge her, but Marissa stands, teetering a little, and says she's got to use the bathroom.

"Yeah, I'd better go, too," her sister says. "We pregnant ladies have to seize every opportunity we can to use the facility." They head inside.

"Pregnant ladies," Andrew says when she's out of earshot. He shakes his head. "I still don't get it." The best I can offer him is a shrug.

When the check comes, I give it a quick scan and take out my wallet. Refuse Tracy's offer to split the tab. "My treat. But thanks." When the girls come back to the table, everyone stands.

On the way out, I sidle up to Ariane and whisper. "She bought a gun?"

"Not yet," she whispers back. "She's applied for a permit."

"What's up with *that*?" I ask. Ariane's about to say something, but she stops when Marissa, ahead of us, slows down and we catch up to her.

Out in the parking lot, everyone hugs everyone else good-bye. Andrew's embrace is the tightest and longest-lasting. What happened during our run yesterday was intense. "Hang in there, Dad," he whispers. I nod. Give him a smile. The kids get in his car, Ariane up front with her brother, Marissa in the back. They wave. Tracy and I wave back. They pull out onto Route 6.

"They're great," Tracy says. "You did a nice job there, Dad." I thank her, manage a smile. She's right; they *are* great kids. But none of them's in great shape. Ari's going it alone with her pregnancy, he's broken up with his girl without ever really saying why. And whatever's going on with Marissa, she's drinking too much. And now she's getting herself a gun? As I stand there, watching them disappear down the road, I wonder how much of the adult lives they're living now, the decisions they're making, have to do with their home life when they were kids. With their parents—one of them unhinged and the other asleep at the wheel.

"Hey?" Tracy says. "You okay?"

"Hm? Yeah, sure. They're not even a mile down the road yet and

I miss them already, that's all. Ariane says I should drive down there. Hang out with them the morning after the wedding."

"Then maybe you should."

"Nah. But this was nice."

"Well, okay then. I've really got to go. Want to get together tonight?"

"Sounds good." We embrace, kiss. She gets in her car and takes off, too.

Driving back to Viveca's, I replay what she just said. *You did a nice job there, Dad.* I shake my head. Tell the guy in the rearview mirror to face up to the truth: that he made those students at the college more of a priority than his own kids. I left them alone with her too much, even though I knew she resented it. And then her resentment had curdled into anger. Rage. Was that why she targeted him? Because he was the male child, and I wasn't around to push down the stairs? Take a mallet to? Was my son just a stand-in for the guy she *really* wanted to hurt? . . . They're still covering for her, even now. That conversation I tried to start with them yesterday went nowhere. Ancient history, Andrew said. The statute of limitations. And I don't believe for a minute Marissa's claim that she doesn't remember it. Even Ari had started to backpedal. "I probably made it sound worse than it was, Daddy." But I saw the way the three of them were looking at one another, the panic on their faces. *Nice job there, Dad.* No. A good father—an alert psychologist—would have read the signs whether they were trying to hide them or not. Would not have left his kids defenseless. Well, he's got a point, I guess: it's history. Nothing I can do about it now. When I get back to the house, I'll put on my trunks and sneakers and head down to Long Nook. Maybe I can run off this sadness that's starting to overtake me. . . .

I think about the run I took down there yesterday with Andrew. When I asked him who broke it off, him or her, he said he did—that it just wasn't going to work out. . . .

"Why not?"

"I don't know, Dad. I don't really want to talk about it. Okay?"

"Sure. But if you do—"

"Yeah, okay. Thanks." He changes the subject—starts talking about his work down there. "Some of the ones coming back are in bad shape."

I tell him about one of the practicums I did when I was working on my degree, counseling Vietnam vets. "Combat takes its toll, no matter what the war is. Takes a toll on the health professionals treating them, too. It did me, anyway. What about you? You handling it okay?"

"Pretty much. Gets to me sometimes—some days worse than others. And the hours, the double shifts, are draining. We're spread pretty thin. But it's worthwhile work, you know? They need help, and when you can give it to them, see the way some of them start to pull out of their depression or whatever, it's . . . I don't know. Gratifying."

I smile at him. "Sounds like you've found your niche."

"Yeah, I guess I have. Took me long enough, huh? All those times I switched my major? Five and a half years of college instead of four? But this is what I really want to do. When I first got stationed there, I was going to go into engine repair. But I kept feeling like it wasn't the right fit for me. So I prayed on it—asked my Higher Power to guide me. And He did. Prayer is powerful, you know that?"

"Can't say that I do, no. I'm one of those damned heathens, remember? But your mother believes in prayer. She told me a while back that she prays every night that they won't ship you over there. That ever worry you? That you might end up in Iraq or Afghanistan?"

He shrugs. "I don't think about it much. And if they do, they do. I went in with my eyes open. I'll go wherever they need me. So Mom still prays, huh? That's kind of surprising."

"Yeah? Why's that?"

"I don't know. I guess I figured with her new lifestyle . . . Casey-Lee's the one who brought me to God. She's pretty religious. Her whole family is. I liked going to church with them, you know? I sort of wish we'd had that kind of foundation when we were kids."

"Well, you did. She made sure each of you kids was christened. I don't know if you remember, but she used to take the three of you to church with her when you were little."

"And then she stopped. Left us home with you on Sunday. I guess what I'm saying is that I wish we'd all gone together. You know. As a family."

"Maybe we should have. But it would have been an empty gesture on my part, Andrew. Don't get me wrong. If you're a believer, then more power to you. And hey, I'd like to believe that some supreme being is up there, making sure everything comes out the way it's supposed to. But my mind just can't go there. I don't know. Maybe it's the kind of work I do. Did, I mean."

"Why? What do you mean?"

"Well, you sit across from patients long enough—hear about incest or rape, or about how some nineteen-year-old's started hearing scary voices in his head, how someone's mother got killed in a car crash because she happened to be in the wrong place at the wrong time—and you begin to doubt that anyone's up there doling out cosmic justice. That it's not all just random. I don't know. Maybe I've just seen too much and heard too much."

"Or maybe you're being arrogant," he says.

I look over at him. "Arrogant? How so?"

"Well, you just said twice that you don't have it figured out. 'I don't know. Maybe it's the kind of work I did. Maybe I've seen too much.' But you sure sound like you think you know. Like you've got the whole thing figured out on your own, so there must not be a Higher Power. That it's all on you. What's that called? Hubris?"

I smile at him, thinking maybe I had that coming. Touché, Andrew.

"The funny thing is, Casey-Lee's family's got a little of that attitude from the other side of things, you know? They read the Bible a certain way and think they've got all the answers. That they know what God wants and what He doesn't, and so everybody should act accordingly."

He's already established the ground rules. I'm not supposed to ask about his broken engagement. But is that part of it? Was this evangelical family he was planning to marry into a little too God-focused for the son of a skeptic and a woman who's about to enter into a gay marriage? Or is that hubris on my part, too?

"All I'm saying, Dad, is that I accept that I don't know. But I have faith that my Lord and Savior does, so I'm putting myself in His hands. Humbling myself to a wisdom that's above and beyond me and praying for His guidance."

Atheism as arrogance? Humility as a door that opens onto faith? I'll have to think about that. What I don't have to think about is how much I love this kid, this son of mine. I reach over and squeeze his shoulder.

"Hey, what's that?" he asks.

"What's what?"

"That thing up ahead at the edge of the water."

When I look, I see what he's looking at: that same carcass I've run past for the last few days, and on my walk with Ariane the day before. "Dead seal," I tell him. "We better give it a wide berth. Doesn't smell too pleasant."

"A shark get him?" he asks.

"Could be. Whatever it was, the gulls have pretty much picked over the leftovers. Now it's the flies' turn." *I glance up at the sky. From the position of the sun, I'd say it's somewhere around four o'clock. We'll have to start back pretty soon.* "Hey, for dinner? How does lobster sound?"

"Sounds great," he says.

"Tracy's coming over," I tell him. "She wants to meet you guys. Hope that's okay." *He nods, not smiling. Says he guesses so. Maybe it's too much at once. Tonight his dad's new girlfriend, tomorrow his mother's wife.*

"You sure? Because I can call her and cancel out if you're not up for it."

"Nah, that's okay. Ari says she's nice. She's up here studying the sharks, right?" *I nod. Ask him how he's feeling about going down there for the wedding. He shrugs.* "I'm still not crazy about the idea, but, hey, it's her life, right? It is what it is."

"Well, I know it'll make her happy that you've made the effort."

"Yeah. She just better not ask me to give her away or anything."

"I doubt she will. And if she does, just tell her you wouldn't be comfortable doing it."

"I just wish you were going, Dad. I get why you wouldn't want to, but, I don't know, it'd just be easier if you were there."

"Yeah, well . . . Tell me. Did your girl and her family know that your mother is marrying a woman?"

"Casey-Lee did. I don't know about her parents. I sure as hell didn't tell them." *He picks up his pace, runs a little ahead of me. When I catch up, he starts talking about Marissa.* "Did you see how bent out of shape *she got when I asked her if someone smacked her? I was only kidding, but from her reaction, I wonder if maybe it did happen."*

"Probably not," I tell him. But now I start wondering again, too.

"I mean, if some guy hurt her and I thought she'd cough up his name, I'd go down there while I'm out here and take care of business. Find him and beat the shit out of him."

"Yeah, that would be a smart move. Then when they hauled you in and let you make a phone call, you could notify your commanding officer that you've been detained by New York's finest. That would go over big. How you doing with that kind of stuff, anyway?"

"What kind of stuff?"

"Managing your anger."

"I'm doing fine with it. Why?"

"Well, it wouldn't be the first time you flew off the handle and led with your fists."

"Yeah, well, anger's justifiable sometimes. You know?"

"Sometimes it is, sometimes it isn't." I probably should have shut my mouth at that point, but I didn't. "Did you ever try and connect the dots between your anger and your mother's? Think that maybe, when you've gone out of control, it's because she used to do that with you?"

"Dammit, Dad. Give it a rest, will you?" He pulls his tank top over his head and throws it in the sand. "Fuckin' hot out here," he says. "I'm going in."

Watching him enter the water, I'm struck by how fit he's kept himself. Broad-shouldered and narrow at the waist, his back well muscled. He really could give some guy a pummeling. When he's up to his knees, he plunges headfirst into a cresting wave. I throw my own shirt on top of his and head in, too. The water's cold at first, but I take a deep breath and go under. By the time I surface again, it feels good. No, better than good. Feels great. Refreshing. Wasn't this one of the reasons why I wanted to come up here? So that this crisp salt water could cleanse me of the past year?

Andrew swims up beside me. "Hope there's no great whites around here," he says. I tell him it's doubtful—that there have been a couple of sightings up here in the waters off Truro, but most of them have been spotted down around Chatham where the seals congregate.

For the next several minutes, we swim side by side, neither of us speaking. "What do you say we head back now?" I finally suggest. "Your sisters are probably wondering where we are."

"Yeah, okay," he says. Back on the beach, we grab our shirts and start jogging back. Then, out of the blue, he says, "I'm going to pray for you, Dad. Ask Jesus to help you."

"Help me do what? See the light and become a believer?"

He shakes his head. "I'm not so sure He cares whether you believe in Him or not. But you're a good man. He knows that. I'm just going to ask Him to help you find peace in your heart."

For the next several steps, I mull over what he's just said. A good man . . . peace in my heart. What happens next is unpremeditated. I pull up short, bend over, and put my hands on my knees. He stops, too. "Dad? You okay?"

It comes spewing out of me like a bellyful of bile: what I let happen that night in Jasmine Negron's apartment, her trumped-up charge of sexual harassment and my colleagues' reaction to it. And then Seamus's suicide and my abrupt resignation, my decision to put the house on the market and move into that dinky little apartment that was making me crazy. "I just never expected that she'd bail on me," I say, my effort to fight back tears a losing battle. "But it's not all on her. I neglected her, took her for granted. She had a right to seek out her own happiness. But with a woman? It's unmoored me, you know? All of it. The divorce, the accusation, quitting my job." I point toward the open sea. "It's like I'm adrift out there. Treading water, getting tired as hell but not knowing what I'm supposed to swim toward. Which way's going to put me back on solid ground."

He squats down beside me, puts his arm around me. "Take it easy. Take some deep breaths," he says. Even in the state I'm in, the irony hits me. How many times have I given kids in crisis this exact same advice?

When I stand up straight again, more or less composed, I swipe my arm across my wet eyes. Look over at him and apologize for my outburst. "You've got enough on your plate without having your old man go to pieces on you. Dumping my crap on top of yours." He says he's glad I told him. Assures me that it's going to be okay. "Yeah? You think so? I hope you're right."

"Maybe this desperation you're feeling is a gift from God," *he says. I look over at him, confused.* "Maybe it's a doorway you've got to step through to get to something new. Something better that's waiting for you and is going to heal your suffering. Like it says in Jeremiah, 'a balm in Gilead.'"

He's proselytizing, I know, but that's okay. "Desperation as a gift, huh? A door? You're getting to be a pretty deep thinker, you know that?"

He smiles. Says no one's ever accused him of that *before. Then he says something that almost sets me off again.* "I love you, Dad."

"I love you, too. Thanks for letting me spill my guts. Just don't say anything to your sisters, okay? Jasmine's not much older than you guys. I don't want them to think their father's a dirty old man."

"They wouldn't think that," *he says.* "But I won't say anything. This is just between you and me. You ready?"

"Yeah, I guess."

"You want to walk the rest of the way back or run?"

"Run," *I say.* "If we're not back soon, they're going to send out a search party."

When we do get back to the girls, the consensus is that we've had enough beach for the day. We head back up the path, shake the sand out of our stuff, get in the car, and go.

Still thinking about the kids' visit, I pull up onto Viveca's driveway. Walking inside, I decide not to go down to the beach after all. I feel too tired to run. And anyway, the place is kind of a mess from their visit. Dishes on the counter and in the sink, sheets balled up at the foot of the stairs—the ones the girls slept on. I was going to make up the bed in the other room up there, but Andrew had ended up sacking out downstairs on the couch. Didn't even go up on the second floor while he was here, I don't think. If he had, I wonder if he'd have recognized those paintings that he and his buddies had pulled out when they were up to no good down at the house out back where Jones and his brother had lived. Probably not. He must have become sexually active pretty soon after that, and real girls' breasts would have been much more interesting than the misshapen ones in those paintings. The floor feels gritty under my sandals—sand from the beach yesterday. I take the upright vac out of the closet. I'll throw the sheets and their towels in the machine and do a wash. Then I'll vacuum up the sand before it scratches her hardwood floors. In a minute, that is. I flop down on the couch. Look over at the end table and spot the red cell phone sitting there. Marissa's. It's plugged into the charger, which is plugged into the wall socket.

Love shack, baby love shack . . . And there's *my* phone. I get up, go into the kitchen. It's on the counter. "Hello?"

"Hi," Annie says. "It's me. I'm calling to see if the kids have left yet."

"Uh, yeah. We went out for a late breakfast. They took off about twenty minutes ago. They should get in somewhere between two and three unless they hit traffic at the bridge." She asks me how the visit went. Fine, I tell her. Great. "You at the house yet?"

En route, she says. She's calling from a rest stop on the Merritt Parkway. Says she's driving up with her housekeeper and her little boy, and that they had to use the restroom.

"Quite an entourage, eh? You three and Viveca."

She says Viveca drove up from the city the night before and is already checked in at Bella Linda—that she wanted to make sure everything was in place for the wedding.

"And you invited the housekeeper and her son? That's nice." She says she *hired* Minnie to help out with things, and that her kid came along because his babysitter ducked out at the last minute. "Ah. So what did you do? Rent a car?" Yes, she says. But she's not driving. Ordinarily she would have, but instead she's hired one of the doormen in her building to take them. "I can't say this too loud, because he's right outside having a smoke. He got fired last weekend for coming in late, and he could really use the extra money. So I said, what the heck. Highway driving makes me nervous anyway."

I picture the doorman I talked to last year when I went down there to the San Gennaro festival. Waited for her and Viveca to come down because I didn't want to go up there to their apartment. He was affable, I remember. Wonder if that's the guy. "Looks like you'll have decent weather tomorrow," I say. "Low eighties they're saying. Low humidity."

"Oh, great. I hadn't thought to check. Well, here comes the entourage, as you say. I guess I'd better go."

"Okay. Oh, and Annie? You weren't thinking of asking Andrew to give you away, were you? Because he said he wouldn't feel comfortable."

"No, no. I'm just so glad he decided to come. I can't wait to see the three of them. . . . You know, Orion, I'd love to see you, too, if you decide at the last minute that you want to change your mind. You could just come out to dinner with us tonight if you don't want to go to the ceremony. Of course, you'd be welcome to come to that, too, if you felt like it. *More* than welcome."

"No, I don't think so. But thanks. Hope it's a great day for you two."

"Thank you, Orion. And thank you for giving me those three kids of ours. I love you for that. I'll always love you."

Loves me but didn't want to stay married to me. Loves her kids but went after one of them with a mallet. "Yeah. Thanks. See ya."

I get up, start the vacuum. The front foyer sure needs it; it's picking up a ton of sand. Then why am I stopping? Turning the damn thing off and yanking the plug? I go back to the living room, sit on the sofa, and close my eyes. *Not even a mile down the road yet and I miss them already. . . . I wish you were going, Dad. It would be easier for me if you were there. . . . We could hang out together Sunday until Andrew and I have to get back to the airport.*

But no. It's too late to change the game plan at this point. And anyway, I'm getting together with Tracy tonight. . . . Still, if I did go down there, stay at the house with her and the kids tonight, it could be a kind of closure. The five of us reconvening there one last time before a buyer comes along. A kind of good-bye to our old life. And Marissa's phone over there: I could bring it to her. I get up, pace. You know what? Fuck it. Maybe I *will* go down there. I'll call Tracy and cancel out on tonight. She'll understand. . . .

Except she's not answering and her voice mail's full. If I'm going to the dinner tonight but not the wedding, do I need to bring a gift? Yeah, probably. But what do you get a couple who has everything? I suppose I could go upstairs and grab one of those paintings I brought up here—one of the small ones. Viveca would sure as hell like that. But no, she'd want to know where it came from, and I don't want to open up *that* can of worms. . . . I could drive up to P'town and find them something there. When the kids and I went up there yesterday, we stopped in front of that shop window and looked at those framed butterflies. They were beautiful—vivid blues and greens, oranges and yellows. *Real* butterflies. Reminded me of those shadow box collages she used to make. And she's always liked butterflies. I doubt Viveca's much of a nature girl, but so what? Annie would like a gift like that. I grab my car keys and go.

Three quarters of an hour later, I'm back with the butterflies. Thank god that place did gift-wrapping. I'll leave it in the car, pack a few things, and start out. I can call them from the road to tell them I'm coming. I've got to try Tracy again, too. And Marissa's phone: I've got to remember to grab that.

After I'm packed, I head downstairs. There's the vacuum cleaner. Well, it'll wait. I'll just leave it out, do the floors when I get back. No one's going to be walking around on that sand while I'm gone. I lock up. Get in the car and back down the driveway. It's a little after one. I should be back in Three Rivers by four, four thirty at the latest.

Out on Route 6, I pass the familiar sights. Rookie's Pizza, Paine's Campground, the Wellfleet Drive-In. I'm excited to get there, but I'd better cool it or I'll get pulled over. They patrol this road pretty regularly.

I'm entering the Orleans roundabout when it dawns on me that I've forgotten Marissa's cell phone. Shit! Should I keep going? No, I'd better go back for it. What's it going to add? Another thirty minutes maybe? I'll still get there in plenty of time for that dinner.

Here they all are again: the drive-in, the campground, Rookie's. Eyes on the road, I reach for my phone. Try Tracy. No answer. She really needs to clear some of those old messages. I take a right at the

Truro Center exit. Another right and then a left puts me onto Pamet Road. From here, I'm another five minutes from that cell phone. In and out and I'll be on my way again.

Driving onto the dirt road that leads to Viveca's, I spot it up ahead through the trees: their truck. Those cleaners. Jesus Christ, I *told* them to call ahead instead of just showing up. And anyway, they were just here three days ago. Do they think I'm *that* much of a slob? Or are they trying to screw the owners by billing them for unnecessary services? Well, too bad if I've kept them waiting. It's their own damned fault.

Except the truck's empty. What's going on? I get out of the car, house key in hand. When I stick it in the lock, the door swings open before I can even turn the knob. There's stuff stacked in the foyer: the Mapplethorpes, some of the sculptures, the Jones paintings I'd put upstairs. What the . . . ? Jesus Christ, they're robbing the place!

I walk into the living room. Scan the bare walls. "Hey!" I yell. She walks into view. I hear footsteps upstairs. Leave, I tell myself. My phone's in the car. I'll block the driveway, call the cops. No, too dangerous. I can drive back down to the Pamet Road and call 9-1-1 from there. Halfway to the front door, I hear him flying down the stairs. Go! Don't look back! But the sudden pain at the small of my back drops me to my knees. What just happened? I look around and see him standing there, gripping the upright vac like it's a baseball bat. See him lifting it over his shoulder. It's coming down toward me. He's aiming for my head. "No!" I scream. And then—

Part IV

A Wedding

Chapter Nineteen

Kent Kelly

Y ou think I want to be this way? That it's a choice? You think I want to be working the kinds of minimum wage jobs that are available to guys with a record like mine? Midnight floor buffer down at the mall, insert-stuffer for the Sunday papers. And even these dead-end jobs had to be negotiated by the employment counselor at the group home I'm in. Now I'm a night shift CNA at Eldredge Eldercare—got my training during my last prison bid. The pay's better: seventy-five cents above minimum wage. In return for my weekly paycheck, half of which I have to fork over for room and board, I empty bedpans, dispose of colostomy bags and other hazardous waste, shine flashlights on the faces of sleeping residents to make sure they're still drawing breath. A few weeks back, the nurse at the desk told me and Raj, another aide, to go down to room seven and clean up Mr. Rasmusson, change his sheets because he'd shit the bed. And after we were done, I looked over at his roommate, Mr. Cavoli— he's a nice old guy, one of my favorite patients—and he was lying there, wide awake. "How you doing, Angelo," I asked him.

"Eh, not so good. I can't sleep."

"Again, huh? You want me to ask the nurse to give you something?"

"Nah, that stuff makes me goofy afterward. If you're not too busy, maybe we can just talk." I told him I was never too busy for him. So I pulled up a chair and listened—let him take me on a tour of the downtown where he'd grown up, the way it was back when he was a boy. It's a funny thing about those eighty- or ninety-year-old brains: they can't remember what happened ten minutes ago, but they have amazing recall of the distant past. "Let's see. There was Ames's butter and cheese store, and then the Chinese restaurant where my mother used to take me for chicken chow mein. Next to that was the Strand Theater, where they gave away free dishes at the Saturday matinees. I was kind of sweet on one of the usherettes that worked there, Elga Swenson. I asked her for a date once, but she said no, her father didn't want her dating roughnecks. I fixed his wagon, though. He'd pick her up after work and sometimes get there early, go in and watch the picture. Still makes me laugh when I think about the way his car was bucking and stalling after I put sugar in his gas tank."

I listened to Mr. Cavoli that night until he began to doze off— until, maybe, he drifted into a dream where he was young again and his whole life was still ahead of him. They're lonely, these old people. Most of their friends have died off, and some of them have families that hardly ever visit. I get pretty close to some of them. Granted, they don't know that my rap sheet says "pedophile," but maybe it wouldn't matter if they *did* know. Maybe they'd just treat me like they find me. Because I'm not a monster. Hey, I've got my flaws. Plenty of them. But I'm more than just a name on the sex offender registry—someone you've got to keep little girls away from. I've got my good points, too. Like I said, I'm not a monster.

Eldredge Eldercare is owned by some company out of Boston. Corporate's careful not to let any of us ex-offenders work days when some visiting family member might see us. Recognize us. Days is when the A Team's on duty: the chatty Spanish moms, the community college kids who work here first shift and take classes at night. Third shift is when us convicted felons report for duty: Shondell (ex-junkie prostitute), Bryan (DUI fatality), Tricia (embezzler, coke addict), Raj (second-degree assault), and me (risk of injury to a minor, kiddie porn). Nadja and Zahra work our shift, too, although their only "crime" is that they're head scarf–wearing Muslims. The rest of us live in halfway houses, report to parole officers. The vampire shift, we call it. When the sun goes down, we rise from our crypts, put on our scrubs, and report for duty. When the moon fades away at daybreak, we punch out, get picked up by our respective group home vans, grab breakfast, and hit the sack.

I didn't used to work crap jobs. I made decent money selling life insurance. It was a family-run agency, and although I wasn't a member of the tribe, I was their top dog, saleswise. Sold rings around the owner's sons and sons-in-law. See, I figured out the con almost immediately. Used my looks and my charisma to seal those deals. What I'd do was befriend the husband first—kid with him a little, talk sports if that's what he was into. Baseball, football: I didn't give a shit about either, but I read the sports page every morning so I could talk the talk, become a Giants or a Patriots fan, dis the Red Sox or the Yankees as the situation called for. And while the man of the house was looking over the policy, I'd look over at the wife and smile. Hold her gaze for maybe two or three seconds more than another salesman might have. And if she held my gaze in return, I knew that I'd pretty much made the sale—that if her hubby was still on the fence, she'd convince him to buy the policy. The flirtatious glances, the body I took pains to keep in shape: it sold more insurance than whatever deal I was offering them on their premium.

Those sales skills? They were transferable. Single moms with little girls: that's the ideal situation. The one useful thing I got from my father was his good genes—an athlete's build, cobalt blue eyes, and a full head of hair. I'm in my fifties now, but my hair's still as thick as it was when I was in my twenties. I dye the top and leave the temples gray. Three hundred sit-ups and push-ups twice a day, plus watching what I eat, keep my chest and abs tight. I've got the same thirty-three-inch waist I've had all my adult life.

Wooing those mothers and their daughters is a process. I'll get behind them in the checkout line at the grocery store and start chatting them up. Then, out in the parking lot, I'll offer to change the tire I punctured after I watched them walk into the store. Next thing you know, I'm eating supper over at their place, taking them out for ice cream. I'm cultivating them both, see? Playing board games and watching videos with the daughter, then sticking around, having a glass of wine or two with the mom—sympathizing with her about how her ex screwed her over. Then I go home, get in bed with a bottle of lotion, and think about the girl: the sprinkling of freckles across her nose, her cute little butt, what her bare chest and her little cherry must look like. . . .

Sometimes I'll take my Polaroids and magazines out of their hiding place and get off that way. At the house I'm in now, my roommate, Daryl, and I have a deal: he doesn't say anything about the stuff I've got stashed up inside our suspended ceiling and I don't say anything about the weed he's got up there. As a matter of fact, I supply Daryl with his weed. He gives me the money and I buy it from Raj down at work. The staff? They're no problem. When you're a veteran of these places, you can pretty much figure out inside of a week who the naïve do-gooders are, who's dumb as rocks, and who's going to be open to bribery.

"Predator," "pedophile," "child molester": yeah, you could call me any of those things. But don't forget "victim" because that was what came first. You think I was born this way? I wasn't. I got fucked up—"emotionally disregulated" as the shrinks put it—the year I was nine. This one therapist-in-training who interviewed me last month—a grad student who was gathering data for some study she was doing about how pedophilia gets kick-started in childhood—she quizzed me for a couple of hours about how I became who I became. "Please be as candid and thorough as you can," she said. I told her some of it: the abridged version, let's say. You can never fully trust shrinks, no matter how sincere they seem. So you withhold, bullshit them, manipulate them a little for your own amusement. But those questions she kept lobbing at me brought it all back, so vividly that it was like I was reliving it. . . .

The trouble started after my father left my mother and me so that he could shack up with his girlfriend and *her* son, puny little Peter Clegg, who was in my class at school. It was confusing, you know? My dad was a mailman and Peter's mother was the postmaster's secretary. That was how their little "romance" started. But at the time, I didn't get any of that. I just assumed that he had left because he liked Peter better than he liked me. What I couldn't figure out was why.

Dad left us high and dry. I was in Cub Scouts, okay? One week Mom was a housewife and our den mother, and the next week she was a grocery clerk down at the First National. That was when I had to start taking the bus over to this woman Irma's house after school.

Irma Cake: she was a foster mother, but she babysat other kids, too. Us after-school kids had to play down in the basement so we wouldn't wake the babies up from their naps or bother her while she was watching her stories on TV. Those babies all must have been heavy sleepers, I guess, because she'd have the volume up so loud that you could hear the television through the fucking floorboards. *Time now for . . . The Edge of Night.* We were only allowed upstairs at snack time, or if we had to use the toilet. And if you needed to tell Irma something while you were up there, you had to wait for a commercial.

Irma's daughter, Tawny, was in charge downstairs. To this day, I fantasize about running into Tawny Cake on the street somewhere and making her pay for the things she did. One time when I was in prison, I woke up smiling from a dream where I'd just plunged a shiv into her heart.

Tawny was older than the rest of us—fourteen or fifteen, maybe. She was a big bruiser and unpredictable as hell. Nice to you one day and a bully the next. On my first day at Irma's, Tawny gave me a handful of Hershey's Kisses. On the second day, I called her Scrawny Tawny, thinking she'd think it was funny. Instead of laughing, she smacked me so hard across the mouth that I cut the inside of my lip on my bottom teeth. She wouldn't let me go upstairs so Irma could look at it, so I just sat there cross-legged on the floor, swallowing back my tears and snot and blood. I never knew from day to day, sometimes from hour to hour, which Tawny I was dealing with.

My mother didn't work on weekends. Sometimes we'd get in the car and go places on Saturday: Wequonnoc Park to look at the animals and swing on the swings, or down to Ocean Beach if it was summer. Once a month or so, we'd drive the forty-five minutes to my cousins' house, the O'Days. Uncle Chick and my mom were brother and sister, and my cousin Donald and I were almost the same age. I liked Donald okay back then, but it bugged me that he was bigger than me, and ten months older, and that *his* father hadn't left *him*. But anyway, whatever Mom and I did on Saturday, by Sunday afternoon I'd start worrying about the next day when I'd have to go back over to Irma's. When I told my mother I didn't want to go there anymore, she said I *had* to go. "These changes are hard for me, too, you know," she said. "Do you think I want to be over at the First National all day, ringing up people's groceries while they watch me like hawks, thinking that I'm out to cheat them? But this is the way things are now, Kent, and we both have to just accept it. And if you don't like it, then call up your father and tell *him* because he's the one who made this mess." When I *did* call Dad, my classmate Peter Clegg was the one who answered. "Who *is* this?" he kept saying. "If you're not going to say anything, then I'm hanging up." And he did, three times in a row. The fourth time, the phone just kept ringing and ringing.

Mornings at school were okay, but once lunch was over, I'd start staring at the wall clock, dreading what was coming. And when the bus driver yanked the door open in front of Irma's, I'd get off as slowly as I could. Irma would appear at the door, holding a baby or a toddler in her arms and calling to me to hurry on in. "How was school today, Kent?" she'd ask.

"Good."

"Okay, down you go then. The girls and Tawny are waiting for you."

The girls, Sandra and Nadine, were both in my grade, but they went to a different school. I didn't like either of them. And I hated Tawny.

There was stuff to play with in the basement, but it was shabby: puzzles with missing pieces, books with all the pictures scribbled on, plastic cowboys and Indians that Irma's dog had chewed before it got run over by a car. The only good thing down there was this can of Lincoln Logs. I'd make a beeline for them, then sit on the cold, damp cement floor and build stuff so I wouldn't have to play dolls with the girls, or get in trouble with Tawny. But I'd be in the middle of making a fort or something when she'd yank me up off the floor and tell me I had to play some stupid game she'd invented. "Twirling" was one. No matter how dizzy you got, we had to keep spinning around in circles until she said we could stop. "Halt!" she'd yell. Then she'd laugh as we staggered like drunks, falling onto the floor or crashing into chairs or walls. If you stopped before she said you could, you had to go through the spanking machine. When Sandra and Nadine spanked you, it didn't hurt, but as you passed under Tawny's legs, she'd whack your butt hard enough to make it sting. After a while, Sandra stopped coming, so it was just Nadine and me. That was when Tawny started making us play "House."

In "House," Nadine was the wife and I had to be the husband. "Hug her," Tawny would order me. "Now call her darling and kiss her." If I cooperated, she'd peel back a roll of Life Savers and let me take two. If I refused, she'd pin me against the floor and tickle me until, unable to breathe, I'd give in. But one day when Tawny told us we had to play "House" again, I dug my heels in. "You do what I say, or else!" she threatened.

"Or else what?" Or else she'd tickle me again, I thought.

"You'll see." When I shook my head, she went upstairs and came back down with an electrical cord and threatened to whip me with it.

"Go ahead," I said. "See if I care." This was a bluff; I was petrified. She chased me around the basement until she had me cornered. Then she yanked down my pants and underpants and lashed my bare butt while Nadine stood there, wide-eyed. "Does that hurt?"

"No, it tickles."

"Yeah? Then how about this?" Several blows later, she had me crying and begging her to stop.

The door at the top of the stairs banged open. "Tawny! What the hell's going on down there?" Irma shouted.

Tawny answered before I could. "Nothing, Ma. Kent's just being a little brat. He's grabbing all the toys and won't share them with Nadine." I would have denied it if she wasn't holding that cord in her fist, ready to whale me some more if I did.

"Then you and Nadine come up and have a snack," Irma said. "And Kent, you can just stay down there by your lonesome for being so selfish."

Halfway up the stairs, Tawny turned back and smirked. "I hope you know there's rats down here. They have red eyes that glow in the dark, and that's the only way you can see them. And when they bite you, you get diseases. This other boy we used to babysit got bit and he *died*." At the top of the stairs, she hit the light switch and the basement went black.

Temporarily blinded, I felt my way to the railing, then crept up to the second step from the top. Blinking back tears, I hugged my knees and looked down, on guard against red-eyed rats.

After I got home that day, my mother wanted to know why I was being such a pouty face. I told her I didn't know. "No? Well, why don't you go take your bath while I start supper?"

While the bathtub was filling up, I undressed and touched my backside because it felt sore and hot. Then I stood up on the toilet and looked over my shoulder in the medicine cabinet mirror. When I saw the ugly red stripes, I started to cry. "Everything okay in there?" Mom called in to me.

"Yes! Don't come in!"

"Well, my goodness, aren't *you* getting modest."

The next day, Tawny ignored me and played all afternoon with Nadine.

The day after that, she snuck upstairs and came down shaking a can of Reddi-wip. "Open your mouths," she told us. When we did, she filled them with whipped cream. Nadine only got one squirt, but I got three. I didn't know why.

That night, when my mother tucked me in, I told her I didn't need anyone to babysit me—that starting on Monday, I could just come home after school, do my homework, set the table, and not get into any trouble. She said maybe we could try that next year when I was in fifth grade, but for now I was too young. "I'd be at the store, watching the clock and worrying about whether or not you were okay. And anyway, if you didn't go to Irma's anymore, you'd never find out about the surprise you're getting."

"What surprise?" I wanted to know.

She said I had to wait and see on Monday. What I imagined was that my father was going to appear at Irma's, take me home, and start living with us again. "Does it have anything to do with Daddy?"

"With Daddy? No, no. It's something else." She reminded me that

I would see my father the next afternoon for our visit. While I was having my visit with him, she said, she was going to get me my surprise and bring it over to Irma's. I begged her for a clue, but she said I'd just have to wait.

When my father picked me up on Saturday afternoon, Peter Clegg was in the car with him. On the way to the movie we were going to, Peter and I had to sit together in the backseat, but neither of us said anything to the other. The movie was *A Night to Remember*, about the sinking of the *Titanic*. I got to sit next to Dad and Peter Clegg sat next to me so we could share the bucket of popcorn. But when the people in the movie started drowning, baby Peter got scared and we had to switch seats. "It's okay, buddy," Dad assured Peter. "It's not real. It's just a movie." He put his arm around him.

"It is *so* real," I leaned over and whispered. "The *Titanic* was a real ship, and all those people really *died*." When Dad got mad at me for making Peter cry, I upended our tub of popcorn and said it was an accident.

My surprise was a little brown gerbil in a cage. The rule was that I couldn't take him home; I could only play with him when I was at Irma's. Mom's plan worked for a while; I stopped complaining about having to go over there. Now, besides the Lincoln Logs, I had my gerbil to play with. I named him Funny because he made me laugh. And that first week, Funny brought me luck. Tawny was gone. She'd gotten sick over the weekend, Irma said, and had to go to the hospital and have her appendix taken out. So it was just me and Nadine downstairs by ourselves. "Can I hold Funny now?" she kept asking me.

"No!" I kept saying. "He's mine." So she had to keep sitting there, watching Funny crawl up and down my arm and eat pellets from my hand.

Then, for no reason, Nadine told me her parents were divorced.

"So?" I said. "What do I care?"

She shrugged. Then she told me my parents were getting a divorce, too.

"No, they're not!" I insisted.

"Yes, they are. Irma told my mother."

"Well, she's wrong then. My father is just on vacation."

"Oh," Nadine said. "You know what? I have a boyfriend."

"Who cares? Stop bothering me."

"You want to know who it is?" I told her I didn't. "It's you," she said.

"It is *not*."

She wanted to know why I didn't want to be her boyfriend. "Because I hate girls, and because you're ugly and have yellow teeth."

She didn't say anything for the next several minutes. Then what she said was, "I hope Tawny dies while she's in the hospital. Don't you?"

We looked at each other for several seconds. Then I nodded. "Here," I said, handing her my gerbil. "You can hold him for one minute, starting now. One thousand one, one thousand two . . ." When I got to one thousand sixty, I put my hand out and demanded that she give him back. She did.

Tawny was still in the hospital the next day. The day after that, she was back home, but she had to lie down on the couch upstairs. But by Thursday, she was back in the basement. She told Nadine and me that while she was in the hospital, a nurse had walked her down to the nursery and let her look at the new babies, and it had given her an idea. "Today when you play 'House,' you two are going to make a baby. Do you know how?" Nadine and I looked at each other, wide-eyed, and shook our heads. "Okay, first of all, you both have to take off all your clothes." Ever the obedient one, Nadine began to undress, but I just stood there, shaking my head. "Okay, suit yourself," Tawny said. She walked over to Funny's cage and took him out. His head was poking out from the hole between her thumb and index finger.

"Put him back!" I said. "You can't touch him! He's mine!"

"He's mine!" she mimicked. She scooped a Lincoln Log off the floor and started tapping it against the top of his head. "Are you going to take your clothes off or not?" she said.

"No!" The tapping got harder and harder.

"Stop crying!" she said. "You're the man, not the lady."

With my fists, I rubbed away my tears. Then I yanked off my sneakers, pulled my polo shirt over my head, and pulled down my pants.

"That's better. Now walk over to your wife and kiss her." I approached Nadine and gave her a peck on the cheek. "On the lips, idiot!" When I just stood there, not doing it, the tapping started again. I kissed Nadine on the lips like she wanted me to. "Did I *tell* you to stop? Do it again, and while you're still kissing her, reach down and touch her cunny."

"Her what?" I asked.

"Boy, you really are stupid, aren't you?" She tossed the Lincoln Log onto the floor, walked over to Nadine, and cupped her hand around the little knob between her legs. I did what she said. Her next order was for Nadine. "Now you touch his thing. Keep doing it until I tell you to stop."

Sometimes, at night in bed, I would reach under my pajamas and touch my pee-pee to make it hard. I liked doing it; it felt nice. But this didn't. When Nadine made it hard, Tawny pointed at it and laughed. She told Nadine to lie on her back on the floor. Then she ordered me to lie down on top of her and move around. "Move around how?" I asked her.

"Like a milk shake in a milk shake maker. Then the baby will start growing inside of her." I was confused. Were we *playing* making a baby, or were we really going to make one? I wasn't about to disobey her, though. As long as I did what she said, she wouldn't hurt Funny.

The next day at school, on my way back from the drinking fountain, I found Peter Clegg's lunch bag in the coatroom, threw it on the floor, and stomped it flat. At afternoon recess, I tripped him during a game of tag. He stumbled, hit the ground, and ripped his pants at the knees. He told the teacher on duty that I'd done it on purpose. "No, I didn't! It was an accident!" I kept insisting until the teacher believed me.

When the bus dropped me off at Irma's that afternoon, her car wasn't in the driveway. The front door was unlocked but no one was around. "Hello?" I kept saying. "Hello?" When I went down to the basement, I was relieved to see that Funny was still alive and well. I grabbed a handful of pellets, took him out of his cage, and stroked his back as he ate. When he pooped on my hand, I walked over to the chair where Tawny always sat and smeared it on the seat.

Where was everyone? I liked nobody else being there, but a little bit didn't like it either because I kept thinking about those red-eyed rats. I was building Funny a Lincoln Log house when the basement door banged open. Nadine was the first one to come into view, then Tawny.

"Where's Irma?" I asked. Tawny said one of the foster babies had a doctor's appointment and she'd taken the other baby, too. "Oh," I said. "Where have you two been?"

"Up in Tawny's room," Nadine said. "Do you like my braids? Tawny braided them." I hadn't until then noticed them. I'd been looking, instead, at the red splotch on her neck.

When I glanced over at Tawny, I saw that she was waiting for my answer. "Yeah," I said. "They're nice."

Later, when we were getting ready to play "House," I saw two more red splotches on Nadine—one on her stomach, and one on the inside of her leg. "Are you getting the measles?" I asked her.

Tawny grabbed onto my shoulder and squeezed. "Haven't you ever heard that curiosity killed the gerbil?" she said. This time when I had to get on top of Nadine and move like a milk shake, I closed my eyes. That made it easier. It even felt a little bit good.

On the bus the next morning, Susan Gibson sat on the seat in front of mine. She was wearing her Girl Scout uniform. I heard her telling Debbie Casey that she'd sold nineteen dollars' worth of Girl Scout cookies, and when she handed in her money at the meeting that afternoon, she was hoping she'd get the pin for being the top seller.

We had an assembly that day, and in the middle of some lady talking about the Indian tribes that used to live in Connecticut, I asked my teacher, Miss Faborsky, if I could go to the boys' room. She asked me if I could wait until the assembly was over. I shook my head. So she let me.

I didn't really have to go. Instead of heading to the boys' room, I returned to our classroom. The lights were off and the coast was clear. I sat down on Susan's seat, reached around in her desk, and found an envelope. Inside was a sheet where she'd written down her cookie order, plus a ten-dollar bill, a five, and four ones. I put everything back in the envelope, then walked over to where Peter Clegg sat, and stuck it inside his desk. Later, when Susan reported that her cookie money was missing, Miss Faborsky made us all stand up, tilt our desks forward so that everything inside fell out onto the floor, and then go stand in a line against the chalkboard. As she walked up and down the rows, examining our piles, she stopped at Peter Clegg's desk and picked up the envelope. "What's this?" she asked Peter. He said he didn't know. She returned the money to Susan and told Peter to go down to the office. After he left the room in tears, Miss Faborsky gave the rest of us a speech about honesty. Whenever her eyes met mine, I nodded. I felt more glad than guilty. Peter hadn't stolen Susan's money, but he *had* stolen my father.

After school, Irma's car was gone again. Grocery shopping this time, Tawny said. We *still* hadn't made our baby, she told us, so we had to try again. It was part of our regular routine now and didn't seem so bad. But this time while I was moving around on top of Nadine, I heard funny noises coming from Tawny. I cracked my eyes open just a little and looked over at her. It took me a few seconds to realize what I was seeing. Her pants were down around her ankles and her knees were wide apart. She was touching herself down there. What struck me more than what she was doing was that she had hair down there, the kind my father had. I'd seen Dad naked a number of times, in the changing room at the community pool, walking bare-butt from his shower to his and Mom's room. But I'd never seen my mother naked. Did ladies grow hair down there, too, the same as men, or was Tawny a freak, like the bearded lady at the carnival? Confused and not wanting to get caught watching her, I closed my eyes again. That was the first time I spasmed while playing "House," dryly but with a kind of painful pleasure. I was more confused than ever.

The next week was February vacation. Mom took the week off from work, so I got to take Funny home with me. By midweek, vacation had gotten boring. Tommy Mankin invited me over to his house one afternoon, and we played football and Crazy Eights, but that was boring, too. Even playing with Funny got boring. I kept thinking about playing "House."

On the Monday after vacation, I got to take Funny to school with me. During show-and-tell, I felt like a big shot answering my classmates' questions: What did he eat? When did he sleep? Peter Clegg asked me the stupidest question of all: weren't gerbils in the same family as mice and rats? I rolled my eyes and told him no.

"Well, actually, Peter's right," Miss Faborsky said. She walked over to the shelf where the World Book Encyclopedias were, pulled out the *R* volume, and flipped through the pages. "Rodents, rodents . . . ," she said. "Ah, here we go." She handed the open book to Roberta Delgado and told her to have a look, then pass it on. When it got to me, I gazed, stunned, at the two-page color spread: mice and squirrels, rats and mole rats, beavers and muskrats. And sure enough, in the company of these others was a gerbil that looked a lot like Funny. Peter Clegg lived close enough to school that he didn't have to take the bus; he rode his bike. And so later that day, after we'd used compasses for an art lesson, I hid mine instead of handing it in. At afternoon recess, I snuck out to the bike rack and punched holes in Peter's tires.

After school, at Irma's front door, I was met by a stranger. "You must be Kent," she said. "I'm Dottie, Irma's friend. She had to go to Tawny's school today, so she asked me to come and stay with youse until she got back."

"Oh. Is Nadine here?" I asked. She said yes, downstairs. She was waiting to show me something.

"Look what I got, Kent!" Nadine said when I was halfway down the basement stairs. Her mother had bought her a gerbil, too—a white one. She'd named her Tammy after that song on the radio. Both Tammy and Funny were out of their cages, chasing each other. They were friends, Nadine said. She picked up her stupid gerbil and put it against her neck. "Stop tickling me," she told it, giggling.

"I hope you know that gerbils are in the same family as rats," I said.

"They are?"

"Yes! So you better hope she doesn't bite you because it would be the same as getting a rat bite." I unbuckled my belt, pulled it away from my dungarees, and threw it on the floor. "Come on," I said. "We're playing 'House.'"

Nadine said she didn't really feel like it.

"Well, *I* do. Come on. Make it snappy!"

A few minutes later, while I was moving against her, our clothes in a pile on the floor, I heard someone say, "Oh, my god! What the hell—" When I looked up, there was Dottie.

That night, while my mother and I were eating supper, the doorbell rang. It was Irma. She was holding Funny's cage. I went to my room and tried as best I could to listen through the crack in the door, but all I could make out was what my mother was saying. "No, no, I understand. Don't worry. I'll figure it out." I thought I was in big trouble. But after Irma left, all Mom said was that she couldn't babysit me anymore because Tawny had taken another after-school job so there'd be no one downstairs to watch Nadine and me. I figured that whatever Tawny's new job was, it had allowed me to dodge a bullet. It wasn't until years later that the truth dawned on me: if Irma had reported what Dottie had seen, she'd lose her license, and with it her income.

For the rest of fourth grade, I had to go over to this weird old lady Mrs. Weingarth's house. Funny lived in my bedroom now, but I played with him less and less and grew to resent having to clean his cage and make sure he had food and fresh water. One afternoon, when I looked in at him, I was shocked to see him lying down with these fat, pink wormy-looking things crawling all over him—six of them! I knew dogs got worms, but I didn't know gerbils got them. Careful not to touch any of them, I lifted Funny out of his cage, then unhooked the bottom tray and carried it into the bathroom. I poked at the slimy pink things with a pencil until each one dropped with a little plunk into the toilet. Then I flushed it. Watching them swirl around in the water and disappear, it suddenly dawned on me that they weren't worms; they were babies. . . . That Funny must be a girl and Tammy must be a boy, instead of the other way around. And that while Nadine and I had been *pretending* to make a baby, our gerbils had made six of them. I kept my mouth shut, though. I didn't tell my mother. And when Funny died a few months later, I wasn't even that sad. I put her stiff little body in a lunch bag and buried her in our backyard as if I was burying everything that had happened in Irma's basement.

When I was in fifth grade, my mother finally let me stay home by myself after school. Left to my own devices, I almost never did my homework, or set the table, or took out the garbage like I had so often promised I would. I mostly just watched TV, built airplane models, and made crank phone calls to strangers whose numbers I called at random. "All your friends think you have bad breath but they don't want to tell you," I'd say. Or "Someone's going to rob your house tonight. You better watch out." When they'd demand to know who was calling, I'd hang up.

When I was in sixth grade, my father got married again—not to Peter Clegg's mother but to another woman named Helene, who had no kids. Dad invited me to the wedding, but it was on a Sunday night and I told him I'd rather stay home and watch *Bullwinkle*. He wasn't a mailman anymore; now he worked for some shipping company. Just before he got transferred to Cincinnati, he took me out to lunch and told me he wanted us to stay in touch. Did I want that, too?

"Not really," I said, hoping he'd notice what a surly little bastard I'd become, thanks to him.

"Well, okay, suit yourself," he said, instead of offering me the objection I was hoping to hear. After he dropped me off back home, I went upstairs to my room and destroyed the Pinewood Derby car he had helped me make in Cub Scouts. Then I cried into my pillow so that Mom wouldn't hear me.

Sometimes on those afternoons between the time I got home from school and the time my mother got home from work, I'd think about Nadine and me playing "House" and diddle myself until the spasm came. During one of those sessions, it changed from dry to wet. After that, I'd do it so often that I'd make my dick sore. I stuffed the balled-up tissues in the pockets of my sports jacket, which I hardly ever wore anymore. Mom didn't go to church much now, and when she did, I made such a stink about going with her that she gave up and let me stay home. By April of that year, I began to sprout pubic and underarm hair. I became the first of my male classmates to shave. I was drinking coffee at breakfast now, and reading the newspaper—the comics and the police report, mostly. I was delighted the morning I read that

Tawny Cake had gotten arrested for something called "aggravated assault," whatever the fuck that was. That was another change: I swore now. Saying the word *fuck* out loud sent a small thrill through me, and saying it in front of my disapproving mother was an added benefit. By the time I was in the ninth grade, I was stealing Mom's smokes and swigging from the bottle of gin she kept hidden in the china closet. I shoplifted candy at the corner store, answered back my teachers. One day, I got so mad at my shop teacher—I can't remember why—that I stormed out of class, grabbed onto the drinking fountain in the hall, and ripped it away from the wall. They suspended me for two weeks and billed my mother for the damage. I never did go back to that school. Mom was at her wits' end by that time and decided that, since my real father had bailed, what I needed was a father *figure*. She went to see her brother, Uncle Chick, and asked him to help. That was when I went to live with the O'Days.

I liked living there okay, although I wasn't crazy about having to share a bedroom with my goody-goody cousin Donald. Mr. Athlete, Mr. Honor Roll. And I got the message that he wasn't that crazy about the arrangement either. But Uncle Chick was pretty cool. Sometimes after school I'd go down to the Shamrock Barbershop where he worked and hang around, watch him cut hair and entertain his customers. Uncle Chick was funny; he was like a comedian or something. He'd tell jokes, make Uncle Brendan's mynah bird that he kept at the shop say stuff. (Uncle Brendan was Uncle Chick and my mother's uncle, my great-uncle. He owned the barbershop and Uncle Chick worked for him.)

Sometimes on Sunday when the rest of the family would go off to church, Uncle Chick would take me fishing, or out to breakfast, or both. We even went ice fishing once, him and me, and I caught a decent-size striped bass. Donald didn't like to fish, plus he always had a lot of homework. He took college prep classes and I was in general studies. If Uncle Chick and I got back from breakfast before the others returned, he'd show me how to fix things around the house. "How'd you like to learn how to use a socket wrench?" he'd go. Or, "How about you and me tackle that leaky faucet in the bathroom?

Yeah? Okay then. Go out to the Merc and get my toolbox." Uncle
Chick's Mercury station wagon had two rows of bench seats up front,
but he had pulled out the third row of seats and set up a kind of por-
table toolshed in the car's way-back, which was pretty cool.

I liked Aunt Sunny, too. She was pretty, and nice to me. And, unlike my own mother, easy to talk to. When she got pregnant, I was the
first person she told. She had come back from the doctor's earlier that
afternoon and I was the only one home, except for my little cousin
Annie, who was taking a nap. "Guess what, Kent?" she said. It made
me feel like kind of a big deal: knowing before anyone else, even Uncle
Chick.

I used to hang around in the kitchen with Aunt Sunny sometimes
and help her make supper—chop up vegetables or whatever, peel potatoes or stir something on the stove. And while we were working together, she'd sometimes ask me my opinions about stuff: civil rights,
whether or not I thought Kennedy was a good president. She made
me think, you know? She always had the radio on in the kitchen, and
I liked the way she'd sing along with the songs they'd play: "Soldier
Boy," "Johnny Angel," and that Patsy Cline song, "I Fall to Pieces."
Patsy Cline was Aunt Sunny's favorite singer. She'd dance sometimes,
too, when the faster songs came on. Annie would wander in, sleepy-
eyed from her afternoon nap, and the two of them would start dancing with each other. "Come on, Kent. You, too!" Aunt Sunny'd say,
and I'd go, "Nah, no thanks," but she'd pull on my hand and make
me. It was silly, but kind of fun: Annie and Sunny and me dancing
in the kitchen. One time, in the middle of us dancing, Sunny said,
"Whoa," and sat down on a kitchen chair. "Come here, you two," she
told Annie and me. "Someone wants to say hello." She lifted up her
shirt, exposing her swollen belly, and had us put our hands on it so we
could feel the baby kicking. It felt weird but kind of cool, too. "Can
we name her Tinkerbell?" Annie asked, but Aunt Sunny laughed and
said it might be a him, not a her. "But I want a little sister," Annie
insisted.

Aunt Sunny kissed her forehead and said it was up to the baby
what it was going to be, not us. But Annie got her wish. Gracie was

born at the end of the summer. Labor Day weekend, it was. Just before school started up again.

Aunt Sunny was always urging me to go to the school dances when Donald went. I tried it once; that was enough for me. I spent the whole night leaning against the wall, or sneaking down to the boys' room to smoke. They had a ladies' choice near the end of the dance—that corny Bobby Vinton song, "Blue Velvet." I stood there, watching all these goody-goody college prep girls cut in on whoever was dancing with Donald. About halfway through the song, this girl Alice from my homeroom asked me to dance, but she was a chub, so I said I didn't know how to slow-dance. I did, though; Aunt Sunny had taught me. God, I hated Donald that night. When we got home, I went to our room while he was in the kitchen getting something to eat, and I grabbed one of his eight billion sports trophies—the one he'd gotten for good sportsmanship in indoor track. It had a little statue of a runner on top, and I decapitated it and put it back on Donald's shelf. Hid the head under my mattress. Donald didn't even notice until a couple of days later. I walked into the room and he was holding his headless trophy. "How did *this* happen?" he wanted to know.

"How the fuck should I know?" I said. He told me to keep my hands off his stuff. "And what if I don't?" I said. "What are *you* going to do about it?"

"Make you sorry you didn't," he said.

"Oh, yeah? You and whose army?" It was a bluff, of course. Donald wasn't just smarter than me; he was also bigger and stronger. He could have taken me easily. The next morning when he and I were eating breakfast, I got up and went over to the fridge. "Hey, cuz, could you pour me some milk?" he asked. I got out a glass, looked over to make sure he wasn't looking, and spit a hawker into the bottom. Then I poured his milk over it and handed it to him. He thanked me and took a sip.

"Don't mention it," I said.

Maybe Donald didn't like me living with his family, but his little sister sure did. After the dismissal bell, Donald would usually stay at school, going to practice or some club meeting, but I'd head back to the O'Days'. "Wanna play dolls with me?" Annie would ask, or "Wanna color in my coloring book?" Sometimes I would, sometimes I wouldn't. If I said no, she'd follow me around the house. "Whatcha doing, Kent? . . . Wanna read me a story? . . . You know what, Kent? Mommy said next year or the year after that my teeth are gonna get wiggly and come out and then a fairy's gonna fly in my window and take them and leave me money. And I think this one's already wiggly. Wanna feel it?"

"You and Annie have gotten to be real pals, haven't you?" Aunt Sunny said once. "She's crazy about you. I hope you realize how good you are with little kids." I liked hearing her say that, and I liked Annie, too. She could be pesty if you weren't in the mood, but I got a kick out of her most of the time. I acted more like her big brother than Donald did.

Having to share a room with Mr. Perfect cut seriously into my jerk-off sessions. They were limited mostly to the times when I went in the bathroom and locked the door, or at night under the covers after the lights were out, or when I could get the lavatory pass at school and beat my meat while looking at the dirty graffiti scrawled all over the walls of the stall. Sometimes, to get myself in the mood, I'd think about Nadine's flat chest and hairless twat, me lying on top of her and gyrating like a fuckin' milk shake. But I didn't think of my little cousin in that way. I just liked Annie because she liked me.

Chapter Twenty

Annie Oh

Minnie and I are seated in back, and Africa is riding up front with Hector. He's a beautiful child: big eyes, long lashes, and that hair that was so popular with blacks back in the 1970s. A "natural," they called it. But the boy is antsy, shifting around in his seat, fingering the buttons on the console. "Sit still up there!" his mother scolds. He unbuckles himself and turns back on his knees. Cups his hand to his mouth and whispers something I don't quite catch. "What you mean you gotta go again? It ain't but twenty minutes since we stopped the last time."

Cause and effect, I feel like saying. Maybe she shouldn't have bought him that big blue slushie at the comfort stop. I reach over the seat and tousle his hair. "It's okay, honey. When a guy's got to go, he's got to go. Right?"

"Uh-huh."

"Don't you 'uh-huh' her," Minnie says. "You say yes, Miz Anna."

"Yes, Miss Anna."

We're in East Hartford now, another forty-five minutes from Three Rivers, still, but just a few miles from the mall. "Hector, why don't you take the Buckland Street exit up ahead? There are plenty of restaurants along there where we can stop."

"Yes, ma'am."

I'm paying Hector and Minnie each a thousand dollars to make this trip. They can both use the money more than I can use their services, but I'm glad I've hired them. With the exception of my kids and a few others, most of the people coming to the wedding are friends and clients of Viveca's. Well, Minnie and Hector are *my* friends, more or less. Approaching the exit, Hector puts on his blinker. Drives the quarter mile and stops at the light. "Chuck E. Cheese!" Africa shouts, his face to the window.

"You keep still," his mother tells him. "We ain't stopping at no Chuck E. Cheese. You just gonna go into wherever Mr. Hector stops so you can do your bidness. This trip ain't about you. You just along for the ride." Africa's bottom lip pokes out, but he doesn't protest.

"This up ahead all right?" Hector asks. I tell him that's fine, and he signals and pulls into the parking lot of a Friendly's.

While his mother hustles Africa inside, I climb out of the backseat to stretch my legs. Hector gets out, too. Lights up. I bum a cigarette from him and do the same. I'm excited about the wedding, but nervous, too. It was stupid of me to try and quit a few days ago. If I need a little nicotine to get through the next few days, then so be it.

I watch Hector as he scans the area. Home Depot, the Olive Garden, Nordstrom's, and Macy's up on the hill. "Welcome to suburbia," I say.

"People here got money. Right, Miss Oh?" I've given up trying to get him to call me Annie. "I read in the *Post* that Connecticut is the richest state. Richer than New York, even."

"Well, the big money's downstate: Greenwich, Darien. This is a more middle-class area. And there's plenty of poverty in Connecticut, too. Especially where we're going." Not that he'll see any of that this weekend. Even scaled down like I requested, the reception is costing Viveca fifty thousand dollars. That's another thing I finally gave up on: paying for half. "Sweetheart, don't worry about it. I can write some of it off as a business expense," she insisted. But two hundred dollars a plate for the wedding supper? Krug champagne at three hundred dollars a bottle? Ridiculous.

A rusty car with a rumbling muffler pulls into the lot. A black girl in a cap and uniform gets out and runs toward the building. Late for work, I figure. Hector's watching her, too. No wonder. She's got a cute little figure. "I worked at one of these Friendly's places once," I tell him. A few days ago, I read a headline in Viveca's *Wall Street Journal*: FRIENDLY'S CHAIN LOSING MARKET SHARE.

"*You* did? I wouldn't have guessed that, Miss Oh."

"No? Why not?"

"Well, you know. I've heard what rents go for in your building."

"Oh, I didn't come from money, Hector. In fact, I was piss poor. Used to be thrilled when the big spenders came in and left a whole dollar for a tip."

"Maybe that's why you're such a good tipper now, huh? Because you remember what it was like."

I smile, shrug. Exhale.

"So you have family coming to your wedding?" he asks.

"New York friends, mostly. But my kids will be there, and my brother and his wife. Oh, and the man who gave me my start as an artist."

"Yeah? Your teacher?"

"No, he was the judge for an art show—the first one I ever entered. When he picked my work for a prize, I was shocked. But that blue ribbon validated me. Encouraged me at a time I was thinking about giving up. He's quite elderly now, but he's coming. I haven't seen him in a long time."

"That'll be nice then, huh? Seeing him again?"

"It will. I'll make sure I introduce you. His name is Mr. Agnello."

Hector's smile fades away. "Yeah, but I was thinking, Miss Oh, that maybe I shouldn't go tomorrow if it's real fancy. I brought a pair of dress pants and my silk shirt with me, but I don't have a suit." I tell him what he's packed will be just fine. That I *want* him to be there. "Okay then. You think they've got an ironing board at that motel we're staying at? Because I just put them in a Safeway bag and they're probably going to be pretty wrinkled."

"That's not a problem, Hector. Tell you what. When you drop me off, come in and I'll press them for you and put them on a hanger. Then you won't have to worry about it."

He shakes his head. "You don't have to do that, Miss Oh."

"It's not a problem. It'll take me all of five minutes."

"No, that's all right. Maybe Minnie can iron them for me."

"Well, we'll figure it out."

"So your kids are coming, huh? That's nice. How many you got?"

We've already had this discussion, but I guess he doesn't remember. "I have three, the same as you. I know you've met my daughter, Marissa." *Your doorman's hot*, I recall her saying, as boy-crazy as ever.

"The one who lives in the city. Right?"

"Uh-huh. And I have a son and another daughter. Ariane's in California and Andrew's stationed down in Texas at Fort Hood."

"He's military?"

"That's right. A lieutenant in the army."

"Nice," he says. He tosses his cigarette on the ground and puts it out with the toe of his shoe. It's the same butterscotch-brown leather I used in the assemblage I sold a few years back: that sad-eyed steer's head I bought from a taxidermist and framed in shoes and coiled leather belts. . . .

"Good news, sweetheart," Viveca says when she calls me at the studio. "I just sold your Wild, Wild West *piece to an investment banker from Wyoming. He came into the gallery and walked right to it without so much as glancing at anything else. I told him forty thousand, figuring I'd go as low as thirty-two or thirty-three. But he sat right down and wrote me a check without even blinking."*

"He's from Wyoming?"

"Uh-huh. Jackson Hole. He said he and his wife are friends with the Cheneys."

"Did he understand that I was making a protest statement?"

"To tell you the truth, that never even came up. But art is in the eye of the beholder, right? And a sale is a sale. Don't work too late tonight, darling. Okay? I asked Carolyn to work a little of her magic, and she's gotten us a nine P.M. reservation at Jean-Georges so that we can celebrate."

Recalling that conversation, the old doubt creeps back into my thinking. We're a mismatch, Viveca and me. Why in the world are we getting married? And why Three Rivers where my old life was? . . . Because we can't get married in New York. And because when we visited Orion that time, she fell in love with the place. The deer, the babbling brook out back. And the painting—the Josephus Jones she's talked about incessantly. No, that's not fair. This isn't about business. It's about us, about Viveca meeting my kids. Oh god, I hope the dinner goes well tonight, never mind the wedding tomorrow. . . .

I would have invited Hector to tonight's get-together—Minnie and her boy, too, if they'd wanted to come—but I didn't think Viveca would want that. So instead I've reserved them rooms at the Best Western on Route 32. I'll give them a little dinner money, too. There's an Applebee's next door and one of those buffet places just down the road in that strip mall. There's an arcade there, too, now that I think of it. Africa will like that. And maybe Hector can check out the casino tonight if he wants to. I can leave him the car. Ride over to the restaurant with Andrew and the girls.

Speaking of who—whom?—maybe they've called. I grab my cell phone out of the car and check to see if they've left me a message. But no. They must still be on the road. I try Marissa's number. She's the one who's always got her cell phone on. . . . But not this time. That's odd. Oh well, they're probably traveling through a dead zone. The service around here can be iffy. At the beep, I leave her a message. "Hi, honey. It's Mom. Just wondering how you guys are doing. Call me when you hear this. Okay?"

Next, I try Viveca. She drove up and checked in at Bella Linda last night because she wanted to go over all the last-minute details with them. She's a little out of her element, not dealing with New Yorkers—a little untrusting that a staff at a rural inn is going to deliver on her expectations. Well, she was the one who wanted quaint, east-of-the-river Connecticut. Rustic décor, sheep grazing in the meadow. If the service is a little more laid-back than Manhattan or Westport, then so be it.

"Hello?"

"Hey, it's me. How's everything going?"

"Fine, sweetheart. Except for the flowers. I distinctly told that florist we wanted calla lilies for the tables, but he said he couldn't get them from his supplier, so he substituted hydrangeas. He got a little defensive when I told them that just wasn't acceptable, so he's called around and located what we wanted from a different company. He's assured me they'll be delivered in time tomorrow." Well, okay. Now she'll have her calla lilies. Why is she giggling?

"What's funny?" I ask.

"Oh, nothing. I'm just a little tipsy, and Lorenzo's sitting here being Lorenzo. He drove up last night, and we're having lunch. You know what a naughty boy he can be. He insisted that we had to have champagne with our salads. Are you at the house yet?" I tell her no, still on the way. Tell her about Africa's having to come along last minute.

"Oh, dear," she says. I can probably guess what she's thinking: that it's not exactly a children's affair. That she *told* me to hire a car service instead of involving our help. "Well, when you get in, let me know and we'll drive over there. I'm dying to show Lorenzo the Josephus Jones. He says he and Marcus might be interested in it, provided we can get your ex to budge on selling it to me. What's the address? Wait a sec. Let me get something to write it down."

Oh, shit. That was Orion's one condition: that she not come over to the house. It seems silly, but I've given him my word. "You know what, Viveca? Why don't you two stay put and let me bring it over there? I uh . . . I haven't been to Bella Linda since they renovated. I'd like to see what they've done."

"All right then. What? Wait a minute, Anna. What did you say, Lorenzo?" More laughter. "Lorenzo said to tell you that we discovered a creamery down the road from here that has homemade peach ice cream." I know the place she's talking about: Blue Slope Dairy, the place with the petting zoo the kids loved. "I've warned him that it's probably got so much butterfat in it, he's going to ruin his boyish figure. Wait a minute, sweetheart. What, Lorenzo? . . . Oh, yes, all right. He says he wants to show you his new tattoo. It's a sunburst circling his navel. Marcus has a matching one. They got them in Chinatown."

"Uh-huh."

"He's been lifting up his shirt all morning to show everyone. The little bumpkin at the front desk got so flustered when he showed her, I thought she was going to need smelling salts, poor thing. Of course, if he keeps eating ice cream while he's here, those abs he's so proud of are going to disappear."

When I look up, I see Minnie hurrying Africa back toward the car. Good god, what has she bought him now? "Okay, I'd better go now, Viveca. I'll call you when we get to the house, and then I'll have Hector drive me over."

"And don't forget to bring the painting," she says.

"I won't."

Minnie swings the back door open and orders Africa to get in back with me and her, and to sit in the middle. When he objects, she warns him not to give her any lip. He's holding one of those waffle cones—two scoops of candy-studded pink ice cream. "That's a big cone for someone your size," I tell him. "What kind did you get?"

"Bubble gum."

"Oh, my. Is it good?" He nods. The sickening sweet aroma of his treat fills the backseat. Minnie orders him to buckle his seat belt, and as he struggles to do so one-handed, his ice cream comes perilously close to falling off the cone and into my lap. "Watch where you're pointing that thing at!" Minnie says. She's armed herself with an inch-thick stack of napkins. "And don't slobber on yourself. I only got two sets of clothes for you, one for today and one for tomorrow. I better not have to be washing out no laundry in the sink."

Hector starts the car and heads out of the parking lot. That cloying bubble gum smell is the same as the amoxicillin I used to have to give my kids when they got ear infections—when I'd be cooped up all day in the house with them, spooning that stuff into them and fighting to keep the thermometer in their mouths. I crack open my window to let in some fresh air. Close my eyes and see, again, that pediatrician's waiting room. What was his name? Dr. McNally—that was it. God, I hated going there. Whoever was sick that visit would sit on my lap, clinging to me, while whoever wasn't sick *yet* played on the floor with all those germy toys and runny-nosed other children. Home again, I'd be managing the sick bay all day long, and then Orion wouldn't get back from work until after I'd gotten the kids down for the night. He'd sit there at the kitchen table, eating his warmed-up supper and looking through the mail and the magazines, nodding and half-listening as I stood there, complaining about what a hellish day I'd had. I can only remember one time when *he* called in and stayed home with the kids when they were sick—the time I got called for jury duty. Sitting in that courthouse all day, among the pool of prospective jurors, was like a vacation. I remember how disappointed I was when, at the last minute, they settled the case and dismissed us. And when I got home, Orion was so put out about his long day tending to their needs, he'd acted like I was supposed to award him a medal for valor. . . . I open my eyes again and look down at my hands. They're fists.

We're not even back on the highway yet, and Africa's already fighting a losing battle against his cone, licking and slurping at the melting ice cream that's dripping onto his shorts. Minnie's looking out the window, watching the stores go by, oblivious. Oblivious, too, to his just having bitten off the pointy end of his cone and begun sucking out the ice cream from the bottom. Andrew used to do the same thing, and it would drive me up the wall.

Andrew: I'm excited to see him, but a lot of my apprehension about the next few days centers around him—how he'll react to Viveca, and she to him if his disapproval is obvious. And now he'll have Lorenzo to deal with, too, I suppose. Lorenzo's such a flirt. Why did he, of all people, have to drive up here early? . . . I just hope Andrew didn't feel he *had* to come because she sent him those plane tickets. If she had only told me she was planning to do that, I would have said it was a bad idea. His conservative Christian fiancée had a ticket, too, but she isn't coming. Is she busy, or is she boycotting?

Hector eases back into the flow of traffic on the interstate. Africa hasn't paid me much attention on this trip, but now that he's riding in back, he's staring at me. Wearing his ice cream mustache and studying me with those big dark eyes of his. Instead of returning my smile, he asks me how old I am. "How old do you think?" I say. "Take a guess."

"Eighty?"

His mother swivels back toward him, mortified. "Miz Anna ain't no eighty! Thass rude! You say you're sorry."

"It's fine, Minnie." I give him a smile. Tell him I'm fifty-two.

"How come you just gettin' married if you old?"

Minnie frowns and opens her mouth again, but I hold up my hand to stop her. "Well, honey, I was married before, but I got divorced. So now I'm marrying somebody else."

"Him?" he asks, pointing up at Hector.

"No, no, the woman I live with. The one your mother works for."

"Oh," he says. "You got kids?"

"Yes, I do. Hector and I were just talking about—"

"They got Xbox?"

"Gee, I don't know. Probably not, though. They're grown-ups. My son is in the army."

His eyes widen. "How many bad guys he kill?"

"Well, he doesn't fight in the wars, honey. He works at a hospital in Texas. Do you know where Texas is?"

He shakes his head. "How come you marrying a lady?"

"Mind your bidness, Africa! Eat your ice cream!"

"No, it's okay. We're getting married because we love each other."

"Oh," he says. No longer interested, he puts the bottom of his cone to his lips and sucks some more. "Hey!" he protests when his mother yanks it away. "Gimme it back, Mama! It's mine!"

"You don't know how to eat a ice cream right, you can go without." She puts her window down and throws the cone out onto the highway. When Africa begins to cry, she asks him if he wants her to *give* him something to cry about. Starts swiping at his mouth with her stack of napkins. "Look at them shorts," she sputters. "You wearin' more than you ate. You ain't been nothin' but trouble this whole trip. I oughta have Mr. Hector pull over and drop you off on the side of the road." I hold my tongue, but what a horrible thing to say to the boy. Was I ever that rough on my kids?

After Africa stops sniveling, the car becomes quiet except for the hum of the tires on the road. Suddenly, I'm jarred by a memory I wish to god hadn't resurfaced. . . .

I'm at the wheel up front and the three kids are in back, the baby strapped into her car seat, finally asleep, and Andrew and Ariane on ei-

ther side of her. They're peevish, both of them. They've been at each other all day, and I'm sick of it. "If you two wake up your sister, you're going to be sorry you did," I warn them.

"You're ugly and stupid," Ariane tells her brother.

"I know you are, but what am I?"

"Ow!" In the mirror, I see them reaching past their little sister and hitting each other. "Mama! Andrew just scratched me!"

"Goddamn you two!" I slam on the brake. Pull off the road and face them. "I've had it with both of you! Get out of the car." They look at each other, shocked. "You heard me. Out!" And when they obey, I gun it. Glimpse their fear in the rearview mirror. Good! Let them be scared for a few minutes. Maybe that will teach them.

Half a mile down the road, I take a right, and then another. One more and I'll be back there. But when I pass a secondhand store I've never seen before, I brake. Put the car in reverse. The baby's still asleep, so I get out with the motor running. This is just the kind of place where I've found some of the raw materials for my best work. GOING OUT OF BUSINESS! a sign in the window says. I don't have time to go inside—I have to get back to the twins—but I can at least take a quick look at the stuff that's out on the sidewalk: used pots and pans, old Life magazines, a rack of clothes, a wooden coat tree. A man comes out and sees me eyeing two hideous-looking animals, dead and stuffed—a weasel of some kind and . . . is it a wolf?

"Coyote," the man says. "And the other one's a fisher cat. There used to be plenty of them around here, but you don't see them much anymore. I can let you have them both for seventy-five bucks. They're worth more." When I shake my head, he says okay, fifty then. I tell him I'm in a hurry but that I'll be back. I run to the car and take off.

Approaching the place where I made them get out, I see a gray station wagon stopped at the side of the road, its directional signal blinking. There's a man squatting beside them, talking to them. Oh god! Oh no! I slam on the brake, fly out of the car, and run toward them, screaming. "Get away from them! Don't you dare talk to my kids!" He stands, hurries back to his car, calling over his shoulder that he was only trying to help them. "What kind of mother leaves her children by the side of the road and—"

"Shut up!" I reach them, grab on to them, hold them tightly to me. "Get out of here before I call the police!"

"Someone ought to call the police on you!*" he shouts back. Slams his car door and takes off, his back tires spitting up gravel, his signal still blinking.*

I was only gone for a few minutes. I only wanted to teach them a lesson. But oh god, what if . . . what if . . . what kind of a mother . . .

I drive away, sobbing. From the backseat, Ariane consoles me. "It's okay, Mama. I told him you were coming back. We won't fight anymore." When I look in the mirror, I see Andrew staring at me, in stunned disbelief still.

Later, sitting at the counter of the five-and-ten, I watch them eat their sundaes. Ask them if they're going to tell their father. They shake their heads. And when, that weekend Orion spells me and I'm free to go off on one of my hunting expeditions, I drive around, looking for that secondhand shop. When I finally find it and pull up to the front, there's nothing out on the sidewalk. I get out of the car, look at the sign in the window. There's a big red ex across the word GOING *and, above it, the word* GONE. *It's dark inside, but in the pile of stuff that hasn't yet been cleared out, I see the coyote and the fisher cat. I'm too late. The piece I've been imagining for the past three days, constructing in my head and sketching out on paper, will never be made. . . .*

My eyes fill with tears. I turn and look out the window so that Minnie won't see. All *she* did was make an empty threat, but I actually left them there and drove off. Tried to scare them. Maybe that man who stopped *was* just trying to help them. I hear him again: *What kind of a mother . . .* A terrible one, that's what kind I was. A mother who was angry and resentful and so focused on her art that . . . They deserved someone better—someone as patient and even-keeled as their father. I probably shouldn't even have had kids. . . . But they turned out all right, didn't they? Survived my mistakes. Oh god, I can't wait to see them. Hug them and hear about their lives. Not so much Marissa; I'm caught up on my New York daughter. Sometimes I wish she'd give me *less* information about what she's up to. Not so the twins: Andrew, who's private and closemouthed the way so many men are, and Ariane, who's always so busy with her work. I'm hungry to see them. To be with the three of them.

"You okay back there, Miss Oh?" Hector asks. Our eyes meet in his rearview mirror. I nod, tell him I'm fine. "You mind if I play some music?"

"No, not at all."

He turns on the radio and finds a Spanish station. "That too loud?"

"No, no. It sounds nice. Salsa, right?"

He nods, smiles back at me. "This is Victor Manuelle. He's one of my favorites. Him and Los Van Van. They're great, too. Nobody makes salsa and merengue music like the Cubans."

"Is that right?" For the next several miles, we listen to the music, the commercials in rapid-fire Spanish.

"See that sign, Africa?" I ask the boy. "Can you read what it says?"

He squints. "Three . . . Rivers . . . whassat next word?"

"Wequonnoc," I tell him.

"Three Rivers, Wequonnoc . . ."

"Nation," his mother says. "Where your brains at, boy?" She turns to me, shaking her head. "What they teachin' them at that school anyway?"

"Three Rivers is where we're going," I tell Africa, overriding his mother's embarrassment. "So that means we're almost there."

He nods. Sticks his finger in his nose and digs around in there until Minnie bats it away. Maybe Viveca was right. I probably should have just hired a car service. This has been one long, difficult ride.

A few minutes later, it gets worse. Africa begins to whimper. "What now?" his mother asks him.

"My tummy hurts." When she tells him to sit still and think about something else, he says he can't. That it *really* hurts. "Mama, I gon' be sick!" And sure enough. His head lurches forward and his little belly begins to heave. When I tell Hector to pull over, he nods. Steers into the right lane and then onto the shoulder. But it's too late. Minnie's grabbed the big straw bag that she's packed their clothes in and opened it wide. She shoves Africa's face down into it and he heaves everything he's been eating and drinking.

"It's all right, baby. It's okay," she says, wiping his face. "You feel better now?" He nods, rests his head against her bosom, and she takes hold of his small hand and closes her own work-worn hand over it. It's the first tenderness she's shown him since we left New York. Hector carries the soiled straw bag around to the back and locks it in the trunk, but the stench lingers. Back on the road again, we ride with the windows open, the wind blowing in our faces.

"This the one?" Hector asks me. I tell him it is, and he takes the exit.

We pass over the bridge and into downtown Three Rivers. It all looks the same: cars lined up at the Dunkin' Donuts drive-thru, people standing at the window of the Dairy Queen where Ariane worked one summer. I'm struck with how much fatter people here are than the ones in weight-conscious Manhattan.

The farther up Main Street we ride, the more I see that things *have* changed. The sporting goods store where we used to buy the kids' sneakers has gone out of business and become a secondhand furniture store. Rosenblatt's is still here, I see, with the same family of chipped-nose mannequins in the window looking out with their vacant eyes. The Fart family, Andrew nicknamed them one afternoon, to the giggling delight of his younger sister. A number of small ethnic food places have opened along the main drag now: Rosa's Tacos, Little Saigon, Jamaican Meat Patties Made Fresh Daily! Probably a result of all the immigrants who work entry-level jobs down at the casino. And for the unemployed, here's a pawnshop. . . . An everything-for-a-dollar store where Blockbuster used to be . . . A check-cashing place that promises WELFARE CLIENTS WELCOME.

At a traffic stop, a haggard man of undeterminable age holds up a cardboard sign: OUT OF WORK. PLEASE HELP ME FEED MY FAMILY. When I reach into my wallet and pull out a ten-dollar bill, he approaches, takes it, and god-blesses me. "At least the bums in Connecticut don't got squeegies," Hector says. Another man hurries across the road in front of us. I recognize him: that guy from the newspaper—the one who owns the place on Bride Lake Road where they found those mummified babies. Remembering that bizarre story, I cringe. The light turns green. We move forward.

After the Stop & Shop, Main Street becomes North Main, and then Sachem Plains Road. Single-family houses give way to farmsteads and wooded lots for sale. It's early still, but some of the leaves have already started turning. Several of the trees look blighted. Approaching our road, we pass the dairy farm where we used to take the kids for hayrides and Halloween pumpkins. Africa grabs his mother's arm. "Look at them giant cows!" he says, pointing to a cluster of Holsteins grazing in the field.

"Giant?" Minnie says. "What you talking about, dummy? They just regular size."

"They bite?"

"Oh, no," I assure him. "Cows are very gentle animals. Would you like Hector to stop so you can get out and get a better look?"

"No!" It's sad that a boy his age has never seen cows before, except maybe in picture books. I guess to a kid who's probably never been out of inner-city Newark before, they must seem more frightening than gunshots or junkies in the streets. Minnie's told me that Africa was with her that time an addict knocked her to the sidewalk and ran off with her purse.

"Take the next right," I tell Hector, and when he does, the car begins its climb up Jailhouse Hill. The Halvorsens have painted their house a different color. It used to be blue and now it's putty gray. The Blackwells have put on an addition. A little boy rides his Big Wheel in old Mrs. Fiondella's driveway. Orion mentioned that she'd died last year, and that a young family had moved in. I smile, recalling the gifts Mrs. Fiondella would leave on our front steps every August: canned tomatoes and peaches; zucchinis the size of caveman clubs; bouquets of basil, the stems wrapped tightly in wet paper towels and aluminum foil. She took a shine to Andrew, especially; after he had shoveled her walkway or raked her leaves, she'd come over and want to pay him.

"No, that's okay," he'd tell her, and she'd follow him until she'd cornered him, waving away his protests and stuffing dollar bills into the pocket of his shirt. With the exception of crabby old Mr. Genovese across the street, there was a sense of community here back then; it was a nice neighborhood for the kids to grow up in. At our place in New York, the guy in the apartment next door barely manages a hello when we step into the elevator together. "The driveway coming up on the left," I tell Hector. "You can pull right in." It's strange to see a Realtor's sign on our front lawn. There's no other car. Andrew and the girls must not have gotten here yet. Maybe they stopped along the way for lunch.

"Where we at?" Africa wants to know. I tell him this was where I used to live. "Who live here now?"

"Just my ex-husband." Minnie tells him to stop being a busybody.

Hector takes out the luggage. Walking up the front steps, I reach into my purse. Finger, at the bottom, the house key which, for some reason, I've never mailed back to Orion. He was surprised when I told him I didn't need the combination to the Realtor's lockbox. "Come on in," I say, swinging open the front door. The three of them enter, wide-eyed and shy.

"How many rooms in this place?" Hector asks.

"Nine."

"Nine rooms for just hisself?" Minnie asks, amazed. She's probably wondering why I'd give up this house to live in a New York apartment, even one as spacious and elegantly appointed as Viveca's.

They follow me into the kitchen. Hector takes out his cell phone to call his sister. He's left his kids with her this weekend and wants to make sure they're behaving, he says. Africa's head swivels back and forth between the den and the counter where the little television is. "That guy who live here got *two* TVs?" he says. "Wow, he *rich.*" I smile, neither confirming nor denying. I open the door to the built-in that holds the ironing board and flop it down. Take out the flat iron and plug it in.

I make a plan. Minnie will iron Hector's wedding clothes while I go downstairs and throw Africa's and her soiled clothes in the washing machine. Minnie says I don't have to do it; she can wash them out in the sink at their motel. But I insist. "They ought to be out of the dryer in, oh, an hour and a half. Hector can stop by later and pick them up." I open the fridge. There's a six-pack of ginger ale in there, a bottle of tonic water. "Who's thirsty?" I ask.

"Me!" Africa says. Hector looks up and shakes his head.

"Minnie? How about you?"

"No, ma'am. Thass a good idea, though. Hidin' the ironing board out of sight like that. I ain't ever seen nothin' like that." When I hand Africa his can of soda, he gulps it down. His mother frowns at him. "Where your manners at?"

"Thank you," Africa says.

"You're welcome, sweetheart. Would you like to watch TV?"

He nods, reaches for the remote. "You got Spike?"

I shrug. What's Spike?

"Never mind no Spike until you go in, use the toilet. That okay, Miz Anna?" Of course, I tell her. Africa says he doesn't have to go. "You do so have to. I know what it mean when you grabbin' yo'self like that. Scoot!"

"He knows better than that," Hector says into the phone. "Is he there? Put him on." Phone in hand, he wanders into the living room.

Minnie licks her finger and touches it to the iron. Picks up the shirt that Hector's brought and places it on the board. It's black, red, yellow, and white—the style that Tony Soprano always wore. "This shirt is louder than a po-leese siren," Minnie says. Amused by her own joke, she grins, then covers her mouth with her hand. She's so self-conscious about those missing front teeth. It's one of the few times I've ever seen her smile. Maybe after Viveca and I get back from Greece, I can give her the money for some new ones.

Africa emerges, the toilet still in midflush. "Get back in there and wash them hands!" Minnie says. He says he washed them. "Don't you be tellin' *me* no stories. And leave the door open so I can see you doin' it." After he's complied, he comes back into the kitchen and picks up the remote. Whizzes past a dizzying number of stations until he finds what he's looking for. I head down to the basement with the vomity clothes.

A few minutes later, nearing the top of the stairs again, I overhear the tail end of a conversation between her and Hector. "Me neither, but I can't say no to no thousand dollars. When we get back, I'm gon' fire that babysitter's ass. Backing out on me like that at the last minute. Hmph."

Blinking back tears, I hear Viveca's reproof: *They don't want to be your friends, Anna. They just want to come to work, do their job, and go home.* Thinking about Viveca reminds me: the Josephus Jones painting I'm supposed to bring over there. I turn around and tiptoe back down the stairs to get it.

But where *is* that painting? Did Orion leave it upstairs after we showed it to her that day? Stash it back up in the attic where we found it? Maybe he's put it in one of these storage cartons.

I look through the boxes without finding it, but in the last one, I find, instead, the old family scrapbook my brother gave me—the one our mother kept. Donald had the photos copied for himself and let me have the originals. I sit, open the album. I haven't looked at it in years.

The first photos are black-and-white Polaroids of Mama and Daddy during what must have been their courtship. In the one where they're kissing, Mama's wearing his big, clunky class ring on a chain around her neck—the ring I'd sometimes finger when I'd sneak into their bedroom and look through their bureau drawers. Did it get thrown out? I wonder. Does Donald have it? It weighed a ton, I remember. . . . In another picture, they're at some kind of carnival or fair. It's summertime. Daddy's in cuffed jeans and a striped T-shirt, the sleeves tight against his biceps. Mama's wearing pedal pushers and a blouse with puffy sleeves and she's carrying a stuffed animal he must have won for her. On the next page there's a color picture, professionally taken. OLAN MILLS, it says in the lower corner. They're at some kind of dress-up affair, posed beneath a trellis decorated with crepe paper and fake-looking flowers. Daddy's in his uniform—his dress whites, so he's already out of high school and in the navy. Mama's wearing a pastel pink semiformal: spaghetti straps, a full skirt. Her heels and wrist corsage match the color of her dress. I lift the picture away from its red corners and look on the back. Mama's handwriting: *Me and Chick at my senior prom, May 25, 1947. The night we got engaged!* Their wedding invitation is on the opposite page. *Mr. and Mrs. Patrick Sullivan request the honour of your presence at the marriage of their daughter, Myrna Cathleen to Mr. Charles O'Day. . . .*

Pictures of their wedding reception, their honeymoon. They both look so young, barely out of their teens. . . . Here's one of Daddy on the deck of a ship, his arms around two other sailors. . . . Mama in a maternity top, Donald as a baby, and then a toddler cross-legged on the floor beneath a sad-looking Christmas tree . . . Daddy standing in front of the barber shop where he used to work with Uncle Brendan . . . Here's me in my christening gown. Me as a two- or three-year-old in a bulky snowsuit . . . Donald and me dressed for Sunday church— Easter, maybe. I swallow hard, studying the one of me sitting on our old living room sofa, holding baby Grace.

I should close the book now. I remember what comes next. The final picture before all the empty pages—the last photo she put in before she and Gracie died. . . .

It's us at Fort Nipmuck—in the picnic area next to the old Indian monument. I remember that day. First we took a hike to Wolf Rock. Then Daddy lit a charcoal fire in one of the little fireplaces and roasted hot dogs. In the picture, we're wearing coats and jackets. The trees are mostly bare, the ground carpeted with leaves. Late October, maybe? Mama's seated at the picnic table holding Gracie on her knee. I'm leaning against her other leg, squint-smiling at the camera the way my own kids used to do. Daddy must have taken this picture because he's not in it. But Donald and Kent are. Don sits on the tabletop to the left of Mama, his high-top canvas sneakers on the bench seat. Kent stands on the other side of her, next to me. His coloring and Andrew's are different, but their eyes, their jawlines: they're the same. It unnerves me to see, once again, how much my son resembles Kent.

If it's October, then Gracie is about two months old. She has five more months to live. Mama, too, although from her peaceful smile, you'd never know it. . . . I force myself to look at him again. Kent, who at the time I adored. I was four when that picture was taken, and now I'm fifty-two. Old, just like Africa said. But I'm my little girl self, too, feeling him pull me out of the freezing water and onto that roof. Pulling me closer to him when we're on the tree limb. I can hear it again: the roar of that rushing black water. . . . But it's all turned out all right, I remind myself again.

Has it? You sure of that?

Go to hell, Kent! Leave me alone!

I slam the scrapbook shut. Get up and shove it back into the box. Kick the box. Kent is just an old picture in a photo album stuck back inside a cardboard box in a home where I no longer even live. For all I know, he may be dead by now. And if he is, then *I'm* the only secret-keeper. What happened will die when I die, and no one else will ever have to know. . . .

I wrap my arms around myself, pace. I don't know how much time has passed when, suddenly, I'm aware of the noises upstairs. Footsteps, voices . . .

The kids are here! They're home!

Chapter Twenty-One

Kent Kelly

T uesday, March 5, 1963: I try not to think about that night, but sometimes I can't help it. A nightmare will take me back there, or something during the day will trigger the memory. The other morning when I got out of work, the van driving me back to the group home passed by some public works guys. They were out early, flushing hydrants, and bam! The sight and sound of that gushing water brought me right back to my aunt and uncle's downstairs apartment on that March night—the worst night of my life. . . .

Aunt Sunny had just given the baby a bottle and gotten her to sleep. "Finally," she said, when she walked out of Annie and Gracie's room. "She's been cranky all day." She went over to the window and looked out at the rain. It had been coming down for two days straight. Walking home from school that afternoon, I'd gotten soaked to the skin.

Uncle Chick and I were parked on the couch, watching *The Untouchables*. Turning to face her husband, Sunny said she was worried about Donald. His indoor track team had had an away meet at Hartford Public, but she'd expected he'd be home long before this. Uncle Chick told her to relax—that the bus driver was probably just taking it slow because of the wet roads. "You look beat, Sun," he said. "Go to bed. I'll stay up and wait for him."

She nodded, kissed him. Bent down and gave me a peck on the cheek. Usually it was Uncle Chick who went to bed first; Aunt Sunny was a night owl like me. Leaving the living room, she was stopped by a blast of tommy-gun fire. On the TV, Eliot Ness's men were riddling Mad Dog Coll's thugs with bullets. Sunny said she didn't know why we wanted to watch this stuff.

"What can we say?" Uncle Chick said. "We're guys."

"Good night, you two," she said, shaking her head.

Uncle Chick was drinking beer, which he usually did at night when he watched TV. There were two empties on the coffee table and he was working on his third. When a commercial came on, he got up to go to the bathroom. As soon as he was out of sight, I picked up his beer, snuck a few quick swigs, and placed it back where the wet ring was. Put my feet up on the coffee table, my hands behind my head. Donald could stay away all night as far as I was concerned. When he came back, Uncle Chick said, "Hey, Numb Nuts. How many times have I told you not to put your shoes up on the furniture?"

"About as many times as Aunt Sunny's told you to use a coaster."

He picked up a pillow and beaned me off the head with it. I was just about to fire it back at him when something caught my eye—a light of some kind moving past the front window. Then there was a pounding at the front door. "What the hell?" Uncle Chick said. He jumped up and ran to the door.

Whoever was out there was talking loud and excited, but I could only make out part of it: "dam," "flood." "Leave *now*!" Uncle Chick ran past me on the way to his and Aunt Sunny's room. "Get Annie!" he ordered me. "Wrap a blanket around her and get in the car."

As I ran into Annie's and Gracie's room, I heard Aunt Sunny's panicked voice. "Is it Donald? Did something happen to Donald?"

When I picked her up, Annie started whimpering, still half-asleep. "It's okay, it's okay," I kept saying. Leaving her room, I almost collided with Uncle Chick, who was hurrying in to get Gracie. "What did I tell you, Kent! Get her in the goddamned car!"

"Okay, okay," I said. "Jesus."

When I got outside, the wind was blowing and the rain was hitting me in the face. Old Mr. and Mrs. Dugas, the next-door neighbors, were hurrying toward their Studebaker. The water rushing through the street was up to my ankles. Annie wanted to know where her mommy was, and I said she was coming, she'd be right out. From the backseat, I watched them running toward us. Uncle Chick was holding the baby, wrapped up in a blanket like Annie. Aunt Sunny was

behind him, struggling to put on her winter coat. The neighbor across
the street called to Chick from his upstairs porch to ask what was going on. "Dam broke up at Wequonnoc Park!" he shouted. "The water's
coming this way!"

Uncle Chick started the Merc, hunched forward, and began gunning it down the hill. Aunt Sunny was up front, next to him, clutching
the baby. When we caught up to the Dugases' car, Uncle Chick laid
on the horn. "Come on! Move it!" he shouted. Instead, their brake
light went on. He drove up onto the sidewalk and tried to pass them,
but there wasn't enough room. "Get going or get the hell out of the
way!" he shouted. Gave the horn another couple of blasts.

"Chick, I'm scared!" Aunt Sunny said. Annie was crying now. The
baby, too. Uncle Chick ordered Aunt Sunny and me to open our windows because the front windshield was fogging up. Then the Merc
stalled, and while Uncle Chick was starting it up again, the Dugases'
car disappeared around the curve. The engine caught and the Mercury shot forward again, but just as we reached the curve, we were
hit from the back by a wall of water. The tires lost contact with the
road and the car started bobbing around, moving every which way instead of straight ahead no matter which way Uncle Chick turned the
wheel. When I looked out the window, a big gray chunk of something
whizzed past us. I saw a tree topple over. I remember feeling scared but
excited, too—like we were on some thrilling, out-of-control carnival
ride. Then something smashed into the back of the car, sending Annie and me flying to the floor and propelling the Merc into a crazy
spin. As I scrambled to get us back up onto our seats, Aunt Sunny
screamed. I looked out the front windshield and recognized the drop-
off we were heading toward—a retaining wall a good fifteen feet high.

The Merc dropped nose-down and we went underwater. The roaring in my ears stopped and everything turned from gray to black.
When I pulled myself and then Annie up into the air pocket at the
rear of the car, I saw that it had landed vertically, its nose underwater,
its back bumper above it. It had somehow come to a stop that way.
I saw, too, that the station wagon's way-back was about a foot and a
half above water. Remembering that Uncle Chick's toolbox was back

there, I lifted myself over the seat back, then pulled Annie up, too. Holding her in one arm, I reached around in the cold black water, feeling among the spilled tools until my hand located Chick's ball-peen hammer. I grabbed it and used it to smash out the back window. When I looked back, I saw that Uncle Chick, Aunt Sunny, and the baby had made it up to the surface, too. Aunt Sunny was coughing and spitting out water, holding Gracie above her head. Uncle Chick was wild-eyed.

As my eyes adjusted to the dark, I could see that the Merc's back bumper was leaning against a long, low building of some kind. If I could climb out and onto the bumper without having the car move forward, the roof would be in reaching distance. "I'm going to climb up there, then I'll pull you guys up," I called back.

"What? What'd you say!" Chick said. The roar of the water rushing past was deafening. I repeated what I'd said, shouting it this time.

"Climb up *where*?" Chick shouted back.

"Onto a roof! The car's leaning against a building and I think I can reach the roof!"

"Save Annie!" Aunt Sunny pleaded.

My hands were wet and shaking from the icy cold, but the pebbly roof shingles gave me some grip, and on my second try I managed to hoist myself up and swing one leg over and onto the roof, then the other. Leaning as far as I dared over the edge, I reached down and coaxed Annie up onto the bumper. Her little fingers curled around mine and I pulled her up one-handed. "I got her!" I shouted. "She's up here on the roof!"

Somehow, Uncle Chick managed to climb out of the back window and onto the bumper with Gracie tucked under his arm. He handed her up to me, grabbed onto the edge of the roof, and pulled himself up. "Come on, Sunny!" he shouted, turning back to his wife. "Climb out as best you can onto the bumper and I'll take it from there!"

She tried once, twice. "I can't do it," she screamed, panic-stricken.

"Yes, you can! I know you can!"

I realized that her soaked winter coat was weighing her down. "Aunt Sunny!" I shouted. "Take your coat off!"

"What? I can't hear you?" I shouted it again, as loud as I could. She heard me that time, because I could see her trembling hand fiddle with the buttons while she held on to the seat back with her other hand. One-handed, she somehow got the coat off her shoulders and pulled the sleeves from her arms. The coat fell away. Lighter now, she managed to get herself halfway out of the back window, but she was still halfway inside. Between her outstretched arm and Uncle Chick's, there was a foot and a half of space.

"Kent, I'm going farther over the edge," Uncle Chick said. "Hold on to my ankles, and when I say pull, you pull with all your mother-fucking might!"

I nodded. "Annie, here," I said, turning to her. "Hold your sister."

She shook her head. Said she was only allowed to hold Gracie when she was sitting on the couch. "Come on! This is different!" I yelled. I held the baby out to her and she took her, bucking and crying, in her arms.

I knelt behind Uncle Chick and grabbed his ankles. "Okay!" I said. But what if I didn't have the strength to do it? What if all three of us got pulled back into that black water? A thought flashed in my mind: I wish Donald were here. We need Donald.

"Okay, I got hold of her!" Uncle Chick shouted. "Now *pull*!"

With my elbows and knees digging into the gritty shingles, I strained and pulled as hard as I could, managing to move myself backward, but only a couple of inches. "Pull, goddamn it! Pull!" Uncle Chick screamed. I clenched my teeth, grunted, and gained another several inches. "That's it! Keep going! Pull!" My arms felt like they'd come right out of the sockets, but when I pulled again, we gained another five or six inches. Aunt Sunny's head came into view. It was working! We were doing it!

"Pull, Kent! Pull!"

As I did, I felt the roof begin to give way under me. Uncle Chick's body slipped forward instead of backward and Aunt Sunny's head disappeared again. "The roof's caving in!" I screamed.

"Okay, let go!" Chick screamed back. "Save the girls, Kent! Save my kids!" On my hands and knees, I watched him slip over the side.

The sound of the roaring water faded away again. I must have gone deaf for a few minutes, because when I looked over at Annie, she was screaming without sound. Afraid that the roof would cave in altogether, I crawled over to her, hugging her body tight against mine. Then I remembered the baby. "Where's Gracie?" I said. My hearing had returned.

"She was slippery," she sobbed. "She wouldn't stop squirming."

Oh, no! I thought, scanning the empty roof. Oh, no! Oh, no! Then I stood and grabbed onto Annie's hand. "Come on," I said. "We've got to get off this thing before it caves." Spotting a tree growing on the far side of the building, I led her across the roof toward it.

I don't remember the particulars of how I got us both up into that tree, but I did. We sat together on one of the bigger limbs, our legs dangling over the side, me with one arm wrapped around Annie's waist and the other arm holding on for dear life to a branch above. Poor Annie. She had long since lost the blanket I'd wrapped her up in and was only wearing her cold, wet pajamas. She was shivering like crazy, and though I couldn't hear them, I could see that her teeth were chattering. The shiny black water was racing beneath us, carrying ice and debris. Carrying little Gracie to who knew where. What did she weigh? Fourteen or fifteen pounds? There was no way in hell she could survive. I unzipped my jacket, pulled Annie tight as I could against my side, and zipped it up again, figuring my body heat might warm her up a little. As best I could, I tried to hold in my sobs so she wouldn't know I was crying for Gracie.

As we waited to be found and rescued, I realized that the rain had finally stopped, and that the moon had come out from behind the clouds. Now I saw exactly where we were, and why the Merc had stopped in that vertical position. After it had pitched itself over that retaining wall, it had landed at the back of the Ford dealership on Franklin Avenue and wedged itself between the long garage we'd climbed on top of and these two huge black oil tanks that sat there, kitty-corner against each other, in front of the car. There, to the right of the tree we were in, was McPadden's Funeral Home, and across the street was Stanley's Market, where I bought my sodas and smokes and stole candy bars. To the left were the grinder shop, the Laundromat, the dry cleaner's where, two days before, I had picked up the long winter coat that Aunt Sunny had worn and later had to shed after it got waterlogged. Just a little ways down the street was the Shamrock Barbershop, where Uncle Chick worked. I found myself wondering if Uncle Brendan's mynah bird had survived the flood.

Annie reached up and tapped me on the shoulder. She said something that I couldn't hear over the noise of the water. "Hmm?" I said. "Say it louder." She wanted to know if the cops were going to make her go to jail because she'd dropped her sister. I thought long and hard. Then I said, "You *didn't* drop her. *I* did. You got that?" She looked up at me, confused. "I had her in my jacket, but she slipped out when we were climbing into this tree."

"No she didn't," she said.

"Yes she did! And I don't want you telling anyone she didn't! Okay?"

We stared at each other for the next several seconds. "Okay," she said. In my whole life, it was the most generous thing I ever did for anyone. Hey, I don't know. Maybe it was the only generous thing I ever did.

"Look!" Annie said a few minutes later. When I followed her gaze, I saw Uncle Chick. He was back on the roof of the garage, creeping toward us on his hands and knees. When he reached the edge, he stood up and leapt, grabbing hold of the tree trunk and then shimmying up and onto a sturdy limb on the other side of ours. He was sobbing, shouting. "I couldn't hold her, Kent! The car moved forward, and when our hands went beneath the water, she slipped from my grip! . . . But Sunny's a strong swimmer. She'll be okay, I *know* she will. . . . But oh, god! What if she . . . ? Oh, god!"

He hadn't yet realized that Gracie wasn't with us. And later, when he did, he rested his head against the tree trunk and wailed.

As the water receded, blocks of ice, smashed cars, and broken tree limbs began to reveal themselves. When we started shouting for help, a guy appeared on the upstairs back porch of the funeral parlor. "I see you!" he called to us. "I'll get help." A few minutes later, he and two men in rain slickers and hip boots—firemen, I guess—came sloshing through the knee-high water toward us. Two of the men were carrying a ladder against their shoulders. They leaned it against the trunk of the tree. One climbed the ladder, got hold of Annie, and climbed down again, the poor kid slung over his shoulder like a sack of potatoes. Uncle Chick and I climbed down after them. For some reason, there were tangles of twine in the fallen tree limbs. The water was now only up to my shins. As I followed the firemen, I kept stumbling on these loose bricks underfoot. They were all over the place.

An ambulance took Annie and me to the hospital, where two nurses treated us for exposure, removing our wet clothes and wrapping us in heated blankets. Another nurse used a rubber squeeze bulb to suck dirty water and mucous from our throats and nostrils. They made us put on these hospital nightgown things and told us we had to stay there overnight for observation. At first, they were going to separate us, but Annie was too scared to let me out of her sight, so they put us in the same two-bed room. When Annie asked the nurses where her mommy was, they gave each other funny looks and said they didn't know but people were looking for her.

They had wanted Uncle Chick to come with us to the hospital, but he'd refused, insisting that he needed to stay and search for his wife and his baby daughter. I think it was around midnight when Donald walked into Annie's and my hospital room. Annie was asleep by then, so the two of us had to whisper. He kept stopping to collect himself in the middle of telling me his story: how the coach's wife was waiting when the track team got back to school. How he hadn't gotten scared until they said he couldn't go home. "Instead, I had to go over to Coach's house until we found out what was going on. Coach called the police station for me. When they finally called back, they said you guys were here. Dad's here, too, you know. They brought him in a little while ago. They let me look in and see him, but they wouldn't let me talk to him yet, because they said he's in shock. Is Ma . . . is she dead, Kent?"

I nodded. "Gracie, too."

He looked mad at first—the way he'd looked the day he discovered that I'd wrecked his trophy. But then he broke down. I pushed over and he got into bed with me, put his arms around me and sobbed, his tears falling against my neck. When he left, about an hour later, he looked more dazed than anything else. He was staying the night at his coach's house.

I couldn't sleep. I kept seeing and hearing the floodwater. Finally, after the second or third time the nurse came in and shined her flashlight in my face, she gave me something to help make me drowsy. When I woke to the sound of birds a little before dawn, I felt, and then saw, Annie asleep against me. Sometime in the middle of the night, she must have climbed out of her bed and up onto mine.

They found Gracie's body first, stuck in some twine-draped tree branches in front of Stanley's Market, just a few hundred feet away from where the Merc had crashed. They didn't find Aunt Sunny's body until that afternoon when Mr. McPadden and his brother began the cleanup at the funeral parlor. It had gotten a lot of damage, both on the main floor where the wakes were and in the basement where the bodies were embalmed and the caskets were stored. It was weird: they found Aunt Sunny on the floor in the casket room, lying face-down in two or three inches of water with her arm sticking straight up. On the radio, I heard Mr. McPadden say that a block of ice had bashed in the basement doors and the water must have carried Aunt Sunny's body inside.

I don't remember getting out of the hospital, or very much about the funeral. Funerals, I mean. Two of them. I remember what the newspaper said, though; all that week, I read every single article about the flood. After all that rain we'd had, the earthen dam holding back Wequonnoc Lake had begun to leak near the base late that afternoon, the paper said, and then, around 10:00 P.M., had collapsed. As the water rushed forward—forty-five million gallons of it, some engineer estimated—the ice on the surface broke into pieces, some of them weighing a ton or more. These were carried along the downward slope, slamming into whatever was in their way with the force of a freight train engine. An old brick mill on Broad Street was in the water's path, and it collapsed under the force of the surge, burying alive four third-shift workers who were at their machines, making rope and twine. Gravity increased the velocity of the debris-strewn water as it raced south, wrecking a number of downtown business-es before passing over the railroad tracks that ran behind the stores and dumping into the Sachem River. From there, the swollen river rushed downstream toward New London, spilling into Long Island Sound. Three Rivers was declared a disaster area, and flags were flown at half-mast for the victims. In all, seven people died: Aunt Sunny and Gracie, those four workers at the twine factory, and a bum who'd been squatting in a lean-to along the riverbank—some colored guy named Rufus Jones. And this was kind of creepy: the paper said that someone else had died that night, too, in a plane crash somewheres else: Aunt Sunny's favorite singer, Patsy Cline.

Uncle Chick had to swallow a bitter pill: the fact that his house had remained watertight. If we'd only stayed put instead of trying to outrun the floodwater, Aunt Sunny and Grace would still be alive. Once the funerals were over, my mother took some vacation days and stayed with us at Uncle Chick's for a week or so. When it was time for her to go back, she called a kitchen table conference with Uncle Chick, Donald, and me. She said it was time for me to come home—that her brother had enough on his plate now without having to worry about me. She volunteered to take Annie, too. Annie would need mothering, she said. Sunny had no sisters and her mother was too sickly to take on the responsibility of a young child. "You helped me out, Chick," she told her brother. "Let me return the favor."

"But what about school?" Uncle Chick said. Mom argued that there were kindergartens in New Britain, too.

Chick was on the verge of agreeing with Mom's plan when Annie, who'd been listening from the next room, burst into the kitchen. "No! I want to stay here with Daddy and Donald and Kent!" she screamed. She threw herself onto the floor and pitched a tantrum. When my mother tried to pick her up and comfort her, she hit her and yelled, "No! Go away! Go home!" Then she crawled on her hands and knees over to me and climbed into my lap.

Uncle Chick said we should probably leave things the way they were for now, and that I didn't need to move back. "Kent's no trouble, Elaine," he told his sister. "In fact, he's a big help. And he and Annie get along good. She's going to have to deal with enough loss without him leaving, too." When I glanced over at Donald, his face was unreadable. Nobody had asked him for his opinion and he hadn't volunteered it, either.

"I'm staying, Mom," I told her. "I can cook, help out around the house, babysit Annie in the afternoon."

"You're still at school in the afternoon," Mom pointed out. "And Annie goes to morning kindergarten. Who's going to take care of her until you get home?" Uncle Chick told her that Annie's bus brought her back at about twelve thirty, when he was home for lunch. He could bring her to the barbershop when lunch was over, and I could pick her up there.

"Yeah, and all's I got last period is study hall," I said. "If Uncle Chick calls the school and explains the situation, they'll let me get excused early."

Didn't I need to study during study hall? my mother asked.

I laughed. "All anyone does in that study hall is yack with each other and play cards. I usually just put my head on the desk and take a nap."

"What about you, Donny?" she said, turning to my cousin. "Could you take care of her some afternoons?"

Donald shook his head. He either had band practice or National Honor Society. "And once baseball season starts, forget it. Coach Covino's a stickler about practice. If you skip, you don't play."

"Well . . . ," Mom said. Reluctantly, she packed her things, hugged the four of us, and drove back to New Britain by herself.

In the weeks that followed, Donald got busier than ever. He didn't even come home for supper half the time. That was his way of coping, I figured. Uncle Chick coped by drinking. His two or three beers a night became a six-pack, a six and a half. When he moved on to the hard stuff, he started going down to the Silver Rail after work instead of coming home. So it was me and Annie at the house a lot of the time—just the two of us. That was when I started touching her in ways I wasn't supposed to.

I didn't really know why I was doing it. All I knew was that Aunt Sunny's death made me angry and sad, and that my little cousin and I shared a secret: that her little sister had died because of her, not me. I had told that lie to protect Annie, but to my surprise, no one really blamed me. It was the circumstances, they all said. I had nothing to feel guilty about. If I hadn't smashed that window and found a way out of the car, we *all* would have died. Not even Donald held Gracie's death against me. "Hey, you tried, man. That's all you could have done. I'm just glad you were there for Annie." He was guilty about not having been there himself, I knew. I could have used that against him, but I didn't. Instead, I used my hands against his little sister. The better part of me knew it was wrong, but the better part of me didn't seem to be in control when we were by ourselves, which was plenty. It was like my hands had a mind of their own.

It started innocently enough. One morning she came into the kitchen while I was cooking us breakfast. Walked over to the stove, put her hands on her hips, and sighed. "Guess what, Kent? I got zema again."

"You got what?"

"Zema. It's real itchy. Want me to go get the cream that Mommy puts on it?" *Used* to put on it, I thought. The poor kid was still struggling to accept the fact that Aunt Sunny's absence from her life was permanent.

"Yeah, go get it," I said, scraping scrambled egg onto her plate. High school started before Annie's school did; the deal was that Uncle Chick was supposed to get her up, feed her, and see her off on the bus. But Chick was already starting to be pretty unreliable, and no one seemed to object if I skipped school. I'd started staying home as often as I went.

When she came back with the cream, I read the back of the tube. "It's *ec*zema, not zema," I said.

"Oh," she said, then pulled her dress up to the waist, revealing the red rash on her thighs.

"Where's your underpants at?" I asked her.

She looked down. "Oops," she said. "I forgot to put them on."

I shook my head. "Good thing your head's screwed on or you'd probably forget that, too."

"That's what Mommy always tells me," she said.

I knelt in front of her, squeezed some of the cream onto my fingers, and rubbed it into her rash. I didn't touch her between her legs, but there it was, and seeing it put me back in Irma's basement, looking at Nadine's. "There," I said. "Feel better?" She nodded. "Okay then. Go put your underwear on, then come back and eat your eggs before they get cold." I glanced at the clock. "Bus is coming in fifteen minutes. You better step on it."

"Okay," she said, and dashed away.

All morning long, I hung around the house and tried not to picture it: Annie's bare thighs, her little pink button. But my mind kept wandering back to what I'd seen when she pulled up her dress. It was weird. A few days earlier, I'd poked around in Donald's stuff and found a dirty magazine: women clutching their tits and fingering their snatches. I had flipped through the pages and gotten off, but it took me a while. But now, thinking about little girls' pussies—Nadine's, Annie's—I went from zero to sixty. I jerked off twice before lunch and once after. What was I? A fucking pervert or something?

When I heard Annie's bus pull up outside, I went to the door and waited for her. I asked her how school was. "Good," she said, "except for when Richard Plante hit me at recess."

"Yeah? Did you tell the teacher?"

She shook her head. Whenever kids squealed, she said, Mrs. Kovacs said she was going to have to take the tattletale out of the closet and make them wear it. "Want to play slapjack?" she asked.

"Yeah, okay. Go get the cards."

She did what she usually did when we played that game: climbed up onto my lap so that she could be the first to slap the jack when I turned over the cards. But she was squirmy that day, and I felt my dick starting to stir. "You're heavy," I said. "Go sit in the chair." I was fighting it.

So I wasn't sure why, during our second game, I asked her how her eczema was. Did she want me to put more cream on her legs? She shook her head. "Okay then. Good." I was part disappointed and part relieved. I let her win. Then I told her she should go watch TV or something because I had to start supper. When she came back in the kitchen a few minutes later, I was peeling potatoes. She asked me if she could peel some, too. I told her no, she was too young to use the peeler. She could hurt herself.

I could hurt her, too, I realized. I had to stop thinking of her in that way.

I spent the next couple of days steering clear of her, which wasn't easy, because she kept shadowing me. "Go play with your Barbies or something, Annie. Scoot. Don't be a pest," I'd tell her, and she'd poke out her bottom lip and walk away. Once when I told her to stop bothering me, she stuck her tongue out and said she didn't even like me anymore, which was bull. "Oh, boo hoo," I said. "I'm so sad."

After we ate supper—it was just the two of us, usually—was when the temptation got the strongest. She'd be in the bathroom, taking her bath, and I'd find myself on the other side of the door, listening and feeling myself up as she sloshed around in there, singing, talking to herself. One night while I was doing that, I heard her cry out in pain. "What's the matter?" I called.

"Stupid tangles!" she said. I opened the door a crack. She was sitting cross-legged in the tub. Her hair was wet and soapy. She had a comb in her hand and was yanking on the snarls. . . . Why not, I thought. The coast was clear. Donald had said he wasn't going to be back until late, and if Uncle Chick wasn't home by now, he was probably down at the Silver Rail, getting shit-faced. I opened the door a little more.

Stay away from her, I told myself, but my brain and my mouth were on different wavelengths. "Need some help?"

"Yes, please."

I swung the door open wide and went in there. "Well, first of all, let's get the shampoo out of your hair," I said. "Close your eyes." I ran some warm water over her head and looked where I wasn't supposed to. "Now give me the comb." I worked it gently through her hair. "There," I said.

I was headed out of the bathroom when I stopped and turned back to face her. I grabbed the bar of soap on the sink and approached her.

"How's that rash of yours?" She said it was all gone. "Yeah? You sure? Because you don't want it to come back again. Why don't I give you a little help washing up down there?" I said. She shook her head.

"I'm a big girl, silly," she said. "I can wash myself."

Okay, *leave*, I begged myself. Go do the dishes. Go watch TV. Instead, I told her if she was doing it the right way, she wouldn't have gotten eczema in the first place. "Let me just show you how to do it right," I said. I grabbed the washcloth and knelt down next to the tub. But as I was reaching between her legs, she pushed her knees together. "What's the matter?" I asked her.

She said her mother had told her not to let anyone touch her in her "private place."

"And she was right," I said. "You shouldn't. But she meant people you don't know, or boys at school, not people you trust. You trust me, right?"

She nodded. The fear in her eyes made my heart pound.

"Okay then. I haven't got all day. Open up." When she did, I soaped up the washcloth and passed it back and forth against the insides of her thighs, then against her little bud. "How does it feel to know you're getting nice and clean down there?" I asked. "Feels good, right?"

She swallowed hard. "I don't know," she said. "Kinda."

"Is the water warm enough? I can make it a little warmer if you like."

She shook her head, blinking back tears. She was so sweet, so pretty. I cupped her chin with my left hand and let the washcloth fall away to the bottom of the tub. Let my fingers take over. "It's okay if it feels good," I said. "It's not a bad thing to feel good while you're getting clean." I was rock hard, pushing myself against the outside of the tub. I leaned toward her and kissed her on the mouth. Closed my eyes and came. When I opened my eyes again, she was staring at me, bewildered. "What's the matter?" she asked.

"Nothing. Why? Come on. Let's get you out of this water before you turn all wrinkly like a raisin." I tickled her under her chin to make her giggle, but she pulled away. "Want me to towel you off?" I said. She shook her head.

After she'd gotten into her nightgown, brushed her teeth, and said her prayers, I tucked her in and began a new chapter of the book I'd started reading her the night before. "More! Read more, Kent! *Please?*" she had begged me. But that night, she didn't even seem to be listening. She interrupted me midsentence to ask where her daddy was.

"He had a meeting to go to," I said. "By the way, I told him about your eczema, and he asked me if I'd show you the right way to wash yourself down there. He'll be glad you know how to clean yourself the right way now, but he said to tell you not to talk to him about it. Because he's kind of shy about stuff like that. But I'm not, so whenever you have questions, you just come to me and I'll answer them for you. Because that's what your daddy wants, and I know it would be what your mommy would want, too. Okay?"

"Okay," she said.

I rose from the chair next to her bed. "Nighty night then."

"Nighty night." I turned off her light and started toward the door. "Kent?"

When I turned back, the moonlight through her window illuminated her silhouette. "Yeah?"

"Today at school, I started thinking about Mommy and I couldn't remember her face at first. But then I could."

"Well, I'll tell you what," I said. "Why don't you take out one of the pictures of her from the photo album and put it in your school bag? Then you can put it in your desk and look at it whenever you need to. Okay?"

She nodded. Gave me a half-smile. "Do you think Mommy watches me up in heaven?" she asked.

I said I was sure she did. "Now if there's nothing else, you'd better get to sleep. Okay?"

But there *was* something else. "Before?" she said. "When I was in the tub? How come you kissed me like that?"

I turned on her light. "Because I love you, Annie. I love you this much." I spread my arms as wide as I could.

"And you love Donald and Daddy, too. Right?"

"Yeah, sure. And I loved Gracie and your mom. But I love you best of all. Now that's enough stalling. See you tomorrow."

"See you tomorrow," she said.

After I left her room, I paced, telling myself I could never touch her that way again. I'd done it once, and that was going to be it. Because I *did* love her. I *did* want to keep her safe. And what if Uncle Chick or Donald found out about what I'd done? That time we'd arm-wrestled at the kitchen table, they'd both taken me in like ten seconds. Either one of them could beat me to a bloody pulp. I said it out loud, as if that made the promise more legit. "Never again. Never, ever."

I was sprawled on the couch watching TV when Donald walked in. "Hey," he said. "Pop home?"

"Not yet. You eat? There's a can of beef stew on the counter."

He said he and some of his friends had gone out for pizza. "Well, I've got a big chem test tomorrow. Guess I'll go study and then hit the sack. Annie okay?" I told him she was fine.

When Uncle Chick staggered in, he nodded in my direction and went to the kitchen for a beer. "What are you watching?" he asked when he came back to the living room and squinted at the TV.

"The news," I said. What the hell else would I be watching at eleven o'clock? He flopped down on the couch next to me, stinking of booze, and the two of us stared at the news footage: the race riots down south, the new pope they'd just picked to replace the one who croaked. "Whassiz name? Cardinal Martini?" Uncle Chick said.

"*Mon*tini."

"Cardinal Martini, dry with a twist." He laughed like what he'd just said was fucking hilarious.

Annie must have been waiting up for him, because when she heard his voice she came out of her room and made a beeline for him. Uh-oh, I thought.

"Hey, Anna Banana," he said. "What are you doing up so late?" She said she couldn't sleep. "No? How come?" She looked right at me when he asked her that, but Uncle Chick was too crocked to notice. I put my finger to my lips.

"I just can't," she said.

"Well, I tell you what. Why don't I tuck you in and sprinkle some magic sleepy dust on you the way Mommy used to. Then you'll go right to sleep." When he stood up, he lost his balance, banging into the coffee table and knocking it over. "Whoopsy daisy," he said. "How'd that get there?"

The last thing I needed was for the two of them to be alone in there, and for her to squeal about bath time. "Magic sleepy dust?" I said. "Gee, that sounds like fun. Can I join you?"

"Sure," Chick said, unaware that Annie was shaking her head no.

Uncle Chick was home on time for the next couple of nights, and over the weekend, Donald was hanging around the house more than usual. But the following Monday evening, it was just the two of us again. I knocked on the door while she was in there, taking her bath. "Hey, you almost out?" I asked. "I've been waiting to take a shower."

The door opened, and her eyes widened when she saw me standing there with just a towel wrapped around me. I was already kind of excited down there. "What's the matter with you?" I said.

"Nothing."

"Then take a picture. It lasts longer. You remember to brush your teeth?" She nodded. "Okay then. Get in bed and I'll tuck you in in a few minutes." As I walked past her toward the tub, I pulled off the towel and let it drop to the floor. I turned the water on, then looked back at her. She was standing in the hall, looking in at me—looking back and forth from my face to where I wanted her to look. "What?" I said, as if my standing there naked was the most normal thing in the world. She shrugged. "Okay then. Scoot. Give me a little privacy." As I got in the shower, I heard the bathroom door bang closed. "Hey!" I shouted. "Leave it open."

"You're spoze to keep it closed," she shouted back.

"Yeah? Who says?"

"My mommy."

"Hey! Come back in here for a second," I told her. When she did, I pulled back the shower curtain to give her another look. "The shower water makes the mirror fog up if the door's closed. Then I can't see what I'm doing when I shave. I could cut myself." I surprised myself— scared myself a little, even—with how easily I'd come up with something on the spot.

"Donald and Daddy shave," she said. "And *they* close the door."

"Well, I guess they don't mind cutting themselves then. But I do." After I was finished, I pulled back the shower curtain, and there she was, sitting cross-legged just outside the door, playing with her Barbies.

"What's up?" I said, walking bare-ass past her toward Donald's and my room. I'd beaten off and was still semi-erect.

"Your pee-pee's big," she said.

"Yeah," I said. When I reached down and touched it, she got up and ran down the hall to her room, abandoning her dolls.

Until that night, I'd always taken my shower just before I went to bed. But now, whenever my uncle and my cousin weren't around, I took it right after she took her bath. She was always making excuses to come into the bathroom while I was in there; it was like a game the two of us were playing. Still, sometimes what was happening scared me. What if the little show I was putting on for her turned into show-and-tell. *If* she told, Uncle Chick would probably kick my ass all the way back to New Britain. And if Donald found out, he'd probably choke me to death first and ask questions later. I was scared of both of them, but more scared that it might be Donald. Still, in a weird way, that was part of the thrill of doing what I was doing. Risking it and getting away with it. I didn't know why.

One night, while I was sleeping, I woke up with Annie poking me on the shoulder. "Hmm? Whassa matter?" I said, still half-asleep. She whispered back that she'd had a bad dream and couldn't wake her daddy up. No surprise there. When Chick came home plastered, he'd usually conk out on the couch with the TV going and still be there in the morning. I squinted over at the blanketed mound in Donald's bed. Heard him snoring. Then I swung my legs to the floor, got up, and went back to her room with her. Crawled into bed and snuggled up against her. It felt nice. I didn't wear pajamas like goody-goody Donald did; I slept in just my underpants. I waited, listening to her breathing until I was pretty sure she'd fallen asleep. Then I reached under her nightgown.

Annie started having a lot of bad dreams after that, and I was always the go-to guy. And on the nights she didn't seek me out, I'd sometimes tiptoe down the hall and get into bed with her anyway. I liked it better when she didn't wake up, because when she did, she'd hold her body stiff as a board and make fists. Sometimes if I got a little too insistent while I was touching her, she'd whimper, and sometimes she'd get so quiet that I'd have to stop and listen so I knew she was still breathing. "Hey?" I'd say.

"What?"

"Nothing. Everything's all right. Go back to sleep."

There was one close call. It happened after one of our nighttime visits. Usually, I'd get right up and tiptoe back to my own bed after I was done, but that night, I fell asleep lying against her and didn't wake up until daybreak. I jumped out of her bed and, leaving her room, ran right into Donald. He was on his way to the bathroom, still half-asleep. "What the hell were you doing in Annie's room?" he asked me.

"What was I *doing*?" I said. "What do you mean, what was I *doing*?" As my mind raced, trying to think of something, I forced myself to look him in the eye. I'd read someplace that that was how store detectives knew if someone was a shoplifter: if they couldn't look their accuser in the eye. "She had a nightmare and got scared," I said. "She woke me up. Said she was too scared to go back to her room by herself."

He just stood there, waiting for more.

"And then I dozed off while I was sitting in that little chair of hers," I said. "I just woke up. Man, my back is killing me."

He wouldn't stop looking at me. I couldn't tell if he was buying it or not.

"It's uh . . . She said she went to your dad first, but she couldn't wake him up." Change the subject, I told myself. Change the fucking subject. "Sleeping it off, I guess. Have you noticed how much he's boozing lately?"

He nodded. "I tried to talk to him about it last weekend, but he got pissed. Told me I should run my own life and he'd run his. . . . Annie should have woken *me* up. I could have—"

"She said she tried to, but you wouldn't wake up either."

That sold it. He suddenly looked guilty "I was up reading until after midnight. We're doing this book *1984* in honors English and I'm way behind. If she gives us a pop quiz before the weekend, I'm fucked."

I nodded sympathetically. Told him Annie's having gotten me up was no problem. "I'm a light sleeper. And anyways, my English teacher shows movies half the time, so I can always grab a nap in class."

He reached up and started rubbing the side of his head. "The thing is, Kent, I can forget about getting a scholarship next year if I don't keep my grades up. My guidance counselor told me colleges look real closely at your grades from junior year. . . . Annie say what her bad dream was about?"

I felt like a louse saying it, but it was him or me. "The flood," I said. "About your mother and Gracie drowning." He winced. Said maybe he'd better talk to her about it. I realized I'd made a tactical error. If he started asking her about a dream she hadn't really had, he might get suspicious all over again. "I wouldn't if I were you, Donny," I said. "She's okay. Why bring it up again?"

He looked relieved. "Yeah, you're right. Look, man, I gotta pee something wicked." And with that, he walked past me and headed down the hall to the bathroom, scratching his ass.

Back in our room, I took a bunch of deep breaths to stop myself from shaking. Then I punched myself in the chest five or six times, hard as I could, for being so goddamned careless.

Later, at breakfast, Donald told Annie he would read to her that night at bedtime. "Okay?" She looked back and forth between the two of us and nodded. He was good for his word. He read to her the next night, too. But after that, it was business as usual again. He wasn't around, and neither was his old man. But yeah, that was the only time I ever came close to getting caught. After that, once I'd gotten what I'd gone into Annie's room for, I always got right up, made sure the coast was clear, and left.

I don't know. Maybe if Irma Cake had told my mother the *real* reason why she wasn't going to babysit me anymore, I wouldn't have had to spend the rest of my life cruising little girls. Or maybe if I *had* gotten caught messing around with Annie—gotten the shit beaten out of me and been kicked out—*that* might have stopped it. It didn't stop, though, partly because I got so good at *not* getting caught, and partly because, along the way, I figured out how to use Annie's and my secret to insure her silence. I began threatening her that if she told on me, I'd have to tell everyone about how Gracie had *really* died. "The cops left *me* alone because I saved everyone else, but that wouldn't help you any if they knew the truth," I assured her. "They'd throw you in jail with bad people and it would be really, really scary." And so what we were doing went on for the next two years. I was a senior by then, and Donald was away at college on a scholar-athlete scholarship. Annie was seven.

The funny thing is, when Protective Services finally *did* pull her out of the house and place her with a foster family, it wasn't because of me. It was because by then her father had turned himself into a hopeless lush. There was a DUI arrest, a disorderly conduct incident down at the Silver Rail. And when Chick started showing up for work drunk first thing in the morning, there were problems at the barbershop, too. He cut a customer so bad while he was shaving him that the guy had to get stitches. Word got out and the shop began to lose business. Another guy got up from the chair in the middle of his haircut because he smelled booze on Chick's breath, and Chick followed him out of the shop and into the street, cursing him out. The last straw was when he took Uncle Brendan's mynah bird out of his cage and, thinking it was funny, opened the door and let him loose. He kept insisting the bird would go off on a little toot and then come right back. He didn't. Uncle Brendan fired him, and when Chick kept showing up for work anyway, good and soused, the cops got called. A few days later, they showed up at the house. Mrs. Dugas next door had called the station after she'd seen Annie walking hand in hand down the street with her father, Chick reeling from one side of the sidewalk to the other. He couldn't even manage to sober up for the authorities' interview, and I guess that was the nail in the coffin.

I went to school one morning and cut out at lunchtime. When I got home, there was a car I didn't recognize parked in front of the house. Two people were in it, a guy behind the wheel and a woman in

the passenger's seat. Uncle Chick was out on the front step, crying his
eyes out.

"What's going on?" I said. "Where's Annie?"

Uncle Chick pointed toward the street. That car was pulling away
from the curb. As I ran out into the street, I saw Annie at the back
window, her face contorted with pain and fear as a woman seated back
there with her tried to make her turn around. I chased the car down
the road until it disappeared around the corner. A few minutes later,
we went back inside, Chick and me. He pulled out a bottle of rotgut,
took a swig, and handed it to me. He kept blubbering, repeating the
same thing over and over. "I failed her, Kent. I loved her so much, but
I failed her." After a while, I realized that he didn't mean Annie. He
meant Aunt Sunny. I felt bad for him but worse for myself. She was
gone. I'd lost her. We *both* got shit-faced that afternoon.

"Kent honey, why didn't you *tell* me how bad he had gotten?" my
mother asked me the night I moved back home.

"Yeah, I guess I should have," I mumbled. The reason I hadn't told
her was because if she butted in, I figured, it might mess up what I
had going with Annie. But now I'd lost her anyway. I didn't realize it
at the time, but I guess I was in mourning. It was as if she'd died, and
I had the same half-sad, half-angry feeling I'd had after Aunt Sunny
and Gracie drowned.

Despite Mom's bugging me about going back to my old school to
finish senior year, I refused. Got my G.E.D. instead. "Same thing," I
told her.

"No it's not, Kent," she said. "You're my only child. I had my heart
set on going to your high school graduation."

"Yeah, well, you'll get over it."

Worried about her brother, Mom called him two or three times a
week. He was usually smashed. He said the people who'd placed Annie in foster care wouldn't tell him where she was. The deal was, he
had to get help with his drinking and prove that he had maintained
sobriety for a year before they'd let him see her. When Mom called
them to get an address, they wouldn't tell her either. Annie was doing

fine, was all they'd say; she was adjusting to her new family and her new school. She had joined the Brownies.

Mom wrote to Donald at college every once in a while. She'd put five or ten bucks in the envelope to help him out. Whenever she left the letters on the counter for me to mail, I'd open them, swipe the cash, and glue the envelope shut again. Whenever *I'd* ask her for money, she'd say no, that I should go look for a job instead of moping around the house all day. The only time Donald ever wrote her back, he said that he hadn't had any contact with his sister either. Later on, we found out that that was a lie. The authorities had determined that Goody Two-shoes was a positive influence in Annie's life. That pissed me off royally. Who'd taken care of her for two years while he was off every night doing his thing? Me, that's who. But as usual, I didn't count.

Mom and I drove over to Three Rivers three or four times to see Uncle Chick, but those visits got to be too hard on her. Either he wasn't around after he said he would be, or else he *was* home, drunk as a skunk. He told her he *couldn't* get sober—that he needed booze to get through his day, given everything and everybody he'd lost. I understood what he meant. For the first couple of months after I moved back, I hardly ever left the house. I just sat around, thinking about what Annie's face had looked like at that back window as they were driving her away.

I finally did get a job, as a fry cook at KFC. I hated it. Hated my boss, Millie. Hated that, no matter how many showers I took, I could never quite get rid of the fried chicken stink on me. The only one of my coworkers I got along with was this woman in her twenties named Karin. She was married, but her husband was a sailor who was out to sea half the time. Karin started flirting with me, but I thought that was all it was until she showed me otherwise. It was during the midafternoon slowdown. Millie had gone to the bank to make a deposit, and both of our coworkers had gone outside to grab a smoke. Karin took me by the hand and led me into the employees' bathroom. Then she locked the door, got down on her knees, and blew me. Ten minutes later, I was back at my station flouring chicken legs.

After that little encounter, Karin started inviting me over to her house to listen to music and shit. There was always beer in her fridge, and her husband had a pretty cool stereo. I'd play stink finger with her until she got off. Then I'd fuck her. It was weird, I guess; any other guy would have kept a situation like that going for as long as he could, but I wasn't any other guy. I was me. Karin was way more into it than I was, and after a while I started telling her I was too busy to go over there. I was more interested in some of the little girls who'd come in with their parents to pick up their chicken dinners than I was in Karin. Nothing ever happened on that front, though. After I'd been working there for six months or so, I quit.

I tried community college for a while. That was where I met Rosemary, a single mom who had a young daughter named Serena. Rosemary had a night class Tuesdays and Thursdays, which was when I'd babysit. Serena was my first little girl since Annie. I was twenty-one; she was nine. She cooperated at first, but then she started balking. Said she was going to tell her mother. Figuring I'd better beat feet before the cops got involved, I raided the envelope where my mom was stashing her Christmas Club money. I threw some of my things together and got on the first bus that pulled into the depot. Got off at Worcester, Mass.

In Worcester, I bunked at the Y and got a job as a janitor there. It was a pretty sweet setup, actually. When the little kids—the Guppies or whatever—were in the locker room with their moms, I'd invent excuses for why I had to go in there and get something or check on something. They caught on, though, and I got fired. From there, I rented a room at a flophouse downtown and picked up a job at Ace Hardware. They assigned me to the warehouse at first, and that sorta sucked, but then they taught me how to use the key-making machine. I'd be out back shelving Sheetrock or lugging bags of sodium crystals, and it would come over the loudspeaker. "Kent to keys, please. Kent Kelly to keys." I'd go inside the store, warm up a little, give my muscles a rest while I was cutting someone a key. One afternoon I made myself a pass key that got me into other tenants' rooms over at the flophouse where I was living now. It was just petty theft: cigarettes, spare change, half-bottles of booze. Nobody at that place had much worth stealing. I was one of the ones they questioned after the manager started getting complaints, but I thought fast and told them I'd seen this junkie down the hall coming out of rooms where she didn't belong. Daisy, her name was. She was a pain in the ass, always knocking on guys' doors to bum smokes or offer sex for money, as if you'd *want* to pay to put your dipstick into that skanky snatch. They must have believed me that she was the thief because they kicked her out. The way I figured it, I was doing the place a public service.

It was depressing living there, though. Lonely. Sundays, when the hardware store was closed, were the worst. I'd lie on my bed and start wondering about how Mom was doing. I'd think about my father who, after he moved to Cincinnati, had called me a grand total of twice. Then I'd think about when I was living with the O'Days, helping Aunt Sunny in the kitchen, hanging out with Uncle Chick. And about the night of the flood. I'd start wondering about Annie—how she was doing now, whether some guy at her foster home might be messing with her. I'd fantasize about finding out who he was and beating him to an inch of his life. Rescuing her. It was fucked-up, I guess: me feeling protective of her, considering some of the shit I'd done. . . .

One Sunday, I went downstairs to the pay phone and called my mother to let her know that I was still alive. She cried at first. Then she started bugging me about where I was. "Please, Kent. What if I got sick and needed to get ahold of you?"

"I'd find out," I assured her, although I didn't know how I would.

"Well, where am I supposed to send your mail then? You've got two or three things from the college and—"

"Just throw it out. I'm not going back there."

"Are you sure, Kent? Maybe you should think about it some more."

"Throw it *out*," I repeated.

"Well, okay, honey, but there's other mail, too. There's something here from the Motor Vehicle. It may be your license renewal."

I told her to throw that away, too—that where I was I got around by bus. To change the subject, I asked her how Uncle Chick was doing. Not good, she said. He'd gone from bad to worse. "So they haven't let him see Annie yet?" No, she said. And they still hadn't given her any information either, other than to say she was doing fine. I looked down at my ragged, bloody finger. Until then, I hadn't realized that I'd been tearing at the skin around the cuticle. "Well, take care, Mom. I gotta go." When she started in about whether or not I was coming home for Thanksgiving, I pretended I was the operator cutting in to say time was up.

"Stop it, Kent. That's *you*," she said.

I hung up. Went outside and walked around for a couple of hours, past all the vacant storefronts, all the shifty-eyed spooks sitting on benches and leaning against the decaying buildings of beautiful downtown Worcester.

Chapter Twenty-Two

Annie Oh

I'm getting ready for bed when Viveca calls, wanting to discuss the evening we've just had—our "rehearsal dinner" without a rehearsal. For Viveca, this is typical. Whenever we come back from an evening out and get into bed, she likes to spoon with the lights out and do a postmortem. But tonight I'm here and she's over there at Bella Linda—in the bridal suite by herself per Orion's wishes.

"Well, they're just wonderful, Anna," she says. "All three of them. And so different from one another—three unique and interesting individuals. You must have been a marvelous mother."

Far from it, I think. But my kids have turned out okay in spite of me.

"And now I'm going to be part of your family, too. Oh, you know what would be lovely? If we could convince the three of them to spend the holidays with us. Their father, too, if he was game. We could take them to the Met, to Rockefeller Center to see the tree. Radio City, even. That Christmas show they do there is tacky, but so what? It would be part of the fun."

"Well, we'll see. They might have plans of their own."

"Yes, of course. It's just that we'd have to make a reservation for Christmas dinner someplace before too long. The best restaurants get booked months in advance for the holidays. I can have Carolyn work on it. Make a reservation for the six of us. We can always adjust the number if we have to."

"Okay, but first things first. Let's get through tomorrow before we start planning for something three months from now."

"No, no, you're right. I'm getting ahead of myself. But I just love the idea of celebrating the holidays as a family. And, of course, the Christmas after this one, there'll be your daughter's little one to share it with." It jolts me back to Ariane's news. When she told us this afternoon, I just stood there, staring at her for several seconds, too stunned to react. "Won't that be fun, sweetheart?"

"Yes, sure. But . . ." Inseminated by a man she's never even seen? It seems so strange.

"But what?"

"No, it's just that Ariane usually stays out there for Christmas. They do a big holiday meal at the place she runs, everything from soup to nuts, and she says the turnout is double what it is on a normal day."

"Well, Anna, her priorities may change after her baby is born. She's such a lovely girl. So earnest and socially conscious. Very Berkeley, that's for sure." My hand grips the phone a little tighter. Was that a put-down? "Tell me. How do you feel about becoming a grandmother?"

"I don't really know yet," I tell her. "With everything that's going on, I haven't had time to process it. But I guess I'm a little nervous about the way it's happened. Ari says she researched the prospective donors, but still. It's kind of like spinning a roulette wheel."

"Well, you've always said how grounded and levelheaded she is. I'm sure it will all be fine. And anyway, it's a different world these days. Women Ariane's age have a lot more options than we did. Well, no. I take that back. Look at us. Tomorrow at this time we'll be legally married. Happy?"

"Yes, of course." And I am. But it's been a long day and I'm exhausted. The clock on the bureau says twelve forty-five. I've got to get some sleep. Hector's dropping Minnie back here at eight in the morning so that she can help out—cook breakfast, give our wedding clothes a pressing. I could do all of it myself, but I've hired her, after all. If I didn't give her things to do, it would be like I was paying her a thousand dollars to attend our wedding.

"And how about that son of yours?" Viveca says. "He's even more handsome in person than he is in pictures. Poor Lorenzo couldn't keep his eyes off of him. I just hope it didn't make Andrew uncomfortable. Has he always been that reserved and serious?"

"More so than he used to be. It's probably his military training. And the kind of work he does—dealing with all those wounded soldiers coming back from the war."

"Yes, I suppose. That must be terribly grim sometimes." I'm relieved that she hasn't seemed to pick up on the possibility that meeting her—seeing us as a couple—is what he may have been reserved and tense about. When Lorenzo made that toast and we kissed, I saw Andrew lock his jaw and look away. Saw Ariane reach over and touch the top of his hand.

"He's nothing like Marissa, that's for sure," Viveca says. "*She* was certainly in rare form tonight."

"Because she had too much to drink. When she and Lorenzo started doing those tequila shots and I suggested she'd had enough, she told me to stop acting so 'momish.'"

"Well, it was a special occasion, after all. And she was fine. A little over-the-top near the end maybe, but nobody minded. Everyone got a kick out of those stories of hers about some of the auditions she's been on. That imitation she did of the asthmatic casting director with the bad toupee was hilarious."

To her, maybe. But I kept hearing desperation in those stories Marissa was telling—all those failed attempts to put herself out there. She worries me. I wonder if Orion noticed anything when she was visiting him.

"Well, it was a lovely evening," Viveca says. "Just the kind of night I'd hoped for." Really? I'd felt like I was walking on thin ice the whole time. "So, are you excited about our big day tomorrow?"

"Yes. I'm nervous, though. I'll be relieved once it's over."

There's an uncomfortable pause on her end. "Not nervous as in, you're having doubts, I hope," she says.

"No, no, of course not." But I've already had one failed marriage. How could I not have doubts? "It's just . . . well, you know how I am. I'm just not comfortable being the center of attention."

She laughs. "Not even at your openings! Remember when that art critic from the *Post* came up from Washington to see your first show? He kept telling you how marvelous your work was, and you kept apologizing for it."

"Don't remind me."

"Well, darling, it's a bride's prerogative to be nervous on the night before her wedding. I just hope you'll be able to relax and enjoy yourself tomorrow. I have some Xanax with me. Maybe you should take one before things get under way tomorrow."

"We'll see," I tell her. "Right now, I just need to get some sleep."

"Of course you do. And I do, too."

"Oh, and about the Jones painting? I was going to look around for it some more when we got back here, but I'm just too tired. I will tomorrow morning, though. Or I could just call Orion and ask him what he did with it."

"No, don't," she says. "I don't want him to think I'm hounding you about it. He's probably dropped it off at an appraiser's and that's where it is. Don't worry about it. Now go get some sleep." She tells me she loves me, I tell her I love her, too, and we end our call.

I walk over to the bureau to put down my phone and, out of habit, check my messages before turning it off. Which is silly, really. Why would the kids be calling me when I've been with them all evening? I've had two missed calls, both from the same number. A 4-0-1 prefix. What is that, Rhode Island? It's probably that same condo company that called me last week. Come for a free weekend in Newport, enjoy the beach and the mansions, and let us sell you a time-share. Damned pests. Didn't cell phones used to be immune from those stupid robo-calls? . . . Orion's kept the same framed photos on the bureau, I see. He and I on our anniversary cruise, the five of us on that whale watch we took. My eyes linger on the kids' high school graduation portraits. God, they look so young. The lighting in the restaurant was dim tonight, but I think I saw some gray in Ariane's hair. Orion's mother went prematurely gray—she probably takes after her. . . . Andrew's hairline has receded a bit, and his face is thinner than it was back then. Makes him look even more like—

No! Don't go there. Chase Kent out of your head or you'll never get to sleep.

I put my hand on the lamp switch, ready to turn it off, then change my mind. There's a stack of magazines on Orion's bedside table. I'm keyed up. I'll read until I get drowsy. I pick up a *New Yorker* and thumb through it. Find an article on Julian Schnabel. That will do.

I pull down the covers and climb into bed. Lie back on the same familiar mattress with its peaks and valleys. The same pearl gray sheets I'd lie against while he nuzzled me, kissed my neck and told me how much he loved me—the predictable preliminaries. I got pregnant with the twins at the first place we lived in, but Marissa was conceived here, in this bed. My mind wanders back to the way Ariane's baby was conceived: in some fertility clinic office, by injection. Why couldn't she have waited? Held out at least until she was in her midthirties? It wasn't inevitable that no one else would come along. She gave up too soon. . . .

These pillows feel different—firm and spongy. Not nearly as comfortable as the goose down pillows we used to have. The kids told me tonight that he's met someone up there on the Cape—a marine biologist who teaches at . . . where was it? The University of Rhode Island? They seemed to like her. Well, good. I'm glad for him. I've worried about Orion. I still don't understand why he gave up his practice so suddenly, or why he's decided to put the house on the market. Well, whatever. If he's rebuilding his life, then good for him. I may have left Orion for Viveca, but I still care deeply about him. I glance over at the pictures on the bureau. We shared a life, for Christ's sake. He's the father of my children. Why wouldn't I still love him?

I punch these stupid new pillows, trying to get more comfortable, but they're unyielding. Why would he have kept everything else the same but gotten new pillows? It doesn't make sense. Okay, stop it, Annie. Just read.

"At Palazzo Chupi, the converted West Village horse stable where artist and film director Julian Schnabel now resides with his . . ." *Three unique and interesting individuals.* She's right. They are. I'm glad she likes them. And no, that comment she made about Berkeley wasn't a

dig. It was just an observation. . . . *Well, it was a special occasion, af-*
ter all. And she was fine. A little over-the-top near the end maybe. Was
it just that, or does she have a drinking problem? She's around alcohol all the time at that bar where she works. . . . *Has he always been*
that reserved and serious? No, just the opposite in fact. I mean, he's
always had a temper, yes, but Andrew's always had that playful side,
too. I smile thinking about how he and Minnie's son hit it off this
afternoon—Andrew coming back down from the attic with his old
Atari or PlayStation or whatever it is. Hooking it up to the TV so that
he and Africa could play video games. Minnie's son was in heaven.
And so was Andrew, for that matter. The two of them whooping
and hollering like they were *both* little kids. But then tonight, sitting
across from Viveca, he seemed so . . . glum. But maybe it didn't have
anything to do with my marrying her. Maybe it *is* his work. Is he playful with his girlfriend? I hope so. I hope she makes him happy. I wish
she had come out here with him. I'd have liked to see the two of them
together. Then I'd know. . . . What did they say that woman's name
was—the one Orion's seeing? Tracy? That's a younger woman's name.
I can't remember knowing any Tracys back when I was in school. That
couldn't have been *her* calling me from Rhode Island, could it? No.
Why on earth would she be calling *me*? It's those time-share people.

"At Palazzo Chupi, the converted West Village horse stable where
artist and film director Julian Schnabel . . ." Ariane came up to bed
when I did, but Marissa and Andrew were still downstairs. Did they
remember to lock up? Orion told me a while back that there'd been
a break-in three or four houses down the hill. He'd said whose house
it was, but I didn't recognize the name. I get up, open the bedroom
door, look down the stairs. The front hall light is still on and I hear
voices—the television, maybe? Did they forget to turn it off? I'd better go down and check.

Standing at the entrance to the living room, I look through the
French doors at the two of them. Marissa's fast asleep on the recliner,
her head flopped back, her mouth wide open. Andrew's slumped on
the couch, watching TV. There are three or four beer bottles on the
coffee table, and he's holding another. After Minnie and Africa left

for their motel, he went out and came back with two six-packs. I walk into the room and sit down beside him. "Hi, honey. What are you watching?"

"Movie," he says, his eyes still on the TV.

I look over at Marissa. "Your sister's dead to the world over there, I see. When did she conk out?"

"About five minutes after this thing started," he says. "She got all excited when it came on, and the next thing I knew, she was in snooze mode."

"Well, it's been a long day. What's the movie?"

"*Pulp Fiction*. I'm a big Tarantino fan." He takes a swig of his beer.

"Quentin Tarantino. Right? I met him at Viveca's gallery last year."

He turns and looks at me. "Really?"

"Uh-huh. But there was a big, noisy crowd and he was talking so fast that I kept missing parts of what he was saying." No reaction. "You'll have to ask Viveca about him. She knows him better than I do. He's bought some pieces from her."

"Yeah? Anything of yours?"

"Oh, no. I doubt my work is his cup of tea. His movies are pretty violent, aren't they?"

"Yup. That's what I like about them."

"Really?" No response. "So. Speaking of Viveca . . ."

His body clenches. He sips his beer. "What about her?"

"Did you . . . do you like her?"

He shrugs. "She's okay, I guess. Why?"

"No reason. I was just wondering. You know, it means a lot to us that you've made the effort to come out for the wedding."

"Does it?"

"Yes, we both appreciate it."

"No problem." And that ends that.

I nod toward the TV. "So what other ones has he done?"

"Tarantino? *Reservoir Dogs* is his best. And uh . . . *Kill Bill, Jackie Brown, Natural Born Killers*."

I tell him I saw that last one. "Part of it, anyway. I couldn't take it, though. It was so brutal, I had to walk out."

He looks at me and laughs.

"What?"

"No, it's just . . . That's a little hypocritical, don't you think? Your stuff's got plenty of violence."

"Some of it has, yes. But—"

"I mean, when I was a little kid, some of it would kind of spook me. One of them, especially. The one where a little paper doll boy was being buried alive by a paper doll woman."

I nod. "His mother. That piece was in my *Grimms' Fairy Tales* series. I'd based it on a strange little story called 'The Stubborn Child.'"

"Yeah, well, whatever it was based on, I'd go to bed and start thinking about it and then I wouldn't be able to sleep."

"Oh, honey. Really? I'm so sorry. You should have said something."

"I did. I woke up Dad and told him. A couple of times, he took me back to bed and stayed with me until I got to sleep. But hey, when I got a little older? I started thinking your work was pretty cool. Actually, it was Jay Jay who convinced me."

"Jay Jay?"

"Yeah. He was over here at the house one rainy day. We were like, maybe, ten or eleven. We were bored, so we went down to the basement to play some darts. And Jay started looking at these sketches you had done that were taped to the wall. And he goes, 'What's up with your mom?' And I was—no offense, Mom, but it was kind of embarrassing, you know? Because the drawings were of a woman cutting some dude's head off. In one of them, she was slicing his neck with a knife, and in another, she was holding up his head."

I nod. "Artemisia."

"Say what?"

"Artemisia Gentileschi. She was an artist from the Renaissance. I'd discovered a painting of hers in a book about baroque art. *Judith Slaying Holofernes*, it was called. I was doing some studies of it. Planning to base a piece on it, which I never ended up following through on. But I can see how, taken out of context, those drawings must have seemed pretty strange. And I'm sorry they embarrassed you."

"Yeah, but let me finish. Jay started complaining about how *his* mother was Mrs. Fuddy Duddy, and how it must be cool to have a mom who was an artist who did stuff like this. And after he said that, I started thinking that, yeah, your artwork *was* pretty cool. So who was Judith, anyway? And what did she have against the poor slob whose head she lopped off?"

"It's from the Old Testament. I'd started reading up on the artist. And apparently this Bible story spoke to her. As a revenge fantasy, I guess. She'd been raped and then publicly humiliated. Blame the victim, you know? Which happened a lot back then."

"Happens a lot now, too. This woman, Jen, that I knew back in basic training? She got raped by her sergeant, and she was afraid to say anything because of that blame-the-victim stuff. And when it did come out, he didn't take the hit for it. She did. They ended up giving her a dishonorable discharge."

I shake my head in disgust. "What I admired about Artemisia's painting was that she was taking back some of the power. Symbolically, I mean. Using her palette and brushes instead of a knife." Gunfire explodes on the television. I glance at the gory murder scene in progress but have to look away. "I guess the difference between me and your friend Tarantino is that I'm *exploring* violence in my work. Not, you know, *glorifying* it. But maybe that's not fair. Like I said, I only saw that one movie of his."

"*Part* of one," he reminds me.

I smile. "Point taken. But what I'm saying is that when I take on the subject of violence, it comes from a different place. I'm exploring justice issues, not just, well, blood for blood's sake. But who knows? Maybe that's what Tarantino's drawing on, too."

"It's personal for you, isn't it?"

I flinch. "Personal? What . . . what do you mean?"

"Isn't it about your childhood? That flood you were in? One time when I was poking around down in your studio, I found this magazine article someone had written about you—about how angry your art is. And one of the things you said in that thing, I still remember, was how 'violent' the water was that night. And hey, your mother and sister drowned. Why *wouldn't* you be angry about a raw deal like that?

I knew a little about your childhood, but I found out a lot more when I read that article."

Not the worst of it, he didn't. I remember how cautious I was with that reporter. What I did and didn't tell her. "Like what, for instance?"

"Well, I knew your mom drowned that night, but I didn't know your baby sister died, too. I didn't even know you *had* a sister. Or that you got put in foster care after your father lost it. Left you in the lurch or whatever."

Left you in the lurch with me.

Stop it! Shut up!

"Well, Andrew, reporters ask a lot of questions, but some of your answers get lost in translation." Change the subject! Change the subject! "But anyway, my childhood is ancient history. So tell me. What do you think about your sister's big news?"

He looks momentarily confused. Then he frowns. "Ariane's you mean? I don't know. Seems more like a Dr. Frankenstein pregnancy than God's plan. In my opinion anyway. But hey, it's her life. Right?"

"Uh-huh. I just hope she doesn't regret it down the line." I repeat what Viveca said over the phone: that Ariane is grounded and level-headed, despite the decision she made. "So she'll make it work, whatever the outcome. I guess both of my twins are in transition, huh? She's having a baby. You're getting married. It's just too bad your fiancée couldn't make it. I was really looking forward to meeting her."

"Yeah, well . . ." He clunks his empty down on the table. Pulls another beer from the carton at his feet. "You know, now that I think about it, Oliver Stone directed *Natural Born Killers*. But Tarantino had something to do with it. Wrote the screenplay, maybe." He points his beer bottle at the TV screen. "Okay, this part's cool," he says. "Watch."

In the movie, a couple is at a nightclub. They've just announced a dance contest. The man doesn't want to compete, but his date insists.

"Isn't that John Travolta?"

"Yeah. Him and Samuel L. Jackson are hired killers. They're hilarious."

Hilarious hired killers? John Travolta and his girlfriend get up to dance. "I like his little ponytail. He's a good dancer, huh? Did you ever see *Saturday Night Fever*?"

He opens his new beer and takes a swig. "Unfortunately."

"That's an old Chuck Berry song they're dancing to. Uncle Donald had the forty-five. He and Mimsy will be here tomorrow. Did I tell you?" He nods. "That's the twist they're doing, by the way. Oh, and now he's doing the swim. Who's playing the girlfriend? She looks familiar, too."

"Uma Thurman. She's his boss's wife, not his girlfriend. There's a great scene coming up where she ODs on something and Travolta starts freaking out. He's supposed to be looking out for her, and if she dies, he's going to be up shit's creek with his boss."

"Oh. But anyway, it's too bad Casey-Lee couldn't come. I was looking forward to meeting her."

"Yeah, you just said that." He grabs a pillow and holds it against his chest. Okay, message received. But when I look back at the TV, a commercial's come on. He grabs the remote and turns down the volume. "I hate it the way they jack up the sound when these stupid ads come on."

In the quiet, I hear Marissa snoring. "Boy, she's really out. Isn't she?"

He glances over at her and shakes his head. "Not surprised after what she put away today."

"Oh, I know. It seemed like every time I looked down at her end of the table tonight, the waiter was refilling her wineglass. And then those tequilas on top of that?"

"Yeah, and she was already feeling no pain when we got here this afternoon. Knocked down a couple of Bloody Marys before we left the Cape this morning, ordered herself a double Jameson at the place where we stopped for lunch."

"Oh my god. Do you think her drinking's becoming a problem?"

"Duh," he says.

"Maybe this acting thing is taking its toll. She's always joking about those auditions she goes to, but it must be pretty stressful."

"Yeah, well. If you want to see stressful, you should see what some of the soldiers I work with are up against. Next to that, going to a bunch of auditions is nothing."

"No, of course not. But still, it can't be easy. Getting her hopes up and then waiting for calls or callbacks, whatever they call them."

"Yeah, and you know that insurance commercial she was in? She said they stopped running it, so there goes that little gold mine of hers. She said she's waiting to hear back on a couple of things now. From casting agents or whatever. When we were up at Dad's, she must have checked her cell about a thousand times an hour. And then, she's such a ditz that she charges the thing and forgets to take it with her when we left. On our way down here, when she realized she forgot it, it was like this big catastrophe. We were in Buzzards Bay by then, just getting off the Cape, and she goes, 'We have to turn around. I left my phone at Dad's.' She got royally pissed at me when I said no. And then she was pissed at Dad when she kept trying to call him on Ari's phone and he wouldn't answer. I was like, 'You know what, Marissa? Maybe he's busy. Maybe the whole world doesn't revolve around you.' She calls me a motherfucker and pouts for the next hour or so. Didn't snap out of it until she got that Jameson in her. Nice language, huh? I guess that's the way New Yorkers talk to each other."

"Well, honey, I imagine you hear that kind of talk at the barracks, too. I don't think it's exclusive to New York."

"Yeah well, I'm just sayin'."

"And you know. She hangs on those callbacks because it's how she makes her living. Even with tips, she can't make much at that waitressing job."

"Then maybe she should change careers. Give up this pie-in-the-sky acting fantasy of hers and get a real job. Stick with something for a change. How many semesters did she have left when she bailed on NYU? After you and Dad shelled out all that money so she could go to school in New York?"

"Two semesters, I think."

"See what I mean? At least if she'd stuck it out, she'd have a degree by now. I mean, yeah, I kind of took the long route, too, but we've all got to grow up sometime—even the twerp. And as far as her drinking?" He repeats what he'd said about his other sister: that it's Marissa's life, her choice to make. That's another thing that's different about Andrew now: this stand-off attitude when it comes to his sisters. They could both get under his skin, but when push came to shove, he was always protective of them—Marissa, especially.

"Maybe before we leave for the wedding tomorrow, you and I should sit her down and talk to her about her drinking," I suggest.

Andrew shakes his head. "You can if you want to, Mom, but I'm staying out of it. When we were up there visiting Dad, I teased her about those bruises she's got and she practically bit my head off."

"Bruises? What bruises?"

"The ones she's hiding under all that makeup. She claims she bumped into something in her kitchen and I said, 'Yeah? In two different places? What really happened? Somebody pop you one?' I was just kidding, you know? But she got pissed and stormed out of the room."

I get up and walk over to her, but I can't see anything in the dim light of the TV. Why hadn't *I* noticed these bruises? "You think someone hit her?"

He shrugs. Says I should ask her myself. "Or Ariane. The two of them had a deep, dark discussion about something after she got all huffy with me. Maybe Ari knows. But you know what, Mom? If she's got an alcohol problem, she's the one who has to deal with it. Not you and me. That's one of the things I learned dealing with the guys who are coming back from the wars—the ones who are numbing themselves with booze or Oxys or whatever. *They've* got to want to stop. You can't make them if they don't want to."

He thinks about something and chuckles. "What?" I say.

"No, I was just thinking about this one guy I work with at the hospital? Pete? He's a maintenance guy—funny as hell. So one time, me and this other psych nurse had just gotten finished subduing a patient who had gone nuts on us? In the middle of a tough withdrawal? And Pete tells us, out of the blue, that he's been sober for twenty-something years. 'Really?' I said. 'Wow, good for you.' And he goes, 'Yeah, I had to because I'm allergic to booze. Every time I got soused, I used to break out in handcuffs.'"

I smile. Gallows humor, I guess. "Well, honey, your sister isn't *that* bad."

"I'm not saying she is. But like I said, she's the one who's got to want to quit. You can't force recovery on someone."

"I'm not talking about forcing her, Andrew. But maybe if I talk to her about it, let her know I'm concerned. And if you want to stay out of it, fine. I guess I should talk to your father. See what he thinks." As if on cue, Marissa scowls and mutters something in her sleep. Her dress is so bunched on one side, I can see her underwear. "Maybe we should try to get her up to bed."

"Nah, just let her sleep it off."

As I sit there watching my daughter, a memory of my father flashes before me: he's in the kitchen, seated at our old dinette set. Slurring his words, whimpering to my aunt about how he should have saved them, how it should have been him who drowned, not Mama. "It runs in the family, you know."

"What does?"

"Alcoholism. My father was a drunk. Did I ever tell you that?"

He shakes his head. "You used to talk about your mother, what she was like. But you never said much about him."

"No? Well, he died before you and Ariane were born. Earlier that same year, in fact. I remember being out to here with you two at his funeral. His drinking wasn't a problem until after . . ."

"The flood?"

I nod. "He felt responsible for their deaths because he couldn't save them. But *I* hadn't died. He could have saved *me*."

Uh-oh. Watch it, Annie.

"From what?"

Not what. Who.

"Oh, honey. Never mind."

"No, what were you just going to say? Tell me."

"What? Oh, just that . . . instead of coming home after work and eating supper with us, putting me to bed, he'd be out at the bars."

"Who's us?"

He's getting warmer.

"Uh . . . what?"

"You said 'instead of eating supper with us.' You mean you and Uncle Donald?"

"Some nights, yes. But your uncle was pretty busy with all his high school activities. He'd be running some club meeting or at practice. He . . . that was how he coped with what had happened, I guess. By staying busy."

"And *how* old were you?"

"When my mother died? Five."

"And they'd just leave you alone? Without a babysitter or anything?"

"Well, no. . . . My cousin was living with us. He'd be there."

"The one who got you guys out of the car that night? Kent?"

You just jumped, Annie. Did he see you jump?

"Uh, yes. Yes, that's right. How did you—?"

"Because we read about it."

"Read about it?"

"Yeah, Ari and me. Whenever we'd ask you about what happened that night, you never seemed to want to go there."

"Oh. Well, honey, those were such painful memories."

"That's what we figured. But Dad never seemed to know much either. So one time, when we were in high school—"

"Who? You and your sister?"

"Yeah. We went to the library—downstairs to the microfilm machine. And we found all that stuff about the flood in the old newspapers. Read your mom's obituary. Saw the pictures of the flood, the one of you and Kent at the hospital after they rescued you."

Is this it? Is this where our secrets—

No! Stay calm. Breathe.

"Whatever happened to him, anyway?"

"I told you. He started drinking and—"

"No, not your father. Kent."

Stop saying his name! "I . . . I don't know, Andrew. They put me in foster care and . . . we lost touch. So I have no idea what happened to him. He moved away. Out of state, I think. And then after my Aunt Elaine died—his mother—after she died . . . He may be dead now, too, for all I know."

Maybe. But I'm still in your head. Aren't I, Annie?

"You should try Googling him. Maybe he's on Facebook or something." Relax those fists! Say something or—"But that must have sucked, huh? Having to go into foster care?"

"What? Yes. The uh . . . the family they put me with was okay, but they had kids of their own. The second family, too. It was hard always feeling like the outsider, the one who didn't belong. I kept hoping my father would straighten himself out and take me back home, but that never happened. It was just a fantasy."

"But he must have come for visits. Right? . . . Mom?"

I shake my head. "No, wait. I did see him once. They set up a visit at the Social Services office. But he was late, and when he finally did show up, he was drunk, so they escorted him out. I saw him for all of five minutes. . . . He sent me Christmas presents a few times at the beginning. Birthday cards. He'd mail them to the agency and they'd forward them to my foster family. But that stopped after a while. Every year I'd wait for them. Run out and get the mail, check the tags on all the presents under the tree."

"How about Uncle Don? Did you see him?"

"Yes, he and I stayed in touch. He'd write me letters, visit during his college vacations. But the only other time I saw my father after he showed up drunk that time was when I was pregnant with you and your sister. He was pretty sick by then. Dying. He kept telling Donald he wanted to see me, so finally I went. We drove to this run-down old welfare hotel in New London where he had a room." A shiver runs through me as I recall that room—the rippy window shades, the filthy sheets and brimming ashtrays. And that smell! "I don't know, honey. I guess I should have gone to see him more often. After I was an adult, I mean. He couldn't help it. It was a disease, right? But . . ."

"What?"

"It was just too hard. For one thing, I was still so angry with him for abandoning me. Choosing booze over his own daughter. And then when I got there that day, he looked so . . . I mean, if I had seen him on the street somewhere, I wouldn't have even recognized him. Would have walked right past him. He'd been so handsome, you know? But now he was just this scrawny, pathetic old . . . And he had this terrible smell. He sat down next to me, took my hand in his and . . . his breath had this sickening sweet, fruity smell to it."

Andrew says a word I don't catch.

"What?"

"Ketoacidosis. We treat some of the older vets at the hospital—the Vietnam flameouts, mostly. A lot of hard-core alkies get that breath. They come in dehydrated, malnourished. Their body can't synthesize glucose so their ketone levels spike. It's a liver problem."

"That's what his death certificate said: liver cancer."

"Makes sense. Hey, I'm sorry, Mom. I always figured you didn't want to talk about things because of the flood. I didn't know about all this other stuff. Must have been hard, huh?"

I nod. "Maybe I should have told you kids more about it if you wanted to know, but I guess I wanted to shield you and your sisters from it. . . . Hey, I made a lot of mistakes, Andrew. I just wasn't a very good mother."

"Yes you were, Mom. Don't say that."

"No, I wasn't. The way I'd fly off the handle—at you, especially."

He smiles. "Yeah, well, I gave you good reason."

"No, you didn't. I remember how scared you looked that day when I pulled over to the side of the road and made you and Ariane get out of the car. . . . And my god, now I find out that even my art-work scared you."

"Yeah, well, your crappy childhood had to come out in some way. Right?" I'm so taken with his kindness, his understanding, that I reach out and touch his cheek. "I mean sure, you had your moments. But you were a damned good mother and don't say you weren't."

Whether I was or I wasn't, I appreciate his saying it. That's something else about my son that's different now: he's more sensitive. I love him so much—I always have—but I need to be done with this conversation. "Look," I tell him. "Your movie's back on."

"Oh, yeah. This is the part I was telling you about. See, she's passed out from whatever she's taken and he can't revive her. Now watch."

On the screen, Uma Thurman is on the floor and they're hovering over her: John Travolta and some shifty-looking couple. The guy fills a syringe and rears back with it. Plunges it into Uma. I turn away. "No, look!" Andrew says. And when I look back, Uma's eyes pop open and she bolts up, like a resurrected corpse. "Awesome, huh?" Why is he laughing? Why is this funny?

He puts his half-drunk beer and the empties back in the carton and stands up. "Okay, that's the scene I was waiting for. I'm beat. Guess I'll hit the hay. You want this on?" The remote's in his hand. When I shake my head, he deadens the TV and the room goes dark.

"Everything's ready up there, honey. I put on sheets for you. And a set of towels on your bureau."

"Okay, thanks. Hey, you all right?"

I nod. Look over at Marissa, cast now in silhouette. "You know what? Let's try and get her upstairs." I stand. Go over to her and put my hand on her shoulder. Give it a little shake. "Marissa?"

"No!" she shouts. "Get away from me!" Her flailing hand hits me on the side of my mouth. It's okay. It doesn't hurt, and anyway she didn't realize what she was doing. She's sound asleep.

"Still a brat," her brother says. "Seriously, Mom. Just leave her alone."

"Okay."

I follow him out of the room and up the stairs. When we reach the top, I tell him good night. Tell him I love him. "Love you, too, Mom," he says. He's at the entrance to the bathroom when he turns back. "Hey, Mom?"

"Hmm?"

"Casey and me? We broke up."

I reach out to him. Place my hand on his arm. "Oh, baby, I'm so sorry. What happened?"

He shrugs. "It just wasn't going to work out."

"Who broke it off? You or—"

"I did. But hey, it's okay. Better to realize it before we got married than afterward. Right?"

"Sure, honey, but—"

"I wasn't going to mention it just before your wedding, you know? But I told Dad when I was up there, so . . ."

"What about your sisters? Do they know?"

He shakes his head. "Don't worry, Mom. I'll live. G'night."

"Good night."

He closes the bathroom door behind him. Poor kid. And poor Marissa, too, passed out down there. I go to the hall closet and grab one of the extra blankets. Go back down and tuck it around her. Do that much at least.

Back upstairs in the bedroom, I turn off the light and crawl between the sheets. Rest my head on these goddamned new pillows. It's no wonder Andrew acted so sullen this evening. It wasn't about Viveca and me. It was about his broken engagement. Oh god, I'm exhausted. I need to get some sleep. . . . *I mean sure, you had your moments. But you were a damned good mother.* Overall, maybe. But I could get so impatient, so frustrated. Half the time, I wanted them to just go away so I could get to my work. And they had to have picked up on that resentment. Kids are perceptive. But it's like he said: they survived. They're all okay in spite of my shortcomings.

Who are you kidding? They're the walking wounded, all three of them. A broken engagement, a Dr. Frankenstein pregnancy. And your third one down there, blacked out. Black and blue. Face it, Annie. I screwed you up, and you screwed them up.

Go to hell. I hope you *are* dead.

And what if I am? Our secrets are still alive. What you and I know that no one else ever found out. That it was you who dropped the baby into that cold, dark water and—

She was crying, bucking against me. And so cold, so slippery. I loved Gracie. I couldn't hold on to her.

Was that it? Or were you jealous of all the attention she was getting?

No! It was an accident.

And what about our other secret? The things we did when we were alone?

The things *you* did. I didn't even understand what was happening. I was just a little girl.

A naughty little girl. Touching me where I wanted you to, letting me touch you.

I missed my mother. I was confused. It was all so confusing. Okay, relax, Annie. Breathe. Go to sleep. . . . But he's right. He damaged me, and I damaged them—the three people I love most in the world. . . . And Orion: I hurt him, too. I was unfaithful to him with Viveca, and now to add insult to injury, I'm marrying her tomorrow in the town where we raised our kids. Where tomorrow our kids will stand there and witness . . . will witness. . . .

What's happening? Why can't I breathe? My lungs need air! Oh god, I feel so sick. What's that noise? Oh god, it's me! I'm shaking so hard that the headboard is banging against the wall. Get out of my room, Kent! Don't touch me! . . . I'm cold. How can I be sweating when I'm freezing cold? Gracie was so cold, so wet. I couldn't hold her. Am I having a heart attack? Is that why my heart is pounding? Why my fingertips are numb?

Scream for help, Annie.

No, I can't! I'll wake them up!

Then get out of bed. Go over to your phone and call for help. Call 9-1-1. But my legs won't move. Why can't I breathe? Is this what drowning feels like? Please, God, don't let me die. I don't want to die like this. Then pray. Yes, that's right. I'll pray. Our Father who art in heaven, hallowed be Thy name. Thy kingdom come, Thy will be done on earth as it is in heaven. Give us this day . . . Give us . . .

Okay, it's passing. I'm up. Walking over to my phone. Turning it on. I watch it light up. Watch my fingers skid along the keys. Press the numbers. Press "send." . . . Why isn't it ringing? Okay, there it goes. Two rings, three, four, five. Answer it, Viveca. *Please* answer it.

"Mmph. Hello? . . . Hello?"

Speak. Say something.

"Who is this? . . . Anna, is that you?"

"Help me." It comes out in a whisper. Did she hear me?

"Anna? What did you just say? Sweetheart, is something wrong?"

"Help me."

And she does. Soothes me with her calming voice. Names it: panic attack. She has me say the address. Says she's going to get up now, get in her car. Put the address into her GPS and come to me. She'll bring the Xanax, she says. She'll be right here. She's coming.

I'm downstairs, waiting at the front window, when I see her headlights. I unlock the door. Open it, let her in, and fall against her, sobbing. "I didn't know what was happening. I thought I was dying."

"It's all right, Anna. I'm here now. Come on. Let's get you up to bed. You're all right now. I'm going to stay with you."

"No, you can't. I promised him."

"It doesn't matter." She takes my hand in hers. "Come with me."

At the base of the stairs, I stop. Look over my shoulder and into the living room. The recliner's empty, the blanket's on the floor. Marissa's woken up and gone to bed.

"Come on now, Anna. Come upstairs. . . . That's it. Now get under the covers. You feel cold. There you go. Good girl. Now just hold on a second. I'll be right back."

She returns from the bathroom with a cup of water. I take the pill she gives me. Swallow it. She gets into bed. Places her body against mine and holds me. Massages my temple with her thumb. "It's all right now, baby. I'm here. You're here with me."

"I was up here, trying to get to sleep, but I started thinking about my kids. Worrying about them, and then, all of a sudden, I couldn't breathe. I thought I was having a heart attack."

"I know, sweetheart. But just try to relax now. Okay?"

"Andrew and I were downstairs. This movie was on, and Marissa—"

"Shssh. Close your eyes and rest."

"He started asking me about when I was a kid. About things I never talk about. And then when I came back up to bed . . . Viveca, there are things that happened when I was little. Bad things."

"Shssh. You can tell me about them, Anna, but right now you just need to relax and go to sleep."

"Okay. Okay, Viveca."

Lying there in the dark, I can't see the photographs on the bureau, but it's as if I can *feel* him looking at me. I'm sorry, Orion. I couldn't keep my promise. I need her here. I'm worried about the kids, Orion. Did you notice anything about them when they visited you? Why did Andrew and his girl break their engagement? It wasn't because of me, was it? Why did Ariane decide to get pregnant that way? She's still young. . . . But okay, Viveca's right. I need to let it all go and get to sleep. And Marissa's gotten herself up to bed. She looked so uncomfortable asleep in that chair. All three of them are down the hall, asleep. And no matter why Ariane got pregnant, her child is growing inside her, its tiny heart beating away. . . . In the quiet, I listen to Viveca's rhythmic breathing. Feel the steady beat of her heart. Her warmth relaxes me, and her arm resting against my back makes me feel safe. I called her, and she came. Took care of me. . . .

I'm starting to doze now. Don't fight it, Annie. Just let it go. . . .

When I wake up, I lie still, confused for a few seconds about where I am. Okay, now I remember. Our bed. The yellow walls, the curtains I hung after he installed the rods. Then it comes back to me: the strange, paralyzing fear that came over me last night. Panic attack, she said. Then she came, brought me up here, got me to sleep. . . .

It's our wedding day! I reach out to touch her, but my hand comes down on the empty mattress. A car starts outside. I get up, go over to the window. Watch her back down the driveway and out into the street. She puts on her headlights. Puts the car into gear and drives away. The sunrise is pretty, a mother-of-pearl pink beyond the trees. . . .

I see it on the bureau: the note in her beautiful, flowing penmanship.

Good morning, darling. I wanted to get up and out of
here before any of the kids woke up—respect the family
boundaries. You were sleeping so peacefully, I didn't have

the heart to wake you up. I'm so sorry you had a bad night, but don't dwell on that. Think about today and all of our tomorrows. I love you, Anna.~ V

And I love her, too. I need her. I want to marry her, go with her to Greece and see the things she wants to show me: those sun-bleached houses built into the hill, the blue Aegean, the red hibiscus against the snow-white fence. My doubts are gone, and I'm filled with hope. The sunrise is beautiful, the sky is clear. It's going to be a beautiful day.

Chapter Twenty-Three

Kent Kelly

At the hardware store, I got promoted to the sales floor. All those fix-it lessons Uncle Chick had given me came in handy, and I was good at selling. I was a natural, they said. Some customer would come in for a can of paint or a package of picture hooks and leave with a quartz heater for their garage or a socket wrench set that was on sale. Impulse buys: that was my specialty once I realized how gullible people could be. I sold this one lady patio furniture in November, and I'm not even talking clearance prices. After a while, I got another promotion: assistant sales manager. They still let me be the key guy, though. There was something about cutting keys that felt satisfying. Years later, when I mentioned that to some court-ordered shrink who was treating me, he said, "Well, Kent, there's something phallic about a key, isn't there? You stick it into a lock and voilà." He was so far off base, I couldn't help laughing at him. For me, it was more about hearing my name over the loudspeaker. "Kent Kelly to the key machine, please. Kent to keys." I was a somebody at that store— the assistant manager and the key guy.

At the flophouse where I lived, this guy Mitch moved into Daisy's old room. He was a tattoo artist. Worked at a storefront place two streets over called Marked Men. (This was before every chick in the universe started getting tattooed.) There was a porn shop next door to Marked Men, and Mitch worked there a couple of nights, too. He was closer to my father's age than mine, but we got to be friends. We'd smoke weed together, play cards, go out for breakfast or to the movies on Sundays, which, like I said, was always the hardest day of the week for me. One Sunday afternoon, he opened up the shop and gave me a tat free of charge—a cobra, its body coiled around my bicep, its hooded head raised and ready to strike. Mitch said a paying customer would have had to fork over seventy-five bucks for it. It hurt like a motherfucker for a day or so, itched for a couple more, but it was worth it. When I wore short sleeves at work, people would ask me to pull up my sleeve so they could see the whole thing. Tell me it was cool. I didn't know Mitch had an ulterior motive until the night we were hanging out in his room doing vodka shots and he reached over and put his hand on my crotch. At first, I was so stunned that I just sat there letting him. But when he went for my zipper, I grabbed his wrist and gave him his hand back. "What's the matter?" he said.

"Nothing. What are you, a fag or something? Because I'm not."

"Don't knock it till you try it," he said. "A guy knows a lot more about what makes another guy feel good than a woman does."

I shook my head. "I'm just not into that kind of action."

A few minutes and a couple of vodkas later, he asked me what kind of action I *was* into. I never would have told him if I wasn't shit-faced.

The next night there was a knock on my door, and when I answered it, there was Mitch. He handed me a magazine called *Young Love*. The porn shop where he pinch-hit kept stuff like that in the back, he said. "Have fun." I stood there, watching him walk down the hall to his room.

The pictures in that magazine excited me, but they shocked me, too. I was pretty streetwise by then but still naïve about some stuff. I guess I'd more or less assumed I was the only guy in the world who liked them that age, but *Young Love* let me know I wasn't. Over the next several days, I looked at it so many times that the binding fell apart.

From there, one thing led to another. Mitch and I had an agreement. He kept me supplied with kiddie porn, and I let him do stuff. I didn't particularly enjoy it, but it was a means to an end. This was years before all that shit became available on the Internet. After I started selling life insurance and could afford a computer, it was like someone had handed me the key to the candy store. At least that was what it was like until those two plainclothes detectives showed up at the door of my condo, read me my rights, and walked out with my hard drive. But that happened a lot later, when I was in my forties and making decent money. The lawyer I hired couldn't get the charges dropped, but he got me off with just a fine. With what he charged me plus what I had to fork over to the government, someone might as well have shoved a gun against my ribs and said, "Stick 'em up." But at least in terms of jail time, I dodged a bullet. Dodged another one in terms of my job. The Duffy Insurance Agency was none the wiser. By then, I had four framed "Sales Manager of the Month" certificates hanging on the wall in my cubicle and four three-hundred-dollar sports jackets hanging in my closet. It didn't much matter if it was out-of-season patio furniture or life insurance policies: I was goddamned good at whatever it was I had to sell.

I've done eight little girls over the years. I have Polaroids of some of them, and memories of every single one. What I'd do was rent apartments in smaller towns but cruise city kids. Get what I wanted and then get back on I-95 and disappear six or seven exits down the highway. I'd zero in on lonely kids for the most part—girls who, in their own way, were as starved for attention as those old folks at Eldredge Eldercare, as neglected as *I* was when I was a kid. This one girl, Lawanda? In Bridgeport? She was the only black kid I ever did. Her mom was a hooker who, when she worked the streets, would give her daughter a few bucks and drop her off at McDonald's. You know how easy it is to pick up a kid when McDonald's is her babysitter?

When you're a grown man who's circling a little girl, you've got to be patient. If you make your move before the kid and her mom both trust you—begin to need you—then it can all go south. But if you bide your time, within a month or so, you're staying the night, going to Wal-Mart with them, giving the kid rides to gymnastics or some other little girl's birthday party. For one thing, the moms whose daughters I'm interested in are struggling to make ends meet— working a job with long hours or, even better, two jobs. And for another thing, they're lonely, too. Starved for attention and romance. So you start pinch-hitting for them if their regular sitter's sick, maybe do a load of laundry if you notice that the hamper's full. When they get

home from work, you rub their aching feet or massage the tension out
of their shoulders, listen to their gripes about their crap-head boss or
their difficult coworker. You tell them they're pretty, and if they try
to dismiss the compliment, you look them straight in the eye and say,
"No, seriously, you are." And they look back at you, hopeful as hell,
blinking back all of their past disappointments. See, I'm lucky because
my diagnosis is Pedophilia, Nonexclusive Type, "nonexclusive" meaning that, although it's little girls who turn me on, I can do the mothers, too, even if I have to think about their daughters to help me cross
the finish line. And when Mom's getting hers on a regular basis, it's
easier for her to stay blind about what might be going on when she's
not there.

Do I feel guilty sometimes? Sure. Like I said, I'm not a monster. Case in point: the day I found out my mother had died and
been buried two weeks earlier, I started banging my head against
the wall, hard as I could. Then I stumbled down the street to the
walk-in clinic. Had to get stitches in my forehead. Hey, I've *known*
monsters—in prison, in a therapy group for sexual predators they
made me go to—and believe me, I'm a different breed than those
guys. The way I look at it, I'm just a guy who needs sex like any other
guy, except that I'm wired a little differently than most, which, when
you think about it, is kind of like having a disability. Think about it.
Most men can go to a bar or go online, pick up some pussy, and be
done with it. Whereas I've got to always be looking over my shoulder,
risking arrest because society's so fucking squeamish and hypocritical about it. You walk through the girls' department of any department store in the country, and they've got the mannequins dressed
up like little sluts. They sell *makeup* for little kids, for chrissake. But
as far as the law's concerned, it's strictly look but don't touch. And
don't kid yourself. Some of these little girls can be pretty seductive.
They'll climb up in your lap and want to cuddle, touch their fingers
to your face so that they can feel how scratchy your whiskers are.
And take it from me: some of these kids, once you've initiated them,
want it, too. Because, hey, sex feels good no matter what age you are.
I gave a ten-year-old an orgasm once and don't tell me I didn't, like

that one facilitator said in one of those groups they made me go to. I mean, who was there? Me or that battle-ax? ...

But yeah, I *do* feel guilty sometimes. Hate myself, even, once the rush is over, especially when they cry. This one guy I knew in prison? Eamon? He *killed* a kid who wouldn't stop crying. His girlfriend's little boy; he flung him headfirst into a wall. Now *there's* a monster for you. And I'm lumped in the same category as *that* sociopath? Uh-uh. No way. The day I picked up the paper and read that Lawanda had been murdered by her mother's meth head boyfriend, I felt so bad about it that I cried like a baby.

This woman Michelle I met when I lived in Stamford was a bit of a cow, but she was also a widow, so there was no ex-husband to contend with. (The exes can be tricky if they're still invested in their kids' lives, or if it wasn't them who wanted the divorce.) Her daughter Lily was a beautiful kid—ten years old, sweet and innocent, with frizzy red hair and tiny pink nipples. Out of all the little girls I've done, Lily came the closest to Annie.

I moved in with them during summertime. The setup was perfect because Michelle played on a softball team. She was their pitcher, and from what I could see, the main reason why her team was leading the league. We'd go to her games in two separate cars. Lily and I would sit in the bleachers and watch for maybe three or four innings. Then I'd take her home and get her ready for bed. Michelle usually went out to a bar with her teammates after their game, so she wouldn't get home until after ten most of the time, and by then I'd have gotten what I wanted and Lily would be asleep.

But I got careless one night. Got a little too rough with Lily, and I was so focused on getting the kid to stop crying about the bleeding that I didn't even realize it had started raining heavily. That the game had been called. I didn't hear Michelle's car pull into the driveway. Didn't hear her enter the house or walk down the hall toward Lily's room. When I looked up, there she was in the doorway, sopping wet, still in her uniform. It got ugly. Lily was screaming, Michelle was screaming and throwing whatever she could grab at me as I hurried toward the door, dressing myself and trying to find my friggin' car keys. She nailed me with these heavy brass bookends. One of them clipped me on the shoulder, the other landed hard against the small of my back. I mean, shit, she was their star pitcher. Trust me, that bitch had an arm on her, and her aim was accurate.

Gunning it back to my place, I made an emergency escape plan. I'd go back to my apartment, throw a few things in a bag, and drive to Providence where Mitch lived. Disappear there for a while. My crucial mistake was stopping at the ATM for cash on the way to my place. I was backing my car out of the driveway when a cruiser pulled in front of it, blocking my way. That was it, and I knew it. The jig was finally up.

I wrote Michelle an impassioned letter, promising that I'd get help and begging her to forgive me, a.k.a. to drop the charges. It came back a week later, unopened. My lawyer told me we should plea-bargain. "The mom's out for blood and they've got the girl's testimony on video. And if I know Judge Dwyer, he'll rule that that kiddie porn prior of yours is admissible. The deck's stacked against you, Kent. Take the deal."

The deal was a ten-year sentence, suspended after seven. I left the courtroom courtesy of DOC and was processed into the society of scumbags at Enfield Correctional. My new peers were rapists, skinheads, arsonists, contract murderers. And trust me, when you enter the hell that's an American prison with a pedophile conviction— when word gets around that a new "short-eyes" has arrived on the compound—you're in for special treatment. At Enfield, I got shanked in the med line, had my food spat on by the servers as I went through the chow line, got beaten up and raped by the tattooed muscleheads who spend their days lifting weights and their shower time meting out a justice system of their own, often with a thumbs-up from the COs, who have it in for us short-eyes, too. "So what the hell do you want *me* to do about it?" one CO asked me when I showed him the turds that some goon had shat onto my mattress. I told him I needed to be moved to a different unit. Two weeks' worth of torment later, a different CO opened my cell door. "Let's go, Kelly," he said. "You're moving."

Finally, I thought. "Where to?"

"Solitary. The deputy warden's issued you a ticket."

"For *what*?"

"For licking your lips and making goo goo eyes at someone's little girl in the visiting room."

"That's bull," I said. "It didn't happen." It didn't!

"Were you in the visiting room Friday afternoon?" I told him I was—that I'd had a legal visit. "Well, then. Come on. Move it." I was innocent, but it was futile to object.

I was in seg for the next ten days. Nothing to do, nothing to read. I was going stir-crazy, thinking about everything from the day I'd flushed those baby gerbils down the crapper to the night of the flood. When they put me back in gen pop, the beat-down I took was so vicious that I lost my left eye. After I got out of the infirmary, I wrote the warden a letter, telling him I was thinking of suing the state and him personally. That was when they transferred me to Gardner, a medium-security facility that houses more drug dealers and white-collar crooks than killers. But there were goons in Gardner, too. "Cyclops," they nicknamed me. Nice, huh? I went along with my counselor's suggestion for survival: pass the word around that I was doing a bid for check-kiting. Whatever prison you're in, you have an easier ride if your fellow felons think you're something other than a child molester. At Gardner, I applied for the nurse's aide program. Waited until I was ten months away from the end of my sentence before I got in.

Annie's a big deal in the art world now; the only time I've seen her since that day they took her away was in a magazine photo. It was back when I was doing time at Gardner, maybe four or five years ago. I'd gone to the prison library to get myself something to read and, by chance, had picked up a dog-eared *Newsweek* from the "help yourself" pile of old magazines. And there she was, in a story about some fancy pants New York art show. It was the name that made me stop turning the pages: Annie Oh. Annie O'Day. . . . I kept staring at the picture of the middle-aged woman posed in front of these "assemblage" things she makes. Different person, I figured. But the more I stared at the woman's face, the more I realized it was her—that this was who she'd turned into. What had I expected? That she'd look the same as she had when she was six or seven? I read the article two or three times before I could wrap my head around what, by chance, I had discovered.

Or *was* it just by chance? Maybe it was a message from that Higher Power everyone was always talking about in the Twelve Steps meetings I went to whenever I needed to get the fuck away from the tier for a while, or when the ridicule about my missing eye got to be too much for me to take. I kept looking at the artwork in back of her which, to me, looked more like a bunch of stuff from the dump than high-priced art that had gotten fuckin' *Newsweek*'s attention. But what did I know about that whole world? I tore out the page, took it back to my cell, and taped it to the wall. From that day until the morning I got released, Annie's face was the first thing I saw in the morning and the last thing I saw before lights-out. I have that picture still—keep it folded up inside my wallet so I can look at it when I want to. Sometimes, still, I'll sit down in front of a piece of paper and, pen in hand, write her name over and over: *Annie, Annie, Annie*

The night I tried to kill myself? I'd gotten out of Gardner and was finishing the rest of my sentence at a halfway house for guys who, like me, are listed on the sexual predator Web site—the kind of home that the Welcome Wagon lady never bothers to go to. I'd been struggling for weeks to resist a new little girl I'd been scoping out. You ever watch those nature shows on cable? Where they show you, say, the way a cheetah will sit and wait, undetected by the herd of deer he's scoping out? And then he'll start focusing on just one of them? *Hyper*focusing until, in his mind, it's just him and the one he's decided he wants? And then, when the time's just right, he goes for it. Runs at it, pounces. *That's* what it's like for me. It's just nature, you know? *My* nature, anyway. Except the difference between me and that cheetah is that he's going to walk away licking his bloody chops and looking for a soft place to lie down and take a nap, and I may be looking at the walls of an eight-by-ten prison cell. . . . It would have been easy in this particular case, too; the kid's mom was a coworker on the janitorial staff down at the mall, and from what I could see, she was asleep at the wheel, parenting-wise. But if I went for it and got caught, they'd send me back to that hellhole or another one just like it for a lot longer than I'd been there the first time, and I knew I wouldn't be able to handle that. So it was like a war going on inside of me: my wanting to have this kid and my fear of having to go back if I got caught. And sharking that kid was driving me crazy. Exhausting me. All the shrinks I'd been to over the years, all the meds they'd put me on, and the truth was that I wasn't fixable. And because I wasn't, I was universally hated. The only person in the world who had really ever loved me was my dead mother. And Aunt Sunny. That's the worst thing in the world: not to have anyone who loves you. And it wasn't even my fault, really. It wasn't like I had chosen this life; it was more like *it* had chosen *me*. So I started thinking, fuck it. Why bother? I just didn't want to take it anymore. That was when I hit on what I thought would be a permanent solution. I walked down to CVS and bought a pack of single-edge razor blades. In the Twelve Step program I was in at the group home, they kept talking about making amends. My sponsor was a former priest and fellow deviant. He liked little boys. I sat down and wrote two letters, one to him and one to all the girls I'd ever "trespassed against." I put both letters on my bed where they'd find them. Then I picked up one of those blades and sliced the veins in both my arms. I cut them vertically instead of across because I'd heard somewhere that that was the way to do it if you were really serious about making the lights go out. But sitting there and watching myself bleed out started scaring me. If there *was* a hell, I was headed there sure as shit after everything I'd done, and maybe it would be worse than prison. And so before I passed out, I picked up the phone and called Father Joe. Sobbed into the receiver that I was scared to die. I guess when push came to shove, I preferred the hell of living inside my skin to the hell of what might come once I slipped out of it.

I spent nine days in the psych hospital. I was depressed, they said. After the new meds kicked in and they released me to the outpatient program, they assigned me to this shrink named Dr. Ronni Banks. There was a motorcycle helmet on her desk and a Honda Gold Wing out in the hospital parking lot. You can never tell about biker chicks.

Some of them are dykes and some of them aren't. I wasn't sure which way the wind blew with Dr. Ronni, but I knew halfway through our first session that I didn't like her. I was in the middle of telling her about my fucked-up childhood: how my father had bailed when I was a kid, how Irma Cake's daughter had "emotionally disregulated" me down in their basement, and that that was the reason I was the way I was. "Wow," she said. "You can really talk the talk, can't you? But let's focus on the future rather than the past, shall we? Let's work on how you can manage your compulsion out in the community. Agreed?"

"Agreed," I said. After I left her office, I asked around about her and found out that she played on the all-girls team.

During our next appointment, she said, "So help me understand then, Kent. First you tell me your actions are impulsive and involuntary. Then you describe a modus operandi that relies on patience and premeditation. So which is it? *Can* you control these urges or *can't* you?"

Now that I knew that neither flirting nor playing the sympathy card about my traumatic childhood was going to work on her, I decided to play the fear card instead. "Jeeze, I don't know, Doc," I said. "I guess I'm like that snake in the Garden of Eden."

She cocked her head. "How so?"

"Well, I'll see some innocent little girl waiting for the school bus, or sitting by herself in the food court at the mall, wearing short shorts and one of those little midriff blouses. And I may start slithering her way. But I know I've got to play her first. Convince her how sweet that apple's going to taste before I can claim my prize."

The skin between her eyebrows buckled with professional concern. "So you're saying that you think of your victim as some sort of . . . reward?"

"Sure. You can relate, can't you? When you rumble up to some lesbo bar on that hog of yours, walk in, and scope out some chick you want to—"

She held up her hand like a traffic cop, but I kept going.

"I mean, 'fess up, Ronni. Are you thinking of her as some fellow human being you can have tea and conversation with, or as that night's lick job?" I pulled my shirtsleeve up to my shoulder so she could see my cobra tattoo. Stuck out my tongue and flicked it up and down at her like a fucking snake.

Dr. Ronni managed to maintain her professional demeanor, but her blinking gave her away: once, twice, three times, four. "We're not discussing me, Kent. We're discussing you," she said. I nodded, smiled. Flicked my tongue at her some more. She glanced at her clock and told me we'd have to continue this discussion next time because our time was up. "No, it isn't," I said. "According to my calculations, we have another seven minutes." Which we did. She stood up anyway, walked to her door, and opened it. I walked out laughing.

When I went to my next appointment, I learned that I'd been reassigned to a male therapist whose name I don't even remember. He was a queer, too—you'd be surprised how many of these jokers in the "helping professions" are—so I was back to flirting. Running my fingers through my hair while we chatted, stroking the insides of my thighs while I played true confessions. At the end of our first meeting, while we were shaking hands, I stroked his knuckles with my fingertips. Just for a second or two. Just enough to stoke his fantasy. With any of these shrinks, you've got to locate the chink in their professional armor so that you can take back some of the power they've got over you. Because if you don't, some of them will go for the jugular. And the next thing you know, instead of telling them a sob story, you're sitting there sobbing for real. And believe me, when that happens, they'll take your vulnerability and run with it.

When I do those girls? It's not that I want to fuck with their heads. It's just that, when it comes over me, I want what I want when I want it. And it's not as if they don't get over it—not as if I've ruined their whole lives. Look at Annie. She sure as hell bounced back. That *Newsweek* article said she was married, living in Connecticut with her husband and kids, and that her work's in demand with art collectors around the country. Which, I assume, means that she must be rolling in the dough by now.

One of the conditions of my parole is that I stay away from the Internet, and you can probably guess why. But not long after I got out of Gardner, I walked from the halfway house to the library downtown, and there it was: an open computer station, far enough away from the front desk for anyone to see what I was looking at. I sat down, my heart racing, and typed in the names of some of the kiddie porn sites I liked. But this filtering software came popping up. It figured: they'd blocked them. Next, on a whim, I Googled "Annie Oh," and all kinds of shit about her art career came up—notices about openings, reviews of shows. I kept clicking on stuff, and eventually I found her street address and phone number. Took her picture out of my wallet, unfolded it, and wrote them down on that old *Newsweek* article.

The first time I called her, I lost my nerve and hung up as soon as it started ringing. The next several times I tried, a man answered—the husband, I figured. That was when I started thinking that maybe, instead of calling and talking to her on the phone, what I might do was hitch a ride over there to Three Rivers and show up at her door. As far as Parole was concerned, I was being a good little boy: staying put, going to work every day, making my curfew. So they took off my ankle bracelet, which more or less gave me the idea. So much had happened since we were kids. I figured she might be glad to reconnect with her long-lost cousin—may have forgiven and forgotten by now. Because, yeah, she was pretty young back then, but hey, I was just a kid myself. Didn't know my ass from my elbow. Plus, I had saved her life that night. And I never *did* tell anyone who was really responsible for Gracie's death; I've kept our secret all these years. I'd like to think those two things count for *some*thing.

But another part of me was afraid that, as soon as she answered the door, she'd slam it in my face. And I couldn't take that. Because out of all the little girls I've done, the only one I ever really loved was Annie. And yeah, the sex was part of it, but so was the closeness we'd shared. To this day, my body remembers what it felt like that night to pull her out of the water and up onto that roof, and then when the two of us were up in the tree, to zip her up inside my jacket to warm her body against mine. And what it felt like to wake up in the hospital the next morning and feel her sleeping against me for safety's sake.

So I decided to risk it. Because I had her address, and hey, she might *not* close the door on me. She might open it and tell me to come in. Make us some coffee and tell me she's glad I came—that she's missed me, too.

I've been there four different times. I go on my day off from the nursing home—Mondays, most of the time, but the last time I went was on a Tuesday. I've got the routine down at this point. I get off at the bus stop downtown, then hoof it out to their neighborhood. Trudge up that big hill where they live, get to the house, and ring the bell. Each time it's been the same: no cars in the driveway, no lights on inside. So I sit on the front steps and wait for a while, an hour or two. Then I give up, walk back down their hill and back to the bus stop. Catch the two o'clock bus back to the group home.

And then? Yesterday? I expected to hear what I'd heard so often when I've called her number—the four rings until the machine kicked in. Instead, someone picked up the phone. Not the husband this time. A female. She has daughters—teenagers, they must be by now—but this was a woman's voice, not a kid's. Annie's voice; it had to be. She was there.

Which is why, this morning, I'm on this three-quarters-empty bus heading over to Three Rivers again. I think my patience may have finally paid off. Because how often do I get a Saturday off? Almost never. And yesterday, it was *her* voice I heard. She's there. So all the ducks are lining up. And if my luck holds out, no one else will be around when I get there: the husband, the kids. It will just be Annie and me, the same as it used to be.

Looking out the window, I catch my own reflection smiling back at me. It's all good, Kent, it seems to be saying. It's all good.

Chapter Twenty-Four

Andrew Oh

Aw, what's the matter? Does the twerp have a big head this morning? Gee, I wonder why."

"Shut up," Marissa says. Clunks her head down on the table, just missing the bottle of Advil. Ariane shoots me a look. Hey, why *should* I shut up after what she knocked down yesterday?

Minnie puts a heaping platter of scrambled eggs on the table, and a plate of English muffins, toasted and buttered. It's like we're in some old black-and-white movie from the 1950s: the colored maid waiting on the white folks. "There ain't no jelly in the 'figerator," she says. "None that I could see."

Ariane says there might be some in the cabinet and gets up to look. Comes back to the table with a jar of strawberry jam and hands it to me. "You want to do the honors, He-Man?" I unscrew the lid for her. "My hero," she says. Marissa snorts into the tabletop.

"So, Minnie, how did you guys make out last night?" I ask her.

"Made out good," she says. "Them motel mattresses were so comfortable that when Hector come by to take Africa for breffest, I had to wake him up."

"Where'd they go?"

"To that IHOP near where we stayin' at. Last time I took that boy to one of them IHOPs, he ate so many chocolate chip pancakes, I thought they were gonna start comin' out of his ears."

"He's a cutie," Ariane says.

"He a handful is what he is," Minnie tells her. "I just hope Hector don't let him eat so many pancakes that he make hisself sick."

Minnie's standing at the counter, grabbing some breakfast, too. I hook my foot around the rung of the empty chair and pull it away from the table. "Come sit down with us," I tell her. "Take a load off."

"Nah, thass okay. I'm good right here, thanks."

"So what time do we have to head over there for the big event?" I ask. Ariane glances at the clock on the wall. In about an hour and a half, she says.

"And what's the plan? Are we all driving over together?" Ariane shrugs, but Minnie knows. She says Hector's picking her up after she's done here—that he's bringing her and Africa to the ceremony and I'm driving my mother and sisters. I wonder what Minnie thinks about this lesbian wedding she's going to witness. I read somewhere that, statistically, blacks tend to be less tolerant of gays than whites are. It's true of the guys in my company; that much I know. "Don't ask, don't tell, and don't shower anywhere near me," LeRoy says whenever the subject comes up, and it never fails to get a laugh. And Donyel told me one of his homeys is doing time for beating a tranny within an inch of his life after he realized the woman he was in bed with was a guy. But who knows? Maybe black women are more tolerant. Either way, Minnie's got to be cool about it, I guess, given who signs her paycheck.

Ariane reaches for the eggs and scrapes most of what's left onto her plate. Takes another muffin, loads on the jam. "This is the most I've eaten in three months," she says. "Hooray for me. My appetite's back."

"Back with a vengeance," I kid her.

Ari laughs, swats me on the arm. "Still a wiseguy," she says.

"Still an asshole," Rissa mumbles.

"You'll feel better if you eat something," Ari tells her. "Coffee and Advil on an empty stomach? Not good." Yeah, it's no wonder she's gotten so skinny. Too skinny, in my humble opinion. Bony arms and legs, tiny little waist.

Marissa raises her head. "Did someone mention coffee?" she says, holding up her mug. Minnie walks over to the table, carafe in hand, and refills it. I slide mine over to her, and she warms me up, too. For

the next several minutes, no one says anything. I guess the three of us
are all mulling over what's in store a little later on. Then, out of the
blue, Ari asks me how my fiancée is doing.

"Casey-Lee?"

"No, your *other* fiancée," Marissa says. I ignore her, but Ari's waiting for an answer.

"She's good. Busy." I'm going for nonchalance, but I'm not sure I'm
pulling it off. Why haven't I told my sisters that the engagement's off?
I was going to when we were driving down from the Cape yesterday,
but then I didn't. I guess I wasn't up for the third degree that would
follow. I'll tell them, though. Tonight maybe, after all the hoopla's over
with. "Lots to do. You know? At the beginning of the school year?"

"Is that why she couldn't come?"

"Hmm? Yeah. Yup."

"So what does she think about Mom marrying Viveca?" Marissa
asks. "Aren't you Bible thumpers all about how marriage has to be between a man and a woman?"

"Yeah, we kind of think that's what Our Lord and Savior had in
mind." She rolls her eyes. "But hey, what do us 'Bible thumpers' know?
We're not nearly as cool and sophisticated as you New Yorkers who
pray to Mammon instead of God."

"Who's Mammon?" she asks.

"Not who. What. Look it up. It's in the Bible."

Ari tries to short-circuit this little exchange we're having. "And
what grade does she teach?"

"Same grade as when you asked me yesterday. Kindergarten."

"Oh, that's right. Well, I'm really looking forward to meeting her."

"Uh-huh." I pick up the jam and ask Minnie if she wants any. She
comes over and takes it from me. Grabs a tablespoon and piles some
onto her muffin. It's like that article I read in class a while back about
the connection between poverty and obesity, the prevalence of diabetes in blacks.

"So what's your Lord and Savior's plan for gays and lesbians?" Marissa says. "Castration? Chastity belts?" I'm trying to think of some

equally smart-ass answer to give her when Mom enters the kitchen, all-business.

"Morning, everyone," she says. She hands Minnie the two dresses on hangers she's holding. "These traveled pretty well. Just a light pressing ought to do it. I have yours here, too, Marissa."

"Jesus, Mom, I *said* I'd bring it down," the twerp snaps.

"Well, now you don't have to. What about your dress, Ariane? Does it need to be ironed?" Ari tells her she's already ironed hers. "Oh, okay. Great. How did you kids sleep last night? Better than me, I hope. When I looked in the bathroom mirror just now, I thought a raccoon was staring back at me."

"I've got some really good shit from Bloomie's that'll cover up those circles no problem," Marissa tells her. "It's super-expensive, but it's worth it."

"Yeah, must be," I say, waving my finger at her neck. Ari kicks me under the table. She knows *some*thing about how the twerp got those bruises, and I plan to pursue it when I get a minute alone with her. Those black-and-blue marks, her weight, her drinking. Bottom line is: I'm worried about Marissa.

Minnie's left her half-eaten breakfast to set up the ironing board, plug in the iron. Over her shoulder she says, "Them eggs must be cold by now. You want me to cook you some new ones, Miz Anna?" Anna is Mom's New York name, I've noticed. Viveca calls her that, too.

Mom says no, then reaches for the last English muffin. Sits down next to Marissa and cups her hand around her shoulder. Asks her how she's feeling.

"Like shit," I say. The twerp gives me the finger.

"All right, you two," Mom says. "Let's not start. Okay?"

"Too late for that," Ariane says. I know I shouldn't, but I pick up the Advil bottle and shake it like a castanet.

"Jesus Christ, would you *stop* it?" Marissa says. "What are you? Twelve years old?"

Ever the peacemaker, Ariane changes the subject to who's taking showers when. "I'll go first," I say. Get up from the table. Mom asks me if I need anything ironed. "Nope, I'm good."

"Are you wearing your uniform, honey?"

"Nah. I tried on that gray suit in my closet. Still fits." When the doorbell rings, I tell them I'll get it.

It's some kid in a Yankees jacket. He's carrying a box. "Florist," he says.

"Just a second," I tell him. All's I've got in my wallet is a bunch of twenties. Well, fuck it. "Here you go," I tell him, handing him one.

He hands me the box and glances down at the twenty. "Hey, thanks, yo," he says.

"Yeah, no problem. I don't usually tip Yankee fans, but what the hell." He grins. Turns and heads back down the front walk.

I bring the flowers into the kitchen. "Oh, good," Mom says. "I was hoping that's who it was." She opens the box, and the girls ooh and ahh at their bouquets.

"There's a boutonnière in here for you, too, Andrew," Mom says.

"Oh, goody. Okay, I'm going up to hit the rain room."

An hour later, Minnie's gone and I'm waiting in the kitchen for the others. The twerp's the first one down. "You look nice," I tell her. "That's a pretty dress. You feeling any better?"

She nods. Tells me Viveca bought the dress for her. "You wouldn't believe how much it cost," she says.

"Yeah, well, your new stepmother's got pretty deep pockets."

"*Our* stepmother," she says. "Seriously, Andrew, you should give her a chance. She and Mom are very happy together."

"Yeah, at Dad's expense."

"Daddy's doing fine," she says. "I just wish he'd answer his fucking phone. I can't believe I forgot mine up there."

"What's the matter? You going through withdrawal?"

Something like that, she says. She's been waiting for a callback from some casting agent. "But he's probably not going to call on the weekend. Right?" I shrug. How should I know? She gets up and goes to the fridge. Takes out the flowers. "You want me to pin your boutonnière on for you?"

"Yeah. Just don't stab me."

"Don't tempt me," she says.

Her hands are shaky, and there's alcohol on her breath. Man, she really *is* becoming a boozer. Either that, or maybe she's not so gung-ho about Mom's wedding as she lets on. Maybe this is a hard weekend for her, too. She pins the flower on, pulls on my lapels, and then stands back to inspect her handiwork.

"Thanks," I say. "So seriously, how *did* you get those bruises?" She rolls her eyes, sticks to her story: she fell in her kitchen, hit the table on her way down. "Were you drunk when it happened?"

"I may have been a little tipsy," she says.

"Then maybe you should cool it on the booze, huh?" She frowns. Tells me she's got everything under control. "Okay, good," I tell her. "And if some other time you get banged up *by* someone—some asshole guy, let's say—"

Tears come to her eyes and she looks away. "Yeah?"

"Then you just pick up that cell phone of yours and let me know so that your big brother can come back and have the pleasure of beating the shit out of him. All right?"

She looks back at me. Smiles. "Okay, I'll keep that in mind. Thanks."

"No problem."

In the silence that follows, I can hear Mom and Ari coming down the stairs. "Well, don't you look handsome," Mom tells me as she enters the room. "And Marissa, you look like you should be on a red carpet somewhere." Mom looks nice, too. Younger than she is. Ariane? Well . . .

"That dress is perfect on you, Mom," Marissa says. There's the usual girl talk: how Mom found her dress at some shop, who the designer is. When Rissa compliments her on the sapphire earrings she's wearing, Mom says they're Viveca's.

"So that takes care of borrowed and blue," Ari says. "What about old and new?" Mom says she just took her stockings out of the package, and that she herself is old—that she feels a little silly being a bride at her age. Marissa says something about how fifty's the new thirty.

"And your dress is vintage," Ari says. "So you're all set: old, new, borrowed and blue."

"Hey, I hate to break up this little hen party, but are you guys noticing the time?" I ask. That gets everyone up and moving toward the front door.

I'm the last one out of the house. Mom and Marissa climb into the back and Ari gets in the front with me. When I start the car, Mom asks me if I remembered to lock up. "Daddy said there was a break-in in the neighborhood a while ago," she says.

"Whose house?" Ari asks. Mom says Dad mentioned the name, but she didn't recognize it. "Must be one of the new families."

I know I locked the front door, but now I'm not sure about the one off the kitchen. "I'll double-check. Be right back," I tell them. I get out of the car, walk around the house to the back and try the door. Yup. Locked up tight. When I get back in the car, I'm hit with the aroma of all those flowers.

On the way over to Bella Linda, Ariane turns around and asks Mom how she's doing. "I'm a little nervous, but fine otherwise."

"Happy?" Ari asks.

"I am, yes. We're very different from one another, but it works somehow. We complement each other." Yeah, and I imagine Viveca thinks so, too. Mom makes all the art and she pockets the commission. But I'm probably just being cynical. . . . Or jealous, maybe. Wasn't that why I broke it off with Casey? Because we didn't "complement" each other? But I wonder if that arrangement stays the same, now that they're getting married. Does Viveca still get her percentage when she sells Mom's work? "I'm just so grateful that you kids took time out of your busy lives to share our day with us," Mom says. "That makes it even more special."

Marissa asks her if she's excited about going to Greece.

"Yes, now I am. At first I wasn't sure about going there for a full month. Being away from my work for that long. But it will still be there when I get back. Right?"

My sisters say it simultaneously. "Right."

Then, out of the blue, Mom says, "Oh, shit!"

I tap the brake. "What?"

"No, honey, it's all right. Keep going. It's just that I promised Viveca I was going to look around for something that's back at the house someplace—a painting that Lorenzo might be interested in buying. But I can look for it later." One of hers? Marissa asks. "No, it's by an artist who used to live in that old cottage out in back."

"Josephus Jones," Ari says. "It's probably not even there, Mama. Daddy took all of those paintings with him up to Viveca's beach house."

"All of what paintings?" Mom asks. "There's only the one."

"No, there's a bunch of them. A couple dozen, maybe."

"What are you guys *talking* about?" Marissa asks. "Who's Josephus Jones?"

"The man who died back there," Ari says. "Remember how we were never allowed to play out in back because someone had drowned in that old well? Daddy told me there was some question about if it was an accident or—"

"Oh, please. Don't even talk about that damned well," Mom says. "It still gives me the creeps. But I don't know what paintings you could be talking about, Ariane. There weren't any others except for the one that we found up in the attic after we moved in. The family that had sold us the house had left it behind. But now he's become quite collectible. Probably because so little of his work survived."

"Well, the ones Daddy has up there did," Ari insists. "And I know they're his, Mama, because his signature's on them."

Is she talking about those paintings that Jay and I used to look at when we went out to that old shack to smoke weed? I can't remember much about them except that there were naked women in some of them. Not exactly *Playboy* centerfolds, but we were what? Fourteen? Fifteen? Boobs were boobs.

Mom says if there were other Josephus Jones paintings at our house, she'd have known about them. And even if there were, why would Dad have taken them up to the Cape with him? "Because the house is on the market," Ariane says. "He said he didn't want strangers walking around the property because they're valuable. And because he didn't want—" She stops midsentence.

"He didn't want what?" Mom says.

"No, nothing. You should just ask Daddy about it."

"Yes, I guess I should. But if there was a stash of valuable artwork hidden away at our place, why wouldn't I have known about it?"

"Because you never went down in the back," I tell her. "Except for the time you busted Jay and me when you caught us up on the roof."

"Don't remind me," she says. "You two could have gotten seriously hurt out there if that thing had collapsed. And that well? The fact that someone might have murdered him? Let's change the subject. Shall we?"

"Yeah, let's," Marissa says. "So Mom, any of Viveca's celebrity clients going to be here today?" Mom says she doesn't remember, and that she might not recognize the names anyway. For the next mile or so, nobody says a thing.

Bella Linda is out on the edge of town, a little after this golf course we're passing. It's still pretty wooded out here. I'm surprised no one's developed the hell out of it yet. Wetlands, maybe. The ground looks a little swampy. . . . Up ahead on the left, I see the sign. Slow down, put my signal on. "Oh, no! The rings!" Mom blurts out. "Andrew, we have to go back to the house. I forgot our rings." Ariane says she doesn't think there's time.

But the clock on the dashboard says 11:29. "Okay, don't sweat it," I tell them. "We've got about half an hour until showtime, right? So let me drop you guys off, and I'll go get them. Be back in twenty minutes, max."

"Oh, honey. Thanks," Mom says. "They're in a little velvet bag on the bureau in Daddy's and my room. It's bluish gray. When I was getting dressed, I put it there so I wouldn't forget. God, how could I be so—Oh, look! There's Mr. Agnello." Two older guys are going up the front steps. The younger one's got the old geezer by the arm.

"Who's Mr. Agnello?" Marissa asks.

"He gave me my start as an artist. Awarded me a 'best in show' when I was thinking about giving up."

"Which one?" Marissa asks. "The old dude or the other one."

"The one with the cane." She puts her window down and calls out to him. "Mr. Agnello!"

When I let them out of the car, Mom runs up to him and gives him a big hug. She'd better cool it. He's so old, he looks breakable. Well, I'd better get going now that I've got a mission to accomplish. I drive down the circular driveway, turn back onto the road, and head back to the house. . . .

Twenty minutes, I told them, but that's optimistic with all this Saturday morning traffic—everyone out running their errands. Well, weddings never start on time anyway. Still, when the old lady in front of me slows down and signals that she's taking a right turn about half a year before she's going to take it, I check the mirror then gun it, passing her on the left. We're not going to get this wedding over with until we get it started, and at this point, that pretty much depends on me.

But naturally, I hit every friggin' red light between here and home. Waiting out the one on South Main Street, I look over at the barbershop where Dad and I used to get our haircuts. I wonder how he's doing up there on the Cape. Maybe he's hanging with Tracy for the day. I hope so. I'd hate to think of him up there alone, stewing about what's going on down here.

It takes me almost fifteen minutes just to get to our road. Halfway up the hill, I pass some little kids at a lemonade stand. They try to flag me down, but I wave and keep going. Sorry, kids. No time. At the crest of the hill, I brake. Turn into our driveway and . . . What the fuck?

Who's *this*? Can't be a burglar. Why would someone who's breaking in be sitting out there on the front steps? Unless he's the lookout. I put the car in park, cut the engine, and get out. He stands up when he sees me coming toward him. What's that he's wearing? An eye patch?

"Help you with something?"

"Is Annie home?" He's gray-haired, skinny.

"Uh, no. No she's not. Who are you?"

He says he's her cousin. "She coming back soon?"

"Not for a while. Was she expecting you?" I already know the answer to that one. If she'd invited him, why would he be here when the wedding's over there? And where's his car? He says no—he wanted to surprise her. They're cousins? That's when it hits me.

"You're not Kent, are you?"

He nods, grins.

"Holy shit. My mom and I were just talking about you last night. You're the one who saved her, right? From that flood?"

"That's right," he says. "Got her out of the car and up into a tree. So you're her son? Yeah, now that I look at you, I can see you got some O'Day in you." He holds out his hand. "Glad to meet you, uh . . ."

"Andrew." We shake. "Glad to meet you, too. And god, Mom's going to be thrilled to see you. She was just saying last night how you guys lost touch with each other. But we've got a complication."

"Yeah? What's that?"

I tell him what's about to go on over there at Bella Linda. "I just came back to get something Mom forgot. Look, why don't you go over there with me? Surprise Mom?" He hesitates, says he's not exactly dressed for a wedding. And he isn't—not for this shindig: frayed gray sweatshirt, stained khaki pants. The guy looks a little down on his luck. "Tell you what," I say. "Come on in. You might be able to wear something of my dad's. It won't be a perfect fit, but I think we can fix you up. We'd better hustle, though. The wedding's supposed to start in another fifteen minutes."

"And it's *her* wedding, you said? I thought she was already married."

"She and my dad are divorced," I tell him. "This is her second marriage. I'll tell you about it on the way over. Come on in."

Dad's clothes don't work out after all; his suit pants are swimming around the guy's ankles, and the waist is way too big. But I get another idea. I'm shorter than Dad, and narrower at the waist. I start taking off the suit I'm wearing, my shirt and tie. We're already going to be a little late getting back there; what's another couple of minutes? By the time I'm dressed in my uniform, he's ready, too. Not a great fit, but it will do. "Think I can skip the tie?" he asks. "I'm not a big one on neckties."

"No problem," I tell him. "Come on. We'd better get over there." We're halfway down the stairs when I remember the goddamned rings. "Go on out," I tell him. "I'll be right there." But when I come down again, I find him looking around in the living room. He didn't pocket anything, did he?

For the first few minutes of the drive over there, the conversation's forced. I think of shit to ask him; he answers in single syllables. After I run out of questions, I turn on the radio to kill the silence. They're playing some dipshit Madonna song. I can see out of the corner of my eye that he's watching me. "So, uh . . . I didn't see any car at the house. How did you get here?"

"Took the bus," he says. "I been meaning to get over and see Annie for a while now, since I moved back to the area. Reconnect with her, you know? But jeeze, I never thought I'd be going to a wedding." A gay wedding at that, I think. I guess I'd better prepare him. But while I'm trying to figure out how to put it, he says, "So you're in the army, looks like."

"Yeah. I'm stationed down in Texas. Fort Hood. I work in the V.A. hospital there. How about you? Ever in the service?"

"Me? Nah." End of subject.

"And how is it you and my mom are related exactly? I know you're cousins, but . . ."

"My mother and Annie's father were sister and brother. So he was my uncle. Uncle Chick."

"And you lived with them for a while, right? Mom's family?"

"Yeah. I was kind of a hellion when I was a kid. My father had taken a powder, and Ma didn't know what to do with me, so she farmed me out. She thought Uncle Chick could straighten me out. He's dead now, isn't he?"

"My grandfather? Yeah, he died before we were born. My two sisters and me, I mean. You'll meet them today. They're already over there."

He nods. "Sad what happened to Uncle Chick. He never got over it after he lost Sunny and the baby. Started hitting the sauce. She was good people, Aunt Sunny. And then he lost Annie, too, on top of that.

I was there the day the state came and got her. He took it hard. We both did. The two of us sat around the kitchen table and got shit-faced drunk. And then, pretty soon after that, I moved back to my mother's. She and I visited him a couple of times, but he was always soused. So after a while, she cut him off. She's dead now, too. But yeah, that was the last time I saw Annie. When they drove her away in that state car."

"Mom doesn't talk much about her childhood, but it must have been rough. All those losses. . . . But hey, you'll see another of your cousins today. My Uncle Donald and his wife are coming to the wedding." The dashboard clock says 12:02. "Must already be there, in fact. We're running a little late."

"To tell you the truth, Donny and I never got along too much when I was living there. We were different types, and he wasn't crazy about my staying with them. Cramped his style, I guess. But Annie and I, we were close. She used to hang all over me. Follow me from room to room. I used to take care of her. Make her supper, read her her stories. I used to spend more time with her than her brother or her father did."

"It was good she had you there," I say.

"Yup. Like I said, she and I were close."

"Well, she's going to be surprised to see you," I tell him. "She was just saying last night that she didn't even know if you were alive still or dead."

"That so? Huh."

When we're within half a mile of the inn, I finally broach the subject. "So tell me. What's your take on gay marriage?" I ask him.

He shrugs. "I don't know. Why?"

"Because Mom's marrying a woman."

"No kidding. *Annie* is?"

"Uh-huh. You have a problem with that?"

Another shrug. "No, not really. She's a big deal artist now, isn't she?"

"Yeah, she's pretty successful. She and her partner—the woman she's marrying—live in New York."

"Oh. Goes with the territory, I guess."

"What do you mean?"

"Well, I've known a couple of artists over the years. Men, not women. And they were both fairies." He turns toward me and smiles. Well, it's more of a leer than a smile, I guess. I'm not sure I like this guy. He's a little weird, and that eye patch is creeping me out a little. But hey, he saved her life that night. So I guess my sisters and I owe our lives to him, too. Not just Mom.

"Okay, we're here," I say, taking the turn into Bella Linda. The parking lot's full now—New York plates, mostly. I find a space and park. We get out, and I hurry toward the front entrance with him behind me. "Where's the fire?" he says. I don't know. Maybe this isn't such a good idea after all. Springing this big a surprise on Mom. Well, too late now if it isn't. But it will be fine. Maybe Uncle Donald won't be thrilled to see him, but I bet Mom will be.

Chapter Twenty-Five

Annie Oh

W hat time is it now?" I ask. Twelve fifteen, Ariane says. I turn to Viveca. "I still can't believe I forgot our rings of all things. It's just that my mind was going in a hundred different directions and—"

"Darling, it's fine. You don't need to keep apologizing."

"That's right," the minister assures me. She wants us to call her Sally, not Reverend Croxford. "I've officiated at a lot of weddings over the years, and I can't remember one of them that began on time." I've talked to her over the phone a few times, read the things she sent us, but this is the first I've seen her in person. She's a large, affable woman—very nice. "It's a bride's prerogative to keep the crowd waiting. This is very fashionable."

"I just hope we're not holding you up," I say.

"Oh, no. I've got to go to my grandson's birthday party at six tonight, so as long as your son gets back before then, we're fine."

"Oh, I'm sure he's not going to take—" I stop when I realize she's kidding. Viveca reaches over and takes my hand, gives it a squeeze.

"Who needs a refill?" Marissa asks, grabbing the champagne bottle she's gone downstairs and gotten so that we can all "chill." Viveca has posted her at the front window of the suite; she's keeping an eye out for Andrew.

"Just a splash," Sally says. She's the only taker.

Marissa obliges, then holds the bottle up to her face. "Might as well finish this off," she says. She pours so much into her own glass that it spills over the top. Takes a slurp and goes back to her post. "Okay, here he is," she says. "God, he changed? No wonder it took him so long. Who's that with him?" Ariane volunteers to go down and get the rings.

"Ask him if he'd like to come up and join us," Viveca says. "Maybe he'd like to escort your mother and me into the ceremony." I remind her that he's already said he'd rather not be in the wedding party. "I know, sweetheart, but maybe he's changed his mind." I shake my head. Suggest that we leave things the way they are. "All right then, sure. It was just a thought."

When Ariane comes back, she gives the rings to Marissa. That's the plan. Per the Unitarian Universalist wedding ceremony, Ari will light the chalice and her sister will present the rings. "Any last-minute questions?" Sally asks. When we shake our heads, she smiles and stands. Straightens the white robe she's wearing and picks up her book. "Okay then, I guess we're good to go. I'll go down and give the musicians their cue. And by the way, may I say that you are two of the loveliest brides I've ever seen. See you down there. Good luck." And with that, she's out the door.

"She's wonderful," Viveca says. "I know I was skeptical about a religious ceremony at first, Anna, but I'm glad you prevailed. If we could take her back to the city with us, I just might start going to services myself." When she suggests that we give ourselves a final check, I follow her to the floor-length mirror and stand behind her.

She looks stunning in her ivory floor-length sheath. I love that slash of coral at the neckline and her matching coral lipstick. It accentuates her Mediterranean complexion. I like this dress of hers even better than the Gaia gown I co-opted for my *Titan Brides* piece. I still can't believe how gracious she was when she got back from her trip and saw that I'd made art out of that expensive designer dress. Why has she picked me to love? I don't deserve her, but I love her so much. "Help me," I said last night, and she came.

"Your turn, darling," she says, stepping aside. And then it's me in the mirror. Viveca was right: my dress is too informal. Too youthful for someone my age. Someone with this middle-aged face. When I put it on this morning, I was so pleased with myself, but now I see how wrong it is. Well, too late now. This is who she's getting.

Ariane hands us our bouquets and Marissa chugs the rest of her champagne. We walk out of the suite. Waiting at the top of the stairs, we hear the crowd and, over it, the signal—they're playing the Brahms. The girls start down. When they near the bottom, Viveca transfers her bouquet from her right hand to her left and takes my hand. "Let's go," she says, and we start down the stairs together.

The room is full. Everyone stands and turns as we enter. Where's Andrew? I can't find him. Oh, there he is, in the second row from the back. And Marissa's right; he *has* changed. He's wearing his uniform. As we make our way down the center aisle, Viveca smiles, acknowledging this guest and that. Not me. I'm looking straight ahead at the minister up in front—focusing on her bright, encouraging smile. When we reach her, she whispers that we should turn around and face our loved ones.

"Love, with all its glories and mysteries, is a gift for which we are grateful," she begins. "And so we light our chalice in honor of the love that burns between Anna and Viveca." Ariane moves toward it, matches in hand. It's different from the chalice the priests use at Mass. More like a bowl than a Holy Grail. Ari lights the match on the third strike. Lights the candle.

"Today we gather in community to witness Anna and Viveca pledge a covenant of sacred matrimony," Sally continues. It would have been nice if Andrew had wanted to stand up here with us, but I understand. I'm just glad he's here. "Marriage embodies all the precious values arising from human companionship. Love is generous and . . ."

I try to stay focused on the words, but I'm distracted. My brother and Mimsy are in the second row, next to Marcus and Lorenzo in their beautifully tailored suits. It looks like Mimsy's put on some weight. And wasn't Donald's hair grayer the last time I saw him? Is he dyeing it now?

"Love nourishes but does not possess. It . . ."

I scan the crowd for Orion. I thought maybe he'd change his mind, but of course he hasn't. Why would he? Still, if he *had* come, then everyone I love would be here in this same room with me. With us. . . . There's Mr. Agnello and his son, four rows back. What's the son's name? When I was talking before to them, Mr. Agnello said he still paints every day. Remarkable. . . . And there, on the opposite side, are Hector, Minnie, and Africa. Africa sticks a finger up his nose, and when Minnie sees it, she reaches over and swats the back of his head. I smile, grateful that they're here. Grateful, too, for Viveca's attention to detail. Everything is so beautiful: the music, the flowers, the way the room is decorated. She insisted on those calla lilies, and here they are. It's all perfect.

"In love, we affirm one another, but we do not dominate."

I recognize several of Viveca's guests—people I've met at dinner parties and openings at her gallery. And there's Carolyn, Viveca's assistant. That must be her husband sitting beside her. I'm glad they've weathered his affair. The man sitting next to Andrew whispers something and Andrew nods in reply. He doesn't look familiar. If I had met him, I would have remembered that eye patch. Probably one of Viveca's eccentric millionaire clients. . . .

I catch the tail end of the minister's reading of that Buddhist prayer I liked. Have I missed that excerpt from *The Prophet* she was planning to read—the one that Viveca and I were supposed to discuss but never did?

"Anna and Viveca, please turn to each other and join hands as you declare your intent." Ariane takes our bouquets from us and we do as the minister says. "And now, Anna, will you please repeat after me?"

My voice sounds softer and more tentative than I'd intended. "I, Anna, join with you, Viveca, in the covenant of marriage." I wish Viveca had gone first. But sentence by sentence, I repeat the rest, careful not to make any mistakes. In contrast to my shaky recitation, Viveca declares her vows in a voice that's strong and sure.

"Do we have the rings?" Sally asks, turning to Marissa.

Marissa? Wake up.

"Oh, sorry," she says. She puts down her bouquet, then upends the velvet bag. Our wedding rings fall onto the palm of her hand. When she gives them to Viveca and me, we slip them onto each other's finger. Sally smiles and speaks about circles of love.

"And so, what love has brought together, let no one break asunder.

For as much as you, Anna and Viveca, have consented to live together in marriage, and have declared the same by this giving and receiving of rings, it is with great pleasure, and by the authority vested in me as a Minister in the State of Connecticut, that I pronounce you wife and wife. I now invite you to seal your marriage with a kiss." Viveca leans in, wet-eyed. Her lips on mine feel tender and loving. Our kiss lasts a few more seconds than might be necessary, but that's okay. I love her, want to keep kissing her because this, more than the rings or the minister's words, is what makes me feel married. The room breaks out in applause. I turn and face them, all these happy faces. Everyone is smiling at us except my son.

The innkeeper steps forward and invites everyone to proceed to the Lavender Room for drinks and canapés while we pose for pictures. "And our wedding couple will join you all in just a few moments."

At the back of the room, I watch Andrew file out with the others. "Want me to go get him?" Marissa asks. I tell her no. He probably needs a drink more than he needs to have his picture taken. The photographer Viveca has imported from New York arranges us the way he wants us and begins to snap away. After he's finished, Viveca gives him further instructions about how she'd like him to photograph the reception.

When we rejoin the gathering for cocktails, there's another round of applause. Viveca and I smile, receive hugs and kisses, best wishes. A waitress appears with champagne in the special flutes Viveca's bought at Tiffany's. The telltale grogginess I've felt from that Xanax last night has finally worn off, so I take a sip. It's dry and delicious. Viveca certainly knows her wine.

Minnie approaches shyly, with Africa clinging to her leg. Hector's behind them. "I ain't ever been to a wedding this fancy before," Minnie tells us. "Them flowers are so pretty." It makes me wish I'd thought to order her a corsage. "Here," I say, handing her my bouquet. "These are for you." When she tries to refuse, I tell her I insist. She takes it in one hand and covers her toothless grin with the other. Then she turns to Africa. "Well? What do you say to Miz Anna and Miz Viveca?"

"'Gratulations," he says. I bend down and, taking him in my arms, plant a kiss on his forehead. "Thank you, sweetheart," I say. He wipes off the kiss as soon as I release him. Hector comes forward and says something to Viveca and me in Spanish—a blessing, I think it is. When he leans in to give Viveca a kiss, she turns her head so far to the side that his lips land on her ear. I reach out and take his rough hands in mine. He kisses me on the cheek.

And now here come Donald and Mimsy. We hug. They hug the girls. I introduce them to Viveca, Hector, and Minnie. "Pietro!" Viveca calls, signaling the photographer. He hurries over and takes a group shot.

"Hey, Africa, did you by any chance have chocolate chip pancakes this morning for breakfast?" Marissa asks.

The boy's eyes widen. "How you know that?" he asks.

She tells him she has magical powers. That she knows all and sees all.

"Pfft," Africa says. "You ain't got no magic powers. You just a lady."

"Oh, yeah? Then how come I know that you like soda? And that you would love one right now? Am I right?" He nods, a little less convinced that Marissa is just some mere mortal. "Better come with me then," she says. When Africa looks up at his mother, she nods permission. Marissa takes his hand and leads him toward the bar.

"If that niece of mine is all-knowing, how come she didn't realize I could use a scotch?" Donald quips. "Ladies?" Mimsy says she'd like a Manhattan and Ariane requests a ginger ale. Ari's starting to show, but that loose dress she's wearing conceals her bump. Well, I guess it's up to her to tell her aunt and uncle her news. "Minnie? Something to drink?" Don asks. She shakes her head, but when he asks her if she's sure, she asks how much they cost.

"They're free," I whisper. "It's open bar."

"Oh, okay then. Gin and ginger."

My brother winces a little, but I don't think Minnie's caught it. "Sure thing," he says. "Minnie, maybe you'd better give me a hand, huh? If I try to carry four glasses, they're going to need a mop."

Minnie nods. Looks hesitantly at the bouquet I've given her. When Ari suggests she put it down on the side table, she does. "Don't let nobody take it," she says, and Ari promises she'll watch it like a hawk. As she and Donald head off toward the bar, Ariane asks Mimsy if Donald has started dyeing his hair.

"Oh yes," she says, rolling her eyes. "I talked him out of buying the sports car but not the Grecian Formula."

The three of us share a mischievous giggle. I look to see if Viveca's amused, too, but she's busy surveying the crowd. "Would you ladies excuse me?" she says. "I think I'd better work the room a little. There are a few people I really should acknowledge. Do you mind, darling?" I tell her no. Ask her if she needs me to go with her. "No, no. You stay here and enjoy your family. We can do a little table-hopping later during the luncheon." And with that, she starts across the room.

I watch as she stops to embrace Andrew who's coming toward us. He returns her hug, stiff as a board. Ariane's watching, too. "How do you think he's doing?" I ask. Fine, she says, but she doesn't get why he changed when he went back to the house. I shrug. Suggest that maybe it makes him feel a little more secure. Viveca moves on and that man with the eye patch approaches Andrew, holding two beers. He hands him one and they clink their bottles. Either Andrew's made a new friend or else he can't shake this guy.

"Hey there, soldier boy," I hear my brother say as he approaches Andrew, his booming voice carrying over the noise of the crowd. Andrew introduces his uncle to his new friend, and my brother says, "Well, I'll be a son of a bitch! Good god, how long has it been?" He shakes the man's hand and pats him on the shoulder. They know each other? From business, must be. Donald does the tax returns for a lot of well-heeled businessmen. But still, it's a coincidence. When I ask Mimsy if she knows him, she says no but that she only helps out at the office part-time.

Now here comes Andrew. He greets his aunt, gives her a kiss. Then he turns to me. "Hey, Mom," he says, holding out his arms. I'm so grateful for his embrace that I don't want to let him go. But when I do, he says something about a surprise. That man who's been shadowing him steps forward.

"Hello, Annie," he says. Bad teeth, salt and pepper stubble. I smile.

Offer him a generic thank-you-for-coming. You'd think if he can afford to buy art from Viveca, he could get himself a decent haircut. "Long time no see, huh?"

What? . . . Who?

"What's the matter? Don't you recognize your long-lost cousin?"

Is it . . . ? No! Not here. Not today. Andrew's saying something, but I can't . . . Don't react, Annie! Don't lose it in front of all these people.

"Kiss for the bride?" When he puts his hand on my shoulder and leans in, puckering, my head jerks back and hits the wall behind me. But it's no use. His lips land on mine, dirtying my kiss from Viveca. I look from Andrew's bewildered face to Ariane's. "Mama?"

"It's *Kent*," Andrew says. "When I went back to the house for . . ." His lips are still moving, but what he's saying is blocked out by a roaring in my ears. The floodwater rushing beneath us. . . . Then I'm back here at Bella Linda but everything has turned gray: Ariane's bouquet, the chattering wedding guests. My mind has gone blank.

He's talking to Mimsy. "And then I was in sales for a while. Insurance. Got so many Salesman of the Month certificates that I started running out of wall space, heh heh."

I'm light-headed. Frantic. I can't stay here, but I can't leave. I have to protect my kids from him. I step forward, putting myself between him and Ariane. "Are you all right, Mama?" she asks me. "You look so pale."

"What? Yes, I'm . . . It's just so hot in here. Why is it so hot?"

"Gee, I was just thinking they should turn the air-conditioning down a little. I'm freezing."

"Oh. You are?" Where's Viveca? Why is everything so gray?

"Yeah, Donny and I shared a room when I went to live with them. But we were like night and day, us two. . . . The honor roll type. Mr. Popular. But I hated school. I was just barely scraping by."

"Do you want to get some air?"

"Some air? Yes, okay. That's a good idea."

"Want me to go with you?"

No, I can't risk that. I'm just barely holding it in. I can't break down in front of my daughter. Or my son. But I have to get them away from him. What if he tells them? Is that why he's come? To let out the secrets I've been so careful to—"Maybe . . . maybe you and Andrew can get me some water. I think if I had a little water."

She laughs, says she thinks she can handle getting a glass of water by herself. "Just go out on the veranda and I'll bring it out to you."

"Isn't that right, Annie?" he says. I can't look at him, so I look at Mimsy. "I was just telling her what a peach your mother was. Aunt Sunny, man. After they made her, they broke the mold." His voice: it's the only thing about him that's the same. "A crying shame what happened to her. And little Gracie, too."

Don't look at me! Don't say her name! Oh god, I'm going to heave. The room is spinning. I cover my mouth. Swallow back the vomit in my throat. Then I'm bumping past the guests, past a waitress holding a tray of—"Excuse me, please! Excuse me!" When I reach the pocket door that closes off the room, I claw at the handle. Throw it open with a bang and rush through the lobby, heading not toward the front door but toward the stairs. Is he following me? Don't look back! Keep going! Get away from him! . . . When I reach the second-floor landing, I run down the hall to Viveca's suite. The door is open. A maid is stripping the bed. "Go!" I shout.

"Yes, ma'am. I just need to—"

"Now!"

I lock the door behind her. Rush into the bathroom and lock that door, too. Lean against it. Alone now, safe, I release my sobs. Take in gulps of air. Then I stagger over to the toilet and vomit into the bowl.

I'm on the floor, whimpering, rocking. I'm six again, lying in the dark. I hear the click of my bedroom door. Feel him get into my bed with me. Feel his hands reach under my nightgown, his breath on the back of my neck. Don't touch me. I won't tell. I promise. Just don't touch me.

Someone's calling my name from far away. I don't answer. "Miss? Could you help us please?" It's Viveca's voice.

"Yes, ma'am. I was finishing up the bed when she . . ."

Then their voices are closer, inside the suite. Coming from the other side of the bathroom door. "Mama?"

"Mom? What's the matter?" Andrew's voice.

"Anna, it's Viveca. Are you all right in there?"

"Is he up here?"

"Who, Mama?" Ari's voice.

"My . . . my cousin."

"No, Mama, it's just us."

"Darling? We're concerned. Please unlock the door."

I reach up behind me. My fingers find the windowsill and I pull myself off the floor. Go over to the door and stare at the knob. "Anna?" I watch my fingers turn the lock, twist the knob.

They're standing there, my three kids and Viveca. But they blur away and I'm back there again. . . . *The roar of the water is in my ears, Gracie's screaming. She's cold and wet, and her body keeps stiffening, pushing against me. I can't see Mama but I can hear her. "I can't, Chick! I can't." Daddy shouts something to Kent and the two of them drop belly-down onto the roof. Kent grabs onto Daddy's ankles and Daddy's head and shoulders disappear over the edge. Then more of him. "Pull!" he keeps screaming. "Pull!" I scream, too, at Gracie. "Stop it! Stop squirming!" But she won't stop. I'm staring so hard at my cousin and my father, Kent's hands gripped around Daddy's ankles, that I don't even notice it at first: that my baby sister has stopped crying, stopped bucking and squirming. When I look down at her, she's not there. My arms are empty. . . .*

And then I'm back again, looking at their worried faces. And I blurt it out. "It wasn't him. It was me." They stare at me, confused. "He didn't drop her like we said. *I* did. She drowned because . . . because . . . *I* dropped her."

"Dropped who, Mama?" Ari says.

"My baby sister. I was holding her and . . . and then she wasn't in my arms anymore. She was in the water, getting carried away."

Viveca holds out her arms, and I step toward her. Fall against her and wail. *If you ever tell them what we're doing, then I'll have to tell on you, Annie. They'll find out what you did and . . .* But he *didn't* tell on me. I've just told on myself. *What's the matter? Don't you recognize your long-lost cousin? Kiss for the bride?* I've heard his voice all my life, but seeing him down there was a hundred times worse. He *hadn't* died. He was back again, smiling, leaning in to kiss me again like ... I couldn't keep it in anymore. I *had* to tell.

They lead me out into the suite, onto the bed. Viveca sits on one side of me, Ariane on the other. Marissa's pulled up a chair. She's facing me. Andrew's standing behind her. Everyone's waiting, looking confused. And so my long-ago memories of that terrible night tumble out: our plunge into the dark water, his pulling me from the back of the car onto that roof, the way she was bucking and screaming in my arms. "I was sopping wet. It was so cold. I think my hands must have gone numb because I didn't even realize ... not until ..."

"*What* water?" Marissa asks. "Mom, what are you *talking* about?"

It's Andrew who answers her. "That flood they were in. The one her mother died in. And her sister."

"What sister? How did I not know she had—?"

"Shut up," Andrew says. "Let her talk."

Viveca takes my hand in hers. "Go on, sweetheart," she says.

"He said ... He said, 'Where's Gracie?' And then the roof started caving in under us, and he grabbed my hand and led me across it. Lifted me up into that tree."

Marissa's mouth is gaping open. Ariane reaches over and brushes the hair off of my cheek. I take the tissues Andrew offers me and wipe my eyes. They have questions. Ask me for clarifications. "He told me he didn't want me to get in trouble. That if he said *he* dropped her ... I was so scared, and it was all so confusing. I don't think I even realized ... I just wanted my mother."

The kids, Andrew in particular, look like they're in such pain that I have to keep looking away from them. I look, instead, at my hands, the fingers of one twisting the ring on the other—the ring Viveca slipped onto my finger downstairs before I realized who he was, that he had come to ruin our wedding. The one I finally face is Viveca. "Our beautiful day," I tell her, sobbing. "I'm so sorry."

She takes me in her arms and holds me. Rocks me back and forth on the bed. "Does my brother know what's going on?" I ask. Marissa says he doesn't—that hardly anyone noticed. That she herself had no idea there was a problem until Ariane came and got her. "Good. Don't say anything to Donald and Mimsy. I don't want them to know. . . . Is he still down there?"

"Uncle Donald?" one of them asks.

"No. *Him.*" I can't say his name. "I want him to go away."

They look at each other. Ariane says, "But, Mama, he came especially to see you. We can't just tell him to leave."

"I can," Viveca says. "Don't worry, Anna. I'll handle it."

I nod. "Thank you." I look from Marissa to Ariane, from Ariane to Andrew. He's the one who looks the most stricken.

Viveca asks me if I can handle going back down and joining our guests once she gets him to go away. "They'll be serving the luncheon soon. We can't just abandon everyone."

I tell her I don't think I can do it—that I'm too shaken up. "I just don't trust myself. I'm sorry. I would if I could but—"

"No, that's all right. We can work around it. But I don't want you to be alone up here either."

She makes a plan. Ariane will stay up here with me, and she, Marissa, and Andrew will go back down and carry on. A stomach flu, they'll tell people. "It came on her out of nowhere. She's sick as a dog, poor thing. Well, things happen. What are you going to do?"

I ask the kids if they're comfortable with that. Both of the girls nod. "Hey, I'm an actor," Marissa says

"Ari, you go down," Andrew says. "I'll stay with her."

She looks at me, then back at her brother. "Okay."

Before they head back down, Viveca gets me a glass of water and hands me another Xanax. "Here, darling. I think you should take one of these." I take the capsule, a sip of water. She takes one, too. Takes a deep breath and puts on a smile. "Okay then," she says. "We'll see you a little later. You try and relax."

At the door, Marissa turns back and asks her brother if he needs something from the bar. "Yeah, bourbon. A double."

"No problem. Be right back."

After they leave, Andrew apologizes for bringing him here. "It's just that last night after you and I were talking about him, and you said you'd lost track of him, I thought you'd *want* to see him, Mom. I didn't know about . . ."

"Of course you didn't. How could you?" I ask him to please go over to the window. I need to make sure that Viveca has gotten him to leave.

"Yeah, all right. Sure." A few minutes later, he says, "Okay, there he goes. He's walking down the driveway."

"Good," I say. "Good riddance."

He looks from the window to me. "You know, Mom, I know his showing up brought all those bad memories back. I get that. But when you think about it, he was only trying to protect you when he said he dropped her."

"*Protect* me? Ha!"

"I'm not saying he should have, necessarily, but think about it. There would have been all kinds of questions. And I mean, hey, you'd just lost your mom. He was probably just trying to spare you the third degree on top of—"

"Bullshit! He made up that story so that—"

Stop it, Annie! Shut your mouth!

He comes over, sits down on the bed. "So that what?"

I look away from him. "Nothing."

"No, what were you going to—?"

"He used it against me."

"Used . . . ?"

"Our secret."

"How? What do you mean?" I look back at him. "Jesus Christ, Mom, *tell* me. I'm just trying to figure this whole thing out."

He's waiting, a plea on his face. "I . . . He made me do things."

"What kind of things?"

"Honey, it's too hard to . . . It was such a long time ago. But when I saw him down there today. When he leaned forward and kissed me . . ."

"Did he molest you or something? Is that what you're saying?" He waits. "Mom?"

It's no use. He's guessed it. I can't sit here and lie to him. "He said . . . he said that if they found out it was me who dropped Gracie, they'd take me away and put me in jail. And that it would be dark and cold. He said jails had rats in them, and that they'd come out at night and crawl all over me. Bite me."

"But dropping your sister was an accident, Mom. You said so yourself before: that it was cold, you were both sopping wet. That you got distracted watching them try to rescue your mother. I can see how, yeah, back then you might have been confused. Scared or whatever. But to keep it a secret all these years? Didn't you ever say, hey, wait a minute—it wasn't my fault. It was the circumstances. Nobody would have blamed me."

I nod. "I *have* told myself that, Andrew. Hundreds of times. But when you're molested at that age, it leaves you with . . . You get stuck. Emotionally, I mean. So yes, as I got older, I could make that rational argument to myself. But my memories weren't rational. They were emotional. A part of me has never stopped being that scared little girl who, if I tell, is going to be put in a jail cell with those rats."

"Yeah, but Mom . . . I mean, what were you? Six? Since when does a six-year-old go to jail?"

"But that was the problem. I was so young that I believed him. My mother was gone, my father wasn't coming home half the time. My brother was always busy with school. So a lot of the time, it was just the two of us in the house. Just me and him. It started during my bath time. He'd—"

"What do you mean *started*? It happened more than once?"

Is this real? Am I really telling him? "It went on for almost two years. It didn't stop until the state pulled me out of the house."

"Two years," he says. He gets off the bed, walks around the room repeating it. "Two *years*?" He comes back and faces me. "When you say he molested you, what . . . What . . . ?"

I hear the sloshing bathwater, see him holding the washcloth. "I didn't understand what was happening. Not at first anyway. He'd come into the bathroom while I was taking my bath and tell me he needed to show me the right way to wash myself. And it . . . went on from there. He'd get excited. Get into the bathtub with me. Tell me to touch it, kiss it." He listens blank-faced. Keeps shaking his head from side to side, as if to shake off the ugly things I'm telling him. "I knew that what we were doing was bad, but that if I didn't keep it a secret, he'd—"

"Mom, don't say 'we.' *He's* responsible for what happened, not you."

I nod. Tell him I understand that now but that I didn't back then—that "we" was the way he kept putting it. "And then . . . And then, he started sneaking into my room in the middle of the night." *His weight on the mattress wakes me up. I feel his hands under my nightgown.* "And then one night, he turned me on my back. Got on top of me and—"

"Mom, *stop*!" he shouts. "Just . . . stop it." His face is flushed. He looks dazed. For the next few minutes, neither of us speaks. He just keeps shaking his head, blinking back tears. When I reach over and place my hand on his shoulder, he bats it away. Oh god, I should have spared him. *Especially* him. Why have I told Andrew of all people? He can't even look at me now that he knows. Looks, instead, at his right foot, his shoe moving back and forth against the carpet. Oh god, my poor son.

"Did they arrest him at least? After they found out?"

"Honey, they *didn't* find out. They took me out of the house because of my father, not him. Kent kept *my* secret and I kept *his*. Until right now. You're the first person I've ever told."

His fists are clenched, his shoe keeps moving backward and forward. "It's just so fucked-up that he got away with it all these years. Did what he did and then never had to pay for it." He looks up from the floor. Looks right at me. "It must have been a relief, right? When the state *did* take you away?"

I shake my head. "I was scared to death when that happened. I didn't trust anyone at that point, especially strangers. What's that thing they say? Better the devil you know than the devil you don't?"

He gets up and goes over to the window. Splays his hands on the sill, rests his forehead against the pane. He speaks to me over his shoulder. "So all these years, you just stuffed it? Didn't even tell Dad?"

"I couldn't, Andrew. Those secrets became a big part of who I was. I just hope . . ."

"Hope what? Say it."

"That now that you know the truth about me, you won't think I'm a horrible person."

"Why would I think that?"

I wish he'd turn around. Wish I didn't have to say it to his broad back.

"Because of what we . . . What *he* . . . Maybe if I had gone to my father. Or Donald. Or told *your* father at some point. He's a psychologist, for Christ's sake. He *deals* with this kind of stuff. It's just that . . ."

"Just what, Mom?"

"I didn't trust men."

"What about Viveca? Does she know?"

"No, not yet. But maybe now that I've told you, I'll be able to risk it. I don't know. I have a lot to think about."

"Yeah," he mumbles. "Me, too."

"Oh, honey. I always thought I'd carry this stuff to the grave. Protect the people I love from all this ugly, dirty . . . And now, of all people, I've told *you*. Burdened *you*."

He says it's okay. He can handle it. "I just can't believe what a stupid shit I was to bring him here today," he says. "Thinking you'd be *glad* to see him."

I assure him he's not to blame—that it was just a horrible coincidence.

"But he just shows up out of the blue? Puts on my suit and rides over here with me? What the fuck? Did he think you were going to have forgotten that any of it ever happened? And now, thanks to me and my stupid idea to bring him here, here we are. Your wedding's going on downstairs, and you're up here with me playing true confessions."

Playing? No. Whatever these last few minutes have been—and whatever happens next—it's not play. . . . I think back to the beginning of this weekend: the ride up here with Minnie and the others, the joy I felt when I heard my kids come in and ran up the basement stairs to see them. And my conversation with Andrew last night, the tenderness I felt for him. Why can't I rewind this whole weekend and start over again?

"Last night?" I say. "When we were watching that movie you like, and you said that my work was violent? I think that was the only way I could get some of it out was through my art. The fear, the anger . . ."

When he turns back and looks at me, his face is flushed. "No it wasn't, Mom. That wasn't the *only* way you got it out."

"I don't . . . Honey, what do you mean?"

"You just said you didn't trust men. Males. Don't you remember the way you used to go off on me?"

I nod. Force myself to face his red face, the way he's glaring at me. "Andrew, I didn't . . . I would never—"

"Yes you would, Mom. You *did*."

Why is he doing this now? Haven't we been through enough? I look away from him. Look over at the doorway where Marissa has just appeared. She's looking from one of us to the other. "Hey?" she says. "What's going on?

He pushes past her, bumping her shoulder and spilling the drink she's holding out to him. "Jesus Christ, knock me over, why don't you?" she says. She looks out into the hallway, then turns back to me. "Where's *he* going?"

Chapter Twenty-Six

Andrew Oh

I start the car. Back out, almost hitting a Porsche with New York plates. *To tell you the truth, Donny and I never got along too much. But Annie and me? We were close. She used to hang all over me.* There's a fire in my head, and I know just exactly how to put it out. I pull onto the road and gun it. He said he came in on the downtown bus, so that must be where he's . . . *Can I kiss the bride?* Jesus Christ, no wonder she freaked. Where are you, motherfucker? You think you got away with it? Guess again.

I pass the golf course. I was up there with her for what? Fifteen minutes? He can't have gotten much farther. *He told me to touch it, kiss it. . . .* You think you can just show up, you sick fuck? Ruin her big day and then crawl back into whatever sewer you crawled out of? Well, you can't, scumbag. And when I find you, payback's gonna be a bitch. . . .

I can feel her hands on my back at the top of the stairs that day. . . . See her in the kitchen, coming at me with that mallet. The blood's pounding in my head. Slow down, asshole! You get pulled over and that piece of crap's going to get an even bigger jump on you. Get away again. I relax my grip on the wheel, flex my fingers. Swivel my head back and forth to loosen the muscles in my neck. I'm past the wooded area now, heading into the more residential stretch. How the hell could he have gotten this far? Did I miss him? Did he see me coming and—No! He *didn't* head back toward the bus station. He went the other way.

I hit the brakes, pull hard to the left. Just miss a tree making the U-turn. Drive off in the opposite direction.

I shoot past the golf course again, then Bella Linda. They must be eating lunch now. And she's up there missing her own . . . I can't stop seeing her face. *She wouldn't stop screaming. I was watching them try to pull my mother onto the roof and then . . .* And that sick fuck uses it against her. Makes it their little secret so that he can—Deer!

I slam the brake and the seat belt holds back my forward thrust. In the state I'm in, I'm lucky I remembered to put it on. I catch my breath. Stare after the goddamned deer as it disappears into the woods on the other side of the road. Jesus, it bolted out so fast I didn't—okay, refocus. Find the fucker.

I drive on, pick up speed again. There's a curve up ahead. Slow down. Breathe. You wrap this car around a tree and—wait! There's someone. Up ahead, walking along the side of the road. Is it . . . ? Yeah, that's him! I stomp on the gas pedal and aim for him, closing the distance between us. But when he looks back and sees it's me, he takes off into the woods. Yeah, you'd *better* run, you fucking coward. Because when I catch you . . . I bump onto the side of the road and slam it in park. Jump out and take off after him.

Where is he? Which way did he go? I stop. Look around. Then I hear leaves crunching, up ahead on the right. "Hey!"

He's fast for his age, but I'm faster, younger. He zigzags around rocks and tree stumps. Runs up a hill. When he reaches the top, he looks back and shouts over his shoulder, "Stay away from me!" He's scared. I can hear it in his voice. Good. He *should* be scared, because once I . . .

I take the hill, spot him again, running down the other side. The undergrowth is getting thicker, the ground's more mucky. Brambles keep pulling at my pant legs. But he's slowing down, too. Must be getting winded by now. Not me. I'm pumped on pure adrenaline.

I'm maybe fifty feet behind him when my shoe gets hooked on a rock and I flop face-first against the wet ground. But I'm up a second or two later and after him again. He looks back and starts shouting some bullshit about how he didn't even know what he was doing. "I was just a mixed-up kid!" *He* was a kid? *He* was? It pisses me off even more. Turbocharges me. Thirty feet behind him, twenty, ten. When I'm within reach, I fly at him. Grab him by the shoulders. Take him down and fall on top of him.

Motherfucker fights back. Pushes me off of him, gets back on his feet and lunges. When he head-bumps me, I try for a headlock but can't get the right grip. He goes for my face. Jams a finger inside my mouth, between my cheek and my teeth, and yanks hard. Hurts like a motherfucker! I try to bite his finger but I can't. His thumb comes at my eye, but I bat it away. Grab him by the wrist. He yanks it back, gets off of me. Tries to take off, but I grab on to his ankle and take him down again. Pin him with an old wrestling move and flip him onto his back. Get on top of him and grab him by the sides of his head. That one eye's looking up at me, crazy scared. "Don't hurt me! I'll press charges, and don't think I won't." Yeah? You think that's going to stop me? "It was her who started it! Crawling up on my lap and—"

"Shut up! Shut the fuck *up*!"

"No, listen to me! You think these little kids are innocent? They're not. They want it just as much as—"

That's what throws me over the edge: him saying that. His head's in my hands and the jagged rock sticking out of the ground next to him seems like a gift from God. I slam his head against it. Once, twice. How does *that* feel, motherfucker? Not sure? Here. Have some more. And what I'm doing feels right and good. Feels fucking *euphoric.* . . .

The next several seconds are a blur, but he's finally stopped resisting. The fight's gone out of him. I stumble onto my feet, coughing, trying to catch my breath. When I look down, his head's flopped to the side of the rock. There's blood and hair on it. That eye patch is riding up on his forehead. He's staring up at me with his one bugged-out eye and there's a hole where the other one's supposed to be. I look away. Start walking deeper into the woods—slowly at first, then faster. Then I'm running away from him. From what I've done.

I don't know how much time passes. Time enough for my breathing to slow down and the blood to stop pounding in my head. My body's soaked in sweat. The inside of my mouth where he clawed at it hurts like a son of a bitch. His blood's on the palms of my hands, my

shirt cuffs, the sleeves of my jacket. He wasn't moving when I got up.
He's probably concussed. Or maybe he was just playing possum. I start
back there because I'd better find out.

Except I can't find him. Did I miss him? Veer too far to the left? Or
did he get up? Get away? . . . No, there he is. And there's the rock. He
hasn't moved. I stand there, about ten feet away from him still, afraid
to approach. Afraid that I've . . . But I have to. I stare down at my feet,
watch them walk toward him.

Without looking at his face, I squat down next to him. Grab his
wrist and check for a pulse. It's faint, but I feel one. At least I think
I do. He's got vitals, needs medical attention. I'm a nurse, aren't I?
Whatever this is going to cost me, I've got to get him some help. I grab
him under the arms and sit him up. Hoist him over my shoulder and,
heaving, teetering, manage to stand up. I wait a couple of seconds and
then start lugging him back toward the car.

He feels light at first. Probably doesn't weigh more than 150. That's
nothing compared to what I lift at the gym. But he gets heavier with
every step, and the ground's uneven and pitchy. I have to keep my knees
from buckling. I can feel his head bumping against the small of my
back. His blood must be staining my uniform. The woods are quiet.
No breeze, no birds. Just my footsteps crunching the dead leaves.

I hear my car before I see it. The engine, the radio. I stand at the
clearing when the car comes into view. Can't just march out there.
Someone could see me and stop. Or call the cops. The driver's side
door's gaping open, and the radio's playing that Fine Young Cannibals
song. *She drives me crazy, and I can't help myself.* . . . My mind ricochets
back to when I was driving him over to the wedding—when I put on
the radio because our conversation had died and the silence was making me uncomfortable. If I hadn't gone back for those rings, none of
this would have ever happened. He would have rung the bell, waited
a while, and then left. We wouldn't have even known he'd been there.
But I *did* go back, and now the bottom's dropped out of everything.
No cars coming either way. It's just me and him. I step out of the
woods and lug him toward the car.

Get the back door open. Slide him off my shoulder and lay him facedown across the seat. God, that gash on the back of his head is ugly. Blunt force trauma. Brain damage, maybe. Jesus.

I get in the front. Close my door, click my seat belt and pull back onto the road. Got to get him to the hospital. I felt a pulse. I'm going to be in *big* trouble if he dies on me. . . . Rage-fueled temporary insanity. But there were extenuating circumstances. Look what I had just found out. And so *what* if he ends up with a TBI? After what he did to her? Then he lays low all these years? Shows up out of the blue? He's lucky he's *got* a pulse, for Christ's sake. . . . *For Christ's sake.* I hear Casey-Lee's voice. *Pray, Andrew. Pray to Our Lord and Savior Jesus Christ.* I nod. That's what I'll do. Driving along, I speak the words out loud. "Have mercy on him, Jesus. Let him survive. And if it's Your will, have mercy on me, too. Please, Jesus? Forgive me my anger, my trespasses."

But there must be a part of me that knows he's dead back there—that that pulse I felt was wishful thinking—because when I see where I am, I realize that I haven't driven to the hospital after all. I've driven home. I take the turn and start up Jailhouse Hill.

When I reach our house, I pull into the driveway. But instead of stopping at the end, I keep going. Drive across the backyard and start down the rutted path out back. Approaching a deep pothole, I brake too hard, too late, and hear the clunk in the back. He's fallen off the seat and onto the floor. Forgive me, Jesus. Please forgive me.

When I get to the brook on this side of the old cottage, I cut the motor. Get out. Hoist him off the floor and back onto the seat. The blood on the back of his head has clotted. Caked up in his hair. I shift the body. His face is gray. His hand is cold to the touch. *Thou shalt not kill.* . . .

I leave him there, hop the brook, and walk over to the well. Stare at the granite slab that covers it. What's my alternative? Turn myself in? Spend the rest of my life stuck in a prison cell when I could be at the hospital·helping people? And what about my parents? My sisters? I wouldn't be the only one suffering if they put me away. Hasn't Mom been through enough? And hasn't Dad? A wife who left him, a son in prison. Should I do this? Can I live with myself if I do?

The slab's even heavier than I figured, but on the second try I manage to lift one end of it enough to jockey it away from the opening. I stare down into the darkness, unable to see the bottom. It's like those black holes I read about: those regions of space-time with a gravitational pull so intense that nothing that gets sucked in ever escapes. I can't escape the fact that I killed him—it's a done deal that I'm going to have to live with for the rest of my life—but why would anyone think to look out here? And who would be looking for him? Does he have a wife or a girlfriend? Kids? A buddy who would miss him? Maybe, maybe not. If he had to take a bus here, he doesn't even own a car. And he looked down-and-out. Maybe he was just a drifter, a loner. The only thing I really know about him is what he did to Mom all those years ago. . . .

I pick up a stone. Toss it in and listen to the plunk. I thought maybe it had gone dry, but it hasn't. What is it? Seven feet deep, maybe? Eight? And the opening's at least two feet wide. That ought to be enough. It's not like he's broad-shouldered. But what if they *do* trace it back to me? Haul me in for questioning? But why would they? Just because he's gone missing doesn't mean I had anything to do with it. . . . And maybe you can find out on the Internet how to beat a polygraph. Everything else is on there. Why not that? And anyway, they're not even admissible. Are they? . . . *Vengeance is mine sayeth The Lord.* I'm already damned for what I've done. I'll pay for it in the next world if I don't in this one.

I go back to the car. Lift the body and carry it in my arms, across the brook and then over to the well. I raise him feet first over the hole and let go. One of his shoulders clears the opening, but the other one doesn't. He's hanging there, crooked and stuck. Okay, Andrew, here's your last chance. You can pull him out again—face up to what you did. Get hauled off to prison. Or not. I stand there, thinking about it, trying to decide. Then I reach down, push on his shoulder. The body drops down with a splash. No going back on my decision now. It's done.

It's a burial, in a way. His mother brought him into the world and I took him out of it. So maybe I should pray for him, pray for his soul.

Except what good would that do him, coming from his killer? Having the guy who bashed in his head stand here and ask Jesus for His Heavenly Mercy. Like I said, I'm damned now. Doomed. From water he came, and to water I've just returned him: prayer-wise, that's about all I can come up with.

My uniform: it's evidence. And so's his bag of clothes on the front-seat floor—the ones he took off when he changed into my suit. I've got to get rid of this stuff. Buy another uniform at the PX when I get back to Texas. I slip out of my shoes, undress down to my skivvies, and then drop them, too. There's no blood on them, but everything I was wearing when I did it is tainted. Everything. I stuff my bloodstained, dirt-caked clothes in there with him. My socks and mud-caked shoes, sopping wet from the brook. His bag of clothes. Then, butt-naked, I struggle the slab back over the well. It takes all the energy I have left. . . .

I walk back to the car and, instead of getting in, stand there, leaning against it, feeling the rapid beating of my heart. My heart's revving, but his has stopped because I stopped it. What if they *did* trace his disappearance back to me? Would they think to look out here? Uncover the well and . . . ? I've got to think this through. Cover up my tracks better than this. That's what murderers do, isn't it? Commit the crime, then cover it up? But I'm going to need more time. Maybe what I can do is call my CO and tell him I've got a family emergency. Get my leave extended. Dad's up there on the Cape, and Mom and my sisters will have taken off by tomorrow. I'm going to have to hold it together until then. There's plenty of rocks out here—that broken-down old stone wall some farmer had put up way back when. I can gather up those rocks and drop them down there. Fill up the shaft as best I can, then come back here with some bags of Sakrete. Mix it, pour it in there, and plug up the well—cement in the evidence. . . . Jesus Christ, I've murdered a man. I'm a murderer. Out of nowhere, I hear the voice of that guy in group when I was in training at Sam Houston—the young private who was torn up with guilt over what he'd done over there in Kandahar. Kicked in the door of that apartment and fired on what he thought was Al-Qaeda, then realized it was a mother and her kids. *Did I kill them or murder them? What would you call it? . . .* I hear another voice—that Vietnam vet who'd pickled himself in alcohol. At first, he didn't want me to work with him, but later on he started trusting me, telling me what it was like back then. *There was this chant they had us say when we were in boot camp. "War is murder, and murder is fun!" And you know something? It* was *fun. I enjoyed wasting those villagers. It was as good as sex. But then after the rush . . .* Now I know what he meant. The rush, the discharge. Those sweet few seconds of calm after the rage spilled out of me. And then it's over, just like he said. You come back down from the high, get up, and deal with the aftermath—clean up the mess you've made. . . .

I'd better go back up to the house. Get showered and dressed before they come back. The last thing I'd need is to drive up from back here and walk into the house naked with his blood on my hands.

I climb into the car, start it. But when I glance in the rearview, I look away. I'm like *what the fuck?* Where did *he* come from? Because I just saw an old black guy leaning against the old cottage. Or did I? . . . Gripping the steering wheel, I force myself to look back again, but no one's there. It was just my imagination. My guilt, screwing with my head already. . . . What *would* you call what I did? Murder? Manslaughter? Justifiable homicide? No, who am I kidding? If it was justifiable, why would I have to hide the body? I put my bare foot to the pedal and the car moves forward. Starts back up the bumpy path.

Back in the house, I take the stairs two at a time. Get in the shower and make the water as hot as I can stand it, as if I can somehow wash away what I've done. What was that Shakespeare play they made us read in high school—the one where the killer's wife can't wash the blood off her hands? *Hamlet,* maybe? *Julius Caesar?* One of those. . . .

I get out, dry off. I can't look in the medicine cabinet mirror. Can't face myself. I get dressed and head back downstairs. Go out to the car with a roll of paper towels and a bottle of kitchen cleaner. I've got to be methodical about it. Thorough. I scrub the blood off the floor, the backseat. At least the seats are leather, not upholstery. I caught a break there. I wipe down the steering wheel, too, in case there are any telltale flakes there—something not visible to the untrained eye. Maybe I've watched too many of those *CSIs*, but I can't take chances. I'm going to have to turn this car back into the rental place. What if, when they go to inspect it, someone spots something I missed? And what if someone *does* report him missing. They could connect the dots back to me. Impound the vehicle and . . . No, that's not going to happen. I can't let it.

When I'm done, I've used up half a bottle of Fantastik and a pile of paper towels. I head back inside. Put the Fantastik back under the sink. Rip the paper towels into pieces and flush them down the crapper, two or three at a time. Any more than that and they could clog up the pipes. When that's done, I head back upstairs, trying to think if I forgot anything—something a forensic scientist might spot. But what? And why would they even be looking at me?

Back in my bedroom, I pull down the shades, pace. Look over at the bookshelf. It's weird the way they kept everything the way it was. It's like a museum of who I used to be. Boxes of Topps and Upper Deck basketball cards, my wrestling and track trophies. I look over at the posters on the wall. Those WWF guys I liked: Mankind, The Rock. The one of that rock group I was so into back then: Rage Against the Machine. Ironic, isn't it? Look where my rage has gotten me. I think about Mom—the way some little thing would trigger it. Set off the rage that was inside her. . . . I hear Dr. Skiles's voice—the thing he sometimes says in group to the guys back from their deployment, the ones who are suffering because of what they saw over there. What they did. *Don't stuff it. This is a safe place to let it out. We're only as sick as our secrets.* And now I know Mom's terrible secret. I'm the *only* one who knows. The only one of her kids whose rage matched hers. And now I have an ugly secret of my own—one that could put me in prison if they found out. Because the difference between me and those guys in group is that I didn't do what I did in combat. It wasn't any act of war. It was revenge, pure and simple—the settling of an old score because of what he did to a little girl who he damaged for life. I look around my room again, wondering what my teenage self would have thought if he could have looked into the future. Known what his adult self would do out in that woods today? . . . Life was so simple back then. All I had to worry about was the next match or meet, whether or not there was going to be a pop quiz on the day when I hadn't done the reading. *Macbeth*: that was the play. The one with the witches and the ghosts. God, that black guy I thought I saw down there for a second. That was weird. *Out, out, damned spot.* Macbeth's wife: that's who it was who couldn't wash off the blood. . . . *"What do you think the blood symbolizes?" Miss Anderman asks us. She's young and inexperienced, just out of college. She waits, a hopeful look on her face that fades away in the long, resentful silence. I feel sorry for her, in a way. I know the answer, but sitting there in my varsity letter jacket, I'm too cool to volunteer it. It's her guilt she can't scrub away. She was the one who wanted the guy killed, who goaded him into doing it, and now she's got to live with herself.* . . . Just like *I'm* going to have to live with *my*self, whether or not they trace his disappearance back to the well out back. *As sick as our secrets.* At least Mom's secrets are finally out. Partially, anyway. And mine is down there, stuffed in a shallow well. I'm facing a life sentence, whether I end up doing time in a prison cell or not.

I flop facedown on my bed, close my eyes, and try to unsee the things flashing in my mind: my mother's face as she realizes who he is. . . . That deer flying out in front of me. . . . Him running ahead of me in the woods, up that hill. I bolt up, remembering what I forgot about: the evidence that's still out there. His blood and hair stuck to that rock. Along with my DNA, most likely. Should I go out to the garage, grab a wire brush and a jug of water? Drive back there and try to find the rock again? Scrub away the evidence that could convict me? But why would they even look out there? No one saw me carrying him out of those woods. The coast was clear. One good rainstorm and his blood will wash away and into the ground. But I'm scared. I wanted to punish him, not kill him. Is this what my life is going to be like from now on? Holding my breath and waiting? In a few days his body's going to start to putrefy. But who would be out there to smell it? Nobody. Some dog, maybe? Some scavenging animal. But once I get it filled up with those rocks. Cemented. . . . I think about the other guy they found out there in that well—that artist who lived in the cottage. *Was* it a murder? If it was, they never got the killer. They couldn't have if it was still a question. . . .

I'm exhausted. My mind, my body. I catch myself dozing off. Wake up with a start. I killed a guy and hid his body. How am I *ever* going to be able to sleep soundly again? Why should I? . . .

I wake to the sound of car doors slamming, voices. I'm groggy, disoriented, and then it hits me like a two-by-four to the head: what I did. They come in. I don't know what time it is, but it's nighttime. It must be. The room is dark. How long have I been out?

Footsteps on the stairs, coming down the hall toward me. My door opens a crack. "Andrew? Are you awake?" Mom's voice. I don't answer. I hear Ariane ask if I'm all right. "He's sleeping," Mom says. The door closes quietly. They go back downstairs.

But a few minutes later, my door opens again and the light goes on. "Hey." It's Marissa. She comes over and sits on my bed. Taps me on the shoulder. "Are you awake?"

"I am now."

"What a day, huh? Are you okay?"

"Not really."

"No, me neither. I can't even wrap my head around it yet. You know?"

"Yeah."

I flip onto my back. See her standing in front of the posters on my wall. "Rage Against the Machine," she says. "Remember when I took that CD of theirs without asking you, and then I scratched it? How mad you got?"

"Uh-huh."

"I guess I really *was* a twerp." She turns around and faces me. "Where did you disappear to today?"

I shrug. Look away. "Nowhere. Just had to get out of there and get my bearings. How's Mom?"

"Fair. But I think it's good that she finally got it out. Can you imagine what it must have been like for her to keep it a secret about her sister all these years? In a way, it explains a lot about her. You know?"

I shake my head. Tell her I don't know anything right now.

"Yeah, like I said, it's a lot to process. But remember when we were kids? How one of us would do something to set her off and she'd go all mental?" At me, mostly. Come after me with something. Hit me hard enough to raise welts. "And then? After she calmed down? Ariane would be all like, 'Don't tell Daddy when he gets home. Okay? Daddy doesn't have to know.'"

"Yeah, I remember. What's your point?"

"That maybe all of those outbursts, all of those secrets we were supposed to keep for her . . . maybe it was all connected to the big secret she was keeping. That it was her, not her cousin, who dropped the baby."

"I don't know, Marissa. Maybe." I just want her to shut up. Leave.

"And it's not like, okay, now that she's finally told us, it's going to be happily ever after. But at least she's got Viveca to help her. She's been great this afternoon, by the way. Kind of . . . I don't know. Motherly." She comes over. Sits on my bed. Why's she staring at me like that? "What happened to you?"

"Nothing. Why? What do you mean?"

"Why is your face all banged up?"

"My face?" I tense. Force myself to keep eye contact.

"Yeah. You've got a scratch under your eye, and a red mark on your forehead. Your mouth looks a little swollen on one side."

I can't do it. Can't look at her. I get off the bed and go over the window so that my back's to her. "No comment."

"Did you go after him? Is that where you went?" I don't answer her. "Ari said she felt sorry for him because Viveca made him leave. But not me. It was kind of creepy the way he had her lie about it. Not admit that she dropped her. I mean, okay, maybe he was trying to cover for her or whatever. I get that. But shit, it was an *accident*. People would have understood. But instead, she's got to sit on it her whole life. Live with the lie. And then he just shows up out of nowhere? Today of all days? Personally, I hope you beat the shit out of him."

I turn and face her. "Don't say anything."

"I won't," she says.

"You promise? I need you to promise me."

"Okay, chill out. I *said* I wouldn't. Remember that time when you got grounded and you snuck out anyway? Went to that concert, and I came down and let you in after you got back? I didn't tell anyone then—not even Ari."

"Stop it. I'm *serious*."

She keeps looking at me, worried now. "Wait here," she says.

She leaves. Returns a minute later. "Come sit down," she says. "This is that cover-up I let Mom use this morning. This stuff's awesome." I sit. She opens the tube and squeezes a little of it onto her finger. Dabs some on my forehead, under my eye, at the corner of my mouth. Spreads it around with her finger. "There," she says. "Good as new. No one would ever know."

"Okay. Thanks."

"Sure. . . . Hey, Andrew? If *I* tell *you* something, do you promise not to say anything?" I nod. "My bruises? I didn't fall. Someone *did* rough me up." I wait. "It was some big deal actor who was in town. This girlfriend of mine knew him. She's . . . well, never mind. I thought it might open a door for me, you know? That he might give me a referral to an agent or whatever. Because acting's all about making connections, okay? So she and I went up to his hotel room and—"

I put up my hand to stop her. There's only so many disclosures I can take in one day. "Spare me the details," I tell her. "Just tell me. Is he still around? You in any danger?"

"Uh-uh. It was a hit-and-run. It was my own stupid fault."

"Yeah, well maybe you should throw in the towel on this acting thing. Take a long look at what it's costing you."

She nods. "Yeah, maybe I should." But in the next second, her expression turns from resignation to hope. "Hey, but you know that old dude who came to the wedding today? The one who gave Mom her start? His son—the one who brought him—works in TV out in Hollywood. Directs a soap opera. So when I told him I'm an actor, he said that they're going to be casting for a new character, an ingenue type that I might be right for. And that if I went out there, he could make sure I got an audition. He gave me his card, told me to call him. I can't afford the flight, but maybe Mom or Viveca will lend me the money. He didn't promise anything, but it might be worth it to take a shot. You know?"

"Marissa . . ."

"I know, I know. But like I said, so much of it is about making connections. Who you know, who you happen to run into."

I'm too weary to come up with a counterargument, and she's going to do what she wants anyway. And besides, I've got bigger problems.

When we hear a car pull up outside, we both look over at the window. Look back at each other. "Who's this?" Marissa says. "I hope it's not that creepy cousin of hers. He wouldn't come back here. Would he?" Car doors slam. Two of them. She gets up and goes over to the window, yanks the shade. "The police? What the hell do they want?"

Me, I think. They want me. But how the hell . . . ? Someone must have seen me carrying the body out of the woods after all. Gotten the license plate. They must have traced it back to the rental car place. Or maybe that guy *was* down there at the cottage. Maybe I *wasn't* just seeing things. "I'm going down," Marissa says. At the doorway, she stops. Looks back at me. "You coming?"

I tell her I'll be right down. Instead, I sit there, watching the blue light winking on and off against my posters. I'm probably going to walk out of here in handcuffs. I reach over to the nightstand. Pick up the pocket Bible I brought with me from Texas. Thumb the pages. It's in Deuteronomy, isn't it? Yeah, here it is. *He that smiteth a man, so that he die, shall be surely put to death. . . .* It's true in a way. Whatever happens, it's going to be the death of my military career, my work at the hospital. I stand up. Walk out of my room and start down the hall. They've got me. What would be the use of denying it? Might as well get this over with.

But when I stop at the top of the stairs and listen, they're not talking about me. Or him. They're saying something about a break-in? Yeah, but that was a while ago. Was there another one? . . . Dad? What?

"—place is owned by, let me see. It's in my notes. . . . A Miss Viveca Christophoulos-Shabbas."

"That's me. He's been staying at my beach house."

What? Helicoptering *who* to Boston? Dad? He's hurt? Was it those sharks? How bad did they get him? Is he going to—

Robbery? An assault? Someone assaulted Dad?

I take the stairs two at a time. What are they *talking* about? What's wrong with my dad?

Part V

Three Years Later

Chapter Twenty-Seven

Orion Oh

She's in the doorway, holding up the phone, waiting for me to notice her. How long has she been standing there? She creeps around here like a ghost, this one. Not like her predecessor, that's for sure. You could hear Carla coming from a couple of rooms away. "I was going to take a message," she says. "But it's your daughter in California. I wasn't sure if—"

"No, that's fine. I was working away so hard in here, I didn't even hear it ringing." I hold out my hand, and she approaches. When I had the sunroom built this past spring, I purposely didn't have an extension put out here. My concentration's compromised enough without a bunch of interruptions. I take the phone from her. Haven't talked to Marissa in over a week. "Hey there, California. What's shaking?"

"Got some news, dude. That's what."

"Yeah? Good news, I hope."

"Yup. They're extending my contract. Looks like I'm going to be gainfully employed as Kendra for another eighteen months."

"Oh, honey, that's terrific. Congrats."

"Yeah, the writers are working on a new plotline. You know Dr. Amos?"

"The one who runs the hospital?"

"Right. So it turns out my character's not just the spunky waitress at the pub. She's also the daughter Dr. Amos never even knew he had. Bianca kept her pregnancy from him and gave me up for adoption."

"Bianca. Is she the one who's been snatched by Somali pirates?"

"Uh-huh. Kidnapped and presumed dead. The actor who plays her is actually off on maternity leave, so they've written her out of the show until February. The way they're handling it is, this letter shows up in her papers, and when Dr. Amos goes through them, that's how he finds out that he has another daughter."

"And why did Bianca keep it from him?"

"I don't know. For spite maybe. Because she's a total bitch."

"Aha." I reach over and click "save." I wrote three new pages this morning, and I'd hate to lose them like I did the last time.

"And you know their other daughter, April?"

"The other waitress at the pub?"

"Right. You know how she and I have become best friends? How April and Kendra have, I mean? The writers are developing a storyline where April gets so threatened by me—by Kendra—that she starts developing this sibling rivalry that begins to make her crazy. So she's going to start plotting to murder me. Meghan? The girl who plays April? She's thrilled because she finally gets to play something other than Miss Goody Two-shoes. But I guess I'm going to survive because, hey, why would they sign me to an eighteen-month contract extension if the writers were going to kill me off?"

I smile. "Well, that's a relief. I wouldn't want to tune in someday and see you getting bumped off, even if it's make-believe."

"Yeah, and dude, you know what's way cool? *Why* they're keeping me? Because of the fan sites. My character is getting a ton of traffic. And my Facebook page has over twelve thousand subscribers. Which is like whoa—for someone who's only been on the show for a year? Daytime Emmy nominations are coming up pretty soon, and Joe says they're submitting a couple of my scenes for consideration as Best Newcomer."

"Well, good luck with that. Joe Agnello's really been your fairy godfather out there in Hollywood, hasn't he? That's one good thing that came out of your mother's wedding. Isn't that where you met him?"

"Uh-huh. Did you hear about his father?"

"Yes, your mother told me. She and Viveca are driving up for the funeral this weekend. Obituary said he was ninety-seven."

"Yeah, he was such a sweet old guy. I talked to him and Joe for quite a while that day at the wedding until . . . well, you know. I was going to try and fly back for the funeral myself. For Joe's sake, you know? But I can't because of the shooting schedule. So I sent him and Shel this awesome food basket from Zingerman's. Bread, cheese, imported chocolates."

"And Shel is . . . ?"

"Joe's partner."

"Ah. Hey, speaking of your character's parentage, aren't Bianca and Dr. Amos both pretty WASP-ish? How is it that they have an almond-eyed daughter?"

"That's come up, actually. Makeup's been experimenting with me—de-emphasizing my Asian looks a little. And the writers will probably deal with it in some way. But come on, dude. Six months from now, I could find out that someone else is my father. Anything's possible in soap opera land."

"Apparently. So anyway, not to change the subject, but how's therapy going? You still thinking about quitting?"

"No. You know how you said I should stick with it a while longer? Well, I'm glad I did because at my last appointment, I had a kind of breakthrough." I ask her if it's anything she wants to tell me about. "Yeah, sure. It's about Mom. My unexpressed anger toward her, you know? Like, when she left you and hooked up with Viveca."

"Really? I knew that Andrew was angry about that. And Ariane at first. But I never realized you were."

"Because I was kind of burying it, I guess. I mean, Viveca was so nice to me. Taking me places, buying me things. And my drinking: I was burying it that way, too. But Dr. Klein helped me realize that when Mom left you, it triggered my own abandonment issues. That I was like projecting or something. It has to do with my childhood stuff."

"So you're saying you felt abandoned as a kid?" I know how *that* feels.

"Well, Andrew and Ariane always had that special twin thing, you know? That bond or whatever," Marissa says. "So I used to feel like the odd kid out sometimes. But it was really more about Mom than them."

"How so?"

"Because she was always so much about her work. Out on her scavenging trips. Down in the basement making art out of them. I'd call down the basement stairs, ask her to come up and make me my lunch, or come up and play a game with me or something. And she'd be like, 'Okay. Just give me ten more minutes.' And then it would be like an hour or more."

"Yeah, well, don't give *me* a free pass. I was just as much of a workaholic as she was."

"Yeah, Dr. Klein asked me about that. But you were away at your job, so that never bothered me. But Mom was at *home*, you know? All she had to do was come upstairs. And this one time? She told me about how Ari and Andrew were a planned pregnancy, but I was an accident."

"A *happy* accident," I tell her. "You were her baby, Marissa. She was just as crazy about you as she was with your sister and brother."

"Yeah, I know. But it was like I had to compete with her art. I'm just saying it was something I *felt*. Not all the time. Just sometimes. But hey, I made out better than her first kid. Right? The one she miscarried." Annie's first pregnancy was another of the secrets she'd kept from me. That one didn't come out until last year, during one of those family sessions we had over the phone with Annie and her shrink. It was the roughest of those conference calls, especially after Marissa disclosed in tears that she'd had an abortion, too. "So yeah," she says now. "I'm still seeing Dr. Klein. He says I'm making progress."

"Sounds like it. Well, good. Keep up the good work. And what about your recovery. How's that going?"

"Great! I'm getting my three-month chip next week."

"Hey, that's wonderful, honey. I'm proud of you."

"Yeah, thanks. Kieran's going to try to rearrange his schedule so he can give it to me. Because he was the one who got me to my first meeting."

"And how's everything going on the Kieran front?"

"Awesome, Daddy. God, if someone had told me a year ago that

I'd be going out with an *actor*, I would have laughed in their face. But Kieran's like the total opposite of most of those narcissistic jerks. His sobriety date's coming up pretty soon, too. He'll have four years. We've been talking lately about my moving in with him when my lease is up in November."

"Really? Big step. You sure you're ready?"

"Pretty sure. Not totally sure yet. We'll see. But we're *good* together, you know? This is the longest relationship I've ever been in."

"Well, that says something. I liked him that weekend you guys came to visit. But proceed with caution. Okay?"

When I look up, the ghost is standing in the doorway again, a sandwich in one hand, a Diet Coke in the other. I point to my desk and she brings them in, puts them down. There's a Post-it on the plate along with the sandwich, reminding me that the transport van is picking me up in another forty minutes. I nod. She nods back and leaves, quiet as a cat. She's nice enough, this new one, but something of an enigma. Well, it's only been a week. I'm sure we'll get to know each other. When I refocus on what Marissa's saying, she's talking about Annie and Viveca's trip to Greece.

"Yeah, they finally get to go on that wedding trip they've been postponing for three years, thanks to me. I've always felt bad about that."

"Well, you shouldn't, Daddy. Mom *wanted* to be there for you. One thing I've learned in my program is that guilt is a wasted emotion, you know? Look back on the past but don't stare." She speaks in these recovery aphorisms all the time now, I've noticed. Day by day. You can't breathe the past or the future, only the present. And as long as she lives by them, fine. But it's like she said the last time we talked: all this newfound happiness of hers rests on a single shot glass that she could pick up in a weak moment. Sabotage herself. It wouldn't be the first time she's done that.

"So what's new with you, dude?" she asks.

"Me? Same old same old: writing, physical therapy. Oh, I've got a new home health care aide. That's new."

"Yeah, I didn't think that was Carmen who answered the phone."

"Carla, you mean? No, she gave her notice a few weeks ago. Moving down to Georgia where her daughter lives. Can't believe how quiet it's been around here since she left."

"Yeah, she was a talker, huh? How's the new one working out?"

"So far so good. She's reserved. Kind of shy, I guess."

"Oh. You know, Mom and Viveca are losing their housekeeper, too."

"Are they?" I grab my soda. Take a sip. Take a bite of my sandwich. Marissa says there was a shooting at their housekeeper's building— that the victim was an eighteen-year-old boy who used to babysit for her son. Got mixed up with a gang, Rissa says. "So Minnie and Africa are moving out of Newark. She has a grown son in Massachusetts and they're going to live with him and his family." The sandwich is liverwurst and Swiss. Mayonnaise instead of the mustard I asked for, but hey. Everyone's got a learning curve. "So, dude, how's your book coming?"

I take another sip of my soda. Swallow. "Good, thanks. I've got all the chapters of the first part outlined. Now I'm starting to flesh them out. I'm waiting for something I ordered on Amazon to get here. A book of oral histories from Chinese immigrants back during that period. I'm looking for specifics. It's all in the details, you know? I was going to tell it chronologically at first. Start with my grandfather's childhood. But now I think the first chapter's going to be about his voyage over here. His misconceptions about where he's headed, his fears of the unknown. And then I'll have him flash back to all that earlier stuff. The backstory, as we authors call it." We authors: I'm being ironic because I'm such a rookie at this, but Marissa doesn't pick up on it.

"Cool," she says. "Hey, dude? I better get off now. Kieran's coming over to help me run my lines for tomorrow's taping and I'm not even dressed yet."

"Yeah, I have to go, too. I've got a one thirty appointment over at the rehab place. Say hi to Kieran for me. And hey, congrats again on your good news. Love you, kiddo."

"Love you, too, Daddy. Hey, tell Ari to call me. I'd ask you to tell

Andrew, too, but it would be wasted breath. I finally got him on Twitter, but half the time he doesn't even answer my tweets."

"Well, he's pretty busy at work."

"No one's that busy, Dad. Okay, bye."

I turn off the phone and sit there, smiling. Marissa had us worried for a while, but she seems to be doing so well these days. Three months sober, a contract extension, a steady boyfriend who's not a jerk. I just hope it lasts. That it's not just a house of cards. I think about my last appointment with poor Seamus, how upbeat he sounded just before he ended his life. But Marissa seems much more mature lately. Annie and I have both noticed it. Why worry about something that might not ever happen?

Half an hour later, I've eaten, moved my bowels and emptied my bladder, gotten rediapered. The toilet stuff's still a little awkward with this new aide, but that will pass. By the time the transport van honks out in the driveway, I'm in my chair and ready to go. She comes up behind me, releases the brake, and wheels me out the door and down the ramp.

Ah, Larry's driving today—the retired cop. Good. He's got a lot more personality than the other, younger ones. "New girl, Doc?" he says. Then to her, "I can take him from here. What's your name, sweetheart?" I can't see her face, but she's probably blushing. Between her shyness and the fact that she's white-haired and fifty or sixty pounds overweight, I'm guessing she hasn't been called "sweetheart" for a while. She tells him her name and he takes hold of the chair. "Just like that old movie, huh? *Johnny Belinda*. That was just on this past weekend. The wife and I watched it. I forget the name of the gal who played her. The one who was married to Ronald Reagan."

"Jane Wyman," she says.

"Yeah, there you go. Jane Wyman. You an old movie fan, too?"

"Yes." That's all he gets out of her. Just a yes.

Larry wheels me onto the lowered ramp and hits the switch. It beeps, I rise. He rolls me into the van, locks the chair in place, and gets back in front. We're off. In another twenty minutes, I'll be doing my arm crank ergometry and resistance training exercises. Not much fun but necessary for my arterial functioning, as Paula reminds me whenever I complain.

"So I was telling the wife about you last time I drove you," Larry tells me, glancing in the rearview mirror. "She said she remembered when it was on the news about your assault. Asked me if they ever caught the son of a bitch who clobbered you. I told her I didn't know but that I'd ask you."

"Yeah, they got him and the girlfriend a couple of months after it happened. They had tried pulling the same deal in Boston, up on Beacon Hill. That was their specialty: preying on temporary residents, people who'd sublet. They'd pass themselves off as brother-and-sister housecleaners helping out their sick mother. But the couple in Boston was smarter than I was. Got suspicious and notified the cops. They caught them in the act, hauling out antiques."

"Put them away, I hope."

"Yeah, he just got sentenced a few months ago. She made a deal with the prosecutor. Testified against him and got off with a lighter sentence. He was the one they really wanted to nail, which they did. He got twenty-five years."

"And you get the rest of your life to live with what he did to you, huh? They should have put the son of a bitch away for good."

"Yeah, well . . ."

"You testify?" I tell him I did. "And how'd that go?"

"It was . . . challenging. Having to face him in court."

"Couldn't they have videotaped you instead?"

"Nope. Law says he had the right to face his accuser."

"Was the bastard able to look you in the eye?"

"On and off, yeah." Jesus, Larry, keep *your* eyes on the road, will you? "Not when the prosecutor had me describe my ordeal after the attack. The fact that they had to put me in a medical-induced coma until the cranial swelling went down. Open up my back so they could get the bone fragments out. They delayed the trial for over two years because I couldn't remember a lot of it at first. But as time went by, more and more of it came back. So between my testimony and the girlfriend's . . ."

"And what about your paralysis? They think the rehab's going to help you get the hell out of that chair eventually?"

"Afraid not. The blow I took injured me above the ninth thoracic vertebra. T-nine, they call it. So that left me with what they call a 'complete' SCI."

"What's an SCI?"

"Spinal cord injury." I forget that not everyone's as well versed in the lingo as I've gotten to be. "There was an outside chance during the first several months that I might regain some of what I lost. But as time went on, it became less and less likely. So what you see is what I got. There are some experimental treatments that they're trying to develop—stem cell transplants, something called 'spine cooling.' So maybe somewhere down the line."

"Yeah, especially with Obama at the wheel. Right? Wasn't Bush against stem cell research?"

"Uh-huh. But federal funding's still pretty limited from what I've read. I haven't given up hope, but I'm not holding my breath either."

"Well, I got to hand it to you, Doc. If it was me, I doubt I'd be as good-natured about it as you are."

I chuckle. "Yeah, well, you should have seen me the first year or so. Nobody accused me of being good-natured back then. And not just about the paralysis, either. Brain injuries can land you in some pretty dark places. Mine sure as hell did."

"Huh." He stops talking after that. It's something I've noticed since the paralysis: you mention depression and it's a conversation killer. Not like when I was in practice. The college kids I saw were always talking about how depressed they were—wallowing in it, some of them. Well, I've done a fair amount of wallowing, too. That first year, especially. I think back to those early tests they did to see if there was any chance that my bladder and bowel function, sexual function, might be coming back. Those pinprick tests to see if I had any feeling in my anus, my penis. *Feel anything just then?*

No.

How about now?

No, nothing.

God, that first year—the worst year of my life. The headaches, the mood swings. My speech was slurred, my memory was compromised. I'd get frustrated because of the disorientation, so then I'd get depressed. Combative. The medical staff, the rehab folks, even the poor janitors who'd come in to mop the floor: whoever would show up in my room wouldn't know from one hour to the next if they were going to have to deal with an ogre or a sad sack. Or Rip Van Winkle. I'd go into deep sleeps sometimes that they'd have to wake me up out of. Then I'd get pissed when they did. Tell them to get the hell out of my room. Leave me alone so that I could get back to sleep. Dream that I could still walk, still run even. I haven't had those kind of dreams for a while now, come to think of it. Guess you'd call that resignation.

But I was lucky, in a way. When they did those initial CT scans up in Boston, they found out that when he clobbered me over the head, my brain had collided with the wall of my skull, but there were no bone fragments floating around in there. If there had been, they would have had to crack open my noggin to get them out. So I caught a break there....

Still, those dark, ugly depressions I kept falling into: that was tough. And not just for me, either. Poor Annie. She was the one who took the brunt of those moods of mine. Just married, and instead of being in New York with Viveca on the weekends, she'd drive up to Boston and stay with me. And not just weekends, either. Sometimes she'd come up on a Wednesday or a Thursday and stay until the following Monday. When the kids visited, I'd try and fake it for their sake. Act positive. But it was taxing, putting on those performances. And after they left, I'd take it out on their mother. Let her have it with both barrels sometimes, as if she was the one who had come at me with that goddamned vacuum cleaner.

I think back to the worst time, the one I'm most ashamed of. It was before Ariane had decided to move back and have the baby here. Before Andrew had made the decision not to re-up. Thanks to Annie, the house had been made handicap-accessible so that I could finally leave that goddamned rehab place I hated and move back home. The ramp outside, the bathroom and kitchen rails, the chair lift so that I could get upstairs, sleep in my room again. Annie'd let her own work go. Had lived back at the house for weeks while she researched equipment, got estimates, hired a contractor and supervised the installations. She was doing my bills, too. Dealing with those arrogant insurance pricks so that I wouldn't have to. Sometimes she'd be on the phone with them for an hour or more. Cajoling them, demanding that they cover this or that, writing letters when they said they wouldn't. Those first two years, she was more like my wife again than my *ex*-wife. She was great to do all that. You'd have thought I'd be grateful. And I *was* grateful when my head was clear. When those dark clouds of gloom would part for an hour or an afternoon and I'd show her a little appreciation. . . .

The fight started the afternoon she got back from dropping Andrew off at the airport. He had come in from Fort Hood for a long weekend. Had called me earlier that week and said he needed to talk to me. *I know you're dealing with all of your own shit, Dad, but if I don't talk to someone, my head's going to explode.* But then, once he was here, he kept *not* telling me and I kept waiting. In fairness, others were around: his mother, my aide, a couple of my old colleagues from the college who had stopped by to see how I was doing. I could tell that something was seriously wrong with Andrew. He'd lost weight. He seemed distracted, edgy. Had trouble making eye contact with both Annie and me. I thought it was odd that he kept going out to the backyard, wandering down the path. . . .

And then, the day he was going back—a couple of hours before it was time for him to head to the airport, time was running out. Carla had left for the day, Ariane was at work, and Annie had gone off to pick up some groceries. It was finally just the two of us. He was sitting slumped in front of the TV, staring at a Celtics game. I told him to turn it off and tell me what the hell was going on—to say what he had flown across the country to say. He looked at me for the next several seconds. Then he aimed the remote and turned off the TV. "When Mom was a little girl?" he began. "After she lost her mother and sister in that flood they were in? You know that cousin who saved her?"

"Uh-huh. I can't remember his name, but—"

"Kent," he said.

"That's right. Kent. What about him?" I waited.

"I'm going to . . . I have to tell you about something Mom told me the day of the wedding. And about something no one else knows about. Something I did that day. And I'm . . . Don't stop me, okay? Because I have to get this all out and I don't . . . Just don't stop me until I'm finished. Okay?"

I nodded. Sat there listening in disbelief.

When he was done, the two of us had just sat there, Andrew sobbing with his hand over his mouth, me trying to get my head around everything he'd just confessed and, at the same time, looking at his suffering, wracking my compromised brain to think of something—anything—to say that might take away his pain. . . .

"Dad, it's like this living nightmare that never lets go of me. I'll be at the barracks, in the shower or lying in bed, and I'll start thinking about it: how I killed him and got away with it. Up to this point, anyway. But it could still happen. Someone might put two and two together and . . . It's just so not who I ever thought I'd be, Dad. A killer, a murderer."

I want to interrupt him, object to what he's saying about himself, but how can I refute it? There's a body hidden down in back inside that well. My son has taken a life.

"I can't eat, can't sleep for shit. And sometimes when I finally do fall asleep, I dream about him. Dream he's alive again, and I'm chasing him, catching up to him—not out in the woods where it happened, but down some street I don't recognize. Or down the corridors of some strange hospital or school or something. . . . At work? I'll be busy with a patient and it'll just come over me. I'll see him sitting out on the front steps that morning when I went back for the rings. See his head flopped to the side, that rock smeared with his blood. And they've started to notice—the docs I work with. I've gotten warnings from two different supervisors. Dr. Champy chewed me out when I got mixed up about the schedule and didn't show up for my shift until after they called. He asked me if I had a drug problem—if that was what was wrong with me. And Dr. Sanders wrote me up after I screwed up some patient's meds. I'm becoming a liability at that place, Dad. I just don't think I can hold it together

anymore. I'm falling apart. I think I'm going to have to tell someone."

And that's when I finally think of something useful to say. "You just did tell someone, Andrew. You told your father. And I want you to promise me that you're not going to tell anyone else. You hear me? Don't you tell another fucking soul."

He just sits there staring at me, not saying anything.

"When it starts getting to you, you're going to pick up the phone and call me. Okay? If you can't sleep, I don't care what the hell time it is, you call me. If it hits you at work? You tell them you need to take a quick break, get yourself out of everyone else's earshot, and dial my number. And I'll answer it, I promise you. From now on, I'll keep my cell with me at all times, no matter where I am. No matter what I'm doing. And when it rings, I'll see that it's you and pick up. Talk you back down from the ledge if you're panicking. Okay? But you have to promise me, Andrew. Not another fucking soul. Not your supervisors, not some buddy of yours, not your mother or your sisters. And most of all, not the police. I'm the only one you should talk to about this. I need you to promise me that."

Fifteen seconds go by, thirty. He's trembling, crying again. And then finally, mercifully, he looks at me and nods. "Yeah, okay, Dad. I promise. . . ."

Larry's just said something up front. I don't know what. "Don't you think so, Doc?" He's looking back at me, waiting for a response.

"Yup," I tell him. "You've got that right. . . ."

Later that afternoon, while she's driving him to the airport, it turns dark outside. Starts raining. It's only three, four o'clock, but it gets as dark as dusk. And the weather inside my head has shifted, too. Those dark clouds have descended, and the fear I've been feeling for my son has curdled into anger. And Annie is who I'm angry with. What he did that day— the way he ran out of there to avenge her, the way he's been suffering ever since—it all comes back to rest on her. It's fucking pathological is what it is. The way she kept me in the dark all those years and then dumped it all out on him. Made our son her confessor. And now his life is ruined, and she's the one who ruined it.

I'm at the front window, staring out at the rain, when I see her drive up. Hear the car door slam. She comes in, takes off her wet coat, shakes

it out on the foyer floor. "Oh, hi," she says. "I didn't see you sitting there.
Boy, it's miserable out. You okay?"

"Yup."

"He checked with the airline on our way up. His flight was on time, so
I guess he's off. I'm going to start supper now. Leftovers okay?"

"Yes." I'm seething. Waiting.

"Orion, can you come in the kitchen with me while I'm getting things
ready? I kind of want to talk to you about Andrew." I tell her I want to
talk with her, too. She's just not going to like what I have to say.

When I wheel myself in there, she's at the fridge, pulling things out.
Her back is turned to me. "Something's up with him," she says. "I think
he's withholding something."

It's not funny—quite the opposite—but I laugh. "Well, he's learned
how to do that from the best, hasn't he?"

She glances over her shoulder at me. "I don't . . . What do you mean?"

"I mean that you're the friggin' queen of withholding. All those secrets
you were so good at keeping when we were married. The way your sister
died that night, what your cousin did to you when you were a kid. Kind
of made the whole marriage a sham, don't you think?"

She stops what she's doing. Turns around and faces me. "How did
you—"

"Because he just told me how you vomited out all your ugly little se-
crets to him that day. Burdened him with all the dirty little things you
never bothered to tell me about."

She looks stunned. Good. She deserves to be. "Orion, I don't really
want to go into all that with you right now. I wish I hadn't told An-
drew that day, but it is what it is. And Millie's been helping me sort
through—"

"Millie? Oh, right. Your shrink. Tell me something, will you? I'm
curious. Have you come clean to her about the abuse yet?" She nods,
mumbles something about how what her cousin did to her is at the crux
of her therapy. "No, no. Not that abuse. I mean the way you used to abuse
our son."

She stares at me, blank-faced. She keeps blinking.

"Pushing him down the stairs so that he ended up with a broken

wrist. Clunking him on the head with a mallet. And Jesus, those were just the things they told me about."

"They?" she says.

"Our kids, Annie. Ariane, mostly. The other two were pretty close-mouthed about it. Still covering for you all these years later. Ari didn't want to tell me either, but I got it out of her. Jesus, you were all about secrets, lies of omission. Weren't you?"

"Orion, can you please just stop now? Because I'm starting to feel like I'm being attacked."

"Speaking of which, you really lucked out that time you clobbered him on the head, huh? No concussion, no TBI. That would have really fucked up your secret-keeping, wouldn't it have?"

She wipes her hands on her apron. Comes over and sits down at the table. "Orion, what's going on here? Where is all this anger coming from?"

"From the gut. That's where. When they came up to see me at Viveca's place that weekend? Before your big gay wedding? That's when I found out. Why'd you do it, Annie? Pick him out of the herd? Make him your victim instead of the girls? Or me?"

She's blinking back tears now. "I didn't . . . I have a temper, Orion. You know that. And sometimes he would—"

"Right. You've got a temper and he's got a penis. Was that what was at the bottom of it? The fact that, of the three of them, it was your male child you needed to victimize?"

"I . . . Stop psychoanalyzing me. And stop making it sound like it was premeditated, because . . . because it wasn't like that. He'd get my goat, press my buttons and I'd just go off. Get a little crazy. And then, afterward, I'd come to my senses and . . . I felt ashamed about those things I did, Orion. Ashamed and guilty."

"But not guilty enough to let me know, apparently. And boy, the kids were in your corner, too, huh? You'd victimize him and then the three of them would feel sorry for you. Close ranks around you, like you were the one who needed to be protected. Wasn't that how it went down, Annie? Poor Mama. She can't help it. She didn't know what she was doing."

"I didn't know! That's what I'm trying to tell you. I'm not justifying it but—"

"*We better not tell Daddy, though. We have to protect her from him. Because he might actually do something. Get her some treatment. Protect us from her rampages.*"

She shakes her head. "*They didn't need to be protected from me. I had my moments, yes, but I was a good mother. I love my kids, Andrew just as much as the girls.*"

"*You think they got off scot-free after all those deceptions you involved them in, Annie? You think they didn't grow up scarred because of all those fucking secrets of yours? Hey, and speaking of secrets, how about the fact that you're a lesbian. That was another thing you kept from me, huh? Boy, that one was a doozy.*"

"*Okay, stop it. Just—*"

"*And me, I was so fucking clueless. Jesus, you'd think a shrink would have been smart enough to catch on after a while, but nope. Not me. I mean, sometimes while I was making love to you, inside of you, I'd open my eyes and look at you. And you'd have that far-off expression like you were someplace else. Like you couldn't wait for me to finish.*"

She shakes her head. "*You're wrong. It wasn't like that for me.*"

"*No? Really? Then how come, nine times out of ten, the only way I could bring you to an orgasm was when I went down on you? Who were you imagining was down there, Annie? What woman were you fantasizing about as you came?*"

She unties her apron and throws it onto the table. Starts to leave the room, then turns around and tries to wound me back. "*I don't care how badly hurt you were up there on the Cape, or how bitter you've become because of it,*" she says. "*I am not going to stand here and have you accuse me unfairly. . . . I come here to help you, Orion. Not so that you can hurl all of these accusations at me. Put me on trial for things that—*"

"*That day you told him about what your cousin did to you? When it was just you and Andrew up there in that room? That was a form of abuse, too. Wasn't it, Annie?*"

"*Stop it! He guessed what Kent did. That's why I told him.*"

"*And then he storms out of there, does what he does, and now—*"

"*What do you mean? He stormed out and did what?*"

"*Nothing. He just . . . Just get out of here, will you? Get in your car and go back to your wife, because it's making me sick to even look at you.*"

I'm not sparing her to be kind. I'd love to hit her with it right about now. She caused it, didn't she? He killed him because of her. She deserves to suffer. It's my son I'm sparing, not her. "*Not another living soul,*" *I told him. And that goes for me, too. If I tell her, she could tell Viveca. Tell his sisters. The more people who know, the more danger he'd be in. The more likely . . .* "*I mean it, Annie. I don't need you to come here every weekend and play nursemaid. In fact, I'd prefer you don't anymore. Just leave. Pack your bag and get the fuck back to New York. Just go.*"

She leaves the room—to do as I've just said, I figure. But I'm wrong. A minute later, she's back in the doorway. "*I am not leaving until tomorrow morning when your aide shows up for her shift,*" *she says.* "*That's the plan, and that's what I'm going to do. But I'm going upstairs now because I don't want to look at you either. I just want to go up and be by myself and try not to think of the things you've just said to me.*"

"*Why not? Because the truth hurts?*"

She doesn't take the bait. An annoying calm has come over her. "*I will leave my door open. Call up the stairs when you want to go to bed. I'll help you get ready, and then I'll stay the night like I planned. You can ring your bell if you need me for anything during the night, the same as always. Because no matter what you've said, what you've accused me of, I am not going to leave you by yourself. No matter how hurtful you've been, I am staying because you need someone to stay.*"

"*Because I'm a fucking gimp? A pathetic cripple that you can condescend to?*"

"*I didn't say that, Orion. You did. Now is there anything you need before I go up?*"

I'm already starting to regret my cruelty toward her, but I sure as hell am not going to apologize. Not yet anyway. I'm just relieved I didn't get so furious with her that I used it as a weapon against her: what he did, where he hid the body.

"*My cell phone,*" *I tell her.* "*It's on the windowsill in the front room. I put it there before when I was looking out at the rain.*" *She asks me who I have to call. "No one. I just want to have it in case someone needs to call me." She gives me a long, inquisitive look, then goes and gets the phone. Comes back, hands it to me, and leaves without another word. I listen to her footsteps on the stairs. . . .*

Why hadn't I laid what Andrew had done at her feet? I mean, she was damned good at keeping secrets. That was her specialty. What was the real reason I hadn't drawn her into it? Maybe because, in spite of everything that had happened, how angry I was at her that day, I was still trying to save her. Still trying to rescue the girl at the dry cleaner's with the flat tire. Wasn't that *my* specialty? Rescuing people? Siobhan, the psych patient, the night when I saved her from choking. All those college kids, up to and including Jasmine that night when she barged into my office because her ex-boyfriend was stalking her. . . .

Maybe that afternoon when I finally *did* confront Annie, spewed all that venom at her, I stopped short of telling her about that body hidden down there in the well because I still loved her. Is that what love is all about for me? Protecting people? Keeping them safe? Or has that always been more about my ego? Pat yourself on the back, Orion. Take a bow, Mr. Knight in Shining Armor. But I wasn't able to save Seamus from slipping a noose around his neck that night and jumping into the stairwell at his dorm. Was too oblivious to save my son from his mother's attacks. Maybe if I had, he wouldn't have developed such a hair-trigger temper himself. Wouldn't have gone after him that day and—no, don't go there again. What good has second-guessing myself about it ever done? . . . *Promise me you're not going to tell anyone else. You hear me? Don't you tell another fucking soul.* I was trying to protect him. Save him from being arrested, convicted, and sent to prison. How many times have I second-guessed myself? Wondered if maybe he *should have* gone to the police? Paid for his crime? Or not. I still haven't been able to decide if I helped him that day or gave him the wrong advice. . . .

But anyway, in the weeks and weekends after I confronted Annie, we made our peace. I apologized for the things I'd said, she for the things she'd done and hadn't done—the secrets she'd kept. I hadn't scared her away after all. And so she had kept returning to the home we had shared so that she could help me. It was ironic, really. Annie had somehow become a better, more honest and forgiving wife than when we were married. So maybe *that's* what love means. Having the capacity to forgive the one who wronged you, no matter how deep the hurt was. At any rate, I'm glad she doesn't know about the corpse that's down there in that well. I've spared her that much.

Up front, Larry's begun talking again. "I'm just curious, Doc. You don't mind my asking, do you?" He's looking at me in the rearview again.

"I'm sorry, Larry. I was someplace else just now. Do I what?"

"Belong to a church."

"Me? No. I'm not religious."

"No? So while you were going through your ordeal, you never prayed?"

"No. Can't say that I did." Who was I going to pray to? Some god I never believed in in the first place? But I'm not about to get into a theological discussion with him.

"Because that's what helped *me* out when I got cancer. Not that what I was up against was as bad as what you went through. I'm not saying that. But once I got done being pissed off at God, I started getting down on my knees and asking for His help. And it worked, you know? So far, anyway. I been cancer free for seven years now."

"Yeah? Good for you."

"Yup. The power of prayer. You can't beat it, far as I'm concerned."

He means well, but I'm in no mood for his proselytizing, so I change the subject. "Looks like we're a little ahead of schedule. Why don't you pull into that Dunkin' Donuts up ahead? Let me buy you a coffee?"

"Sounds good, Doc," he says. "But only if *I'm* buying. And don't give me an argument, either. I insist."

Fifteen minutes later, we've had our caffeine and he's wheeling me into rehab. Paula, the therapist I work with, is out front talking with the receptionist. "Well, look who's here," she says. "How are you doing today, handsome?"

"Handsome." "Sugar." "Sweetheart." I used to resent this chummy familiarity. Just because I couldn't walk or park myself on the toilet seat anymore, they didn't need to condescend to me. But after a while, I realized they were just being friendly, not assuming that my TBI had rendered me stupid. "Handsome, huh? Which one of us you talking to? Me or him?"

She looks from me to Larry and winks. "Oh, both of you cutie pies," she quips. I crane my neck back at Larry. Tell him he'd better go back out to the van and get his shovel so we can deal with this bullshit she's slinging.

They both laugh. "Speak for yourself, Doc," Larry says. "Me, I can't wait to get up every morning because I get better-looking every day."

"Oh, brother," Paula says. "Well, what do you say, Orion? You ready for your workout?"

"Ready as I'll ever be." I sigh. And with that, she rolls me into the torture chamber. Sandie's working with an amputee who's gotten a prosthetic leg and Kathy's passing a beach ball back and forth with a gray-haired woman with a contorted face. Stroke, I figure.

The transport guys? They don't wait for you. They drop you off, then move on to their next assignment. After your appointment's over, the receptionist calls the company for a pickup and you sit and wait. Patience is a virtue, my mother always used to say, and if that's the case, I guess I must be pretty virtuous by now, whether I pray or not. Paula added a few new exercises this time, and I struggled with them. I'm spent. Itching to get home and maybe grab a nap. But by the time Javier, one of the younger drivers, strolls in, I've been parked and waiting for over an hour like a bag of groceries. It's futile to complain, so I keep my mouth shut. "Hey there, Javier. How's it going?"

"Going good," he says. Whistling, he releases the brake and wheels me out into the midafternoon sunshine. He spends most of the drive home mumbling into his cell phone. They're not supposed to use them unless it's the dispatcher who's called. But I'm guessing that's not who he's talking to, unless the dispatcher's name is Babe. "Yeah, I hear you, babe. I'm just saying. . . ."

When we get to Jailhouse Hill, he signals and takes the turn. Halfway up the hill, we pass a kid learning to master her two-wheeler, her dad running alongside her. Twenty years ago, that was Ariane and me. Her brother got the hang of it right away, but not Ari. Skinned knees, tears . . .

Javier pulls into the driveway. Hops out. As he's lowering my chair to the ground, I see my aide coming around from the backyard. It's the second time this week that she's done that. A couple of days ago, I looked out and saw her coming up the path from down where the cottage is. Makes me uneasy that she might be poking around down there. Not that I think she suspects anything, or that she'd be able to lift off that granite slab. And Andrew says if anyone did go nosing around, look down the well, all they'd see is rocks and cement. But still. What's drawing her back there? "Getting a little fresh air?" I ask her as she approaches us. She nods. Looks a little guilty unless it's my imagination, which it very well might be. Still, I'd better keep an eye on her. Or call up the agency and tell them she's not working out. I won't say anything to Andrew, though. He's jumpy enough about what's back there. No need to get him worked up over nothing.

Javier drives off and she wheels me around to the front. Pushes the chair up the ramp and inside. She asks me if I'm going back to work. "Nah, I think I'll just watch a little TV—see what my buddy Dr. Oz has to say today. You start supper yet?" She says she's got something simmering in the Crock-Pot. Asks if Andrew's coming over to eat tonight. "Not that I know of. It'll just be Ariane, Dario, and me."

As if on cue, Ari and her boy burst through the front door. She's carrying the mail in one arm, his backpack in the other. "Package for you, Dad," she says. "Looks like something from Amazon."

"Oh, good. I've been waiting for a book I ordered." I turn to my grandson. "Hey there, buddy. What's up?" He holds up something he made in day care: a drawing with crayon scribbles and glued-on doo-dads. "Wow, this is cool," I tell him. "You're an artist just like Grandma. Do you think we should send this to her and Grandma Viveca?" (Gamma and Gamma Bibeca, he calls them. I'm Bumpa.)

He shakes his head. Says it's for me.

"Is it? Gee, thanks. Then maybe we should put it on the refrigerator, huh?" He nods emphatically, crawls up onto my lap. This kid has done more for my recovery than all the doctors and therapists combined. I ask his mother how things went at the group home today. Chaotic, she says. "Business as usual, eh?" She rolls her eyes and smiles. Ari loves her work, though. She's crazy about those Down syndrome adults she supervises. Last year she did some fund-raising and took them all to Disney World.

"Come on, kiddo," she tells Dario. "Let's put you in a clean pair of big boy pants." When he whines that he wants to stay down here with Bumpa, she reminds him that he had an accident in the car and needs to get changed. His toilet training's going pretty well overall, but he's still having slip-ups from time to time. He slides off my lap and follows his mother out of the room.

It's funny how things have worked out. The way my two daughters have exchanged coasts. Marissa's moved out to California and Ariane's come back home. Eight months pregnant when she finally made that decision. Thank god I hadn't sold this place after all. I'd taken it off the market even before Andrew told me what had happened the day of the wedding.

Out in the hallway, I hear Dario talking to "Bewinda." They've really taken to each other, those two. The only time I see her smile is when he's around. I remarked the other day how good she is with him. Asked her if she had any kids of her own. She said no. No children, never married—that she took care of her mother until she died and then went into home health care. Guess I'll hold off for a while on calling the agency. So what if she's wandering around the property? I'm sure it's got nothing to do with that well.

"Dr. Oh?" she says. I jump a little. Like I said, she moves around here like a ghost. "Can I get you anything?" She's got the feather duster in her hand.

"No thanks, Belinda. I'm good."

She nods, then heads toward the living room. She dusts that room more than any of the others, I've noticed. Noticed, too, how she always stops and looks at that painting over the fireplace—the only one of Joe Jones's that I've held on to. I wheel myself out of the den and join her in there.

"What do you think?" I ask her. "You like that painting?" She nods. When I tell her it's Adam and Eve beneath the Tree of Life, she nods. Says she reads her Bible every night and every morning. "You know, the artist who painted it has a connection to this place. You've seen that dilapidated old cottage down in back, on the other side of the brook? He used to live out there once upon a time. He and his brother. They worked for the builder who lived in this house."

"Oh," she says. "He did?"

"Uh-huh. Josephus Jones. That's him in the painting. Adam, I mean. It's a self-portrait. He put himself in a lot of his paintings."

"Oh." What's she looking so uncomfortable about?

"Sad story, really. He died young. Left a lot of his paintings behind, in that cottage. Never could interest anyone in them while he was alive, but now his work has gotten pretty valuable. Before his time, maybe. I've sold most of the paintings that were down there. I could have gotten a lot for this one, too. It's the largest one he ever did, far as anyone knows. But I couldn't quite bring myself to part with it. Kind of figured it belonged here rather than in a museum or in someone's private collection."

She opens her mouth to speak, then stops herself. "You looked like you were about to say something just then," I note.

She looks back at the painting. "I knew him," she says.

"Jones? Really? How?"

She says she used to work downtown in the library when she was in high school, and that he would come in to read the newspapers and magazines. And that he'd talk with her when she was working the front desk.

"No kidding. What was he like?"

"He was a nice man. Very kind."

"So you were friends?"

She shakes her head. "I just knew him from the library. That's all."

"From what I heard, there was some speculation about how he

died—whether or not it was an accident. Some suspicion that some-one might have killed him. Ever hear anything along those lines?" She shakes her head. She's got that same guilty look she had earlier when I saw her coming back up the path. The feather duster's shaking in her hand. "This is probably just idle gossip, but I heard somewhere along the way that they suspected his brother might have done him in. That the brother's wife lived down there at the cottage with them, and there might have been some hanky-panky going on between her and Joe. And that the brother—"

"Excuse me, but I better go check on dinner," she says. Looking more upset than guilty now, she rushes out of the room.

I sit there, thinking. Wondering. Is that why she's gone down in back those times? Because she knew Joe Jones? Maybe they *were* friends, and she just doesn't want to admit it. A lot of the locals around here are pretty set in their ways, about race along with everything else. It probably would have been frowned upon back when she was grow-ing up: a high school girl having a black man for a friend. I suddenly remember something the woman from her agency told me: that she was going to assign me someone else, but that Belinda asked her for this placement. She had told the boss that she'd grown up on Jail-house Hill and thought it would be nice to come back here to work. Were they neighbors, her and Joe? And if so, why wouldn't she have told me that?

"Dr. Oh?" Jesus, she's just done it again—appeared out of nowhere and spooked me.

"Yes?"

"There was nothing going on between him and his brother's wife. That was just a rumor." I look at her, studying her expression. She looks defensive, maybe even angry.

"Oh. Okay." I open my mouth to ask her how she knows, but before I can get my question out, she turns and goes. Subject closed. She's a mystery, this one. . . .

A few minutes later, I hear her and Dario in the kitchen, singing and playing. "Ashes, ashes. We all fall DOWN!" Laughter from both of them. That kid must be magical, that's all I can say. He pulled me out of the quicksand of my anger and depression. And now another miracle: he's made the ghost giggle.

That night, in bed, I start reading the book I got in the mail, underlining some of the best details, scribbling notes in the margins for later referral. Then I stop. Put the cap back on my pen and think about why I'm doing this. . . .

I had started writing during the long months of my recovery as a way of stimulating my brain and dealing with unfinished business. I'd been reflecting about my life, everything that had happened. And thinking back to my childhood—writing about it—I had run up against a familiar wall. Behind that wall, as impenetrable as ever, was Francis Oh. Who had he been, this father who had disowned me, denied my existence? She was exhausted the day she disclosed all this—three or four days before she died. . . .

"At first, he tried to deny that Francis was the father. How did I know this child was his son's? 'Because your son is the only man I've ever been with,' I told him. I could tell he believed me, but he still wouldn't tell me how to find Francis!" And so I reveal something that up until then I've been withholding from her: that, in one of my subsequent visits to Grandpa Oh's restaurant, he gave me my father's contact information. And that I had held on to it for years before I mustered up the courage to write to him. And when I finally did, my letter came back to me unopened a few weeks later with the word deceased *scrawled across the front. She stares at me for the next several seconds, then sighs and says, "Well, all right then. That ends that."*

But it hadn't ended it—not for me. He had escaped again, permanently this time—this father who had denied my existence, and whose existence I had denied in return as a defense mechanism. I hated him more than ever.

Yet in the months after my assault, when my brain functioning had returned and I faced the fact that my paralysis was permanent, I printed out that photo of the Oh family reunion my cousin had sent me, stared at the sober-looking boy in the striped shirt, and wrote down in a notebook the few things I knew about him: that he had been a skinny kid, a college student who'd studied math, and, later, had been an accountant. That he had liked gangster movies. Smoked Viceroys. When I put down my pen, I stared at the quarter of a page that my writing had taken up and the three-quarters of a page of blank space. It seemed hopeless. But then I picked up the pen again and scrawled a page and a half of questions about Francis Oh. What had his childhood been like? Had he enjoyed baseball and Big Band music? Why had he settled in Dayton, Ohio? Did he have other children? Not that she knew or her sister Doris knew of, Ellen had e-mailed back when I queried her about the possibility that I had half-siblings. Later, I bought an old Dayton city directory on eBay and found the listing for Francis and Alice Oh. No mention of offspring. Apparently, I was my father's one and only child.

Eventually, I came to believe that if I wanted to break through the fortress Francis Oh was hiding behind, then maybe the chink in the wall—no pun intended—was the grandfather I had known only slightly. I had two photographs of Henry Oh: the one taken shortly after he'd arrived in America and the one of him among his family at that California reunion. I also had my in-person memories of Grandpa Oh: his lined, unsmiling face. The way he would scan the open room of his big, noisy dim sum palace, overseeing his staff of dour waitresses wheeling their carts. The way he would stop tableside to chat with customers he knew, go back and forth through the swinging doors of the restaurant's kitchen.

But I'd been blocked for a while in my efforts to bring Grandpa Oh's story to life—jammed up to the point that I started thinking about giving up. Henry Oh began to seem as elusive as his son, Francis. But then I read an article in the *Times,* "Your Brain on Fiction," and what a gift! The article talked about studies that examined how the language of fiction—metaphors, sensory details, emotional fireworks between characters—activates different parts of a reader's brain. It said brain scientists at Emory and in Canada and Europe—Spain, I think it was—had studied the MRIs of subjects when they read fiction and found out that the olfactory cortex and the motor cortex were being stimulated in the same way as if these subjects were experiencing the real deal: smelling, feeling textures, running away from bad guys. And that narrative—the opportunity to get inside a character's head and think what he's thinking and feeling—takes the reader beyond the boundaries of his own experiences and hones his ability to empathize. I tore that article out of the paper, reread it a few times, and then bam! It hit me. What if, instead of writing *about* my grandfather, I *became* him? Traveled back in time and simulated his life as he was living it? And so I crossed over the border from nonfiction to fiction, and the floodgates opened up. I pinned that picture of Grandpa Oh my cousin had sent me to the bulletin board over my desk, the one of him when he was a pigtailed adolescent who'd just entered the country. Started tapping into his hopes and fears, his homesickness. And now it's a ritual. Every morning when I start my work, I stare into those dark eyes of his and ask him to take me back into his life. And most days, it works. Transports me into "the zone" so that, for the next two or three hours, I get to climb out of my own skin and into his. Zip it up the way Ariane zips Dario into his sleeper when she gets him ready for bed. My guess is that *my own* motor cortex and sensory cortex must be lighting up while I'm writing. Because the writer has to live the vicarious experience before the reader can. Right?

Is it any good, this novel I'm constructing? Will it ever get published? Probably not. But at least when I'm finished, a document will exist. Something that, should they ever want to pick it up and read it, my kids will be able to know that their ancestor was more than the stereotypical Chinaman who came here and worked hard to achieve his version of the American dream. Grandpa Oh looks so stoic and unreadable in that early photo, so unattainable. But I've gotten inside his head. I know him now—a version of him, at least. I can see behind those inscrutable eyes. And maybe this process will help me to come back full circle to my original goal. Help me to crack the mystery of my *own* inscrutable father—if not the factual Francis Oh, then a fictional construction of who he might have been. . . .

It's another big part of what saved me—pulled me out of my anger and despair about the brain stuff, the paraplegia. Not to mention the despair that Andrew's confession had left me with. I went down for the count for a while after he unburdened himself that day. Got stuck in a depression so dark and deep that it might as well have been *me* down there in that well. The SSRIs didn't touch it: Zoloft, Luvox, Lexapro. . . . After I gave Tracy her walking papers—told her I didn't *want* her to waste the rest of her life taking care of an invalid, and that in some ways I wished she hadn't even found me alive that night—I started flirting with the idea of suicide. Considered how I might do it, looked again and again at the Hemlock Society's Web site. I couldn't do it, though. Couldn't saddle my kids with the aftermath—Andrew, especially. I'd kept my promise to him. Kept that cell phone with me day and night. What if I did myself in, and a minute or so later, he called me? Needed my help? . . .

And hey, this may not be the kind of life I ever imagined for myself, but I'm resigned to the fact that it *is* a life. I've got my writing, my daughter and her son here with me, Andrew living nearby. Every morning when Dario comes into my bedroom sleepy-eyed and climbs up into bed with me—with his Bumpa—I thank my lucky stars that I'm still around. That that SOB up there on the Cape *didn't* kill me that day when he went after me, or that I *didn't* finish what he started when I thought there was no way out. That it was all just hopeless.

I get through another thirty or forty pages of *Chinese Immigration 1868–1892: Oral Histories*, then start to get drowsy. Put the book on the night table. I'll read some more in the morning before Annie and Viveca get here. Mr. Agnello's funeral is at ten, Annie said, so they'll be by sometime around noon and bring lunch. I'll have to remember to tell Viveca what Belinda said: that she knew Josephus Jones. Or maybe I shouldn't tell her. If I did, Viveca would want to speak to her, give her the third degree about him. And I don't think Belinda would appreciate . . . I don't think . . . I'm starting to doze. I reach over and turn out the light. That's enough for today. Get some sleep.

Chapter Twenty-Eight

Orion Oh

O rion?"

   "In here!"

     "Where's here?"

"I'm out in the sunroom." I glance at the clock. It's almost one thirty.

They enter, both of them in black, one as lovely as the other. "Sorry we're so late," Annie says. "Are you starving?"

"No, no. How was it?"

"Lovely," Viveca says. "The music, the eulogy his son gave. It was a wonderful tribute, very touching but humorous, too," Viveca says. "He obviously loved his father very much."

"We went out to the cemetery for the interment and were going to come over here from there," Annie says. "But when Joe invited us to the luncheon, he said he had set up a display—old family photos and several of Mr. Agnello's paintings. So I kind of wanted to see it. That's why we're so late."

"Not a problem," I tell her. "You ate then?" She says they didn't.

Viveca stands, suggests that Annie and I visit while she gets lunch ready. After she's out of earshot, I shoot Annie a look of mock surprise. "She cooks?"

"We picked up deli," she says. "Be nice. Where is everyone?"

"My aide has the rest of the day off, and Ariane and Dario went to some kiddie carnival at the mall. Andrew's working today, gets out at five. He's stopping over then."

Her smile fades away. "How's he doing?"

I shrug. "I'm not sure, really. He says he's okay, but other than going to work and going to the gym, he doesn't seem to have much of anything else. Except for the casino. He goes down there two or three times a week."

"By himself?"

"Far as I know."

She shakes her head. "Remember all the friends he used to have? Jay Jay, Josh, Luke. Those boys practically lived here."

"Well, most of those guys have left the area by now. Gotten married, had kids. Remember Patrick Stanton, Andrew's wrestling buddy? I ran into his dad at the bank a while ago. He told me Pat's started his own tourist business in Kenya. Runs wild game tours or something."

"Gee," she says. "What about Andrew's drinking? He was slurring his words the other night when I called him."

"I don't really know, Annie. He'll have a couple of beers when he's over here, but that's about it. Not sure what he does when he goes back to his place. But yeah, this lone wolf stuff worries me, too. The way he's isolating himself."

"And I take it he's not seeing anyone. Every time I ask him about girlfriends, he changes the subject."

"Nope, no girlfriends. Ariane tried to fix him up with someone she knows, but he told her no. I've talked to him about maybe getting on one of those matchmaking sites, but he says he's not interested."

"What do you think it's about? His broken engagement?"

"I doubt it. That was what? Three years ago? And the breakup was his decision, not hers." This is starting to make me uncomfortable, so I change the subject. "I tell you one thing, though. He's crazy about that nephew of his, and vice versa. When he comes over here for supper, Dario sticks to him like Velcro. Andrew got his old Matchbox cars down from the attic a while back, and the two of them will get down on the rug and play. Crash the cars into each other. Dario's really into those demolition derbies of theirs. Makes the sound effects. *Rrrum-rrrum, rrrum.* Crash!"

She smiles. "Boys will be boys."

Viveca appears in the doorway. "Either of you want coffee?"

"I do." We say it simultaneously. I tell her Belinda's set it up before she left. That all she has to do is hit the "on" button.

"Got it," Viveca says, then disappears.

"So how are things going with you two?" I ask Annie. Fine, she says. "Your trip to Greece is coming up pretty soon, huh? *Finally.*"

"Now don't start that again," she says. "There was no way I was going off on a trip abroad when things were so touch and go with you. Viveca either. She was worried about you, too."

I nod. "Worried enough to let me borrow you back that first year. I think you spent more time in the hospital and at that rehab place than you did with her. And I know from Marissa that it was an issue—all the time you were spending here. That there was even some talk about a separation."

"Well, we weathered that, Orion," she says. "Every marriage goes through its rough patches. You know that. In therapy? One of the things I had to work on—learn to put to rest—was my guilt about our comfortable lifestyle. The fact that I'd come from nothing and she hadn't. It was a roadblock between us that I had to take down. And Viveca is generous in her own way. But we're fine now. Better than we've ever been, in fact."

I nod, smile. "Well, I'll tell you one thing. She saved my ass financially with those sales of the Jones paintings that the cops recovered. I don't know how I would have paid off all those bills otherwise. And the fact that she took a reduced commission on them? That was above and beyond. Was that your idea or hers?"

"Hers. But those sales have paid off for her, too, prestige- and publicity-wise. The gallery's been doing brisk business ever since—even in *this* economy."

"Good for her then—for both of you. So, onward to Mykonos then. You looking forward to it?"

"Very much so. There are some amazing ruins on Delos, the island next to Mykonos, that I can't wait to see. The Sacred Lake, the Minoan Fountain, the Meeting Hall of the Poseidonists."

"The Poseidonists? As in the god of the sea?"

"Uh-uh. They worshipped him. I've started planning a new series with a water theme. Oceans, rivers, rain. I'm thinking of calling it *We Are Water*. What do you think?"

"Nice," I tell her. "Sounds promising."

"I've done some preliminary sketches, but it's all just conceptual and open-ended at this point. I kind of want to see what feeds me once I'm over there. But that's enough about *my* work. What about yours? How's your book coming along?"

"Pretty good. Did I tell you I've decided to turn it into a novel?"

She nods. "Last time we talked. Well, whenever you want to show it to me, I'd love to read it. Have Ariane or Andrew read any of it?"

"No. I'm not ready for that yet."

She frowns. "You know what I think the trouble with Andrew is? Why he's isolating himself? I don't think he's ever gotten over that shooting at Fort Hood. He worked with that doctor, you know. The one who killed all those people."

"Yeah, I do know that." But I also know that what's eating away at Andrew is another killing. A hidden corpse.

"That was the worst day of my life," Annie says. "When I heard about those shootings down there? I sat in front of the television, almost as if I were in a trance or something. Then I got ahold of myself—told myself I had to *do* something. So I put my coat on and walked down to the Church of the Most Precious Blood. Got down on my knees and prayed harder than ever before that Andrew wasn't one of that maniac's victims."

"Church of the Most Precious Blood—why does that sound familiar?"

"It's in Little Italy. Remember the San Gennaro festival?"

"Ah," I say. "That's it."

"I'd been going there all along. Not for Mass, but during odd hours when the church was empty, or almost empty. And I'd kneel and ask God to keep him safe—to not let him have to go over there to Afghanistan or Iraq. And then, suddenly, not even that hospital in Texas was safe. After I left the church and went back to the apartment? The day of the shootings? When I heard his voice on the message machine—

heard him say that he wasn't even scheduled to go in that day—I just stood there and wailed." Just thinking about that scare has brought her to tears again. "I can't tell you how relieved I was when he decided not to reenlist—to get out of the army and move back here to help you. I cried when I heard that news, too. I tell you one thing, Orion. I know you don't believe in the power of prayer, but I sure do."

The power of prayer: someone else said the same thing to me recently. Can't remember who.

Viveca calls in to us. "Everything's just about ready. Anna, could you come in and set the table?"

Annie gets up, comes over to my wheelchair. "Shall we go in?" I tell her I need to check on something first. I don't. I just need a minute by myself. When she says she'll be back after she sets the table, I remind her that I can wheel myself in there—that I'm not a *quadri*plegic. "Right," she says. Gives me a wink and walks out.

Alone, I sit there, thinking again about the real reason why our son has unplugged from everything except his work. I'm still the only one he's told about what happened that day—what he did, where the body is. It must only be a skeleton now. *I have to tell someone, Dad. It's like my head is going to explode if I don't. . . .* Poor Andrew: the burden he has to live with. But what good would it have done if he'd turned himself in? The guy was a pedophile—had gone to prison for doing to some other little girl what he had done to Annie. And he'd been a loner, apparently. There's never been anything on the Internet about his having gone missing—nothing I've ever found anyway. I still check from time to time. But whenever I Google the guy, all that ever comes up is the stuff about his arrest and conviction for having molested that other poor kid.

Sometimes I wish Andrew *hadn't* told me. It's not easy keeping his secret. But at least he's not suffering in a prison somewhere. He's doing good, useful work with those psych patients. *Helping* people instead of stagnating in some shit-hole cell. And at least he's got me to share a little of the weight of his secret. Talk him down when he goes into those panics about it. And thanks to the anti-anxiety meds they put him on, he's not having them as much lately.

"Orion?"

"Yup. Coming."

After lunch, Viveca says she wants to walk down in back and look at the cottage where Joe Jones used to live and paint. "Would you like to come with me, darling?" she asks. Annie says no, that she'll stay and do the dishes.

"The ground's probably going to be mushy down there after that rain we had yesterday," I tell Viveca. "If I were you, I'd take off those heels you're wearing and put on Ari's Timberlands. They're over there by the door."

She nods. "Good idea." When she's ready to go, I kid her about her fashion statement: her fancy tailored suit and those scuffed-up hiking boots. She laughs, strikes a model's pose. Feels good to kid with her a little.

"Watch out for that well down there," Annie tells her. I flinch when she says it, but it goes undetected.

After the dishes are done, Annie pours us more coffee and sits at the table with me. "So," I say. "Sounds like your old pal Mr. Agnello got a pretty nice send-off, eh?"

She nods, says the Mass was concelebrated by the bishop and two other priests. I ask her if it's weird being a Catholic these days, given the church's position on gay marriage. "A little," she says. "But once a Catholic, always a Catholic. It's like saying I'm not going to be Irish anymore."

I nod. "What about Communion? Do you partake?"

"I do. I'm not about to let a bunch of old men dictate what I can or can't do. Those are their rules, not God's. I joined the Unitarian church in our neighborhood a while back, and I go to services there mostly. But I go to Mass when the spirit moves me. My relationship with God is between Him and me."

"Atta girl," I tell her. "What about all those pedophile scandals? That must hit home, too, I imagine. Fuel a little of your anger about priests."

She looks away from me and nods. She's been in therapy ever since all her secrets came tumbling out, but I can see it's still hard for her—what happened the night of the flood, and then what happened after it.

The front door bangs open. Footsteps, big and little, come hurrying toward us. "Well, hi, Dario!" Annie says, dropping to her knees and grabbing him, giving him smooches. When she lets him go, he takes the balloon animal his mother's holding. "Gamma, look!" he says.

"Oh, cool! What is it? A lion?"

He shakes his head. "A doggie."

"And where did you get it?"

"A funny man made it for me."

"A clown," Ari reminds him.

Annie takes it from him. "And what does the doggie say?"

"Woof woof."

She makes it bob back and forth. "Hello, Dario. I'm your doggie. Woof woof woof." His giggling is infectious.

The visit goes well. Chinese takeout for dinner was Andrew's idea. He picked it up and brought it over after work. It's been nice to see him interact so easily with Viveca this time. Little by little, he's let go of his resentment toward her, too. Makes it easier for his mother—for all of us, really. When Dario comes back down from his bath, his hair's slicked back and he's zipped up in his nubby yellow sleeper. "We thought Gamma and Gamma Viveca might like to read him a story before he goes to bed," Ari says.

"Oh, yes indeed," Viveca says. "Shall we read one of the ones we brought you?" His head bobs up and down. "This one," he says, pulling *The Very Hungry Caterpillar* from the stack on the table.

"Good choice," Annie says. "Come on then." She picks him up. "Mmm, you smell delicious. I think I'll eat you up." When she nuzzles his neck, he screams with delight because it tickles. The three of them head upstairs.

The twins start tackling the cleanup. It's good to see Andrew in such a good mood tonight, the two of them bantering back and forth like old times. "Uh-oh. Whose phone is that?" I ask.

Ariane says it's hers and digs around in her purse. "Hello?" From the gist of the conversation, there seems to be a problem over at the group home.

"They going back to the city tonight or staying over?" Andrew asks me.

Going back, I tell him. They should be taking off pretty soon. When his sister gets off the phone, she says she has to go over there to straighten something out. "Can you stay?" she asks her brother.

"Sure," he says. "I was going to stick around anyway. Help Papa Bear over here with his nighttime stuff."

"Okay, great. I'll just run up and say good-bye to Mama and Viveca."

A year ago, I might have gotten miffed about Ariane's assumption that I couldn't have babysat Dario by myself, but I'm less sensitive about that kind of thing now. Learning to let go of the small stuff has helped me with my recovery. Reminds me of that bracelet Ariane always wears: the one someone gave her on a plane once. Change what you can, accept what you can't, and be smart enough to know the difference.

Viveca comes downstairs first and heads into the living room. When I wheel myself in there, I see her standing in front of Joe Jones's painting of the Tree of Life. "Anytime you change your mind, Orion," she says.

"No, no. This one's a keeper."

"Speaking of keepers, I'll let you in on a little secret," she says. She tells me *she's* the one who purchased Jones's *The Cercus People*. For Annie, she says. Their anniversary's coming up just before they leave for Greece, and she's going to surprise her with it. "It's such an important part of her history as an artist that I thought she should have it."

"Yeah, but you shouldn't have had to *buy* it. After all those other sales you brokered at that reduced commission? I would have been happy to give it to you. Why don't you let me write you a check?"

"I wouldn't think of it," she says. "Nor would I have thought to charge you a straight commission on those other sales. I wanted to find *some* way to help you out after what happened, Orion, and that was what I could do."

"That, and letting me borrow Annie back all those weeks at the beginning. And all those weekends afterward."

She reaches over and pats my shoulder. Smiles. I think back to the day when Annie told me she and Viveca had fallen in love. That she wanted a divorce. Angry and in pain, I had made Viveca the rich bitch, the mercenary predator who had stolen my wife. Suspected she was more interested in Annie's art sales than she was in Annie. But Annie had already begun to let go of me by the time she moved to New York, and it's not like I was the blameless victim in that. We'd been growing apart, taking each other for granted. I'd done nothing to turn things around; I'd just let her float away. But at the time, I couldn't admit that. It was easier to think of myself as Viveca's victim than to cop to my own culpability. So I had cast her as the villain. But if it was convenient for me to think that way back then, it wasn't really fair. Viveca's got her good points as well as her less desirable ones, just like the rest of us. Like me, for example. And the truth is, they really do love each other. I can admit that now. Viveca isn't Cruella De Vil after all. She never was.

When Annie comes back down, she reports that Dario's fast asleep, sucking his thumb. She says they'd better be going. Good-bye hugs, good-bye kisses. When I suggest that they take some of the leftover Chinese with them, Viveca asks me if I'm kidding. Reminds me that their apartment is four blocks up from Chinatown.

After they leave, Andrew asks if I want to watch some TV or head upstairs and get ready for bed. I tell him I think I'll hit the sack; that this evening has been fun, but I'm beat. He nods, releases the brake on my chair, and wheels me toward the stairs. I put my arms around his neck and he pulls me up and onto the chair lift. Hits the button. I rise.

When I'm done in the bathroom, I wheel myself down the hall to check in on Dario. Andrew's in there, watching him sleep. He and I exchange smiles and he wheels me into my bedroom. Like the pro he is, he transfers me from the chair onto my bed. Sits down and starts kneading my feet to promote my circulation. My paralysis still strikes me as strange sometimes: the way I can see him working on my feet but can't feel a thing. I still dream sometimes that I can walk. "How about a back rub?" Andrew asks. I shake my head, tell him I'll pass. "Okay then. Let me fix you up and let you get some shut-eye."

He goes over to the closet and gets a fresh Depends. Takes off the one I've been wearing, then sponges and powders me down there. "Funny how we've exchanged roles," I tell him.

"Hmm?"

"I used to diaper *you*."

He smiles, nods. Out of the blue, he asks me if I miss sex.

"Sometimes. The closeness more than the act itself, I guess. Touching, caressing. Spooning against another warm body. And boobs. I really miss boobs."

"Yeah, boobies are good." He asks me if I ever hear from Tracy.

"Uh-huh. She called me from Key West last week. She's on sabbatical down there."

"Was that why you two broke up? Because of . . . you know?"

"That was a concern. Sure. It was my decision, not hers. Wouldn't have been fair to her, you know? Why should someone who's in her sexual prime have to be tethered to a guy who's dead below the waist?"

"Yeah, but if she's still calling you . . ."

"No, no. Tracy's moved on, more power to her. When we talked last week, she mentioned that she's seeing someone down there—a guy who runs a charter fishing boat."

"Yeah? How'd you feel when she said that?"

"Oh . . . made me a little sad, to tell you the truth. But it's for the best. It's like something Marissa said to me this morning when I talked to her: you can look back on the past. Just don't stay stuck there. What about you?"

"What about me what?"

"Don't *you* miss sex? I mean, hey, I'm an old geezer. But a young guy like you—"

"Dad, don't start," he says. "I already got the pitch from Mom tonight about how I should be dating. And anyway, who says I don't have sex? What do you think the Internet's for?" He means it as a joke, but I can't muster a smile. This self-imposed loneliness of his breaks my heart.

"Not the same thing," I tell him. "What's your resistance about? The secret you're keeping? Because there were extenuating circumstances. And if you put yourself out there, you might find someone who you could trust and—"

"And what? Saddle her with it? Or hook up with someone, marry her, and not ever tell her what I did that day? Keep my deep, dark secret from her like Mom kept hers from you? Marriage is about trust, isn't it? Open communication?"

"But that's what I'm saying, Andrew. Maybe if you find the right girl—"

"Yeah, and what if after a couple of years of being married, she decides *I'm* not the right *guy*? That she wants a divorce? It would be a pretty juicy piece of ammunition for her to use against me. Wouldn't it? The fact that I killed a guy and stuffed him down a well?"

He finishes diapering me in silence. Yanks my sweatpants back on and pulls the covers up. I can tell he's pissed. "Are you mad at me?" I ask him.

"No. I just wish you and Mom and Marissa would stop harping on me about getting a girlfriend. And that Ari would stop trying to fix me up."

"Okay, kiddo. Got it. I'll lay off."

"Good." He walks over to the door and turns back. "Anything else you need?" I shake my head. "Okay then. Get some sleep."

I reach over and tap the book I've been reading. "Yeah, I think I'll read a little while first."

"Okay. G'night then."

"Night. And Andrew? Thanks."

"Sure. No problem."

"Not just for helping me tonight," I say. "For everything. Moving back here, hanging out with me. I'm not sure what kind of shape I'd be in right now if I didn't have your support."

He nods, gives me a sad smile, and says it again. "No problem, Dad. Thanks for your support, too. You want your door open or closed?"

"You can leave it open." He nods again and leaves.

I open my book, stare at the page I'm on for the next few minutes without really reading. . . . It's theoretical: this ex-wife who's going to turn around and betray him. But I can understand his hesitation, his fear. I think about that bumper sticker I read in the parking lot yesterday when Belinda ran into the pharmacy to get my prescriptions: JUST BECAUSE YOU'RE PARANOID DOESN'T MEAN SOMEONE'S *NOT* OUT TO GET YOU. When I look up, he's at the door again. "Hey," he says.

"Hey. What's up?"

"I was just thinking. Got a proposition for you."

"Oh, yeah? What's that?"

"I'm off this coming Tuesday and Wednesday. What do you say the two of us take a road trip?"

"Sounds intriguing," I say. "Got any particular destination in mind?"

"Yeah, I was thinking maybe . . . the Cape."

I flinch. "Return to the scene of the crime? Nah, I don't think so, buddy. But thanks for the offer."

"No, listen. We could steer clear of Viveca's. But what if we drove up there, got a motel room in Wellfleet or P'town? I could drive you over to Long Nook Beach. Haven't you always said it's your favorite place?"

"Used to be," I tell him.

"The crowds will be gone by now, and the weather's still nice. We could go up there, stay overnight, and come back the next day."

He stands there, looking at me. Waiting. "Let me think about it," I tell him. Okay, he says. I can let him know.

I give up on reading. Put my book down. When I close my eyes I can see it: the view when you look down there from the top of the dune, the sandbar that forms when it's low tide. I can hear it, too— the crack of the surf, the waves rolling in. . . . When I reach over to turn off my light, it's smiling at me: that little soapstone dolphin my Grandpa Valerio carved for me when I was a kid. I pick it up, smile back at it. . . . Maybe we *can* go up there. Being at their trial and testifying against them didn't give me any closure, and neither did their conviction. But this might. Going up there with Andrew, being able to look out at the ocean again. I don't know, though. Like I said, I'll have to think about it.

Chapter Twenty-Nine

Orion Oh

We arrive at Long Nook at about one in the afternoon. It's a warm, overcast day, but the rain we hit on the drive up has stopped. The parking lot's empty. Andrew swings into the spot up front and cuts the engine. I tell him my handicapped tag is back at the motel inside the bag Belinda packed. He laughs, scanning the empty lot. Says he doesn't think it's much of an issue.

He gets out of the car and grabs the folding patio chair he's thrown in the back. Jogs up the path with it and unfolds it up at the top. The wheels on my chair won't work in the sand, so the plan is that he'll carry me up there and put me in the folding chair. That way, I can look out at the ocean below. When he comes back down, he opens my door, swings my legs around. "Ready?"

"Yep." I put my arms around his neck and he lifts me up and over his shoulder like I'm a sack of potatoes. When we reach the top of the dune, he bends his knees and slides me down onto the chair. "Houston, we have landed," I joke, but Andrew, born after the space race, doesn't get it.

I look out on the horizon. Gray sky, choppy gray-green waves. The sea breeze feels good against my face, my arms. I fill my lungs with ocean air. A sunny day would have been nicer, but this is still pretty damned terrific.

Andrew sits down on the ground beside me and hugs his knees. "Nice," he says. "I think this may be my favorite place, too."

I tell him about the whale Ariane and I saw from this same vantage point three years ago. Back when I had working legs and a new girlfriend, I think. Back before Andrew took another man's life and it changed the course of his own. . . . Okay, but what have you *gained* since then? I ask myself. It's something I used to advise my university patients to do to combat self-pity: replace negative thoughts with positive ones. So, okay, what *have* I gained? Well, my work on the novel. My grandson. . . . And this road trip. This time with my son. Despite how hard it's been to keep his secret, and to see how much keeping it has limited his life, it's brought us closer. Andrew and I are closer now than we've ever been.

"Hey," he says. "You want to go down by the water?"

I shake my head. "Don't forget, my friend. What goes down must come back up again. I'd probably give you a heart attack halfway back up."

"Pfft. What do you weigh now? One-sixty-five? One-seventy? Piece of cake compared to what I'm lifting at the gym. And I can stop and rest if I need to. Which I won't. Come on, Papa Bear. Let's do it."

He stands up, lifts me out of the chair. Carries me in his arms the way I used to carry him when he was a boy—when he'd fall asleep coming home from someplace and I'd lift him out of the car and bring him up the stairs to bed. Now we're like some screwed-up version of the *Pietà*, the child cradling the broken parent instead of vice versa. But no, that would make me Jesus, and I'm not that by a long shot. I didn't die for my own sins, let alone everyone else's. I'm still here. "You okay?" I ask him. He says he's fine.

When we reach the bottom, he says, "Where to?"

"Maybe a little closer to the water?"

"You got it."

He puts me down about six feet up from the high-water mark. We sit side by side in the sand, looking out at the ocean, neither of us speaking. A few minutes later, he stands up, pulls his shirt over his head. "Can't resist," he says.

"Go for it."

"You want to come in?"

"No thanks. I'm good right here."

"Just wish I'd thought to bring some trunks."

When I suggest that he just drop his drawers and go skinny-dipping, he looks up and down the beach, back at the path. I laugh. Tell him what he told me up there in the parking lot—that it's not much of an issue with just the two of us. He nods, shucks his clothes, and heads in.

Looking at his naked body, I think back to the day he was born. Ariane had been birthed with no complications, but not him. The umbilical cord had wrapped itself around his neck, and we didn't know if he was going to make it or not. But then the doctor had somehow saved him from strangulation and he had emerged from his mother's body squalling and blue. The nurse had cut the cord and placed him in my arms. Cradling him, I watched him breathe in oxygen and turn pink. Looked at the little nub between his legs and thought, wow, a son. I've got a son. Seeing him now, I realize that blessing is something my own father deprived himself of, and for the first time in my life, I pity him his loss, his cowardice. And pitying him robs him of his power over me. He never got to see his son grow up the way I have. . . . I recall Andrew's skinny frame when he was a kid, his teenage body after he started lifting weights and getting some muscle definition. Now he's got a grown man's body, solid and muscular. Powerful. So powerful that he killed a man. . . .

He goes in up to his knees, then takes the plunge. When he comes up again, the water's up to his chin. I smile at his dolphinlike swimming—the way he goes under, comes up for air, shakes his head, and submerges again. I think of something I read recently, I forget where. *A life I didn't choose chose me.* That's true for both of us. . . .

When he comes out, walks back to me, he's shivering a little. "How was it?" I ask him. Awesome, he says. He towels off, pulls his underwear and jeans back on, and sits down beside me. When I ask him about the tattoo on his shoulder, he says he got it the night before he left Fort Hood.

"Those are Chinese characters, aren't they?" He nods. "What's it say?"

"Says, *love wins.*"

To hide my sorrow, I smile. "No matter which way our lives turn out. Right?" He doesn't answer me. We both stare out at the water, neither of us feeling the need to speak. But a minute or so later, when I look over at him, I see that his eyes are closed and his lips are moving. Is he praying? Does Andrew still pray? And if he does, for what? Forgiveness from his god? Salvation for the soul of his victim? I look back at the ocean and think about what his mother told me: how she prayed for his safety every single day when he was in the service. Sometimes I wish *I* could believe in some bigger scheme of things the way people of faith do—some merciful overseer who you could pray to, ask things of. Can't do it, though. But even if I can't pray—can't express my gratitude to some higher power up there in the sky—it doesn't mean I'm *not* grateful, because I am. Grateful that he *wasn't* at work the day that shrink lost it and went on his shooting rampage. That he *wasn't* deployed over there to either of those wars. He's here beside me, as safe as any of us ever gets to be.

"Where'd you just go?" he asks.

"Hmm?"

"You look like you were deep in thought just now," he says.

"Oh. Well . . . I was just thinking about your mother."

"Yeah? What about her?"

I'm not going to get into the god thing with him, so I come up with something else. "She's pretty excited about some new art project she's planning. Going to work on it over there in Greece."

"Is that the one she told me about? Where she uses yarn or whatever to connect her life to that painter who used to live out back on our property?"

"Oh, you mean 'Josephus's Thread.' No, she finished that one. You remember that Greek myth about the labyrinth? How the hero—Theseus, I think his name was—goes in there, kills the Minotaur, and then gets out again, thanks to Ariadne's thread? So he won't stay lost in the maze forever?"

He shrugs. Asks who Ariadne is.

"The king's daughter. She gives him a skein of thread so he can save himself after he slays the monster. He unwinds it as he walks through the maze and then follows it back to the entrance. Your mom's proud of that piece. Says it's the most directly autobiographical one she's ever done. I guess the point she's making is that Joe Jones's art not only led her to make her own, but that it also led her to being able to confront what happened during her childhood. Slay *those* monsters, okay? The flood, the abuse. She says that piece came out of all of the therapy she's done." I think about the monster Andrew killed on her behalf. How he hid the body in the same place where Jones was killed. How he's entwined in Josephus's thread, too, but may never get himself out of the maze *his* life has become.

"It's all Greek to me," he says. "So she's working on another one now?"

"Yeah. Says she might call it *We Are Water*."

His face darkens. "Is this one going to be about that flood, too?"

"No, I don't think so. I guess the other one dealt with that, pretty much. Allowed her to move on. From what I gather, this next one is going to be about the gods and goddesses, the mysteries of the Aegean. She's excited about some ruin she's going to check out while she's over there. An altar built by some group that worshipped the sea."

"Yeah?" He picks up a flat stone. Stands and scales it into the surf.

"It's true when you think about it, I guess."

"What is?"

"We *are* water."

He nods. "Sixty to seventy percent, if I remember my physiology textbooks. And the brain's something like *eighty*-five percent."

The brain, I think. That miraculous, mysterious organ. One part of mine is blocking me from using my legs, and another part is helping me to reconnect with my grandfather—to hear his voice, listen to his story. And who knows? Maybe my father will finally begin to speak to me, too. "Yeah, but that's not what I meant," I tell my son.

He looks at me, waiting. And so I open my mouth and try to articulate what it is I *do* mean. "All of life came from the ocean, right? Even us. We flip-flopped out of the water, grew feet and bigger brains, stood up and started walking. Makes sense, doesn't it? For the first nine months of our lives, we float underwater. Then we hit the cold air, the glaring light of day, and start crying salty tears. Begin the lifelong challenge of trying to figure out why we're here, what it all means."

"Getting pretty philosophical in your old age," he says. "Aren't you?"

"Maybe. But think about it. We *are* like water, aren't we? We can be fluid, flexible when we have to be. But strong and destructive, too." And something else, I think to myself. Like water, we mostly follow the path of least resistance. Wasn't that what I advised Andrew to do the day he confessed what he'd done: told him to shut his mouth about it? Take the path of least resistance?

"You know what I've always liked?" he says. "The *sound* of water. It's, I don't know, kind of comforting or something. You know? Rain on the roof, rivers flowing. I always liked listening to the brook out in back of our house—the way it gushed during the spring thaw, trickled in summer if there hadn't been much rain. And the ocean. Close your eyes and listen for a minute, Dad."

I do what he says, taking in the sound of the breaking waves, the surf lapping the shore. When I open my eyes again, he's looking at me. "I've been wrestling with something," he says. "Praying on it. Asking God for clarity."

"About what?" I ask, although I already know what he's going to say.

"I've been thinking lately about turning myself in."

I want to open my mouth, make the case again about why he shouldn't. Rescue him from what will happen to him if he does. But I'm not my son's knight in shining armor or anyone else's; I've given up that conceit. And whether or not I've let my license to practice expire, this time I'm Dr. Oh as well as Dad. Isn't that what the best therapists do? Hold their tongues and listen? Let the sufferer follow his own path out of the labyrinth?

"I haven't decided yet, though," he says. "I keep going back and forth."

I ask him the question I'm not sure I want him to answer. "You leaning more one way than the other?"

"Depends on which hour you're talking about," he says.

I look away from him then, look out at the rolling waves and think about umbilical cords, nooses, the skeins of string that tangle and connect us. If he *does* go to the police, *does* end up in prison, maybe he'll save himself from this choked-up life he's been living. Be able to breathe again like he did the morning of his birth when the cord between his mother and him that had sustained him for nine months now was strangling him. When I look back at him, I tell him to do what his gut tells him to. Wish him luck making his decision.

He smiles at me. Doesn't speak at first. And when he finally does, he says what he said to me the last time we were at this beach, when we stopped in the middle of that run we took. "I love you, Dad."

I reach over and take his hand in mine. Squeeze it. "I love you, too."

"Fuckin' hot out here, huh?" he says. "Now that the sun's out?" Shielding my eyes, I look up at the sky. When *did* the sun come out? Before? Just now? I hadn't even noticed. "Come on," he says. "Let's cool off."

And without another word, he gets up, stands over me, and lifts me onto my useless puppet's leg. Scoops me up in his strong arms and walks us toward the glittering water. Blinking back tears, holding on to Andrew's tattooed shoulder, I gaze at the horizon. Together—father and son, the atheist and the believer, we enter the churning, mysterious sea.

Gratitude

I'm enormously grateful to my wise and thoughtful editor, Terry Karten, and my genial and gracious literary agent, Kassie Evashevski, for their help and guidance in helping me to make this a better book.

My appreciation also extends to the following writers whose critical feedback was important to the development of this story: Denise Abercrombie, Doug Anderson, Jon Anderson, Bruce Cohen, Susan Cole, Janet Dauphin, Doug Hood, Careen Jennings, Leslie Johnson, T. C. Karmel, Pam Lewis, Sari Rosenblatt, Amanda Smith, Ellen Zahl, and the women of the York Correctional Institution writing group.

Warm thanks to painters and educators Joseph Gualtieri and Mary Ann Hall for their guidance and inspiration with regard to all things artistic.

This story was informed in part by a devastating 1963 flood that occurred in my hometown of Norwich, Connecticut. For their connection to and generous sharing of information about that tragedy, I am grateful to the following: Tony Orsini, Tom Moody, Jim Moody, Sean Moody, Tony Longo, Norah Kaszuba, Frances and Dick Buckley, Dennis Riley, Bill Zeitz, and the good folks of D'Elia's Bakery.

Thanks to the following who shared their time and information on a variety of subjects, or who connected me to people who informed aspects of this story: Steven Dauer, Laura Durand, Mary Kay Kelleher, Fran Kornacki, and Melody Knight Leary.

A nod of appreciation to my faithful office assistants, Amanda Smith and Joe Darda, and for their guidance and moral support, Justin Manchester, Charley Correll, Mark Hand, and Hilda "Prosperine" Belcher. As always, thanks to my good and faithful friend Ethel Mantzaris.

The publication of a novel requires teamwork, and I salute the Harper team, the best in the business, especially Michael Morrison, Jonathan Burnham, Kathy Schneider, Leslie Cohen, Tina Andreadis, Lydia Weaver, Leah Wasielewski, Milan Bozic, Fritz Metsch, Sarah Odell, Shelly Perron, Kate Walker, and the entire sales crew.

Special thanks to my bride of the past thirty-five years and the love of my life, Christine Lamb.

Finally, it is my sincere hope that this novel honors the lives and acknowledges the untimely deaths of Ellis Ruley (1882–1959) and Margaret "Honey" Moody (1938–1963).

Suggestions for further reading:

Thomas R. Moody, Jr.'s *A Swift and Deadly Maelstrom: The Great Norwich Flood of 1963, A Survivor's Story* (Bloomington, IN: XLibris, 2013).

Glenn Robert Smith and Robert Kenner's *Discovering Ellis Ruley: The Story of an American Outsider Artist* (New York: Crown, 1993).

A Note from Wally Lamb

The deaths by gunfire of children and their teachers at the Sandy Hook Elementary School in Newtown, Connecticut, occurred as I was readying this novel for publication. I invite readers who are so inclined to join me in my response to this unfathomable tragedy by contributing to one or both of the following. Thank you.

Brady Campaign to Prevent Gun Violence: www.bradycampaign.org

National Alliance on Mental Illness: www.nami.org

Wally Lamb is the author of four previous novels, including the *New York Times* and national bestseller *The Hour I First Believed*, and *Wishin' and Hopin'*, a bestselling Christmas novella. His first two works of fiction, *She's Come Undone* and *I Know This Much Is True*, were both number one *New York Times* bestsellers and selections of Oprah's Book Club. Lamb edited *Couldn't Keep It to Myself* and *I'll Fly Away*, two volumes of essays from students in his writing workshop at York Correctional Institution, a women's prison in Connecticut, where he has been a volunteer facilitator for fifteen years. He lives in Connecticut with his wife, Christine. The Lambs are the parents of three sons.